THE CLASSIC BOOK OF SCIENCE FICTION

EDITED BY
GROFF CONKLIN

WITH A NEW FOREWORD BY
GEORGE GESNER

BONANZA BOOKS • NEW YORK

This 1982 edition is published by Bonanza Books,
distributed by Crown Publishers, Inc.
h g f e d c b a

Manufactured in the United States of America

Library of Congress Cataloging in Publication Data

Main entry under title:

The Classic book of science fiction.

   Originally published as: Big book of
science fiction. New York : Crown, 1950.
   1. Science fiction. I. Groff, Conklin,
1904-1968. II. Big book of science fiction.
PN6120.95.S33C5   1982   813'.0876'08   81-12232
ISBN 0-517-35726-7   AACR2

CONTENTS

FOREWORD

It has been a long and arduous journey for science fiction, sprouting from the early visionaries of centuries past to pulp magazines and fandom of the mid-1900s to the widely accepted genre of literature it is today.

The Classic Book of Science Fiction by Groff Conklin is a brilliant assortment of science fiction stories from the mid-1900s that bridges the gap between the days of prototype science fiction and the present.

It is difficult to pinpoint when science fiction originated because it is a form of writing that encompasses a wide range of ideas and incorporates many styles of literature. One school of thought takes it back to the sixth and seventh centuries B.C., when the Greek poet Homer presented the *Odyssey*, considered to be one of the earliest prototypes of science fiction. The use of the imaginary voyage theme and its heroic character qualify this work for a place in the history of science fiction and fantasy. One can easily include ancient mythology and tales of folklore with their use of themes such as heroes, fantasy, supernatural, monsters, immortality, and utopias.

Others will point to the names of Francis Bacon, Johannes Kepler, Francis Godwin, and Cyrano de Bergerac of the seventeenth century. These men, once again, used the idea of the voyage, but they were starting to incorporate scientific ideas. A pioneering spirit drove them to experiment in search of cause and effect. Bacon, a philosopher and statesman, wrote *New Atlantis* and conducted countless experiments. One of these experiments led to his death. In gathering snow for an experiment in cryonics—preserving the flesh of a bird in frozen conditions—he caught a fatal chill. Kepler, the famous German astronomer, wrote *Somnium*, a combination of scientific theory based on his lunar observations and a fictional account of life on the moon. This piece ranks him as one of the true inaugurators of the genre. Godwin made his contribution to the field with *The Man in the Moone: or a Discourse of a Voyage Thither by Domingo Gonsales the Speedy Messenger*. Cyrano de Bergerac may be well known for his deft swordsplay and spindly nose, but to the history of science fiction he is known for his work *L'autre monde*, known today as *Other Worlds*, which included *Voyage to the Moon*.

The eighteenth century brought about the rise of the novel and formal realism. Out of this period came Jonathan Swift's *Gulliver's Travels*, Daniel Defoe's *Robinson Crusoe*, and Voltaire's *Micromégas*. In the early nineteenth century Edgar Allan Poe and Mary Shelley were very influential, melding scientific supposition into their Gothic romances. Another school of thought credits Mary Shelley with the first science fiction novel, *Frankenstein: or, The Modern Prometheus*. This Gothic horror novel combined elements of humanism and scientific ideas such as galvanism. She laid the groundwork for such science fiction themes as monsters and androids, discovery and invention, and conceptual breakthrough. Another of her works, titled *The Last Man*, was also an important prototype for science fiction in that it featured themes of destruction and survival. Many cite this romance as the starting point for the use of the holocaust theme. This century also saw a flurry of mainstream writers such as Nathaniel Hawthorne, Mark Twain, Robert Louis Stevenson, Bulwer Lytton, and Herman Melville moving out of their genre to do works in the science fiction vein.

The mid-1800s produced one of the two founding fathers of science fiction by the name of Jules Verne. Although Verne wrote many non-science fiction books, his fame rests on his visions of the near future and his use of the fantastic voyage theme. His name was further glorified when his works fell into popular domain and filmmakers struck gold with 20,000 *Leagues Under the Sea, Around the World in 80 Days, From the Earth to the Moon, The Mysterious Island, Journey to the Center of the Earth,* and other works.

H. G. Wells, the other founding father, made his name around the turn of the century. There is no doubt about whether Wells deserves that title. Romantic visions of worlds to come, visitors from other worlds, and almost every theme to be incorporated into modern science fiction can be attributed to this man. By this time there was already an avalanche of writers in the genre with no signs of slowing down.

In the year 1926 a man named Hugo Gernsback founded the first science fiction magazine—*Amazing Stories.* In this magazine he coined the term *scientifiction,* which gave the world a label for the style of writing that had evolved through all those years and was suddenly erupting with major force. Various science fiction magazines, novels, and films followed with intense proliferation. This era of time is commonly referred to as The Golden Age of Science Fiction. One of the anthologies of the period was *The Classic Book of Science Fiction* edited by Groff Conklin. In this book, formerly titled *The Big Book of Science Fiction,* Conklin scoured countless pulp magazines for well-written stories by both established names and promising new talents. Conklin certainly deserves his title as a master anthologist, and this work further exemplifies that distinction. Some of the names in this volume have disappeared from view in later years, but most of the names still exist at the forefront of science fiction today.

Conklin divided his book into six thematic parts: (1) Inventions, Dangerous and Otherwise; (2) Wonders of Earth and Man; (3) From Outer Space; (4) Adventures in Dimension; (5) Far Traveling; and (6) World of Tomorrow. Part One includes the tale "The Diminishing Draft" by onetime *New York Times* science editor Waldemar Kaempffert. Although the scientific idea hardly seems plausible, even more so now than in 1918 when it was written, it is still a wonderful romance with just enough suspense and inventive thought to be suitable for inclusion. Kaempffert uses the age-old theme of "great and small," a very popular idea implemented in many fantasy tales. Another important theme discussed here is that of transmutation. This is an idea that has fascinated readers throughout science fiction history. It plays an important role in Horace L. Gold's "A Matter of Form." This story of a man whose brain is transplanted into the body of a dog showcases Gold as a brilliant writer. Gold straddles two genres (science fiction and detective fiction) masterfully. Unfortunately many people don't associate Gold with his writing, since his reputation rests on his renown as editor of the leading science fiction magazine of the fifties, *Galaxy Science Fiction*, as well as numerous other anthologies. Also included in this section is Ward Moore, an American novelist who wrote mainstream fiction. Moore received distinction for his novel *Bring the Jubilee*, in which he suggests a hypothetical alternative world where the South wins the Civil War. In this book he offers "Peacebringer," a story about a misdirected messiah.

Part two features "Defense Mechanism," the first story published by Katherine MacLean. She uses her psychology background to good use, implementing a communication theme with the device of telepathy. This is a theme that seems to be a trademark of several of her stories. In 1971 MacLean won a Nebula Award for her short story "The Missing Man." Also included is "Margin for Error," an engrossing story of paranoia and intellect written by Lewis Padgett. Padgett is one of the pseudonyms used by Henry Kuttner, who was married to writer C. L. Moore and often collaborated with her. Together they contributed a wealth of material under pseudonyms as well as their own names.

Mack Reynolds's debut story, "The Isolationist," opens up the third section. He injects considerable political thought into this story of a patriotic farmer and the outerspace invaders he confronts. Reynolds has been a prolific writer best known for his Section G novels, which include *Planetary Agent X* and *Dawnman Planet*. "Nobody Saw the Ship" is the of William F. Jenkins, better known as Murray Leinster. Leinster who was known as the Dean of Science Fiction, won a Hugo Award in 1956 for his novelette *Exploration Team*, but he is best remembered for the quality of writing he contributed to science fiction magazines. Theodore Sturgeon has always been concerned with the human element in his works, and "Mewhu's Jet" is no exception in this highly romanticized tale of a young visitor from another world. Sturgeon has never been known for hard science fiction, but his psychological romances have been much appreciated. Sturgeon won the Hugo and Nebula awards for his short story "Slow Sculpture" in 1971. He scripted two "Star Trek" episodes—"Shore Leave" and "Amok Time"—and he was awarded the 1954 International Fantasy Award for *More Than Human*. This master of human relationships and love has always been one of the most popular writers of this genre. Another tender and touching story closes out the section. "Dear Devil" by Eric Frank Russell is a story about a Martian poet who earns the love of a new colony of earthmen. The British writer won a Hugo for his short story "Allamagoosa."

Part Four of *The Classic Book of Science Fiction* features a wealth of excellent stories by lesser known names. Noel Loomis wrote "The Long Dawn" about a prehistoric man cast into the future, and Green Peyton wrote "Ship That Turned Aside." This is a marvelous voyage piece using devices of time and dimensional travel. It is also a splendid example of a "robinsonnade," a science fiction theme coined in reference to Defoe's classic work *Robinson Crusoe*. The section ends with "E for Effort" by T.

FOREWORD ix

L. Sherred. Time has proven this piece—about an invention that allows
one to see the past and present and the power associated with it—to be one
of the more popular short stories ever to be written. It's been included in
several recent anthologies.

The fifth section includes one of the choices for all-time best science
fiction stories as selected by the Science Fiction Writers of America; it is
included in the Science Fiction Hall of Fame. "Arena" by Fredric Brown
relates the story of a galactic war that must be settled in single combat
between a human and an alien. Many viewers of *"Star Trek"* may notice
that this story was adapted for one of their segments called "Arena." Brown
earned his reputation as a detective fiction writer, but his humorous
science fiction has won him acclaim with such works as *What Mad
Universe* and *Martians, Go Home*. We once again return to Roger Bacon,
or, we should say, he returns to us in "The Roger Bacon Formula" by
Fletcher Pratt, author of many fantasy novels including *The Blue Star*.
This tale hints that Bacon's experiments were a lot more successful than
history will account for. The narrator-protagonist meets Bacon in Greenwich Village and through one of his formulas finds himself transported to
Venus. Lester del Rey achieved much of his stature as an editor and the
namesake for Del Rey Books, but he is also known for some excellent short
stories, such as "Nerves" and the entry in this book, "The Wings of
Night." The 1977 Nebula Grand Master Award winner for lifetime
achievement in science fiction was Clifford D. Simak. This celebrated
writer's awards include a Jupiter in 1977 for *A Heritage of Stars*, Hugos for
Way Station in 1964 and "The Big Front Yard" in 1959. His most impressive
piece of work is *City* (1952), built upon stories he wrote the previous
decade, including "Desertion" about a man and his dog communicating in
the pastoral setting of Jupiter.

The last section includes a piece exclusive to the Golden Age period, by
Jules Verne, called "In the Year 2889." It is not a sterling work of art, but
Verne's prophetic visions once again never cease to amaze. Ray Bradbury is
one of the most creative minds in science fiction. Anyone who can lay claim
to *The Martian Chronicles, Fahrenheit 451,* and *The Illustrated Man* without a doubt has his name etched in the scrolls of science fiction history.
The story included here, "Forever and the Earth," deals with a disen-
chanted short story writer of the future who looks back in time to commission the legendary author Thomas Wolfe from his deathbed to do a new
work of literature. While this enables the writer's literary desires to be
rekindled, he enables Wolfe to see a glimpse of the future. Best-selling
author John D. MacDonald, best known for his novels of intrigue and his
Travis McGee series, is included here with his strange tale called "The
Miniature." Another giant name in science fiction and fantasy is also
included. Fritz Leiber seems to have cornered the market on awards as his
novels *The Big Time* and *The Wanderer* were awarded Hugos. Also awarded
with Hugos plus the Nebula were "Gonna Roll Those Bones," "Ship of
Shadows," and "Catch that Zeppelin." Another Hugo winner was his
novella *Ill Met in Lankhmar*. In this book he offers a psychological tale of

world power called "Sanity." The book closes with "Not with a Bang" by Damon Knight. This well-known editor and writer (winner of the Jupiter for "I See You") lends us this "Adam and Eve" tale about the last two living people on Earth.

One can sense by the listing of the previous authors with their awards and accomplishments that this is a book of extraordinary talent and vision. It is proof to Conklin's mastery of the subject that he unearthed forgotten stories and new talent looking for the strangely prophetic and the peculiarly modern. There has always been a flurry of skepticism and antagonism surrounding the genre, but certainly nobody can deny that it is important modern literature. As Conklin said, "Fantasies based upon extrapolation of scientific or quasi-scientific ideas are definitely with us at least for as long as our society is based upon a complex technology. The genre will continue to grow sturdily with the growth of interest in, and understanding of, scientific and technological matters." *The Classic Book of Science Fiction* is a stepping stone for science fiction, a bastion of literature whose time has come.

New York   GEORGE GESNER
1982

ACKNOWLEDGMENT

No one ever really edits a book alone. The number of friendly advisers and critics who have had a hand in shaping the contents of this new collection is much too large for listing here. On the other hand, there are a few people who have had more than a correspondential function in the organization of the *Big Book*, and to them I want to give a bow:

To the Bronx High School of Science Science Fiction Club, and particularly to Ezra Shahn, Stephen Taller and Morton Sternheim, for their helpful, informed and enthusiastic cooperation;

To Sam Moskowitz, for the well-deserved criticism which he gave *The Treasury* in one of the science fiction fan magazines;

To Bob Tucker, publisher of *The Science Fiction Newsletter*, for suggestions and support;

To Julie Unger, most generous of science fiction booksellers, for his contributions of otherwise unobtainable copies of rare magazines;

To Fred Pohl, calmest and least ulcer-ridden of literary agents, for numerous kindnesses;

To L. Jerome Stanton, Horace Gold, Theodore Sturgeon, Will (Murray Leinster) Jenkins, and Willy Ley for advice and assistance;

And finally to Lucy, my amiable wife, who did so much of the hard work on permissions and so on, even though her enthusiasm for science fiction *still* remains something less than unbounded.

New York   GROFF CONKLIN
June 1950

PART ONE

Inventions, Dangerous and Otherwise

Thomas McMorrow

MR. MURPHY OF NEW YORK

"NEW YORK," said Cohen bitterly, "is dying of enlargement of the heart."

"Well said," I nodded, surveying this czar of an industry employing two hundred and fifty thousand New Yorkers.

"The great building, the skyscraper," he continued with a touch of fanaticism, "is a natural and necessary feature of a modern city! How can keymen meet one another otherwise? If they're going to be miles apart and communicate only by televistor, why, you don't need a city at all. The reason why Canabec is the new metropolis of North America——"

"By George," exclaimed Mr. Bligh, of Canabec, making a show of consulting his watch, "if I miss the St. Lawrence express on the Controlane, I'll not get home till this afternoon. Don't let me hurry you, gentlemen, but if you've decided to do this thing, let's do it. As I've told you, I can give you ten acres, which will be enough to house your industry for all purposes; you are aware that we will require you to go up not less than one hundred floors, 60 per cent to be residential. But I dare say that Mr. Craig here"—looking at me—"who is going to build for you, is familiar with our code."

"Quite," I said curtly, and readdressed myself to Cohen: "Were you in New York when the Americus Tower fell?"

"I had my residence on the roof of the Americus," interposed the futile Mr. Murphy, producing blue prints, "and the coziest home I ever lived in. If you'll give me your attention now, Mr. Craig, I'll show you what I want you to build for me in the way of a residence atop your new Central Unit in Canabec, and I'll take a twenty-year lease at eighty thousand per year."

He was of just enough importance to us to be admitted to the fringes of our conference, but that wasn't Mr. Murphy's conception of his status. He had a great deal of inherited money.

"You weren't at home, I take it, Mr. Murphy," said Cohen soberly, "when the Americus fell?"

"Oh, I would have been killed!" expostulated Mr. Murphy. "As a matter of fact, gentlemen, I was at my shore home in Maine." He became weightily informative. "I was in the recreation hall of my place there, superintending the refinishing of the bowling alley—Mrs. Murphy and I are both very fond of bowling—when my man Rogers came to me with a sheet from the Radio News, and showed me the flash from New York to the general effect that the Americus Tower had fallen. I took it very easily at first; it seemed more likely to me that the news service had been misinformed than that so unprecedented an event had come to pass. 'Nonsense, Rogers!' I said, dismissing it as lightly as that. However, gentlemen, later in the day—Rogers had come to me about twenty-three o'clock—Mrs. Murphy came home to lunch from the country club, and the first thing she said to me, gentlemen, was 'Darius, have you heard——'"

"That the Americus Tower has fallen," finished Cohen. We were on a topic of inexhaustible interest to New Yorkers, but Mr. Murphy was taking us too far afield, as usual.

"Ah, exactly!" said Mr. Murphy, turning approving blue eyes on the black-browed manufacturer. "Or in effect, Mr. Cohen."

"Post mortem, gentlemen," said Mr. Bligh restively. He looked out my window at moribund New York. It was the fall of the Americus Tower that brought about your Safe-and-Sane Law, limiting the height of buildings to ten stories, but that law was justified in any event. Your skyscrapers were creating such a traffic problem——"

"No such thing!" snapped Cohen. "Pardon me, Mr. Bligh. I'll tell you what created that traffic problem—it was our transportation system. Go back there to 1930, when the building of skyscrapers really began in earnest, and see what they were doing about transportation. They were building the first Hudson River bridge, for one thing, and landing it in New York at One Hundred and Seventy-eighth Street. There's city planning for you—who wanted to go to One Hundred and Seventy-eighth Street? The commuters wanted to go to the midtown, and they had to travel about seven miles down through Manhattan Island to get there. I suppose it was easier to land away up there—which reminds me of a new joke I heard last night on the Home Circuit. . . . Do you subscribe to the Home Circuit, Mr. Bligh? They have all the latest. . . . About an intoxicated man who lost his watch one night on Fourteenth Street, but went to look for it on Forty-second because the light was better up there. Ha-ha! . . . That was the bridge; and look at the way they ran the city into debt by building north-and-south subways, all long haul, when they could have run short lines into Long Island and Jersey and made the city spread east and west. What gave you people the jump on us, in my opinion——"

"You New Yorkers," sighed Mr. Bligh. "Let's get to business, gentlemen, please."

"In my opinion," repeated Cohen, "Canabec is the world center today because she had the vision to accommodate herself to facts. Skyscrapers

—absolutely! But mostly residential—that's the point. Canabec, with six million population, has no traffic problem. Her people live where they work, and that's the end of it. We were working toward it here, until the fall of the Americus gave the little people their chance."

He brooded. "We had executive ability, but no imagination. We spent a billion dollars to bring water into the city, emptying puddles a hundred miles away, when the vast Hudson River was right beside us! When the last puddle was drained dry, somebody noticed the Hudson and thought of narrowing it at Spuyten Duyvil and raising it above salt-water level. Why, it's only two years since we used to sewer into it. New York wasn't a city; it was a big Indian village."

"Gas-proof casements and an aerating plant," said Mr. Murphy. "I must insist on that, the same as I had in my home on the Americus Tower, because with Russia only six hours away, you never can tell. It might have been all right when the United States was the only great nation, but now there are three—four, if you count Canada—and I was reading an article in last Sunday's paper describing the next war, and it was enough to make a man thoughtful. And Mrs. Murphy won't have glass curtain walls; she says it never gives the same sense of privacy. She says she can't have every Tom, Dick and Harry looking into her apartment, as they do when somebody leaves the cap off the televistor. There's that; and also——"

"Mr. Craig, you're a builder," said Cohen. "I've often wondered if there was anything in that talk about the iron erectors planning to wreck the Americus Tower because the builder had been a strike-breaker out West."

"Poppycock. You mean that they put the steel frame together in such a way that it would collapse later? It couldn't be done, Mr. Cohen. We had a building department in New York, with a competent force of inspectors, and the company that made the building loan had its own inspectors. And I knew the steel engineer who designed that job, and he was one of the best. His plans are still on file with the city."

"I understand that you saw the building go down, Mr. Craig."

"I did," I said, with slowly kindling enthusiasm for an oft-told tale. "And it was only the mercy of heaven that I didn't go down with it, because I was one of the tenants. . . . If you remember, the building fell on the day that the first Controlane landed in New York, and that's why so few people were killed—only a hundred odd. Almost everybody had gone over to see the ship come down on the landing field on Welfare Island in the East River. You'll remember that it was a Saturday, and the mayor proclaimed a municipal holiday, suspending business.

"I was over there on the Queensboro Bridge at eleven o'clock that morning, talking to a chap who told me a lot about the new ship and what a wonderful advance in transportation it was; it wasn't much bigger than old Robert Fulton's first steamboat. He told me about the lanes of control, and how the ship is lifted and propelled by power sent through the air by the stations; he said that those stations could lift a locomotive and train of cars and drive them through the air, and I was old-fashioned enough to marvel.

"There was some delay, and I didn't wait to see the ship arrive. If I recall what the trouble was, the power wasn't selective at that time, and some skylarkers were throwing things down from the bridge into the power lane for the fun of watching them vanish as the power seized them and flung them across the ocean. Word came that the ship was being held in Islip, England, until the bombardment was stopped. Fortunately, the cushion was working over there and nobody was seriously hurt, except in his dignity; the American Ambassador, in the midst of his speech, was hit with watermelon rind, and then came cucumbers and other edibles, none very choice or welcome. The New York police came up on the bridge to stop the rowdies' sport, and somebody cried out that the bridge was getting into the lane, and there was a panic. Somebody jostled me while somebody else snatched my watch, and I decided to go back to my office and to see the ship another day.

"I walked, of course. That was the quickest way to get around New York in those days, just before they gave out the taxi franchise. You remember the streets? Wheel to wheel—twice as many cars as could be accommodated, and everybody free to add still another. They didn't have then even the thousand-dollar license fee to operate a private car within the five boroughs."

"All cure and no prevention," rasped Cohen. "That was New York."

"I came up Forty-second Street and looked over at the Americus Tower across Bryant Park, and wished I owned it; it was a magnificent property. It was two hundred feet wide at the base, by half the block, and ninety stories high; an office building only six months old and with a gross rental of three million dollars a year. A very sweet proposition, I thought enviously, and Tweed is a lucky dog—Tweed, you remember, was the owner. One big success like that building, I thought, and I'd be satisfied. Tweed had chosen a fine neighborhood—a neighborhood of professional clubs. His building towered over them all; ninety stories of tapestry brick and Indiana limestone, with the new gold-plated gambrel roof, not a flaw nor a hair-line crack, all rented and pulling for Tweed like a Percheron.

"A dirt truck was staggering up out of the lot adjoining the Americus on the east. A new skyscraper was to go there; the excavator was working on a bonus against time, and he wasn't bothering with the Controlane ship.

"I was at Forty-second Street and Fifth Avenue, and was stepping from the curb to cross the street when I heard that first crash. It wasn't so loud; a door banged beside me would have startled me more. There was a rumbling as of a subway train heard over-ground."

I paused to light a cigarette. It was an old story, but one of unfailing interest to New Yorkers, with the fascination of the unsolved and perhaps unsolvable. The quiet streets of Manhattan could be fairly covered with the paper that has been blackened with discussions of the fall of the Americus Tower.

"Twelve rooms and five baths," said Mr. Murphy, "and you can use all the glass you like in the bathrooms. Suction glass, isn't it, Mr. Craig? We had a studio living room thirty-five feet long and twenty feet high; I think nothing has quite the tone of a real high ceiling. But don't forget the gas-proof casements closing all openings to the air. Mrs. Murphy and I couldn't rest in peace if we thought we might be smothered in our beds. Who could, now, really?

"Pardon me, Mr. Craig; I didn't intend to interrupt you. Yes, we were at our shore place in Maine when the building fell. We had left our home atop the Americus in the middle of May, and had been some six weeks at the shore when this terrible thing happened. How little we think! I can still see Mrs. Murphy waiting for me at the elevator. 'Darius,' she said, 'are you positively sure you closed and fastened all the windows, and left all the interior doors open? You are so absent-minded.' We had been troubled with mice, and when you're troubled with mice it is very wise to leave open all the interior doors in your home when going away, or the little villains will gnaw through the doors. You can prevent that sort of thing by using steel doors, but I don't think they're ever quite the same as fireproofed wood. So cold and institutionlike. Don't you think so?"

"Yes, indeed, Mr. Murphy. . . . And then came that steady and deafening grinding and squealing. My eyes were on the Americus, and I can tell you they popped. The windows of the showrooms on the ground floor were gone; I hadn't seen them go, nor heard them; you could hear nothing but that merciless grating and wrenching. The limestone ashlar between window openings fell out and I saw red iron. The building was—— Up shot my gaze to the roof. The shining surfaces up there seemed to be undulating in the sunlight.

"The building was—— The great Americus Tower—— No, I didn't believe it. Like our friend Mr. Murphy here, though with less excuse, I couldn't believe it. I stood there. The three stories of ashlar were undulating, buckling, and they seemed as pliable and elastic as rubber. They didn't disintegrate; they didn't fall. And then they fell—three stories of cut limestone—into the street. But so incredulous was I that they seemed to fall slowly, like sheets of paper wafting down.

"The building was falling. The Americus Tower was falling. The brickwork of the whole twenty-fifth floor—some say it was first the eighteenth, but I say it was the twenty-fifth—came away and swept down, slowly, floating. It was a steel-bearing job, of course; the walls were carried on the steel.

"The Americus was tilting. Its façade was dissolving. I claim that the steel failed first at the twenty-fifth floor. No matter now, but it was once thought very important, before the public took the bit in its teeth and brought in the verdict in advance of the evidence. I testified to it, telling what I saw; let other people tell what they saw. The façade below the twenty-fifth floor seemed to stand still while the upper twenty floors bowed toward the street. And then the whole vast fabric moved from its place in the sky—moved outward, slowly, so slowly; gathering speed.

"I turned and bolted for dear life. I never ran so; I didn't feel myself running; I was only intent on getting away, and I everlastingly got! I shot up Fifth Avenue. Flashing a look about, to see whence destruction would rush upon me now, I saw the people on the Elevated station on Sixth Avenue, agape, hands in air. I met a man last February in Sebring who was on that Elevated station that day; he told me that he was not conscious of being frightened, but that his heart stopped beating. I wasn't like that; I was stampeded. I'm told that the air was full of a vast roaring and whistling, but I didn't hear it. When the Americus came flailing down across Bryant Park and the blocks north—Mr. Murphy's private residence landed in Forty-fifth Street, knocking a ten-story loft into a cocked hat—the noise was heard in Irvington-on-the-Hudson and in Summit, in New Jersey; but I didn't hear it, upon my word. I was running.

"I was pretty heavy then, and I lost my first burst about Forty-fifth Street; a policeman had me by the shoulder. I was sobbing so for breath that I couldn't talk. I knew him and he knew me, and he told me that he thought I was running away after setting off a bomb, but he didn't tell me until months later, and then it had come out in the investigation that he had fired a shot at me. All he said at first was, 'It's Mr. Craig.'

" 'Did you see it?' I gasped.

" 'What? I heard it, God knows. What was it?'

"We were up to our ankles in water that was pouring down Forty-fifth Street; a main had been broken evidently. The street was level with water from building line to line.

" 'Let's go back,' I urged. And with him beside me, I ran the other way, as if a wave had caught me and swept me to Forty-fifth Street and was now receding with equally compelling sweep.

"Yes, there are a great many people in New York who have the mayor's holiday and the ballyhoo over the new Controlane to thank for their lives. Seven thousand people would have been at work in the Americus that was now lying across Bryant Park like a wrecked and beached steamer. Not since the last earthquake below a modern city has anyone seen the like; and not even then, let me say. Why, sixty years ago, at San Francisco, the steel-framed buildings stood; the outcry against them after the Americus disaster was reactionary panic. As well condemn steel ships because of the Titanic or Burgundia sinkings; the Burgundia was ninety thousand tons, and it went down like a tin cup. An accident is an accident, and such will happen to the end of time. The Americus disaster might have been much worse. I believe not more than a hundred and fifty people were killed in all, which was wonderful luck, speaking from the viewpoint of the rest of us.

"It took the Northard and the Hennesy wrecking companies four months to cut up the wreck and ride it away; they were two weeks clearing Forty-fifth Street of the metal roof. The Metropolitan, I understand, realized only two thousand dollars from the sale of the roof as junk—something queer about that. The Tyng process for deep mining had knocked the bottom out of the price of roofing metal, but scrap gold was still worth a dollar ten a pound; and there was the aluminum alloy. However, that's a small matter; I mention it because it was wrangled over during the investigation."

"That was a great investigation," said Cohen. "Some of those witnesses should have left the chamber under arrest, for they certainly violated the P. & P. Act."

"Publicity," I nodded. "Harrigan's testimony, that such a time was made over, is a fair example—barefaced publicity for the new striated steel process. I myself had sometimes thought that designers were going too far in lightening structural steel, but I'm no steel engineer, and I guess Hendricks knew his business; he designed the Americus steel. He exposed Harrigan's animus later on when he proved that the eccentrically loaded columns were braced laterally, bringing the thrust below the bracing; and that was accepted practice. As for the carrying capacity, those columns were rolled steel, and it's sound construction to impose a working stress per square inch of sectional area of ten tons. Harrigan's stuff was all laboratory stuff, theorizing; practice is what I go by, and I don't want anybody to stand around and tell me how to pick up the mule's hind foot, especially if he's selling crutches."

"They believed Harrigan."

"I tell you he was selling the striated steel process! Go look at the fifty-story Federal Building on Mail Street, and you'll see so-called settlement cracks. Settlement cracks, my eye; they're caused by the buckling of the striated steel columns. The material has tremendous tensile strength, and is fine for framing and connecting—trimmers, headers and tail beams—but I'd prefer even cast iron for compression. I'm no steel engineer, but I'm betting my money every day on my notions of construction. The steel didn't fail until the Americus was away out of plumb—when the masonry flaked off—and then it began at the splice plates. That was what let in the lurid yarn about the erectors neglecting to rivet.

"Excited and puzzled people will listen to anything; you remember the amateur detective who rushed in and told them that the first-floor columns were not steel at all but cast pottery! What started the wheels in his head was my testimony that the building had failed first at the street; that pointed inquiry at the base columns, and it was discovered that one of them had been eaten nearly through by sulphuric acid. The explanation was that a canister of the acid had leaked into the channel; the tenants of the ground floor were industrial chemists."

"Gentlemen, gentlemen," said Mr. Bligh.

"I believe, Mr. Craig," said Mr. Murphy, spreading his blue prints, "that you builders calculate your costs by the cubic foot; correct me if I err. Now, including the observation room and garage, I had about one hundred and ten thousand cubic feet in my residence atop the Americus Tower, and if I pay you eighty thousand dollars per year——"

"Hendricks insisted to the day of his death that the bearing stresses had shifted. He was the best steel engineer in New York, but he got his reputation, of course, by shaving the margin of safety. Any dub can design steel if he is given a free hand to thicken it, but the engineer who gets the business is the one who can lighten it. When the Americus was built, steel was selling for about a hundred per ton erected, and a difference of a thousand tons was worth saving. I do think his 40 per cent aluminum alloy was too much, in columns, but it was accepted practice.

"The steel failed somewhere, changing into thrusts what were meant to be compressions. Steel-framed buildings will stand a shaking, such as by earthquake, much better than an old-style, wall-bearing job, but they won't stand a lateral thrust so well. Speaking of wartime risks, like Mr. Murphy, a bomb exploding by a masonry wall will knock a hole in it and let the rest of the wall stand, but if that bomb knocked out a column of a steel-bearing job, the whole building would pull that way. That's my opinion, though I'm no engineer. Hendricks said that the loadings had shifted, bringing stresses to bear on columns that they weren't designed to carry, but he couldn't explain how it came about. His plans are still on file, and many competent engineers have passed on them."

"What about the foundations?"

"There was a looose end. That excavation beside the Americus might have had something to do with the catastrophe. Too bad that the excavator and all his men were killed when the gable wall fell on them. Dan Derry, better known as Dynamite Dan, was the excavator. He had been shooting several holes at a time, and that's not so wise, because an unexploded charge is likely to be left in the rock. If he detonated a forgotten charge under one of the piers of the Americus Tower, it might have brought the building down. The footings were examined after the water was pumped out, but nothing was learned."

"The water?" said Mr. Murphy, frowning.

"The main intake had been broken, naturally."

"Mrs. Murphy——"

"The footings were on bed rock and there was no evidence that they had shifted. You remember the report of the investigating committee; after reviewing all the guesses, they favored that of a theorizing engineer and guessed with him that the collapse was due to fatigue of materials."

"In other words," smiled Cohen, "they brought in a verdict of death by suicide; that the Americus Tower had become tired of life."

"May I venture to hope, gentlemen," said Mr. Bligh, "that we may soon find time to attend to our affair? If you can use this ten acres at Canabec——"

"Now there's an idea," said Mr. Murphy brightly. "Perhaps you can settle a domestic controversy, Mr. Craig. I have often debated with Mrs. Murphy—and not always in the best of temper—her use of my razors.

"Take a razor. If you use the same razor all the time, it grows fatigued and will not hold an edge. Lay it aside and let it rest, and it will pick up again. Or again, you have watched a man breaking a rock with a sledge; he hits it a dozen times without effect, and then the next blow breaks it apart."

"How interesting! You'll pardon me, Mr. Bligh, but I've always been tremendously interested in science."

"Fatigue of materials, Mr. Murphy," said I, "is a subject as to which scientists are still somewhat in the dark. They know it's a fact. And we may take it as a fact that if there was no margin of safety in the Americus Tower, if the steel was loaded to the limit of its strength, it would hold for a certain time and then get tired and let go."

"What you say about the water main having burst, Mr. Craig," said Mr. Murphy intently, "bears out my own contention at the time. Following the disaster, the city presented me with a perfectly preposterous bill for water, and I had to make an affidavit that I had not been in residence at the Americus Tower for a matter of at least six weeks. You can't imagine how insistent and disobliging the chaps were."

Cohen took the contracts that Mr. Bligh was thrusting at him, glanced at them and laid them down. "Skyscrapers, Mr. Craig!"

"Positively," said I. "A necessity of modern business; the big unit."

"What were you telling me, Mr. Bligh, about the Education Law in Canabec?"

"We're up-to-date," said Mr. Bligh contentedly. "Our young people must leave the schools and find gainful employment at the age of eighteen."

"I was twenty-four when I graduated from college," said Mr. Murphy. "Surely, Mr. Bligh, a boy can't complete the study of Latin, Greek——"

"Nor Sanskrit, either, Mr. Murphy; and every argument for the universal study of Latin and Greek holds for Sanskrit. It's the basic language and has a great literature. And, to most people, astrology is a more colorful and interesting study than the higher mathematics, and just as useful. You people made the mistake of letting professional educators decide what the children should learn; by limiting the school age we persuade our people to take interest in the education of their children and to see that their time isn't wasted. You people let lawyers make your laws, teachers control your education, soldiers plan your military establishment, and the general population plan your cities."

"Say rather the taxpayers," amended Cohen. "It was the majority of taxpayers who took advantage of the fall of the Americus to clap on a height limit. Their interests, certainly, were being injured by the erection of skyscrapers. That the process was inevitable, biological, was no satisfaction to them. We are builders, like ants—your Canabec is still not as tall in proportion as the cities raised by African ants; our cities are part of our life processes, and while we may ameliorate their effects on the individual, we cannot choke down the biological human urge to federate, to coöperate, to build—skyscrapers!"

"Surely you don't compare a human being to an ant, Mr. Cohen," objected Mr. Murphy. "He's ever so much more intelligent, you know."

"Which?"

"Eh? The human being! My goodness."

"Unproved, Mr. Murphy. First comes division of labor, then adaptation to the job, and then division of thinking. The ants have gone the whole route."

Cohen was extravagant, bitter, inclined to gibe; I knew what he was feeling. I, too, was a New Yorker of many generations, and I had come to see my city slipping toward decay. The country dweller finds a dearness in the familiar hill and stream; even the tree—mere springing vegetable—that shades his house is dear to him. Would not his pride be greater, more deeply to be wounded, if his people had builded every foot of that landscape, if that tree were a giant edifice raised by his people? Cohen and I, obeying the will to live which is stronger than love, fiercer than pride, were here to arrange for a vast migration to the city that was supplanting our incomparable New York.

"It is not a matter of sentiment," exclaimed Cohen, as if sensible of my thoughts. "The big building is a necessity and ordained! If we live we must grow; other times, other ways. Not a thing did they allege against the skyscraper that was the skyscraper's fault. Congestion of traffic? But the big building immobilizes traffic, gathers a multitude of people in one place. They say it turns the street into a canyon; but doesn't it turn the house into a hill? It's all morbid opposition to change; people want things to be as they are, as they were. Look at our antique collectors—my wife paid six thousand dollars yesterday for a brass bed, *circa* 1910; and she puts in our living room, where I have the best electric heating, an antique oil stove that smells to high heaven. Gordongin bottles with those quaint bootleg labels, phonograph records, cuspitoons and door keys. She calls me a barbarian. I have no love for the beautiful and artistic."

"Your wife collects G. G. bottles, Mr. Cohen?" said Mr. Murphy with new respect. "I'd love to have her opinion on the few that I've got hold of; I believe they are authentic bootleg, but there is so much faking done nowadays. Has she any American Scotch bottles? I have one with Just Off the Ship blown in the glass, and the dealer gave me his word——"

"Now, gentlemen, please," breathed Mr. Bligh. "Do remember that I'm a thousand miles from home and haven't had any lunch yet. Well, I shall have to call up." He took out his pocketell. "Are you there? Billy calling. . . . Hello, Molly! I just called you to say that I can't possibly get home—— What's that, sweetheart? . . . Oh, no, no. . . . But I say that I am not! I am in New York at a conference. . . . Yes, business. . . . Why don't I—— Now, Molly, how can you ask me to be so rude? . . . Oh, very well, my dear; in a moment." He turned to us, coloring, and said, "Will you permit?" We were married men ourselves; we smiled and got to our feet and bowed to his lady when she appeared; her eyes swept us vigilantly. "I'm sorry this had to happen, gentlemen," said Mr. Bligh, blanking her. "May we proceed now with our affair?"

"I know how you feel, Mr. Bligh," said Mr. Murphy, "and I speak as a fellow sufferer and not a physician. Last week I went down to the Chesapeake for a day's sport—clam digging. Nothing of any size in these waters but jellyfish, and I can't see them as game. I had a good day and got my full bag and was showing the shelly beauties to Mrs. Murphy when I chanced to lay down my pocketell and forgot it there. I tell you I caught it proper when I arrived home for being out of sight so long; besides losing a first-chop pocketell. It isn't as though I were often forgetful. A great game country, that. Robins, moles, even woodchuck. And frogs? In plenty. It's the sort of country our ancestors——

"But that reminds me, Mr. Craig, of something that's been bothering me off and on for the last twenty years, ever since I got that ridiculous bill from the city for a hundred thousand cubic feet of water. It's not of the least importance, I'm sure, but if the money was due and owing, I'd pay it even yet. You are quite sure the main was broken?"

"Certainly. . . . Mr. Cohen, we might as well get to it. If we sign up at once, I'll take the St. Lawrence express with Mr. Bligh, together with my superintendent, and I'll put an air blast into the lot tomorrow morning. You'll have to decide at once whether you'll use brick or glass; on that point, the mason machinists are talking strike against the new machines that lay a thousand bricks a minute. Glass will cost you a little more, but you don't need windows, and you have in every way a more modern building."

"I like brick walls for the homes," said Cohen. "Brick seems more homelike somehow. Lay up thirty-five floors in glass, and the upper sixty-five in brick. What about the lighting?"

"The good old lumen bulb is still my first choice. If I were you, I'd leave the Radio-light alone for the present; the service is very unsatisfactory more than three hours after sunset. For heating we'll use Silver Bar, the same as you have in your own home; the first cost is high, but then it becomes cheap and foolproof."

"We shall use gaslight and steam," said Mr. Murphy with innocent vanity. "These modern inventions are all a bit vulgar, don't you think? Give me the soft and mellow flickering of the gas mantle and the cheerful knocking of the steam in the radiators! It may cost quite a little more, but—I don't know; we like antique effects. They give a home such atmosphere. And we have authentic Hoover Period radiator inclosures for all the rooms." He smiled cozily. "It's a small matter, Mr. Craig, but I'm glad to be assured that I turned off the water in that bathtub in our residence in the Americus Tower. Mrs. Murphy always insisted that I didn't, and I always insisted that I did. And while we were still debating, the building fell down, so that it seemed that the issue would never be decided between us."

Cohen poised the pen; the responsibility of the moment pressed on him. It was fifteen years since New York had ceased to grow; twelve since it had registered its first loss in population. The movement away, to cities that had not adopted the arbitrary height limit, had slowly gathered volume, but ours would be the first large-scale desertion. It would be imitated.

"Our fault," he said, striving for definition, "was rating administration too highly; our chosen leader was the able executive. Executive ability didn't make America the first power on earth, and didn't save the other nations. It was imagination! It was private enterprise. Imagination is the gift of the few, and private enterprise welcomes it. Government—administration—does not welcome imagination, is hostile to it. Government expresses the mind of the unimaginative majority, and its first article of faith is that it is perfect. Private enterprise built New York, made it the world city; and then, because of a small catastrophe, it was shouldered aside, and the unimaginative majority, with its faces to the past, took charge. No more integration; no more striving upward; no more skyscrapers."

"But, Mr. Cohen," said Mr. Murphy with irritating patience, "there were great cities before there were skyscrapers. Look at London; look at Paris, Rome."

"They have their skyscrapers now," said Mr. Bligh. "And they always did build as high as they could. The modern building was impossible before the invention of the lift, the elevator. Even so, Rome had its ten and twelve story buildings—they must have had noble legs in those days. Well, Mr. Cohen?"

Cohen dipped pen in ink. "Look at the blood and tears that went into the building of the pyramids. And for what? One of the earliest stories of our race is of the men who tried to build a tower to reach the sky. I dare say they were stopped by the local taxpayers whose caves wouldn't rent any more."

I had been doing some figuring. "This may be of only historical value," I said, looking at the result, "but we're making history here. Mr. Murphy, you say that the city sent you a bill for a hundred thousand cubic feet of water? That water couldn't have come from the broken main or it wouldn't have registered on your meter."

"The city conceded that the meter had been put out of order by the crash, Mr. Craig, when I pointed out to them that my residence had been shut up for more than six weeks."

"You shut it up good and tight, did you?"

"Oh, yes. Mrs. Murphy——"

"Mrs. Murphy, of Chicago," murmured Cohen, catching my point. His black eyes were intent.

"Of New York, Mr. Cohen. . . . Yes, I made everything fast. I was in my room, drawing my bath—we'd sent the servants ahead—when my man Rogers sent down word that Washington Travel had notified him of an approaching disturbance, and that we'd better get going. Dressing rapidly——"

"Where was your bathroom?"

"On the mezzanine." He turned to his blue prints again. "We had five bathrooms in all. But I think, for our new residence at Canabec——"

"If you were drawing your bath," I said sternly, "you must have stopped the waste. And you think that, perhaps, you went away and left the water running."

"A mere surmise, Mr. Craig. But why are you so pressing? If you think that I should pay this bill even now——"

I drew a breath. "A hundred thousand cubic feet of water, gentlemen, weighs more than three thousand tons. In my opinion, though I'm no engineer, the steel frame designed by Hendricks would not have stood under a superimposed load of three thousand tons—not without buckling somewhere. If it would stand any such overloading, Hendricks didn't know his business. It's late in the day to reopen the investigation into the fall of the Americus Tower."

"Probably too late," said Cohen briskly, snatching the televistor, "but we can get an expert opinion in twenty minutes as to the engineering problem. . . . Hello, let me have the Building Department, and then the City Commissioner! . . . Remain here, please, Mr. Murphy. It seems that you kicked over the lamp, but perhaps the city is not yet destroyed. If there's a chance of scrapping the New York height limit within a reasonable time, and letting us build here as we should and must, my industry isn't moving to Canabec."

"Gentlemen, gentlemen!" exclaimed Mr. Bligh, of Canabec, vexedly.

Waldemar Kaempffert

THE DIMINISHING DRAFT

"WELL, I've engaged an assistant," I announced to my wife one day at luncheon.

"I am glad of that. You have been working much too hard. Who is he?"

"It isn't a 'he,'" I replied as carelessly as I could. "It's Jeanne Briand."

"But why Jeanne Briand? What qualifications has she? What does she know of biochemistry?" she inquired, too searching, I thought, in that high-pitched, staccato voice of hers which latterly had grated on me.

"She's taken her master's degree," I explained as best I could, "and besides she had a course in biology under Calhoun."

Mr. Kaempffert is better known today as science editor of *The New York Times* than as a science fiction writer.

The wife of a university professor may not be versed in the subject with which his name is identified, but she knows that academic standards are high. Knows that a vivacious, copper-haired, laughing-eyed girl who has dabbled in a few textbooks and chased butterflies with a net is not ordinarily given an important post in a famous biochemical laboratory.

"I think you might have taken young Mitchel or some other postgraduate in your department."

That was all we said. She suspected something. There was no question of it.

And so Jeanne was duly installed in my home laboratory. I made it very plain to her that she must keep regular hours, also that she must conduct herself as my assistant and not as the woman whom I loved and whom I hoped to wed.

From the first I had my misgivings. It was Jeanne who conceived the idea of working in the laboratory with me—not I. She was as out of place among my instruments and reagent bottles as a wood nymph.

It is needless to dwell on the circumstances that swayed us, needless to recount here how difficult it was to part whenever we had passed an hour together, needless to picture the dreamy longing that hung over us both until our hands and lips touched again. That is a characteristic of every week-old love.

"Please let me help you in your work," she pleaded over and over again. "I want to be near you always. Let me do anything—anything. I can keep the instruments clean. I can write down your notes. It is unbearable to see you only like this, once in a long while. Let me work with you in the laboratory."

"But you forget," I reasoned, "that the laboratory where I do most of my work is in my own house. And I am married. Some day we shall be together always. Think of the risks that we would run. We can't have a scandal. Sooner or later we would be discovered."

I had intended to make a clean breast of the whole affair to my wife and free myself from my marital ties in the conventional way, even though it meant the end of my university career. But Jeanne could not and would not wait. A man of stronger will than mine would have yielded. The desire to have her ever near me, to see the winsome smile on her face, to sense her presence in the same room, moved me more than her arguments. In short, I yielded.

Scientifically speaking, she was all but useless in the laboratory. She had some talent for drawing, and so I employed her in making diagrams for my treatise on "Experimental Evolution."

She radiated femininity. She had an elfish way of interrupting me in my work. At the most critical stage in dissecting the head of an insect under the glass, she would come up and stroke my hair or kiss the nape of my neck. If I reproved her, she wept, which meant much kissing away of her tears and mollifying her with the endearments that all lovers automatically invent on the spur of the moment. And yet, she honestly tried to help me, simply because of her slavish devotion to me.

Although she needed constant supervision, her drawings were excellent. Indeed, they soon justified her presence in my laboratory in the eyes of the entire university.

It was about a fortnight after she became my nominal assistant that I assigned to her the task of making a series of sketches to demonstrate the effect of baroturpinol on parameba.

I may mention in passing that parameba is a microscopic animal—a mere cell—found in stagnant ponds, and that in a dilute solution of baroturpinol the whole structure of the creature undergoes a remarkable change. It was I who discovered the effect of baroturpinol on microorganisms of the parameba class. Immersed in baroturpinol the few cells of which parameba is composed dwindle and dwindle under the microscope until finally the organism, still keeping its own shape, disappears.

I had completely misinterpreted this disappearance of microorganisms under the action of baroturpinol. I thought that they merely disintegrated. It was Jeanne who taught me otherwise.

One day, while she was engaged in making the drawings which would show the progressive disappearance of parameba, Jeanne exclaimed, "They've come back again!"

"Who has?" I questioned, thinking that she was talking of people whom we knew. Besides, I was engrossed in correcting the proofs of a scientific paper.

"Why, the parameba. I can't understand it!"

A glance convinced me that she was right. In less than a minute I saw a specimen literally grow under my eyes into a full-fledged parameba. I can liken the proceeding only to the coming of an object toward one, with all the attendant increase in size that the movement implies.

Perhaps I may make myself clearer if I say that the restoration of parameba, as I saw it then and many times after, was like a railway train traveling toward one from the distance. At first a far speck is visible; then the outline of a locomotive engine can be distinguished; and at last a huge machine and thundering cars threaten to crush one out of existence.

But that was not all. *Parameba came back alive!* Every biologist and chemist supposed that baroturpinol was a deadly poison. At all events, I had noticed that when any microorganism was brought into contact with even a trace of baroturpinol, all activity ceased. Death seemed necessarily to precede the process of shrinking. I could hardly believe my eyes when I saw my resuscitated parameba moving about with that characteristic tumbling motion by which it is so well known.

"What have you been doing?" I asked.

"Just what you told me to do."

"Dear, dear Jeanne," I said, taking her two hands in mine. "Do you know that you have made what may prove to be a very important discovery in biology? Do you know that you may have upset the whole theory of life?"

She clapped her hands. But at the time the wonderful scientific significance of what she had seen was lost to her. She saw that I approved of her, and she was happy.

But what did this astonishing revival of parameba mean? Over and over again I watched for the return of specimens under the microscope. Parameba would not return. I questioned Jeanne closely; I even watched her prepare a few slides herself, hoping that she had unconsciously departed from the routine that I had prescribed and had contaminated the baroturpinol in a way that would explain everything.

At last she remembered. She had touched the slide with a little glass rod in order to shift it on the stage of the instrument. The rod did not seem clean. She thought to improve matters by wiping it. A painstaking and conscientious laboratory worker would have used a piece of sterile cotton. Jeanne used her pocket handkerchief. It was clear enough that that little piece of linen was strangely linked with the accidental revivification of parameba.

My deduction was confirmed when I, too, experimented with the handkerchief. I deposited a single drop of stagnant water on a clean glass slide. Under the powerful lens I saw parameba tumbling about. Then I added a drop of baroturpinol (one gram of baroturpinol to a cubic centimeter of distilled water is the proportion, as every one knows), and at once all activity ceased. Apparently killed, the specimens of parameba began to shrink in that curious manner upon which I had already dilated. I took a glass rod and wiped it on Jeanne's handkerchief. First making sure that parameba had quite disappeared, I touched the little drop of moisture on the slide. My guess was right. It was Jeanne's handkerchief. Parameba came rushing back to life as startlingly as at first.

The handkerchief had been definitely linked with the phenomenon, but I was in the dark as much as ever. What mysterious properties had this little piece of fabric that it should thus divert the whole course of modern biochemistry?

"Tell me, Jeanne," I said, "did your handkerchief touch anything here —some solution?"

"No, I'm sure."

"But you must have done something with it. Feel. It's a little damp."

"I wiped my eyes with it," she admitted reluctantly. "I had been crying at something that you said."

I did not stop to inquire what it was that I had said. A light dawned on me. Her tears had so uncannily brought back parameba to life! And tears—what are they, when stripped of all sentiment, but salt water?

A spectroscopic analysis of Jeanne's handkerchief convinced me that common salt had the property of bringing back parameba to life.

Dozens of experiments showed that almost any solution of salt would answer; the stronger it was the more quickly did life triumph over death.

And now began an investigation which was a strange mixture of scientific research and love-making. To Jeanne it was like a play. She was very much bored when I would repeat tests perhaps twenty-five or fifty times simply to be sure of my results. But when we experimented with a new organism, she was all eagerness, all dancing eyes and clapping hands.

It was Jeanne who made the discovery in the first place, and Jeanne who developed its full possibilities. She had no well-considered plan of work; she simply allowed her impulses, her girlish whims to sway her.

"I want things to happen," she would say, as I tried to explain to her how time-wasting was this unscientific, haphazard, blind plunging into a new and unexplored field. And yet, through her insatiable desire for excitement, her dramatic interest, we found out what really happened when higher organisms were subjected to the action of baroturpinol.

As for me, I confined myself entirely to simple-celled organisms, all so small that they cannot be seen with the naked eye. Here, I thought, was enough work to engage me for years. But that was too tame for Jeanne. She had the imagination and the daring that seem to accompany scientific ignorance.

I kept a little aquarium in one corner of the laboratory—a spawning glass jungle of fresh-water life. It was a never-ending source of entertainment for her. I have known her to sit for an hour at a time watching crayfish crawl lazily along on the bottom, or a school of tiny goldfish fighting for a crumb that she had mischievously tossed in.

One day—it was about two months after she came to me—she ran to me all radiant, holding a bowl at the bottom of which were two or three tiny golden flakes. They were so small that I had to hold the bowl against the window and view them by transmitted light.

"What have we here?" I asked, wondering what new fancy had seized her.

"Goldfish," she said.

"Nonsense," I retorted.

"Yes, they are," she insisted. "I took some Japanese goldfish from the aquarium and dropped them into baroturpinol, and they all shrank up like this."

If the original discovery of parameba's disappearance and return had startled me, how shall I describe the stupefaction that this announcement called forth? I saw at once what I had only guessed at before. Parameba had shrunk beyond the limits of visibility under the microscope, which accounted for its utter disappearance. But the goldfish, being much larger, had shrunk until each became perhaps the size of a dot on the letter "i."

I gazed at the girl with increasing wonder. Never would it have occurred to me to leap at once from simple microscopic organisms to so high a form of life as a fish. On the other hand, I must say that it was my academic timidity, if I may so call it—my systematic way of proceeding stepwise from one experiment to another—that had led to the original misconception of baroturpinol's effect.

To every physician and every biologist in the world, baroturpinol was simply a germicide. True, Tilden, who had discovered it, had noticed that it had a curious puckering effect on living tissue, for which reason it had been condemned as quite useless as a substitute for mercury bichloride, phenol, and similar agents, and had been adopted simply as a convenient and cheap hospital sterilizer. And now comes my Jeanne, my capricious, dancing, playful Jeanne, a mere trifler in science, and at once uncovers the hidden possibilities of a completely misunderstood compound, not because she is a biologist, but because she simply wants to be amused.

Obviously it was my business to find out whether, like the microscopic organisms that I had thus far examined, the baroturpinoled goldfish would be revivified by a solution of common salt. I decanted the liquid in the bowl, washed the inanimate, shimmering flakes in distilled water, and then filled the bowl with a solution of salt.

The drama of parameba's return to life was repeated on a more striking scale. Very slowly the dead creatures began to expand. Soon they assumed their normal shapes—not, I repeat, that they had lost them by shrinking, but simply that the curves of their bodies were developed. It was not until they had regained their full size that life itself returned.

To me the thing was as startling as if a man, who had been poisoned by prussic acid, and who had been pronounced dead, were to open his eyes, get up, and walk. I took some pains to explain all this to the intensely amused Jeanne, and I repeated the experiment with a particularly large goldfish which I abstracted from the aquarium. I made no impression whatever upon her. She promptly christened the fish "Lazarus" when he came back to life, and adopted him as a pet.

This impulsiveness of hers, this reckless disregard of all system and plan, could this be a form of mental activity which I had been wrong in regarding rather lazily as showing only an average order of intellect? Some one has defined intuition as a swift deduction from present facts. If that be so—I am no psychologist—then we must reckon with intuition as well as with the slower and more deliberate methods of reasoning in scientific research.

If Jeanne was anything she was intuitive. I felt that I must credit her with powers that were denied me. After all it was she, and not I, who had stumbled upon the amazing action of baroturpinol. I had done little beyond repeating her fanciful experiments under rigorous scientific control. She showed me the stars, as it were; I merely counted them.

The possession of a common secret strengthened the tie between Jeanne and myself. It was as if we had found some beautiful, priceless gem which we had decided to keep for ourselves and never to show to the world. We lost all self-control. In the beginning we had maintained a semblance of formality. She kept regular laboratory hours, coming in the morning at nine and leaving at about five in the afternoon. It was always "Professor Hollister" and "Miss Briand" when we spoke to each other before others.

But in truth the hours that we spent together in the laboratory each day heightened our love for each other, made us more and more indispensable to each other. It became so difficult for us to leave each other that we even went into the woods together for specimens to be experimented with in the laboratory. These specimens she could easily have gathered for me quite alone. The university students and the villagers began to talk about us.

It was my wife, of course, who imparted that information to me.

"You are making yourself ridiculous," she announced.

"Indeed? How?"

"Every one is talking about you."

I pretended not to understand. An attempt of mine to divert her attention from a topic which it made me uneasy to discuss failed ignominiously.

"Even the postmaster in the village comments on your conduct with Jeanne Briand. Everyone stopped talking when I came to the regular sewing-circle yesterday, and looked at me in a pitying sort of way. If you have no consideration for yourself, at least consider me."

I got up and stalked out of the room. I was neither polite nor brave.

The time had come for action. I could not go on in this way. A scandal was inevitable, and the best that I could now do was to mitigate it in some way. Jeanne and I must separate until such time as I could free myself with the aid of the divorce courts. I must tell her.

She read in my face that something was wrong when I stepped into the laboratory late that afternoon.

"You are in trouble, dear," she said. "What is it? Tell me."

And then I told her of the conversation with my wife, of the utter impossibility of concealing our true relations much longer.

"We must separate, Jeanne; it's only for a little while—until I am free. And then we shall come back to each other again, and we will work together in the laboratory not as professor and assistant, but as man and wife."

She burst into tears. Never before had I seen a human being in such distress. She was convulsed with anguish, so that her whole body shook. I took her in my arms and did my best to soothe her.

"It will only be for a little while," I repeated over and over again. It was all that I could think of, all that I could say.

The sun had long since set, and the laboratory was soon quite dark. We sat together on the couch in the corner in close embrace, Jeanne's head on my shoulder.

"You must rest," I said, and laid her on the couch and sat beside her.

She half murmured, half moaned something and let me do with her as I would.

How long she lay there I did not realize at the time. Hour after hour slipped by. At last it struck me that we could not stay thus all night—that I must take Jeanne home.

"Come," I admonished her, "we must go now. It is very late."

I helped her to her feet, pressed a button, and turned on the electric light. She was as limp as a drooping flower, all numb and listless. I walked to the closet and took her hat from its peg.

As I did so I heard footsteps in the corridor leading to the laboratory. Who could this be?

Completely unnerved as I was, distracted by Jeanne's despair, I was incapable of thinking clearly. It was one in the morning by the laboratory clock. Jeanne never stayed in the laboratory later than six. No one must find her here now.

In my ordinary senses the fall of a footstep in the corridor would not have disturbed me. Now I acted automatically and with cowardly absurdity. I ran to the door and locked it instead of flinging it open wide.

There came a knock.

If some one had leveled a pistol at me and threatened to shoot me, I could not have been more alarmed. Jeanne, too, was frightened. We looked at each other questioningly, two helpless lovers.

"Let me in," shrilled a voice outside. It was my wife's. From what she had told me earlier in the day, I inferred that she must have been watching Jeanne like a cat, and that she carefully noted when the girl came and went. Where to find her now she knew only too well.

Concealment was useless.

"What do you want?" I asked.

A flood of impassioned accusations followed, in which Jeanne was referred to as "that woman," with much incoherent repetition of the phrase "wrecked home." The situation was damning.

Months ago I had decided that the divorce proceedings should be free from the usual scandal. But what a ghastly story this would make in the newspapers! I could read the suggestive headlines and the salaciously worded account of the manner in which my wife had trapped me—a university professor. The sensational newspapers in particular would rejoice in the opportunity of pillorying the supposedly academic scientist and of exposing him as if he were a libertine in cap and gown.

It was Jeanne who saved us. I stood like one paralyzed, not knowing what to do. It was the rustle of her skirt that brought me to my senses. I turned around just in time to see her raise a beaker of baroturpinol to her lips and pour it down.

I know that I cried out, for there was a sudden cessation of the clamor outside the door. I rushed to Jeanne's side. Good Heavens! What would the effect be?

Never had we experimented with baroturpinol on anything higher than a fish. She lost consciousness in my arms. I thought she was dead. She was pallid and stiff, as if *rigor mortis* had set in. Then came over her that change which I had observed under the microscope and in the test tube. Her form dwindled and dwindled in my arms as if it were slipping from me, until at last I held nothing but her limp clothes.

It was as if both her soul and her body had drifted away from the room. As if she had slipped out of her earthly fabric like a butterfly from its chrysalis. I dropped the bundle on the floor and began to grope within it. Somewhere within these folds I knew must be the shrunken body of my Jeanne.

At last I found it—a little white form. I slipped it into my pocket. The clothes and hat I stuffed into a chest.

My courage had returned now. I stepped to the door, unlocked it and flung it wide open. My wife entered, and with her a maid whom she evidently brought as a witness. Her lips were tightly drawn; her eyes were mere slits. If ever there was an infuriated woman bent on vengeance, it was she.

She looked about her. Under other circumstances her astonishment would have been comical. All this furtive watching, all these clamorous accusations—all for nothing? She darted to the closet in which Jeanne would hang her hat and coat and I my laboratory aprons, convinced that Jeanne was hidden there. She threw back the door with such violence that the knob indented the plaster wall.

"Where is she? What have you done with her?" she screamed.

"You see that you are mistaken; there is no one here."

She saw that further inquiry would be useless. Outwitted but not deceived, she swept angrily out of the room. I locked the door after her.

I sat down at the laboratory table, took out of my pocket the thing that had once been my Jeanne, and placed it before me. My eyes were blurred with tears. So this was all that was left to me of Jeanne. This was the price of my weakness and my cowardice! She was dead now, and I felt as if I had been an accomplice in her suicide.

There comes an interval in every grief, an interval of calm, during which all mundane affairs seem trivial and even one's own misery becomes petty. It is as if one had passed out of a long, dark, narrow passageway into a vast open twilight beyond. In one of those intervals of calm I regained sufficient control of myself to examine the white remnant of Jeanne.

The thing that to my fevered touch had felt like a mere shapeless mass when I hastily thrust it into my pocket, revealed itself as a little statuette of wondrous beauty. It seemed carved out of ivory, this exquisite, miniature, frozen Jeanne. What would not Cellini have given if he could have shaped a figure so beautiful?

Everything was white except the hair, her eyebrows, and the lashes of her closed eyes. The lips were delicately tinted like a budding rose, but they had not the rich color of pulsating life. As for her hair, it still lay in tiny coils about her head, a mass of twisted, coppery brown. Jeanne must have been in the act of falling when I caught her in my arms. One foot of the little figure was raised, and it seemed as if she were about to sink down on one knee.

A sculptor would have marveled at the mere material of which this rare work of art had been fashioned. It seemed like wax; yet it had nothing of the oiliness of wax to the touch. Could it be ivory? It was too exquisitely white.

And then the wonderful perfection of its detail! I was afraid to touch the lashes of the eyes, lest I should break them. And the little ears, how finely they were modeled! The little hands and feet, how scrupulously every curve and line and hollow had been preserved! And the dear body of her, how plastic for all its lifeless rigidity!

For the first time in my life I understood the ecstatic ravings of artists when they endeavored to reveal to others the beauty that is so evident to them. Beauty such as this left one inarticulate.

The face perplexed me—or rather its expression. Jeanne was all gaiety and animation. But this reduction of herself suggested nothing of that. How could it? Jeanne was motion personified, flitting hither and thither like a butterfly. These placid features, with no trace of the smile that lit up the dearest face in the world, were still and cold.

The aspect of this precious, pallid beauty, all that was left to me of Jeanne, overcame me. I know that I sobbed, and I am not ashamed to own it. I vowed to myself that I would preserve this remnant of her, this visible evidence of her self-sacrifice, as a thing to be worshiped. I would enshrine it in some secret, fitting way; it would be my holy of holies.

Dawn was breaking. I washed my hot, fevered face and held a water-soaked towel to my swollen eyes for a few minutes. Fresh air and a long walk would do me good, I thought. I wrapped the white figure tenderly in cotton, dropped it into my pocket, and then walked out into the open.

I must have wandered about in a stupor. For the life of me I cannot now tell where I went or how I returned. I know that the sun was well up in the heavens when I found myself in and went to my room. In the afternoon I had to give a lecture on Mendel's laws to the senior class in biology. I flung myself down on the bed, dressed as I was, hoping that I might snatch an hour's sleep, so that I might not appear too manifestly beside myself with grief.

I must have dozed, for I was awakened by a knock at the door. It was the maid. I was wanted at the telephone.

"Say that I can't be disturbed," I directed her.

"She says it's very important," was the reply.

"Who does?"

"Miss Briand's landlady."

My state of mind can be imagined when I say that I could not divine why Jeanne's landlady wished to speak to me on the telephone. I found out quickly enough when I answered.

Did I know where Miss Briand was? asked the voice over the telephone. She had not been at home all night, and it was now past noon. Was she at the laboratory yesterday? When did she leave? Should her disappearance be reported to the police?

I could tell from her voice that the woman was concerned more about herself than about Jeanne. She ran a respectable house, she insisted again and again. She did hope nothing had happened which would compromise her on her establishment. I reassured her as best I could and promised her that I would look into the matter of Jeanne's disappearance and communicate with her again.

Her reference to the police startled me. It brought me to my senses. It had not occurred to me before that a human being cannot step out of existence, as it were, unchallenged. Suppose the police were to descend on the laboratory and investigate!

What could I say? No one would believe me, of course, if I told the truth. About the experiments with parameba and how they had led step by step to Jeanne's undoing. Even if I summoned the best experts, even if they confirmed my discoveries, what biologist would be bold enough to administer baroturpinol to a human being and prove that even the highest forms of life yielded to the strange influence of that mysterious compound? And what human being, short of a madman, could be found who would willingly sacrifice himself? Good Heavens!

And then there were Jeanne's clothes. They would surely be found in the chest.

I sank into a chair. My whole body was bathed in a perspiration of fright. Suppose that I were accused of murder? A divorce scandal was bad enough, but a murder, a murder—

Lecturing was out of the question. I telephoned to the university that illness would prevent me from attending and that the class was to be dismissed. I had to think this out; I must gain time. My case was clearly desperate.

All at once a ray of hope flashed upon me. Why not try salt? If parameba, a sea-urchin, a goldfish—and a fish is, after all, not so very low in the scale of evolution—can be restored to their natural proportions and to life, why not a human being? Yes, perhaps the salt solution would save me and bring back my Jeanne to me.

But what reason had I to suppose that because a few animals could be reduced and expanded at will, I might bring Jeanne back to life? Suppose that the little statuette should return to life, but to remain a mere miniature of Jeanne? That was too horrible!

Worse still, suppose that the figure should reassume the girl's natural shape, but that no spark of life would reanimate the body? What then? I should be worse off than ever. The white remnant of her that I carried with me could be hidden. The clothes in the chest, too, could be disposed of. No one could prove that Jeanne was really dead.

But a lifeless body—

I fled into the laboratory. If ever a man was on the verge of madness, it was I. Tormented by grief at the loss of Jeanne and stricken with terror at the prospect of arrest, I felt like a wild beast at bay.

I longed for some simple-minded, practical, unscientific friend to whom I could turn for counsel in my need. I knew the difference between a holothurian and a jellyfish, but in the cloistered university I had lost track of human hearts and problems. However, my problem was my problem; I alone could solve it.

It came to me very clearly at last that I owed it to Jeanne to make some effort at resuscitating all that was left of her. The resolution was more easily made than carried out. Where should I conduct this momentous experiment?

The laboratory naturally suggested itself first. I dismissed the thought almost at once. There was no vessel large enough to hold a human body, and suspicion might be aroused if I had one brought in. I might go to a hotel and engage a room and bath; the bathtub would surely serve the purpose.

But suppose that the little figure of Jeanne should swell and magnify, and suppose that life should not return. I would have to explain the presence of a corpse in my room—the corpse of a woman who had played a part in my life and for whom the police were searching. That would help neither Jeanne nor me. Better a thousand times that she should remain in my pocket than that!

Finally I came to the conclusion that I must go to some lonely place by the sea. Had we not discovered early in our investigations that any solution of salt, even seawater, performed the miracle of bringing back to life organisms which had been diminished by baroturpinol? Besides, would it not be easy to dispose of the corpse if life did not return?

I looked at my watch. It was just half past three. Glaston-by-the-Sea was three hours' distant by the railway. If I left this afternoon, by night all my doubts and fears would be dispelled.

I had not slept in twenty-four hours. Some rest I must have. My nerves were so unstrung that I could feel my eyelids quivering; I could hardly touch a book or an implement without dropping it.

So I went into my room, and bathed, and threw myself down on the bed to catch what little sleep I could.

Glaston-by-the-Sea is a fishing village comprising nothing more than a dozen houses. In front of it lies the ocean; in back tower cliffs of limestone. The sand stretches on either side of the village for miles and miles. Walk ten minutes away from the village and you might as well be in the Desert of Sahara for any signs of human life that you can see.

I knew the coast well; many a specimen had I collected among the rocks as the tide went out.

It was dark when I alighted from the train, four miles from Glaston. The full moon was rising in the east—a great round, yellow topaz that crept higher and higher in the sky. I had not counted on a bright night.

To carry out a hazardous experiment in the aspect of that cold, luminous disk seemed too public. It was so like a round, inscrutable face that looked down at me in benignant curiosity. Then it occurred to me how strangely fascinated Jeanne had always been by the full moon. How she had longed for the time when we might watch it rise together in some such lonely place as this, shut off from the strife and the clamor and the prying eyes of the world. I am not superstitious, but it did seem as if that great ball in the sky might be a good omen.

At about ten o'clock I reached the shore two miles above Glaston, for I had carefully avoided the village. It was flood tide. The sea was dappled with opalescent ripples. Now and then a swelling wave would roll up on the sands and the water would tumble reluctantly back again in a vast expanse of foam. Only the rhythmic wash of a smooth sea broke the silence of that moonlit solitude.

Jeanne's clothes and hat I had brought with me in a traveling bag. I took them out and spread them on the beach just as I imagined she would have arranged them herself in her chamber.

Now that I thought of it, this idea of coming to Glaston and making an heroic attempt to bring Jeanne back to life seemed like a stroke of genius. What if the experiment did fail? What if the reduced image of herself did resume its normal shape, but without coming back to life? I could leave the corpse on the sands. It would seem as if she had died in some inexplicable way.

Here were her clothes all neatly arranged, testifying mutely in my behalf. There was no sign of violence.

One by one I took off my own clothes and laid them down beside Jeanne's. Very, very carefully I unwrapped the parcel in which I had carried her about. I feared that I might break off a strand of hair or nick a foot or hand.

Holding the figure in my outstretched hands as if it were a sacred image, I walked into the sea straight toward the moon, my face uplifted. This was more than a scientific experiment. Human life, human happiness, human love were at stake.

Now that I look back at the events of that unforgettable night, the whole proceeding must have seemed more like a religious ceremony than a frantic man's desperate effort to save the thing that he held most precious. Surely no worshiper who had ever entered an ancient Egyptian temple was more reverentially hopeful than I, nor more innocently expectant of a miracle that would sweep away all earthly doubts and reveal the hand of destiny itself pointing toward the light.

Slowly the water rose to my knees, to my waist, and at last to my breast. It lapped the frail figure in my hand. I clutched the thing lest it should slip from my grasp. How long I stood thus, shoulder-high in the waves, I do not know. Perhaps it was only five minutes, perhaps as long as a quarter of an hour.

I know that I was stricken with terror for a time, for the figure in my hands might have been made of stone for any change that I could feel.

Was I to fail? Was Jeanne hopelessly, irretrievably dead?

Then a moment came when the figure seemed to slip in my hands. I grasped it tighter lest I should lose it. Still it slipped—slipped as a fish slips in the hands. Now I realized what was happening. Jeanne was growing, literally growing in my crooked fingers! I almost swooned.

Even if the swelling miniature were not the most precious thing in the world to me, even if it did not mean happiness and life itself, I would have found it difficult to retain my self-control. Very, very slowly the figure grew to the size of a child. I had to hold it in my arms now; it was not only larger, but perceptibly heavier.

A doubt assailed me. Would it stop growing? I prayed that it might keep on.

Presently it grew so large that I could no longer hold it in my arms alone. I walked back a few steps and lowered the figure so that its feet touched the bottom. But I saw to it that it was completely immersed, fearful lest some monstrous effect might be produced if even a shoulder were dry and could not grow with the rest.

In half an hour, I should judge, what had been apparently an exquisite statuette, something that I could carry in my pocket, had become the full-sized form of my Jeanne. But it was still hard. There was no feeling of yielding flesh—nothing but the rigidity of so much clay.

For that I had been prepared by the observation that I had made in my laboratory. Life returned to a shrunken organism slowly, almost hesitantly.

At last I felt Jeanne soften in my arms. She was a thing of flesh now. Her form had become supple and flexible; I could feel it as so much tissue.

And then the miracle of miracles happened! Her bosom heaved; she sighed; her eyes opened. She moaned, and stared at me, utterly bewildered. Her mind could not orient itself at first. In a dim way she seemed to realize who I was.

I could feel her arms tighten about my neck, and so I carried her to the beach, in the most ecstatic and exalted state in which I have ever been.

I told my wife everything—everything of the initial experiments with parameba and the goldfish, everything except Jeanne's bold swallowing of the baroturpinol in a critical situation and of her subsequent miraculous reanimation. Jeanne meant all to me; and my wife had ceased to be, if I may say so, what she never was. I wanted a divorce, and I said so frankly.

"So this is to be the end?" she sobbed bitterly.

"I see no other way. To remain as we are, and to pretend that all is as it should be between us, would mean misery for both of us. It is better that we should part."

"But what if I should refuse? Is it right that you should begin a new and happy life and that I, after all these years, should drift about aimlessly and wretchedly? This home is mine as much as yours. I made it what it is, and shall I give up everything for a woman whom I hate?"

There was much more in the same vein. I had not counted on this. It was partly bitter hatred of Jeanne that swayed her and partly wounded pride.

It had never occurred to me before that marriage means more to a woman than the building of a nest and the gratification of the mating instinct. In her scheme of existence the conventions or vanities of married life are enormously important. Her conjugal rights, the social status brought about by the mere act of marriage, are to her what his patent of nobility is to a duke—something not to be relinquished without a struggle.

My wife refused point-blank to divorce me.

"But that is senseless," I argued. "If I stay here, our life will be a mere travesty; if I leave you and go my own way you will not be unhappier. What do you gain by refusing?"

"You can't marry a woman who has ruined my life, and whom I hate. By refusing to divorce you I destroy her. No decent man or woman will befriend her, knowing what she is to you."

With that she flounced out of the room.

This turn of events I had not foreseen. I knew that divorce meant the end of my university career, and for that I was fully prepared. But to have the finger of scorn pointed at the woman I loved—

I am a social being. Companionship means much to me, and it meant as much to Jeanne. For a few months we might be sufficient to ourselves. Then would come a time when I would wish to spend an evening with congenial friends, and Jeanne with women who give teas and form organizations for the uplifting of the poor and unenlightened.

What then? I could hardly venture to cross the thresholds of those temples of purity and virtue whither I would eventually be drawn, and on my arm a woman whose relations to me were regarded as scandalous.

And she—she would undoubtedly be rebuffed if she sought to enter the circle within which she now moved so freely.

You see that a scientist can be far more practical in his reasoning than the world supposes. After all, his whole training teaches him how to deal with facts.

I was to meet Jeanne that evening in a dense grove, near a little farm-house about half a mile from the end of the trolley-line. Ever since her astonishing restoration we had arranged to see each other there three times a week. Her return to the laboratory was out of the question for the time being.

There she was at the appointed time and place, looking very demure in a neat white dress which she had made herself. She saw that I was troubled, and I told her at once the outcome of the afternoon's parley.

Either she would not or she could not see the situation in its true light. Was I not everything in her life? She was more than willing to forego ordinary social intercourse if she could only work and live with me. A thousand reasons she advanced to prove how unnecessary the outer world must be to us.

She was a born romanticist, living perpetually in a fairy castle on a mountaintop capped with silvery clouds. In that atmosphere there is no time; Jeanne lived only in the present. I could hope for no practical assistance from her. I must reason this problem out for myself.

So I changed the topic at the first opportunity, and we passed the rest of the evening in the usual lighthearted way.

During these meetings we talked chiefly of the romantic possibilities of baroturpinol.

"How simple and cheap it would be for us to travel," she would ramble on. "You could carry me in your pocket just as you did to Glaston; or I could pack you away in my handbag and take you with me. If I had a friend, I might even have myself sent to you by parcel-post. Salt water you can get everywhere."

Of course I smiled at this, but I'm not so sure that Jeanne was not serious.

That was the last I ever saw of her.

Two days later I was to keep my tryst with Jeanne for the third time that week. I was in the grove at the appointed hour. She did not come. Was she detained? Or was she ill? I fretted and fumed, hoping that each figure that loomed up in the darkness (for the grove was near the road) might be Jeanne. At eleven o'clock I gave up all hope of seeing her that night.

My wife met me as I opened the door of my house.

"May I speak to you a moment?" she asked.

I hung up my hat and followed her into her own room. She took from her safe a little box and laid it on her dressing-table. Next she raised a window which opened on a paved court below. It was clear she was following a well-thought-out plan of action.

"I believe you wish to say something to me," I said to relieve my suspense.

"Yes." Nothing more.

She untied the box, concealed it from me as she did so. Presently she turned around, holding in her hand an envelope.

"Read this," she said. "It came yesterday."

The envelope had been steamed open. It was addressed to me in Jeanne's handwriting.

"And so you open and read my letters?" I queried angrily.

"When I suspect that they concern me, I do," she retorted coolly.

I reproduce it here. That letter and a lock of hair that she once gave me are all that I have of Jeanne.

Dearest Dick:

I have been thinking so much of that wonderful night on the beach at Glaston—the night when I was born again on the bosom of the sea, just as if I were another Aphrodite. How beautiful it was to awaken and find myself looking at you by the light of the moon! I want to live all that over again, to come back from oblivion and find myself clinging to you.

If I were to ask you, I know that you would never consent to my becoming a dead image of myself again. You would suspect my motive if I were to ask you for some baroturpinol. So I have bought what I need. If you will come to meet me in the grove beyond the farm at the usual time on Friday, you will find only a little white Jeanne in the midst of her clothes.

Put her in your pocket and take her with you to Glaston next Monday. The moon will then be full.

Jeanne

Was I frightened? I can hardly say. It was as if some one had struck me a blow. I was stunned.

Intuitively I sensed the diabolical thing that my wife had done. I had told her enough of my first experiments; the rest Jeanne's letter made sufficiently plain.

"When I read this," she explained, all the while standing, "I understood everything. I know now what happened in the laboratory that afternoon when I knocked at the door.

"Now, listen carefully to what I say. I have told you that I hate this woman, that I will not permit her to take from me what is rightfully mine. Late this afternoon I went to the place that she mentions in her letter. I did not know just when she was to meet you, and I didn't care. It was merely a matter of waiting. I hid myself behind some bushes and watched.

"A little while after sunset I saw her down the road. She came into the grove and sat down on the grass. Then she took off her hat and laid it beside her. She sat very quietly, looking down the road through the trees. At first I thought that she was afraid and that she would not take the solution at all. Then I realized why she did nothing. She was waiting for you.

"She was clever! She was not going to run the risk of leaving a heap of clothes in a grove an hour before you came, with the chance of arousing the curiosity of some boy who might wander into the grove. She would wait until she saw you far away. You would reach her just at the right moment. So it proved. I could see you myself fully a quarter of a mile away; it was still quite light. She never took her eyes off the road. I think she must have seen you before I did. She opened her handbag and took out a bottle before I caught my first glimpse of you.

"The next I knew, she had placed the bottle to her lips and drained it off. I turned away. I didn't want to see her shrivel up before my very eyes. A quarter of a minute, I thought, would be about long enough for her to shrink. So I counted fifteen and turned around. Where she had sat was only a heap of clothes.

"There was not a second to lose now. You were almost at the grove. I crawled out of the bushes and gathered up everything, clothes, hat, and all. Then I ran away from the place just as you were about to enter."

All the while she had been handling the box. I knew what it contained, and my brain was feverishly busy devising and rejecting, over and over again, plans to get it away from her; by stealth if possible, by force if necessary. I should have leaped from my seat at once and seized her, but I sat still, dazed, as if in a kind of hypnotic trance.

"And here is your Jeanne," she almost screamed as she took out a white, sitting figure. "You will never, never have her again. I take her so, and this—*this* is what I do to her!"

This time I did act. I leaped to my feet, knocked over the table that she had so ingeniously placed to obstruct me, and rushed at her.

But I was too late.

She was at the open window.

She raised her hand high above her head, posed there for a fraction of a second, the very incarnation of hate and vengeance. Then she dashed the white thing upon the stone pavement of the court below.

I heard it break into a hundred pieces as it struck.

WARD MOORE

PEACEBRINGER

THE first mention of Isaiah MacAdam did not, of course, carry that soon to be famous name—indeed, the name did not yet exist—and the small notice in the local papers, too insignificant to be aired on the radio or carried by press wires, did not hint its connection with that strange figure whose shadow was so soon to be cast over the entire world.

Like this: *Los Angeles: An outlying branch of the Bank of America was robbed today under circumstances which have baffled the police. At 11:25 A.M. all employees of the branch and three depositors present at the time experienced a feeling of extreme lassitude followed almost immediately by loss of consciousness. All present awoke, as from a deep sleep, between 11:40 and 11:45. It was discovered that bills and coins in the tellers' cages were missing, though no checks, money orders or securities had been touched. Apparently no attempt had been made to enter the vault which was standing open. The police have grilled all employees and the three depositors, but the only discrepancy in their statements is the assertion of a guard that there were four, not three, depositors at 11:25. Announcement of an arrest is expected shortly. The loss is approximately $11,000.*

That was the beginning. The few who saw the story laughed and no doubt said it was a clever conspiracy by the clerks and tellers with three outside accomplices. Everyone was more interested in the newest phase of the cold war.

This story first appeared under a different title; the one it now bears is the author's own choice. In Mr. Moore's words, "The story was retitled by *Amazing Stories* 'Sword of Peace,' which I thought much less apt, not only out of the usual writer's touchiness over his own work, but because the peace-sword synthesis is an indirect New Testament allusion and my story used quotations from Isaiah."

The next episode caught the attention of many more, both because of its more spectacular nature and because it was coupled by the papers with the first, and played up. The Los Angeles Federal Reserve Bank was held up under identical circumstances. Of course, "held up" is a misnomer; everyone in the huge building went to sleep about ten in the morning, not to revive till almost three. Messengers, visitors, salesmen, business people entering on errands between those times found, as soon as they went through the massive doors, clerks and porters slumped as though dead or drugged. Before they could raise an alarm, they too experienced a sense of weakness followed by unconsciousness. They too awoke, without any ill aftereffects, within a few minutes of the original victims. This time the loss was nearly $3,000,000.

There was no question of conspiracy here. Some of the most trusted officers of the Federal Reserve, men of impeccable character and distinguished repute, were among the anesthetized. It was robbery, not a doubt of it, robbery under baffling and frightening circumstances. Someone had discovered a new technique in larceny, and if the highwayman could repeat his feat, as it seemed he could, no bank in the world was safe from his mysterious depredations.

Many attempts were made to explain the trick of the robberies. Mass hypnosis was the most popular, but this was discounted by the latecomers' falling under the spell as surely as those there all along. Rays, electronic impulses, invisible gases were all offered as solutions to the enigma. Scientists were interviewed respectfully if uncomprehendingly on their opinion of what Winchell called "the current doughziness" and the interviews were printed on the front pages. The Attorney-General announced that every effort of the FBI would be engaged to probe the mystery and put the perpetrator in the Federal Penitentiary.

I was then, as I had been for some time, research chemist at Ribbon Plastics, one of the largest manufacturers of gadgets and war materials in the country. Mr. Joseph Ribbon, president of the corporation, summoned me to his office. "You're a scientist—what's this all about?"

"Well, Joe," I began—nearly all the employees of Ribbon Plastics called the boss Joe; I don't know exactly why, for he was neither likable nor friendly, and there was a rumor he wrote poetry in secret, but it was a custom, perhaps to make up for our substandard pay—"well, Joe, I don't know that my being a scientist helps. I've been working a long time on cellulose and its products; nothing there to explain this."

"If these robberies keep up we'll be out of business; money'll be worth a dime. Anarchy! Chaos! No market for plastics!"

"Sorry I can't help you," I said cheerfully, and went back to my laboratory. I put a fresh pot of coffee on the electric plate—I like it fresh and often—lit a cigarette, and opened the afternoon paper. If Ribbon Plastics was on the way out, I might as well take it easy while I still had a job.

The front page was almost evenly divided between the latest U.S.-Soviet tension and more speculations about the "daylight sleep robberies." I glanced through the news section, read the comics attentively, and then, in sardonic mood, turned to the want ads, something I hadn't done for fifteen years. Four solid columns were devoted to a single ad—mostly white space, for the text was short, though large and black.

MEN, WOMEN & CHILDREN
INTERESTED IN
WORLD PEACE
WORLD GOVERNMENT
WORLD SANITY.
PERMANENT JOBS FOR ALL
TOP PAY TO START
EXPERIENCE IMPOSSIBLE
THEREFORE UNNECESSARY
PERSONS OF GOODWILL
APPLY TO ADAM
BOX 131313

Well, well, I thought, maybe I won't have to worry after all; there seems to be a position for me with Mr. Adam. I must say he's reckless with his cash. To tell the truth, I wasn't greatly impressed, certain it was some freakish stunt by one of the irresponsibles who bob up periodically in our great city.

But the words "World Peace" and "World Government" for some reason set me thinking, perhaps because my mind was idle at the moment, back five or six years, when there were two of us in the research department at Ribbon Plastics. Oh, plenty of others have been a little crazy on the subject of universal peace and global federation, but I don't think I'd ever known one quite so fanatical as Ira Atz. Good wood chemist too, one of the best—between ourselves, and strictly out of earshot of Joe Ribbon, I wasn't even in the same class—Ira had just two interests in life. One was the eradication of nationalism, the other was lignin. That was his specialty, lignin research. He was bound and determined to prove that lignin was the most important part of wood; my cellulose was nothing but a toy, a by-product; lignin was the tree itself. And he was going to do things with lignin, make it produce everything coal tar did and a lot more. Lignin was going to change the world—a one-world, without nations or boundaries.

I hadn't seen Ira for a couple of years—not since Joe Ribbon fired him personally. If Ira had been smart, like me, he would have kept Joe happy with a new "discovery" every now and then that Ribbon Plastics could market for a few hundred thousand. But he was a pigheaded idealist, intent only on finding out what made lignin tick, down to the last chemical combination. So, full of world federation and wood chemistry, he went out of our lives.

Of course I forgot about good old Ira immediately. Next day there was another big robbery, this time netting $400,000. And Mr. Adam's ad disappeared. Instead, a news item announced that the paper's offices had been swamped with mail and the appeal would not be run again until the volume of letters slowed.

For almost a month there were no new developments. Joe Ribbon's blood pressure eased, business went on, and I decided it didn't matter about Mr. Adam's advertisement since I still had a job after all. Then there occurred the affair at Lockheed.

The holdup of the giant aircraft factory, a plant covering many acres and employing thousands of workers, was instantly acknowledged the most amazing criminal act of the century. The magnitude of the operation, the boldness of the scheme, the precision of the execution and the nature of the loot caught the public imagination as the bank robberies had not. In daylight, this great plant, situated in a populous industrial district, was entered by an unknown number of persons; guards, clerks, workers and executives were sent into the now notorious coma, and every finished aircraft flown off into the blandly expressionless sky. It was as spectacular as it was incredible.

But while there was no sign of the vanished planes, there were, for the first time, faint clues on the scene of the outrage. Clues pointing to nothing tangible, but at least partially dispelling the more fantastic theories, such as those predicating invisible men or visitors from other planets using strange powers.

Some of the guards stated that just before the moment of drowsiness they were approached by strangers who did not appear to have proper credentials to enter the factory and who seemed to be stalling for time before stating their business. Several guards spoke, not too certainly, of a sensation of dampness prior to being overcome. And two employees who were strongly allergic to sedatives reported themselves violently sick afterward. This was the only time the anesthetic had produced an ill-effect.

Meager clues, nothing to set against apprehension that shook the whole country. Martial law was declared in Los Angeles County, enormous rewards were posted for the apprehension of the robbers; the army, marines, State Guard, the FBI and many other agencies of government were put on full time duty tracking down the criminals.

In the excitement one newspaper reporter's work got rude treatment; what was to have been a front-page story was buried in the second section. Like many others, the reporter had been interested in the want ad inserted by Mr. Adam a month before. But his interest was professional; he smelled a story in it. He had therefore written to the box number, first finding out from the ad-taker that it had been paid for by one I. Adam, with an address in the Edendale district. Hanging around the classified desk as inconspicuously as possible, he saw the contents of the box—a bulging mailsack—picked up by a uniformed messenger who carried it to a long-abandoned and condemned factory building on North Broadway. Questioned by the reporter afterward, the messenger said the order had come in by telephone and he had delivered the sack to an ordinary-looking man of perhaps between thirty and forty who gave him a dollar tip.

The newsman hesitated whether to bluff his way into the factory or wait for a possible reply to his letter of application. He decided to wait; late that night his phone rang.

"This is Adam."

"Yes, Mr. Adam."

"Not Mister, just Adam."

"Yes . . . Adam?"

"That's better now: you're serious about a fulltime job for peace and world government?"

"Oh yes, M—Adam."

"Good. Married?"

"No, sir."

"No 'sirs'—just Adam. Member of the national guard or military reserve?"

"No . . . Adam."

"Religion?"

"Does that matter?" asked the reporter.

"If you mean, do certain affiliations bar employment, the answer is no. But we have many duties, not all similar, and Muslims, say, might prefer activities not agreeable to Quakers."

"Episcopalian," said the reporter briefly.

"Can you be here at seven tomorrow morning?" Adam named the North Broadway address.

Next morning, still regretting his curtailed sleep, the reporter found two or three hundred applicants in front of the factory, as well as sightseers, cops keeping order, and fellow journalists. He resigned himself to hours of waiting, when a hitherto unnoted loudspeaker said hollowly, "All bona fide applicants came in and wait. Applicants with appointments only." The line started moving inside the empty building, dusty and echoing.

The applicants cracked the usual feeble jokes, shuffled feet, looked half hopeful, half sheepish. Outside, the loudspeaker droned, "No more interviews till two o'clock. No more interviews till two o'clock. No more . . ." It was evidently a transcription, and a nervewracking one.

The feature story described how the men and women were sifted into smaller and smaller groups by means of questions from another loudspeaker until finally he found himself in a tiny office, bare and dusty as the rest of the building. Facing him was a man who made the messenger's "ordinary looking" seem remarkably accurate. Possibly just under forty, of medium height, on the lean side of plumpness, light brown or dark blue eyes behind glasses, fair complexion, small nose, rounded chin, a few gray hairs—there was nothing to make him stand out from hundreds of thousands. He spoke brusquely, not giving the impression of arrogance, but rather of being inescapably pressed for time.

The questions were the usual ones, interspersed with others less customary. Was he free to travel? Willing to take orders? Any orders? Any orders at all? How sincere was his desire for world peace? Willing to risk his life for it? The reporter got the impression the questions were intended to assay his sincerity as well as his value, but that the questioner was no trained psychologist. In five minutes the interview was over; the newsman was told he would be notified if he were wanted. He felt somehow he had failed to past a test.

That was about all, except for checking the various loose ends, which was what had delayed the printing of the story. The factory had been rented to a Mr. Ivan Adam on the understanding it would be vacated on short notice and not used industrially. Mr. Adam had paid three months' rent in cash, offered no references, never asked for any refund although the factory was used only for a week. The Edendale address was an apartment house where no Adam, Adams, or similar name was known. All Ivan Adams or Adamses the reporter was able to run down were positively not the man on the phone or in the dusty office. He did succeed in reaching some of the other applicants, but their stories only duplicated his. He guessed these were, like himself, weeded out; those accepted by Adam not being available.

Well, I thought, finishing this pointless report, the paper must be hard up for copy. Like others I promptly forgot the want ad and its aftermath.

But not the Lockheed holdup and its consequences. The first few times the stolen planes, identifiable by their lack of CAA numerals, landed at airports for gas, attempts were made for prolonging the refuelling while the authorities were called to struggles with the pilots and shots by zealous attendants. All were baffled by sudden drowsiness, followed by sleep. No worthwhile identifications were secured; the pilots seemed of all ages and types.

It was one of those hot, cloudless September days when the deafeningly blue sky screams for some contrast to relieve its monotonous uniformity, that sophisticated watchers, mostly small boys, were startled by something new in the way of skywriting over the air of Los Angeles. Those who could anticipate every word of an Honest John announcement and knew the proper placing of the dot in Pepsi Cola were at a loss to identify the white smoke.

GR

The watchers were fascinated. A new advertiser, possibly a new product. Bets were made as the plane zoomed for the next letter.

GREAT

Great what? Everybody asked. Great bargain? Great car? Great drink? Impatience was hard to control as the plane spelled out SHALL.

Great shall . . . ? Maybe a new car. Great Shall. Some began to remember faint rumors that the Shall Oil Company was putting out a car to boost its gas sales.

GREAT SHALL BE

This made no sense at all; opinion was divided between theories that the skywriter had his copy mixed up, that he was practising, or drunk. However they continued to watch tolerantly while the first letters expanded into unintelligibility and the plane went on doggedly spelling out:

GREAT SHALL BE THE PEACE OF THY CHILDREN

Everyone sighed relievedly. A nut. A religious fanatic. A screwball defiling with biblical quotations skies sacred to the immortal quips of advertisers. There was general satisfaction among the audience in labelling the skywriter and some annoyance at time wasted with such absurdities. Several camera enthusiasts directed lenses upward. When some of these pictures were published it was found the plane carried bogus CAA markings—that it was one of the planes stolen from Lockheed.

The discovery produced a terrified bewilderment. Bank robbers with a new method of undermining the rights of property were a monstrous evil; religious nuts who quoted the prophet Isaiah—the source of the words was established even before they faded—were funny, but there was nothing funny about larceny, nothing naughty about reproducing the phrases of the Old Testament. The inconsistency first confused and then enraged the man in the street; if "Isaiah," as the gang leader became popularly known, could have been identified and seized he would have been lynched with righteous dispatch.

It was soon clear that "Isaiah" guessed the public temper, for there were no more sacred texts written in the Southern California sky. The mobilization of jet fighters which had been prepared mercilessly to shoot down the pious bandit waited idly on the ground. But he brought himself into wider notice another way.

The usual Sunday afternoon crowd shuffled slowly and a trifle self-consciously toward the door of the Columbia Broadcasting studio on Sunset Boulevard. In an hour Jack Benny's coast-to-coast broadcast would be on, and those ambitious enough to squeeze inside would see and hear the comedian in person instead of having to listen through their radios.

The lucky ones filed into the seats. They were properly warmed up with commercials, community singing, musical numbers, and jokes left over from last week's program. But no sooner was the "on the air" flashed and the famous line, "Hello again" delivered than the audience fell into a sound sleep. That this was not due to any failure of Mr. Benny's wit was confirmed by the entire cast as well as the staff of CBS joining them in slumber.

All over the country, listeners—the corners of their mouths ready with expectant smiles—were startled by "'Hear, ye that are far off, what I have done; and yet that are near, acknowledge my might.' This is Adam, Adam, the peacebringer. My time is short, but the world's time is shorter still. I won't say another war will end civilization; you have heard that too often, and anyway it is questionable if civilization exists. But another war will destroy the earth, at least as far as animal life goes. As long as national sovereignty and all its trappings—armies, navies, flags; diplomats, jealousies and rivalries—continue, war is unavoidable. We have seen how nations cling to their selfish prerogatives and yield only to force. I, Adam, have that force, and I shall use it to make the world into a single nation.

"I urge you, wherever you are, to join me. Many of you have friends who are already peacebringers, devoted as I am to this cause. They will approach everyone they believe ready; these will reach further out to *their* friends. Those who join with us will be well paid; in money now, in peace, happiness, prosperity and liberty soon. You need have no scruples; the domination of the world for peace will be accomplished without the taking of a single life or the injuring of a single individual. I have the means to put anyone, anywhere, into a state of suspended animation for any length of time; thus all resistance will be overcome without hurt.

"One final word. I have no personal ambitions. I desire neither to be world dictator nor world prime minister. On the day of universal peace Adam will disappear, along with the last flag, the last battleship and the last bomb."

If there had been excitement before, there was frenzy now. Even before the transcription had whirled through its last groove police converged on the great studio. They pushed their way through the crowd outside, who had no idea of what was going on, past the portals, to find ushers, scattered like ninepins, sleeping stiffly where they had fallen. The auditorium of the Jack Benny show was packed with a mass of slumberers; on the stage the comedian and his company were slumped over chairs or microphones. On a turntable the platter still revolved aimlessly, the needle scratching obstinately round and round a voiceless groove. There were no signs of Adam or his accomplices.

Accomplices he must have had, for it would take at least five to replace the honest technicians and see that the broadcast went through. A cordon was instantly thrown around the building to prevent anyone leaving before establishing satisfactory identification. While the network program was continued from New York with a soothing organ recital, the police went through the auditoriums, control rooms and offices, where, besides a few souvenirs, all they found were sleepers. Or possibly, as they admitted later, the guilty ones pretended to be asleep.

It was true, when the effects of the potion wore off after half an hour and identifications were made, they picked up many miscellaneous offenders, including traffic law violators for whom bench warrants had long been out, but none who could reasonably be suspected of complicity in the outrage.

The scene was searched eagerly for clues. The record was scrutinized not only for fingerprints, but for origin. But the prints were smudged, suggesting the use of gloves, and the disk was a common make, sold by the thousand. The law was no nearer solution than before.

Isaiah Adam's purpose in interrupting the Benny broadcast succeeded. Monday's paper was largely devoted to Adam, his predecessors —like Savonarola—theories of the nature of his hypnotic agent, and a recounting of his earlier adventures, including the want ad and the investigations of the curious reporter. It also ran a strong editorial urging that something be done.

I suppose everyone expected a lull after the Jack Benny episode; I know I did. But though Adam might not be a trained psychologist in the opinion of the reporter, he was enough of one not to give the world a moment to forget him. I say the world, for by this time other countries too were concerned with what he would do next.

As Adam had promised, mysterious phone calls began coming to all sorts of people, people connected by no obvious ties, who had no particular social, economic, political or ideological classifications. I suppose we heard only of the unsuccessful calls by the Peacebringers when patriotic and indignant citizens reported the messages to the police. The ones which recruited the recipients into Adam's organization were naturally not publicized; the dupes instead busying themselves finding still newer adherents.

And now came the period of the less spectacular raids. There was no duplication of the Lockheed raid or the seizure of CBS. Banks continued to be looted in spite of precautions, but we were becoming hardened to that. More frequently small factories, printshops, binderies suffered. The theft of much electronic equipment led authorities to believe that the building of one or more portable radio stations was in progress, and this was confirmed shortly afterward by the sudden interpolation into popular programs of quotations from Isaiah. The moment of respectful silence following a commercial would be rudely shattered by, "Let the people renew their strength: let them come near; then let them speak." Pianissimo passages during symphonies were backgrounds not only for the coughs of those sufferers from chronic bronchitis who find concert halls the most congenial infirmaries, but for the thundering of, "Come near, ye nations, to hear; and hearken, ye people; let the earth hear, and all that is therein; the world, and all things that come forth of it. For the indignation of the Lord is upon all nations, and his fury upon all their armies. . . ."

Efforts to locate these mobile units by triangulation were unavailing, though flying squads were on constant alert. Irate listeners wrote furious letters and hastily organized groups badgered the Federal Communications Commission. The Un-American Activities Committee reported that Isaiah Adam was the notorious Soviet agent Ivan Adamin, and demanded he be cited for contempt, tried for subversion, imprisoned for conspiracy and deported for sedition. Prominent figures stated that the free enterprise system was threatened, and the continued downward fluctuations of the stock market were attributed to him.

In this atmosphere of angry helplessness the arrest of an extremely obscure individual whose name, fittingly enough, was Jack Smith, was, at least for a moment, the grasping of something tangible. Smith made a crash landing with his two-engined plane on an airfield beside the Mississippi near Memphis. Attendants came rushing up. The pilot climbed out; as he faced them they began to feel drowsy, and relaxed, sleeping, to the ground. They did not come to for twenty minutes.

When they did they wasted no time speculating over the disabled plane or looking vaguely around for the vanished pilot, but sprinted to phone the authorities, who now exerted themselves as they never had in cases of mere murder, lynching, race riots or other minor crimes. Roadblocks were set up, the area was scouted from the skies, every inch of ground was combed for the fugitive.

When Smith was found he submitted quietly to arrest and search. The mystified police, who had been momentarily expecting the familiar symptoms of stupefaction, could only surmise that he had discarded in his flight whatever means of inducing sleep the Peacebringers carried about with them, for nothing suggesting a container of gas, drugs, or anything similar was found on his person. Refusing to talk, he was lodged in the Memphis jail.

As the news that a follower of Isaiah Adam had been taken was shouted over the air and screamed in the headlines, the damaged plane was inspected with the utmost scientific thoroughness. As suspected, it was one of the stolen Lockheed planes, with false numerals on the wings, and it contained a powerful radio transmitter and a stock of Adam's transcriptions. But there was no sign of whatever produced the hypnosis, and the fingerprints, which were many, did not check with those on file of any known criminal.

No amount of questioning evoked anything from the prisoner beyond the admission that he was indeed a Peacebringer, and a dissertation—cut short with a blackjack by an impatient questioner—on the urgent need of everyone there joining Adam. He was put in a cell, awaiting the arrival of experts from Washington. Next morning the jailers, turnkeys and policemen woke from an unexpected and uninvited nap to find the cell door open and the prisoner gone.

In the midst of the uproar over the escape of Smith, with its inevitable charges of negligence and corruption, Isaiah Adam acted again. After the Jack Benny affair every precaution was taken against another such, but as Adam demonstrated his independence of actual entrance into the studios this watchfulness was gradually relaxed. This provided the opportunity for the interruption of a soap opera sniffling its way—

by transcription—through its midweek catalepsy. Housewives, busy with vacuum cleaner and handkerchief, were startled in the midst of episode 517 of "Dick and Peter" to hear the voice of Adam, a voice rapidly becoming as familiar as the only slightly flatter tones of President Truman.

"'This is the way, walk you in it.' There is no other road to survival except the road of peace and world federation. The time has not quite come for Adam to give final warning, but it is proper to make an example to show that Adam is serious. For years there has been civil war in Greece. Listen to Adam, world: Within three months Adam will bring peace there."

Of course the speech was cut off the air before it was half given, but it was reproduced in the papers and showered over the country in the first of the Peacebringers' propaganda leaflets. Although Adam's threat of imposing peace on Greece was taken as just another evidence of insanity, there was general delight in the prospect of being relieved, if only temporarily, of his presence. He could hardly expect to stop the fighting by remote control; while he was about his quixotic errand there would be no more inexplicable bank robberies, interrupted programs, jail deliveries, or daylight sleeps.

Naturally every care was taken to prevent his departure from the United States or his arrival in Southern Europe. If private citizens were to be allowed to go around stopping wars at will, the whole structure of society might be irrevocably injured. But since no one had the remotest notion of who Isaiah Adam was or what he looked like, the embargo was difficult.

That he slipped through the cordon anyway, the world learned by a spectacular event. On June 22, the Royal Hellenic arsenal at Piraeus was destroyed in a bold "daylight sleep" raid, following the familiar pattern. Guards crumpled under the mysterious drug, as did the workers there, and while they were bemused the Peacebringers took every shell, rifle, machine gun, bomb and lethal weapon in the place and tossed them into the Aegean. Millions of dollars' worth of American-made equipment was lost in a few hours.

Before the raging and astonished Greek authorities had time to catch their breath and execute more than a dozen "accomplices"—all of whom had been going unimaginatively about their various businesses while the raid took place—the scene shifted to the actual battlefront. Whole companies, regiments even, of government troops were overcome by the soporific, and while lying around in unmartial sleep, deprived of their weapons.

While the Athenian police and detachments of the army searched the ruins of the Acropolis for the headquarters of the Peacebringers, great gaps were thus made in the defense wall protecting the kingdom from the incursion of the rebels. Through these gaps disaffected Greeks, Albanians, Macedonians, Bulgars, Jugoslavs and Russians poured.

Adam was denounced over a panicky radio and the royal family prepared to move to Crete or even Egypt.

But as the invaders moved triumphantly down the Peloponnesos, they too encountered the eerie power of Adam. Squads, platoons, battalions, found themselves suddenly overcome by irresistible drowsiness —usually in proximity to some innocently gaping peasants—only to awake, disarmed and helpless in enemy territory. But instead of being, as they naturally expected, beset by ferocious government troops brandishing the most improved American weapons, they encountered only bewildered soldiers as helpless and munitionless as themselves. The victims, after a period of mutual suspicion, gave up the attempt to prolong the conflict with fists and rocks, fraternized and found common cause in the outrage to their belligerent virility perpetrated by the Peacebringers. By the time the last rifle was broken and the last machine gun destroyed, the former enemies had united in a single implacable cause; to exterminate the foreign meddler who had dared to insult Hellenic manhood.

The Greek interlude radically changed the status of Adam—or Isaiah MacAdam as he was now beginning to be called. Exactly how this permanent name evolved is uncertain, though both *Time* and *The Saturday Review of Literature* speculated at length on its origin. Perhaps the natural sensibility of ordinary folk revolted against the conjunction of vowel sounds, instinctively intruding strong consonants between, or a sense of propriety tried to bring the name more into harmony with common usage. Amateur philologians disputed whether the MacAdam had been bestowed because of its association with roads in view of the Peacebringers' harping on "the way," or if it did not spring from a notion that his thriftiness with human life was Scottish. At any rate, from a purely American criminal, a sort of glorified gangster with a scientific secret to implement his refusal to harm those at his mercy, he became an international menace.

Nations which had been on the iciest of diplomatic terms began wary conversations regarding common action against Isaiah MacAdam. Nicaragua and Costa Rica, fearing he might choose to hypnotize their raiding parties, agreed on a mutual defense in the event of his appearance in Central America. India and Pakistan hastily concluded an amicable union, and the Dutch made overtures to the Indonesians for an armistice effective until he was disposed of.

The public opinion polls, which had formerly inquired only, "How would you go about trapping Adam?," now asked, "What do you think of Isaiah MacAdam's methods?" The results were headed, U.S. OVERWHELMINGLY CONDEMNS MACADAM. 89.04% answered "approve," six percent replied "disapprove," while 23.0001% had never heard of him. Lest these figures cause confusion, the analysts showed conclusively that only .00000007% of the citizens—or ten and one half persons—really backed the Peacebringers. Publication of this figure brought immediate demand for the arrest of these ten and a fraction who must constitute the entire organization. The only obstacle to this step was the original one—no one could identify the criminals.

Apparently the miscreants themselves were unaffected by the polls, or else the cockiness engendered by the Greek venture made them callous. Now the purpose of the earlier looting of the printshops became apparent as the country was flooded with all sorts of written propaganda. Leaflets, pamphlets and books choked the mails; when the Postmaster General threatened to declare MacAdam's matter unmailable he was defied—over the radio—and told any such action would result in complete disruption of all mail service through periodic stupefaction of the postal employees.

So Americans continued to receive not only the Book of Isaiah and copies of *Union Now,* but accounts of the end of the Greek civil war, tracts on peace, arguments showing what could be done with the money presently spent on armament and copies of Gandhi's Autobiography. After a month of this bombardment, MacAdam made his expected radio broadcast.

"'Make an uproar, O ye peoples, and ye shall be broken in pieces; and give ear, all ye of far countries; gird yourselves, and ye shall be broken in pieces. Take counsel together, and it shall come to nought; speak the word, and it shall not stand; for God is with us.' This is Adam, or if you prefer, Isaiah MacAdam. The time has come for serious consideration. I have demonstrated fully that I have the power to keep my word, also that I have no personal ambition. I could have made myself dictator of the Balkans, yes, of all Europe if I had wanted. But all I wish is an end to war, a beating of swords into plowshares, and spears into pruning hooks, so that 'nation shall not lift up sword against nation, neither shall they learn war any more.' I know this is what you are looking for too—what do you profit by wars or national sovereignty?

"The United States is the greatest and most powerful country in the world, so it is fitting it should lead the way—be the first to disarm utterly. It is also proper that the seat of the new world government be here, perhaps in Kansas, the geographical center of the continent. On the first of the coming year, then, the present government of the United States will be abolished and delegates from all over the world will meet in Lawrence, Kansas, to form a new authority for the entire globe. By that time the disarming of the country will be complete, you will have begun to enjoy the benefits of peace: lower taxes, freedom from anxiety, the beginning of the end of obstacles to free trade—so naturally you will be eager to bring these benefits to the rest of the world.

"I urge the present authorities to cooperate with me rather than try the futile job of hindering. On this account I am allowing a week before I begin my work, for Congress and the President voluntarily to disband the armed forces and take steps to supersede the Constitution with a temporary charter for the world. I hope they will see the advisability of doing this freely instead of waiting for me to move first."

Among the many whose fright was turned into panic by this ultimatum was my employer, Joe Ribbon. His answer to the threat of Isaiah
MacAdam's rule—for in spite of his disclaimer nearly everyone was
convinced he was about to gas the entire population, appropriate their
property and make them his slaves—was to close down Ribbon Plastics,
including the research department, indefinitely. "What's the use of
staying in business? No more military contracts; besides, that fellow
can go anywhere, like the invisible man. Maybe he'll come around and
inspect my books." Mr. Ribbon had a morbid horror of anyone but himself being intimate with his books; the thought shocked his commercial
modesty.

"No," he said emphatically, "Ribbon Plastics closes as of now; we'll
reopen when that fellow is dead or in jail where he belongs. Anybody
wants his job back in a hurry better get busy and catch Mr. Mac-
Adam."

That night I was sitting in the little two-room apartment on Beverly
Boulevard where I had lived for years, drinking cup after cup of coffee
and wondering about the future. It was not just the closing down of the
plant which distressed me; I was long since independent of the wage
Joe Ribbon paid me. But I had patented several improvements in high
explosives and invested the royalties in the companies which manufactured them. If Ribbon Plastics was but the first to close, if Mac-
Adam's mad plans were carried through, what did the future hold for
me? My gloomy speculations were interrupted by the doorbell.

Certain it was some explorer who had lost his way looking for
Eloise, Jane or Yvette, or perhaps a friendly poker game or a dispenser
of marijuana, I went, not too agreeably, to the door.

"Hello, Jeunas. Looking the same as ever; you haven't changed a bit
in years."

The hallway was soot black; I was standing in the lighted doorway.
Whoever was out there could see me, but I could distinguish nothing
more than a looming blur. "Who is it?"

"Such hospitality! Aren't you going to ask me in?"

"Oh come in, come in. At least then I can see who you are."

He accepted my grudging invitation and closed the door behind him.
It took me almost a full minute to recognize him, he had changed so in
the few years since I had seen him last. His face was still commonplace,
but impressed on its prosaic planes were deep lines, his hair was shot
with gray, and there was a turbulent, impatient look behind the masking
glasses.

"Ira!" I exclaimed, "Ira Atz!"

He smiled at me with some of his old-time good humor. "You were
expecting maybe Isaiah MacAdam?" he mimicked.

I knew then, and was amazed that I could have been so obtuse all
this time. I had had all the clues. I had even, I remembered, thought of
my old colleague when I first read the want ad which later proved to

be the work of Isaiah MacAdam. But I never put two and two together till this moment.

"I shouldn't have said that," he remarked, settling himself easily in my one comfortable chair, leaving me only the other which had an unyielding back and seat. "At least not yet. But of course I thought you'd guessed."

"No," I answered stupidly. "No, I never guessed."

"No matter." He cracked his fingers, a new habit. "You know now; that's the important thing. Oh, you can't imagine what it's like to be isolated like this: to walk on the street and know you're passing men and women who would scream with terror if they guessed your identity; yes, and turn you in to the police the next moment. Ishmael, not Isaac nor Isaiah."

He cracked his fingers again and looked around the room carefully. We had never been close friends, our only contact was in the laboratory of Ribbon Plastics. I did not understand what brought him to me.

"To have power," he went on, "absolute power, such as no one ever had before, and realize that imbecile mankind is only afraid you will use it for their good. Can you imagine it? Not that you will destroy them, for that's what they've always approved and admired, rushing to sacrifice their lives for the Hitlers and Stalins and Napoleons and Alexanders. What a joke!"

He had changed, changed vastly. The old Ira was intense, but his intensity had been that of determination. This nervous man seemed consumed with angry despair. I could hardly believe that the man who had calmly ordered the United States to commit suicide, who was so clearly master of the world, should be in a mood of furious protest against injustice. What more could he want?

"You didn't exactly have to—" I began.

"Of course I had to! What choice had I? To sit around waiting for the statesmen to finish the work thus far so nobly advanced of making the planet uninhabitable."

"But, Ira, you're a wood chemist and a good one. Why couldn't you stick to your own work?"

"I did, I have, I am. Is science a device for making Joe Ribbon more money? Or is it something to make men live better, longer, more happily? Am I to cultivate 'pure' science on the island of Bikini? Or in a world Bikini? Surely you must have realized by this time that the world is as much a part of our laboratory as the tables and retorts under our hands? And that you cannot do your work in a laboratory threatened by immediate danger, with the walls cracking and the ceiling about to fall in?"

The same old Ira after all, I thought; spouting, dreaming, impractical —I pulled my thoughts up. Not entirely impractical.

"More than anything else," he said, "I've missed having someone like you around I could talk shop to, someone who'd appreciate that paxide is not the end product, but merely a trivial by-product of lignin—"

"Paxide? Is that what you call your sleeping gas?"

"Gas? Oh come, surely you weren't taken in by these Sunday supplemen analysts? Paxide isn't a gas. It's a liquid."

"A liquid! Then gas masks . . ."

"Not a bit of use in the world. Paxide is absorbed through the pores as well as the mouth or nose. The only thing effective against it is an antidote already present in the body. And like all the lignin derivatives it is many times as efficient as the coal tar products. Paxide is spectacular, but when it has done its work it will have only a limited use as a general anesthetic because it is simply a superior aspirin. But lignyon—forty times as strong as nylon . . ."

He went on and on, extolling the wonders of lignin, just as he used to when he was working for Joe Ribbon. Only then it had been conjecture; now it was knowledge. That, I thought, is why I never recognized his voice in the broadcasts; that is the great mark of the change in him. The voice was still commonplace and flat—it would always be that—but it had deepened, become more incisive, more assured.

He was telling me now of his life after he was fired from Ribbon Plastics. Improvident, impractical, without a dime, he determined nevertheless to devote himself exclusively to his lignin research. He borrowed, begged, stole even, to keep going; was hungry and dirty most of the time. He solved problem after problem, living and working in an abandoned garage, developing products industrialists would have paid millions for, but which he would not sell in what he called "an uncivilized and childish world." Paxide was the last by-product, in his opinion an unimportant one, but he recognized instantly that it was the one which would enable him to use the others properly. And what he meant by that phrase was to give them away freely, once he had united and pacified the world.

He broke off abruptly. "Of course you're with us?"

"With you?" Suddenly the man in front of me was no longer good old Ira Atz, but Isaiah MacAdam, the world menace. What happened when a confessed gangster asked you casually if you were with him— and you said no? "I . . . I don't know . . ."

"You don't know? Good God, man—where have you been all this time? Thanks to paxide the human race faces the prospect of peace and sufficiency for the first time in its existence. How can you not know whether you're with us or not?"

"I don't question your aims, Ira," I temporized, "but your methods—"

"—are illegal? What an old stickler you are! They may be illegal now, but the world government will make them legal all right. It'll have to, to justify its birth."

"I wasn't thinking entirely of legality. I keep remembering the businesses that have failed because of you—"

"Name one. I never exploited small firms; none of the banks that contributed went broke."

"Perhaps not, but there were certainly drastic changes after some of your . . . exploitations, and many employees were fired."

"I sent them money. We traced them down and saw that they didn't suffer."

"It was other people's money."

"Whose isn't? Don't tell me Joe Ribbon made his the hard way."

"Ribbon closed up, you know—on your account. I'm out of a job."

"You can name your own salary when you come in with us."

"And there were the Greeks shot after the raid at Pireaus."

"Yes. Vile and stupid. And I blame myself for not taking precautions. But what about the lives saved by the ending of the war? Doesn't that balance?"

"Not for the executed and their families."

"Then you won't come in?"

I had no intention of being forced either to refuse or accept. The man was a fanatic and there was no telling to what lengths he might go if crossed. "I can't imagine what you need me for. You must have chemists, and better ones, in plenty."

"Of course we have; scientists from every field, cellulose experts too. It isn't a matter of need at all. I just want somebody around who knows Ira Atz the man, and not Isaiah MacAdam, the conquering genius."

I continued to roll with his punches, desperate to avoid committing myself one way or the other. Naturally I had no intention of throwing my lot with his, but I dared not let him know it. "How can I get in touch with you?" I asked finally.

"I'll get in touch with you. No one knows where I am to be found; no one can be put to the temptation to betray me."

After he left, I puzzled my problem for a long time, solacing myself with fresh coffee. Nothing but an antidote already in the body. "A superior aspirin," he had said. Absently I poured another cup. Nothing but an antidote—

"Coffee!" I shouted aloud. "Coffee!"

It was three o'clock. I put down the cup that had done its revelatory work; my mind was made up. I didn't stop to pack a bag, change my clothes, or telephone anyone. I walked over to the taxi stand at First and Vermont and woke a hackie. "Municipal Airport," I said.

I have little recollection of the trip to Washington. I'm sure I was too excited to sleep, too intense to strike up conversations. And I have only a vague memory of the delays and annoyances before I got through the barriers of officialdom to the head of the FBI. In spite of the times I'd already told my story, the cross-examinations I had wearily submitted to, and the consequent opportunities I later learned had certainly been used to verify my bona fides, I had once more to repeat myself.

"But how do you know this Ira Atz is really Isaiah MacAdam? There are all sorts of unbalanced characters eager for notoriety; men and women who will do anything, confess any crime, to get into the head-lines. How do you know your friend Ignatz—"

"Ira."

"—isn't lying?"

"Because his story checks. With his history as a nut on the subject of one world as well as a wood chemist. And even if it didn't, wouldn't it be worth following up? Or don't you really want to stop Isaiah Mac-Adam?"

He leaned back in his chair and looked at me thoughtfully across the desk. "To be frank, there are many of us—even here in the Federal Bureau of Investigation—who don't. Idealists who have been taken in by MacAdam and are prepared to help him, at least by inaction, if not overtly as Peacebringers."

"In that case—" I began.

"But I am not one of them. Like yourself, my interests are . . . patriotic."

"Then if you catch Ira and put him behind bars—"

"Suppose we do. I don't think it would be easy, but suppose we do. Remember what happened when they caught one of his men once, Bill Jones—"

"Jack Smith, I think."

"An alias, probably. Well, if we got MacAdam, first thing some of his gang would be around with this gas—"

"Liquid. Paxide is a derivative of lignin."

"—and before you could say 'peace on earth, good will to men,' they'd have him out again."

"Not if his guards are inoculated with an antidote beforehand."

"You'll excuse my scepticism, but I have no proof your antidote will work."

"Damn it, man!" I cried in exasperation, "I've had no time to conduct tests and no samples of paxide available if I had. But surely it's worth taking a chance."

It was impossible to understand the apathy and inertia pervading Washington and, indeed, the whole country during that week of grace given by Isaiah MacAdam. All seemed resigned to—or was it possible, anxious for?—the threatened ruin of cherished institutions. I cannot even say my report and suggestions met with polite indifference. Indifference, yes; politeness, no.

I stayed on however, much as I begrudged the terrific expense of the capital and raged against the blank wall of imbecility. I don't think I hoped any longer to convince anyone in authority or to reach the ear of an official not bogged down in stupor. I stayed because there was nothing else to do.

The balance of the week passed. Then it was Sunday.

I want to make it clear that no one expected a miracle, such as a change of heart on the part of MacAdam, or the sudden intervention of Superman. Everyone knew he would keep his word and begin the destruction of American defenses as soon as the time limit expired. Most people agreed his first blow would be against one of the atom-bomb plants.

Evidently his mania demanded a more spectacular gesture: he chose to begin with the navy. Shortly after 3 A.M.—midnight in California—shore sentries fell into the typical paxide coma, launches were seized, and the great fleets boarded. The destroyers in San Diego, battleships and cruisers off San Pedro or San Francisco Bay, the Atlantic Fleet lined up like sitting ducks in the Hudson, were all taken over by the Peace-bringers. Their numbers must have been ridiculously underestimated by the newspapers, to say nothing of their discipline, for they not only took over all except the few vessels at Pearl Harbor—confederates even boarded ships on goodwill missions in European ports—but the shore installations of the searchlights, radar and communications as well. The night watches were anesthetized by paxide before they could challenge the invaders from the seized launches, and the sleeping crews sprayed with the same soporific.

Most of the sailors were on shore-leave; even so it must have been a terrific task to bundle the unconscious seamen into the launches, make many trips to the docks and back, piling up helpless navy personnel like cords of wood, and then finally opening the seacocks on the magnificent vessels and decamping before dawn.

Daylight—and the astonished, awakening sailors, incredulous on the docks and wharves where they had been dumped, saw only empty water where the proud navy had vanished. But not vanished entirely, for in the shallower anchorages, when the ships had not listed too far, the tops of the tripod masts still showed steadfastly above the waves. Isaiah MacAdam had demonstrated his power and his hatred of the weapons of war beyond any doubt.

Early in the morning, while the telegrapher at Zwingle, Iowa, was under the spell of paxide, a telegram addressed simply "To the American People" was sent out from his key. "I have not spoken in secret."

I was sitting in my tiny hotel-room, alternately cursing the pigheadedness of the authorities who could have easily prevented this disaster had they listened to me, and wondering if it was not yet too late to accept Ira's offer after all, when the phone rang. It was the head of the FBI.

"Can you come immediately?"

"Yes," I answered bitterly, "now that the horse is stolen."

"Never mind that. There will be a car at your hotel door by the time you get downstairs. Wait for nothing. This is urgent."

Exactly what I'd been telling him for a week.

We raced through the silent, empty length of Constitution Avenue, siren wide open. I don't know whether I had expected mourning crowds, or curious crowds, riotous or angry crowds, but I know I must have expected crowds of some kind to demonstrate their shock and awareness, for this Sunday calm scandalized me. Apathy in the face of MacAdam's threat was bad enough; indifference to his deed was simply unbelievable.

The Chief was waiting for me in the doorway of his office. He wasted no time on preliminaries. "How long will it take to prepare 100,000 doses of antidote?"

"How many assistants can I have?"

"All you want—the entire medical and public health service—and as many laboratories as you need."

"Two days. But what about picking up Ira Atz?"

"Can't find him. Been trying since the first day you suggested. No, we're going to have to do it the hard way."

For the next forty-eight hours I worked like a maniac, but at the end of that time, thanks to the simplicity of the formula, we had not 100,000 dosages, but three times as many. They were instantly flown to all vital army posts, airbases, munitions depots and atom plants. No one could know where Isaiah MacAdam would strike next.

But though no one could know, speculation and panic reached unprecedented heights, and the convulsions of a nation with a dreadful wound was a horrible sight. Hardly a store or factory opened on Monday morning; the banks and stock market remained closed; great mobs, recovering from their impassiveness of the day before, paraded through the streets. The churches were open; in some, prayers were offered for the confusion of this enemy, in others Isaiah MacAdam was proclaimed savior of the world. For the first time there were open mass meetings of Peacebringers, and hundreds of thousands of deluded men and women testified their devotion.

The rest of the world experienced the same fright and perturbation in only slightly less degree. MacAdam had kept his promise of action; after the United States was completely disarmed it would be their turn. Nothing, it seemed, could stop him from fulfilling his dream of one world, helpless against his imposed unification.

On Tuesday he moved again, and again, despite all calculations, it was at an unanticipated point. Instead of striking at a military installation, with characteristic brazenness he attacked the very heart of the government—the Capitol itself—with Congress in session and the President in his room there waiting to address them.

Almost at the stroke of noon, well-dressed strangers approached the military police stationed around the building. Asked some trivial question, the guards suddenly became aware of a vapor in the air like very fine rain, although it was a cloudless day, and realized that the strangers were now holding small vessels in their hands from which protruded nozzles like those of an atomizer spray. Also, the strangers were looking surprised and disconcerted.

Not more than two or three of the MP's grasped the situation, but these few acted instantly. As a routine order, the guards, like everyone on sentry duty, had been immunized with injections of caffein that morning; MacAdam's sleep-inducing liquid affected them no more than drops of tapwater.

Shouting a warning, the MP's lowered their rifles to the ready. There was no struggle; the disguised Peacebringers, unable to conquer their dismay at the first failure of the hitherto invincible paxide, continued futilely to spray the air. Dozens of bystanders collapsed into sleep before the astonished attackers were arrested, bayoneted, or shot.

Among the captured was Ira Atz himself, evidently unable to resist being present at what was to have been his greatest triumph. He seemed dazed and sullen when I was rushed over to identify him. He refused to talk; indeed, he had so far changed from his old self that he spat in my face, thus showing himself, I thought, a poor loser. They hustled him off before a lynch mob could form; he was tried shortly after and sentenced to so many consecutive terms that it would require many, many life-times for him ever to be free again.

And that, except for one little incident, ends my part in the story of Isaiah MacAdam. Joe Ribbon promptly reopened his plastics factory. The armament industry boomed as never before, what with a whole navy to replace. The FBI finally found Ira's laboratory with its wealth of lignin derivatives, products which have made fortunes for the for-ward-looking companies now manufacturing them, particularly those almost magic materials which were made into uniforms, heavy duty tires for army vehicles, and casings for atom bombs.

As a precaution against any of the Peacebringers still at large repeat-ing their leader's scheme the world now takes daily injections of caffein, that simple antidote suggested to me by my fondness for coffee; and if this has led to an increased mortality from heart conditions, it is a small price to pay for our freedom to prepare to defend ourselves from whatever malcontent nations may be getting ready to attack us.

Oh yes, my last appearance in the drama. I suppose I keep forgetting it because of a slightly unpleasant blunder. I was awarded a special medal by Congress for my part in capturing Isaiah MacAdam, and pre-sented with $30,000 from a grateful nation. The President announced the award in a nationwide radio address. It was a very proud moment.

Only he kept making one slip. My name, as you know, is the good old Huguenot one of Jeunas. All through the fulsome talk, the chief executive kept substituting a d for the n.

———————

HORACE L. GOLD

A MATTER OF FORM

GILROY'S telephone bell jangled into his slumber. With his eyes grimly shut, the reporter flopped over on his side, ground his ear into the pillow and pulled the cover over his head. But the bell jarred on.

When he blinked his eyes open and saw rain streaking the windows,

Mr. Gold is the editor of a new magazine, GALAXY-*Science Fiction,* which should appear on the newsstands before this book is published.

he gritted his teeth against the insistent clangor and yanked off the receiver. He swore into the transmitter—not a trite blasphemy, but a poetic opinion of the sort of man who woke tired reporters at four in the morning.

"Don't blame me," his editor replied after a bitter silence. "It was your idea. You wanted the case. They found another whatsit."

Gilroy instantly snapped awake. "They found another catatonic!"

"Over on York Avenue near Ninety-first Street, about an hour ago. He's down in the observation ward at Memorial." The voice suddenly became low and confiding. "Want to know what I think, Gilroy?"

"What?" Gilroy asked in an expectant whisper.

"I think you're nuts. These catatonics are nothing but tramps. They probably drank themselves into catatonia, whatever that is. After all, be reasonable, Gilroy; they're only worth a four-line clip."

Gilroy was out of bed and getting dressed with one hand. "Not this time, chief," he said confidently. "Sure, they're only tramps, but that's part of the story. Look . . . hey! You should have been off a couple of hours ago. What's holding you up?"

The editor sounded disgruntled. "Old Man Talbot. He's seventy-six tomorrow. Had to pad out a blurb on his life."

"What! Wasting time whitewashing that murderer, racketeer—"

"Take it easy, Gilroy," the editor cautioned. "He's got a half interest in the paper. He doesn't bother us often."

"O. K. But he's still the city's one-man crime wave. Well, he'll kick off soon. Can you meet me at Memorial when you quit work?"

"In this weather?" The editor considered. "I don't know. Your news instinct is tops, and if you think this is big— Oh, hell . . . yes!"

Gilroy's triumphant grin soured when he ripped his foot through a sock. He hung up and explored empty drawers for another pair.

The street was cold and miserably deserted. The black snow was melting to grimy slush. Gilroy hunched into his coat and sloshed in the dirty sludge toward Greenwich Avenue. He was very tall and incredibly thin. With his head down into the driving swirl of rain, his coat flapping around his skinny shanks, his hands deep in his pockets, and his sharp elbows sticking away from his rangy body, he resembled an unhappy stork peering around for a fish.

But he was far from being unhappy. He was happy, in fact, as only a man with a pet theory can be when facts begin to fight on his side.

Splashing through the slush, he shivered when he thought of the catatonic who must have been lying in it for hours, unable to rise, until he was found and carried to the hospital. Poor devil! The first had been mistaken for a drunk, until the cop saw the bandage on his neck.

"Escaped post-brain-operatives," the hospital had reported. It sounded reasonable, except for one thing—catatonics don't walk, crawl, feed themselves or perform *any* voluntary muscular action. Thus Gilroy had not been particularly surprised when no hospital or private surgeon claimed the escaped post-operatives.

A taxi driver hopefully sighted his agitated figure through the rain. Gilroy restrained an urge to hug the hackie for rescuing him from the bitter wind. He clambered in hastily.

"Nice night for a murder," the driver observed conversationally.

"Are you hinting that business is bad?"

"I mean the weather's lousy."

"Well, damned if it isn't!" Gilroy exclaimed sarcastically. "Don't let it slow you down, though. I'm in a hurry. Memorial Hospital, quick!"

The driver looked concerned. He whipped the car out into the middle of the street, scooted through a light that was just an instant too slow.

Three catatonics in a month! Gilroy shook his head. It was a real puzzler. They couldn't have escaped. In the first place, if they had, they would have been claimed; and in the second place, it was physically impossible. And how did they acquire those neat surgical wounds on the backs of their necks, closed with two professional stitches and covered with a professional bandage? New wounds, too!

Gilroy attached special significance to the fact that they were very poorly dressed and suffered from slight malnutrition. But what was the significance? He shrugged. It was an instinctive hunch.

The taxi suddenly swerved to the curb and screeched to a stop. He thrust a bill through the window and got out. The night burst abruptly. Rain smashed against him in a roaring tide. He battered upwind to the hospital entrance.

He was soaked, breathless, half-repentant for his whim in attaching importance to three impoverished catatonics. He gingerly put his hand in his clammy coat and brought out a sodden identification card.

The girl at the reception desk glanced at it. "Oh, a newspaperman! Did a big story come in tonight?"

"Nothing much," he said casually. "Some poor tramp found on York and Ninety-first. Is he up in the screwball ward?"

She scanned the register and nodded. "Is he a friend of yours?"

"My grandson." As he moved off, both flinched at the sound of water squishing in his shoes at each step. "I must have stepped in a puddle."

When he turned around in the elevator, she was shaking her head and pursing her lips maternally. Then the ground floor dropped away.

He went through the white corridor unhesitantly. Low, horrible moans came from the main ward. He heard them with academic detachment. Near the examination room, the sound of the rising elevator stopped him. He paused, turning to see who it was.

The editor stepped out, chilled, wet and disgusted. Gilroy reached down and caught the smaller man's arm, guiding him silently through the door and into the examination room. The editor sighed resignedly.

The resident physician glanced up briefly when they unobtrusively took places in the ring of internes about the bed. Without effort, Gilroy peered over the heads before him, inspecting the catatonic with clinical absorption.

The catatonic had been stripped of his wet clothing, toweled, and rubbed with alcohol. Passive, every muscle absolutely relaxed, his eyes were loosely closed, and his mouth hung open in idiotic slackness. The dark line of removed surgical plaster showed on his neck. Gilroy strained to one side. The hair had been clipped. He saw part of a stitch.

"Catatonia, doc?" he asked quietly.

"Who are you?" the physician snapped.

"Gilroy . . . *Morning Post.*"

The doctor gazed back at the man on the bed. "It's catatonia, all right. No trace of alcohol or inhibiting drugs. Slight malnutrition."

Gilroy elbowed politely through the ring of internes. "Insulin shock doesn't work, eh? No reason why it should."

"Why shouldn't it?" the doctor demanded, startled. "It always works in catatonia . . . at least, temporarily."

"But it didn't in this case, did it?" Gilroy insisted brusquely.

The doctor lowered his voice defeatedly. "No."

"What's this all about?" the editor asked in irritation. "What's catatonia, anyhow? Paralysis, or what?"

"It's the last stage of schizophrenia, or what used to be called dementia præcox," the physician said. "The mind revolts against responsibility and searches for a period in its existence when it was not troubled. It goes back to childhood and finds that there are childish cares; goes further and comes up against infantile worries; and finally ends up in a prenatal mental state."

"But it's a gradual degeneration," Gilroy stated. "Long before the complete mental decay, the victim is detected and put in an asylum. He goes through imbecility, idiocy, and after years of slow degeneration, winds up refusing to use his muscles or brain."

The editor looked baffled. "Why should insulin shock pull him out?"

"It shouldn't!" Gilroy rapped out.

"It should!" the physician replied angrily. "Catatonia is negative revolt. Insulin drops the sugar content of the blood to the point of shock. The sudden hunger jolts the catatonic out of his passivity."

"That's right," Gilroy said incisively. "But this isn't catatonia! It's mighty close to it, but you never heard of a catatonic who didn't refuse to carry on voluntary muscular action. There's no salivary retention! My guess is that it's paralysis."

"Caused by what?" the doctor asked bitingly.

"That's for you to say. I'm not a physician. How about the wound at the base of the skull?"

"Nonsense! It doesn't come within a quarter inch of the motor nerve. It's *cerias flexibilitas* . . . waxy flexibility." He raised the victim's arm and let go. It sagged slowly. "If it were general paralysis, it would have affected the brain. He'd have been dead."

Gilroy lifted his bony shoulders and lowered them. "You're on the wrong track, doc," he said quietly. "The wound has a lot to do with his condition, and catatonia can't be duplicated by surgery. Lesions can cause it, but the degeneration would still be gradual. And catatonics can't walk or crawl away. He was deliberately abandoned, same as the others."

"Looks like you're right, Gilroy," the editor conceded. "There's something fishy here. All three of them had the same wounds?"

"In exactly the same place, at the base of the skull and to the left of the spinal column. Did you ever see anything so helpless? Imagine him escaping from a hospital, or even a private surgeon!"

The physician dismissed the internes and gathered up his instruments preparatory to harried flight. "I don't see the motive. All three of them were undernourished, poorly clad; they must have been living in substandard conditions. Who would want to harm them?"

Gilroy bounded in front of the doctor, barring his way. "But it doesn't have to be revenge! It could be experimentation!"

"To prove what?"

Gilroy looked at him quizzically. "You don't know?"

"How should I?"

The reporter clapped his drenched hat on backward and darted to the door. "Come on, chief. We'll ask Moss for a theory."

"You won't find Dr. Moss here," the physician said. "He's off at night, and tomorrow, I think, he's leaving the hospital."

Gilroy stopped abruptly. "Moss . . . leaving the hospital!" he repeated in astonishment. "Did you hear that, chief? He's a dictator, a slave driver and a louse. But he's probably the greatest surgeon in America. Look at that. Stories breaking all around you, and you're whitewashing Old Man Talbot's murderous life!" His coat bellied out in the wash of his swift, gaunt stride. "Three catatonics found lying on the street in a month. That never happened before. They can't walk or crawl, and they have mysterious wounds at the base of their skulls. Now the greatest surgeon in the country gets kicked out of the hospital he built up to first place. And what do you do? You sit in the office and write stories about what a swell guy Talbot is underneath his slimy exterior!"

The resident physician was relieved to hear the last of that relentlessly incisive, logical voice trail down the corridor. But he gazed down at the catatonic before leaving the room.

He felt less certain that it was catatonia. He found himself quoting the editor's remark—there definitely *was* something fishy there!

But what was the motive in operating on three obviously destitute men and abandoning them; and how had the operation caused a state resembling catatonia?

In a sense, he felt sorry that Dr. Moss was going to be discharged. The cold, slave-driving dictator might have given a good theory. That was the physician's scientific conscience speaking. Inside, he really felt that anything was worth getting away from that silkily mocking voice and the delicately sneering mouth.

At Fifty-fifth Street, Wood came to the last Sixth Avenue employment office. With very little hope, he read the crudely chalked signs. It was an industrial employment agency. Wood had never been inside a factory. The only job he could fill was that of apprentice upholsterer, ten dollars a week; but he was thirty-two years old and the agency would require five dollars immediate payment.

He turned away dejectedly, fingering the three dimes in his pocket. Three dimes—the smallest, thinnest American coins—

"Anything up there, Mac?"

"Not for me," Wood replied wearily. He scarcely glanced at the man.

He took a last glance at his newspaper before dropping it to the sidewalk. That was the last paper he'd buy, he resolved; with his miserable appearance he couldn't answer advertisements. But his mind clung obstinately to Gilroy's article. Gilroy had described the horror of catatonia. A notion born of defeat made it strangely attractive to Wood. At least, the catatonics were fed and housed. He wondered if catatonia could be simulated—

But the other had been scrutinizing Wood. "College man, ain't you?" he asked as Wood trudged away from the employment office.

Wood paused and ran his hand over his stubbled face. Dirty cuffs stood away from his fringing sleeves. He knew that his hair curled long behind his ears. "Does it still show?" he asked bitterly.

"You bet. You can spot a college man a mile away."

Wood's mouth twisted. "Glad to hear that. It must be an inner light shining through the rags."

"You're a sucker, coming down here with an education. Down here they want poor slobs who don't know any better . . . guys like me, with big muscles and small brains."

Wood looked up at him sharply. He was too well dressed and alert to have prowled the agencies for any length of time. He might have just lost his job; perhaps he was looking for company. But Wood had met his kind before. He had the hard eyes of the wolf who preyed on the jobless.

"Listen," Wood said coldly, "I haven't a thing you'd want. I'm down to thirty cents. Excuse me while I sneak my books and toothbrush out of my room before the super snatches them."

The other did not recoil or protest virtuously. "I ain't blind," he said quietly. "I can see you're down and out."

"Then what do you want?" Wood snapped ill-temperedly. "Don't tell me you want a threadbare but filthy college man for company—"

His unwelcome friend made a gesture of annoyance. "Cut out the mad-dog act. I was turned down on a job today because I ain't a college man. Seventy-five a month, room and board, doctor's assistant. But I got the air because I ain't a grad."

"You've got my sympathy," Wood said, turning away.

The other caught up with him. "You're a college grad. Do you want the job? It'll cost you your first week's pay . . . my cut, see?"

"I don't know anything about medicine. I was a code expert in a stock-broker's office before people stopped having enough money for investments. Want any codes deciphered? That's the best I can do."

He grew irritated when the stranger stubbornly matched his dejected shuffle.

"You don't have to know anything about medicine. Long as you got a degree, a few muscles and a brain, that's all the doc wants."

Wood stopped short and wheeled.

"Is that on the level?"

"Sure. But I don't want to take a deadhead up there and get turned down. I got to ask you the questions they asked me."

In face of a prospective job, Wood's caution ebbed away. He felt the three dimes in his pocket. They were exceedingly slim and unprotective. They meant two hamburgers and two cups of coffee, or a bed in some filthy hotel dormitory. Two thin meals and sleeping in the wet March air; or shelter for a night and no food—

"Shoot!" he said deliberately.

"Any relatives?"

"Some fifth cousins in Maine."

"Friends?"

"None who would recognize me now." He searched the stranger's face. "What's this all about? What have my friends or relatives got to do—"

"Nothing," the other said hastily. "Only you'll have to travel a little. The doc wouldn't want a wife dragging along, or have you break up your work by writing letters. See?"

Wood didn't see. It was a singularly lame explanation; but he was concentrating on the seventy-five a month, room and *board*—food.

"Who's the doctor?" he asked.

"I ain't dumb." The other smiled humorlessly. "You'll go there with me and get the doc to hand over my cut."

Wood crossed to Eighth Avenue with the stranger. Sitting in the subway, he kept his eyes from meeting casual, disinterested glances. He pulled his feet out of the aisle, against the base of the seat, to hide the loose, flapping right sole. His hands were cracked and scaly, with tenacious dirt deeply embedded. Bitter, defeated, with the appearance of a mature waif. What a chance there was of being hired! But at least the stranger had risked a nickel on his fare.

Wood followed him out at 103rd Street and Central Park West; they climbed the hill to Manhattan Avenue and headed several blocks downtown. The other ran briskly up the stoop of an old house. Wood climbed the steps more slowly. He checked an urge to run away, but he experienced in advance the sinking feeling of being turned away from a job. If he could only have his hair cut, his suit pressed, his shoes mended! But what was the use of thinking about that? It would cost a couple of dollars. And nothing could be done about his ragged hems.

"Come on!" the stranger called.

Wood tensed his back and stood looking at the house while the other brusquely rang the doorbell. There were three floors and no card above the bell, no doctor's white glass sign in the darkly curtained windows. From the outside it could have been a neglected boardinghouse.

The door opened. A man of his own age, about middle height, but considerably overweight, blocked the entrance. He wore a white laboratory apron. Incongruous in his pale, soft face, his nimble eyes were harsh.

"Back again?" he asked impatiently.

"It's not for me this time," Wood's persistent friend said. "I got a college grad."

Wood drew back in humiliation when the fat man's keen glance passed over his wrinkled, frayed suit and stopped distastefully at the long hair blowing wildly around his hungry, unshaven face. There—he could see it coming: "Can't use him."

But the fat man pushed back a beautiful collie with his leg and held the door wide. Astounded, Wood followed his acquaintance into the narrow hall. To give an impression of friendliness, he stooped and ruffled the dog's ears. The fat man led them into a bare front room.

"What's your name?" he asked indifferently.

Wood's answer stuck in his throat. He coughed to clear it. "Wood," he replied.

"Any relatives?" Wood shook his head.

"Friends?"

"Not any more."

"What kind of degree?"

"Science, Columbia, 1925."

The fat man's expression did not change. He reached into his left pocket and brought out a wallet. "What arrangement did you make with this man?"

"He's to get my first week's salary." Silently, Wood observed the transfer of several green bills; he looked at them hungrily, pathetically. "May I wash up and take a shave, doctor?" he asked.

"I'm not the doctor," the fat man answered. "My name is Clarence, without a mister in front of it." He turned swiftly to the sharp stranger. "What are you hanging around for?"

Wood's friend backed to the door. "Well, so long," he said. "Good break for both of us, eh, Wood?"

Wood smiled and nodded happily. The trace of irony in the stranger's hard voice escaped him entirely.

"I'll take you upstairs to your room," Clarence said when Wood's business partner had left. "I think there's a razor there."

They went out into the dark hall, the collie close behind them. An unshaded light bulb hung on a single wire above a gate-leg table. On the wall behind the table an oval, gilt mirror gave back Wood's hairy, unkempt image. A worn carpet covered the floor to a door cutting off the rear of the house, and narrow stairs climbed in a swift spiral to the next story. It was cheerless and neglected, but Wood's conception of luxury had become less exacting.

"Wait here while I make a telephone call," Clarence said.

He closed the door behind him in a room opposite the stairs. Wood fondled the friendly collie. Through the panel he heard Clarence's voice, natural and unlowered.

"Hello, Moss? . . . Pinero brought back a man. All his answers are all right. . . . Columbia, 1925. . . . Not a cent, judging from his appearance. . . . Call Talbot? For when? . . . O. K. . . . You'll get back as soon as you get through with the board? . . . O.K. . . . Well, what's the difference? You got all you wanted from them, anyhow."

Wood heard the receiver's click as it was replaced and taken off again. Moss? That was the head of Memorial Hospital—the great surgeon. But the article about the catatonics hinted something about his removal from the hospital.

"Hello, Talbot?" Clarence was saying. "Come around at noon tomorrow. Moss says everything'll be ready then. . . . O. K., don't get excited. This is positively the last one! . . . Don't worry. Nothing can go wrong."

Talbot's name sounded familiar to Wood. It might have been the Talbot that the *Morning Post* had written about—the seventy-six-year-old philanthropist. He probably wanted Moss to operate on him. Well, it was none of his business.

When Clarence joined him in the dark hall, Wood thought only of his seventy-five a month, room and board; but more than that, he had a job! A few weeks of decent food and a chance to get some new clothes, and he would soon get rid of his defeatism.

He even forgot his wonder at the lack of shingles and waiting-room signs that a doctor's house usually had. He could only think of his neat room on the third floor, overlooking a bright back yard. And a shave—

Dr. Moss replaced the telephone with calm deliberation. Striding through the white hospital corridor to the elevator, he was conscious of curious stares. His pink, scrupulously shaven, clean-scrubbed face gave no answer to their questioning eyes. In the elevator he stood with his hands thrust casually into his pockets. The operator did not dare to look at him or speak.

Moss gathered his hat and coat. The space around the reception desk seemed more crowded than usual, with men who had the penetrating look of reporters. He walked swiftly past.

A tall, astoundingly thin man, his stare fixed predatorily on Moss, headed the wedge of reporters that swarmed after Moss.

"You can't leave without a statement to the press, doc!" he said.

"I find it very easy to do," Moss taunted without stopping.

He stood on the curb with his back turned coldly on the reporters and unhurriedly flagged a taxi.

"Well, at least you can tell us whether you're still director of the hospital," the tall reporter said.

"Ask the board of trustees."

"Then how about a theory on the catatonics?"

"Ask the catatonics." The cab pulled up opposite Moss. Deliberately he opened the door and stepped in. As he rode away, he heard the thin man exclaim: "What a cold, clammy reptile!"

He did not look back to enjoy their discomfiture. In spite of his calm demeanor, he did not feel too easy himself. The man on the *Morning Post*, Gilroy or whatever his name was, had written a sensational article on the abandoned catatonics, and even went so far as to claim they were not catatonics. He had had all he could do to keep from being involved in the conflicting riot of theory. Talbot owned a large interest in the paper. He must be told to strangle the articles, although by now all the papers were taking up the cry.

It was a clever piece of work, detecting the fact that the victims weren't suffering from catatonia at all. But the *Morning Post* reporter had cut himself a man-size job in trying to understand how three men with general paralysis could be abandoned without a trace of where they had come from, and what connection the incisions had on their condition. Only recently had Moss himself solved it.

The cab crossed to Seventh Avenue and headed uptown.

The trace of his parting smile of mockery vanished. His mobile mouth whitened, tight-lipped and grim. Where was he to get money from now? He had milked the hospital funds to a frightening debt, and it had not been enough. Like a bottomless maw, his researches could drain a dozen funds.

If he could convince Talbot, prove to him that his failures had not really been failures, that this time he would not slip up—

But Talbot was a tough nut to crack. Not a cent was coming out of his miserly pocket until Moss completely convinced him that he was past the experimental stage. This time there would be no failure!

At Moss's street, the cab stopped and the surgeon sprang out lightly. He ran up the steps confidently, looking neither to the left nor to the right, though it was a fine day with a warm yellow sun, and between the two lines of old houses Central Park could be seen budding greenly.

He opened the door and strode almost impatiently into the narrow, dark hall, ignoring the friendly collie that bounded out to greet him.

"Clarence!" he called out. "Get your new assistant down. I'm not even going to wait for a meal." He threw off his hat, coat and jacket, hanging them up carelessly on a hook near the mirror.

"Hey, Wood!" Clarence shouted up the stairs. "Are you finished?"

They heard a light, eager step race down from the third floor.

"Clarence, my boy," Moss said in a low, impetuous voice, "I know what the trouble was. We didn't really fail at all. I'll show you . . . we'll follow exactly the same technique!"

"Then why didn't it seem to work before?"

Wood's feet came into view between the rails on the second floor.

"You'll understand as soon as it's finished," Moss whispered hastily, and then Wood joined them.

Even the short time that Wood had been employed was enough to transform him. He had lost the defeatist feeling of being useless human flotsam. He was shaved and washed, but that did not account for his kindled eyes.

"Wood . . . Dr. Moss," Clarence said perfunctorily.

Wood choked out an incoherent speech that was meant to inform them that he was happy, though he didn't know anything about medicine.

"You don't have to," Moss replied silkily. "We'll teach you more about medicine than most surgeons learn in a lifetime."

It could have meant anything or nothing. Wood made no attempt to understand the meaning of the words. It was the hint of withdrawn savagery in the low voice that puzzled him. It seemed a very peculiar way of talking to a man who had been hired to move apparatus and do nothing but the most ordinary routine work.

He followed them silently into a shining, tiled operating room. He felt less comfortable than he had in his room; but when he dismissed Moss's tones as a characteristically sarcastic manner of speech, hinting more than it contained in reality, his eagerness returned. While Moss scrubbed his hands and arms in a deep basin, Wood gazed around.

In the center of the room an operating table stood, with a clean sheet clamped unwrinkled over it. Above the table five shadowless light globes branched. It was a compact room. Even Wood saw how close everything lay to the doctor's hand—trays of tampons, swabs and clamps, and a sterilizing instrument chest that gave off puffs of steam.

"We do a lot of surgical experimenting," Moss said. "Most of your work'll be handling the anæsthetic. Show him how to do it, Clarence."

Wood observed intently. It appeared simple—cut-ins and shut-offs for cyclopropane, helium and oxygen; watch the dials for overrich mixture; keep your eye on the bellows and water filter—

Trained anæsthetists, he knew, tested their mixture by taking a few sniffs. At Clarence's suggestion he sniffed briefly at the whispering cone. He didn't know cyclopropane—so lightning-fast that experienced anæsthetists are sometimes caught by it—

Wood lay on the floor with his arms and legs sticking up into the air. When he tried to straighten them, he rolled over on his side. Still they projected stiffly. He was dizzy with the anæsthetic. Something that felt like surgical plaster pulled on a sensitive spot on the back of his neck.

The room was dark, its green shades pulled down against the outer day. Somewhere above him and toward the end of the room, he heard painful breathing. Before he could raise himself to investigate, he caught the multiple tread of steps ascending and approaching the door. He drew back defensively.

The door flung open. Light flared up in the room. Wood sprang to his feet—and found he could not stand erect. He dropped back to a crawling position, facing the men who watched him with cold interest.

"He tried to stand up," the old one stated.

"What'd you think I'd do?" Wood snapped. His voice was a confused, snarling growl without words. Baffled and raging, he glared up at them.

"Cover him, Clarence," Moss said. "I'll look at the other one."

Wood turned his head from the threatening muzzle of the gun aimed at him, and saw the doctor lift the man on the bed. Clarence backed to the window and raised the shade. Strong noonlight roused the man. His profile was turned to Wood. His eyes fastened blankly on Moss's scrubbed pink face, never leaving it. Behind his ears curled long, wild hair.

"There you are, Talbot," Moss said to the old man. "He's sound."

"Take him out of bed and let's see him act like you said he would." The old man jittered anxiously on his cane.

Moss pulled the man's legs to the edge of the bed and raised him heavily to his feet. For a short time he stood without aid; then all at once he collapsed to his hands and knees. He stared full at Wood.

It took Wood a minute of startled bewilderment to recognize the face. He had seen it every day of his life, but never so detachedly. The eyes were blank and round, the facial muscles relaxed, idiotic.

But it was his own face—

Panic exploded in him. He gaped down at as much of himself as he could see. Two hairy legs stemmed from his shoulders, and a dog's forepaws rested firmly on the floor.

He stumbled uncertainly toward Moss. "What did you do to me?" he shouted. It came out in an animal howl. The doctor motioned the others to the door and backed away warily.

Wood felt his lips draw back tightly over his fangs. Clarence and Talbot were in the hall. Moss stood alertly in the doorway, his hand on the knob. He watched Wood closely, his eyes glacial and unmoved. When Wood sprang, he slammed the door, and Wood's shoulder crashed against it.

"He knows what happened," Moss's voice came through the panel.

It was not entirely true. Wood knew something had happened. But he refused to believe that the face of the crawling man gazing stupidly at him was his own. It was, though. And Wood himself stood on the four legs of a dog, with a surgical plaster covering a burning wound in the back of his neck.

It was crushing, numbing, too fantastic to believe. He thought wildly of hypnosis. But just by turning his head, he could look directly at what had been his own body, braced on hands and knees as if it could not stand erect.

He was outside his own body. He could not deny that. Somehow he had been removed from it; by drugs or hypnosis, Moss had put him in the body of a dog. He had to get back into his own body again.

But how do you get back into your own body?

His mind struck blindly in all directions. He scarcely heard the three men move away from the door and enter the next room. But his mind suddenly froze with fear. His human body was complete and impenetrable, closed hermetically against his now-foreign identity.

Through his congealed terror, his animal ears brought the creak of furniture. Talbot's cane stopped its nervous, insistent tapping.

"That should have convinced even you, Talbot," he heard Moss say. "Their identities are exchanged without the slightest loss of mentality."

Wood started. It meant— No, it was absurd! But it did account for the fact that his body crawled on hands and knees, unable to stand on its feet. It meant that the collie's identity was in Wood's body!

"That's O. K.," he heard Talbot say. "How about the operation part? Isn't it painful, putting their brains into different skulls?"

"You can't put them into different skulls," Moss answered with a touch of annoyance. "They don't fit. Besides, there's no need to exchange the whole brain. How do you account for the fact that people have retained their identities with parts of their brains removed?"

There was a pause. "I don't know," Talbot said doubtfully.

"Sometimes the parts of the brain that were removed contained nerve centers, and paralysis set in. But the identity was still there. Then what part of the brain contained the identity?"

Wood ignored the old man's questioning murmur. He listened intently, all his fears submerged in the straining of his sharp ears, in the overwhelming need to know what Moss had done to him.

"Figure it out," the surgeon said. "The identity must have been in some part of the brain that wasn't removed, that couldn't be touched without death. That's where it was. At the absolute base of the brain, where a scalpel couldn't get at it without having to cut through the skull, the three medullæ, and the entire depth of the brain itself. There's a mysterious little body hidden away safely down there—less than a quarter of an inch in diameter—called the pineal gland. In some way it controls the identity. Once it was a third eye."

"A third eye, and now it controls the identity?" Talbot exclaimed.

"Why not? The gills of our fish ancestors became the Eustachian canal that controls the sense of balance.

"Until I developed a new technique in removing the gland—by excising from beneath the brain instead of through it—nothing at all was known about it. In the first place, trying to get at it would kill the patient; and oral or intravenous injections have no effect. But when I exchanged the pineals of a rabbit and a rat, the rabbit acted like a rat, and the rat like a rabbit—within their limitations, of course. It's empiricism—it works, but I don't know why."

"Then why did the first three act like . . . what's the word?"

"Catatonics. Well, the exchanges were really successful, Talbot; but I repeated the same mistake three times, until I figured it out. And by the way, get that reporter on something a little less dangerous. He's getting pretty warm. Excepting the salivary retention, the victims acted almost like catatonics, and for nearly the same reason. I exchanged the pineals of rats for the men's. Well, you can imagine how a rat would act with the relatively huge body of a man to control. It's beyond him. He simply gives up, goes into a passive revolt. But the difference between a dog's body and a man's isn't so great. The dog is puzzled, but at any rate he makes an attempt to control his new body."

"Is the operation painful?" Talbot asked anxiously.

"There isn't a bit of pain. The incision is very small, and heals in a short time. And as for recovery—you can see for yourself how swift it is. I operated on Wood and the dog last night."

Wood's dog's brain stampeded, refusing to function intelligently. If he had been hypnotized or drugged, there might have been a chance of his eventual return. But his identity had been violently and permanently ripped from his body and forced into that of a dog. He was absolutely helpless, completely dependent on Moss to return him to his body.

"How much do you want?" Talbot was asking craftily.

"Five million!"

The old man cackled in a high, cracked voice. "I'll give you fifty thousand, cash," he offered.

"To exchange your dying body for a young, strong, healthy one?" Moss asked, emphasizing each adjective with special significance. "The price is five million."

"I'll give you seventy-five thousand," Talbot said with finality. "Raising five million is out of the question. It can't be done. All my money is tied up in my . . . uh . . . syndicates. I have to turn most of the income back into merchandise, wages, overhead and equipment. How do you expect me to have five million in cash?"

"I don't," Moss replied with faint mockery.

Talbot lost his temper. "Then what are you getting at?"

"The interest on five million is exactly half your income. Briefly, to use your business terminology, I'm muscling into your rackets."

Wood heard the old man gasp indignantly. "Not a chance!" he rasped. "I'll give you eighty thousand. That's all the cash I can raise."

"Don't be a fool, Talbot," Moss said with deadly calm. "I don't want money for the sake of feeling it. I need an assured income, and plenty of it; enough to carry on my experiments without having to bleed hospitals dry and still not have enough. If this experiment didn't interest me, I wouldn't do it even for five million, much as I need it."

"Eighty thousand!" Talbot repeated.

"Hang onto your money until you rot! Let's see, with your advanced angina pectoris, that should be about six months from now, shouldn't it?"

Wood heard the old man's cane shudder nervelessly over the floor.

"You win, you cold-blooded blackmailer," the old man surrendered.

Moss laughed. Wood heard the furniture creak as they rose and set off toward the stairs.

"Do you want to see Wood and the dog again, Talbot?"

"No. I'm convinced."

"Get rid of them, Clarence. No more abandoning them in the street for Talbot's clever reporters to theorize over. Put a silencer on your gun. You'll find it downstairs. Then leave them in the acid vat."

Wood's eyes flashed around the room in terror. He and his body had to escape. For him to escape alone, would mean the end of returning to his own body. Separation would make the task of forcing Moss to give him back his body impossible.

But they were on the second floor, at the rear of the house. Even if there had been a fire escape, he could not have opened the window. The only way out was through the door.

Somehow he had to turn the knob, chance meeting Clarence or Moss on the stairs or in the narrow hall, and open the heavy front door—guiding and defending himself and his body!

The collie in his body whimpered baffledly. Wood fought off the instinctive fear that froze his dog's brain. He had to be cool.

Below, he heard Clarence's ponderous steps as he went through the rooms looking for a silencer to muffle his gun.

Gilroy closed the door of the telephone booth and fished in his pocket for a coin. Of all of mankind's scientific gadgets, the telephone booth most clearly demonstrates that this is a world of five feet nine. When Gilroy pulled a coin out of his pocket, his elbow banged against the shut door; and as he dialed his number and stooped over the mouthpiece, he was forced to bend himself into the shape of a cane. But he had conditioned his lanky body to adjust itself to things scaled below its need. He did not mind the lack of room.

But he shoved his shapeless felt hat on the back of his head and whistled softly in a discouraged manner.

"Let me talk to the chief," he said. The receiver rasped in his ear. The editor greeted him abstractedly; Gilroy knew he had just come on and was scattering papers over his desk, looking at the latest. "Gilroy, chief," the reporter said.

"What've you got on the catatonics?"

Gilroy's sharply planed face wrinkled in earnest defeat. "Not a thing, chief," he replied hollowly.

"Where were you?"

"I was in Memorial all day, looking at the catatonics and waiting for an idea."

The editor became sympathetic. "How'd you make out?" he asked.

"Not a thing. They're absolutely dumb and motionless, and nobody around here has anything to say worth listening to. How'd you make out on the police and hospital reports?"

"I was looking at them just before you called." There was a pause. Gilroy heard the crackle of papers being shoved around. "Here they are— The fingerprint bureau has no records of them. No police department in any village, town or city recognizes their pictures."

"How about the hospitals outside New York?" Gilroy asked hopefully.

"No missing patients."

Gilroy sighed and shrugged his thin shoulders eloquently. "Well, all we have is a negative angle. They must have been picked damned carefully. All the papers around the country printed their pictures, and they don't seem to have any friends, relatives or police records."

"How about a human-interest story," the editor encouraged; "what they eat, how helpless they are, their torn, old clothes? Pad out a story about their probable lives, judging from their features and hands. How's that? Not bad, eh?"

"Aw, chief," Gilroy moaned, "I'm licked. That padding stuff isn't my line. I'm not a sob sister. We haven't a thing to work on. These tramps had absolutely no connection with life. We can't find out who they were, where they came from, or what happened to them."

The editor's voice went sharp and incisive. "Listen to me, Gilroy!" he rapped out. "You stop that whining, do you hear me? I'm running this paper, and as long as you don't see fit to quit, I'll send you out after birth lists if I want to.

"You thought this was a good story and you convinced me that it was. Well, I'm still convinced! I want these catatonics tracked down. I want to know all about them, and how they wound up behind the eight-ball. So does the public. I'm not stopping until I *do* know. Get me?

"You get to work on this story and hang onto it. Don't let it throw you! And just to show you how I'm standing behind you . . . I'm giving you a blank expense account and your own discretion. Now track these catatonics down in any way you can figure out!"

Gilroy was stunned for an instant. "Well, gosh," he stammered, confused, "I'll do my best, chief. I didn't know you felt that way."

"The two of us'll crack this story wide open, Gilroy. But just come around to me with another whine about being licked, and you can start in as copy boy for some other sheet. Do you get me? That's final!"

Gilroy pulled his hat down firmly. "I get you, chief," he declared manfully. "You can count on me right up to the hilt."

He slammed the receiver on its hook, yanked the door open, and strode out with a new determination. He felt like the power of the press, and the feeling was not unjustified. The might and cunning of a whole vast metropolitan newspaper was ranged solidly behind him. Few secrets could hide from its searching probe.

All he needed was patience and shrewd observation. Finding the first clue would be hardest; after that the story would unwind by itself. He marched toward the hospital exit.

He heard steps hastening behind him and felt a light, detaining touch on his arm. He wheeled and looked down at the resident physician, dressed in street clothes and coming on duty.

"You're Gilroy, aren't you?" the doctor asked. "Well, I was thinking about the incisions on the catatonics' necks—"

"What about them?" Gilroy demanded alertly, pulling out a pad.

"Quitting again?" the editor asked ten minutes later.

"Not me, chief!" Gilroy propped his stenographic pad on top of the telephone. "I'm hot on the trail. Listen to this. The resident physician over here at Memorial tipped me off to a real clue. He figured out that the incisions on the catatonics' necks aimed at some part of their brains. The incisions penetrate at a tangent a quarter of an inch off the vertebræ, so it couldn't have been to tamper with the spinal cord. You can't reach the posterior part of the brain from that angle, he says, and working from the back of the neck wouldn't bring you to any important part of the neck that can't be reached better from the front or through the mouth.

"If you don't cut the spinal cord with that incision, you can't account for general paralysis; and the cords definitely weren't cut.

"So he thinks the incisions were aimed at some part of the base of the brain that can't be reached from above. He doesn't know what part or how the operation would cause general paralysis.

"Got that? O. K. Well, here's the payoff:

"To reach the exact spot of the brain you want, you ordinarily take off a good chunk of skull, somewhere around that spot. But these incisions were predetermined to the last centimeter. And he doesn't know how. The surgeon worked entirely by measurements—like blind flying. He says only three or four surgeons in the country could've done it."

"Who are they, you cluck? Did you get their names?"

Gilroy became offended. "Of course. Moss in New York; Faber in Chicago; Crowninshield in Portland; maybe Johnson in Detroit."

"Well, what're you waiting for?" the editor shouted. "Get Moss!"

"Can't locate him. He moved from his Riverside Drive apartment and left no forwarding address. He was peeved. The board asked for his resignation and he left with a pretty bad name for mismanagement."

The editor sprang into action. "That leaves us four men to track down. Find Moss. I'll call up the other boys you named. It looks like a good tip."

Gilroy hung up. With half a dozen vast strides, he had covered the distance to the hospital exit, moving with ungainly, predatory swiftness.

Wood was in a mind-freezing panic. He knew it hindered him, prevented him from plotting his escape, but he was powerless to control the fearful darting of his dog's brain.

It would take Clarence only a short time to find the silencer and climb the stairs to kill him and his body. Before Clarence could find the silencer, Wood and his body had to escape.

Wood lifted himself clumsily, unsteadily, to his hind legs and took the doorknob between his paws. They refused to grip. He heard Clarence stop, and the sound of scraping drawers came to his sharp ears.

He was terrified. He bit furiously at the knob. It slipped between his teeth. He bit harder. Pain stabbed his sensitive gums, but the bitter brass dented. Hanging to the knob, he lowered himself to the floor, bending his neck sharply to turn it. The tongue clicked out of the lock. He threw himself to one side, flipping back the door as he fell. It opened a crack. He thrust his snout in the opening and forced it wide.

From below, he heard the ponderous footfalls moving again. Wood stalked noiselessly into the hall and peered down the well of the stairs. Clarence was out of sight.

He drew back into the room and pulled at his body's clothing, backing out into the hall again until the dog crawled voluntarily. It crept after him and down the stairs.

All at once Clarence came out of a room and made for the stairs. Wood crouched, trembling at the sound of metallic clicking that he knew was a silencer being fitted to a gun. He barred his body. It halted, its idiot face hanging down over the step, silent and without protest.

Clarence reached the stairs and climbed confidently. Wood tensed, waiting for Clarence to turn the spiral and come into view.

Clarence sighted them and froze rigid. His mouth opened blankly, startled. The gun trembled impotently at his side, and he stared up at them with his fat, white neck exposed and inviting. Then his chest heaved and his larynx tightened for a yell.

But Wood's long teeth cleared. He lunged high, directly at Clarence, and his fangs snapped together in midair.

Soft flesh ripped in his teeth. He knocked Clarence over; they fell down the stairs and crashed to the floor. Clarence thrashed around, gurgling. Wood smelled a sudden rush of blood that excited an alien lust in him. He flung himself clear and landed on his feet.

His body clumped after him, pausing to sniff at Clarence. He pulled it away and darted to the front door.

From the back of the house he heard Moss running to investigate. He bit savagely at the doorknob, jerking it back awkwardly, terrified that Moss might reach him before the door opened.

But the lock clicked, and he thrust the door wide with his body. His human body flopped after him on hands and knees to the stoop. He hauled it down the steps to the sidewalk and herded it anxiously toward Central Park West, out of Moss's range.

Wood glanced back over his shoulder, saw the doctor glaring at them through the curtain on the door, and, in terror, he dragged his body in a clumsy gallop to the corner where he would be protected by traffic.

He had escaped death, and he and his body were still together; but his panic grew stronger. How could he feed it, shelter it, defend it against Moss and Talbot's gangsters? And how could he force Moss to give him back his body?

But he saw that first he would have to shield his body from observation. It was hungry, and it prowled around on hands and knees, searching for food. The sight of a crawling, sniffing human body attracted disgusted attention; before long they were almost surrounded.

Wood was badly scared. With his teeth, he dragged his body into the street and guided its slow crawl to the other side, where Central Park could hide them with its trees and bushes.

Moss had been more alert. A black car sped through a red light and crowded down on them. From the other side a police car shot in and out of traffic, its siren screaming, and braked dead beside Wood and his body.

The black car checked its headlong rush.

Wood crouched defensively over his body, glowering at the two cops who charged out at them. One shoved Wood away with his foot; the other raised his body by the armpits and tried to stand it erect.

"A nut—he thinks he's a dog," he said interestedly. "The screwball ward for him, eh?"

The other nodded. Wood lost his reason. He attacked, snapping viciously. His body took up the attack, snarling horribly and biting on all sides. It was insane, hopeless; but he had no way of communicating, and he had to do something to prevent being separated from his body. The police kicked him off.

Suddenly he realized that if they had not been burdened with his body, they would have shot him. He darted wildly into traffic before they sat his body in the car.

"Want to get out and plug him before he bites somebody?" he heard.

"This nut'll take a hunk out of you," the other replied. "We'll send out an alarm from the hospital."

It drove off downtown. Wood scrambled after it. His legs pumped furiously; but it pulled away from him, and other cars came between. He lost it after a few blocks.

Then he saw the black car make a reckless turn through traffic and roar after him. It was too intently bearing down on him to have been anything but Talbot's gangsters.

His eyes and muscles coördinated with animal precision. He ran in the swift traffic, avoiding being struck, and at the same time kept watch for a footpath leading into the park.

When he found one, he sprinted into the opposite lane of traffic. Brakes screeched; a man cursed him in a loud voice. But he scurried in front of the car, gained the sidewalk, and dashed along the cement path until he came to a miniature forest of bushes.

Without hesitation, he left the path and ran through the woods. It was not a dense growth, but it covered him from sight. He scampered deep into the park.

His frightened eyes watched the carload of gangsters scour the trees on both sides of the path. Hugging the ground, he inched away from them. They beat the bushes a safe distance away from him.

While he circled behind them, creeping from cover to cover, there was small danger of being caught. But he was appalled by the loss of his body. Being near it had given him a sort of courage, even though he did not know how he was going to force Moss to give it back to him. Now, besides making the doctor operate, he had to find a way of getting near it again.

But his empty stomach was knotted with hunger. Before he could make plans he had to eat.

He crept furtively out of his shelter. The gangsters were far out of sight. Then, with infinite patience, he sneaked up on a squirrel. The alert little animal was observant and wary. It took an exhaustingly long time before he ambushed it and snapped its spine. The thought of eating an uncooked rodent revolted him.

He dug back into his cache of bushes with his prey. When he tried to plot a line of action, his dog's brain balked. It was terrified and maddened with helplessness.

There was good reason for its fear—Moss had Talbot's gangsters out gunning for him, and by this time the police were probably searching for him as a vicious dog.

In all his nightmares he had never imagined any so horrible. He was utterly impotent to help himself. The forces of law and crime were ranged against him; he had no way of communicating the fact that he was a man to those who could possibly help him; he was completely inarticulate; and besides, who could help him, except Moss? Suppose he did manage to evade the police, the gangsters, and sneaked past a hospital's vigilant staff, and somehow succeeded in communicating—

Even so, only Moss could perform the operation!

He had to rule out doctors and hospitals; they were too routinized to have much imagination. But, more important than that, they could not influence Moss to operate.

He scrambled to his feet and trotted cautiously through the clumps of brush in the direction of Columbus Circle. First, he had to be alert for police and gangsters. He had to find a method of communicating —but to somebody who could understand him and exert tremendous pressure on Moss.

The city's smells came to his sensitive nostrils. Like a vast blanket, covering most of them, was a sweet odor that he identified as gasoline vapor. Above it hovered the scent of vegetation, hot and moist; and below it, the musk of mankind.

To his dog's perspective, it was a different world, with a broad, distant, terrifying horizon. Smells and sounds formed scenes in his animal mind. Yet it was interesting. The pad of his paws against the soft, cushioned ground gave him an instinctive pleasure; all the clothes he needed, he carried on him; and food was not hard to find.

While he shielded himself from the police and Talbot's gangsters, he even enjoyed a sort of freedom—but it was a cowardly freedom that he did not want, that was not worth the price. As a man, he had suffered hunger, cold, lack of shelter and security, indifference. In spite of all that, his dog's body harbored a human intelligence; he belonged on his hind legs, standing erect, living the life, good or bad, of a man.

In some way he must get back to that world, out of the solitary anarchy of animaldom. Moss alone could return him. He must be forced to do it! He must be compelled to return the body he had robbed!

But how could Wood communicate, and who could help him?

Near the end of Central Park, he exposed himself to overwhelming danger.

He was padding along a path that skirted the broad road. A cruising black car accelerated with deadly, predatory swiftness, sped abreast of him. He heard a muffled *pop*. A bullet hissed an inch over his head.

He ducked low and scurried back into the concealing bushes. He snaked nimbly from tree to tree, keeping obstacles between him and the line of fire.

The gangsters were out of the car. He heard them beating the brush for him. Their progress was slow, while his fleet legs pumped three hundred yards of safety away from them.

He burst out of the park and scampered across Columbus Circle, reckless of traffic. On Broadway he felt more secure, hugging the buildings with dense crowds between him and the street.

When he felt certain that he had lost the gangsters, he turned west through one-way streets, alert for signs of danger.

In coping with physical danger, he discovered that his animal mind reacted instinctively, and always more cunningly than a human brain.

Impulsively, he cowered behind stoops, in doorways, behind any sort of shelter, when the traffic moved. When it stopped, packed tightly, for the light, he ran at topnotch speed. Cars skidded across his path, and several times he was almost hit; but he did not slow to a trot until he had zigzagged downtown, going steadily away from the center of the city, and reached West Street, along North River.

He felt reasonably safe from Talbot's gangsters. But a police car approached slowly under the express highway. He crouched behind an overflowing garbage can outside a filthy restaurant. Long after it was gone, he cowered there.

The shrill wind blowing over the river and across the covered docks picked a newspaper off the pile of garbage and flattened it against the restaurant window.

Through his animal mind, frozen into numbing fear, he remembered the afternoon before—standing in front of the employment agency, talking to one of Talbot's gangsters—

A thought had come to him then: that it would be pleasant to be a catatonic instead of having to starve. He knew better now. But—

He reared to his hind legs and overturned the garbage can. It fell with a loud crash, rolling down toward the gutter, spilling refuse all over the sidewalk. Before a restaurant worker came out, roaring abuse, he pawed through the mess and seized a twisted newspaper in his mouth. It smelled of sour, rotting food, but he caught it up and ran.

Blocks away from the restaurant, he ran across a wide, torn lot, to cover behind a crumbling building. Sheltered from the river wind, he straightened out the paper and scanned the front page.

It was a day old, the same newspaper that he had thrown away before the employment agency. On the left column he found the catatonic story. It was signed by a reporter named Gilroy.

Then he took the edge of the sheet between his teeth and backed away with it until the newspaper opened clumsily, wrinkled, at the next page. He was disgusted by the fetid smell of putrifying food that clung to it; but he swallowed his gorge and kept turning the huge, stiff, unwieldy sheets with his inept teeth. He came to the editorial page and paused there, studying intently the copyright box.

He set off at a fast trot, wary against danger, staying close to walls of buildings, watching for cars that might contain either gangsters or policemen, darting across streets to shelter—trotting on—

The air was growing darker, and the express highway cast a long shadow. Before the sun went down, he covered almost three miles along West Street, and stopped not far from the Battery.

He gaped up at the towering *Morning Post* Building. It looked impregnable, its heavy doors shut against the wind.

He stood at the main entrance, waiting for somebody to hold a door open long enough for him to lunge through it. Hopefully, he kept his eyes on an old man. When he opened the door, Wood was at his heels. But the old man shoved him back with gentle firmness.

Wood bared his fangs. It was his only answer. The man hastily pulled the door shut.

Wood tried another approach. He attached himself to a tall, gangling man who appeared rather kindly in spite of his intent face. Wood gazed up, wagging his tail awkwardly in friendly greeting. The tall man stooped and scratched Wood's ears, but he refused to take him inside. Before the door closed, Wood launched himself savagely at the thin man and almost knocked him down.

In the lobby, Wood darted through the legs surrounding him. The tall man was close behind, roaring angrily. A frightened stampede of thick-soled shoes threatened to crush Wood; but he twisted in and out between the surging feet and gained the stairs.

He scrambled up them swiftly. The second-floor entrance had plate-glass doors. It contained the executive offices.

He turned the corner and climbed up speedily. The stairs narrowed, artificially illuminated. The third and fourth floors were printing-plant rooms; he ran past; clambered by the business offices, classified advertising—

At the editorial department he panted before the heavy fire door, waiting until he regained his breath. Then he gripped the knob between his teeth and pulled it around. The door swung inward.

Thick, bitter smoke clawed his sensitive nostrils; his ears flinched at the clattering, shouting bedlam.

Between rows of littered desks, he inched and gazed around hopefully. He saw abstracted faces, intent on typewriters that rattled out stories; young men racing around to gather batches of papers; men and women swarming in and out of the elevators. Shrewd faces, intelligent and alert—

A few had turned for an instant to look at him as he passed; then turned back to their work, almost without having seen him.

He trembled with elation. These were the men who had the power to influence Moss, and the acuteness to understand him! He squatted and put his paw on the leg of a typing reporter, staring up expectantly. The reporter stared, looked down agitatedly, and shoved him away.

"Go on, beat it!" he said angrily. "Go home!"

Wood shrank back. He did not sense danger. Worse than that, he had failed. His mind worked rapidly: suppose he *had* attracted interest, how would he have communicated his story intelligibly? How could he explain in the equivalent of words?

All at once the idea exploded in his mind. He had been a code translator in a stockbroker's office—

He sat back on his haunches and barked, loud, broken, long and short yelps. A girl screamed. Reporters jumped up defensively, surged away in a tightening ring. Wood barked out his message in Morse, painful, slow, straining a larynx that was foreign to him. He looked around optimistically for someone who might have understood.

Instead, he met hostile, annoyed stares—and no comprehension.

"That's the hound that attacked me!" the tall, thin man said.

"Not for food, I hope," a reporter answered.

Wood was not entirely defeated. He began to bark his message again; but a man hurried out of the glass-inclosed editor's office.

"What's all the commotion here?" he demanded. He sighted Wood among the ring of withdrawing reporters. "Get that damned dog out of here!"

"Come on—get him out of here!" the thin man shouted.

"He's a nice, friendly dog. Give him the hypnotic eye, Gilroy."

Wood stared pleadingly at Gilroy. He had not been understood, but he had found the reporter who had written the catatonic articles! Gilroy approached cautiously, repeating phrases calculated to sooth a savage dog.

Wood darted away through the rows of desks. He was so near to success— He only needed to find a way of communicating before they caught him and put him out!

He lunged to the top of a desk and crashed a bottle of ink to the floor. It splashed into a dark puddle. Swiftly, quiveringly, he seized a piece of white paper, dipped his paw into the splotch of ink, and made a hasty attempt to write.

His surge of hope died quickly. The wrist of his forepaw was not the universal joint of a human being; it had a single upward articulation! When he brought his paw down on the paper, it flattened uselessly, and his claws worked in a unit. He could not draw back three to write with one. Instead, he made a streaked pad print—

Dejectedly, rather than antagonize Gilroy, Wood permitted himself to be driven back into an elevator. He wagged his tail clumsily. It was a difficult feat, calling into use alien muscles that he employed with intellectual deliberation. He sat down and assumed a grin that would have been friendly on a human face; but, even so, it reassured Gilroy. The tall reporter patted his head. Nevertheless, he put him out firmly.

But Wood had reason to feel encouraged. He had managed to get inside the building, and had attracted attention. He knew that a newspaper was the only force powerful enough to influence Moss, but there was still the problem of communication. How could he solve it? His paw was worthless for writing, with its single articulation; and nobody in the office could understand Morse code.

He crouched against the white cement wall, his harried mind darting wildly in all directions for a solution. Without a voice or prehensile fingers, his only method of communication seemed to be barking in code. In all that throng, he was certain there would be one to interpret it.

Glances *did* turn to him. At least, he had no difficulty in arousing interest. But they were incomprehending looks.

For some moments he lost his reason. He ran in and out of the deep, hurrying crowd, barking his message furiously, jumping up at men who appeared more intelligent than the others, following them short distances until it was overwhelmingly apparent that they did not understand, then turning to other men, raising an ear-shattering din of appeal.

He met nothing but a timid pat or frightened rebuffs. He stopped his deafening yelps and cowered back against the wall, defeated. No one would attempt to interpret the barking of a dog in terms of code. When he was a man, he would probably have responded in the same way. The most intelligible message he could hope to convey by his barking was simply the fact that he was trying to attract interest. Nobody would search for any deeper meaning in a dog's barking.

He joined the traffic hastening toward the subway. He trotted along the curb, watchful for slowing cars, but more intent on the strewing of rubbish in the gutter. He was murderously envious of the human feet around him that walked swiftly and confidently to a known destination; smug, selfish feet, undeviating from their homeward path to help him. Their owners could convey the finest shadings and variations in emotion, commands, abstract thought, by speech, writing, print, through telephone, radio, books, newspapers—

But his voice was only a piercing, inarticulate yelp that infuriated human beings; his paws were good for nothing but running; his pointed face transmitted no emotions.

He trotted along the curbs of three blocks in the business district before he found a pencil stump. He picked it up in his teeth and ran to the docks on West Street, though he had only the vague outline of a last experiment in communication.

There was plenty of paper blowing around in the river wind, some of it even clean. To the stevedores, waiting at the dock for the payoff, he appeared to be frisking. A few of them whistled at him. In reality, he chased the flying paper with deadly earnestness.

When he captured a piece, he held it firmly between his forepaws. The stub of pencil was gripped in the even space separating his sharp canine fangs.

He moved the pencil in his mouth over the sheet of paper. It was clumsy and uncertain, but he produced long, wavering block letters. He wrote: "I AM A MAN." The short message covered the whole page, leaving no space for further information.

He dropped the pencil, caught up the paper in his teeth, and ran back to the newspaper building. For the first time since he had escaped from Moss, he felt assured. His attempt at writing was crude and unformed, but the message was unmistakably clear.

He joined a group of tired young legmen coming back from assignments. He stood passively until the door was opened, then lunged confidently through the little procession of cub reporters. They scattered back cautiously, permitting him to enter without a struggle.

Again he raced up the stairs to the editorial department, put the sheet of paper down on the floor, and clutched the doorknob between his powerful teeth.

He hesitated for only an instant, to find the cadaverous reporter. Gilroy was seated at a desk, typing out his article. Carrying his message in his mouth, Wood trotted directly to Gilroy. He put his paw on the reporter's sharp knee.

"What the hell!" Gilroy gasped. He pulled his leg away startledly and shoved Wood away.

But Wood came back insistently, holding his paper stretched out to Gilroy as far as possible. He trembled hopefully until the reporter snatched the message out of his mouth. Then his muscles froze, and he stared up expectantly at the angular face, scanning it for signs of growing comprehension.

Gilroy kept his eyes on the straggling letters. His face darkened angrily.

"Who's being a wise guy here?" he shouted suddenly. Most of the staff ignored him. "Who let this mutt in and gave him a crank note to bring to me? Come on—who's the genius?"

Wood jumped around him, barking hysterically, trying to explain.

"Oh, shut up!" Gilroy rapped out. "Hey, copy! Take this dog down and see that he doesn't get back in! He won't bite you."

Again Wood had failed. But he did not feel defeated. When his hysterical dread of frustration ebbed, leaving his mind clear and analytical, he realized that his failure was only one of degree. Actually, he had communicated, but lack of space had prevented him from detailed clarity. The method was correct. He only needed to augment it.

Before the copy boy cornered him, Wood swooped up at a pencil on an empty desk.

"Should I let him keep the pencil, Mr. Gilroy?" the boy asked.

"I'll lend you mine, unless you want your arm snapped off," Gilroy snorted, turning back to his typewriter.

Wood sat back and waited beside the copy boy for the elevator to pick them up. He clenched the pencil possessively between his teeth. He was impatient to get out of the building and back to the lot on West Street, where he could plan a system of writing a more explicit message. His block letters were unmanageably huge and shaky; but, with the same logical detachment he used to employ when he was a code translator, he attacked the problem fearlessly.

He knew that he could not use the printed or written alphabet. He would have to find a substitute that his clumsy teeth could manage, and that could be compressed into less space.

Gilroy was annoyed by the collie's insistent returning. He crumpled the enigmatic, unintelligible note and tossed it in the wastebasket, but beyond considering it as a practical joke, he gave it no further thought.

His long, large-jointed fingers swiftly tapped out the last page of his story. He ended it with a short line of zeros and dashes, gathered a sheaf of papers, and brought it to the editor.

The editor studied the lead paragraph intently and skimmed hastily through the rest of the story. He appeared uncomfortable.

"Not bad, eh?" Gilroy exulted.

"Uh—what?" The editor jerked his head up blankly. "Oh. No, it's pretty good. Very good, in fact."

"I've got to hand it to you," Gilroy continued admiringly. "I'd have given up. You know—nothing to work on, just a bunch of fantastic events with no beginning and no end. Now, all of a sudden, the cops pick up a nut who acts like a dog and has an incision like the catatonics. Maybe it isn't any clearer, but at least we've got something actually happening. I don't know—I feel pretty good. We'll get to the bottom—"

The editor listened abstractedly, growing more uneasy from sentence to sentence. "Did you see the latest case?" he intrrupted.

"Sure. I'm in soft with the resident physician. If I hadn't been following this story right from the start, I'd have said the one they just hauled in was a genuine screwball. He goes bounding around on the floor, sniffs at things, and makes a pathetic attempt to bark. But he has an incision on the back of his neck. It's just like the others—even has two professional stitches, and it's the same number of millimeters away from the spine. He's a catatonic, or whatever we'll have to call it now—"

"Well, the story's shaping up faster than I thought it would," the editor said, evening the edges of Gilroy's article with ponderous care. "But—" His voice dropped huskily. 'Well, I don't know how to tell you this, Gilroy."

The reporter drew his brows together and looked at him obliquely. "What's the hard word this time?" he asked, mystified.

"Oh, the usual thing. You know. I've got to take you off this story. It's too bad, because it was just getting hot. I hated to tell you, Gilroy; but, after all, what the hell. That's part of the game."

"It is, huh?" Gilroy flattened his hands on the desk and leaned over them resentfully. "Whose toes did we step on this time? Nobody's. The hospital has no kick coming. I couldn't mention names because I didn't know any to mention. Well, then, what's the angle?"

The editor shrugged. "I can't argue. It's a front-office order. But I've got a good lead for you to follow tomorrow—"

Savagely, Gilroy strode to the window and glared out at the darkening street. The business department wasn't behind the order, he reasoned angrily; they weren't getting ads from the hospital. And as for the big boss—Talbot never interfered with policy, except when he had to squash a revealing crime story. By eliminating the editors, who yielded an inch when public opinion demanded a mile, the business department, who fought only when advertising was at stake, Gilroy could blame no one but Talbot.

Gilroy rapped his bony knuckles impatiently against the window casement. What was the point of Talbot's order? Perhaps he had a new way of paying off traitors. Gilroy dismissed the idea immediately; he knew Talbot wouldn't go to that expense and risk possible leakage when the old way of sealing a body in a cement block and dumping it in the river was still effective and cheap.

"I give up," Gilroy said without turning around. "I can't figure out Talbot's angle."

"Neither can I," the editor admitted.

At that confession, Gilroy wheeled. "Then you *know* it's Talbot!"

"Of course. Who else could it be? But don't let it throw you, pal." He glanced around cautiously as he spoke. "Let this catatonic yarn take a rest. Tomorrow you can find out what's behind this bulletin that Johnson phoned in from City Hall."

Gilroy absently scanned the scribbled note. His scowl wrinkled into puzzlement.

"What the hell is this? All I can make out of it is the A.S.P.C.A. and dog lovers are protesting to the mayor against organized murder of brown-and-white collies."

"That's just what it is."

"And you think Talbot's gang is behind it, naturally." When the editor nodded, Gilroy threw up his hands in despair. "This gang stuff is getting too deep for me, chief. I used to be able to call their shots. I knew why a torpedo was bumped off, or a crime was pulled; but I don't mind telling you that I can't see why a gang boss wants a catatonic yarn hushed up, or sends his mob around plugging innocent collies. I'm going home . . . get drunk—"

He stormed out of the office. Before the editor had time to shrug his shoulders, Gilroy was back again, his deep eyes blazing furiously.

"What a pair of prize dopes we are, chief!" he shouted. "Remember that collie—the one that came in with a hunk of paper in his mouth? We threw him out, remember? Well, *that's the hound Talbot's gang is out gunning for! He's trying to carry messages to us!*"

"Hey, you're right!" The editor heaved out of the chair and stood uncertainly. "Where is he?"

Gilroy waved his long arms expressively.

"Then come on! To hell with hats and coats!"

They dashed into the staff room. The skeleton night crew loafed around, reading papers before moping out to follow up undeveloped leads.

"Put those papers down!" the editor shouted. "Come on with me—every one of you."

He herded them, baffled and annoyed, into the elevator. At the entrance to the building, he searched up and down the street.

"He's not around, Gilroy. All right, you deadbeats, divide up and chase around the streets, whistling. When you see a brown-and-white collie, whistle to him. He'll come to you. Now beat it and do as I say."

They moved off slowly. "Whistle?" one called back anxiously.

"Yes, whistle!" Gilroy declared. "Forget your dignity. Whistle!"

They scattered, whistling piercingly the signals that are supposed to attract dogs. The few people around the business district that late were highly interested and curious, but Gilroy left the editor whistling at the newspaper building, while he whistled toward West Street. He left the shrill calls blowing away from the river, and searched along the wide highway in the growing dark.

For an hour he pried into dark spaces between the docks, patiently covering his ground. He found nothing but occasional longshoremen unloading trucks and a light uptown traffic. There were only homeless, prowling mongrels and starving drifters; no brown-and-white collie.

He gave up when he began to feel hungry. He returned to the building hoping the others had more luck, and angry with himself for not having followed the dog when he had the chance.

The editor was still there, whistling more frantically than ever. He had gathered a little band of inquisitive onlookers, who waited hopefully for something to happen. The reporters were also returning.

"Find anything?" the editor paused to ask.

"Nope. He didn't show up here?"

"Not yet. Oh, he'll be back, all right. I'm not afraid of that." And he went back to his persistent whistling, disregarding stares and rude remarks. He was a man with an iron will. He sneered openly at the defeated reporters when they slunk past him into the building.

In the comparative quiet of the city, above the editor's shrills, Gilroy heard swiftly pounding feet. He gazed over the heads of the pack that had gathered around the editor.

A reporter burst into view, running at top speed and doing his best to whistle attractively through dry lips at a dog streaking away from him.

"Here he comes!" Gilroy shouted. He broke through the crowd and his long legs flashed over the distance to the collie. In his excitement, empty, toneless wind blew between his teeth; but the dog shot straight for him just the same. Gilroy snatched a dirty piece of paper out of his mouth. Then the dog was gone, toward the docks; and a black car rode ominously down the street.

Gilroy half started in pursuit, paused, and stared at the slip of paper in his hand. For a moment he blamed the insufficient light, but when the editor came up to him, yelling blasphemy for letting the dog escape, Gilroy handed him the unbelievable note.

"That dog can take care of himself," Gilroy said. "Read this."

The editor drew his brows together over the message. It read:

$$\ldots;\ldots;\cdot;\quad;\ldots;\cdot;\ldots\text{''}\ldots\cdot;\cdot;\quad;\ldots\text{''}\ldots\ldots;\cdot;\ldots;\cdot;\cdot;\text{''}\ldots;\quad\ldots;\text{''}\ldots\text{''};\ldots\quad\text{''}\ldots;\quad\text{''};\text{''}\cdot;$$

"Well, I'll be damned!" the editor exclaimed. "Is it a gag?"

"Gag, my eye!"

"Well, I can't make head or tail of it!" the editor protested.

Gilroy looked around undeterminedly, as if for someone to help them. "You're not supposed to. It's a code message." He swung around, stabbing an enormously long, knobbed finger at the editor. "Know anyone who can translate code—cryptograms?"

"Uh—let's see. How about the police, or the G-men—"

Gilroy snorted. "Give it to the bulls before we know what's in it!" He carefully tucked the crudely penciled note into his breast pocket and buttoned his coat. "You stick around outside here, chief. I'll be back with the translation. Keep an eye out for the pooch."

He loped off before the editor could more than open his mouth.

In the index room of the Forty-second Street Library, Gilroy crowded into the telephone booth and dialed a number. His eyes ached and he had a dizzy headache. Close reasoning always scrambled his wits. His mind was intuitive rather than ploddingly analytical.

"Executive office, please," he told the night operator. "There must be somebody there. I don't care if it's the business manager himself. I want to speak to somebody in the executive office. I'll wait." He lolled, bent into a convenient shape, against the wall. "Hello. Who's this? . . . Oh, good. Listen, Rothbart, this is Gilroy. Do me a favor, huh? You're nearest the front entrance. You'll find the chief outside the door. Send him into the telephone, and take his place until he gets through. While you're out there, watch for a brown-and-white collie. Nab him if he shows up and bring him inside. . . . Will you? . . . Thanks!"

Gilroy held the receiver to his ear, defeatedly amusing himself by identifying the sounds coming over the wire. He was no longer in a hurry, and when he had to pay another nickel before the editor finally came to the telephone, he did not mind.

"What's up, Gilroy?" the editor asked hopefully.

"Nothing, chief. That's why I called up. I went through a military code book, some kids' stuff, and a history of crypotography through the ages. I found some good codes, but nobody seems to've thought of this punctuation code. Ever see the Confederate cipher? Boy, it's a real dazzler—wasn't cracked until after the Civil War was over! The old Greeks wound strips of paper around identical sticks. When they were unrolled, the strips were gibberish; around the sticks, the words fell right into order."

"Cut it out," the editor snapped. "Did you find anything useful?"

"Sure. Everybody says the big clue is the table of frequency—the letters used more often than others. But, on the other hand, they say that in short messages, like ours, important clues like the single words 'a' and 'I,' bigrams like 'am,' 'as,' and even trigrams like 'the' or 'but,' are often omitted entirely."

"Well, that's fine. What're you going to do now?"

"I don't know. Try the cops after all, I guess."

"Nothing doing," the editor said firmly. "Ask a librarian to help."

Gilroy seized the inspiration. He slammed down the receiver and strode to the reference desk.

"Where can I get hold of somebody who knows cryptograms?" he rasped.

The attendant politely consulted his colleagues. "The guard of the manuscript room is pretty good," he said, returning. "Down the hall—"

Gilroy shouted his thanks and broke into an ungainly run, ignoring the attendant's order to walk. At the manuscript room he clattered the gate until the keeper appeared and let him in.

"Take a look at this," he commanded, flinging the message on a table.

The keeper glanced curiously at it. "Oh, cryptogram, eh?"

"Yeah. Can you make anything out of it?"

"Well, it looks like a good one," the guard replied cautiously, "but I've been cracking them all for the last twenty years." They sat down at the table in the empty room. For some time the guard stared fixedly at the scrawled note. "Five symbols," he said finally. "Semicolon, period, comma, colon, quotation marks. Thirteen word units, each with an even number of symbols. They must be used in combinations of two."

"I figured that out already," Gilroy rapped out. "What's it *say?*"

The guard lifted his head, offended. "Give me a chance. Bacon's code wasn't solved for three centuries."

Gilroy groaned. He did not have so much time on his hands.

"There're only thirteen word units here," the guard went on, undaunted by the Bacon example. "Can't use frequency, bigrams or trigrams."

"I know that already," Gilroy said hoarsely.

"Then why'd you come to me if you're so smart?"

Gilroy hitched his chair away. "O. K., I won't bother you."

"Five symbols to represent twenty-six letters. Can't be. Must be something like the Russian nihilist code. They can represent only twenty-five letters. The missing one is either 'q' or 'j,' most likely, because they're not used much. Well, I'll tell you what I think."

"What's that?" Gilroy demanded, all alert.

"You'll have to reason *a priori,* or whatever it is."

"Any way you want," Gilroy sighed. "Just get on with it."

"The square root of twenty-five is five. Whoever wrote this note must've made a square of letters, five wide and five deep. That sounds right." The guard smiled and nodded cheerfully. "Possible combinations in a square of twenty-five letters is . . . uh . . . 625. The double symbols must identify the lines down and across. Possible combinations, twenty-five. Combinations all told . . . hm-m-m . . . 15,625. Not so good. If there's a key word, we'll have to search the dictionary until we find it. Possible combinations, 15,625 multiplied by the English vocabulary—that is, if the key word *is* English."

Gilroy raised himself to his feet. "I can't stand it," he moaned. "I'll be back in an hour."

"No, don't go," the guard said. "You've been helping me a lot. I don't think we'll have to go through more than 625 combinations at the most. That'll take no time at all."

He spoke, of course, in relative terms. Bacon code, three centuries; Confederate code, fifteen years; war-time Russian code, unsolved. Cryptographers must look forward to eternity.

Gilroy seated himself, while the guard plotted a square:

:	"	,	.	:	
a	b	c	d	e	;
f	g	h	i	j	;"
k	l	m	n	o	,
p	r	s	t	u	.
v	w	x	y	z	:

The first symbol combination, two semicolons, translated to "a," by reading down the first line, from the top semicolon, and across from the side semicolon. The next, a semicolon and a comma, read "k." He went on in this fashion until he screwed up his face and pushed the half-completed translation to Gilroy. It read:

"akdd kyoiztou kp tbo eztztkprepd"

"Does it make sense to you?" he asked anxiously.

Gilroy strangled, unable to reply.

"It could be Polish," the guard explained, "or Japanese."

The harassed reporter fled.

When he returned an hour later, after having eaten and tramped across town, nervously chewing cigarettes, he found the guard defended from him by a breastwork of heaped papers.

"Does it look any better?" Gilroy asked hoarsely.

The guard was too absorbed to look up or answer. By peering over his shoulder, Gilroy saw that he had plotted another square. The papers on the table were covered with discarded letter keys; at a rough guess, Gilroy estimated that the keeper had made over a hundred of them.

The one he was working with had been formed as the result of methodical elimination. His first square, the guard had kept, changing the
positions of the punctuation marks. When that had failed, he altered his
alphabet square, tried that, and reversed his punctuation marks once
more. Patient and plodding the guard had formed this square:

,	.	;	"	:	
z	u	o	j	e	,
y	t	n	i	d	.
x	s	m	h	c	;
w	r	l	g	b	"
v	p	k	f	a	:

Without haste, he counted down under the semicolon and across
from the side semicolon, stopping at "m." Gilroy followed him, nodding
at the result. He was faster than the old guard at interpreting the semicolon and comma—"o." The period and semicolon, repeated twice, came
to "ss." First word: "moss."

Gilroy straightened up and took a deep breath. He bent over again
and counted down and across with the guard, through the whole message, which the old man had lined off between every two symbols. Completed, it read:

```
;;|;,|.;|.;|   ;,|.:|:,|."|::|..|;,|:,|   ;,|;,|   ..|";|;,|   :;|::|..|::|..|;,|;,|."|.;|.;|
m o s s        o p e r a t e d        o n        t h e        c a t a t o n i c s

..|::|;"|:"|;,|..|   ".|.;|   ":|".|;,|::|;,|:;|".|;,|"""|   ";|".|;;|   .:|."|;,|..|:;|.;|..
t a l b o t       i s        f i n a n c i n g          h i m       p r o t e c t

;;|:,|   ":|."|;,|;;|   ..|";|:,|;;
m e        f r o m        t h e m
```

"Hm-m-m," the guard mused. "That makes sense, if I knew what it
meant."

But Gilroy had snatched the papers out of his hand. The gate clanged
shut after him.

Returning to the office in a taxi, Gilroy was not too joyful. He rapped
on the inside window. "Speed it up! I've seen the sights."

He thought, if the dog's been bumped off, good-by catatonic story!
The dog was his only link with the code writer.

Wood slunk along the black, narrow alleys behind the wholesale fruit
markets on West Street. Battered cans and crates of rotting fruit made
welcome obstacles and shelters if Talbot's gangsters were following him.

He knew that he had to get away from the river section. The gangsters
must have definitely recognized him; they would call Talbot's headquarters for greater forces. With their speedy cars they could patrol the
borders of the district he was operating in, and close their lines until he
was trapped.

More important was the fact that reporters had been sent out to search
for him. Whether or not his simple code had been deciphered did not

matter very much; the main thing was that Gilroy at last knew he was trying to communicate with him.

Wood's unerring animal sense of direction led him through the maze of densely shadowed alleys to a point nearest the newspaper office. He peered around the corner, up and down the street. The black gang car was out of sight. But he had to make an unprotected dash of a hundred yards, in the full glare of the street lights, to the building entrance.

His powerful leg muscles gathered. He sped over the hard cement sidewalk. The entrance drew nearer. His legs pumped more furiously, shortening the dangerous space more swiftly than a human being could; and for that he was grateful.

He glimpsed a man standing impatiently at the door. At the last possible moment, Wood checked his rush and flung himself toward the thick glass plate.

"There you are!" the editor cried. "Inside—quick!"

He thrust open the door. They scurried inside and commandeered an elevator, ran through the newsroom to the editor's office.

"Boy, I hope you weren't seen! It'd be curtains for both of us."

The editor squirmed uneasily behind his desk, from time to time glancing disgruntledly at his watch and cursing Gilroy's long absence. Wood stretched out on the cold floor and panted. He had expected his note to be deciphered by then, and even hoped to be recognized as a human being in a dog's body. But he realized that Gilroy probably was still engaged in decoding it.

At any rate he was secure for a while. Before long, Gilroy would return; then his story would be known. Until then he had patience.

Wood raised his head and listened. He recognized Gilroy's characteristic pace that consumed at least four feet at a step. Then the door slammed open and shut behind the reporter.

"The dog's here, huh? Wait'll you take a look at what I got!"

He threw a square of paper before the editor. Wood scanned the editor's face as he eagerly read it. He ignored the vast hamburger that Gilroy unwrapped for him. He was bewildered by Gilroy's lack of more than ordinary interest in him; but perhaps the editor would understand.

"So that's it! Moss and Talbot, eh? it's getting a lot clearer."

"I get Moss's angle," Gilroy said. "He's the only guy around here who could do an operation like that. But Talbot— I don't get his game. And who sent the note—how'd he get the dope—where is he?"

Wood almost went mad with frustration. He could explain; he knew all there was to be known about Talbot's interest in Moss's experiment. The problem of communication had been solved. Moss and Talbot were exposed; but he was as far as ever from regaining his own body.

He had to write another cipher message—longer, this time, and more explicit, answering the questions Gilroy raised. But to do that— He shivered. To do that, he would have to run the gang patrol; and his enciphering square was in the corner of a lot. It would be too dark—

"We've got to get him to lead us to the one who wrote the message," Gilroy said determinedly. "That's the only way we can corner Moss and Talbot. Like this, all we have is an accusation and no legal proof."

"He must be around here somewhere."

Gilroy fastened his eyes on Wood. "That's what I think. The dog came here and barked, trying to get us to follow him. When we chased him out, he came back with a scrawled note about a half hour later. Then he brought the code message within another hour. The writer must be pretty near here. After the dog eats, we'll—" He gulped audibly and raised his bewildered gaze to the editor. Swiftly, he slipped off the edge of the desk and fumbled in the long hair on Wood's neck. "Look at that, chief—a piece of surgical plaster. When the dog bent his head to eat, the hair fell away from it."

"And you think he's a catatonic." The editor smiled pityingly and shook his head. "You're jumpy, Gilroy."

"Maybe I am. But I'd like to see what's under the plaster."

Wood's heart pumped furiously. He knew that his incision was the precise duplicate of the catatonics', and if Gilroy could see it, he would immediately understand. When Gilroy picked at the plaster, he tried to bear the stabbing pain; but he had to squirm away. The wound was raw and new, and the deeply rooted hair was firmly glued to the plaster. He permitted Gilroy to try again. The sensation was far too fierce; he was afraid the incision would rip wide open.

"Stop it," the editor said squeamishly. "He'll bite you."

Gilroy straightened up. "I could take it off with some ether."

"You don't really think he was operated on, do you? Moss doesn't operate on dogs. He probably got into a fight, or one of Talbot's torpedoes creased him with a bullet."

The telephone bell rang insistently. "I'd still like to see what's under it," Gilroy said as the editor removed the receiver. Wood's hopes died suddenly. He felt that he was to blame for resisting Gilroy.

"What's up, Blaine?" the editor asked. He listened absorbedly, his face darkening. "O. K. Stay away if you don't want to take a chance. Phone your story in to the rewrite desk." He replaced the receiver and said to Gilroy: "Trouble, plenty of it. Talbot's gang cars are cruising around this district. Blaine was afraid to run them. I don't know how you're going to get the dog through."

Wood was alarmed. He left his meal unfinished and agitated toward the door, whimpering involuntarily.

Gilroy glanced curiously at him. "I'd swear he understood what you said. Did you see the change that came over him?"

"That's the way they react to voices," the editor said.

"Well, we've got to get him to his master." Gilroy mused, biting the inside of his cheek. "I can do it—if you're in with me."

"Of course I am. How?"

"Follow me." Wood and the editor went through the newsroom on the cadaverous reporter's swift heels. In silence they waited for an elevator, descended to the lobby. "Wait here beside the door," Gilroy said. "When I give the signal, come running."

"What signal?" the editor cried, but Gilroy had loped into the street and out of sight.

They waited tensely. In a few minutes a taxi drew up to the curb and Gilroy opened the door, sitting alertly inside. He watched the corner behind him. No one moved for a long while; then a black gang car rode slowly and vigilantly past the taxi. An automatic rifle barrel glinted in the yellow light. Gilroy waited until a moment after it turned into West Street. He waved his arms frantically.

The editor scooped Wood up in his arms, burst open the door, and darted across the sidewalk into the cab.

"Step on it!" Gilroy ordered harshly. "Up West Street!"

The taxi accelerated suddenly. Wood crouched on the floor, trembling, in despair. He had exhausted his ingenuity and he was as far as ever from regaining his body. They expected him to lead them to his master; they still did not realize that he had written the message. Where should he lead them—how could he convince them that he was the writer?

"I think this is far enough," Gilroy broke the silence. He tapped on the window. The driver stopped. Gilroy and the editor got out, Wood following indecisively. Gilroy paid and waved the driver away. In the quiet isolation of the broad commercial highway, he bent his great height to Wood's level. "Come on, boy!" he urged. "Home!"

Wood was in a panic of dismay. He could think of only one place to lead them. He set off at a slow trot that did not tax them. Hugging the walls, sprinting across streets, he headed cautiously downtown.

They followed him behind the markets fronting the highway, over a hemmed-in lot. He picked his way around the deep, treacherous foundation of a building that had been torn down, up and across piles of rubbish, to a black-shadowed clearing at the lot's end. He halted passively.

Gilroy and the editor peered around into the blackness. "Come out!" Gilroy called hoarsely. "We're your friends. We want to help you."

When there was no response, they explored the lot, lighting matches to illuminate dark corners of the foundation. Wood watched them with confused emotions. By searching in the garbage heaps and the crumbling walls of the foundation, they were merely wasting time.

As closely as possible in the dark, he located the site of his enciphering square. He stood near it and barked clamorously. Gilroy and the editor hastily left their futile prodding.

"He must've seen something," the editor observed in a whisper.

Gilroy cupped a match in his hand and moved the light back and forth in the triangular corner of the cleared space. He shrugged.

"Not around there," the editor said. "He's pointing at the ground."

Gilroy lowered the match. Before its light struck the ground, he yelped and dropped it, waving his burned fingers in the cool air. The editor murmured sympathy and scratched another match.

"Is this what you're looking for—a lot of letters in a square?"

Wood and Gilroy crowded close. The reporter struck his own match. In its light he narrowly inspected the crudely scratched encoding square.

"Be back in a second," he said. It was too dark to see his face, but Wood heard his voice, harsh and strained. "Getting flashlight."

"What'll I do if the guy comes around?" the editor asked hastily.

"Nothing," Gilroy rasped. "He won't. Don't step on the square."

Gilroy vanished into the night. The editor struck another match and scrutinized the ground with Deerslayer thoroughness.

"What the hell did he see?" he pondered. "That guy—" He shook his head defeatedly and dropped the match.

Never in his life had Wood been so passionately excited. What *had* Gilroy discovered? Was it merely another circumstantial fact, like his realization that Talbot's gangsters were gunning for Wood; or was it a suspicion of Wood's identity? Gilroy had replied that the writer would not reappear, but that could have meant anything or nothing. Wood frantically searched for a way of finally demonstrating who he really was. He found only a negative plan—he would follow Gilroy's lead.

With every minute that passed, the editor grew angrier, shifting his leaning position against the brick wall, pacing around. When Gilroy came back, flashing a bright cone of light before him, the editor lashed out.

"Get it over with, Gilroy. I can't waste the whole night. Even if we do find out what happened, we can't print it—"

Gilroy ignored him. He splashed the brilliant ray of his huge five-celled flashlight over the enciphering square.

"Now look at it," he said. He glanced intently at Wood, who also obeyed his order and stood at the editor's knee, searching the ground. "The guy who made that square was very cautious—he put his back to the wall and faced the lot, so he wouldn't be taken by surprise. The square is upside-down to us. No, wait!" he said sharply as the editor moved to look at the square from its base. "I don't want your footprints on it. Look at the bottom, where the writer must've stood."

The editor stared closely. "What do you see?" he asked puzzledly.

"Well, the ground is moist and fairly soft. There should be footprints. There are. *Only they're not human!*"

Raucously, the editor cleared his throat. "You're kidding."

"*Gestalt,*" Gilroy said, almost to himself, "the whole is greater than the sum of its parts. You get a bunch of unconnected facts, all apparently unrelated to each other. Then suddenly one fact pops up—it doesn't seem any more important than the others—but all at once the others click into place, and you get a complete picture."

"What are you mumbling about?" the editor whispered anxiously.

Gilroy stooped his great height and picked up a yellow stump of pencil. He turned it over in his hand before passing it to the editor.

"That's the pencil this dog snatched before we threw him out. You can see his teethmarks on the sides, where he carried it. But there're teethmarks around the unsharpened end. Maybe I'm nuts—" He took the dirty code message out of his inside breast pocket and smoothed it out. "I saw these smudges the minute I looked at the note, but they didn't mean anything to me then. What do you make of them?"

The editor obediently examined the note in the glare of the flash. "They could be palmprints."

"Sure—a baby's," Gilroy said witheringly. "Only they're not. We both know they're pawprints, the same as are at the bottom of the square. You know what I'm thinking. Look't the way the dog is listening."

Without raising his voice, he half turned his head and said quite casually, "Here comes the guy who wrote the note, right behind the dog."

Involuntarily, Wood spun around to face the dark lot. Even his keen animal eyes could detect no one in the gloom. When he lifted his gaze to Gilroy, he stared full into grim, frightened eyes.

"Put that in your pipe," Gilroy said tremulously. "That's his reaction to the pitch of my voice, eh? You can't get out of it, chief. We've got a werewolf on our hands, thanks to Moss and Talbot."

Wood barked and frisked happily around Gilroy's towering legs. He had been understood!

But the editor laughed, a perfectly normal, humorous, unconvinced laugh. "You're wasting your time writing for a newspaper, Gilroy—"

"O. K., smart guy," Gilroy replied savagely. "Stop your cackling and tell me the answer to this—

"The dog comes into the newsroom and starts barking. I thought he was just trying to get us to follow him; but I never heard a dog bark in long and short yelps before. He ran up the stairs, right past all the other floors—business office, advertising department, and so on—to the newsroom, because that's where he wanted to go. We chased him out. He came back with a scrawled note, saying: 'I am a man.' Those four words took up the whole page. Even a kid learning how to write wouldn't need so much space. But if you hold the pencil in your mouth and try to connect the bars of the letters, you'd have letters something like the ones on the note.

"He needed a smaller system of letters, so he made up a simple code. But he'd lost his pencil. He stole one of ours. Then he came back, watching out for Talbot's gang cars.

"There aren't any footprints at the bottom of this square—only a dog's pawprints. And there're two smudges on the message, where he put his paws to hold down the paper while he wrote on it. All along he's been listening to every word we said. When I said in a conversational tone that the writer was standing behind him, he whirled around. Well?"

The editor was still far from convinced. "Good job of training—"

"For a guy I used to respect, you certainly have the brain of a flea.

Here—I don't know your name," he said to Wood. "What would you do if you had Moss here?"

Wood snarled.

"You're going to tell us where to find him. I don't know how, but you were smart enough to figure out a code, so you can figure out another way of communicating. Then you'll tell us what happened."

It was Wood's moment of supreme triumph. True, he didn't have his body yet, but now it was only a matter of time. His joy at Gilroy's words was violent enough to shake even the editor's literal, unimaginative mind.

"You still don't believe it," Gilroy accused.

"How can I?" the editor cried plaintively. "I don't even know why I'm talking to you as if it could be possible."

Gilroy probed in a pile of rubbish until he uncovered a short piece of wood. He quickly drew a single line of small alphabetical symbols. He threw the stick away, stepped back and flashed the light directly at the alphabet. "Now spell out what happened."

Wood sprang back and forth before the alphabet, stopping at the letters he required and indicating them by pointing his snout down.

"T-a-l-b-o-t w-a-n-t-e-d a y-o-u-n-g h-e-a-l-t-h-y b-o-d-y M-o-s-s s-a-i-d h-e c-o-u-l-d g-i-v-e i-t t-o h-i-m—"

"Well, I'll be damned!" the editor blurted.

After that exclamation there was silence. Only the almost inaudible padding of Wood's paws on the soft ground, his excited panting, and the hoarse breathing of the men could be heard. But Wood had won!

Gilroy sat at the typewriter in his apartment; Wood stood beside his chair and watched the swiftly leaping keys; but the editor stamped nervously up and down the floor.

"I've wasted half the night," he complained, "and if I print this story I'll be canned. Why, damn it, Gilroy— How do you think the public'll take it if I can't believe it myself?"

"Hm-m-m," Gilroy explained.

"You're sacrificing our job. You know that, don't you?"

"It doesn't mean that much to me," Gilroy said without glancing up. "Wood has to get back his body. He can't do it unless we help him."

"Doesn't that sound ridiculous to you? 'He has to get back his body.' Imagine what the other papers'll do to that sentence!"

Gilroy shifted impatiently. "They won't see it," he stated.

"Then why in hell are you writing the story?" the editor asked, astounded. "Why don't you want me to go back to the office?"

"Quiet! I'll be through in a minute." He inserted another sheet of paper and his flying fingers covered it with black, accusing words. Wood's mouth opened in a canine grin when Gilroy smiled down at him and nodded his head confidently. "You're practically walking around on your own feet, pal. Let's go."

He flapped on his coat and carelessly dropped a battered hat on his craggy head. Wood braced himself to dart off. The editor lingered.

"Where're we going?" he asked cautiously.

"To Moss, naturally, unless you can think of a better place."

Wood could not tolerate the thought of delay. He tugged at the leg of the editor's pants.

"You bet I can think of a better place. Hey, cut it out, Wood—I'm coming along. But, hell, Gilroy! It's after ten. I haven't done a thing. Have a heart and make it short."

With Gilroy hastening him by the arm and Wood dragging at his leg, the editor had to accompany them, though he continued his protests. At the door, however, he covered Wood while Gilroy hailed a taxi. When Gilroy signaled that the street was clear, he ran across the sidewalk with Wood bundled in his arms.

Gilroy gave the address. At its sound, Wood's mouth opened in a silent snarl. He was only a short distance from Moss, with two eloquent spokesmen to articulate his demands, and, if necessary, to mobilize public opinion for him! What could Moss do against that power?

They rode up Seventh Avenue and along Central Park West. Only the editor felt that they were speeding. Gilroy and Wood fretted irritably at every stop signal.

At Moss's street, Gilroy cautioned the driver to proceed slowly. The surgeon's house was guarded by two loitering black cars.

"Let us out at the corner," Gilroy said.

They scurried into the entrance of a rooming house.

"Now what?" the editor demanded. "We can't fight past them."

"How about the back way, Wood?"

Wood shook his head negatively. There was no entrance through the rear.

"Then the only way is across the roofs," Gilroy determined. He put his head out and scanned the buildings between them and Moss. "This one is six stories, the next two five, the one right next to Moss's is six, and Moss's is three. We'll have to climb up and down fire escapes and get in through Moss's roof. Ready?"

"I suppose so," the editor said fatalistically.

Gilroy tried the door. It was locked. He chose a bell at random and rang it vigorously. There was a brief pause; then the tripper buzzed. He thrust open the door and burst up the stairs, four at a leap.

"Who's there?" a woman shouted down the stair well.

They galloped past her. "Sorry, lady," Gilroy called back. "We rang your bell by mistake."

She looked disappointed and rather frightened; but Gilroy anticipated her emotion. He smiled and gayly waved his hand as he loped by.

The roof door was locked with a stout hook that had rusted into its eye. Gilroy smashed it open with the heel of his palm. They broke out onto a tarred roof, chill and black in the overcast, threatening night.

Wood and Gilroy discovered the fire escape leading to the next roof.

They dashed for it. Gilroy tucked Wood under his left arm and swung himself over the anchored ladder.

"This is insane!" the editor said hoarsely. "I've never done such a crazy thing in my life. Why can't we be smart and call the cops?"

"Yeah?" Gilroy sneered without stopping. "What's your charge?"

"Against Moss? Why—"

"Think about it on the way."

Gilroy and Wood were on the next roof, waiting impatiently for the editor to descend. He came down quickly but his thoughts wandered.

"You can charge him with what he did. He made a man into a dog."

"That would sound swell in the indictment. Forget it. Just walk lightly. This damned roof creaks and lets out a noise like a drum."

They advanced over the tarred sheets of metal. Beneath them, they could hear their occasionally heavy tread resound through hollow rooms. Wood's claws tapped a rhythmic tattoo.

They straddled over a low wall dividing the two buildings. Wood sniffed the air for enemies lurking behind chimneys, vents and doors. At instants of suspicion, Gilroy briefly flashed his light ahead. They climbed up a steel ladder to the six-story building adjoining Moss's.

"How about a kidnap charge?" the editor asked as they stared down over the wall at the roof of Moss's building.

"Please don't annoy me. Wood's body is in the observation ward at the hospital. How're you going to prove that Moss kidnaped him?"

The editor nodded in the gloom and searched for another legal charge. Gilroy splashed his light over Moss's roof. It was unguarded.

"Come on, Wood," he said, inserting the flashlight in his belt. He picked up Wood under his left arm. In order to use his left hand in climbing, he had to squeeze Wood's middle in a strangle hold.

The only thing Wood was thankful for was that he could not look at the roof three stories below. Gilroy held him securely, tightly enough for his breath to struggle in whistling gasps. His throat knotted when Gilroy gashed his hand on a sharp sliver of dry paint scale.

"It's all right," Gilroy hissed reassuringly. "We're almost there."

Above them, he saw the editor clambering heavily down the insecurely bolted ladder. Between the anchoring plates it groaned and swayed away from the unclean brick wall. Rung by rung they descended warily, Gilroy clutching for each hold, Wood suspended in space and helpless—both feeling their hearts drop when the ladder jerked under their weight.

Then Gilroy lowered his foot and found the solid roof beneath it. He grinned impetuously in the dark. Wood writhed out of his hold. The editor cursed his way down to them.

He followed them to the rear fire escape. This time he offered to carry Wood down. Swinging out over the wall, Wood felt the editor's muscles quiver. Wood had nothing but a miserable animal life to lose, and yet even he was not entirely fearless in the face of the hidden dangers they were braving. He could sympathize with the editor, who had everything to lose and did not wholly believe that Wood was not a dog. Discovering a human identity in an apparently normal collie must have been a staggeringly hard fact for him to swallow.

He set Wood down on the iron bars. Gilroy quickly joined them, and yanked fiercely at the top window. It was locked.

"Need a jimmy to pry it open," Gilroy mused. He fingered the edges of the frame. "Got a knife on you?"

The editor fished absent-mindedly through his pockets. He brought out a handful of keys, pencil stubs, scraps of paper, matches, and a cheap sheathed nail file. Gilroy snatched the file.

He picked at the putty in the ancient casement with the point. It chipped away easily. He loosened the top and sides.

"Now," he breathed. "Stand back a little and get ready to catch it."

He inserted the file at the top and levered the glass out of the frame. It stuck at the bottom and sides, refusing to fall. He caught the edges and lifted it out, laying it down noiselessly out of the way.

"Let's go." He backed in through the empty casement. "Hand Wood through."

They stood in the dark room, under the same roof with Moss. Wood exultantly sensed the proximity of the one man he hated—the one man who could return his body to him. "Now!" he thought. *"Now!"*

"Gilroy," the editor urged, "we can charge Moss with vivisection."

"That's right," Gilroy whispered. But they heard the doorknob rattle in his hand and turn cautiously.

"Then where're you going?" the editor rasped in a panic.

"We're here," Gilroy replied coolly. "So let's finish it."

The door swung back; pale weak light entered timidly. They stared down the long, narrow, dismal hall to the stairs at the center of the house. Down those stairs they would find Moss—

Wood's keen animal sense of smell detected Moss's personal odor. The surgeon had been there not long before.

He crouched around the stairhead and cautiously lowered himself from step to step. Gilroy and the editor clung to banister and wall, resting the bulk of their weight on their hands. They turned the narrow spiral where Clarence had fatally encountered the sharpness of Wood's fangs, down to the hall floor where his fat body had sprawled in blood.

Distantly, Wood heard a cane tap nervously, momentarily; then it stopped at a heated, hissed command that scarcely carried even to his ears. He glanced up triumphantly at Gilroy, his deep eyes glittering, his mouth grinning savagely, baring the red tongue lolling in the white, deadly trap of fangs. He had located and identified the sounds. Both Moss and Talbot were in a room at the back of the house—

He hunched his powerful shoulders and advanced slowly, stiff-legged, with the ominous air of all meat hunters stalking prey from ambush. Outside the closed door he crouched, muscles gathered for the lunge, his ears flat back along his pointed head to protect them from injury. But they heard muffled voices inaudible to men's dulled senses.

"Sit down, doc," Talbot said. "The truck'll be here soon."

"I'm not concerned with my personal safety," Moss replied tartly. "It's merely that I dislike inefficiency, especially when you claim—"

"Well, it's not Jake's fault. He's coming back from a job."

Wood could envision the faint sneer on Moss's scrubbed pink face. "You'll collapse any minute within the next six months, but the acquisitive nature is as strong as ever in you, isn't it, Talbot? You couldn't resist the chance of making a profit, and at a time like this!"

"Oh, don't lose your head. The cata-whatever-you-call-it can't talk and the dog is probably robbing garbage cans. What's the lam for?"

"I'm changing my residence purely as a matter of precaution. You underestimate human ingenuity, even limited by a dog's inarticulateness."

Wood grinned up at his comrades. The editor was dough-faced, rigid with apprehension. Gilroy held a gun and his left hand snaked out at the doorknob. The editor began an involuntary motion to stop him. The door slammed inward before he completed it.

Wood and Gilroy stalked in, sinister in their grim silence. Talbot merely glanced at the gun. He had stared into too many black muzzles to be frightened by it. When his gaze traveled to Wood his jaw fell and hung open, trembling senilely. His constantly fighting lungs strangled. He screamed, a high, tortured wail, and tore frantically at his shirt, trying to release his chest from crushing pressure.

"An object lesson for you, Talbot," Moss said without emotion. "Do not underestimate an enemy."

Gilroy lost his frigid attitude. "Don't let him strangle. Help him."

"What can I do?" Moss shrugged. "It's angina pectoris. Either he pulls out of the convulsions by himself—or he doesn't. I can't help. But what did you want?"

No one answered him. Horrified, they were watching Talbot go purple in his death agony, lose the power of shrieking, and tear at his chest. Gilroy's gun hand was limp; yet Moss made no attempt to escape. The air rattled through Talbot's predatory nose. He fell in a contorted heap.

Wood felt sickened. He knew that in self-preservation doctors had to harden themselves, but only a monster of brutal callousness could have disregarded Talbot's frightful death as if it had not been going on.

"Oh, come now, it isn't as bad as all that," Moss said acidly.

Wood raised his shocked stare from the rag-doll body to Moss's hard, unfearful eyes. The surgeon had made no move to defend himself, to call for help from the squad of gangsters at the front of the house. He faced them with inhuman prepossession.

"It upsets your plans," Gilroy spat.

Moss lifted his shoulders, urbanely, delicately disdainful. "What difference should his death make to me? I never cared for his company."

"Maybe not, but his money seemed to smell O. K. to you. He's out of the picture. He can't keep us from printing this story now." Gilroy pulled a thin folded typescript from his inside breast pocket and shoved it out at Moss.

The surgeon read it interestedly, leaning casually against a wall. He came to the end of the short article and read the lead paragraph over again. Politely, he gave it back to Gilroy.

"It's very clear," he said. "I'm accused of exchanging the identities of a man and a dog. You even describe my alleged technique."

" 'Alleged!' " Gilroy roared savagely. "You mean you deny it?"

"Of course. Isn't it fantastic?" Moss smiled. "But that isn't the point. Even if I admitted it, how do you think I could be convicted on such evidence? The only witness seems to be the dog you call Wood. Are dogs allowed to testify in court? I don't remember, but I doubt it."

Wood was stunned. He had not expected Moss to brazen out the charge. An ordinary man would have broken down, confronted by their evidence.

Even the shrinking editor was stung into retorting: "We have proof of criminal vivisection!"

"But no proof that I was the surgeon."

"You're the only one in New York who could've done that operation."

"See how far that kind of evidence will get you."

Wood listened with growing anger. Somehow they had permitted Moss to dominate the situation, and he parried their charges with cool, sarcastic deftness. No wonder he had not tried to escape! He felt himself to be perfectly safe. Wood growled, glowering hatred at Moss. The surgeon looked down contemptuously.

"All right, we can't convict you in court," Gilroy said. He hefted his gun, tightening his finger on the trigger. "That's not what we want, anyhow. This little scientific curiosity can make you operate on Wood and transfer his identity back to his own body."

Moss's expression of disdain did not alter. He watched Gilroy's tensing trigger finger with an astonishing lack of concern.

"Well, speak up," Gilroy rasped, waving the gun ominously.

"You can't force me to operate. All you can do is kill me, and I am as indifferent to my own death as I was to Talbot's." His smile broadened and twisted down at the corners, showing his teeth in a snarl that was the civilized, overrefined counterpart of Wood's. "Your alleged operation interests me, however. I'll operate for my customary fee."

The editor pushed Gilroy inside and hurriedly closed the door. "They're coming," he chattered. "Talbot's gangsters."

In two strides Gilroy put Moss between him and the door. His gun jabbed rudely into Moss's unflinching back. "Get over on the other side, you two, so the door'll hide you when it swings back," he ordered.

Wood and the editor retreated. Wood heard steps along the hall, then a pause, and a harsh voice shouted: "Hey, boss! Truck's here."

"Tell them to go away," Gilroy said in a low, suppressed tone.

Moss called, "I'm in the second room at the rear of the house."

Gilroy viciously stabbed him with the gun muzzle. "You're asking for it. I said tell them to go away!"

"You wouldn't dare to kill me until I've operated—"

"If you're not scared, why do you want them? What's the gag?"

The door flung open. A gangster started to enter. He stiffened, his keen, battle-trained eyes flashing from Talbot's twisted body to Moss, and to Gilroy, standing menacingly behind the surgeon. In a swift, smooth motion a gun leaped from his armpit holster.

"What happened to the boss?" he demanded hoarsely. "Who's he?"

"Put your gun away, Pinero. The boss died of a heart attack. That shouldn't surprise you—he was expecting it any day."

"Yeah, I know. But how'd that guy get in?"

Moss stirred impatiently. "He was here all along. Send the truck back. I'm not moving. I'll take care of Talbot."

The gangster looked uncertain, but, in lieu of another commander, he obeyed Moss's order. "Well, O. K. if you say so." He closed the door.

When Pinero had gone down the hall, Moss turned to face Gilroy. "You're not scared—much!" Gilroy said.

Moss ignored his sarcastic outburst. "Where were we?" he asked. "Oh, yes. While you were standing there shivering, I had time to think over my offer. I'll operate for nothing."

"You bet you will!" Gilroy wagged his gun forcefully.

Moss sniffed at it. "That has nothing to do with my decision. I have no fear of death, and I'm not afraid of your evidence. If I do operate, it will be because of my interest in the experiment." Wood intercepted Moss's speculative gaze. It mocked, hardened, glittered sinisterly. "But, of course," Moss added smoothly, "I will definitely operate. In fact, I insist on it!"

His hidden threat did not escape Wood. Once he lay under Moss's knife it would be the end. A slip of the knife—a bit of careful careless- ness in the gas mixture—a deliberately caused infection—and Moss would clear himself of the accusation by claiming he could not perform the operation, and therefore was not the vivisectionist. Wood recoiled, shaking his head violently from side to side.

"Wood's right," the editor said. "He knows Moss better. He wouldn't come out of the operation alive."

Gilroy's brow creased in an uneasy frown. The gun in his hand was a futile implement of force; even Moss knew he would not use it—could not, because the surgeon was only valuable to them alive. His purpose had been to make Moss operate. Well, he thought, he had accomplished that purpose. Moss offered to operate. But all four knew that under Moss's knife, Wood was doomed. Moss had cleverly turned the victory to utter rout.

"Then what the hell'll we do?" Gilroy exploded savagely. "What do you say, Wood? Want to take the chance, or keep on in a dog's body?"

Wood snarled, backing away.

"At least, he's still alive," the editor said fatalistically.

Moss smiled, protesting with silken mockery that he would do his best to return Wood's body.

"Barring accidents," Gilroy spat. "No soap, Moss. He'll get along the way he is, and you're going to get yours."

He looked grimly at Wood, jerking his head significantly in Moss's direction.

"Come on, chief," he said, guiding the editor through the door and closing it. "These old friends want to be alone—lot to talk over—"

Instantly, Wood leaped before the door and crouched there menacingly, glaring at Moss with blind, vicious hatred. For the first time, the surgeon dropped his pose of indifference. He inched cautiously around the wall toward the door. He realized suddenly that this was an animal—

Wood advanced, cutting off his line of retreat. Mane bristling, head lowered ominously between blocky shoulders, bright gums showing above white curved fangs, Wood stalked over the floor, stiff-jointed, in a low, inexorably steady rhythm of approach.

Moss watched anxiously. He kept looking up at the door in an agony of longing. But Wood was there, closing the gap for the attack. He put up his hands to thrust away—

And his nerve broke. He could not talk down mad animal eyes as he could a man holding a gun. He darted to the side and ran for the door.

Wood flung himself at the swiftly pumping legs. They crashed against him, tripped. Moss sprawled face down on the floor. He crossed his arms under his head to protect his throat.

Wood slashed at an ear. It tore, streaming red. Moss screeched and clapped his hands over his face, trying to rise without dropping his guard. But Wood ripped at his fingers.

The surgeon's hands clawed out. He was kneeling, defenseless, trying to fight off the rapid, aimed lunges—and those knifelike teeth—

Wood gloated. A minute before, the scrubbed pink face had been aloof, sneering. Now it bobbed frantically at his eye level, contorted with overpowering fear, blood flowing brightly down the once scrupulously clean cheeks.

For an instant, the pale throat gleamed exposed at him. It was soft and helpless. He shot through the air. His teeth struck at an angle and snatched— The white flesh parted easily. But a bony structure snapped between his jaws as he swooped by.

Moss knelt there after Wood had struck. His pain-twisted face gaped imbecilically, hands limp at his sides. His throat poured a red flood. Then his face drained to a ghastly lack of color and he pitched over.

He had lost, but he had also won. Wood was doomed to live out his life in a dog's body. He could not even expect to live his own life span. The average life of a dog is fifteen years. Wood could expect perhaps ten years more.

In his human body, Wood had found it difficult to find a job. He had been a code expert; but code experts, salesmen and apprentice workmen have no place in a world of shrinking markets. The employment agencies are glutted with an oversupply of normal human intelligences housed in strong, willing, expert human bodies.

The same normal human intelligence in a handsome collie's body had a greater market value. It was a rarity, a phenomenon to be gaped at after a ticket had been purchased for the privilege.

"Men've always had a fondness for freaks," Gilroy philosophized on their way to the theater where Wood had an engagement. "Mildly amusing freaks are paid to entertain. The really funny ones are given seats of honor and power. Figure it out, Wood. I can't. Once we get rid of our love of freaks and put them where they belong, we'll have a swell world."

The taxi stopped in a side street, at the stage entrance. Lurid red-and-yellow posters, the size of cathedral murals, plastered the theater walls; and from them smirked prettified likenesses of Wood.

"Gosh!" their driver gasped. "Wait'll my kids hear about this. I drove the Talkin' Dog! Gee, is that an honor, or ain't it?"

On all sides, pedestrians halted in awe, taxis stopped with a respectful screech of brakes; then an admiring swarm bore down on him.

"Isn't he *cute?*" women shrieked. "So *intelligent*-looking!"

"Sure," Wood heard their driver boast proudly, "I drove him down here. What's he like?" His voice lowered confidentially. "Well, the guy with him—his manager, I guess—he was talkin' to him just as intelligent as I'm talkin' to you. Like he could understand ev'y word."

"Bet he could, too," a listener said definitely.

"G'on," another theorized. "He's just trained, like Rin-tin-tin, on'y better. But he's smart all right. Wisht I owned him."

The theater-district squad broke through the tangle of traffic and formed a lane to the stage door.

"Yawta be ashamed ayehselves," a cop said. "All this over a mutt!"

Wood bared his fangs at the speaker, who retreated defensively.

"Wise guy, huh?" the mob jeered. "Think he can't understand?"

It was a piece of showmanship that Wood and Gilroy had devised. It never failed to find a feeder in the form of an officious policeman and a response from the crowd.

Even in the theater, Wood was not safe from overly enthusiastic admiration. His fellow performers persisted in scratching his unitching back and ears, cooing and burbling in a singularly unintelligent manner.

The thriller that Wood had made in Hollywood was over; and while the opening acts went through their paces, Wood and Gilroy stood as far away from the wings as the theater construction would permit.

"Seven thousand bucks a week, pal," Gilroy mused over and over. "Just for doing something that any mug out in the audience can do twice as easily. Isn't that the payoff?"

In the year that had passed, neither was still able to accustom himself to the mounting figures in their bank book. Pictures, personal appearances, indorsements, highly fictionized articles in magazines—all at astronomical prices—

But he could never have enough money to buy back the human body he had starved in.

"O. K., Wood," Gilroy whispered. "We're on."

They were drummed onto the stage with deafening applause. Wood went through his routine perfunctorily. He identified objects that had been named by the theater manager, picking them out of a heap of piled objects.

Ushers went through the aisles, collecting questions the audience had written on slips of paper. They passed them up to Gilroy.

Wood took a long pointer firmly in his mouth and stood before a huge lettered screen. Painfully, he pointed out, letter by letter, the answers to the audience's questions. Most of them asked about the future, market tips, racing information. A few seriously probed his mind.

White light stabbed down at him. Mechanically, he spelled out the simple answers. Most of his bitterness had evaporated; in its place was a dreary defeat, and dull acceptance of his dog's life. His bank book had six figures to the left of the decimal—more than he had ever conceived of, even as a distant Utopian possibility. But no surgeon could return his body to him, or increase his life expectancy of less than ten years.

Sharply, everything was washed out of sight: Gilroy, the vast alphabet screen, the heavy pointer in his mouth, the black space smeared with pale, gaping blobs of faces, even the white light staring down—

He lay on a cot in a long ward. There was no dreamlike quality of illusion in the feel of smooth sheets beneath and above him, or in the weight of blankets resting on his *outstretched* body.

And independently of the rest of his hand, his *finger* moved in response to his will. Its nail scratched at the sheet, loudly, victoriously.

An interne, walking through the ward, looked around for the source of the gloating sound. He engaged Wood's eyes that were glittering avidly, deep with intelligence. Then they watched the scratching finger.

"You're coming back," the interne said at last.

"I'm coming back." Wood spoke quietly, before the scene vanished and he heard Gilroy repeat a question he had missed.

He knew then that the body-mind was a unit. Moss had been wrong; there was more to identity than that small gland, something beyond the body. The forced division Moss had created was unnatural; the transplanted tissue was being absorbed, remodeled. Somehow, he knew these returns to his natural identity would recur, more and more—till it became permanent—till he became human once more.

PART TWO

Wonders of Earth and of Man

MORRISON COLLADAY

THE PLANETOID OF DOOM

JIM and I weren't feeling very cheerful. We were both out of a job, and that year it wasn't easy to pick up new ones. The supply boat from New Orleans had just left with our engineering crew. There were some odds and ends of work to finish up, and we were going to camp out on an old "gazzoleen" tub tied up in a bayou near the mouth of the Mississippi for the next couple of weeks. The mosquitoes were pretty bad, and we would have to cook our own meals; but our salaries would go on for that additional time, so things might have been worse.

We were both one year out of engineering school. We had been bossing a crew in the Louisiana marshes, spotting salt domes for one of the big oil companies. When you locate a salt dome in that part of the country, you can pretty nearly figure that there is oil underneath. Finding the salt domes is easy enough by present-day methods. You set off dynamite charges in the ground at measured distances from a central point, and then time the arrival of the vibrations. That's all there is to it, except making the necessary calculations from the date.

We had figured on our jobs lasting another year, and we thought we were sitting pretty. The corporation furnished food and shelter for its employees and there was no way of spending money down there in the swamps, so we saved most of our salaries. Then the oil market went blooey and headquarters began to cut expenses. At least we got our two weeks' notice, and that's more than a good many others got.

The "gazzoleen" was tied up to the dock in front of the deserted corrugated iron warehouse. Beyond were several shacks on stilts, in which the men had lived. It seemed pretty lonely after having a gang around for nine months. Jim was polishing up a theodolite while I read whatever looked interesting in the bunch of New Orleans newspapers the supply boat had left. After you get used to doing without papers, they don't seem as important as when they come to you a couple of times a day.

I saw the headline in the New Orleans *States*—"Planetoid to Approach Close to Earth," but it didn't excite me. I can't get a copy of the paper, but the account went something like this:

"A new planetoid has been discovered with a parabolic orbit which will probably bring it closer to the earth than any heavenly body has hitherto come. It is traveling at such great speed that astronomers have so far found it difficult to chart its course accurately." There was more of it, but that was the important part.

"Hope it doesn't hit us during the next two weeks," said Jim. "This would be a swell place in a tidal wave, I don't think!"

Isolated as we were, we heard nothing more about the planetoid until the night it fell into the Gulf of Mexico somewhere on a line between Yucatan and the mouth of the Mississippi River. People in the rest of the world where there were daily newspapers were told of its rapid approach toward the earth. I judge efforts were made not to alarm them more than was necessary, but as the thirteenth of June approached, they were prepared for something to happen. Of course, we were not.

It was just our good luck that the old "gazzoleen" tub we were living in was built so she was practically unsinkable. Some humorist had painted the name *Gazelle* on her stern. She was about thirty feet long, eight feet beam, and built as heavily as a scow. There was a deckhouse forward where Jim and I slept. The engine was in the stern, bolted to a deck of extra heavy planking reinforced with iron. The hull could be entered through only one hatchway flush with the deck. Below, forward, was a compartment for the more valuable tools and equipment, aft, was another compartment for dynamite. Now both of these were empty, the stuff they contained having been transferred to the supply boat.

When the hatchway was closed, about the only thing that could have sunk the old tub was the dynamite, should it go off. A hurricane or a tidal wave might sweep away the light deckhouse and even tear loose the exposed engine, but anyone below would be safe, unless he smothered to death. If the *Gazelle* had been built like an ordinary boat, Jim and I would have been fish food on the thirteenth of June, like most of the other inhabitants of the southeastern part of the United States.

It was not long after the discovery of the planetoid that astronomers decided it was likely to hit the earth. They were unable to agree as to the probable effects of the collision because of the unknown factors of size, speed at moment of contact, and whether point of contact would be a continent or an ocean. There was general agreement that the visitor was small as planetoids go—not more than ten miles in diameter and possibly not more than five. It was also generally agreed that the collision would occur somewhere within the tropics.

One astronomer predicted that "the air and water at the point of contact would be instantly consumed and dissipated and a considerable region of the earth's surface raised to incandescence. It might happen that diffusion of noxious gases from sudden combustion of hydro-carbon compounds would so vitiate the atmosphere as to render it unsuitable for breathing." Another asserted that the entrance into the atmosphere of an object traveling at the high speed of the planetoid must cause air waves so powerful as to produce all the effects of a disastrous earthquake.

The newspapers republished accounts of the fall, in 1908, of a great meteorite in Yenesei Province in Central Siberia. This meteorite was supposed to have weighed not more than a hundred and forty tons, yet it devastated hundreds of square miles of country.

It was one o'clock in the morning of June thirteenth that the planetoid hit the earth. We had gone to bed, but it was too hot to sleep even though we had brought our army cots out on deck. We were lying there smoking and talking about what we were going to do when we got away from the salt marshes and the mosquitoes and the loneliness. . . .

Suddenly a wave of green light flashed up from the western horizon and spread across the sky. We tumbled from our cots in less time than it takes to tell about it. I noticed that the unearthly color made Jim look like a corpse with purple lips and holes for eyes. It must have been only a fraction of a second until a great incandescent green sphere shot into view.

It rushed across the sky, growing larger as it approached until it looked four times the size of the sun. Behind it swept a fan-like green tail. Then, as we watched it, the sphere seemed to expand instantaneously in a tremendous explosion, and the whole sky became a blazing furnace. The shock threw me violently to the deck.

Jim shouted at me, but my ears were ringing so I could not understand him. He saw that I was half dazed and dragged me below. He had just succeeded in fastening down the hatch cover when we heard the shriek of the oncoming wind. There was a crash and the boat turned halfway over. Jim was flung down on top of me and a second later we were both thrown against the side.

"That was the warehouse," Jim shouted above the tumult outside.

There was another interval of seconds before the tidal wave reached us. We heard a new sound above the roar of the wind, and then there was plenty of action for a few minutes. Comparing impressions afterward, we decided that the tidal wave must have swept the wreckage of the warehouse away and then rolled the *Gazelle* over several times, finally leaving her right side up, fortunately for us.

We were pretty badly bruised by the time the more violent motion subsided. It was evident that the boat was being swept to some unknown destination at immense speed. However, we were afloat and neither of us had any bones broken. We concluded that there was nothing for us to do except wait until we stranded somewhere. We made ourselves as comfortable as possible in the darkness and finally I fell asleep.

I was wakened by a sudden jar and realized that we were no longer moving.

"I guess we're aground," I said.

"Feels like it," answered Jim. "The water's going down. The boat's beginning to tip."

We waited an hour before we took a chance on opening the hatch.

By that time the *Gazelle* was lying on her side as if she had been hauled up on shore. We were almost too stiff to walk when we climbed out and got the first glimpse of our extraordinary surroundings.

Extending as far as we could see was a lake of troubled water of a peculiar greenish color, from which rose great buildings. In a moment I realized that we were gazing over a submerged New Orleans. I knew the business section of the city fairly well and I saw that the *Gazelle* had landed on the roof of the Federal Reserve Bank, one of the lower buildings surrounded by skyscrapers.

The water was now receding rapidly. Though it was still dark except for a pale moon, it seemed curious that we saw no people and that there were no lights in the buildings. Nobody could sleep through what had happened that night, and New Orleans was a city of nearly half a million.

Jim and I stared at each other. "Where do you suppose all the people are?" I asked.

"Drowned in bed, most of them, I guess. They're keeping awfully quiet if they're alive."

I realized then that one of the things that made the scene so ghostly was the absolute silence. There was not a sound except an occasional gurgle from the retreating water. We stood for fifteen minutes at the edge of the roof, watching for some sign of life.

"No use waiting here, doing nothing," said Jim at last. "We'd better go after help."

"We can't unless we find another boat," I answered. "It'll be flooded here for weeks with the drainage pumps out of commission. All of this country is from ten to twenty feet lower than the river. There's no place for the water to go."

We reasoned that there was a good chance of finding a usable boat along the docks. We solved the problem of getting there by putting together a raft of partitions and office furniture from an adjoining building, which we entered through a smashed skylight. The distance to the docks wasn't great and both of us were strong swimmers, but there was something extremely unpleasant-looking about that green water. It wasn't as it became twenty-four hours later, but even now it looked slimy and iridescent and seemed to be in constant motion as though it were full of crawling things.

When we paddled our raft down Canal Street we had no idea of danger. Even when the piece of a door frame I was using for an oar was suddenly seized and dragged from my hands, we thought an alligator washed into the city from the swamps was being playful.

Jim sculled the craft to the ramp which led to the ferry house at the foot of Canal Street. We climbed over the railing and waded through a couple of feet of water which still covered the floor into the waiting room. Here was a scene of desolation, and two or three bodies—the first we had seen.

The two-decker ferryboat had sunk in her slip, but the pilot house and hurricane deck were now above water. One of the two lifeboats was smashed to kindling, but the other was serviceable after we had bailed it out with fire buckets.

We pushed the lifeboat over the side and started down the river with one pair of oars which I found in the pilot house. In that current oars were not of much use except to steer. The Mississippi was swollen by the water draining from thousands of square miles of the valley inundated by the tidal wave. We swept past the city docks, keeping our eyes open for a launch with a serviceable motor. Apparently none of the hundred or so vessels tied up at the docks or anchored in the river had escaped disaster. We could see the masts and superstructures of those sunk in the comparatively shallow water near shore.

It was not a cheerful scene. The flood was carrying toward the sea the wreckage of hundreds of towns as well as countless bodies of human beings and animals.

We floated down to Belle Chasse before we found what we wanted. There at the docks used by the Seatrain, a ferry which carried loaded freight cars to Cuba, we found on a gondola a thirty-foot cabin launch with the engines of a rum runner. It had been carefully loaded for shipment and was undamaged by the tidal wave. Not a drop of water had penetrated to the cabin or hull.

With the equipment at the dock it was a simple job to get the boat into the water. Her gasoline tanks were empty, of course, but we found gas pumps above water, so that was soon remedied. We broke into freight cars until we had secured enough supplies of every imaginable kind to last several weeks. One of the most important things we came pretty near forgetting altogether. I thought about it just as we were getting ready to cast off for our trip up the river.

"Water!" I exclaimed. "What are we going to drink?"

"Gosh, I never thought of that," said Jim, frowning. "We certainly can't drink this green stuff. It's beginning to smell worse than sewage, and the Lord knows what it tastes like."

We spent another hour breaking into more freight cars before we came across a shipment of bottled water.

It was beginning to grow dark, and if we had been sensible we would have stayed where we were until morning. But we were both anxious to get started after help. It seemed hardly possible that a city of five hundred thousand people could be wiped out by any catastrophe without leaving some survivors.

By this time the river had fallen below the tops of the levees. Back of the levees the country was covered with a stagnant green lake about twelve or fifteen feet deep, from which the upper stories of buildings that had not been washed away projected. During the entire day we had seen no sign of another human being.

Just as we started the engine, three planes appeared in the sky. As we chugged away upstream they saw us.

"Must be trying to signal," said Jim as they dipped and circled around.

We watched, but we couldn't make out what they wanted, if they were really trying to signal us. Presently they winged away toward the north.

It was when it grew dark that we got the first sight of the curious phenomenon which has puzzled scientists as much as anything connected with the destruction of the planetoid. Against the darkness a delicate shimmer of iridescent green flame seemed to rise from the water for about ten feet. It wasn't flame, of course, for we were surrounded by it and the temperature remained constant. We sailed in a sea of this palpitating green light, extending as far as we could see in every direction. When we approached downtown New Orleans the buildings in the business section stood out against a blue-black sky, bathed in pale green radiance.

We reached the foot of Canal Street and tied up the launch at the concrete steps which descend from the top of the levee to the river. This is where the pleasure boats used to take on their passengers. Beyond lay the coffee dock, usually lined with vessels from all parts of the world. Tonight they were resting on the bottom of the river. We could see their masts and smokestacks by the greenish flames which played over the surface of the water.

At the foot of Canal Street the land gradually rises for two blocks until it reaches the height of the levee, forming an elevated plaza paved with concrete, which was now above water. Jim and I stood at the edge of the plaza looking down the green lake which two days before the city had boasted was the widest and best lighted street in the world.

There seemed to be nothing we could do at least until daylight. We were turning away when Jim caught a glimpse of the boys.

"I see somebody!" he exclaimed excitedly. "Look—that second-floor window of the Custom House."

"Where?" I asked, staring at the immense granite building two blocks away with its multitude of windows.

"Look where I'm pointing—the second window from the corner on the second floor. There's two of them, two boys."

Now I saw them. They were sitting on the window sill, apparently planning to jump into the water a few feet below and swim to us.

"I guess they'll make it all right," said Jim a little doubtfully. "It isn't much of a swim."

As he spoke, one of the boys lowered himself into the water. He struck out strongly and had nearly reached the buildings on the opposite side of North Peters Street when suddenly he began to scream.

We saw that the water all around him was in violent commotion. He was struggling and his screams became shriller. Then something pulled him under and he didn't come up again.

Jim and I looked at each other with white faces—at least, I saw his was white and I felt sick enough.

"Stay where you are!" we yelled to the other boy who was still perched on the window ledge.

"It was all over so quick we couldn't do anything," I said. "Suppose it was an alligator?"

Jim shrugged his shoulders. "Might have been. Maybe a big gar. You can't tell what's been washed up from the bottom of the Gulf of Mexico. We'll have to go after that other boy."

We found a life raft on the Bienville Street dock. It wasn't very heavy and we dragged it down to the flooded street. The boy was still crouched on the sill of the second-floor Custom House window. Of the other boy there was no sign when we passed the corner where he had disappeared.

He was a very frightened youngster when we reached him. The raft was about eight feet below the window ledge on which he was perched and he was afraid to lower himself so I could get hold of him.

"Gee, suppose I fall in?" he said.

"You won't," I assured him. "I'll catch you."

A life raft looked pretty flimsy to him, I guess, after what had happened. Finally we got him down safely and started back the way we had come.

We had gone a little more than half the distance back to the plaza when the raft gave a sudden lurch and then righted itself. If it had been a boat it probably would have overturned. The boy yelled and I whirled around just as an appalling-looking creature reared itself out of the water.

The part that was visible was like a huge snake a foot in diameter and six feet long, terminating in a head which was nearly all mouth filled with wicked-looking teeth. This head darted toward the boy. I struck at it with my paddle, but that bounced off the rubber-like, muscular neck.

Jim whipped out his forty-five automatic and let go all the shots in the magazine. A body big around as a barrel leaped convulsively out of the water and then fell back. It was immediately the center of a swirling commotion. Other sharp-pointed jaws with razor-sharp teeth were tearing it to pieces.

We poled the raft along close to the buildings and got back to the plaza before the spotted morays—which is what we were afterward told they were—turned their attention to us again.

After he had had something to eat, the boy told us his story. His name was Joe Waters and he was fifteen years old. He had run away from his home in Columbus, Ohio, to see the world and had got stranded in New Orleans when he couldn't find a job. The boy who was drowned was a chance acquaintance who had taught him how it was possible to live without money.

The two of them had escaped from the tidal wave by the merest accident. The fourth floor of the Custom House, erected back in 1840 or thereabouts, had never been completed inside. It was a good place to sleep, except for lack of light and air, if the boys could dodge the watchman on the lower floors. After they reached the unused stairway—

through a hole in the wire netting which was supposed to keep intruders away—there was no one to disturb them.

The night of the tidal wave they were sleeping in this place, and while the three lower floors of the building were flooded, very little water penetrated to the tightly closed fourth floor. They were wakened by the noise, but were too frightened to try to get away until the following night. They had nothing to eat and they were starting on a foraging expedition when we first saw them climbing out of a window. They thought that the water had gone down enough for them to swim or wade to one of the small restaurants in the next block. Joe was about to follow the other boy into the water when he saw the ferocious head of a moray appear above the surface. He thought it must be an alligator and shouted a warning. The swimmer glanced over his shoulder and evidently figured he could make the buildings on the opposite side of the street, for he kept on. He was within a few feet of safety when he was pulled under.

"There was hundreds of 'em," said Joe, "and they just et him up alive!"

We began our night journey up the flooded and lightless Mississippi with Jim at the wheel and me nursing the engine. We expected, each time we rounded a bend, to meet rescue vessels on their way to New Orleans. When daylight came without our seeing anything afloat on the river except our own boat, we began to realize that the catastrophe had been much greater and more widespread than we had imagined.

"Funny the government hasn't sent help," I said as the morning wore on.

"Sent it from where?" asked Jim. "For all we know, every boat this side of St. Louis was sunk."

It wasn't until we reached Natchez, two hundred miles from New Orleans, that we saw any signs of life. Natchez proper is situated on a high bluff. Natchez-Under-the-Hill had been gradually falling into the river for years, and the tidal wave completed its destruction. We tied up to the remains of a dock and in a few minutes were in touch with the outside world again.

The low-lying regions around the city had suffered the fate of the rest of the lower valley. Cellars and ground floors of buildings had been flooded and that was about the extent of the damage. We were the first to bring news from the south and our arrival caused a good deal of excitement. All telegraph lines were down, but there was a local radio station and the rest of the world had been inquiring frantically for news of New Orleans.

The newspaper men took charge of us for the next few hours. A flash was sent out telling of our arrival and the news we brought of the destruction of life in the lower valley. Preparations for a relief expedition were under way a few minutes afterward. Memphis, three hundred miles from Natchez, was the nearest point from which it could start. The United States Engineering District headquarters had a number of vessels there, used in levee work, which had been battered about considerably but which were perfectly serviceable. They were quickly loaded with supplies. Within two hours after we landed at Natchez they were on their way down the river with a hastily gathered corps of doctors and nurses, and troops for police duty.

Before long, news reached Natchez from Washington that the Red Cross would take charge of the New Orleans situation. After we had answered all the questions of the newspaper men, we tried to find out what had happened to the rest of the world when the planetoid fell, but very little seemed to be known. The tidal wave had swept up the Mississippi Valley as far as St. Louis, converting the low country behind the levees into great lakes. It came so suddenly that the inhabitants of the lower valley were unable to escape and most of them apparently had perished.

The water which flooded the upper part of the valley was not so heavily charged with the mysterious green substance, and the phosphorescent flames which played over its surface were not so spectacular as they were in the New Orleans section. The river in front of Natchez was rapidly assuming its normal yellow shade.

No word had been received from Florida and the lower Atlantic coast region. Even before we brought the tragic news, the gravest fears had been felt for the low-lying Gulf states as well as for Mexico, Yucatan, Central America, the Canal Zone, the northern coast of South America and the islands of the Caribbean Sea. All cables were out of commission and it had been impossible to get any response from radio stations in this territory.

Jim and I went aboard the *General Pershing*, the first of the rescue vessels to arrive at Natchez the next day. The *General Pershing* was one of the awkward-looking, three-story-hotel constructions used by the United States engineers in their levee operations. It would accommodate, in a pinch, a couple of thousand persons, I imagine.

When we looked back, after we had started down the river, we could see following us a procession of boats and barges, all part of the rescue fleet.

We discovered that the greenish flood water contained more dangerous inhabitants than spotted morays. We were opposite Kenner, a small town a few miles from New Orleans, and we were eating lunch when we heard a commotion on the upper deck. Mississippi boats of the type of the *General Pershing* are built with the lower decks almost entirely enclosed. No space is wasted on passages outside the staterooms, the windows of which look directly over the water.

At first we paid no attention to the noise, but suddenly a man began screaming. Jim and I and most of the others at the tables rushed up the stairs. By the time we reached the upper deck the man was dying.

We crowded around while a couple of physicians worked over him. In a minute or two his writhing stopped. The distorted face, lips drawn back halfway to the ears, swollen tongue thrust between the exposed teeth, eyes protruding from their sockets as if they were about to pop out, became rigid.

"He's gone," said one of the doctors as he released his grasp of the victim's arms, while the other put his hypodermic away. Suddenly it dawned on me that I'd never seen anything at all like the ten-foot greenish snake lying on the deck with its head mashed to pulp. One of the officers moved its thick body with his foot.

"What is it?" I asked him.

"A sea snake," he answered. "Never saw one before, except in the Indian Ocean. Deadly as a cobra. Sometimes the water there is full of them. Don't know as I ever saw one as big as this fellow, though. We seem to have run into a lot of them."

I noticed for the first time that around the rail, about a dozen feet apart, were men armed with clubs. Every few seconds one of them would bend over the rail and strike at something.

"More of them trying to get aboard?" Jim asked.

The officer nodded. "Never knew them to try to board a ship before."

Jim gazed over the rail, then he turned and beckoned to me. "Pretty, isn't it?" he asked grimly. I looked down at the water. The river seemed to be full of snakes, trying to climb up the sides of the vessel like great worms. Most of them fell back into the water before they got very far and the others were beaten off by the sailors.

I wondered what was going to happen after it got too dark to see the snakes. I noticed Colonel Lounsbury, who was in charge of the expedition, in consultation with several of the engineers. Shortly afterward men began stringing rows of wire around the outside of the railing. When they had finished, notices were posted warning passengers that the wires would be heavily charged with electricity.

Presently the current was turned on and we leaned over the rail to watch the effect. The snakes seemed to be as thick as ever and not at all discouraged by the reception they had been getting. From where we were we could see eight or ten of them crawling up the side. All except three fell back into the water before they got far. The three kept on coming until they struck the four parallel wires. Then there was a flash accompanied by a little smoke.

"I guess that takes care of them," said Jim.

"Sure, but what are we going to do when we land?" I asked. "Suppose they're in New Orleans as they are here?"

"If they are," he said slowly, "there won't be much use landing anyway. That sailor died ten minutes after he was bitten."

Soon afterward we entered the crescent which the river forms around the city. Suddenly the odor of death and corruption swept over us in a great wave. It was so strong it made me gasp. Colonel Lounsbury summoned Jim and me to the pilot house.

"Did you see any of these sea snakes in New Orleans?" he asked.

We shook our heads. "Of course, we weren't looking for them," said Jim.

"They make the job we've got ahead of us a nasty one," said the Colonel. "No way of keeping them from attacking small boats, so far as I can see. Most of the city under water when you left—hadn't drained off much?"

"I don't believe it could drain off," I said. "Where could it drain to? The river and the lake are both higher than the city."

Colonel Lounsbury nodded. "The only way, I guess, is to get the pumps going. I can't figure how we'll do it, unless we find some of the city engineers alive."

We were passing the blocks of white buildings along the levee comprising the Second District flood control base. They seemed intact, though the government vessels along the levee had been sunk. Colonel Lounsbury examined them through field glasses. His face was grim as he put the glasses away.

"See anyone?" I asked.

He shook his head. "No use landing there. If any of the boys were alive, they'd have signalled us."

There were no signs of life on shore as we continued on our way toward the foot of Canal Street, which was to be the base for whatever rescue operations were possible.

The other vessels following us down the river received their orders by radio. Thus they were able to prepare for the sea snakes before they were attacked. When we were a little above Canal Street we edged in beside the levee between the Algiers ferry and the coffee dock. Ordinarily there would have been room for several vessels our size at the concrete embankment, but now we had to avoid the sunken hulks with only their masts sticking out of the water.

Colonel Lounsbury radioed the vessels following us to anchor where they were and wait further orders. He wasted no time. Five minutes after we had tied up, a landing party of twelve, including Jim and me, started ashore.

The first thing I noticed was that the water in Canal Street had receded nearly to the Custom House. There was no wind and the smell of decay which hung over the city was almost overpowering. Scattered along the street where the receding water had left them were many human bodies and parts of bodies. Beyond the Custom House the green flood looked more unhealthy and repulsive than ever, though the phosphorescent flames were not visible in daylight.

Colonel Lounsbury scanned the city through his field glasses. "Looks bad," he said. "Still we've got to be certain. We'll get a couple of the lifeboats down here and see what we can find."

"What about the sea snakes?" asked one of the civilian members of the party.

"Well, what about them?"

"Suppose they attack the lifeboats?" persisted the man.

"It'll be damn unpleasant, but what of it? We've got to find out whether there's anybody alive in the city, and there isn't any other way." He looked at his watch. "Who wants to go along?"

Half an hour later, two of the ship's lifeboats were floating in the water-filled street. Those of us who were going piled in and we started out Canal Street, keeping a close watch for signs of life. We figured if there were any survivors, we would find them in the hotels or office buildings, the upper stories of which had been above the tidal wave.

Most of the principal hotels and big buildings were within a block or two of Canal Street. St. Charles Street and Royal Street, on opposite sides of Canal Street, were only two blocks away from where we launched the boats.

We turned up St. Charles toward the St. Charles Hotel, a red brick structure covering the block between Common and Gravier Streets. We found the lobby of the hotel was still flooded to a depth of six or seven feet. There was no way of getting through the doors except by swimming, and naturally no one was foolish enough to attempt that. Finally Jim and I climbed to the top of the glass portico which extended out from the main entrance. We pulled up after us Colonel Lounsbury, and Professor Ames who was in charge of the scientific end of the expedition. The rest of the party remained in the boats.

We made our way to the mezzanine floor of the building through a broken window. It was evident at first glance that the water had left no one alive in this part of the hotel. We found the same conditions as we climbed to floor after floor until we reached the topmost one. Here there was an especially strong odor of decay, and a moment later we saw why. Scattered around the corridors and rooms were curious-looking bodies. As we got a first glimpse of them from the head of the stairs, I for one was not sure they were human. As soon as I went closer I saw why. They were only parts of bodies. Most of the flesh had been torn from the bones.

"Gosh!" exclaimed Jim. "Something's been eating them!"

"Maybe it was the spotted morays again," suggested Colonel Lounsbury.

Professor Ames, who had been examining the bodies, shook his head. "Those people weren't killed in the water. You can tell that by the clothing. It looks to me as if they had escaped the tidal wave and were attacked afterward when they thought they were safe."

"What's that?" asked Jim suddenly.

Shouts and yells were coming up from below. We rushed to the windows and saw the men we had left in the boats fighting with what at first I thought were a new kind of enormous sea snakes. They were fifty or sixty feet long, had red fins down their backs and heads like horses. Lifting themselves partly out of the water they seized whatever was nearest their huge jaws. Their teeth sheared through an oar as if it were made of paper. During the few seconds we were at the windows I saw one of them snap at a man who dodged and the jaws closed on the side of the boat. Unbelievable as it sounds, a semicircular piece was bitten out of the thick planking.

There seemed to be hundreds of writhing bodies outlined under the water by the red fins. Some of the men in the boats began to shoot while others tried to climb the portico supports to reach the mezzanine floor of the hotel, as we had done.

The four of us at the windows had been paralyzed with astonishment for the few seconds while this was going on. Then with one impulse we tore down the stairs. I'm not sure what we expected to do. There was no possible way of fighting the creatures. If we had reached the mezzanine floor in time we might have pulled some of the victims up to safety. As it was, when we climbed out on the portico and looked down, there was nothing in sight except the two empty boats and floating oars.

It was necessary for us to recover one of the boats to get back to the ship. There was no current in the flooded streets, so they had not drifted far away. First we tried fastening a couple of sash weights to the end of a rope and tossing the weights into the boat. Several times we thought we had succeeded and so we would if the weights had caught around one of the seats. Finally the professor suggested tying together a couple of the long poles they used in the hotel for raising and lowering windows. This did the work and we drew the boat up to the wall.

Meanwhile the horse-headed creatures, which Professor Ames called *regalecus glesne,* had disappeared and the water was quiet.

"Might as well take a chance now as later," said Colonel Lounsbury. "That suit the rest of you?"

We all assented.

"Let's go then," he said, lowering himself into the boat. We followed him. We fished four oars out of the water and rowed away from the neighborhood as quietly as possible. Instead of going back to Canal Street we turned into Common, which ran along one side of the hotel. Directly ahead of us and only three blocks away was the part of Canal Street which was above water, Common running into it at an angle.

We had almost reached this point of comparative safety when we saw the first of the animals which science has been entirely unable to account for. All of the other creatures that came with the green water were larger forms of species which were previously known. The creature that we now saw gazing at us from the roof of a low building fifty yards ahead was like nothing except the prehistoric monsters which scientists have labelled tyrannosaurs.

Professor Ames saw it first. "Stop!" he exclaimed. "Look up on that roof on the left, halfway down the block."

We stopped quickly enough when we saw what he was pointing to. Its body was partly concealed by adjoining buildings, but we saw enough not to want to go nearer. It looked like an alligator twenty or thirty feet long, with six or seven-foot rear legs built for jumping and tiny front legs. It had a tail that was a cross between an alligator's and a kangaroo's. The middle of its body was thicker than an alligator and the head larger. It was watching us as it crouched on the roof, ready to spring when we got near enough.

"Row backwards," said the Colonel, "and keep cool."

I don't suppose any of us felt very cool as the boat slowly backed until it reached Magazine Street. We were able to keep our eyes on the animal in front of us, but we hadn't any idea how many more there might be in the neighborhood.

"I'd swear it was a tyrannosaur," said Professor Ames, "if the species hadn't been extinct for millions of years."

The tyrannosaur, or whatever it was, didn't attempt to leap into the water and pursue us, as we figured it probably would. We decided afterward that it had been feeding on dead bodies until it was torpid. I suppose there is not much doubt that the only thing that saved us from the fate of the other members of the party was that the thousands of carnivorous creatures under and above water had been feeding until they were no longer hungry.

We turned up Magazine Street one block to Gravier and started to row again in the direction of the levee. We had reached South Peters Street when the boat struck an obstruction and stopped.

"We must be aground," said Jim, sticking his oar down into the water to measure its depth.

Suddenly the boat was lifted into the air as if it weighed no more than a feather. We were pitched sprawling into the green water as it overturned. I struggled to my feet and found that I had landed on the loading platform of a warehouse with the water not much above my knees. The Professor and the Colonel were also safe on the platform, but Jim was some distance away, swimming toward us.

A great slimy tentacle covered with sucking discs rose from the water and wrapped itself around the empty boat.

"Hurry, Jim!" I shouted, starting toward him.

"Keep back!" he yelled.

I saw another of the tentacles was reaching for him just under the surface. Fortunately there was a curved iron hook with a handle sticking in the top of a bale of cotton near me. I seized it and swung at the tentacle as it was closing around him. The sharp hook went right through the slimy cylinder and I was nearly dragged under before I could let go.

Jim caught hold of me and we backed up against the wall.

"Come this way!" I heard the Colonel shout.

I looked around and saw that he and Professor Ames were climbing an outside fire escape. We hurried toward them, but it isn't possible to make much speed through water even knee deep. However, we reached the fire escape safely and climbed to the third floor where the two men were waiting for us.

"Whew!" exclaimed the Colonel. "That was the narrowest squeeze yet. I thought Jim here was a goner and I wouldn't have given much for your chances either."

"But what was it?" I asked. "It looked like another of the snakes, only bigger, with suckers all over it."

He silently pointed to a building across the street and a little farther down. There in a double doorway were the bulbous body and enormous staring eyes of a great octopus. Several of its tentacles were partly out of water and they were at least forty feet long.

For the moment we were apparently safe. The eyes of the octopus remained fixed balefully, but it made no effort to come after us.

Our immediate problem was to reach the docks only a few hundred feet away, but there was still a stretch of the green water between, and now we had no boat. We made our way through a trapdoor to the roof of the building, carrying with us a coil of rope. The buildings in the block were of different heights, but by using the rope we reached the one on the corner nearest the river without a great deal of difficulty. This was a warehouse filled with baled cotton and closed up tightly with iron shutters to avoid the possibility of fire. At first it looked as if we were not going to get inside, but we finally found a window opening on a fire escape, with the shutters unbolted.

The water in front of the warehouse was only about three feet deep and shallowed rapidly over the railroad tracks to the concrete ramp which led to the coffee dock a hundred yards away. Still, after our recent experiences we didn't feel like wading through it.

Jim thought of the plan which we carried out. We rolled bales of cotton from the warehouse and built a dry road—and it wasn't as easy as it sounds. A bale of cotton weighs five hundred pounds. The Colonel and the Professor were willing enough to help, but they weren't of much use for heavy manual work.

When the road was completed to the ramp Jim and I were pretty tired. We had put down the last bale when the tyrannosaurs attacked us. Jim saw them first.

"My gosh, look what's coming!" he yelled to me.

They were swimming down Gravier Street, thirty or forty of them, and looked like immense alligators with their heads elevated several feet above the surface. As we raced toward the warehouse where the Colonel and the Professor were waiting, unconscious of this new danger, the tyrannosaurs caught a glimpse of us. Fortunately they paused for a minute to watch us.

Then they raised themselves from the shallow water on their rear legs and tails and leaped forward like giant kangaroos. We hadn't far to go, but we reached the warehouse entrance pretty nearly in a dead heat with the animals. They were so close, as we slid the iron-sheathed doors shut, that one of them got his nose pinched and set up a most tremendous bellowing.

The only light on the ground floor of the building came through the door, and after it was closed we had to feel our way around. We located the other two men by their voices and managed to reach the second floor window through which we had entered the building. We decided to go back to the roof and try to signal the ship with our guns. We remembered that the tyrannosaurs must be able to climb, because the first one we had seen was crouching on a Common Street roof. Some of them might be waiting for us at the top of the fire escape.

As it turned out, we needn't have worried, for the roofs were clear. We gazed down into the street and saw some of the great animals swimming around in the green water. Others were crouching in the shallows, perhaps watching for us to come out of the building. Half a dozen had climbed the ramp which leads to the docks. These last were now crouched close to the ground, watching intently something which we couldn't see.

"Maybe some of the boys are coming to hunt us," said the Colonel anxiously. "I wish we could let them know what they're up against."

A couple of minutes later we saw fifteen or twenty men advancing cautiously along the railroad tracks now barely covered with water. They had evidently seen the tyrannosaurs, which had so far made no effort to attack them.

Colonel Lounsbury fired his gun into the air quickly, three times in succession.

The advancing party paused and looked around. The Colonel fired again and this time they saw us.

The noise infuriated the tyrannosaurs. Those surrounding the warehouse began another desperate attempt to reach us. They even tried to climb the bare walls. A couple of them succeeded in getting as far as the awning over the loading platform.

The animals on the ramp leaped to the tracks. The rescue party apparently had no arms except their automatics. There was a moment of confusion and then the pistols began to bark.

We found out afterward that a tyrannosaur could be killed if a bullet entered its skull between the eyes or, if it was standing, a little below and to the right of the left foreleg. The bullets from an army forty-five automatic would penetrate the thick scales which covered the body, but except at these two points would not stop the creature in time to be of much service to the man attacked.

The six maddened tyrannosaurs plunged into the compact group and in less than ten seconds three of the men were dead, practically torn to pieces. A few seconds later two of the saurians dropped into the shallow water, disabled. The rain of bullets at close range was producing its effect. A third rolled over and the survivors, screaming like wounded elephants, turned tail and fled.

The bellowing of the wounded tyrannosaurs stirred up the rest of the herd. They began to roar and the men rushing around the corner in pursuit got a glimpse of them. One look was enough. They turned and dashed up the ramp toward an open door in the coffee dock. The tyrannosaurs leaped in pursuit, covering thirty feet in a jump. One of them got inside before the men slid the door shut. The others seemed maddened at the sight of their dead and dying companions. They tore down a shed and raced up and down the railroad tracks trying to find a way into the dock building.

We had watched this battle, unable to help. Now the animals were between us and the dock, so there was nothing for us to do at the moment except stay where we were.

"We won't have to wait long," said Colonel Lounsbury. "They'll bring machine guns next time."

Half an hour later one of the sliding doors in the coffee dock was pushed back and we saw the shields of two machine guns in the opening.

The tyrannosaurs had quieted down by this time and at first they didn't pay any attention to the new enemies. Suddenly one of the machine guns began to chatter as its muzzle was directed toward a group of the beasts crouched under the wall of the Anheuser-Busch Building.

They leaped up bellowing as the stream of bullets stung them. At first they ran around in bewilderment, but then the noise attracted their attention to the guns. Two of them were disabled by this time, but the others started toward their attackers. The rest of the herd joined them and they looked more like pictures I have seen of charging buffaloes than anything else I can think of.

"The guns'll never stop them!" exclaimed Jim.

The Colonel, watching with grim face, said nothing.

Both machine guns were firing now and every steel-jacketed bullet must have found its mark in the dense group of animals. Some of those in front fell and impeded the progress of those behind. Meanwhile as they got closer to the guns the execution became more deadly.

They were within forty feet of the doorway as near as I could judge when the slaughter became too much for them. Those that were able turned and fled, leaving at least half their number dead or disabled on the ground.

We watched the survivors until they were out of sight. Then we hurried across the path of cotton bales to meet our rescuers who were busily engaged in despatching the wounded tyrannosaurs. The specimens now at the New York Museum of Natural History and at the Smithsonian were those killed in this battle.

Before night the news of what had happened to our landing party and the condition of things in New Orleans was speeding to all parts of the world. Colonel Lounsbury was in communication with Washington and later with the commanders of the other vessels of the rescue fleet lying in the Mississippi. It was quite certain that the members of our landing party who had disappeared were dead. As far as we were able to determine, there was no one left alive in New Orleans.

I assume that some plan was agreed on that night for further exploration of the devastated area, but if so, it was never carried out. Before morning the great question was whether we were going to save our own lives.

Jim and I were very tired and we went to bed as soon as we could get away from the newspaper men on board the *General Pershing*. I don't know how long I had been asleep when I was wakened by being thrown from my berth to the stateroom floor. I sat up, dazed, to see Jim staring at me from the lower berth.

"Hurt?" he asked.

"Guess not," I answered, feeling over myself gingerly. "But gosh, what threw me out?"

He shook his head. "I don't know. I was asleep and whatever it was woke me up. There it is again."

There was a sudden shock as if the boat had gone aground while it was moving pretty fast.

I grabbed my trousers and shoes and rushed out, with Jim following. The cabins were filled with excited men, none of whom seemed to know what was happening. I made for the upper deck. Suddenly there was another shock which sent me reeling against a wall.

"Earthquake!" yelled one of the stewards as he ran by.

I reached the upper deck just as the engines started and the vessel began to move away from the levee. It was a ghastly enough scene on which I gazed. The stirring up of the water had increased its phosphorescence; the green flames were leaping fifteen and twenty feet in the air. While on the water we felt an earthquake shock only occasionally, on shore they must have been nearly continuous. There was a constant roar of falling masonry. The tall buildings swayed as if they were pasteboard in a high wind. The walls covering the steel frames began to crash. The American Bank Building went first, the masonry peeling off a floor at a time. As it was rapidly becoming a gaunt twisted skeleton, the tower of the Hibernia Building crashed.

We were several hundred feet from the levee when everyone was thrown to the deck by another shock. This must have been worse on shore, for the sound of falling buildings increased to an ear-splitting roar. As I pulled myself to my feet I saw the great coffee dock and the concrete levee to which we had been moored gently slide into the river.

An onrushing wave picked up the *General Pershing* and swept her toward the Algiers shore. If it had happened five minutes before, when she was broadside to the levee, it would have been the end of another good boat. As it happened, we were headed toward the channel and the wave hit our stern, poured over the upper deck, smashed a lot of windows and rolled on, leaving us behind.

In a few minutes the boat was again under control and slowly moving up the river. Ahead of us we could see the searchlights of the other vessels of the fleet, all fleeing from the danger zone. I glanced back toward the doomed city in time to see the steel frame of the American Bank Building sway farther and farther to one side. Then suddenly it wasn't there!

While I was watching I heard an exclamation of alarm from behind me. I whirled around in time to see a great column of flame leap into the air in the south. It was impossible to judge at night its distance from where we were, but we found out later that it was the first of the volcanoes which rose that night from the floor of the Gulf of Mexico. The column of flame extending five or six miles into the sky was not steady but had a regular pulsation. Each time it leaped upward a great crescent of golden light seemed to leave it and float away into the heavens.

The earthquake shocks were becoming more frequent, about two or three a minute, with a severe one every five or six minutes. The engines were under forced draught, but it was hard to tell how much progress we were making. The current seemed to be becoming more rapid. On both banks the levees were sliding into the river. There was a good chance of the channel becoming blocked or too shallow for our fairly deep draught vessels as the river spread over the surrounding country.

A second column of flame rose into the air not far from the first. This was followed by others until there were six of them extending across the southern horizon. Dark gray sand began to fall on the deck in a heavy shower. At the same time electrical phenomena occurred. There were continuous lightning flashes in the south; St. Elmo's fire appeared all over the vessels, every sharp point was surrounded by a glow.

I happened to wonder about the time and glanced at my watch. It was eight o'clock in the morning and still as dark as midnight. I found out afterward that the darkness that day extended over half of the United States. It was not until several hours later, fortunately for us, when we had progressed some distance up the river, that the great earthquake occurred which levelled most of the buildings south of the Ohio River and east of the Rocky Mountains.

It came without warning after we thought the worst was over. I was knocked unconscious and have no idea how long I was out. At that I was more fortunate than most of the others aboard. Several were killed and a great many seriously injured.

When consciousness gradually came back to me I saw that the vessel was lying on her side with the decks sloping at an angle of forty-five degrees. I dragged myself to the rail and looked down on a sea of mud. The river had disappeared. A hundred yards away there was a great chasm through which I could hear water roaring.

There was still something wrong about the scene and I couldn't tell what it was. I rubbed my hand across my eyes, and then I knew. There was the hundred yards of mud, in which thousands of fish were struggling, between the vessel and the brink of the chasm—but the chasm had no other side. Beyond the stretch of mud was nothing! It was as if there you stepped off the end of the earth.

I'd had a nasty knock on the head and I guess what I saw didn't make me feel any better. Anyhow, I went out again.

When I next opened my eyes, Jim was bending over me.

"Gosh, I'm glad you're all right!" he exclaimed. "You had me scared for a while."

I sat up and the first thing I noticed was that the deck was level again. "Are we afloat?" I asked.

He nodded. "We sure are, and you won't believe you're awake when you see what's happened."

"I don't want to look," I said. "I saw it before."

"Come on," he insisted. "You never saw anything prettier."

I stared at him. "Prettier!" I repeated. Then I realized that the sun was shining from a bright blue sky. There was a tang of salt in the air. I could hear the throb of the engines.

Jim helped me to my feet and I looked around. I rubbed my hand over my eyes again. No mud, no river, no land, nothing as far as I could see except blue sea ruffled by the wind into waves topped with tiny whitecaps.

"Where are we?" I demanded, turning to Jim.

"Somewhere in the Mississippi Valley below Natchez, or where Natchez was."

"What does it mean?" I asked blankly.

He shrugged his shoulders. "You can guess as well as anybody else. All we know is that the Gulf of Mexico now covers all the Mississippi Valley. There was the earthquake, the land sank and the ocean rushed in."

"Well," I said, slowly looking around, "it looks as if we'd had grandstand seats for the biggest thing that ever happened."

This was intended to be a narrative of the personal experience of two who happened to see more of the Great Catastrophe than most of those who survived. Therefore I have made no attempt to take sides in the scientific controversies that have raged since. However, in regard to one subject our experiences give a certain weight to our views.

Most scientists believe that there was some quality of the green substance deposited in the water by the planetoid that almost miraculously stimulated growth. Our adventures with immense sea creatures apparently support this theory. On the other hand, certain scientists claim that the tidal wave washed up over the southern portion of the United States creatures that ordinarily live in the depths of the Gulf of Mexico and the Caribbean Sea. They have produced records of sea snakes as large as any that attacked us, ribbon fish larger than those we encountered, and against our estimate of forty-foot tentacles for the octopus, they produce a record of portions of a dead one washed ashore with tentacles that must have originally been at least sixty feet long.

Nevertheless, those of us who actually encountered the monsters in New Orleans believe they were abnormal.

It seems incredible that the planetoid, so insignificant in size when compared with the earth, should have caused the death of millions of people and submerged a considerable part of the North American continent. It really produced both of these effects indirectly. The tidal wave was so enormously destructive because the inhabitants of the southern United States were living practically at sea level. Any convulsion severe enough to produce a great tidal wave might easily have been equally destructive.

The increase in tension of the crust of the earth and the great earthquake, followed by the subsidence of the Mississippi Valley, restored a condition which probably existed in the prehistoric past. The inland sea covering the Mississippi valley possesses many advantages over the turbulent uncontrollable river. A large part of the land which disappeared consisted of malarial swamps which were probably irreclaimable.

The world is going on as if the catastrophe had never occurred. Sometimes Jim and I almost doubt it ourselves. Then we go to the New York Museum of Natural History or to the Smithsonian at Washington and gaze at the stuffed tyrannosaurs we saw killed on the New Orleans docks.

W. ALEXANDER

ONE LEG TOO MANY

AS Dr. Wentworth stood on the steps of his residence awaiting the arrival of his chauffeur with the car, he watched with a speculative eye a young man cutting the grass of his well-kept lawn. The chap, he thought, was about twenty-five, and strong, for he pushed the heavy lawn-mower with ease, although somewhat handicapped by a wooden leg which occasionally sank deep into a soft spot on the lawn.

"Good morning, William," greeted the doctor, approaching him across the springy sward. "You seem to be working hard this warm morning. By the way, how long is it since you lost your leg?"

"Good morning, Doctor," answered the young man, with a wide smile, which exposed a beautiful set of white teeth, and also a cavity where a molar was missing. "It is about eight years since I lost my leg. It was crushed in a railroad accident and amputated about four inches below the knee."

"How would you like to have a new leg?" asked the doctor.

"Oh, you mean one of those new-fangled artificial legs with joints and all that? I guess that would be fine. I see fellows walking around with them and you can hardly tell they are artificial, but I understand they are very expensive."

"Well, that is not just what I mean; but suppose you drop in to see me tonight about eight and we will talk it over."

"Mr. William Hall to see you by appointment, sir," Haskins, Dr. Wentworth's man, with a bit of a sniff, announced that evening, as the doctor sat reading in his library.

"Very well, Haskins," the doctor replied. "Show him in and see that I am not disturbed for the next hour."

"Come in, William," called the doctor when the young man appeared, looking well groomed in a neat brown suit. "Make yourself comfortable in that easy chair. You will find smokes of various kinds on the stand beside you."

After William had touched a match to a long, slim cigar and had settled back comfortably in his chair, Dr. Wentworth asked:

"How long have you lived here, William?"

"Almost five years. I came here from Dancerville, Iowa, about a year after my accident. I had been living with my father on a farm just outside the village, but we quarreled and I left home."

"How much schooling have you had?"

"High school and one year in college."

"Then you have probably read enough," said the doctor, "not to be too startled at what I am about to say to you. You know that science has made immense progress in the past twenty-five years, more perhaps than was made in the previous two hundred years.

"A few years ago I became convinced that the human body should be able to replace by new growth a lost limb, as do crustaceans such as the lobster, shrimp, crawfish, and many others. After some investigation I concluded that the lobster was the best adapted for the purpose of my experiments, as it grew a lost leg or claw much more quickly than the others.

"My first effort was to learn what part peculiar to these creatures caused the new growth. For this purpose I secured from a French scientist, a friend of mine, an X-ray moving picture machine and a projector, that I might note on the film any changes in the lobster's interior while the new growth was taking place. It was in this way that I learned of a ductless gland which became intensely active the minute a claw or leg was lost. This gland immediately swelled to twice its normal size and emitted a constant flow of hormones into the bloodstream until the claw was fully grown, then it subsided to normal size and apparently lay dormant."

"This is all very interesting, Doctor," interrupted William, "but a little over my head. What, for instance, are hormones?"

"Roughly speaking," explained the doctor, "hormones is the name given to the secretion of ductless glands—glands with no outlet—which is sent through the bloodstream to rejuvenate some part of the body. As you are probably aware, gland transplantation from animals to the human body has been carried on with more or less success for some time. It occurred to me that if this new-growth gland could be transplanted from the lobster to a human body, it would function in the same way and for the same purpose, thereby causing a new limb to grow on the human body where one had been lost by accident.

"The chief difficulty was to find a method to transplant successfully a living gland from a lobster—a cold-blooded arthropod—to a warm-blooded animal, under which head a human body would come. After a number of failures I succeeded in transplanting a gland to a guinea-pig's leg. I reduced the blood temperature in the guinea-pig by partially shutting off blood circulation in the leg and packing it in ice until the gland had thoroughly knitted to the animal's tissue. My next successful operation was to transplant a gland from a lobster to a male and female guinea-pig, as I was anxious to find if the gland would be transmitted to their young.

"While I was awaiting developments in this operation, the first guinea-pig lost three toes in an accident and when they quickly grew out again, I knew my experiment had opened a vast field of possibilities. Later I found that the progeny of the pair of guinea-pigs had inherited the gland and the ones I now have are the tenth generation and the gland in them is almost twice the size of the gland originally transplanted from the lobster.

"I am now ready to carry my experiment to its conclusion, that is, transplant a gland from a guinea-pig to a man. I am inviting you to participate in this experiment with me. If it is successful—which I have no reason to doubt—you will again have two sound legs; if unsuccessful, you will be no worse off physically and I will make you a present of five thousand dollars to assuage your disappointment. What do you say?"

"You almost take my breath away!" exclaimed the astonished William. "If I did not know of your reputation for performing operations that seemed like miracles, I would call it all a fairy tale, but I am prepared to believe that a doctor who can transfer vital parts from one person to another can do almost anything. I am ready to take a chance with you. When do you wish to operate and how long will I be laid up?"

"I will make the gland transplantation tomorrow, and unless my calculations are wrong, your new leg should be fully grown in thirty days."

The first and second efforts were failures, as the gland refused to amalgamate with the tissues of William's body. In the third operation Dr. Wentworth filled the incision, in which the gland was to nestle, with Dr. Zambi's famous Collodiansy and in thirty-six hours it had adhered to the surrounding tissue and was functioning as perfectly as though it were an integral part of William's body. Then the doctor removed the skin from the end of the leg-stump and all was ready for the expected growth.

It was with fascination and almost awe that Wentworth and William watched the leg grow by inches day after day, until at the end of thirty-five days William had two as fine a pair of legs as any sturdy young man could desire. While watching the developments of the operation, the doctor and William had become very friendly. On the day he was to be dismissed from the hospital, Dr. Wentworth asked William:

"What are your plans for the future, William?"

"I am going to look for a job, sir," he answered. "Something better than pushing a lawn-mower. With my wooden leg I was too diffident to go after anything better, but now with two good legs, I feel that I can tackle more."

"I am badly in need of a secretary," remarked the doctor. "I wonder if you would care for the position? You could handle it nicely, your chief duties being to relieve me of the many minor details connected with my work that now harass me."

"Thank you, Doctor," replied William, gratefully, "I don't know of a position that I would like better. Since I have been here in the hospital I have read many of your medical books, especially those telling of your wonderful operations. It seems to me that your success with my leg opens vast possibilities in surgery. It seems logical that from now on, when a patient is about to be operated on for the removal of some part, a gland will first be transplanted to the patient. Then after the diseased part or organ is removed, the gland will quickly cause a new and healthy part to re-grow. I have been keeping a surprise for you, Doctor. Do you remember the cavity in my mouth where I had lost a molar? Look at it now."

The doctor looked and was startled to note that the cavity was now filled with a new tooth.

"That is surprising," said Dr. Wentworth. "If the gland will cause one new tooth to grow, it could also cause a whole set of teeth to grow, replacing those removed. And as you suggest, it should cause internal parts to grow where those diseased had been removed."

William had been with Dr. Wentworth for six months, when he entered the library one night very much excited.

"Doctor," he cried, "read this letter which I just received."

The doctor took the letter and read:

Dancerville, Iowa, April 10, 1926.

Mr. William Hall,
San Diego, Cal.
Dear Sir:

Your father died some five months ago, since which time I, as executor under the will, have made every effort to locate you, as you are named as sole heir. I learned today that you had been seen in San Diego some time ago, so am addressing this letter to that point in hopes of reaching you.

You may not be aware that your father left an estate of considerable value, approximately half a million dollars, oil having been found on the home farm shortly after you left. If this letter reaches you, wire me at once when you will arrive here.

Yours truly,
James Ralston,
Executor, Estate of Frank B. Hall.

"That certainly is wonderful news, William," said the doctor heartily. "Did you wire Mr. Ralston?"

"Just going to do so now. Can I leave for Dancerville tomorrow morning, sir?"

"Surely, William," answered the doctor, looking at him with affection. "I am going to miss you badly, but I am happy in your good fortune."

"Oh, you are not going to lose me, Doctor," replied William. "I have become too much interested in your work to leave you now. This money will enable me to take the medical course I have wanted."

Ten days later Dr. Wentworth received the following telegram from William, dated at Dancerville:

"Executor refuses to turn estate over to me, claiming that I am an impostor. Says the William Hall who is the heir has but one leg, while I have two. Explained about operation, but he just laughed. Have brought suit for possession of estate, case comes to trial next Monday. Can you be here to help me prove that I am I?"

The doctor wired William that he would be there and commenced at once to arrange with his assistants for the care of his patients.

On the following Monday, when William's attorney put Dr. Wentworth on the stand, he told of his experiments and eventual operation on William, which produced the growth of a new leg. When he had finished his recital, he saw that Judge Long, before whom the case was being tried, and also the spectators in the court-room, were incredulous. He even fancied he heard a titter ripple through the room.

"Doctor, if doctor you be," said the judge, shaking a finger at him in wrath, "that is the most preposterous story to which this court has ever been forced to listen. There is evidently a conspiracy here to defraud the real William Hall of his inheritance. Grow a new leg indeed! You should be indicted for perjury and I shall bring the matter to the notice of the Grand Jury."

Dr. Wentworth was greatly embarrassed and, as he watched the finger the angry judge was shaking at him, he absently noted that the first joint was missing. As he listened to the scathing denunciation of the judge, he was filled with rage to think that these small-town ignoramuses should doubt his word. Then he was seized with an inspiration, a method of proving the truthfulness of his story.

"Your Honor," he asked, "may I have a word with you in private?"

The judge nodded and he mounted the rostrum to his side and whispered to him for a moment. Judge Long was seen to shake his head vigorously, but still the doctor whispered. At last the judge was seen to nod and Dr. Wentworth walked from the room, a half smile on his lips.

Judge Long glared about the room for a moment as though seeking a culprit on whom he could vent his wrath, then seeing none, pounded on his desk with his gavel and said: "This case is postponed for ten days. Clerk, call the next case."

Ten days later the case was again called for trial and the attorney for the defense at once put on the stand a number of witnesses. First came the doctor who had amputated William's leg and the nurse who attended him. Then the claim-agent of the railroad who had settled William's claim against the company. Next came a dentist who testified to pulling a molar tooth for William Hall. Finally several neighbors were put on the stand who had known William after his accident. They all testified that the plaintiff closely resembled William Hall, but were sure he had but one leg.

The attorney for the defense, in concluding his summing up of his case, said: "Your Honor, we feel that we have made our case. We submit that this is the most brazen attempt of an impostor that we have ever witnessed. While it is true that the plaintiff does closely resemble the missing William Hall, he has one leg too many to qualify. We rest our case."

The attorney for William Hall, the plaintiff, stated that they really had but one witness, Dr. Wentworth, and as the Court had already heard his testimony, they felt it unnecessary to again put him on the stand. Therefore they rested their case.

Judge Long arose and leaned on his desk, peering over the top of his glasses at the spectators in the court-room. His chin whiskers were slightly a-tremble and an odd smile played about his lips. After a moment of silent gazing he spoke: "In the past ten days this Court has looked into the record of Dr. Wentworth, the only witness of the plaintiff, and found to its astonishment that he is a scientist of international renown. He has performed many operations that to the lay-mind appear little short of miracles. Ten days ago this Court, in its ignorance and small-town bigotry, spoke to this honorable gentleman in a manner for which it now most humbly offers its apologies. I say to you that a monument should be built for this man to commemorate the relief he has brought to suffering humanity with his wonderful operations.

"This Court finds for the plaintiff and instructs that the defendant, James Ralston, shall at once turn over the estate in question to the plaintiff, William Hall."

After a dramatic pause, Judge Long raised his right hand in the air, index finger extended, and cried: "There is the evidence that convinced this Court."

The spectators, familiar for years with the sight of the judge's finger with the first joint missing, now gazed with astonishment at that same finger with the first joint three-fourths grown and almost half of a new nail showing.

Miles J. Breuer, M.D.

THE MAN WITH THE STRANGE HEAD

A MAN in a gray hat stood halfway down the corridor, smoking a cigar and apparently interested in my knocking and waiting. I rapped again on the door of Number 216 and waited some more, but all remained silent. Finally my observer approached me.

"I don't believe it will do any good," he said. "I've just been trying it. I would like to talk to someone who is connected with Anstruther. Are you?"

"Only this." I handed him a letter out of my pocket without comment, as one is apt to do with a thing that has caused one no little wonderment:

> "Dear Doctor": it said succinctly. "I have been under the care of Dr. Faubourg who has recently died. I would like to have you take charge of me on a contract basis, and keep me well, instead of waiting till I get sick. I can pay you enough to make you independent, but in return for that, you will have to accept an astonishing revelation concerning me, and keep it to yourself. If this seems acceptable to you, call on me at 9 o'clock, Wednesday evening. Josiah Anstruther, Room 216, Cornhusker Hotel."

"If you have time," said the man in the gray hat, handing me back the letter, "come with me. My name is Jerry Stoner, and I make a sort of living writing for magazines. I live in 316, just above here."

"By some curious architectural accident," he continued, as we reached his room, "that ventilator there enables me to hear minutely everything that goes on in the room below. I haven't ever said anything about it during the several months that I've lived here, partly because it does not disturb me, and partly because it has begun to pique my curiosity—a writer can confess to that, can he not? The man below is quiet and orderly, but seems to work a good deal on some sort of clockwork; I can hear it whirring and clicking quite often. But listen now!"

Standing within a couple of feet of the opening which was covered with an iron grill, I could hear footsteps. They were regular, and would decrease in intensity as the person walked away from the ventilator

---

This story, although a little primitive in concept for modern tastes, is interesting as a precursor of tales such as "No Woman Born," by Catherine L. Moore, which was one of the most popular selections in *The Treasury of Science Fiction* (Crown Publishers, 1948).

opening below, and increase again as he approached it; were interrupted for a moment as he probably stepped on a rug; and were shorter for two or three counts, no doubt as he turned at the end of the room. This was repeated in a regular rhythm as long as I listened.

"Well?" I said.

"You perceive nothing strange about that, I suppose," said Jerry Stoner. "But if you had listened all day long to just exactly that you would begin to wonder. That is the way he was going on when I awoke this morning; I was out from 10 to 11 this forenoon. The rest of the time I have been writing steadily, with an occasional stretch at the window, and all of the time I have heard steadily what you hear now, without interruption or change. It's getting on my nerves.

"I have called him on the phone, and have rung it on and off for twenty minutes; I could hear his bell through the ventilator, but he pays no attention to it. So, a while ago I tried to call on him. Do you know him?"

"I know who he is," I replied, "but do not remember ever having met him."

"If you had ever met him you would remember. He has a queer head. I made my curiosity concerning the sounds from his room an excuse to cultivate his acquaintance. The cultivation was difficult. He is courteous, but seemed afraid of me."

We agreed that there was not much that we could do about it. I gave up trying to keep my appointment, told Stoner that I was glad I had met him, and went home. The next morning at seven he had me on the telephone.

"Are you still interested?" he asked, and his voice was nervous. "That bird's been at it all night. Come and help me talk to the hotel management." I needed no urging.

I found Beesley, the hotel manager, with Stoner; he was from St. Louis, and looked French.

"He can do it if he wants to," he said, shrugging his shoulders comically; "unless you complain of it as a disturbance."

"It isn't that," said Stoner; "there must be something wrong with the man."

"Some form of insanity——" I suggested; "or a compulsion neurosis."

"That's what I'll be pretty soon," Stoner said. "He is a queer gink anyway. As far as I have been able to find out, he has no close friends. There is something about his appearance that makes me shiver; his face is so wrinkled and droopy, and yet he sails about the streets with an unusually graceful and vigorous step. Loan me your pass key; I think I'm as close a friend of his as anyone."

Beesley lent the key, but Stoner was back in a few minutes, shaking his head. Beesley was expecting that; he told us that when the hotel was built, Anstruther had the doors made of steel with special bars, at his own expense, and the windows shuttered, as though he were afraid for his life.

"His rooms would be as hard to break into as a fort," Beesley said as he left us; "and thus far we do not have sufficient reason for wrecking the hotel."

"Look here!" I said to Stoner; "it will take me a couple of hours to hunt up the stuff and string up a periscope; it's an old trick I learned as a Boy Scout."

Between us we had it up in about that time; a radio aerial mast clamped on the window sill with mirrors at the top and bottom, and a telescope at our end of it, gave us a good view of the room below us. It was a sort of living room made by throwing together two of the regular-sized hotel rooms. Anstruther was walking across it diagonally, disappearing from our field of view at the further end, and coming back again. His head hung forward on his chest with a ghastly limpness. He was a big, well-built man, with a vigorous stride. Always it was the same path. He avoided the small table in the middle each time with exactly the same sort of side step and swing. His head bumped limply as he turned near the window and started back across the room. For two hours we watched him in shivering fascination, during which he walked with the same hideous uniformity.

"That makes thirty hours of this," said Stoner. "Wouldn't you say that there was something wrong?"

We tried another consultation with the hotel manager. As a physician, I advised that something be done; that he be put in a hospital or something. I was met with another shrug.

"How will you get him? I still do not see sufficient cause for destroying the hotel company's property. It will take dynamite to get at him."

He agreed, however, to a consultation with the police, and in response to our telephone call, the great, genial chief, Peter John Smith was soon sitting with us. He advised us against breaking in.

"A man has a right to walk that way if he wants to," he said. "Here's this fellow in the papers who played the piano for 49 hours, and the police didn't stop him; and in Germany they practice making public speeches for 18 hours at a stretch. And there was this Olympic dancing fad some months ago, where a couple danced for 57 hours."

"It doesn't look right to me," I said, shaking my head. "There seems to be something wrong with the man's appearance; some uncanny disease of the nervous system—Lord knows I've never heard of anything that resembles it!"

We decided to keep a constant watch. I had to spend a little time on my patients, but Stoner and the chief stayed, and agreed to call me if occasion arose. I peeped through the periscope at the walking man several times during the next twenty-four hours; and it was always exactly the same, the hanging, bumping head, the uniformity of his course, the uncanny, machine-like exactitude of his movements. I spent an hour at a time with my eye at the telescope studying his movements for some variation, but was unable to be certain of any. That afternoon I looked up my neurology texts, but found no clues. The next day at 4 o'clock in the afternoon, after not less than 55 hours of it, I was there with Stoner to see the end of it; Chief Peter John Smith was out.

As we watched, we saw that he moved more and more slowly, but with otherwise identical motions. It had the effect of the slowed motion pictures of dancers or athletes; or it seemed like some curious dream; for as we watched, the sound of the steps through the ventilator also slowed and weakened. Then we saw him sway a little, and totter, as though his balance were imperfect. He swayed a few times and fell sidewise on the floor; we could see one leg in the field of our periscope moving slowly with the same movements as in walking, a slow, dizzy sort of motion. In five more minutes he was quite still.

The Chief was up in a few moments in response to our telephone call.

"Now we've got to break in," he said. Beesley shrugged his shoulders and said nothing. Stoner came to the rescue of the hotel property.

"A small man could go down this ventilator. This grill can be unscrewed, and the lower one can be knocked out with a hammer; it is cast-iron."

Beesley was gone like a flash, and soon returned with one of his window-washers, who was small and wiry, and also a rope and hammer. We took off the grill and held the rope as the man crawled in. He shouted to us as he hit the bottom. The air drew strongly downwards, but the blows of his hammer on the grill came up to us. We hurried down stairs. Not a sound came through the door of 216, and we waited for some minutes. Then there was a rattle of bars and the door opened, and a gust of cold wind struck us, with a putrid odor that made us gulp. The man had evidently run to open a window before coming to the door.

Anstruther lay on his side, with one leg straight and the other extended forward as in a stride; his face was livid, sunken, hideous. Stoner gave him a glance, and then scouted around the room—looking for the machinery he had been hearing, but finding none. The chief and I also went over the rooms, but they were just conventional rooms, rather colorless and lacking in personality. The chief called an undertaker and also the coroner, and arranged for a post-mortem examination. I received permission to notify a number of professional colleagues; I wanted some of them to share in the investigation of this unusual case with me. As I was leaving, I could not help noting the astonished gasps of the undertaker's assistants as they lifted the body; but they were apparently too well trained to say anything.

That evening, a dozen physicians gathered around the figure covered with a white sheet on the table in the center of the undertaker's work room. Stoner was there; a writer may be anywhere he chooses. The coroner was preparing to draw back the sheet.

"The usual medical history is lacking in this case," he said. "Perhaps an account by Dr. B. or his author friend, of the curious circumstances connected with the death of this man, may take its place."

"I can tell a good deal," said Stoner; "and I think it will bear directly on what you find when you open him up, even though it is not technical medical stuff. Do you care to hear it?"

"Tell it! Go on! Let's have it!"

"I have lived above him in the hotel for several months," Stoner began. "He struck me as a curious person, and as I do some writing, all mankind is my legitimate field for study. I tried to find out all I could about him.

"He has an office in the Little Building, and did a rather curious business. He dealt in vases and statuary, book-ends and chimes, and things you put around in rooms to make them look artistic. He had men out buying the stuff, and others selling it, all by personal contact and on a very exclusive basis. He kept the stock in a warehouse near the Rock Island tracks where they pass the Ball Park; I do not believe that he ever saw any of it. He just sat in the office and signed papers, and the other fellows made the money; and apparently they made a lot of it, for he has swung some big financial deals in this town.

"I often met him in the lobby or the elevator. He was a big, vigorous man and walked with an unusually graceful step and an appearance of strength and vitality. His eyes seemed to light up with recognition when he saw me, but in my company he was always formal and reserved. For such a vigorous-looking man, his voice was singularly cracked and feeble, and his head gave an impression of being rather small for him, and his face old and wrinkled.

"He seemed fairly well known about the city. At the Eastridge Club they told me that he plays golf occasionally and excellently, and is a graceful dancer, though somehow not a popular partner. He was seen frequently at the Y.M.C.A. bowling alleys and played with an uncanny skill. Men loved to see him bowl for his cleverness with the balls, but wished he were not so formally courteous, and did not wear such an expression of complete happiness over his victories. Bridley, manager of Rudge & Guenzel's book department, was the oldest friend of his that I could find, and he gave me some interesting information. They went to school together, and Anstruther was poor in health as well as in finances. Twenty-five years ago, during the hungry and miserable years after his graduation from the University, Bridley remembered him as saying:

" 'My brain needs a body to work with. If I had physical strength, I could do anything. If I find a fellow who can give it to me, I'll make him rich!'

"Bridley also remembers that he was sensitive because girls did not like his debilitated physique. He seems to have found health later, though I can find no one who remembers how or when. About ten years ago he came back from Europe where he had been for several years, in Paris, Bridley thinks; and for several years after this, a Frenchman lived with him. The city directory of that time has him living in the big stone house at 13th and 'G' streets. I went up there to look around, and found it a double house, Dr. Faubourg having occupied the other half. The present caretaker has been there ever since Anstruther lived in the house, and she says that his French companion must have been some sort of an engineer, and that the two must have been working on an invention, from the sounds she heard and the materials they had about. Some three or four years ago the Frenchman and the machinery vanished, and Anstruther moved to the Cornhusker Hotel. Also at about this time, Dr. Faubourg retired from the practice of medicine. He must have been about 50 years old, and too healthy and vigorous to be retiring on account of old age or ill health.

"Apparently Anstruther never married. His private life was quite obscure, but he appeared much in public. He was always very courtly and polite to the ladies. Outside his business he took a great interest in Y.M.C.A. and Boy Scout camps, in the National Guard, and in fact in everything that stood for an outdoor, physical life, and promoted health. In spite of his oddity he was quite a hero with the small boys, especially since the time of his radium hold-up. This is intimately connected with the story of his radium speculation that caused such a sensation in financial circles a couple of years ago.

"About that time, the announcement appeared of the discovery of new uses for radium; a way had been found to accelerate its splitting and to derive power from it. Its price went up, and it promised to become a scarce article on the market. Anstruther had never been known to speculate, nor to tamper with sensational things like oil and helium; but on this occasion he seemed to go into a panic. He cashed in on a lot of securities and caused a small panic in the city, as he was quite wealthy and had especially large amounts of money in the building-loan business. The newspapers told of how he had bought a hundred thousand dollars worth of radium, which was to be delivered right here in Lincoln—a curious method of speculating, the editors volunteered.

"It arrived by express one day, and Anstruther rode the express wagon with the driver to the station. I found the driver and he told the story of the hold-up at 8th and 'P' streets at eleven o'clock at night. A Ford car drove up beside them, from which a man pointed a pistol at them and ordered them to stop. The driver stopped.

"'Come across with the radium!' shouted the big black bulk in the Ford, climbing upon the express wagon. Anstruther's fist shot out like a flash of lightning and struck the arm holding the pistol; and the driver states that he heard the pistol crash through the window on the second floor of the Lincoln Hotel. Anstruther pushed the express driver, who was in his way, backwards over the seat among the packages and leaped upon the hold-up man; the driver said he heard Anstruther's muscles crunch savagely, as with little apparent effort he flung the man over the Ford; he fell with a thud on the asphalt and stayed there. Anstruther then launched a kick at the man at the wheel of the Ford, who crumpled up and fell out of the opposite side of the car.

"The police found the pistol inside a room on the second floor of the Lincoln Hotel. The steering post of the Ford car was torn from its fastenings. Both of the hold-up men had ribs and collar-bones broken, and the gunman's forearm was bent double in the middle with both bones broken. These two men agreed later with the express driver that Anstruther's attack, for suddenness, swiftness, and terrific strength was beyond anything they had dreamed possible; he was like a thunderbolt; like some furious demon. When the two men were huddled in black heaps on the pavement, Anstruther said to the driver, quite impersonally: "'Drive to the police station. Come on! Wake up! I've got to get this stuff locked up!'

"One of the hold-up men had lost all his money and the home he was building when Anstruther had foreclosed a loan in his desperate scramble for radium. He was a Greek named Poulos, and has been in prison for two years; just last week he was released——"

Chief Peter John Smith interrupted.

"I've been putting two and two together, and I can shed a little light on this problem. Three days ago, the day before I was called to watch Anstruther pacing his room, we picked up this man Poulos in the alleyway between Rudge & Guenzel's and Miller & Paine's. He was unconscious, and must have received a terrible licking at somebody's hands; his face was almost unrecognizable; several ribs and several fingers on his right hand were broken. He clutched a pistol fitted with a silencer, and we found that two shots had been fired from it. Here he is——"

A limp, bandaged, plastered man was pushed in between two policemen. He was sullen and apathetic, until he caught sight of Anstruther's face from which the chief had drawn a corner of the sheet. Terror and joy seemed to mingle in his face and in his voice. He raised his bandaged hand with an ineffectual gesture, and started off on some Greek religious expression, .and then turned dazedly to us, speaking painfully through his swollen face.

"Glad he dead. I try to kill him. Shoot him two time. No kill. So close——" indicating the distance of a foot from his chest; "then he lick me. He is not man. He is devil. I not kill him, but I glad he dead!"

The Chief hurried him out, and came in with a small, dapper man with a black chin whisker. He apologized to the coroner.

"This is not a frame-up. I am just following out a hunch that I got a few minutes ago while Stoner was talking. This is Mr. Fournier. I found his address in Anstruther's room, and dug him up. I think he will be more important to you doctors than he will in a court. Tell 'em what you told me!"

While the little Frenchman talked, the undertaker's assistant jerked off the sheet. The undertaker's work had had its effect in getting rid of the frightful odor, and in making Anstruther's face presentable. The body, however, looked for all the world as though it were alive, plump, powerful, pink. In the chest, over the heart, were two bullet holes, not bloody, but clean-cut and black. The Frenchman turned to the body and worked on it with a little screw-driver as he talked.

"Mr. Anstruther came to me ten years ago, when I was a poor mechanic. He had heard of my automatic chess-player, and my famous animated show-window models; and he offered me time and money to find him a mechanical relief for his infirmity. I was an assistant at a Paris laboratory, where they had just learned to split radium and get a hundred horse-power from a pinch of powder. Anstruther was weak and thin, but ambitious."

The Frenchman lifted off two plates from the chest and abdomen of the body, and the flanks swung outward as though on hinges. He removed a number of packages that seemed to fit carefully within, and which were on the ends of cables and chains.

"Now—" he said to the assistants, who held the feet. He put his hands into the chest cavity, and as the assistants pulled the feet away, he lifted out of the shell a small, wrinkled emaciated body; the body of an old man, which now looked quite in keeping with the well-known Anstruther head. Its chest was covered with dried blood, and there were two bullet holes over the heart. The undertaker's assistants carried it away while we crowded around to inspect the mechanism within the arms and legs of the pink and live-looking shell, headless, gaping at the chest and abdomen, but uncannily like a healthy, powerful man.

Katherine MacLean

DEFENSE MECHANISM

THE article was coming along smoothly, words flowing from the typewriter in pleasant simple sequence, swinging to their predetermined conclusion like a good tune. Ted typed contentedly, adding pages to the stack at his elbow.

A thought, a subtle modification of the logic of the article began to glow in his mind, but he brushed it aside impatiently. This was to be a short article, and there was no room for subtlety. His articles sold, not for depth, but for an oddly individual quirk that he could give to commonplaces.

While he typed a little faster, faintly, in the echoes of his thought, the theme began to elaborate itself richly with correlations, modifying qualifications, and humorous parenthetical remarks. An eddy of especially interesting conclusions tried to insert itself into the main stream of his thoughts. Furiously he typed along the dissolving thread of his argument.

"Shut up," he snarled. "Can't I have any privacy around here?"

The answer was not a remark, it was merely a concept: two electro-chemical calculators pictured with the larger in use as a control mech, taking a dangerously high inflow, and controlling it with high resistance and blocs, while the smaller one lay empty and unblocked, its unresist-ant circuits ramifying any impulses received along the easy channels of pure calculation. Ted recognized the diagram as something borrowed from his amateur concepts of radio and psychology.

"All right. So I'm doing it myself. So you can't help it!" He grinned grudgingly. "Answering back at your age!"

Under the impact of a directed thought the small circuits of the idea came in strongly, scorching their reception and rapport diagram into his mind in flashing repetitions, bright as small lightning strokes. Then it spread and the small other brain flashed into brightness, reporting and repeating from every center. Ted even received a brief kinesthetic sensation of lying down, before it was all cut off in a hard bark of thought that came back in the exact echo of his own irritation.

"Tune down!" it ordered furiously. "You're blasting in too loud and jamming everything up! What do you want, an idiot child?"

Ted blanketed down desperately, cutting off all thoughts, relaxing every muscle, but the angry thoughts continued coming in strongly a moment before fading.

"Even when I take a nap," they said, "he starts thinking at me! Can't I get any peace and privacy around here?"

Ted grinned. The kid's last remark sounded like something a little better than an attitude echo. It would be hard to tell when the kid's mind grew past a mere selective echoing of outside thoughts, and be-came true personality, but that last remark was a convincing counter-feit of a sincere kick in the shin. Conditioned reactions can be efficient.

All the luminescent streaks of thought faded and merged with the calm meaningless ebb and flow of waves in the small sleeping mind. Ted moved quietly into the next room and looked down into the blue-and-white crib. The kid lay sleeping, his thumb in his mouth and his chubby face innocent of thought. Junior—Jake.

It was an odd stroke of luck that Jake was born with this particular talent. Because of it they would have to spend the winter in Con-necticut, away from the mental blare of crowded places. Because of it Ted was doing free-lance in the kitchen, instead of minor editing be-hind a New York desk. The winter countryside was wide and wind-swept, as it had been in Ted's own childhood, and the warm contacts with the stolid personalities of animals through Jake's mind were al-ready a pleasure. Old acquaintances—Ted stopped himself skeptically. He was no telepath. He decided that it reminded him of Ernest Thompson Seton's animal biographies, and went back to typing, dis-missing the question.

It was pleasant to eavesdrop on things through Jake, as long as the subject was not close enough to the article to interfere with it.

Five small boys let out of kindergarten came trouping by on the road, chattering and throwing pebbles. Their thoughts came in jumbled together in distracting cross currents, but Ted stopped typing for a moment, smiling, waiting for Jake to show his latest trick. Babies are hypersensitive to conditioning. The burnt hand learns to yank back from fire, the unresisting mind learns automatically to evade too many clashing echoes of other minds.

Abruptly the discordant jumble of small boy thoughts and sensations delicately untangled into five compartmented strands of thoughts, then one strand of little boy thoughts shoved the others out, monopolizing and flowing easily through the blank baby mind, as a dream flows by without awareness, leaving no imprint of memory, fading as the children passed over the hill. Ted resumed typing, smiling. Jake had done the trick a shade faster than he had yesterday. He was learning reflexes easily enough to demonstrate normal intelligences. At least he was to be more than a gifted moron.

A half hour later Jake had grown tired of sleeping, and was standing up in his crib, shouting and shaking the bars, when Martha hurried in with a double armload of groceries.

"Does he want something?"

"Nope. Just exercising his lungs." Ted stubbed out his cigarette and tapped the finished stack of manuscript contentedly. "Got something here for you to proofread."

"Dinner first," she said cheerfully, unpacking food from the bags. "Better move the typewriter and give us some elbow room."

Sunlight came in the windows and shone on the yellow table top and glinted on her dark hair as she opened packages.

"What's the local gossip?" he asked, clearing off the table. "Anything new?"

"Meat's going up again," she said, unwrapping peas and filets of mackerel. "Mrs. Watkin's boy, Tom, is back from the clinic. He can see fine now, she says."

He put water on to boil and began greasing a skillet while she rolled the filets in cracker crumbs. "If I'd had to run a flame thrower during the war, I'd have worked up a nice case of hysteric blindness myself," he said. "I call that a legitimate defense mechanism. Sometimes it's better to be blind."

"But not all the time," Martha protested, putting baby food in the double boiler. In five minutes lunch was cooking.

"Whaaaa—" wailed Jake.

Martha went into the baby's room, and brought him out, cuddling him, and crooning, "What do you want, Lovekins? Baby isn't hungry yet, is ims. Baby just wants to be cuddled, doesn't baby."

"Yes," said Ted.

She looked up, startled, and her expression changed, became withdrawn and troubled, her dark eyes clouded in difficult thought.

Concerned, he asked, "What is it, honey?"

"Ted, you shouldn't—" She struggled with words. "I know it is handy to know what he wants, whenever he cries. It's handy having you tell me, but I don't— It isn't right somehow. It isn't *right*."

Jake waved an arm and squeaked randomly. He looked unhappy. Ted took him and laughed, making an effort to sound confident and persuasive. It would be impossible to raise the kid in a healthy way if Martha began to feel he was a freak. "Why isn't it right? It's normal enough. Look at E. S. P. Everybody has that, according to Rhine."

"E. S. P. is different," she protested feebly, but Jake chortled and Ted knew he had her. He grinned, bouncing Jake up and down in his arms.

"Sure it's different," he said cheerfully. "E. S. P. is queer. E. S. P. comes in those weird accidental little flashes that contradict time and space. With clairvoyance you can see through walls, and read pages from a closed book in France. E. S. P., when it comes, is so ghastly precise it seems like tips from old Omniscience himself. It's enough to drive a logical man insane, trying to explain it. It's illogical, incredible, and random. But what Jake has is just limited telepathy. It is starting out fuzzy and muddled and developing toward accuracy by plenty of trial and error, like sight, or any other normal sense. You don't mind communicating by English, so why mind communicating by telepathy?"

She smiled wanly. "But he doesn't weigh much, Ted. He's not growing as fast as it says he should in the baby book."

"That's all right. I didn't really start growing myself until I was about two. My parents thought I was sickly."

"And look at you now." She smiled genuinely. "All right, you win. But when does he start talking English? I'd like to understand him, too. After all I'm his mother."

"Maybe this year, maybe next year," Ted said teasingly. "I didn't start talking until I was three."

"You mean that you don't want him to learn," she told him indignantly, and then smiled coaxingly at Jake. "You'll learn English soon for Mummy, won't you, Lovekins?"

Ted laughed annoyingly. "Try coaxing him next month or the month after. Right now he's not listening to all these thoughts, he's just collecting associations and reflexes. His cortex might organize impressions on a logic pattern he picked up from me, but it doesn't know what it is doing any more than this fist knows that it is in his mouth. That right, Bud?" There was no demanding thought behind the question, but instead, very delicately, Ted introspected to the small world of impression and sensation that flickered in what seemed a dreaming corner of his own mind. Right then it was a fragmentary world of green and brown that murmured with wind.

"He's out eating grass with the rabbit," Ted told her.

Not answering, Martha started putting out plates. "I like animal stories for children," she said determinedly. "Rabbits are nicer than people."

Putting Jake in his pen, Ted began to help. He kissed the back of her neck in passing. "Some people are nicer than rabbits."

Wind rustled tall grass and tangled vines where the rabbit snuffled and nibbled among the sun-dried herbs, moving on habit, ignoring the abstract meaningless contact of minds, with no thought but deep content.

Then for a while Jake's stomach became aware that lunch was coming, and the vivid business of crying and being fed drowned the gentler distant neural flow of the rabbit.

Ted ate with enjoyment, toying with an idea fantastic enough to keep him grinning, as Martha anxiously spooned food into Jake's mouth. She caught him grinning and indignantly began justifying herself. "But he only gained four pounds, Ted. I have to make sure he eats something."

"Only!" He grinned. "At that rate he'd be thirty feet high by the time he reaches college."

"So would any baby." But she smiled at the idea, and gave Jake his next spoonful still smiling. Ted did not tell his real thought, that if Jake's abilities kept growing in a straight-line growth curve, by the time he was old enough to vote he would be God, but he laughed again, and was rewarded by an answering smile from both of them.

The idea was impossible, of course. Ted knew enough biology to know that there could be no sudden smooth jumps in evolution. Smooth changes had to be worked out gradually through generations of trial and selection. Sudden changes were not smooth, they crippled and destroyed. Mutants were usually monstrosities.

Jake was no sickly freak, so it was certain that he would not turn out very different from his parents. He could be only a little better. But the contrary idea had tickled Ted and he laughed again. "Boom food," he told Martha. "Remember those straight-line growth curves in the story?"

Martha remembered, smiling. "Redfern's dream—sweet little man, dreaming about a growth curve that went straight up." She chuckled, and fed Jake more spoonfuls of strained spinach, saying, "Open wide. Eat your boom food, darling. Don't you want to grow up like King Kong?"

Ted watched vaguely, toying now with a feeling that these months of his life had happened before, somewhere. He had felt it before, but now it came back with a sense of expectancy, as if something were going to happen.

It was while drying the dishes that Ted began to feel sick. Somewhere in the far distance at the back of his mind a tiny phantom of terror cried and danced and gibbered. He glimpsed it close in a flash that entered and was cut off abruptly in a vanishing fragment of delirium. It had something to do with a tangle of brambles in a field, and it was urgent.

Jake grimaced, his face wrinkled as if ready either to smile or cry. Carefully Ted hung up the dish towel and went out the back door, picking up a billet of wood as he passed the woodpile. He could hear Jake whimpering, beginning to wail.

"Where to?" Martha asked, coming out the back door.

"Dunno," Ted answered. "Gotta go rescue Jake's rabbit. It's in trouble."

Feeling numb he went across the fields, through an outgrowth of small trees, climbed a fence into a field of deep grass and thorny tangles of raspberry vines, and started across.

A few hundred feet into the field there was a hunter sitting on an outcrop of rock, smoking, with a successful bag of two rabbits dangling near him. He turned an inquiring face to Ted.

"Sorry," Ted told him rapidly, "but that rabbit is not dead yet. It can't understand being upside down with its legs tied." Moving with shaky urgency he took his penknife and cut the small animal's pulsing throat, then threw the wet knife out of his hand into the grass. The rabbit kicked once more, staring still at the tangled vines of refuge, then its nearsighted baby eyes lost their glazed bright stare and became meaningless.

"Sorry," the hunter said. He was a quiet-looking man with a sagging, middle-aged face.

"That's all right," Ted replied, "but be a little more careful next time, will you? You're out of season anyhow." He looked up from the grass to smile stiffly at the hunter. It was difficult. There was a crowded feeling in his head, like a coming headache, or a stuffy cold. It was difficult to breathe, difficult to think.

It occurred to Ted then to wonder why Jake had never put him in touch with an adult. After a frozen stoppage of thought he laboriously started the wheels again and realized that something had put them in touch with the mind of the hunter, and that was what was wrong. His stomach began to rise. In another minute he would retch.

Ted stepped forward and swung the billet of wood in a clumsy sidewise sweep. The hunter's rifle went off and missed as the middle-aged man tumbled face first into the grass.

Wind rustled the long grass and stirred the leafless branches of trees. Ted could hear and think again, standing still and breathing in deep, shuddering breaths of air to clean his lungs. Briefly he planned what to do. He would call the sheriff and say that a hunter hunting out of season had shot at him and he had been forced to knock the man out. The sheriff would take the man away, out of thought range.

Before he started back to telephone, he looked again at the peaceful, simple scene of field and trees and sky. A memory of horror came into clarity. The hunter had been psychotic.

Thinking back, Ted recognized parts of it, like faces glimpsed in writhing smoke. The evil symbols of psychiatry, the bloody poetry of the Golden Bough, that had been the law of mankind in the five hundred thousand lost years before history. Torture and sacrifice, lust and death, a mechanism in perfect balance, a short circuit of conditioning through a glowing channel of symbols, an irreversible and perfect integration of traumas. It is easy to go mad, but it is not easy to go sane.

"Shut up!" Ted had been screaming inside his mind as he struck. "Shut up."

It had stopped. It had shut up. The symbols were fading without having found root in his mind. The sheriff would take the man away out of thought reach, and there would be no danger. It had stopped.

The burned hand avoids the fire. Something else had stopped. Ted's mind was queerly silent, queerly calm and empty, as he walked home across the winter fields, wondering how it had happened at all, kicking himself with humor for a suggestible fool, not yet missing—Jake.

And Jake lay awake in his pen, waving his rattle in random motions, and crowing "glaglagla gla—" in a motor sensory cycle.

He would be a normal baby, as Ted had been, and as Ted's father before him.

And as all mankind was "normal."

Lewis Padgett

MARGIN FOR ERROR

FERGUSON had had this feeling before, though never so strongly. Until now the faint qualms he sometimes felt had fluttered through his mind and vanished too quickly to be recognizable. That was because he had never before talked with a Benjamin Lawson.

This time the qualms hovered, lingered—took focus and forced themselves up through the layers of the mind to his awareness. He had to free them and give them a name.

A name? But there was no name for qualms like these.

Is there some proverb that points out the tendency of social crises to create a man who can deal with them? Ferguson groped briefly for a literary peg to hang his baffling suspicions on. Failing for the moment, he crushed down the uneasiness and looked dubiously at Benjamin Lawson's face. The qualms sank docilely enough. They had been recognized. They could wait, now.

All Ferguson brought back with him from that brief excursion into

Henry Kuttner, one of the most popular of all science fiction writers, has never appeared in a Crown-Conklin anthology. However, he probably does not mind, since Lewis Padgett, one of his pseudonymous alter-egos, has been in all three: *The Best, The Treasury,* and the *Big Book.*

the realms of the submerged mind was the knowledge that there was about Lawson something not to be trusted, and a suddenly much strengthened respect for his own hunches. Reason played no part in it. Ferguson *knew*—in effect—but he did not quite know that he knew.

For many years, he realized, he had been anticipating this. He had expected the coming of . . . of—

Of Benjamin Lawson.

He remembered how it had started.

In an office of ILC, a televisor screen buzzed a peremptory signal and turned bright red. Mr. Greg Ferguson, whose qualifications for vice president were unusual, turned on the descrambler automatically and winked at his guest. Before A.C.—Atomic Control—Ferguson would certainly have been a criminal, but in ILC he was an integrated, useful member of society. The fact that there were four hundred and ninety-nine other vice presidents never troubled him.

ILC stood for the Federal Bureau of Insurance, Lotteries, and Crèches.

"Mr. Ferguson marked as free," a voice said. "Request attention to apparent swindle attempt."

"Little the poor fool knows," Ferguson remarked. "Cagliostro himself couldn't swindle ILC. But they certainly try." He watched the screen fade to a blue-and-yellow design, a symbol of a playback.

Mr. Daniel Archer beamed. By profession he was a Fixer, which was a combination of attorney, publicity agent, sociologist, and secretary. He worked for a politician named Hiram Reeve, which was why he had called on Ferguson and listened for half an hour to the vice president's low-key boasting about how ILC worked.

"Wagner—" the televisor said.

"Tell that robot he needs a vacation," Ferguson ordered. "Not Wagner. Ben Lawson. That right, Mr. Archer?"

Archer nodded. "He's the one. Of course there may be nothing in it, but we never take chances. At least I don't."

Ferguson pondered while the visor screen turned pink with embarrassment, flashed rapidly through a selective color-wheel, and hunted for Ben Lawson's playback. This wasn't the first time a Fixer had asked Ferguson's advice. Fixers by definition were thorough investigators. They had to be, in order to keep their patrons in power. And there was less pork-barrel rolling than one might have expected, since good Fixers were always in demand, and they had the right to switch allegiance whenever they decided that their patrons' tactics conflicted with sound sociology. Archer was a fat, sardonic little man, but he had clever eyes.

"Wagner," Ferguson said, while they waited. "That was a simple case, open and shut. I used straight Operation Suicide on him. He had it all figured out. Except that he wasn't sure he could take out the policy—"

"Don't they all wonder that, when they're working an angle?"

Ferguson decided that Archer was playing dumb. Well, let him. Ferguson himself was always happy to explain the workings of ILC and his own job. The fact that he was also justifying himself had never occurred to him.

"Yes. And Wagner was surprised when we O.K.'d his application. Double idemnity covering suicide in any shape or form. I gather he's been trying to cut his throat ever since. Incidentally, he wants to take out an accident and liability policy now; seems he's got worried about accidental death since he isn't covered for it."

"Will he get the policy?"

"Why not? I told you the average percentages. We can't lose on accident, Mr. Archer. We can't lose. Here's Lawson's playback; let's catch it."

A gleam came into Archer's mild eyes. He leaned forward to watch the screen. It showed an office in an ILC bureau in a distant city. A clerk—an ordinary front man—was rising from his chair as the client entered. Ferguson touched a stud in the auxiliary screen and watched it with half his vision while pertinent data, recorded and correlated by robot machines, flashed into view.

Brain radiations normal . . . no important glandular stimulus . . . adrenals normal . . . body temperature constant at 98.8 correct for client after mild exercise . . .

"Confident," Ferguson said. "He's got something all worked out. The perfect crime—he thinks. He's the one?"

Archer nodded. They studied the client. He was a perfectly ordinary young man, who might have been stamped out with a matrix labeled *Specimen of Younger Generation, Male, Sound in Wind and Limb.* He was simply a big, blond youngster, with blue eyes, a pleasant smile, and, presumably, not a worry in the world.

Through the screen the clerk said, "Mr. Lawson?"

"That's right. Ben Lawson."

"Please sit down. How can I help you? Not a crèche registration, I suppose—unless you're married?"

Lawson smiled. "Me married? Not for quite a while yet. I'll let you know in plenty of time before the kids come along."

The clerk laughed dutifully. "Then it's insurance or lottery. We've got the Pimlico, the Queensland Royal Blue, the Irish—"

"I don't gamble," Lawson said. "It's insurance. Can I take out insurance to cover these possibilities?" He pushed a slip of paper across the desk.

The clerk said, "We insure everything that isn't antisocial, sir. We insure against fire, failure, fraud, felony, fright, fits, flaying, fleabites—" It was a familiar gag at ILC. But now the clerk had glimpsed the list. He slowed down and stopped. He frowned, gave Lawson a quick glance, and said, "You say you don't gamble?"

"Well, I suppose you could call insurance a gamble, couldn't you? What's the matter? Have I put down anything antisocial on my list?"

The clerk hesitated. "We've got our own arbitrary rules about antisociability, sir. Homicide is, of course, but we insure against homicide. And against most crimes, except when the client's too poor a risk. You understand, there has to be a complete examination—"

"I'm healthy, I think."

"Not only you, sir. There has to be a survey into your background, your environment, your associates—"

"Complicated, huh?" Lawson asked.

The clerk swallowed and looked at the list again. "Kicking a policeman," he said, rather faintly. "That . . . ah . . . seems to be the mildest item you want to be insured against."

"Would that be antisocial, by your rules?"

"I can't answer that offhand. However, all these . . . items . . . seem rather unlikely, don't they? I should think you would be better advised to select other policies. We would be happy to make up a selection for you after our personal survey has been completed, something perhaps more suitable—"

"Oh, suit yourself," Lawson said. "Those are the policies I want, though. If I can't get them, I'll have to think of something else. I made quite a list, in case some of the items weren't acceptable to ILC. But I haven't exhausted the possibilities."

"Putting phenylthiourea in the city reservoir," the clerk murmured. "You want to be insured against . . . ah . . . putting phenylthiourea in the city reservoir?"

"That's right," Lawson said cheerfully.

"Oh. Is this a toxic substance?"

"Nope."

"Do you have any intention of putting phenylthiourea in the city reservoir?"

"That's what I want to be insured against," Lawson said, looking wide-eyed and innocent.

"I see," the clerk said, coming to some conclusion. "Would you mind answering our routine questionnaire now? An appointment will be made as soon as we've completed our survey."

"I suppose the premiums would be low enough for me to handle?"

"They'd vary."

"I haven't got much money," Lawson said. "Still I guess something could be worked out." He smiled slowly. "O.K., the questionnaire?"

"You can use this visor," the clerk said, making an adjustment. "If you'll signal when you're finished . . . here's the button—"

The clerk went out. The visor began taking qualitative and quantative pictures of Lawson, stereoscopic and fluoroscopic. It said briskly, with the inflexibly arrogant tone of a robot-mechanism, "Full name, please, last name first."

"Lawson, Benjamin."

"Age?"

"Twenty-one."

"Date of birth?"

"April ninth, Twenty—"

Back at local headquarters Ferguson pressed a few buttons, studied a blowup from the "Encyclopaedia Britannica" that flipped on the screen, and nodded at Archer.

Archer said, "What's—"

"It's a chemical compound, it says here, made up of carbon, hydrogen, nitrogen and sulphur. Seven out of ten people find it bitter as the devil. The other three find it tasteless. It's a matter of gene inheritance, dominant or recessive."

"Toxic?"

"Anything is, in large enough quantities, including H_2O. People get drowned, don't they? But why put phen . . . phenylthiourea in the city reservoir? Why not arsenic, if he's homicidal?"

"Is he?"

"We don't know yet. We're getting the survey made now. Very odd. Slightly ridiculous. When people try to outsmart ILC, they usually work it out with careful logic, doing their best to cover up what they really intend. This guy Lawson is practically telling us what he's intending. Don't ask me if we'll accept him as a client; it all depends on the survey."

"Kicking a policeman," Archer said dreamily, his face placid and his eyes shrewd. "What else did he have on his list?"

"Here it is on the visor. Peculiar. He not only wants financial coverage, but he wants our scot-free clause. He doesn't want to suffer any legal consequences."

"You arrange that, don't you? You're a Federal Bureau. If he kicks a policeman—"

"If we issue the policy," Ferguson said grimly, "he's certainly not going to be able to kick a policeman. I'll see to that. Maybe this boy thinks he can outsmart ILC, but he's not going to outsmart me."

"A personal matter?" Archer said, looking at Ferguson intently.

"Sure, that's why I'm a socially integrated individual. I can channel my impulses into constructive canals, instead of destructive ones. I'm rather proud of my resourcefulness, Mr. Archer, and proud of ILC. I'm using my mind to its full capacity here—and where else could I do that? Except perhaps as a Fixer."

"Thank you," Archer said politely. "If you can put my mind at rest about Ben Lawson, I'll be grateful. So far it's what they used to call a maggot—a whim. But I've never yet met an altruist who wasn't getting something out of his altruism himself. Lawson—"

But Ferguson was brooding over Lawson as an enemy of ILC. "Phenylthiourea, eh?" he said. "I'll fix his wagon."

The foundations for the Bureau were necessarily laid in Chicago, Alamogordo, and Hiroshima. It was built on the instability of an atom. The Atomic War occurred at the right time and at the wrong time. If the global warhead had exploded in the mid-forties, the result would have been catastrophe, devastation, and red ruin. It didn't. If it had exploded after atomic energy had been perfected and production methods sufficiently improved and speeded up, the result would have been, in all likelihood, a fine opportunity for future civilizations to develop on the outlying planets, with the Earth as a secondary Sun. The difference was, very roughly, the difference between a pistol with one cartridge in the chamber and a pistol with a full clip. But when the level of world thought had returned to customary post-war standards—meaning a cheerfully optimistic concept that the next dip on the roller coaster either didn't exist or wouldn't come in our time—then presently saturation point was reached. International politics and national economics were going down while atomic science went up. Luckily the bottom was reached before the top. There was an Atomic War, neither as mildly cataclysmic as it might have been in 1946 nor as finally thorough as it would have been decades later. It merely depopulated most of the planet.

But that, of course, was inevitable.

It was also inevitable for the race to rebuild. One advantage of the utter breakdown was the factor that specialization became difficult and union important. Biologists, psychologists, physicists, and sociologists were forced to work together, by virtue of pure necessity. Physically they decentralized, but mentally they became federalists in thought and action. Miraculously a sufficiently stable world government was worked out. At first it was concentrated in a small area north of Mauch Chunk, Pennsylvania, but it spread. Knowledge of technology still existed, which helped a great deal. But there was the immense problem of rebuilding.

One answer lay in eliminating the difficulty of children. Infanticide would have solved the immediate problem but scarcely the racial one. Having children was encouraged, because of the increase in sterility and freak mutants and the decrease in normal births. Still, it became necessary to solve the vital difficulty of general immaturity.

In a word, not many people continued to mature after they had children. At least one parent began to slow down, never achieving full mental maturity.

Unlike the gorilla—

For some reason Ferguson felt nervous and expounded at length to Archer, who listened with every appearance of great interest. Perhaps this was because Ferguson himself had now entered into the Fixer's calculations. At any rate, Archer listened.

"Man is immature," Ferguson said. "Any naturalist or biologist can prove that. Or any sociologist, for that matter." He conveniently forgot that his guest owned a degree in sociology. "Our cranial sutures aren't knit, our habit-patterns aren't adult, the physical proportions of our bodies—well, we're built physically like the immature gorilla. And we act that way, too. We're a social race. We like physical contact, compet-

itive games, horseplay—generally speaking. I'll admit that immaturity
is what gives us our drive; we're insecure, so we experiment. The mature gorilla doesn't need to. He's perfectly adjusted to his environment
—he's got his feeding-ground and his harem, and about his only real
danger is from young bulls who want his harem. He's bad-tempered
and perfectly self-sufficient. Lord knows we're not, or we wouldn't
throw so many parties!"

"ILC is trying to mature the race," Archer said, half-questioningly.

"Children are a handicap in our culture," Ferguson said. "The male
gorilla drives his kids away when they begin growing. And they can
fend for themselves; they're equipped to do that, in the jungle. But
civilization has made a deadlier jungle. One that only a nominal adult
can cope with. No provision was made for the young of the species;
that was left as an individual problem. The result was a culture in
which the male was dominant and women enslaved. Oh, very roughly—
but rearing children in pre-atomic cities was a full-time job. Wastage!"

Archer moistened his lips.

"Have a drink," Ferguson suggested. "Want to dial me a Scotch and
soda, while you're at it?" He waited, watching the great curved sweep
of the window. He gestured, and at the signal the soft rhythm of
color-patterns gathered like a folding curtain and ran down like water
and was gone, revealing the view beyond. The city was small in population but large in area, and there were a great many parks.

This is the way it should be, Ferguson thought. *This is safe.*

So you had a convalescent world—a basically healthy organism but
susceptible to a good many figurative diseases. People with a suscepti-
bility to cancer should avoid continual irritation of tissue. Cancer is
uncontrolled pathological cell-growth. Controlled cell-growth is normal
and beneficial. Similarly—atomics.

Avoid irritation.

People, in fact, lived pretty much as they wanted to under ILC. They
couldn't have everything, naturally. Neuroses couldn't be eliminated
overnight. But the Atomic War was the equivalent of electric shock
therapy. *En masse,* ILC used a palliative plan. Individually—ILC
insured.

Not everything. There are no Utopias. Even supermen would have
superproblems. There was an iron hand, but the velvet glove was the
textile people loved to touch. The atomic cancer was arrested by drastic
surgery; yet it had filtered through the bloodstream. So in lieu of a real
answer, ILC avoided irritation. ILC kept the world-patient from catching other ailments that might cause irritation. Anything could build to
a sociological infection which could in turn make the cancer break out
again. As long as the race was healthy, it was medium safe.

That applied to Greg Ferguson, too.

ILC made certain of that. No irritations would arise for him—the
formula said—that couldn't be adjusted. Ferguson was a crooked peg
in a crooked hole. Conceivably he was less mature—or, rather, more

immature—than most; conceivably he needed the safety-factor, the stability, the certain security which the symbol of ILC represented to him.

In fact, he did need that. Badly.

You can't rebuild the world in a day. There was plenty of technological knowledge, but not many people. That meant an all-out effort. So ILC cut down the factors that retarded maturation. The group had to be large to support research workers not immediately productive, and if one-half of every couple had to rear a batch of children, the potential manpower was halved. So the children were placed in crèches. The young gorilla can survive in a jungle—young children were given the equivalent of a safe jungle. A crèche—and the parents didn't have the responsibility, and could continue their maturing process.

The Federal Bureau of Insurance, Lotteries and Crèches made that possible. It was impossible to finance the crèches by taxation; the government wanted to avoid irritation, not augment it. And the Lotteries helped a great deal, but Insurance was the real answer. It was the place where steam was blown off. It was the answer man. It was where budding neuroses were caught. People take out insurance, by and large, because of neuroses, and in the old days they had good reason. Under ILC practically anything was insurable. A man wants insurance against something he's afraid will happen, or something he wants to happen. Often it is a socially or personally pathological matter.

The adult gorilla, however, needs no insurance.

"Here's a case—potential psychosis of a client."

Ferguson shifted a visor screen down. A man's face appeared. He looked normal.

Archer raised his eyebrows.

"He wants insurance against infectious disease," Ferguson explained. "The premium's rather high on that, obviously. We still haven't licked all the mutated bugs, though the race built up strong resistance after the biological battles. But look at his survey and see what you get."

Information fled madly across the screen while Archer waited.

"Well?"

"I don't see anything special," the Fixer said.

"No? You don't see why the guy may presently want suicide insurance?"

"Mm-m. Suicide. Why? He's well integrated. Useful, happy—"

"Any unusual purchases? Try the chemist's list."

"Oh. Green soap. Germicides. A UV portal—"

"Two of 'em, one for his office, one for his home. The guy is working straight toward a lovely case of misophobia. That should mean fear of mice but it means fear of dirt. The rest is routine, for the psych crew. I gather the initial irritant occurred when he was home on a visit from his crèche, as a kid. Spilled some gunk on his sister and hurt her. His parents made the wrong kind of a fuss. He's got a guilt complex. Eventually he may hear voices from the woodwork telling him he's sinned. You see?"

"Ah," Archer said, "does he get his policy—this potential misophobe?"

"Of course. Why not? When he gets his final exam is where the gimmick comes in."

"The hypnosis . . . oh, yes. I'd like to know more about that."

"Well," Ferguson said, "it's the reason why this particular client will be a good risk instead of a poor one. We'll cure him and channel his neuroses at the same time. Barring genuine accident—the percentages will be in our favor. They wouldn't be otherwise, because of the guy's submerged death-wish. Eventually he'd purposely expose himself to some contagious disease, without knowing anything about it consciously. He wants to be punished. Misophobia, ha."

"Report on Benjamin Lawson," the televisor announced.

"Good," Ferguson said. "Shoot it across."

Lawson was twenty-one years and one week old. He was absolutely normal. Even his minor deviations during his training period were merely normal. Had they been absent, that would have been supicious and worth investigation. All children put frogs in their teachers' desks, provided the frogs are available. Rodents, insects, or reptiles will do at a pinch.

On his twenty-first birthday Lawson had had the choice of several jobs for which he was prepared. His field seemed to be general integration; he had studied everything omnivorously but rather casually. However, he had taken advantage of the month-long vacation period optional to all graduates, and stayed home most of the time, visiting his parents, who were mildly pleased to have him. He read a great many newstapes, and he interviewed a government councilor named Hiram Reeve, suggesting that Reeve introduce an immaturity pension bill at the next session. That accounted for Archer's presence; Archer was Hiram Reeve's Fixer.

"Detail," said the televisor. "Lawson proposed the inverse of an old-age pension. All children would become eligible at birth and continue to draw the pension until reaching biological maturity. Councilor Reeve agreed to present such a bill—"

"But he won't," Ferguson said to himself. "Campaign promises, eh?"

"Within the last two years Lawson has studied these subjects: biology, mutation, biological time and entropic time, endocrinology, psychology, pathology, sociology, and the philosophy of humor. His studies were intensive rather than casual. There seems to—"

"Skip to his home life, for the last few days," Ferguson requested. "What's he reading there?" He leaned toward the screen, but the instant closeup view made his motion unnecessary. Sprawled languidly in a relaxer, the cheerful Mr. Lawson was immersed in Joe Miller's Joke Book.

Some days later, Lawson called at ILC by appointment and this time he saw Greg Ferguson, who had flown in an hour earlier to superintend the final exams. Certain preparations were necessary. In the old days a company might not issue fire insurance on a tenement until the owner put up fire escapes, so ILC stipulated that psychic fire escapes must be built on every client. Moreover, ILC built them.

"You understand, Mr. Lawson," Ferguson said, "the policies become invalidated if at any time you should refuse to return for additional examinations, should we decide they're necessary."

"Oh, sure. That's all right. But do I get my insurance?"

"You want a separate policy to cover each contingency?"

"Yes. If I can afford the premiums on them all."

"You've got twenty-five policies here," Ferguson said. "They cover quite a range. The premiums would vary, naturally. It would be a poor risk for us to insure you against turning your ankle—we'd rather insure you against being rained on, since we can control the weather these days. You've got quite an extreme range here, everything from orange crop failure in Florida to snakebite. Crops don't fail, incidentally."

"Well, not through climatic conditions," Lawson said, "but weren't there some mutated boll weevils that ruined the cotton in South Carolina a few years ago?"

Ferguson nodded. "You're betting on the chance of a similar mutation hitting Florida oranges, then?"

"I guess I'm betting against chance, in a way. Some of these policies are pretty sure to pay off."

"Do you think so?" Ferguson asked. "Remember, you'll have some heavy premiums to pay—and betting against chance is a dangerous business."

"May I—?" Lawson examined the figures Ferguson handed him. He whistled. "That fifth one's plenty expensive. Why's that?"

"Insurance against your purposely giving somebody hay fever? Difficulty of proof, for one thing, but mainly there are too many virus mutations these days. The allergies are tricky. We'll insure you on that score, of course, but it'll cost you money. Why do you want to give somebody hay fever?"

"I want to be insured *against* doing that, Mr. Ferguson," Lawson said blandly. "But I don't think I can afford that one. Still, the other items—" He computed rapidly in his head. "I suppose I could scrape up first premiums."

Ferguson watched the young man. By now he knew Ben Lawson, inside and out. He knew his heredity and his habit patterns. He knew how and why the client worked. And there was absolutely nothing suspicious about Lawson, except Archer's hunch.

And that wasn't actionable.

So he merely said, "Mr. Lawson, I'm bound to give you a warning. If you can pay only the first premiums, you're going to lose your money and your insurance—unless you take a job and make some more dough."

"Nobody *has* to take a job."

"People get hungry if they don't. Even if they apply for the dole, they work it out in man-hours of labor."

"Oh?" Lawson said.

"The insurance we issue is sound. We underwrite, and we pay, when required. But I want to warn you that our losses are due almost entirely to the laws of uncontrollable chance. When the personal factor enters into the question—we don't lose. In your case the personal factor applies completely. There's no way in which you could accidentally put phenylthiourea in the city reservoir."

"No way at all?"

"The chances are astronomical. You haven't found a way to upset the laws of chance, have you?"

"Wouldn't you know it by now if I had? You check pretty thoroughly."

Ferguson nodded. "That's correct. If you get at the reservoir, it'll be due to your own personal impulse. You know that's impossible, or it will be."

"Impossible?"

"Nearly so. The hypnosis treatment is more effective than most people realize. We're going to condition you so you *can't* do any of the things you're insuring against."

"Well, that's fine," Lawson said. "I certainly wouldn't want to put phenylthiourea in the city reservoir, would I?"

Watching the young man, Ferguson had an inexplicable moment of *déjà vu;* and he stayed motionless and silent, because he didn't like such things, and let free association—by which is meant selective association —flow through his mind. Presently he had it, though he had to go back to the days of his gauche adolescence. It was very much like the times when he was in an Upper Crèche, immature, facing an adult who made him feel awkward and ignorant—an adult who knew so many more of the rules than he did.

He studied Lawson. There was nothing overt to account for this— except the equivalent of the curious behavior of the dog in the nighttime. Lawson wasn't apparently up to anything. Lawson seemed to feel perfectly at ease. And even though the hypnotic treatment was guaranteed, including the inevitable margin for error, Ferguson felt a slight qualm near his liver. His solar plexus. The great nerves gather there, working in harmony with the brain-mechanism that was government *per se*—and so Ferguson sensed a threat, and that hinted at an opening abyss at his feet.

ILC was the cornerstone. The alternative was the only real personal devil that had ever been created—the threat of uncontrolled atomics. But then sanity and logic, which have betrayed so many people in the past, came back, and he knew that one man couldn't upset the applecart. Especially this wide-eyed youth.

Cocky fledgling. He'd just broken the shell of his crèche egg. Naturally he felt competent to cope with anything. He'd always coped with whatever had existed within his eggshell. But that shell had been a barrier, keeping the wrong things out.

"There is one point," Ferguson said. "Your dreams."

"What about them?"

"Our experts have queried that angle. Especially the hypnogogic visions. But up to three years ago your recorded dreams followed a regular pattern, with variations. Since then—"

"They don't?"

"Oh, they do. They follow a pattern. But *without* variations."

"That just means I'm a type, doesn't it? A real norm?"

Ferguson scowled. "The norm's an arbitrary figure. Are you trying to kid me?"

"I'm sorry. I underestimated you. I know the theoretical norm would be pretty much of a monster. It's a handy semantic term. Even if norms exist, they can't stay that way under environmental pressures."

"So. Either you've been lying about your dreams for the last few years, or you haven't."

"Nobody's complained."

"People look for different things. In the crèches they look for one thing. Here we look for another."

"If I'm a bad risk, you can turn me down."

"Oh, no," Ferguson said flatly. "We seldom turn down a client. We allow margins; we pay off when necessary. We insure. If we could control the uncertainty factor, we could just charge a flat sum to work miracles. As it is, in the majority of cases we don't have to pay off. Because we have our hypnotic treatment as extra insurance—our own. But when we do pay, we want to know why. We've got a close schedule of statistics, and they have to check. Apparently you're not antisocial. You've no latent criminal tendencies that we can discover. You're a normal man for your age." Ferguson stopped, a curious qualm going through him at his own words. He realized that he didn't believe what he had just said. He *knew*, with a flat, impossible conviction, that Lawson was not—*normal*.

There was no evidence. Not even the item that had brought Archer in on the case. Suppose, Ferguson thought, he should ask Lawson, "Why did you request Councilor Reeve to back an immaturity pension?" He would get an answer, but not a satisfactory one. For Lawson would not have profited by such a pension. He was legally, mentally, and physically mature. So his plea to the councilor had been, apparently, simple altruism, and far from logical, since the young of the species already had the equivalent of an immaturity pension under the present system.

Ferguson listened with detachment to the new note of annoyance in his own voice.

"Sometimes people think they can swindle ILC," he said. "They never succeed."

It was a key word he had thrown. Ferguson waited. The young man grinned.

"It seems to me," he said, "that you take yourselves awfully seriously, if you don't mind my saying so. If I'd plotted out a solemn method to fake an accident or something, you wouldn't have bothered. As long as life is real and earnest, you don't object, but one touch of humor and you think I'm going to reach CM and explode in your face."

Ferguson tightened his mouth. After a moment he said, "We'll take a chance. What policies do you want?"

"Well—I think we'll forget about these three. The premiums are too high. I'll take the rest—twenty-two policies, I make it. All right?"

"You can afford to pay two premiums on each, then—exclusive of the three you've thrown out. Why not choose fewer, so you can be sure they won't lapse before you get a job?"

Lawson said, "Well, if I picked two or three and they paid off, I couldn't get the others afterward at the same rate, could I?"

"Obviously not. We'd have to allow—"

"I'll take them all, then, except the three I can't afford."

"Thank you," Ferguson said, but he didn't mean it.

"It's perfectly obvious what he intends to do," Ferguson said. "He'll try to get us to pay off on one policy so he can continue to pay all the other premiums. And whenever his bank account runs low, he'll cash in on another policy. Kick a policeman or something. What a low idea of humor."

Archer took a long time to answer. He closed his eyes, apparently considered the whole problem, opened them again, and inquired, "Do you staff officers in ILC have psychiatric checkups?"

"Now I'm crazy. Is that it?"

"It's easier to believe that than to think one man could upset your whole organization so easily. Why jump to the unlikeliest conclusion before you've checked on the likelier ones? I know ILC has paid off on insurance before, but always in line with the law of averages."

They were in Ferguson's office overseeing Lawson's hypnosis, which, according to the visor, was progressing according to schedule. So far there had been no hitch. Lawson was a fair hypnotic subject, even without the drug. He had gone into test catalepsy, and reacted in a normal manner. He had gone through the usual routine of firing a blank cartridge at a psychiatrist, which might have meant that (a) he was homicidal, or (b) he unconsciously realized the gun was loaded with blanks, or (c) he abhorred psychiatrists. Rechecks indicated that the second was true. He had also been instructed to swipe a dollar from an attendant's pocket, and that meant nothing either. Barter is the basic; currency is necessarily a symbol, and what a dollar meant to Lawson was difficult to discover.

Psychiatry is as exact and inexact a science as mathematics. Once you realize that it's possible to create a whole new system of mathematics at need, you realize that ordinary math is accurate only when the rules are followed. But if you use the rules of one system to solve the problems of another system, there may arise some difficulty. The psychiatrists working on Lawson were not bollixed, but Ferguson thought they might not know it if they were.

And yet he had nothing to work on except a hunch.

Hunches are exact sciences, though, once you get away from fairy tale concepts. So-called prescient dreams can be accurate. A wish-fulfillment dream may certainly be prescient; it's at least a half and half gamble. Ferguson's hunch came from his unconscious, which had the hopes and fears of all his years. He had achieved security against tremendous odds, for in the twentieth century he would have been a miserably unhappy specimen. To him ILC symbolized security, which he vitally needed. A threat to ILC was, very definitely, a threat to himself. And, like most other men, he had the buried nightmare psychosis of the ultimate chain reaction.

ILC did mean status quo, in a way. The people in charge allowed for stress and strain and flux, of course; environment makes a vast amount of difference in precision measurements—of metal, for example. If you kept the human race in a vacuum under glass, status quo would be practicable. As it was—

"He makes me nervous," Ferguson said inadequately. "A hunch is no evidence, but—"

"What's the matter? Think he's a superman?" Archer asked ironically.

Ferguson considered his nails. "You're not serious."

"Well—it's unlikely."

"I've done a lot of research from time to time on just that subject," Ferguson said. "Sometimes I've wondered . . . Why the devil are *you* checking up on Lawson if you're so sure he's harmless?"

"I don't take chances. A good Fixer is like an aneroid barometer. Sensitive. I've got certain specialized training and skills. When there's the equivalent of a variation in atmospheric pressure, I notice it, and I like to find out what the cause was. I've been on a lot of wild-goose chases, but—I don't take chances."

"It's no coincidence that we're working on the same problem," Ferguson said. "You noticed the result and I guess I noticed the cause. We've each got a directional fix on Lawson—he's the cross-bearing. Like a storm brewing in the Antarctic. It's as though you noticed a falling barometer in Wisconsin while I noticed a thermal at the South Pole. Well— Lawson makes me feel funny. And Lawson asked your patron to back a bill, which is where you came in. Hiram Reeve must have had a lot of screwball bills proposed to him before this."

"But never altruistically."

"What—never?"

"I meant never. Sometimes you have to dig deep to find the payoff, but it's always there. There's compensation involved, always, psychologically anyway. You'll find that disinterested reformers aren't as disinterested as they appear—if you check up on their personal warps. People who want to save the world, Mr. Ferguson, generally have a plush-seated throne picked out for themselves in the brave new one. But Lawson's proposition was apparently altruistic, and I want to make sure he had a selfish motive for proposing his immaturity pension idea. Then I can relax."

"It's just a job to you, then?"

"I like to do my job. That's why I'm working for Reeve—he's the most competent politico around. If there were a better one, I'd change allegiance. But right now—apparently I'm looking for normality in Lawson and you're looking for abnormality."

"He's normal," Ferguson said. "Notice that reaction chart."

They examined the televisor. Lawson was being conditioned against kicking a policeman.

"Will it work?" Archer asked.

"Impossible to tell. We depend a great deal on implanting fear of consequences. But we insure against consequences. In lab conditions, Lawson might very well refrain from kicking a policeman, because he unconsciously knows he wouldn't get his policy if he did. But once he's insured—the policy guarantees against consequences. There's always a margin for error."

Across the screen moved a jiggling green line that meant Lawson refrained from kicking the equivalent of a policeman.

Three days later Lawson threw phenylthiourea into the reservoir. He did it within range of one of the watchdog telephoto lenses, set up in a ring around the water supply, and first he held up the labeled bottle so there would be no mistake. Thereafter he laughed hilariously and went away.

"I want protection against a homicidal impulse," Ferguson said to the ILC psychiatrist. "Probably it's got a paranoid base. There's a client out to git me."

"Out to git you, is he?" the psychiatrist said. "What's he been up to?"

Ferguson told him. "There's nothing yet," he ended. "Not even a neurosis, as far as I know. But I worry about the guy. He's taken out twenty-two policies, and—I'm afraid of how I may start to feel later."

"Identification with ILC. I expect we can get rid of that feeling. Sublimate it or something. Remove the cause. Oh, well. One swallow doesn't make a dipsomaniac. We'll put you through the routine, Ferguson."

"I keep thinking of mature gorillas. A nice therapy would be for me to take a hunting trip and shoot male gorillas. I don't know. This could lead to claustrophobia and agoraphobia. Fear of open spaces, I mean, not fear of crowds. Then I'd have to spend my time like those figures in one of those little houses that foretell weather. Keep dashing in and out. What about a nice padded cell with walls that expand and contract?"

"What about a sedative?" the psychiatrist countered. "The trouble with you staff boys, as a matter of fact, is that the minute you get a hangnail you think it's a major psychosis. These minor things generally adjust themselves automatically. We keep complete, up-to-date charts of all the staff, and we know a great deal more about you than you think.

You're all right. Just to keep you happy, we'll go through the routine and make sure you're not a lycanthrope—though you wouldn't be holding down the job you do if you hadn't achieved integration."

"But what about Lawson?" Ferguson inquired plaintively.

That was, of course, already taken care of. Naturally ILC called Lawson in for re-examination. He came willingly enough, apparently suppressing a mild amusement at the whole proceeding. Ferguson had a deep-rooted conviction that the psychiatrists would discover nothing. All his old qualms and fears combined to tell him that whatever Lawson had was beyond the range of ILC's precision instruments to discover. The only real way to detect his variation from the norm would be to correlate the effect he had on other bodies—the way Pluto's existence was suspected before it was actually discovered.

But Lawson's psychological pattern came safely within the extreme range of normality.

He had a high resistance-quotient; so had many other people. Repeated treatments of sodium pentothal failed to break down all his barriers—that wasn't a wholly unfamiliar phenomenon. He lay on the couch, doped with the hypnotic drug, and answered questions in a way that entirely failed to satisfy Ferguson.

"How did you feel when you threw phenylthiourea into the reservoir?" they asked him.

"I felt good," Lawson said.

"Did you remember that we had agreed you couldn't throw phenylthiourea into the reservoir?"

Silence.

They repeated the query.

"No," Lawson said.

"Could you kick a policeman?"

"No."

There wasn't much they could do about it that hadn't already been done. They gave him supplementary hypnotic treatments, reinforcing the conditioning even more thoroughly than before. But he was written down under Margin for Error. He was a rare type, yet he came within the limits of normality. If he had extensions beyond that norm—the psychiatrists couldn't detect them. Ferguson thought he had. Convincing other people was another matter. ILC had quite as much evidence on its side as he had on his—if you could call it evidence. Apparently it wasn't. And the points that really convinced Ferguson himself were intangibles, on which he could produce no evidence at all. Sometimes he himself felt doubt, but in the end he always swung back to the blind, illogical conviction that was part of his mind by now. Hypersensitivity? Was that the answer? He had for many years been interested in the subject of the theoretical superman, and there had been times when, looking askance at someone or other, he had wondered—

But never before had he felt conviction. With a part of his brain that seemed to be as specialized and infallible as radar—a sensitivity apparently only he possessed, he *knew*. He had always, deep within him, expected that some day the theoretical would become the practical. Now he thought that it had happened. But how could he convince anyone who did not already have this same conviction springing from an inner perception to which even he could give no name? He might as well announce the second coming of the Messiah. People would dismiss him as a crank, at best. Public disbelief would in effect invalidate the truth—if it were true. There had never been but one man who could safely have claimed to be Napoleon—and even he, without sufficient evidence, might expect to be certified. Before the time of Galileo, Ferguson told himself, there must have been a number of lunatics who, among their other delusions, were convinced that the Earth went round the Sun.

Margin for Error would not exist if a good many people did not fall into that particular classification. To choose one case arbitrarily looked like simple eccentricity on Ferguson's part. He had no arguments anyone could understand. He was a pre-Galilean convinced of the Earth's orbit. And he had no telescopic apparatus an ordinary human could use.

What could he do about it?

Only what he had already done.

The psychiatrists could help up to a certain point—the limit of visibility on their figurative telescopes. But he dared not tell them all he suspected, for fear of being tagged as a psychotic himself. In effect he had to psychoanalyze himself, a notoriously difficult task—and try to segregate and analyze the nameless, certain sense that told him what Lawson was.

Meanwhile Benjamin Lawson went placidly about his business.

Having latched onto a good deal of money from ILC, as the result of his escapade at the reservoir, he deposited it with an investment broker and rented a small cottage fully equipped by Services. He seemed to want to avoid responsibility. There was an odd air of *playing* to his life. Food, prepared and hot, arrived, a week's supply at a time, and Lawson had only to push a button, make his selection, and eat. Then he pushed another button and the service disappeared for automatic cleansing. Since the house was functional, there were no dust-catchers, and air conditioning and electronic gadgets took care of the inevitable filth that occurs everywhere except in a hard vacuum. There was a playground-resort a few hundred miles away, and Lawson often flew there to ski, play tennis, have a vigorous game of skatch, or swim. He bought thousands of books and book-reels and read omnivorously. He had a chemical laboratory and other laboratories, all purely amateur. He had a great deal of fun making soap, and only the chlorophyl-deodorizer-units saved the bungalow from becoming a stench and an abomination.

He didn't do any work.

A year later he kicked a policeman. His money was running low.

Ferguson was doing pretty well. A hitherto-unrealized psychosis had been uncovered, involving a forgotten infancy-wish for the Moon; and by a remarkable series of associations, involving green cheese, butter, and bread, it had resolved itself into the father-image, which was familiar enough to be handled by even the stupidest psychiatrist. Ferguson called on his father, an ancient and unregenerate oldster who spent most of his time collecting dirty limericks, and was conscious of no particular reaction, except a feeling of mild boredom when his antique sire insisted on repeating every limerick he knew at least three times. He was left with a conviction that his father needed psychoanalysis, and he went back to work mentally cleansed and integrated, he felt.

Then Lawson kicked the policeman.

"But that was over two years ago," Archer said into the televisor. "I remember you were all steamed up about it then. Still, it's been two years! Lawson hasn't collected on any more policies, has he?"

"That's not the point," Ferguson said, a muscle in his cheek twitching. "Everyone but me has forgotten about Lawson—he's down in the files as just another case. I called to see if you'd lost interest, too."

Archer made a noncommittal sound.

Ferguson looked at him across the miles. "I'd be willing to bet," he said, "that you've got Lawson's name on your calendar for a future checkup."

Archer hesitated. "All right," he said. "You win. But it's simply routine; I've checked on him every six months. I do that with a good many people—I told you once I don't take chances. Luckily I've got a competent staff, so I can afford the time. But it's just routine."

"It may be routine with your other cases," Ferguson said, "but don't tell me it's only that with Lawson."

Archer smiled. "I know you've got a phobia about him. Is there anything new?"

Ferguson looked thoughtfully at Archer, wondering how much of his motive he should reveal at this time. He decided to stick to the facts.

"You know what I believe, Archer. I haven't any proof. He has been careful never to do anything that would give him away. Neither has he shown any indication of what he intends to do when he does use his— powers. I think I've found out why."

"Could it be simply because he's a normal man without any special powers?" Archer asked gently.

"No, it couldn't! I'll tell you what it really is. He's still a child."

"At twenty-three?"

Ferguson smiled. "Do you know the ages of all your routine cases that well?"

"Well, go on," Archer said, shrugging.

"I've been studying his case very thoroughly. I've made charts and graphs from the information I've gathered, and I've showed them to specialists. I've got opinions and I've made comparisons. Lawson's activity-patterns are those of a twelve-year-old child—with variations. Intellectually he's not twelve years old, but his recreations—his periods of relaxation, when the intellectual centers of the brain aren't exclusively in control—that's when the important factors begin to show. He thinks like an adult, but he plays like a child. It's delayed maturation; it must be."

"So you believe he'll turn into a superman when he grows up?"

"That's why he went to your patron Reeve when he graduated from his crèche. It's the immaturity pension angle. He wasn't as altruistic as he seemed; by his own standards he was immature at the time. He still is. He's simply waiting until he grows up."

"Then what? He'll conquer the world?"

"I think he could if he wanted to." Ferguson considered Archer's face on the screen. "Well?" he said.

"What do you expect me to say to that?"

"I'm waiting for you to cross Lawson's name off your list. If your only interest in him has been curiosity about the altruism angle, you can check him off as of now. Are you going to?"

Archer paused a fraction of a second too long before he said, "Sure."

"That means you're not going to. You're too accurate a barometer to dismiss me as a crackpot entirely."

"You keep leaving me with nothing to say except go on."

Ferguson said, "I've got a phobia, I'll admit that. I've been living with it for a long time now. I don't like it. It's like living with one leg and no prosthetic device—I can get used to it, but my own adjustment won't help the rest of the world. I'm going to make Lawson furnish proof that will convince you and everybody else that he's—what he is. I'll need your help. He's made some good investments. That's why he hasn't yet needed to collect on any of those other policies he got originally. I'm beginning to think he took out so many just to disarm suspicion, so he could remain within the Margin for Error if he had to break two or three. He's broken two. He's been investigated. If he broke a third, I think other people besides me might begin to worry and wonder. I want him to break another. It's time people did begin to worry. This is where you come in. If Lawson's investments went wrong, he'd need more dough. I want them to go wrong. That's more your line than mine. What do you say?"

"What's in it for me?" Archer asked.

"You can stop worrying about that memo on your calendar—one way or the other. I promise that if nothing happens I'll never bother you again about it." That was the end of what Ferguson said aloud. In his own mind he finished the sentence. "—but I won't have to. Lawson will!"

Lawson was not likely to take that lying down. Ferguson did not expect vindictiveness from the boy; Lawson would be above petty revenge. But he could not afford to let a thing like this happen unchecked; Ferguson meant Lawson to know that this was a deliberate attack. And if Lawson was what Ferguson believed him to be, he could not afford to let the knowledge of his superior potentialities be spread abroad. If guns are being fired at you, you spike those guns. There need be nothing vindictive about it—but self-preservation must be as strong in the immature superman as it is in any other organism.

One of two things would happen; Lawson would collect on another policy, which would put him perilously close to the outside limits of Margin for Error. ILC would worry and wonder, remembering the suspicions Ferguson had already planted. Lawson could scarcely afford to break his hypnosis a third time openly. The alternative could only be an overt retaliation on his attackers; that was what Ferguson hoped for with part of his mind. It would be the more certain way of proving his case. And Archer had to be in on it. In a perfunctory way Ferguson was sorry he had to drag Archer into this. He would have had no objection to staking himself out alone as bait for the tiger if it would do any good. But no tethered goat has ever killed a tiger yet, alone. Ferguson had already established himself too firmly as a crackpot in the minds of those whose opinions mattered. If he could pull Archer down with him, Archer would have to fight back against the superman, or go under. Corroborative evidence from a man like Archer would have some weight with the authorities.

Ferguson watched Archer's face anxiously. He saw the decision hang in the balance for an interminable chain of seconds. Then Archer nodded.

"I'll see what I can do," he said.

Ferguson let out his breath in a long sigh.

The ease with which Lawson thought of a third alternative was infuriating. He did neither of the things Ferguson expected. Instead, he took out insurance on the *Nestor*, a luxury liner on the Earth-Moon run, and since a great many people wanted similar policies—it was almost a lottery, in view of an epidemic of meteor swarms—no attention was aroused at ILC. Besides, the usual Margin for Error had been allowed. The *Nestor* blasted off three days after its announced time for departure, which gave it a sufficient safety factor and caused dozens of people to cancel their policies.

So the *Nestor* avoided the meteor swarms, but ran into an atomic warhead which had been orbiting in free space for years, awaiting the fatal appointment.

The *Nestor* was running on atomic fuel. The great ship blazed white for an instant and disintegrated.

So did Ferguson. Not literally, of course; not with the spectacular finality of the ship.

Perhaps the worst part was the waiting. He was almost certain that Lawson knew what had been intended, and why, and who was responsible.

But nothing happened.

There was no yardstick. Ferguson didn't know what to expect because he didn't know Lawson's limitations. Ferguson might, unknown to himself, be walking straight toward an apparently accidental demise, hours or days from now, as final as that of the *Nestor*. It seemed fairly obvious that Lawson had foreseen that final rendezvous between the ship and the wandering warhead in its orbit. Was there a rendezvous ahead for Ferguson? Or was he being ignored? He didn't know which thought he liked less.

His work began to suffer. He wasn't eating well these days, which might have brought on his headaches. He overheard his secretary complaining that he was developing a temper like a bear, but he knew that was the wrong simile; the adult gorilla exhibited tendencies more like what Ferguson was feeling now. Irritation, a desire for solitude, above all suspicion. It was the suspicion that bothered him most.

After he had made the third major mistake in a row in office routine he took a vacation by request. He was more glad than sorry when the request came through—not that he thought a vacation would help to solve his problem—you can't negate a fact like Lawson by ignoring it—but he was at least relieved of the troublesome suspicion which had been developing to major proportions of late.

He was suspicious of new clients.

He kept remembering Lawson's aggressively normal face and manner in their first interview. And now he read behind every application the potential for—

A second Lawson.

For six months he tried to run away from a nightmare. The Himalaya Playground didn't help. Specialized occupational therapy didn't help either. Nor did the Moon. Ferguson found the satellite bleak and unfriendly, even at the stimulating Shady Glen north of Tycho. When he looked up at the clouded disk of Earth in the sky, he kept thinking the masses of light and dark had the shape of Lawson's face. It covered the whole planet, just as the shadow of Lawson had covered all of Ferguson's life by now. Lawson watched him unwinkingly from above.

Time on the Moon has a different quality from time on Earth. He had to count up laboriously sometimes to discover how long it had been since he left ILC. He had a reason for wondering, because there was a message he expected. A message from Archer. Before he left Earth, he had asked Archer to notify him in case anything developed. A good many months must have gone by, though here on the Moon they didn't seem so long. But no message came.

When he saw the dull colors of winter spreading down from the pole, he knew his six-months' period was up and he would have to think about going back soon. And now he had to face it; he was afraid to go back, until he heard from Archer. Eventually he undertook the considerable expense of a person-to-person call. It was not, after all, an expense. The call could not be completed. Archer had disappeared.

It was hard to check from this far away, but apparently the Fixer's office had been closed some months ago, and there was no forwarding number. By the time Ferguson's reservation for the return trip came up, he knew what he had to do.

If he had gone straight home, things might have worked out quite differently. But at that time of year the space liner was operating between Tycho and a port in South Africa. An old compulsion which had been haunting Ferguson for some time now saw its chance and broke out of all control.

For a long while he had wanted very much to kill a gorilla. It was not as irrational as it sounded. Psychiatrically speaking, he knew it involved symbolism and displacement. Emotionally, he knew what face he would see across the sights of the gun when he found his gorilla. It had to be an adult male.

With all the resources of his time, this wasn't difficult to arrange; but the disgraceful ease with which the telephoto analyzers located a specimen, the simplicity of driving the sullen brute into an ambush with supersonics, the facility with which Ferguson, in his fast, armored Hunter, shot his quarry, left the man completely dissatisfied. Men had killed gorillas before. It proved nothing. It didn't prove the point that bothered him.

Sight and memory of the gorilla's face, in death, stayed with him. The monster had been mature, for his species. Antisocial and dangerous. But dangerous only to whatever intruded into his domain.

With a mature superman, Ferguson thought, human progress might stop. A superman would not feel insecurity, that goad which has always driven mankind. A superman would be a law unto himself. Would he behave like an anthropomorphic god, lending a helping hand to Homo sapiens, or would mankind seem to him as alien and unimportant as a savage tribe?

Lesser breeds without the law—

But the world belonged to man. Not to Lawson. ILC was the law. ILC was the fortress. Without ILC's stability, there would be no protection. *I'm not safe any more,* Ferguson thought. *I could never stand alone. Maybe that merely means racial immaturity; ILC does stand in loco parentis, but it's always been that way—man has always wanted an All-Father image—*

Ferguson turned in the rifle, but he kept the pistol.

There was so difficulty about locating Lawson. He still lived in the same cottage. But he seemed to be looking slightly older. He nodded cheerfully to Ferguson when the latter came in.

"Hello," he said.

Ferguson took out the gun and aimed it at Lawson.

Lawson looked scared, or pretended to.

"Don't," he said hastily. "I can explain. Don't shoot me."

His apparent fright was the only thing that stopped Ferguson's finger on the trigger.

"You don't need to be afraid of me," Lawson assured him in a soothing voice. "Please put down that gun."

"I know all about you. You're dangerous. You could conquer the world if you wanted to."

"I doubt it," Lawson said, his fascinated stare on the gun muzzle. "I'm not really a superman, you know."

"You're not ordinary Homo sapiens."

"Now look. I know a good deal about you, too. You could hardly expect me not to after what's happened. A man's investments don't all go haywire at once unless somebody's been manipulating the market against him."

"So that's what happened to Archer." Ferguson's voice rose. "I suppose I can expect the same thing, whatever it is."

"Archer? You must mean Reeve's Fixer. So far as I know, he's going about his business as usual." Lawson was eying his adversary warily. "You're the problem right now," he said. "You're not going about *your* business; you're going about mine. I wish you'd lay off, Ferguson. I know what you're thinking, but honestly, I'm not doing anyone any harm. Maybe you have reason for some of your conclusions about what you call my superpowers, but there's nothing miraculous about them. It . . . it's just—"

"It's what?" Ferguson demanded as the other man hesitated.

"Call it a—way of thinking. That's as close as I can come to explaining what it is I've got. I just don't make mistakes. Not ever."

"You made one when you let me come in just now, with a gun in my pocket."

"No, I didn't," Lawson said.

There was a pause.

He went on. "Suppose I tell you a little about it. You were partly right, you know, in what you've been saying about me. I am immature. Normally, I'd never have known I wasn't mature at twenty-one. There weren't any standards of comparison. But this—thing—in my mind helped there. It isn't prescience, it's just a . . . a way of thinking. You might call it precision and knowledge of precision tactics. An ability to disassociate the personality from pure thought. I can disassociate logic from emotion, you see—but that's only part of it. Before I graduated from the crèche, I knew it would take a good many years before I really matured."

"You're not human. You don't give a care about human beings."

Lawson said, "Look at it this way. Long ago, there was child labor. Kids were put to work in mines and factories when they were ten—or even before that. How could they reach normal maturity under those conditions? They needed normal childhood, with the right facilities. I had the same problem, with a maturation delayed years beyond the time of everybody else. I couldn't take a job—any job. I could have coped with the requirements, of course, but it would have—warped me. Even before I got my particular ability fully developed, I had a sort of protective instinct pointing out the right direction to take—generally. Just as a new-hatched chicken runs from danger. I *needed* a normal childhood —one that would be normal for me."

"I suspected what you were."

"Because of what you are," Lawson said gently.

Ferguson blinked. "You're antisocial and dangerous," he said. "Your record shows that. You wrecked the *Nestor.*"

"You know better than that. You're trying to make me a personal devil."

"You insured the *Nestor,* and the *Nestor* ran into an atomic warhead in space. What about logics of probability?"

"What about logic?" Lawson countered. "I can think and integrate without emotional bias when necessary, that's all. It's not prescience. It was a matter of hard work, research, astronomy, historical study, and integration. I found out the exact time of the *Nestor's* departure, I found records of spaceships that had noted radiations in certain areas above the stratosphere. I checked on what atomic shells were fired during the Atomic War. I don't think any ordinary human would have had the patience or the speed to do the integration I did, but—it's simply hard work, plus extensions of the brain that have always been shackled before."

"You can foretell the future?"

"Given the factors, I can formulate the probable final equation—yes. But as for this special talent of mine—I can't tell you. All I can say is that technology has its limits, but the human mind hasn't. We've gone tremendously far with technologies—so far that we nearly killed ourselves with atomics because we didn't know how to use nuclear fission. But every weapon creates the man to use it—and to hammer it into a plowshare. I'm a mutation. Eventually we'll know how to handle atomics without danger—"

"*We?*"

"I'm the first. But there are others like me in the crèches now. Immature as yet. But my brothers will grow—"

Ferguson thought of the gorilla.

Lawson said, "I know how to think. I'm the first man in the world who ever knew how to do that. I'll never need a psychiatrist. I don't think I'll ever make a mistake, because I can really think impersonally, and there's nobody who's ever been able to do that before. That's the basis of the future—not technologies that people misuse, but people who can use technology. Right now, there are over eighty children in crèches who have that special factor for logic in their minds. It's a dominant mutation. We don't want to rule; we'll never want that. It's only autocrats who need power—those who tag groups as 'little people' so that by comparison they'll be big people. My job, just at present, is to see that my brother mutants get the immaturity pension they need. I must provide that money somehow. I can do it; I've worked out some methods—"

"Nevertheless I'm going to kill you," Ferguson said. "I'm afraid of you. You could rule the world."

"Madmen rule," Lawson said. "Sane men work, directionally. Atomics have to be controlled; that's one step. It takes pure, sane thought to handle that. And I'm the first truly sane man who has ever existed on Earth."

"Like that gorilla I shot yesterday? He was integrated. He was vicious and touchy and static. He had his feeding-ground and his harem, and that was enough for him. He wanted no progress and needed none. That's maturity for you. Progress stops—the world stops. You're a dead end, Lawson—and in a minute you'll just be dead."

"Do you think you can kill me?"

"I don't know. Probably not, if you're a superman. But I'm going to try."

"And if you fail?"

"Probably you'll kill me. Because if you don't, I'll spread the word, and you'll be lynched—some day. At least, I'll talk. If that's the only weapon I have against you."

"Animals kill," Lawson said. "Men kill. I don't kill."

"I do," Ferguson said, and squeezed the trigger.

Nothing happened.

When the room steadied about him again, he was seated in a deep chair, staring at the gun on the floor where he had dropped it. For the moment it didn't matter why he had failed—why the gun had failed. The fact of failure was enough.

Lawson had been intolerably kind. He had a vague feeling that Lawson had gone away somewhere to fetch him a drink. His time sense was unsteady again. Perhaps that was because he had so newly returned from the Moon. Whatever the reason, his sense of urgency was gone.

Then on the wall he saw the television panel, and an urgency woke again in him in a new direction. Archer. Archer could give him the answer. If Archer were still alive.

With no recollection of motion he found himself before the screen, steadying himself with braced hands on the base, giving the familiar call number for the office where Archer no longer worked. He got from the exchange the same information his lunar call had elicited—office closed, no forwarding address. He tried Archer's home, with the same lack of result. Then he tried the office of Hiram Reeve, the politician who had been Lawson's patron, and here he found the right answer.

"ZX 47-6859. That's a private number, Mr. Ferguson. ILC will keep it confidential, of course?"

Ferguson promised, and blanked the face out quickly. His voice was a little unsteady as he repeated the ZX number. It seemed incredible that Archer's plump face should dawn so clearly and promptly in the screen. Ferguson had pictured him as dead or destroyed in some subtler way, with so many vivid variations as applied to himself, that he tried stupidly to reach out and touch the screen for reassurance. The surface was cold and smooth beneath his fingertips, but Archer jumped back and laughed, putting up a futile hand to shield his eyes from the imagined blow.

"Hey, what's the idea?" he demanded.

"Are you all right, Archer? Where are you? What's happened?"

"Sure I'm all right," Archer said. "What about you? You don't look too good."

"I don't feel too good. But I've got proof. He's admitted it!"

"Hold on a minute. Let's get this straight. I know you just got back from the Moon, but—"

"I'm at Lawson's house. I've confronted him with the evidence." Ferguson made a great effort and forced his mind into co-ordinated thought. So much depended on what he was able to put across in the next few sentences. He could not afford weakness yet. "Lawson's admitted everything I've been telling you," he said. "It was all true. For a while I almost thought I was going crazy, but now Lawson admits it—listen, Archer, he admits it! You've got to help me! I realize my record's bad—I knew, but I couldn't convince anybody, and it nearly drove me off my rocker. I suppose I've been sounding psychotic for a long time now, but they'll listen to you. They've got to—because I tried to shoot Lawson, and I couldn't. Somebody will have to do something quick." He paused, drew a deep breath, and said harshly, "There are eighty more of *them*. Do you hear that, Archer? They're growing up. They're going to take over. I know how that sounds, but you've got to believe me. Give me a chance to prove it! Could you get here fast? How far away are you? It all depends on you; Archer, please don't fail me!"

Archer smiled. It was borne in upon Ferguson's mind that he looked like a different man now. Somehow in the last six months he had shed his reserve, his wariness, and seemed completely relaxed and confident. But a slight shadow darkened his look of jovial content when he answered.

"I can get there right away," he said. "Hold on." He turned away from the screen. Ferguson saw the back of his head as he crossed the room and opened a door in the far wall. He heard the door open. Beyond the opening door he had a brief glimpse of a tiny, distant room in which a tiny, distant man stood with his back to the door, looking into a televisor screen. Very small and clear on that miniature screen he saw a miniature duplicate of a man opening a door upon a room in which a man stood facing a televisor screen—

It was the sound of the opening door that rescued him from the plunge through abyss after diminishing abyss of infinite duplication. He heard the door opening twice, once in the screen and once in the wall behind him. When he turned, Archer was crossing the threshold.

This time it was a long while before the room stopped turning. "I'm sorry," Archer said. "I should have warned you. I guess I just didn't think. Things have been happening pretty fast around here."

"What things? What happened? What are you doing here?"

"I work here," Archer said.

"You—*work here?*"

"I've changed my patron. No law against that, is there? I worked for Reeve as long as I thought he was the best man. But now I'm working for Ben Lawson. He's the best—man."

Ferguson made an inarticulate sound. "You traitor," he said wildly.

"To what?"

"Your own species!"

"Oh, very likely," Archer said blandly. "Still, I know where I'm most useful. And I like to be useful. It's none of our business to sit in judgment, is it?"

"Of course it's our business! Who will if we don't? I—"

Archer interrupted. "It doesn't matter whether we do or don't. You saw what happened when you tried to shoot Lawson."

Ferguson had entirely forgotten the pistol. Now he crossed the room unsteadily, picked it up, and broke it open. The cartridges were blanks.

"All hunters are required to return their weapons after they've come back from expeditions," Archer said pedantically. "ILC's policy is to avoid irritation, so nobody tried to take that pistol away from you at Uganda Station. However, blank cartridges were substituted. Lawson knew what would happen. It took him seven hours of fast calculation and logic to work out the inevitable probability, including the psychological factor that involved your personal reactions—but you see the result. You can't kill him. He can always work out what's going to happen."

"Man, you can't—" Ferguson found himself becoming incoherent. He stopped, drew a painfully long breath, and began again, with an attempt at control. "You can't be such a fool! Maybe I've failed to kill Lawson—alone. But that doesn't mean that both of us, together . . . the resources of ILC . . . the whole human race would band together to destroy Lawson if they knew—"

"Why should they destroy him?"

"Self-preservation!"

"That instinct failed the race," Archer said softly, "when it made the first atomic bomb. Status quo is only a stop-gap. The single answer now is not a new control for atomics, but a new kind of man. A mature man."

"The mature gorilla—"

Archer interrupted. "Yes, I know. You've had that phobia in mind for a long time. But you're thinking like an immature gorilla yourself, aren't you?"

"Of course I am. The whole race is at that stage. That's what frightens me. Our entire culture is based on progress rising out of competition and co-operation. If a really mature mind should take over, all progress would stop."

"You really don't see the answer to that?" Archer said.

Ferguson opened his mouth for what he realized would be only repetition. He wasn't getting anywhere with Archer; he was making no impression. All he could do was repeat what he had already said. "Like a child," he thought wildly. "Repetition, not logical argument. Only—"

They could no longer communicate with one another. It was as though Archer had changed over to a new and incomprehensible standard of thinking. The barrier between them was as tangible as the surface of a televisor screen. They could see one another through it, but they could no longer touch.

Ferguson's shoulders sagged a trifle as he gave up the attempt at communication. He turned toward the door, hesitating. He glanced back with a new wariness at this man who was suddenly an enemy.

What, he wondered, were Archer's orders from Lawson? Surely they couldn't afford to let him go. He groped in vain for an understandable parallel. In this situation a normal human would have shot him as he went out the door, or locked him safely away where he could do them no harm. But Lawson had never operated with normal human weapons like these. Lawson's weapons—

Archer said suddenly, "You're free to go whenever you like. One thing, though. Listen, Ferguson. Lawson tried to take out another policy with your company today, and was turned down. It looked like a poor risk. I thought you ought to know."

Ferguson could read nothing in Archer's face. The barrier still stood between them. He thought there was more than met the ear behind that statement, but he knew that he could only wait. He went out through the door and down the walk, in the bright yellow sunshine of his familiar world. It was a world that depended on him for its salvation. And a world he could not save because it would not heed his warning.

Flickers of hope rose irrationally in his mind. Had Archer, after all, been trying to tell him that Lawson was fallible? If ILC had refused a policy, it might mean that their suspicions were roused at last. It might mean that he had not lost the battle after all. Perhaps they would listen now. Rapidly he began to calculate how long it would take him to get back to headquarters—

But between him and his calculations kept swimming the recollection of the liner *Nestor* and the derelict warhead, moving closer and closer in uncharted space toward the rendezvous that only Lawson had foreseen.

Two hours later Ferguson closed the door of his office behind his secretary's somewhat indignant back, and glanced with a sigh of relief around the small, empty room. He knew he hadn't done his cause any good by his unswerving course through the building, brushing aside the surprised greetings of what friends he had left after the last two years. The most important thing in the world just now was solitude. He locked the door and turned to his private visor screen.

"Get me the current file on Benjamin Lawson," he said. "Recently he applied for a policy that was refused. I want to know why." He waited impatiently, drumming on the resilient plastic frame with unsteady fingers.

"Hello, Mr. Ferguson," the screen said pleasantly. "Glad you're back. There's been nothing new on Lawson since you left, but I'll send the file up right away."

"Don't bother, then. I want to know about this new policy. Hurry it up, can't you?" He heard his voice rise shrilly, and with an effort forced it to more normal tones.

There was a moment's silence. Then the face said, with a shade of embarrassment, "Sorry, Mr. Ferguson; that seems to be under TS."

"What do you mean?" he asked irritably, and before she could speak— "Never mind, never mind. Thanks." He snapped the switch.

They had never pulled TS on him before. Top Secret stuff was technically limited to the three highest-ranking officers of the company, though actually staff members of Ferguson's rank honored such rules more by their breach than by their observance.

I mustn't let it throw me, he said silently. *I can't let it throw me.* And after a moment he knew what he could do. There were three men whose televisor screens would automatically reply to a TS query. He made two calls before he found an empty office. It was lunch time, fortunately for him.

He unlocked his door, went down the corridor to the emergency stairs, and climbed three floors. On the way he formulated a plausible enough tale, but he didn't need to use it. By a stroke of better luck than had attended him so far, the first vice president's office was empty. He closed and locked the door behind him, and switched on the screen for one-way visual.

"Give me the latest TS on Benjamin Lawson."

"Well, that's that," Archer said.

Lawson lay back in his chair, lifted the trumpet to his lips, and blew a long clear note at the ceiling. It might have been a note of derision at the human race, but Archer did not choose to read that into it. He knew Lawson too well—or he thought he did.

"It's a pity," Archer went on. "I was sorry we had to do it, but he wouldn't leave us any other out."

"Does it bother you?" Lawson asked, squinting at him over the rim of the trumpet's horn. Reflected in the brass Archer saw his own distorted face and the shadow of worry on it.

"I suppose it does, a little," he said. "But it couldn't be helped."

"It's not as if we'd planted a booby-trap on him," Lawson pointed out. "We only arranged for him to know the truth."

Archer laughed shortly. "Misused semantics. Truth sounds innocuous, doesn't it? And yet it's the deadliest thing you could ask any human to face. Or any superhuman, either, I should think."

"I wish you wouldn't call me superhuman," Lawson said. "You sound like Ferguson. I hope *you* don't think I want to conquer the world."

"I tried to tell him you didn't, but by then he was seeing a superman behind every tree, and there was nothing I could say that would make sense to him."

Lawson slid further down into the chair and ran through a brief series of riffs. The room was full of clear resonance for a moment. Before it died away Lawson put aside the trumpet and said, "I don't suppose it would make sense to anybody brought up on anthropomorphic thinking."

"I know. It took me a long time to come around. And I suppose it was only by identifying my interests with yours that I was able to see it."

"Ferguson went to extremes, but the two things he was so afraid of are the conclusions any anthropomorphic thinker would arrive at if he knew the truth about me and the other eighty in the crèches. He was perfectly right, as far as he went, about the parallel between gorilla and human maturation, of course. The immature gorilla is naturally a gregarious, competitive critter. That's part of its growing up. That's progress, if you like. In the crèches, we kids used to think our football and baseball and skatch scores were the most important things in the world— the goal was to win. But the real idea was to develop us physically and teach us mental and social co-ordination, things we'd need when we grew up. You don't see grown men taking things like that so seriously."

Archer said, "Yes—but try making Ferguson see the parallel! Or any other anthropomorphic thinker."

"Progress as men see it," Lawson said pedantically, "is not an end in itself; it is as much a means to an end as any schoolboy's game."

Archer grinned. "Paragraph 1, Chapter 1, Primer for the New Race," he suggested. "There's no use trying to explain that to Ferguson. He has a big blind spot on that side of his mind. His whole culture's based on the idea of competition and progress. It's his god. He'd fight to the last ditch before he'd admit his . . . his football score isn't the last great hope of the race of men."

"He has fought to the last ditch," Lawson said. "He's in it now. We can dismiss Ferguson." He regarded his trumpet thoughtfully and said, "Paragraph 1, Sentence 2. When the end has been achieved, the means is no longer of any value. We know this is so, but never try to tell it to a human." He paused and winked at Archer. "Your case is the exception, of course," he observed politely. "Paragraph 1, Sentence 3. Never blame the human for that. We can't expect him to admit that his whole culture is no more than a childish game to which there must be an end if the game is to serve any purpose. Never look down on humans—they laid the foundations for us to build on, and we know no more than they what shape that building will take."

Archer was silent, a hint of deference in his manner. This was the only subject which he had ever seen Lawson approach seriously. "Paragraph 2," Lawson went on, scowling at the trumpet. "Never attack a human except in self-defense and then destroy him quickly and completely. Humans think autistically; they will always be convinced you want to rule their world. Their egotism will never let them admit the truth. We have no need of their toys; we must put away childish things."

There was a brief silence. Then Archer said, "We ought to get that primer on paper before very long; we'll be needing it."

"Maybe we ought to dedicate it to Ferguson," Lawson suggested sardonically, as he picked up the trumpet and delicately fingered the keys.

The clear note of the horn vibrated through the room again.

"You make me think of Joshua," Archer told him.

Lawson grinned. "Gabriel," he said succinctly.

Ferguson leaned tensely toward the screen. It flickered, and a voice said, "Report on policy refused November 4th to applicant Benjamin Lawson—" The voice went on, and Ferguson listened for a stunned moment and then refused to listen.

This is the chain reaction, he told himself, in the delicate, controlled silence of his mind, while the voice spoke on unheeded from the screen. This is the personal devil that every man has feared since the first Bomb fell. But we've watched for the wrong reaction. This is fission no one expected, fission between the old race and the new. No one knows but me—and Archer—and I'll never be able to give the warning—

This was defeat. There was no use fighting any longer. He saw failure and disaster before him, the control of all Earth wrested from human hands and Lawson lording it like Nero over a populace of slaves. For Ferguson was an autistic thinker to the last. He saw Progress at full stop, and that was the last abyss of all, for beyond it his narrowing mind could see nothing but the dark. The last barriers of his defense went down, and he let himself listen to the words that the screen was repeating.

The screen said:

"Lawson desired to insure against the possibility of ILC officer Gregory Ferguson becoming insane. Since investigation shows that Ferguson has already exceeded the Margin for Error allowable for developing paranoid psychoses—"

Moving through uncharted space, the liner *Nestor* and the derelict warhead crashed once more in the infinite darkness of Gregory Ferguson's mind. After that, there was white incandescence.

All thinking stopped.

PART THREE

From Outer Space

MACK REYNOLDS

ISOLATIONIST

THE first attempt on the part of members of the Galactic Union to open communications with Planet K3LT14, known to its inhabitants as Earth, or Terra, was made by a benevolent society of the Aldebaran System. Although the Aldebarans were acquainted with the fact that Terra had not as yet reached a civilization development of even DQ-14, and was, consequently, far from prepared to enter the Galactic Union, they had become alarmed at the experiments in nuclear fission which the Terrans were making. The society feared that the energetic new race might destroy itself before reaching maturity. . . .

To begin with, I was probably feeling more crotchety than usual as a result of my trip into Harvey. Alone on the farm, and with more work than I can handle myself, I sometimes forget my bitterness; but my monthly trip to town often upsets me for days afterwards. Perhaps I was more tolerant when I was younger and Ruth and the boys were still alive.

I'd got through my business without trouble and had stopped off in a restaurant before heading home. I should have known better. The food was cooked on an electric stove and came mostly from cans. In the corner stood a garishly painted music box, covered with neon lights that flickered and flowed until I felt my eyeballs were about to pop out. Over and over it played something about a room full of roses, and from time to time suffering patrons got up and put money into it, like sacrifices to the God of Clamor. They didn't even change the tune; they kept playing the same one as if they were hypnotized.

At first I thought the man sitting next to me was staring at my beard. I ignored him, figuring that if he wanted to scrape his face raw with a razor every day, that was his business, but I'd leave my face the way nature planned it to be. However, he finally spoke up. "You're Alex Wood," he said, "aren't you? With a farm about twenty miles out of town?"

This is the only story in this book which the editor has altered in any way. His appreciation and thanks are gratefully extended to Mr. Reynolds for permitting the slight variations, none of which changed the essence of this engaging and thoughtful little tale.

I nodded.

He flashed me a professional smile and stuck out his hand to be shaken. So I shook it and dropped it, saying, "What're you selling?"

He laughed, the way salesmen do, and explained, "My name is Brown, and my line is radio. I . . ."

I snorted. "I think radios ought to be taxed. Personally, I wouldn't have one in my house." I went back to my food.

You'd think I had told him I was a cannibal. "Why not?" he said. "Practically everybody—"

I stopped eating again and said patiently, as if I were talking to a youngster, "Because if I had a radio somebody might turn it on, and then I'd have to listen. A radio is worse than electric lights."

He blinked his eyes; his little salesman's mustache twitched. "What's wrong with electric lights?"

I wiggled a finger at him. "They turn night into day, which automatically turns day into night. You wind up with nothing accomplished except that you've missed the best hours of the twenty-four by spending the dawn in bed."

He wrinkled up his forehead as if he didn't know what I was talking about, but was afraid to tell me I was crazy because he still had some hopes of selling me something.

I didn't bother going further. What was the use? Like nearly everybody else, he probably thought that the "gifts" of science were wonderful and that we were heading for the promised land on a streamlined bus.

"I'm not interested in installing any electrical gadgets on my farm," I told him, and returned to the adulterated stuff they call food in town restaurants.

He was beginning to get irritated, the way they do when they see they are not going to make a sale. "You aren't much in favor of progress, are you?" he asked, with a patronizing tone to his voice.

I sighed disgustedly and said, "Look, son, everybody's in favor of progress, just like everybody's against sin. The difference is in what you mean by progress. Now take automobiles . . ."

He sneered. "Well, they get you there quicker, and they don't . . ."

I raised my voice a little. "And what do you do when you get there? Anything worth while? For a hundred years people have been trying to 'get there quicker' so busily that they haven't had time to figure out something worth doing when they arrive. Everybody is going as fast as they possibly can—and getting nowhere. These new thousand-mile-an-hour airplanes can reach anywhere on the earth's surface in twelve hours. But what's accomplished by all that speed? Stomach ulcers!"

He took a drink of his coffee, looking over the rim of his cup at me as though I were an enemy saboteur, or something like that. "Among other things," he said in a measured tone, "it has military advantages."

I began to boil. "Making it easier to kill people, eh? Did it ever occur to you that if our scientists spent the time and money they did on the atom bomb on cancer research, there probably wouldn't be any cancer today?"

He didn't answer, but shrugged his shoulders, slapped some change down on the counter, got up and left, looking back over his shoulder at me as if I were a combination of a lunatic loose from an asylum and a member of some Fifth Column.

All the way back to the farm I thought up things I could have said to him, emphasizing where our modern trend is taking us. We have developed a tremendous science, true, but we have found no way to control it. Frankenstein's monster was a juvenile delinquent compared to what we are creating with our scientific developments. We are heading for complete destruction unless a miracle comes along to save us—and I don't believe in miracles.

I was so upset that night, thinking over this discussion, that I didn't get to sleep until late. As a result, it was nearly dawn when I woke up, just in time to see the thing come down from the sky.

I sat up quickly in bed as I saw it up in the heavens from the bedroom window. I thought at first it might be a meteorite. But when it got closer, I could see that I was wrong. It was built something like a fat cigar, and was shooting fire from its fore end like a Fourth of July roman candle. Its speed was falling off quickly; and, as it neared the ground, it slowed up still more until, when it finally touched, it did so almost gently, just beyond a little rise in the ground.

I suddenly realized that it must have landed right in the midst of my corn. I jumped from the bed, hurried into my trousers, and ran over to the closet for the shotgun. I rammed two buckshot shells into the breech and was out the door and crossing the fields in less than a minute, half dressed and with my shoelaces trying to trip me up as I ran.

I could hear Betty and Beth stomping in terror in their stalls, and the chickens squawking as though a coyote were in with them.

It was too much. I try to tell myself that I don't mind other people having their cars, their electric devices, and even their airplanes. But when they seek me out on my isolated little farm, where I've tried so hard to escape the world I once knew, and land one of their fantastic new experimental rocket ships in my corn—

As I expected, a good acre and more of my best golden bantam was nothing more than smoldering stubble. I strode through it on a half-run, and pounded on what appeared to be the door of the thing with the butt of my shotgun.

I still can't say whether it would be proper to call it a jet plane. It was considerably larger than any craft of the sort I'd seen. But then, though I'm not much up on current developments, I understand the government is spending billions of dollars on the making of such hellish devices. At any rate, hardly anybody can keep up with all the latest types of flying machines.

It must have reached nearly a hundred feet into the air. Its wings were short and stubby. The metal—I guess it must have been metal—on the outside had a queer shimmering look, something like an old mirror that had had a considerable amount of the mercury on its back damaged. In spite of all the flame it had been shooting out, even the metal around the vents where the flames came from did not seem to be hot. I touched one of them with a finger; it felt cool.

I thumped on the door again, still in a rage. As poor as I am, this invention of "progress" had to destroy nearly half of my sweet corn crop.

The door still did not open, and I half walked, half stumbled around the thing. It was as big as a small barn. I could not help but wonder how it ever got up into the air. What a sample of man's ability! If he only would turn his genius to human advancement instead of to instruments of war and machines for over-production, and all the rest!

. . . By the time I had circled the big ship, the door had begun to move, slowly. When an actual crack finally appeared, there was a sudden blast of air, as though the pressure inside had been greater than that outside. I stood there watching, my shotgun under my arm, waiting to read the riot act when the drivers of this vehicle showed their faces.

Suddenly the door swung free, and there they were, three of them staring down at me.

Perhaps my scorn of individuals who make war their profession, even in times of peace, colored my outlook; but it seemed to me, in the half light of the early morning, that they were the weirdest specimens I'd ever seen. Even their clothes were monstrous, but I suppose they were what you'd expect flyers who go up in high-level planes would have to wear. They certainly were the most incredible garments I had ever laid eyes on.

I glared at the three grimly, waiting for some kind of apology or explanation. Not that I was expecting to accept their excuses; I was ready to tell them exactly what I thought of them.

The first of them, probably the commanding officer, stared at me, and at the ground around me, for a full minute before saying anything. He was a tall man, without a hair on his head, and his eyes were much more piercingly bright than ordinary. He looked out of place on a military ship, it seemed to me, as though he were really a dreamer or a philosopher, not someone who would spend his life working on super-bombers to kill off his fellow man.

He said, finally, "Greetings. This is Terra, is it not?"

A foreigner!

You could tell from the way he talked. He had the heaviest accent I had ever heard; I could hardly understand him. I have always thought it was bad enough that the government should put thousands of Americans to work figuring out new ways of killing, but that they should hire foreigners to help them seems too much to me.

I never have heard of any town called Terra. I snorted, holding myself in check. "This is Harvey, North Dakota, or rather, it's about twenty miles outside of Harvey." I was about to light into them, but they threw me off by putting their heads together and jabbering away in some foreign language.

Finally the leader turned back to me again and said, "We are from Borl, in the Aldebaran System. We bring you greetings and well wishes from—"

It was then that I began to get really angry. "So you're *all* foreigners! At first I thought you were some Americans with an experimental plane, but now I see I was wrong. You're *foreign* military people. Ships like this are never built for peaceful purposes. You come here in your big, fast-flying bomber, pretending to be friendly. Probably next year you'll come back for another visit, carrying atom bombs or even some poisons to spoil our crops."

He tried to stop me, but I went on, too wound up to interrupt myself just because he raised his hand. "You come down blasting away with your hellish ship of destruction, scaring my stock half to death, ruining my best sweet corn, and then you have the gall—"

I don't think he understood half of what I was saying, but he interrupted me before I could catch my breath.

"You don't understand," he said, frowning a little. "We have come to give you the advice and guidance of a more advanced people, and to help you—"

I broke in on him again. Even if he was telling the truth and not just more propaganda, I was still in a fury.

"Advice!" I yelled at him. "Advice! Keep your valuable advice! I have been getting more crazy advice from Washington than I know what to do with, without some foreign wiseacres starting in. How to plant, what to plant, when to plant, how to fertilize, how to put in electricity, how to do this and that and the other thing. And then what happens? First they teach you how to grow tremendous crops, and then they make you destroy them! How many potatoes to pour kerosene on, what crops to plow under, what acres to leave fallow and get paid for it, what pigs to shoot, what fruit trees to chop down!"

Everything of the past forty years seemed to flash in front of me. All the results of their quick-growing technology and their lack of knowing what to do with it. Their making of more and more products with the new machines, without having places to sell them all. And the whole thing finally blowing up with wars over colonies and sources of raw materials, like oil, and markets where they could dump their surplus manufactured goods. I thought of the loss of Johnny in the first world war, and of Cris in the second, of Ruth's death by cancer, and of the crazy stock market collapse and the depression in the thirties which drove us away from the cities and my profession as a teacher, out to the simplicities of the country, and a farming life; and I realized that their insane science is still growing and growing, and a sane way of using the things it discovers is yet to be figured out. And I remembered that they are preparing for the next war just as fast as they possibly can. Their science be hanged!

Finally I stopped for breath.

The commander of the group was beginning to get pretty pale with anger himself by this time. "This is an incredible indignity!" he said. "Haven't you considered the fact that we have gone to endless difficulties in making this journey here and in studying your fantastic language by using your radio emanations? And then to land on your barbarian . . ."

That set me going again. I was too wrought up to make much sense in what I was saying, but I yelled back as loudly as I could. "Fantastic language! Who told you you could talk it? It's all a man can do to understand your gibberish! And what do you mean—barbarian? The real savages are you professional soldiers and you technicians who work overtime making death-dealing machines!"

I realized I was talking so loud and so fast that probably he couldn't understand me, so I slowed down. "*If you don't like this country, why don't you go back where you came from?*"

He stared at me for a long time without saying anything. "That seems an excellent suggestion," he said finally. "Obviously, we made a mistake in coming at all." His eyes seemed to shoot sparks at me, he was so angry. Then suddenly he turned and went back in his ship and slammed the door behind him as hard as he could. I could hear the machinery working inside it again, making it air-tight.

I recalled what the blast from its exhausts, or whatever they were, had done to my corn, so I dashed back to get out of the way. A few minutes later the big ship flashed blinding flames from its bottom, and lifted sluggishly from the ground. It gained speed slowly, then faster, then with a roar it streaked up and disappeared into the sky. It was a terrible thing to watch, I thought. Something like a skyrocket, a youngster's toy, developed into an instrument of war that could destroy cities in an instant!

I plodded back to the house, exhausted, knowing myself for the old, tired, disillusioned, bitter man that I am. I felt no hope for myself or for the human race. Only a miracle could save this world of ours from self-destruction—and I don't believe in miracles.

. . . *Unfortunately, the Aldebaran expedition was a failure, being received with open hostility and belligerence. At the time some criticism was made of the group's leader, on the grounds that he had left Terra after being influenced adversely by but one inhabitant of the backward planet. Be that as it may, Terra was not visited again until two hundred decals later, following several atomic wars. There were no members of the species homo sapiens left by then.*

— From the Encyclopaedia Galactica.

MURRAY LEINSTER

NOBODY SAW THE SHIP

THE landing of the Qul-En ship, a tiny craft no more than fifteen feet in diameter, went completely unnoticed, as its operator intended. It was armed, of course, but its purpose was not destruction. If this ship, whose entire crew consisted of one individual, were successful in its mission then a great ship would come, wiping out the entire population of cities before anyone suspected the danger.

But this lone Qul-En was seeking a complex hormone substance which Qul-En medical science said theoretically must exist, but the molecule of which even the Qul-En could not synthesize directly. Yet it had to be found, in great quantity; once discovered, the problem of obtaining it would be taken up, with the resources of the whole race behind it. But first it had to be found.

The tiny ship assigned to explore the Solar System for the hormone wished to pass unnoticed. Its mission of discovery should be accomplished in secrecy if possible. For one thing, the desired hormone would be destroyed by contact with the typical Qul-En ray-gun beam, so that normal methods of securing zoological specimens could not be used.

The ship winked into being in empty space, not far from Neptune. It drove for that chilly planet, hovered about it, and decided not to land. It sped inward toward the sun and touched briefly on Io, but found no life there. It dropped into the atmosphere of Mars, and did not rise again for a full week, but the vegetation on Mars is thin and the animals mere degenerate survivors of once specialized forms. The ship came to Earth, hovered lightly at the atmosphere's very edge for a long time, and doubtless chose its point of descent for reasons that seemed good to its occupant. Then it landed.

It actually touched Earth at night. There was no rocket-drive to call attention and by dawn it was well concealed. Only one living creature had seen it land—a mountain lion. Even so, by midday the skeleton of the lion was picked clean by buzzards, with ants tidying up after them. And the Qul-En in the ship was enormously pleased. The carcass, before being abandoned to the buzzards, had been studied with an incredible competence. The lion's nervous system—particularly the mass of tissue in the skull—unquestionably contained either the desired

Like Henry Kuttner, who has only appeared in my anthologies under the name of Lewis Padgett, Will Jenkins has never been published in a Conklin science fiction collection; but Murray Leinster, his Mr. Hyde, has been in all three Crown titles. Mr. Jenkins is the uncrowned Dean of science fiction writers, for he has been producing good science fiction at a fast clip ever since 1918.

hormone itself, or something so close to it that it could be modified and the hormone produced. It remained only to discover how large a supply of the precious material could be found on Earth. It was not feasible to destroy a group of animals—say, of the local civilized race—and examine their bodies, because the hormone would be broken down by the weapon which allowed of a search for it. So an estimate of available sources would have to be made by sampling. The Qul-En in the ship prepared to take samples.

The ship had landed in tumbled country some forty miles south of Ensenada Springs, national forest territory, on which grazing-rights were allotted to sheep-ranchers after illimitable red tape. Within ten miles of the hidden ship there were rabbits, birds, deer, coyotes, a lobo wolf or two, assorted chipmunks, field-mice, perhaps as many as three or four mountain lions, one flock of two thousand sheep, one man, and one dog.

The man was Antonio Menendez. He was ancient, unwashed, and ignorant, and the official shepherd of the sheep. The dog was Salazar, of dubious ancestry but sound worth, who actually took care of the sheep and knew it; he was scarred from battles done in their defense. He was unweariedly solicitous of the wooly half-wits in his charge. There were whole hours when he could not find time to scratch himself, because of his duties. He was reasonably fond of Antonio, but knew that the man did not really understand sheep.

Besides these creatures, among whom the Qul-En expected to find its samples, there were insects. These, however, the tiny alien being disregarded. It would not be practical to get any great quantity of the substance it sought from such small organisms.

By nightfall of the day after its landing, the door of the ship opened and the explorer came out in a vehicle designed expressly for sampling on this planet. The vehicle came out, stood on its hind legs, closed the door, and piled brush back to hide it. Then it moved away with the easy, feline gait of a mountain lion. At a distance of two feet it was a mountain lion. It was a magnificent job of adapting Qul-En engineering to the production of a device which would carry a small-bodied explorer about a strange world without causing remark. The explorer nested in a small cabin occupying the space—in the facsimile lion—that had been occupied by the real lion's lungs. The fur of the duplicate was convincing; its eyes were excellent, housing scanning-cells which could make use of anything from ultraviolet far down into the infra-red. Its claws were retractable and of plastic much stronger and keener than the original lion's claws. It had other equipment, including a weapon against which nothing on this planet could stand, and for zoological sampling it had one remarkable advantage. It had no animal smell; it was all metal and plastics.

On the first night of its roaming, nothing in particular happened. The explorer became completely familiar with the way the controls of the machine worked. As a machine, of course, it was vastly more powerful than an animal. It could make leaps no mere creature of flesh and blood could duplicate; its balancing devices were admirable; it was, naturally, immune to fatigue. The Qul-En inside it was pleased with the job.

That night Antonio and Salazar bedded down their sheep in a natural amphitheatre and Antonio slept heavily, snoring. He was a highly superstitious ancient, so he wore various charms of a quasi-religious nature. Salazar merely turned around three times and went to sleep. But while the man slept soundly, Salazar woke often. Once he waked sharply at a startled squawking among the lambs. He got up and trotted over to make sure that everything was all right, sniffed the air suspiciously. Then he went back, scratched where a flea had bitten him, bit—nibbling—at a place his paws could not reach, and went back to sleep. At midnight he made a clear circle around his flock and went back to slumber with satisfaction. Toward dawn he raised his head suspiciously at the sound of a coyote's howl, but the howl was far away. Salazar dozed until daybreak, when he rose, shook himself, stretched himself elaborately, scratched thoroughly, and was ready for a new day. The man waked, wheezing, and cooked breakfast; it appeared that the normal order of things would go undisturbed.

For a time it did; there was certainly no disturbance at the ship. The small silvery vessel was safely hidden. There was a tiny, flickering light inside—the size of a pin-point—which wavered and changed color constantly where a sort of tape unrolled before it. It was a recording device, making note of everything the roaming pseudo-mountain lion's eyes saw and everything its microphonic ears listened to. There was a bank of air-purifying chemical which proceeded to regenerate itself by means of air entering through a small ventilating slot. It got rid of carbon dioxide and stored up oxygen in its place, in readiness for further voyaging.

Of course, ants explored the whole outside of the space-vessel, and some went inside through the ventilator-opening. They began to cart off some interesting if novel foodstuff they found within. Some very tiny beetles came exploring, and one variety found the air-purifying chemical refreshing. Numbers of that sort of beetle moved in and began to raise large families. A minuscule moth, too, dropped eggs lavishly in the nest-like space in which the Qul-En explorer normally reposed during space-flight. But nothing really happened.

Not until late morning. It was two hours after breakfast-time when Salazar found traces of the mountain lion which was not a mountain lion. He found a rabbit that had been killed. Having been killed, it had very carefully been opened up, its various internal organs spread out for examination, and its nervous system traced in detail. Its brain-tissue, particularly, had been most painstakingly dissected, so the amount of a certain complex hormone to be found in it could be calculated with precision. The Qul-En in the lion shape had been vastly pleased to find the sought-for hormone in another animal besides a mountain lion.

The dissection job was a perfect anatomical demonstration; no instructor in anatomy could have done better, and few neuro-surgeons could have done as well with the brain. It was, in fact, a perfect laboratory job done on a flat rock in the middle of a sheep-range, and duly reproduced on tape by a flickering, color-changing light. The reproduction, however, was not as good as it should have been, because the tape was then covered by small ants who had found its coating palatable and were trying to clean it off.

Salazar saw the rabbit. There were blow-flies buzzing about it, and a buzzard was reluctantly flying away because of his approach. Salazar barked at the buzzard. Antonio heard the barking; he came.

Antonio was ancient, superstitious, and unwashed. He came wheezing, accompanied by flies who had not finished breakfasting on the bits of his morning meal he had dropped on his vest. Salazar wagged his tail and barked at the buzzard. The rabbit had been neatly dissected, but not eaten. The cuts which opened it up were those of a knife or scalpel. It was not—it was definitely not!—the work of an animal. But there were mountain-lion tracks, and nothing else. More, every one of the tracks was that of a hind foot! A true mountain lion eats what he catches; he does not stand on his hind paws and dissect it with scientific precision. Nothing earthly had done this!

Antonio's eyes bulged out. He thought instantly of magic, Black Magic. He could not imagine dissection in the spirit of scientific inquiry; to him, anything that killed and then acted in this fashion could only come from the devil.

He gasped and fled, squawking. When he had run a good hundred yards, Salazar caught up to him, very much astonished. He overtook his master and went on ahead to see what had scared the man so. He made casts to right and left, then went in a conscientious circle all around the flock under his care. Presently he came back to Antonio, his tongue lolling out, to assure him that everything was all right. But Antonio was packing, with shaking hands and a sweat-streaked brow.

In no case is the neighborhood of a mountain lion desirable for a man with a flock of sheep. But this was no ordinary mountain lion. Why, Salazar—honest, stout-hearted Salazar—did not scent a mountain lion in those tracks. He would have mentioned it vociferously if he had, so this was beyond nature. The lion was *un fantasmo* or worse; Antonio's thoughts ran to were-tigers, ghost-lions, and sheer Indian devils. He packed, while Salazar scratched fleas and wondered what was the matter.

They got the flock on the move. The sheep made idiotic efforts to disperse and feed placidly where they were. Salazar rounded them up and drove them on. It was hard work, but even Antonio helped in frantic energy—which was unusual.

Near noon, four miles from their former grazing-ground, there were mountain-peaks all around them. Some were snow-capped, and there were vistas of illimitable distance everywhere. It was very beautiful indeed, but Antonio did not notice; Salazar came upon buzzards again.

He chased them with loud barkings from the meal they reluctantly shared with blow-flies and ants. This time it wasn't a rabbit; it was a coyote. It had been killed and most painstakingly taken apart to provide at a glance all significant information about the genus *canis,* species *latrans,* in the person of an adult male coyote. It was a most enlightening exhibit; it proved conclusively that there was a third type of animal, structurally different from both mountain lions and rabbits, which had the same general type of nervous system, with a mass of nerve-tissue in one large mass in a skull, which nerve-tissue contained the same high percentage of the desired hormone as the previous specimens. Had it been recorded by a tiny colored flame in the hidden ship —the flame was now being much admired by small red bugs and tiny spiders—it would have been proof that the Qul-En would find ample supplies on Earth of the complex hormone on which the welfare of their race now depended. Some members of the Qul-En race, indeed, would have looked no farther. But sampling which involved only three separate species and gave no proof of their frequency was not quite enough; the being in the synthetic mountain lion was off in search of further evidence.

Antonio was hardly equipped to guess at anything of this sort. Salazar led him to the coyote carcass; it had been neatly halved down the breastbone. One half the carcass had been left intact; the other half was completely anatomized, and the brain had been beautifully dissected and spread out for measurement. Antonio realized that intelligence had been at work. But—again—he saw only the pad-tracks of a mountain lion, and he was literally paralyzed by horror.

Antonio was scared enough to be galvanized into unbelievable energy. He would have fled gibbering to Ensenada Springs, some forty miles as the crow flies, but to flee would be doom itself. The devils who did this sort of work liked—he knew—to spring upon a man alone. But they can be fooled.

The Qul-En in the artificial mountain lion was elated. To the last quivering appendage on the least small tentacle of its body, the pilot of the facsimile animal was satisfied. It had found good evidence that the desired nervous system and concentration of the desired hormone in a single mass of nerve-tissue was normal on this planet! The vast majority of animals should have it. Even the local civilized race might have skulls with brains in them, and, from the cities observed from the stratosphere, that race might be the most numerous fair-sized animal on the planet!

It was to be hoped for, because large quantities of the sought-for hormone were needed; taking specimens from cities would be most convenient. Long-continued existence under the artificial conditions of civilization—a hundred thousand years of it, no less—had brought about exhaustion of the Qul-Ens' ability to create all their needed hormones in their own bodies. Tragedy awaited the race unless the most critically needed substance was found. But now it had been!

Antonio saw it an hour later, and wanted to shriek; it looked exactly like a mountain lion, but he knew it was not flesh and blood because it moved in impossible bounds. No natural creature could leap sixty feet; the mountain-lion shape did. But it was convincingly like its prototype to the eye. It stopped, and regarded the flock of sheep, made soaring progression to the front of the flock, and came back again. Salazar ignored it. Neither he nor the sheep scented carnivorous animal life. Antonio hysterically concluded that it was invisible to them; he began an elaborate, lunatic pattern of behavior to convince it that magic was at work against it, too.

He began to babble to his sheep with infinite politeness, spoke to blank-eyed creatures as *Senor* Gomez and *Senora* Onate. He chatted feverishly with a wicked-eyed ram, whom he called *Senor* Guttierez. A clumsy, wabbling lamb almost upset him, and he scolded the infant sheep as Pepito. He lifted his hat with great gallantry to a swollen ewe, hailing her as *Senora* Garcia, and observed in a quavering voice that the flies were very bad today. He moved about in his flock, turning the direction of its march and acting as if surrounded by a crowd of human beings. This should at least confuse the devil whom he saw. And while he chatted with seeming joviality, the sweat poured down his face in streams.

Salazar took no part in this deception. The sheep were fairly docile, once started; he was able to pause occasionally to scratch, and once even to do a luxurious, thorough job on that place in his back between his hind legs which is so difficult to reach. There was only one time when he had any difficulty. That was when there was a sort of eddying of the sheep, ahead. There were signs of panic. Salazar went trotting to the spot. He found sheep milling stupidly, and rams pawing the ground defying they had no idea what. Salazar found a deer-carcass on the ground and the smell of fresh blood in the air and the sheep upset because of it. He drove them on past, barking where barking would serve and nipping flanks where necessary—afterward disgustedly tonguing bits of wool out of his mouth.

The sheep went on. But Antonio, when he came to the deer-carcass, went icy-cold in the most exquisite of terror; the deer had been killed by a mountain lion—there were tracks about. Then it, too, had been cut into as if by a dissector's scalpel, but the job was incomplete. Actually, the pseudo-mountain lion had been interrupted by the approach of the flock. There were hardly blow-flies on the spot as yet. Antonio came to it as he chatted insanely with a sheep with sore eyes and a halo of midges about its head, whom he addressed as *Senorita* Carmen. But when he saw the deer his throat clicked shut. He was speechless.

To pass a creature laid out for magical ceremony was doom indubitable, but Antonio acted from pure desperation. He recited charms which were stark paganism and would involve a heavy penance when next he went to confession. He performed other actions, equally deplorable; when he went on, the deer was quite spoiled for neat demonstration of the skeletal, circulatory, muscular and especially the nervous system and brain-structure of genus *cervus*, species *dama*, specimen an adult doe. Antonio had piled over the deer all the brush within reach, had poured over it the kerosene he had for his night-lantern, and had set fire to the heap with incantations that made it a wholly impious sacrifice to quite nonexistent heathen demons.

Salazar, trotting back to the front of the flock after checking on Antonio and the rear-guard, wrinkled his nose and sneezed as he went past the blaze again. Antonio tottered on after him. But Antonio's impiety had done no good. The tawny shape bounded back into sight among the boulders on the hillside. It leaped with infinite grace for impossible distances. Naturally! No animal can be as powerful as a machine, and the counterfeit mountain lion was a machine vastly better than men could make.

The Qul-En now zestfully regarded the flock of sheep. It looked upon Salazar and Antonio with no less interest. The Qul-En explorer was an anatomist and organic chemist rather than a zoologist proper, but it guessed that the dog was probably a scavenger and that the man had some symbiotic relationship to the flock.

Salazar, the dog, was done a grave injustice in that estimate. Even Antonio was given less than he deserved. Now he was gray with horror. The blood in his veins turned to ice as he saw the false mountain lion bounding back upon the hillside. No normal wild creature would display itself so openly. Antonio considered himself both doomed and damned; stark despair filled him. But with shaking hands and no hope at all, he carved a deep cross on the point of a bullet for his ancient rifle. Licking his lips, he made similar incisions on other bullets in reserve.

The Qul-En vehicle halted. The flock had been counted; now to select specimens and get to work. There were six new animal types to be dissected for the nervous organ yielding the looked-for hormone. Four kinds of sheep—male and female, and adult and immature of each kind—the biped, and the dog. Then a swift survey to estimate the probable total number of such animals available, and—

Antonio saw that the devil mountain lion was still. He got down on one knee, fervently crossed himself and fed a cross-marked bullet into the chamber of his rifle. He lined up the sights on the unearthly creature. The lion-facsimile watched him interestedly; the sight of a rifle meant nothing to the Qul-En, naturally. But the kneeling posture of the man was strange. It was part, perhaps, of the pattern of conduct which had led him to start that oxidation process about the deer-specimen.

Antonio fired. His hands trembled and the rifle shook; nothing happened. He fired again and again, gasping in his fear. And he missed every time.

The cross-marked bullets crashed into red earth and splashed from naked rock all about the Qul-En vehicle. When sparks spat from a flint pebble, the pilot of the mountain lion realized that there was actual danger here. It could have slaughtered man and dog and sheep by the quiver of a tentacle, but that would have ruined them as specimens. To avoid spoiling specimens it intended to take later, the Qul-En put the mountain-lion shape into a single, magnificent leap. It soared more than a hundred feet up-hill and over the crest at its top; then it was gone.

Salazar ran barking after the thing at which Antonio had fired, sniffed at the place from which it had taken off. There was no animal smell there at all. He sneezed, and then trotted down again. Antonio lay flat on the ground, his eyes hidden, babbling. He had seen irrefutable proof that the shape of the mountain lion was actually a fiend from hell.

Behind the hill-crest, the Qul-En moved away. It had not given up its plan of selecting specimens from the flock, of course, nor of anatomizing the man and dog. It was genuinely interested, too, in the biped's novel method of defense. It dictated its own version of the problems raised, on a tight beam to the wavering, color-changing flame. Why did not the biped prey on the sheep if it could kill them? What was the symbiotic relationship of the dog to the man and the sheep? The three varieties of animal associated freely. The Qul-En dictated absorbed speculations, then it hunted for other specimens. It found a lobo wolf, and killed it, verified that this creature also could be a source of hormones. It slaughtered a chipmunk and made a cursory examination. Its ray-beam had pretty well destroyed the creature's brain-tissue, but by analogy of structure this should be a source also.

In conclusion, the Qul-En made a note via the wavering pin-point of flame that the existence of a hormone-bearing nervous system, centralized in a single mass of hormone-bearing nerve-tissue inside a bony structure, seemed universal among the animals of this planet. Therefore it would merely examine the four other types of large animal it had discovered, and take off to present its findings to the Center of its race. With a modification of the ray-beam to kill specimens without destroying the desired hormone, the Qul-En could unquestionably secure as much as the race could possibly need. Concentrations of the local civilized race in cities should make large-scale collection of the hormone practical unless that civilized race was an exception to the general nervous structure of all animals so far observed.

This was dictated to the pin-point flame, and the flame faithfully wavered and changed color to make the record. But the tape did not record it; a rather large beetle had jammed the tape-reel. It was squashed in the process, but it effectively messed up the recording apparatus. Even before the tape stopped moving, though, the record had become defective; tiny spiders had spun webs, earwigs got themselves caught. The flame, actually, throbbed and pulsed restlessly in a cobwebby coating of gossamer and tiny insects. Silverfish were established in the plastic lining of the Qul-En ship; beetles multiplied enormously in the air-refresher chemical; moth-larvae already gorged themselves on the nest-material of the intrepid explorer outside. Ants were busy on the food-stores. Mites crawled into the ship to prey on their larger fellows, and a praying-mantis or so had entered to eat their smaller ones. There was an infinite number of infinitesimal flying things dancing in the dark; larger spiders busily spun webs to snare them, and flies of various sorts were attracted by odors coming out of the ventilator-opening, and centipedes rippled sinuously inside—

Night fell upon the world. The pseudo-mountain lion roamed the wild, keeping in touch with the tide of baa-ing sheep now headed for the lowlands. It captured a field-mouse and verified the amazing variety of planetary forms containing brain-tissue rich in hormones. But the sheep-flock could not be driven at night. When stars came out, to move them farther became impossible. The Qul-En returned to select its specimens in the dark, with due care not to allow the man to use his strange means of defense. It found the flock bedded down.

Salazar and Antonio rested; they had driven the sheep as far as it was possible to drive them, that day. Though he was sick with fear and weak with horror, Antonio had struggled on until Salazar could do no more. But he did not leave the flock; the sheep were in some fashion a defense—if only a diversion—against the creature which so plainly was not flesh and blood.

He made a fire, too, because he could not think of staying in the dark. Moths came and fluttered about the flames, but he did not notice. He tried to summon courage. After all, the unearthly thing had fled from bullets marked with a cross, even though they missed; with light to shoot by, he might make a bull's-eye. So Antonio sat shivering by his fire, cutting deeper crosses into the points of his bullets, his throat dry and his heart pounding while he listened to the small noises of the sheep and the faint thin sounds of the wilderness.

Salazar dozed by the fire. He had had a very hard day, but even so he slept lightly. When something howled, very far away, instantly the dog's head went up and he listened. But it was nowhere near; he scratched himself and relaxed. Once something hissed and he opened his eyes.

Then he heard a curious, strangled *"Baa-a-a."* Instantly he was racing for the spot. Antonio stood up, his rifle clutched fast. Salazar vanished. Then the man heard an outburst of infuriated barking; Salazar was fighting something, and he was not afraid of it, he was enraged. Antonio moved toward the spot, his rifle ready.

The barking raced for the slopes beyond the flock. It grew more enraged and more indignant still. Then it stopped. There was silence. Antonio called, trembling. Salazar came paddling up to him, whining and snarling angrily. He could not tell Antonio that he had come upon something in the shape of a mountain lion, but which was not—it didn't smell right—carrying a mangled sheep away from its fellows.

He couldn't explain that he'd given chase, but the shape made such monstrous leaps that he was left behind and pursuit was hopeless. Salazar made unhappy, disgusted, disgraced noises to himself. He bristled; he whined bitterly. He kept his ears pricked up and he tried twice to dart off on a cast around the whole flock, but Antonio called him back. Antonio felt safer with the dog beside him.

Off in the night, the Qul-En operating the mountain-lion shape caused the vehicle to put down the sheep and start back toward the flock. It would want at least four specimens besides the biped and the dog, but the dog was already on the alert. The Qul-En had not been able to kill the dog, because the mouth of the lion was closed on the sheep. It would probably be wisest to secure the dog and biped first —the biped with due caution—and then complete the choice of sheep for dissection.

The mountain-lion shape came noiselessly back toward the flock. The being inside it felt a little thrill of pleasure. Scientific exploration was satisfying, but rarely exciting; one naturally protected oneself adequately when gathering specimens. But it was exciting to have come upon a type of animal which would dare to offer battle. The Qul-En in the mountain-lion shape reflected that this was a new source of pleasure—to do battle with the fauna of strange planets in the forms native to those planets.

The padding vehicle went quietly in among the wooly sheep. It saw the tiny blossom of flame that was Antonio's campfire. Another high-temperature oxidation process . . . It would be interesting to see if the biped was burning another carcass of its own killing. . . .

The shape was two hundred yards from the fire when Salazar scented it. It was upwind from the dog; its own smell was purely that of metals and plastics, but the fur, now, was bedabbled with the blood of the sheep which had been its first specimen of the night. Salazar growled. His hackles rose, every instinct for the defense of his flock. He had smelled that blood when the thing which wasn't a mountain lion left him behind with impossible leapings.

He went stiff-legged toward the shape. Antonio followed in a sort of despairing calm born of utter hopelessness.

A sheep uttered a strangled noise. The Qul-En had come upon a second specimen which was exactly what it wished. It left the dead sheep behind for the moment, while it went to look at the fire. It peered into the flames, trying to see if Antonio—the biped—had another carcass in the flames as seemed to be a habit. It looked—

Salazar leaped for its blood-smeared throat in utter silence and absolute ferocity. He would not have dreamed of attacking a real mountain lion with such utter lack of caution, but this was not a mountain lion. His weight and the suddenness of his attack caught the operator by surprise, the shape toppled over. Then there was an uproar of scared bleatings from sheep nearby, and bloodthirsty snarlings from

Salazar. He had the salty taste of sheep-blood in his mouth and a yielding plastic throat between his teeth.

The synthetic lion struggled absurdly. Its weapon, of course, was a ray-gun which was at once aimed and fired when the jaws opened wide. The being inside tried to clear and use that weapon. It would not bear upon Salazar; the Qul-En would have to make its device lie down, double up its mechanical body, and claw Salazar loose from its mechanical throat with the mechanical claws on its mechanical hind-legs. At first the Qul-En inside concentrated on getting its steed back on its feet.

That took time, because whenever Salazar's legs touched ground he used the purchase to shake the throat savagely. In fact, Antonio was within twenty yards when the being from the ship got its vehicle upright. It held the mechanical head high, then, to keep Salazar dangling while it considered how to dislodge him.

And it saw Antonio. For an instant, perhaps, the Qul-En was alarmed. But Antonio did not kneel; he made no motion which the pilot—seeing through infra-red-sensitive photocells in the lion's eyeballs—could interpret as offensive. So the machine moved boldly toward him. The dog dangling from its throat could be disregarded for the moment. The killing-ray was absolutely effective, but it did spread, and it did destroy the finer anatomical features of tissues it hit. Especially, it destroyed nerve-tissue outright. So the closer a specimen was when killed, the smaller the damaged area.

The being inside the mountain lion was pleasantly excited and very much elated. The biped stood stock-still, frozen by the spectacle of a mountain lion moving toward it with a snarling dog hanging disregarded at its throat. The biped would be a most interesting subject for dissection, and its means of offense would be most fascinating to analyze. . . .

Antonio's fingers, contracting as the shape from the ship moved toward him, did an involuntary thing. Quite without intention, they pulled the trigger of the rifle. The deeply cross-cut bullet seared Salazar's flank, removing a quarter-inch patch plastic and metal, hit a foreleg. Although that leg was largely plastic, what metal it contained being mostly magnesium for lightness, there were steel wires imbedded for magnetic purposes. The bullet smashed through plastic and magnesium, struck a spark upon the steel.

There was a flaring, sun-bright flash of flame, a dense cloud of smoke. The mountain-lion shape leaped furiously and the jerk dislodged the slightly singed Salazar and sent him rolling. The mountain-lion vehicle landed and rolled over and over, one leg useless and spouting monstrous, white, actinic fire. The being inside knew an instant's panic; then it felt yielding sheep-bodies below it, thrashed about violently and crazily, and at last the Qul-En jammed the flame-spurting limb deep into soft earth. The fire went out; but that leg of its vehicle was almost useless.

For an instant deadly rage filled the tiny occupant of the cabin where a mountain-lion's lungs should have been. Almost, it turned and opened the mouth of its steed and poured out the killing-beam. Almost. The flock would have died instantly, and the man and the dog, and all the things in the wild for miles. But that would not have been scientific; after all, this mission should be secret. And the biped . . .

The Qul-En ceased the thrashings of its vehicle. It thought coldly. Salazar raced up to it, barking with a shrillness that told of terror valorously combatted; he danced about, barking.

The Qul-En found a solution. Its vehicle rose on its hind legs and raced up the hillside. It was an emergency method of locomotion for which this particular vehicle was not designed, and it required almost inspired handling of the controls to achieve it. But the Qul-En inside was wholly competent; it guided the vehicle safely over the hilltop while Salazar made only feigned dashes after it. Safely away, the Qul-En stopped and deliberately experimented until the process of running on three legs developed. Then the mountain lion, which was not a mountain lion, went bounding through the night toward its hidden ship.

Within an hour, it clawed away the brush from the exit-port, crawled inside, and closed the port after it. As a matter of pure precaution, it touched the "take-off" control before it even came out of its vehicle.

The ventilation-opening closed—very nearly. The ship rose quietly and swiftly toward the skies. Its arrival had not been noted; its departure was quite unsuspected.

It wasn't until the Qul-En touched the switch for the ship's system of internal illumination to go on that anything appeared to be wrong. There was a momentary arc, and darkness. There was no interior illumination; ants had stripped insulation from essential wires. The lights were shorted. The Qul-En was bewildered; it climbed back into the mountain-lion shape to use the infra-red-sensitive scanning-cells.

The interior of the ship was a crawling mass of insect life. There were ants and earwigs, silverfish and mites, spiders and centipedes, mantises and beetles. There were moths, larvae, grubs, midges, gnats and flies. The recording-instrument was shrouded in cobweb and hooded in dust which was fragments of the bodies of the spiders' tiny victims. The air-refresher chemicals were riddled with the tunnels of beetles. Crickets devoured plastic parts of the ship and chirped loudly. And the controls —ah! the controls! Insulation stripped off here; brackets riddled or weakened or turned to powder there. The ship could rise, and it did. But there were no controls at all.

The Qul-En went into a rage deadly enough to destroy the insects of itself. The whole future of its race depended on the discovery of an adequate source of a certain hormone. That source had been found. Only the return of this one small ship—fifteen feet in diameter—was needed to secure the future of a hundred-thousand-year-old civilization.

And it was impeded by the insect-life of the planet left behind! Insect-life so low in nervous organization that the Qul-En had ignored it!

The ship was twenty thousand miles out from earth when the occupant of the mountain lion used its ray-beam gun to destroy all the miniature enemies of its race. The killing beam swept about the ship. Mites, spiders, beetles, larvae, silverfish and flies—everything died. Then the Qul-En crawled out and began to make repairs, furiously. The technical skill needed was not lacking; in hours, this same being had made a perfect counterfeit of a mountain lion to serve it as a vehicle. Tracing and replacing gnawed-away insulation would be merely a tedious task. The ship would return to its home planet; the future of the Qul-En race would be secure. Great ships, many times the size of this, would flash through emptiness and come to this planet with instruments specially designed for collecting specimens of the local fauna. The cities of the civilized race would be the simplest and most ample sources of the so-desperately-needed hormone, no doubt. The inhabitants of even one city would furnish a stop-gap supply. In time—why—it would become systematic. The hormone would be gathered from this continent at this time, and from that continent at that, allowing the animals and the civilized race to breed for a few years in between collections. Yes . . .

The Qul-En worked feverishly. Presently it felt a vague discomfort; it worked on. The discomfort increased; it could discover no reason for it. It worked on, feverishly. . . .

Back on Earth, morning came. The sun rose slowly and the dew lay heavy on the mountain grasses. Faraway peaks were just beginning to be visible through clouds that had lain on them overnight. Antonio still trembled, but Salazar slept. When the sun was fully risen he arose and shook himself; he stretched elaborately, scratched thoroughly, shook himself again and was ready for a new day. When Antonio tremblingly insisted that they drive the flock on toward the lowlands, Salazar assisted. He trotted after the flock and kept them moving; that was his business.

Out in space, the silvery ship suddenly winked out of existence. Enough of its circuits had been repaired to put it in overdrive. The Qul-En was desperate, by that time. It felt itself growing weaker, and it was utterly necessary to reach its own race and report the salvation it had found for them. The record of the flickering flame was ruined. The Qul-En felt that itself was dying. But if it could get near enough to any of the planetary systems inhabited by its race, it could signal them and all would be well.

Moving ever more feebly, the Qul-En managed to get lights on within the ship again. Then it found what it considered the cause of its increasing weakness and spasmodic, gasping breaths. In using the killing-ray it had swept all the interior of the ship. But not the mountain-lion shape. Naturally! And the mountain-lion shape had killed specimens and carried them about. While its foreleg flamed, it had even rolled on startled, stupid sheep. It had acquired fleas—perhaps some from Salazar—and ticks. The fleas and ticks had not been killed; they now happily inhabited the Qul-En.

The Qul-En tried desperately to remain alive until a message could be given to its people, but it was not possible. There was a slight matter the returning explorer was too much wrought up to perceive, and the instruments that would have reported it were out of action because of destroyed insulation. When the ventilation-slit was closed as the ship took off, it did not close completely; a large beetle was in the way. There was a most tiny but continuous leakage of air past the crushed chitinous armor. The Qul-En in the ship died of oxygen-starvation without realizing what had happened, just as human pilots sometimes black out from the same cause before they know what is the matter. So the little silvery ship never came out of overdrive. It went on forever, or until its source of power failed.

The fleas and ticks, too, died in time; they died very happily, very full of Qul-En body-fluid. And they never had a chance to report to their fellows that the Qul-En were very superior hosts.

The only entity who could report told this story and was laughed at. Only his cronies, ignorant and superstitious men like himself, could believe in the existence of a thing not of earth, in the shape of a mountain lion that leaped hundreds of feet at a time, which dissected wild creatures and made magic over them, but fled from bullets marked with a cross and bled flame and smoke when such a bullet wounded it.

Such a thing, of course, was absurd!

Theodore Sturgeon

MEWHU'S JET

"WE INTERRUPT this program to announce—"

"Jack! Don't jump like that! And you've dropped ashes all over your—"

"Aw, Iris, honey, let me listen to—"

—at first identified as a comet, the object is pursuing an erratic course through the stratosphere, occasionally dipping as low as—"

This story, like all of Sturgeon's, is a particularly remarkable accomplishment for a man who is circulation promotion expert for Time-Life-Fortune! Of course, he did not have that job when he wrote the story, and one can only hope that having the job will not inhibit him from writing more that are just as good.

"You make me nervous, Jack! You're an absolute slave to the radio. I wish you paid that much attention to me."

"Darling, I'll argue the point, or pay attention to you, or anything in the wide world you like when I've heard this announcement; but please, *please* LET ME LISTEN!"

"—*dents of the East Coast are warned to watch for the approach of this ob*—"

"Iris, don't—"

Click!

"Well, of all the selfish, inconsiderate, discourteous—"

"That will do, Jack Garry! It's my radio as much as yours, and I have a right to turn it off when I want to!"

"Might I ask why you find it necessary to turn it off at this moment?"

"Because I know the announcement will be repeated any number of times if it's important, and you'll shush me every time. Because I'm not interested in that kind of thing and don't see why I should have it rammed down my throat. Because the only thing you ever want to listen to is something which couldn't possibly affect us. But mostly because you *yelled* at me!"

"I did *not* yell at you!"

"You *did!* And you're yelling *now!*"

"Mom! Daddy!"

"Oh, Molly, darling, we woke you up!"

"Poor bratlet. Hey—what about your slippers?"

"It isn't cold tonight, Daddy. What was that on the radio?"

"Something buzzing around in the sky, darling, I didn't hear it all."

"A spaceship, I betcha."

"You see? You and your so-called science-fiction!"

"Call us a science-faction. The kid's got more judgment than you have."

"You have as little judgment as a seven-year-old child, you mean. And b-besides, you're turning her a-against me!"

"Aw, for Pete's sake, Mom, don't cry!"

At which point, something like a giant's fist clouted off the two-room top story of the seaside cottage and scattered it down the beach. The lights winked out, and outside, the whole waterfront lit up with a brief, shattering blue glare.

"Jacky, darling, are you hurt?"

"Mom, he's bleedin'!"

"Jack, honey, say something. *Please* say something."

"Urrrrgh," said Jack Garry obediently, sitting up with a soft clatter of pieces of falling lath and plaster. He put his hands gently on the sides of his head and whistled. "Something hit the house."

His red-headed wife laughed half-hysterically. "Not really, darling." She put her arms around him, whisked some dust out of his hair, and began stroking his neck. "I'm . . . frightened, Jack."

"You're frightened!" He looked around, shakily, in the dim moonlight that filtered in. Radiance from an unfamiliar place caught his bleary gaze, and he clutched Iris' arm. "Upstairs . . . it's gone!" he said hoarsely, struggling to his feet. "Molly's room . . . Molly—"

"I'm here, Daddy. Hey! You're squeezin'!"

"Happy little family," said Iris, her voice trembling. "Vacationing in a quiet little cottage by the sea, so Daddy can write technical articles while Mummy regains her good disposition—without a phone, without movies within miles, and living in a place where the roof flies away. Jack—what hit us?"

"One of those things you were talking about," said Jack sardonically. "One of the things you refuse to be interested in, that couldn't possibly affect us. Remember?"

"The thing the radio was talking about?"

"I wouldn't be surprised. We'd better get out of here. This place may fall in on us, or burn, or something."

"An' we'll all be kilt," crooned Molly.

"Shut up, Molly! Iris, I'm going to poke around. Better go on out and pick us a place to pitch the tent—if I can find the tent."

"Tent?" Iris gasped.

"Boy oh boy," said Molly.

"Jack Garry, I'm not going to go to bed in a tent. Do you realize that this place will be swarming with people in no time flat?"

"O.K.—O.K. Only get out from under what's left of the house. Go for a swim. Take a walk. Or g'wan to bed in Molly's room, if you can find it. Iris, you can pick the oddest times to argue!"

"I'm not going out there by myself!"

Jack sighed. "I should've asked you to stay in here," he muttered. "If you're not the contrariest woman ever to— Be quiet, Molly!"

"I didn't say anything."

Meeew-w-w!

"Aren't you doing that caterwauling?"

"No, Daddy, truly."

Iris said, "I'd say a cat was caught in the wreckage except that cats are smart and no cat would ever come near this place."

Wuh-wuh-muh-meeee-ew-w-w!

"What a dismal sound!"

"Jack, that isn't a cat."

"Well, stop shaking like the well-known aspen leaf."

Molly said, "Not without aspen Daddy's leaf to do it."

"Molly! You're too young to make bad puns!"

"Sorry, Daddy. I forgot."

Mmmmmew. Mmm—m-m-m.

"Whatever it is," Jack said, "it can't be big enough to be afraid of and make a funny little noise like that." He squeezed Iris' arm and, stepping carefully over the rubble, began peering in and around it. Molly scrambled beside him. He was about to caution her against making so much noise, and then thought better of it. What difference would a little racket make?

The noise was not repeated, and five minutes' searching elicited nothing. Garry went back to his wife, who was fumbling around the shambles of a living room, pointlessly setting chairs and coffee tables back on their legs.

"I didn't find anyth—"

"YIPE!"

"Molly! What is it?"

Molly was just outside, in the shrubbery. "Oh . . . oh— Daddy, you better come quick!"

Spurred by the urgency of her tone, he went crashing outside. He found Molly standing rigid, trying to cram both her fists in her mouth at the same time. And at her feet was a man with silver-gray skin and a broken arm, who mewed at him.

"—Guard and Navy Department have withdrawn their warnings. The pilot of a Pan American transport has reported that the object disappeared into the zenith. It was last seen eighteen miles east of Normandy Beach, New Jersey. Reports from the vicinity describe it as traveling very slowly, with a hissing noise. Although it reached within a few feet of the ground several times, no damage has been reported. Inves—"

"Think of that," said Iris, switching off the little three-way portable. "No damage."

"Yeah. And if no one saw the thing hit, no one will be out here to investigate. So you can retire to your downy couch in the tent without fear of being interviewed."

"Go to sleep? Are you mad? Sleep in that flimsy tent with that mewing monster lying there?"

"Oh heck, Mom, he's sick! He wouldn't hurt anybody."

They sat around a cheerful fire, fed by roof shingles. Jack had set up the tent without much trouble. The silver-gray man was stretched out in the shadows, sleeping lightly and emitting an occasional moan.

Jack smiled at Iris. "Y'know, I love your silly chatter, darling. The way you turned to and set his arm was a pleasure to watch. You didn't think of him as a monster while you were tending to him."

"Didn't I, though? Maybe 'monster' was the wrong word to use. Jack, he has only one bone in his forearm!"

"He has what? Oh, nonsense, honey! 'Tain't scientific. He'd have to have a ball-and-socket joint in his wrist."

"He *has* a ball and socket joint in his wrist."

"This I have to see," Jack muttered. He picked up a flash lantern and went over to the long prone figure.

Silver eyes blinked up at the light. There was something queer about them. He turned the beam closer. The pupils were not black in that light, but dark-green. They all but closed—from the sides, like a cat's. Jack's breath wheezed out. He ran the light over the man's body. It was clad in a bright-blue roomy bathrobe effect, with a yellow sash. The sash had a buckle which apparently consisted of two pieces of yellow metal placed together; there seemed to be nothing to keep them together. They just stayed. When the man had fainted, just as they found him, it had taken almost all Jack's strength to pull them apart.

"Iris."

She got up and came over to him. "Let the poor devil sleep."

"Iris—what color was his robe?"

"Red, with a . . . but it's *blue!*"

"Is now. Iris, what on earth have we got here?"

"I don't know. I don't know. Some poor thing that escaped from an institution for . . . for—"

"For what?"

"How should I know?" she snapped. "There must be some place where they send creatures that get born like that."

"Creatures don't get born like that. Iris, he isn't deformed. He's just different."

"I see what you mean. I don't know why I see what you mean, but I'll tell you something." She stopped, and was quiet for so long that he turned to her, surprised. She said slowly, "I ought to be afraid of him, because he's strange, and ugly, but—I'm not."

"Me, too."

"Molly, go back to bed!"

"He's a leprechaun."

"Maybe you're right. Go on to bed, chicken, and in the morning you can ask him where he keeps his crock of gold."

"Gee." She went off a little way then stood on one foot, drawing a small circle in the sand with the other. "Daddy."

"Yes, Molly-m'love."

"Can I sleep in the tent tomorrow, too?"

"If you're good."

"Daddy obviously means," said Iris acidly, "that if you're *not* good he'll have a roof on the house by tomorrow night."

"I'll be good." She disappeared into the tent.

"For kids," Jack said admiringly, "it never rains tomorrow."

The gray man mewed.

"Well, old guy, what is it?"

The man reached over and fumbled at his splinted arm.

"It hurts him," said Iris. She knelt beside him and, taking the wrist of his good arm, lifted it away from the splint, where he was clawing. The man did not resist, but lay and looked at her with pain-filled, slitted eyes.

"He has six fingers," Jack said. "See?" He knelt beside his wife and gently took the man's wrist. He whistled. "It *is* a ball and socket."

"Give him some aspirin."

"That's a good . . . wait." Jack stood pulling his lip in puzzlement. "Do you think we should?"

"Why not?"

"We don't know where he comes from. We know nothing of his body chemistry, or what any of our medicines might do to him."

"He . . . what do you mean, where he comes from?"

"Iris, will you open up your mind just a little? In the face of evidence like this, are you going to even attempt to cling to the idea that this man comes from anywhere on this earth?" Jack said with annoyance. "You know your anatomy. Don't tell me you ever saw a human freak with skin and bones like that! That belt buckle—that material in his clothes . . . come on, now. Drop your prejudices and give your brains a chance, will you?"

"You're suggesting things that simply don't *happen!*"

"That's what the man in the street said—in Hiroshima. That's what the old-time aeronaut said from the basket of his balloon when they told him about heavier-than-air craft. That's what—"

"All right, all right, Jack! I know the rest of the speech. If you want dialectics instead of what's left of a night's sleep, I might point out that the things you have mentioned have all concerned human endeavors. Show me any new plastic, a new metal, a new kind of engine, and though I may not begin to understand it, I can accept it because it is of human origin. But this . . . this man, or whatever he is—"

"I know," said Jack, more gently. "It's frightening because it's strange, and away down underneath we feel that anything strange is necessarily dangerous. That's why we wear our best manners for strangers and not for our friends—but I still don't think we should give this character any aspirin."

"He seems to breathe the same air we do. He perspires, he talks . . . I think he talks—"

"You have a point. Well, if it'll ease his pain at all, it may be worth trying. Give him just one."

Iris went to the pump with a collapsible cup from her first-aid kit, and filled it. Kneeling by the silver-skinned man, she propped up his head, gently put the aspirin between his lips, and brought the cup to his mouth. He sucked the water in greedily, and then went completely limp.

"Oh, oh. I was afraid of that."

Iris put her hand over the man's heart. "*Jack!*"

"Is he . . . what is it, Iris?"

"Not dead, if that's what you mean. Will you feel this?"

Jack put his hand beside Iris'. The heart was beating with massive, slow blows, about eight to the minute. Under it, out of phase completely with the main beat, was another, an extremely fast, sharp beat, which felt as if it were going about three hundred.

"He's having some sort of palpitation," Jack said.

"And in two hearts at once!"

Suddenly the man raised his head and uttered a series of ululating shrieks and howls. His eyes opened wide, and across them fluttered a translucent nictitating membrane. He lay perfectly still with his mouth open, shrieking and gargling. Then, with a lightning movement, he snatched Jack's hand to his mouth. A pointed tongue, light-orange and four inches longer than it had any right to be, flicked out and licked Jack's hand. Then the strange eyes closed, the shrieks died to a whimper and faded out, and the man relaxed.

"Sleeping now," said Iris. "Oh, I hope we haven't done anything to him!"

"We've done something. I just hope it isn't serious. Anyhow, his arm isn't bothering him any. That's all we were worried about in the first place."

Iris put a cushion under the man's oddly planed head, touched the beach mattress he was lying on to see that he would be comfortable. "He has a beautiful mustache," she said. "Like silver. He looks very old and wise, doesn't he?"

"So does an owl. Let's go to bed."

Jack woke early, from a dream in which he had bailed out of a flying motorcycle with an umbrella that turned into a candy cane as he fell. He landed in the middle of some sharp-toothed crags which gave like sponge rubber. He was immediately surrounded by mermaids who looked like Iris and who had hands shaped like spur gears. But nothing frightened him. He awoke smiling, inordinately happy.

Iris was still asleep. Outside, somewhere, he heard the tinkle of Molly's laugh. He sat up, looked at Molly's camp cot. It was empty.

Moving quietly, so as not to disturb his wife, he slid his feet into moccasins and went out.

Molly was on her knees beside their strange visitor, who was squatting on his haunches and—

They were playing patty-cake.

"Molly!"

"Yes, Daddy."

"What are you trying to do? Don't you realize that that man has a broken arm?"

"Oh gosh, I'm sorry. Do you s'pose I hurt him?"

"I don't know. It's very possible," said Jack Garry testily. He went to the alien, took his good hand.

The man looked up at him and smiled. His smile was peculiarly engaging. All of his teeth were pointed, and they were very widely spaced. "Eeee-yu mow madibu Mewhu," he said.

"That's his name," Molly said excitedly. She leaned forward and tugged at the man's sleeve. "Mewhu. Hey, Mewhu!" And she pointed at her chest.

"Mooly," said Mewhu. "Mooly—Geery."

"See, Daddy?" Molly said ecstatically. "See?" She pointed at her father. "Daddy. Dah—dee."

"Deedy," said Mewhu.

"No, silly! Daddy."

"Dewdy."

"Dah-dy!"

Jack, quite entranced, pointed at himself and said, "Jack."

"Jeek."

"Good enough. Molly, the man can't say 'ah.' He can say 'oo' or 'ee' but not 'ah.' That's good enough."

Jack examined the splints. Iris had done a very competent job. When she realized that instead of the radius-ulna development of a true human, Mewhu had only one bone in his forearm, she had set the arm and laid on two splints instead of one. Jack grinned. Intellectually, Iris would not accept Mewhu's existence even as a possibility; but as a nurse, she not only accepted his body structure but skillfully compensated for its differences.

"I guess he wants to be polite," said Jack to his repentant daughter, "and if you want to play patty-cake, he'll go along with you, even if it hurts. Don't take advantage of him, chicken."

"I won't, Daddy."

Jack started up the fire and had a green-stick crane built and hot water bubbling by the time Iris emerged. "Takes a cataclysm to get you to start breakfast," she grumbled through a pleased smile. "When were you a boy scout?"

"Matter of fact," said Garry, "I was once. Will modom now take over?"

"Modom will. How's the patient?"

"Thriving. He and Molly had a patty-cake tournament this morning. His clothes, by the way, are red again."

"Jack—where does he come from?"

"I haven't asked him yet. When I learn to caterwaul, or he learns to talk, perhaps we'll find out. Molly has already elicited the information that his name's Mewhu." Garry grinned. "And he calls me 'Jeek.'"

"Can't pronounce an 'r,' hm?"

"That'll do, woman. Get on with the breakfast."

While Iris busied herself over breakfast, Jack went to look at the house. It wasn't as bad as he had thought—a credit to poor construction. Apparently the upper two rooms were a late addition and had just been perched onto the older, comparatively flat-topped lower section. The frame of Molly's bed was bent beyond repair, but the box spring and mattress were intact. The old roof seemed fairly sound, where the removal of the jerry-built little top story had exposed it. The living room would be big enough for him and Iris, and Molly's bed could be set up in the study. There were tools and lumber in the garage, the weather was warm and clear, and like any other writer, Jack Garry was very much attracted by the prospect of hard work for which he would not get paid, as long as it wasn't writing. By the time Iris called him for breakfast, he had most of the debris cleared from the roof and a plan of action mapped out. It would only be necessary to cover the hole where the stairway landing had been, and go over the roof for potential leaks. A good rain, he reflected, would search those out for him quickly enough.

"What about Mewhu?" Iris asked as she handed him an aromatic plate of eggs and bacon. "If we feed him any of this, do you think he'll throw another fit?"

Jack looked at their visitor, who sat on the other side of the fire, very close to Molly, gazing big-eyed at their breakfasts.

"I don't know. We could give him a little, I suppose."

Mewhu inhaled his sample, and wailed for more. He ate a second helping, and when Iris refused to fry more eggs, he gobbled toast and jam. Each new thing he tasted he would nibble at, blink twice, and then bolt down. The only exception was the coffee. One taste was sufficient. He put it down on the ground and very carefully, very delicately overturned it.

"Can you talk to him?" Iris asked suddenly.

"He can talk to me," declared Molly.

"I've heard him," Jack said.

"Oh, no. I don't mean *that*," Molly denied vehemently. "I can't make any sense out of that stuff."

"What do you mean, then?"

"I . . . I dunno, Mommy. He just—talks to me, that's all."

Jack and Iris looked at each other. "Must be a game," said Iris. Jack shook his head, looking at his daughter carefully as if he had not really seen her before. He could think of nothing to say, and rose.

"Think the house can be patched up?"

"Oh sure." He laughed. "You never did like the color of the upstairs rooms, anyway."

"I don't know what's gotten into me," said Iris thoughtfully. "I'd have kicked like a mule at any part of this. I'd have packed up and gone home if, say, just a wall was gone upstairs, or if there were just a hole in the roof, or if this . . . this android phenomenon arrived suddenly. But when it all happens at once—I can take it all!"

"Question of perspective. Show me a nagging woman and I'll show you one who hasn't enough to worry about."

"You'll get out of my sight or you'll have this frying pan bounced off your yammering skull," said Iris steadily. Jack got.

Molly and Mewhu trailed after him as he returned to the house, stood side by side goggling at him as he mounted the ladder.

"Whatsha doing, Daddy?"

"Marking off the edges of this hole where the stairway hits the place where the roof isn't, so I can clean up the edges with a saw."

"Oh."

Jack roughed out the area with a piece of charcoal, lopped off the more manageable rough edges with a hatchet, cast about for his saw. It was still in the garage. He climbed down, got it, climbed up again, and began to saw. Twenty minutes of this, and sweat was streaming down his face. He knocked off, climbed down, doused his head at the pump, lit a cigarette, climbed back up on the roof.

"Why don't you jump off and back?"

The roofing job was looking larger and the day seemed warmer than it had. Jack's enthusiasm was in inverse proportion to these factors. "Don't be funny, Molly."

"Yes, but Mewhu wants to know."

"Oh, he does. Ask him to try it."

He went back to work. A few minutes later, when he paused for a breath, Mewhu and Molly were nowhere to be seen. Probably over by the tent, in Iris' hair, he thought, and went on sawing.

"Daddy!"

Daddy's unaccustomed arm and shoulder were, by this time, yelling for help. The dry soft-wood alternately cheesed the saw out of line and bound it. He answered impatiently, "Well, what?"

"Mewhu says to come. He wants to show you something."

"Show me what? I haven't time to play now, Molly. I'll attend to Mewhu when we get a roof over our heads again."

"But it's for you!"

"What is?"

"The thing in the tree."

"Oh, all right." Prompted more by laziness than by curiosity, Jack climbed back down the ladder. Molly was waiting. Mewhu was not in sight.

"Where is he?"

"By the tree," she said with exaggerated patience, taking his hand. "Come on. It's not far."

She led him around the house and across the bumpy track that was euphemistically known as a road. There was a tree down on the other side. He looked from it to the house, saw that in line with the felled tree and his damaged roof were more broken trees, where something had come down out of the sky, skimmed the tops of the trees, angling closer to the ground until it wiped the top off his house and had then risen up and up—to where?

They went deeper into the woods for ten minutes, skirting an occasional branch or fallen treetop, until they came to Mewhu, who was leaning against a young maple. He smiled, pointed up into the tree, pointed to his arm, to the ground. Jack looked at him in puzzlement.

"He fell out of the tree and broke his arm," said Molly.

"How do you know?"

"Well, he just did, Daddy."

"Nice to know. Now can I get back to work?"

"He wants you to get the thing in the tree!"

Jack looked upward. Hung on a fork two-thirds of the way up the tree was a gleaming object, a stick about five feet long with a streamlined shape on each end, rather like the wingtip tanks of a P-80. "What on earth is that?"

"I dunno. I can't— He tol' me, but I dunno. Anyway, it's for you, so you don't . . . so you don't—" She looked at Mewhu for a moment.

The alien's silver mustache seemed to swell a little. "—so you don't have to climb the ladder so much."

"Molly—how did you know that?"

"He *told* me, that's all. Gosh, Daddy, don't be mad. I don't know how, honest; he just did, that's all."

"I don't get it," muttered Jack. "Anyhow—what's this about that thing in the tree? I'm supposed to break my arm too?"

"It isn't dark."

"What do you mean by that?"

Molly shrugged. "Ask him."

"Oh. I think I catch that. He fell out of the tree because it was dark. He thinks I can get up there and get the whatzit without hurting myself because I can see what I am doing. He also flatters me. Or is it flattery? How close to the apes does he think we are?"

"What are you talking about, Daddy?"

"Never mind . . . why am I supposed to get that thing, anyway?"

"Uh—so's you can jump off the roof."

"That is just silly. However, I do want a look at that thing. Since his ship is gone, that object up there seems to be the only artifact he brought with him except his clothes."

"What's an artifact?"

"Second cousin to an artichoke. Here goes nothin'." And he swung up into the tree. He had not climbed a tree for years, and as he carefully chose his way, it occurred to him that there were probably more efficient ways of gaining altitude. An escalator, for example. Why didn't escalators grow on trees?

The tree began to shiver and sway with his weight. He looked down once and decided instantly not to do it again. He looked up and was gratified to see how close he was to the object he was after. He pulled himself up another three feet and was horrified at how far away it was, for the branches were very small up here. He squirmed upward, reached, and his fingers just brushed against the shank of the thing. It had two rings fastened to it, he noticed, one each side of the center, large enough to get an arm through. It was one of these which was hung up on a branch. He chinned himself, then, with his unpracticed muscles cracking, took one hand off and reached.

The one-hand chinning didn't come off so well. His arms began to sag. The ring broke off its branch as his weight came on it. He was immediately surrounded by the enthusiastic crackling of breaking shrubbery. He folded his tongue over and got his teeth on it. Since he had a grip on Mewhu's artifact, he held on . . . even when it came free. He began to fall, tensed himself for the bone-breaking jolt he would get at the bottom.

He didn't get it.

He fell quite fast at first, and then the stick he was holding began to bear him up. He thought that it must have caught on a branch, by some miracle—but it hadn't! He was drifting down like a thistle seed, hanging from the rod, which in some impossible fashion was supporting itself in midair. There was a shrill, faint *whooshing* sound from the two streamlined fixtures at the ends of the rod. He looked down, blinked sweat out of his eyes, looked again. Mewhu was grinning a broad and happy grin, and Molly was slack-jawed with astonishment.

The closer he came to the ground the slower he went. When, after what seemed an eternity, he felt the blessed pressure of earth under his feet, he had to stand and *pull* the rod down. It yielded slowly, like an eddy current brake. Dry leaves danced and whirled under the end pieces.

"Gee, Daddy, that was wonderful!"

He swallowed twice to wet down his dry esophagus, and pulled his eyes back in. "Yeah. Fun," he said weakly.

Mewhu came and took the rod out of his hand, and dropped it. It stayed perfectly horizontal, and sank slowly down to the ground, where it lay. Mewhu pointed at it, at the tree, and grinned.

"Just like a parachute. Oh, *gee*, Daddy!"

"You keep away from it," said Jack, familiar with youthful intonation. "Heaven knows what it is. It might go off, or something."

He looked fearfully at the object. It lay quietly, the hissing of the end pieces stilled. Mewhu bent suddenly and picked it up, held it over his head with one hand. Then he calmly lifted his feet and hung from it. It lowered him gently, butt first, until he sat on the ground, in a welter of dead leaves; for as soon as he picked it up, the streamlined end pieces had begun to blast again.

"That's the silliest thing I ever saw. Here—let me see it." It was hovering about waist-high. He leaned over one of the ends. It had a fine round grille over it. He put out a hand. Mewhu reached out and caught his wrist, shaking his head. Apparently it was dangerous to go too near those ends. Garry suddenly saw why. They were tiny, powerful jet motors of some kind. If the jet was powerful enough to support a man's weight, the intake must be drawing like mad—probably enough to snap a hole through a man's hand like a giant ticket-puncher.

But what controlled it? How was the jet strength adjusted to the weight borne by the device, and to the altitude? He remembered without pleasure that when he had fallen with it from the treetop, he had dropped quite fast, and that he went slower and slower as he approached the ground. And yet when Mewhu had held it over his head, it had borne his weight instantly and lowered him very slowly. And besides—how was it so stable? Why didn't it turn upside down and blast itself and passenger down to earth?

He looked at Mewhu with some increase of awe. Obviously he came from a place where the science was really advanced. He wondered if he would ever be able to get any technical information from his visitor—and if he would be able to understand it. Of course, Molly seemed to be able to—

"He wants you to take it back and try it on the roof," said Molly.

"How can that refugee from a Kuttner opus help me?"

Immediately Mewhu took the rod, lifted it, ducked under it, and slipped his arms through the two rings, so that it crossed his back like a water-bucket yoke. Peering around, he turned to face a clearing in the trees, and before their startled eyes, he leaped thirty feet in the air, drifted away in a great arc, and came gently to rest twenty yards away.

Molly jumped up and down and clapped her hands, speechless with delight. The only words Garry could find were a reiterated, "Ah, no!"

Mewhu stood where he was, smiling his engaging smile, waiting for them. They walked toward him, and when they were close, he leaped again and soared out toward the road.

"What do you do with a thing like this?" breathed Jack. "Who do you go to, and what do you say to him?"

"Le's just keep him for a pet, Daddy."

Jack took her hand, and they followed the bounding, soaring silver man. A pet! A member of some alien race, from some unthinkable civilization—and obviously a highly trained individual, too, for no "man in the street" would have made such a trip. What was his story? Was he an advance guard? Or—was he the sole survivor of his people? How far had he come? Mars? Venus?

They caught up with him at the house. He was standing by the ladder. His strange rod was lying quiet on the ground. He was fascinatedly operating Molly's yo-yo. When he saw them, he threw down the yo-yo, picked up his device, and slipping it across his shoulders, sprang high in the air and drifted down to the roof. "Eee-yu!" he said, with emphasis, and jumped off backward. So stable was the rod that, as he sank through the air, his long body swung to and fro.

"Very nice," said Jack. "Also spectacular. And I have to go back to work." He went to the ladder.

Mewhu bounded over to him, caught his arm, whimpering and whistling in his peculiar speech. He took the rod and extended it toward Jack.

"He wants you to use it," said Molly.

"No, thanks," said Jack, a trace of his tree-climbing vertigo returning to him. "I'd just as soon use the ladder." And he put his hand out to it.

Mewhu, hopping with frustration, reached past him and toppled the ladder. It levered over a box as it fell and struck Jack painfully on the shin.

"I guess you better use the flyin' belt, Daddy."

Jack looked at Mewhu. The silver man was looking as pleasant as he could with that kind of a face; on the other hand, it might just possibly be wise to humor him a little. Being safely on the ground to begin with, Jack felt that it might not matter if the fantastic thing wouldn't work for him. And if it failed him over the roof—well, the house wasn't *very* tall.

He shrugged his arms through the two rings. Mewhu pointed to the roof, to Jack, made a jumping motion. Jack took a deep breath, aimed carefully, and, hoping the gadget wouldn't work—jumped.

He shot up close to the house—too close. The eave caught him a resounding thwack on precisely the spot where the ladder had just hit him. The impact barely checked him. He went sailing up over the roof, hovered for a breathless second, and then began to come down. For a moment he thought his flailing legs would find purchase on the far edge of the roof. He just missed it. All he managed to do was to crack the same shin, in the same place, mightily on the other eave. Trailing clouds of profanity, he landed standing—in Iris' wash basket. Iris, just turning from the clothes line, confronted him.

"Jack! What on earth are you . . . get out of that! You're standing right on my wash with your dirty . . . *oh!*"

"Oh oh!" said Jack, and stepped backward out of the wash basket. His foot went into Molly's express wagon, which Iris used to carry the heavy basket. To get his balance, he leaped—and immediately rose high in the air. This time his luck was better. He soared completely over the kitchen wing of the house and came to earth near Molly and Mewhu.

"Daddy, you were just like a bird!"

"I'm going to be just like a corpse if your mother's expression means what I think it does." He shucked off the "flyin' belt" and dove into the house just as Iris rounded the corner. He heard Molly's delighted "He went *that* way" as he plowed through the shambles of the living room and out the front door. As the kitchen door slammed he was rounding the house. He charged up to Mewhu, snatched the gadget from him, slipped it on and jumped. This time his judgment was faultless. He cleared the house easily although he came very near landing astride the clothesline. When Iris, panting and furious, stormed out of the house, he was busily hanging sheets.

"Just what," said Iris, her voice crackling at the seams, "do you think you're doing?"

"Just giving you a hand with the laundry, m'love," said Jack.

"What is that . . . that object on your back?"

"Another evidence of the ubiquity of the devices of science-fiction," said Jack blandly. "This is a multilateral, three-dimensional mass adjuster, or pogo-chute. With it I can fly like a gull, evading the cares of the world and the advances of beautiful redheads, at such times as their passions are distasteful to me."

"Sometime in the very near future, you gangling hatrack, I am going to pull the tongue out of your juke box of a head and tie a bowknot in it." Then she laughed.

He heaved a sigh of relief, went and kissed her. "Darling, I am sorry. I was scared silly, dangling from this thing. I didn't see your clothes basket, and if I had I don't know how I'd have steered clear."

"What is it, Jack? How does it work?"

"I dunno. Jets on the ends. They blast hard when there's a lot of weight pushing them toward the earth. They blast harder near the earth than up high. When the weight on them slacks off a bit, they throttle down. What makes them do it, what they are using for power—I just wouldn't know. As far as I can see, they suck in air at the top and blow it out through the jets. And, oh yes—they point directly downward no matter which way the rod is turned."

"Where did you get it?"

"Off a tree. It's Mewhu's. Apparently he used it for a parachute. On the way down, a tree branch speared through one of these rings and he slipped out of it and fell and broke his arm."

"What are we going to do with him, Jack?"

"I've been worrying about that myself. We can't sell him to a sideshow." He paused, thoughtfully. "There's no doubt that he has a lot that would be of value to humanity. Why—this thing alone would change the face of the earth! Listen—I weigh a hundred and seventy. I *fell* on this thing, suddenly, when I lost my grip on a tree, and it bore my weight immediately. Mewhu weighs more than I do, judging from his build. It took his weight when he lifted his feet off the ground while holding it over his head. If it can do that, it or a larger version should be able, not only to drive, but to support an aircraft. If for some reason that isn't possible, the power of those little jets certainly could turn a turbine."

"Will it wash clothes?" Iris was glum.

"That's exactly what I mean! Light, portable, and more power than it has any right to have—of *course* it'll wash clothes. And drive generators, and cars, and . . . Iris, what do you *do* when you have something as big as this?"

"Call a newspaper, I guess."

"And have a hundred thousand people peeking and prying all over the place, and Congressional investigations, and what all? Uh . . . *uh!*"

"Why not ask Harry Zinsser?"

"Harry? I thought you didn't like him."

"I never said that. It's just that you and he go off in the corner and chatter about multitude amputation and debilities of reactance and things like that, and I have to sit, knit—and spit when I want someone's attention. Harry's all right."

"Gosh, honey, you've got it! Harry'll know what to do. I'll go right away."

"You'll do nothing of the kind! With that hole in the roof? I thought you said you could have it patched up for the night at least. By the time you get back here it'll be dark."

The prospect of sawing out the ragged hole in the roof was suddenly the least appealing thing in the world. But there was logic and an "or else" tone to what she said. He sighed and went off, mumbling something about the greatest single advance in history awaiting the whim of a woman. He forgot he was wearing Mewhu's armpit altitudinizer, and only his first two paces were on the ground. Iris hooted with laughter at his clumsy walking on air. When he reached the ground, he set his jaw and leaped lightly up to the roof. "Catch me now, you and your piano legs," he taunted cheerfully, ducked the lancelike clothes prop she hurled at him, and went back to work.

As he sawed, he was conscious of a hubbub down below.

"Dah—dee! Mr-r-roo ellue—"

He sighed and put down the saw. "What is it?"

"Mewhu wants his flyin' belt!"

Jack looked at the roof, at the lower shed, and decided that his old bones could stand it if he had to get down without a ladder. He took the jet-tipped rod and dropped it. It stayed perfectly horizontal, falling no slower and no faster than it had when he had ridden it down. Mewhu caught it, deftly slipped his splinted arm through it—it was astonishing how careful he was of the arm, and yet how little it inconvenienced him—then the other arm, and sprang up to join Jack on the roof.

"What do you say, fella?"

"Woopen yew weep."

"I know how you feel." He knew that the silver man wanted to tell him something, but couldn't help him out. He grinned and picked up the saw. Mewhu took it out of his hand and tossed it off the roof, being careful to miss Molly, who was dancing back to get a point of vantage.

"What's the big idea?"

"Dellihew hidden," said Mewhu. "Pento deh numinew heh." And he pointed at the flyin' belt and at the hole in the roof.

"You mean I'd rather fly off in that thing than work? Brother, you got it. But I'm afraid I have to—"

Mewhu circled his arm, pointing all around the hole in the roof, and pointed again to the pogo-chute, indicating one of the jet motors.

"I don't get it," said Jack.

Mewhu apparently understood, and an expression of amazement crossed his mobile face. Kneeling, he placed his good hand around one of the little jet motors, pressed two tiny studs, and the casing popped open. Inside was a compact, sealed, and simple-looking device, the core of the motor itself, apparently. There seemed to be no other fastening. Mewhu lifted it out and handed it to Jack. It was about the size and shape of an electric razor. There was a button on the side. Mewhu pointed at it, pressed the back; and then moved Jack's hand so that the device was pointed away from them both. Jack, expecting anything, from nothing at all to the "blinding bolt of searing, raw energy" so dear to the science-fiction world, pressed the button.

The gadget hissed, and snuggled back into his palm in an easy recoil.

"That's fine," said Jack, "but what do I do with it?"

Mewhu pointed at Jack's saw cut, then at the device.

"Oh," said Jack. He bent close, aimed the thing at the end of the saw cut, and pressed the button. Again the hiss, and the slight, steady recoil; and a fine line appeared in the wood. It was a cut, about half as thick as the saw cut, clean and even and, as long as he kept his hand steady, very straight. A fine cloud of pulverized wood rose out of the hole in the roof, carried on a swirl of air.

Jack experimented, holding the jet close to the wood and away from it. He found that it cut finer the closer he got to it. As he drew it away from the wood, the slot got wider and the device cut slower until at about eighteen inches it would not cut at all. Delighted, Jack quickly cut and trimmed the hole. Mewhu watched, grinning. Jack grinned back, knowing how he would feel if he introduced a saw to some primitive who was trying to work wood with a machete.

When he was finished, he handed the jet back to the silver man, and slapped his shoulder. "Thanks a million, Mewhu."

"Jeek," said Mewhu, and reached for Jack's neck. One of his thumbs lay on Jack's collarbone, the other on his back, over the scapula. Mewhu squeezed twice, firmly.

"That the way you shake hands back home?" smiled Jack. He thought it likely. Any civilized race was likely to have a manual greeting. The handshake evolved from a raised palm, indicating that the saluter was unarmed. It was quite possible that this was an extension, in a slightly different direction, of the same sign. It would indeed be an indication of friendliness to have two individuals present their throats, each to the other.

Mewhu, with three deft motions, slipped the tiny jet back into its casing, and holding the rod with one hand, stepped off the roof, letting himself be lowered in that amazing thistle-down fashion to the ground. Once there, he tossed the rod back. Jack was startled to see it hurtle upward like any earthly object. He grabbed it and missed. It reached the top of its arc, and as soon as it started down again the jets cut in, and it sank easily to him. He put it on and floated down to join Mewhu.

The silver man followed him to the garage, where he kept a few pieces of milled lumber. He selected some one-inch pine boards and dragged them out, to measure them and mark them off to the size he wanted to knock together a simple trapdoor covering for the useless stair well; a process which Mewhu watched with great interest.

Jack took up the flying belt and tried to open the streamlined shell to remove the cutter. It absolutely defied him. He pressed, twisted, wrenched, and pulled. All it did was to hiss gently when he moved it toward the floor.

"Eek, Jeek," said Mewhu. He took the jet from Jack, pressed it. Jack watched closely. Then he grinned and took the cutter.

He swiftly cut the lumber up with it, sneering gayly at the ripsaw which hung on the wall. Then he put the whole trap together with a Z-brace, trimmed off the few rough corners, and stood back to admire it. He realized instantly that it was too heavy to carry by himself, let alone lift to the roof. If Mewhu had two good hands, now, or if— He scratched his head.

"Carry it on the flyin' belt, Daddy."

"Molly! What made you think of that?"

"Mewhu tol' . . . I mean, I sort of—"

"Let's get this straight once and for all. How does Mewhu talk to you?"

"I dunno, Daddy. It's sort of like I remembered something he said, but not the . . . the words he said. I jus' . . . jus'—" she faltered, and then said vehemently, "I don't *know*, Daddy. Truly I don't!"

"What'd he say this time?"

She looked at Mewhu. Again Jack noticed the peculiar swelling of Mewhu's silver mustache. She said, "Put the door you jus' made on the flyin' belt and lift it. The flyin' belt'll make it fall slow, and you can push it along while . . . it's . . . fallin'."

Jack looked at the door, at the jet device, and got the idea. When he had slipped the jet-rod under the door, Mewhu gave him a lift. Up it came; and then Mewhu, steadying it, towed it well outside the garage before it finally sank to the ground. Another lift, another easy tow, and they covered thirty more feet. In this manner they covered the distance to the house, with Molly skipping and laughing behind, pleading for a ride and handing the grinning Mewhu a terrific brag.

At the house, Jack said, "Well, Einstein Junior, how do we get it up on the roof?"

Mewhu picked up Molly's yo-yo and began to operate it deftly. Doing so, he walked around the corner of the house.

"Hey!"

"He don't know, Daddy. You'll have to figger it out."

"You mean he could dream up that slick trick for carrying it out here and now his brains give out?"

"I guess so, Daddy."

Jack Garry looked after the retreating form of the silver man, and shook his head. He was already prepared to expect better than human reasoning from Mewhu, even if it was a little different. He couldn't quite phase this with Mewhu's shrugging off a problem in basic logic. Certainly a man with his capabilities would not have reasoned out such an ingenious method of bringing the door out here without realizing that that was only half the problem.

Shrugging, he went back to the garage and got a small block and tackle. He had to put up a big screw hook on the eave, and another on the new trapdoor; and once he had laboriously hauled the door up until the tackle was two-blocked, it was a little more than arduous to work it over the edge and drag it into position. Mewhu had apparently quite lost interest. It was two hours later, just as he put the last screw in the tower bolt on the trapdoor and was calling the job finished, that he heard Mewhu begin to shriek again. He dropped his tools, shrugged into the jet stick, and sailed off the roof.

"Iris! Iris! What's the matter?"

"I don't know, Jack. He's . . . he's—"

Jack pounded around the house to the front. Mewhu was lying on the ground in the midst of some violent kind of convulsion. He lay on his back, arching it high, digging his heels into the turf; and his head was bent back at an impossible angle, so that his weight was on his heels and his forehead. His good arm pounded the ground, though the splinted one lay limp. His lips writhed and he uttered an edgy, gasping series of ululations quite horrible to listen to. He seemed to be able to scream as loudly when inhaling as when exhaling.

Molly stood beside him, watching him hypnotically. She was smiling. Jack knelt beside the writhing form and tried to steady it. "Molly, stop grinning at the poor fellow!"

"But—he's happy, Daddy."

"He's what?"

"Can't you see, silly? He feels—good, that's all. He's laughing!"

"Iris, what's the matter with him? Do you know?"

"He's been into the aspirin again, that's all I can tell you."

"He ate four," said Molly. "He loves 'em."

"What can we do, Jack?"

"I don't know, honey," said Jack worriedly. "Better just let him work it out. Any emetic or sedative we give him might be harmful."

The attack slackened and ceased suddenly, and Mewhu went quite limp. Again, with his hand over the man's chest, Jack felt the strange double pulsing.

"Out cold," he said.

Molly said in a strange, quiet voice, "No, Daddy. He's lookin' at dreams."

"Dreams?"

"A place with a or'nge sky," said Molly. He looked up sharply. Her eyes were closed. "Lots of Mewhus. Hunderds an' hunderds—big ones. As big as Mr. Thorndyke." (Thorndyke was an editor whom they knew in the city. He was six feet seven.) "Round houses, an' big airplanes with . . . sticks fer wings."

"Molly, you're talking nonsense!" said her mother worriedly. Jack shushed her. "Go on, baby."

"A place, a room. It's a . . . Mewhu is there and a bunch more. They're in . . . in lines. Rows. There's a big one with a yella hat. He—keeps them in rows. Here's Mewhu. He's outa the line. He's jumpin' out th' windy with a flyin' belt." There was a long silence. Mewhu moaned.

"Well?"

"Nothin', Daddy—wait! It's . . . all . . . fuzzy. Now there's a thing, a kinda summerine. Only on the ground, not in the water. The door's open. Mewhu is . . . is inside. Knobs, and clocks. Pull on the knobs. Push a— Oh. *Oh!* It hurts!" She put her fists to her temples.

"Molly!"

Molly opened her eyes and said, quite calmly, "Oh, *I'm* all right, Mommy. It was a thing in the dream that hurt, but it didn't hurt *me*. It was all a bunch of fire an' . . . an' a sleepy feeling, only bigger. An' it hurt."

"Jack, he'll harm the child!"

"I doubt it," said Jack.

"So do I," said Iris, wonderingly, and then, almost inaudibly, "Now, why did I say that?"

"Mewhu's asleep," said Molly suddenly.

"No more dreams?"

"No more dreams. Gee. That was—funny."

"Come and have some lunch," said Iris. Her voice shook a little. They went into the house. Jack looked down at Mewhu, who was smiling peacefully in his sleep. He thought of putting the strange creature to bed, but the day was warm and the grass was thick and soft where he lay. He shook his head and went into the house.

"Sit down and feed," Iris said.

He looked around. "You've done wonders in here," he said. The litter of lath and plaster was gone, and Iris' triumphant antimacassars blossomed from the upholstery. She curtsied. "Thank you, m'lord."

They sat around the card table and began to do damage to tongue sandwiches. "Jack."

"Mm-m?"

"What was that—telepathy?"

"Think so. Something like that. Oh, wait'll I tell Zinsser! He'll never believe it."

"Are you going down to the airfield this afternoon?"

"You bet. Maybe I'll take Mewhu with me."

"That would be a little rough on the populace, wouldn't it? Mewhu isn't the kind of fellow you can pass off as your cousin Julius."

"Heck, he'd be all right. He could sit in the back seat with Molly while I talked Zinsser into coming out to have a look at him."

"Why not get Zinsser out here?"

"You know that's silly. When we see him in town, he's got time off. Out here he's tied to that airport almost every minute."

"Jack—do you think Molly's quite safe with that creature?"

"Of course! Are you worried?"

"I . . . I am, Jack. But not about Mewhu. About me. I'm worried because I think I should worry more, if you see what I mean."

Jack leaned over and kissed her. "The good old maternal instinct at work," he chuckled. "Mewhu's new and strange and might be dangerous. At the same time Mewhu's helpless and inoffensive, and something in you wants to mother him, too."

"There you really have something," said Iris, thoughtfully. "He's as big and ugly as you are, and unquestionably more intelligent. Yet I don't mother you."

Jack grinned. "You're not kiddin'." He gulped his coffee and stood up. "Eat it up, Molly, and go wash your hands and face. I'm going to have a look at Mewhu."

"You're going in to the airport, then?" asked Iris.

"If Mewhu's up to it. There's too much I want to know, too much I haven't the brains to figure out. I don't think I'll get all the answers from Zinsser, by any means; but between us we'll figure out what to do about this thing. Iris, it's *big!*"

Full of wild, induced speculation, he stepped out on the lawn. Mewhu was sitting up, happily contemplating a caterpillar.

"Mewhu."

"Dew?"

"How'd you like to take a ride?"

"Hubilly grees. Jeek?"

"I guess you don't get the idea. C'mon," said Jack, motioning toward the garage. Mewhu very, very carefully set the caterpillar down on a blade of grass and rose to follow; and just then the most unearthly crash issued from the garage. For a frozen moment no one moved, and then Molly's voice set up a hair-raising reiterated screech. Jack was pounding toward the garage before he knew he had moved.

"Molly! what is it?"

At the sound of his voice the child shut up as if she were switch-operated.

"Molly!"

"Here I am, Daddy," she said in an extremely small voice. She was standing by the car, her entire being concentrated in her protruding, faintly quivering lower lip. The car was nose-foremost through the back wall of the garage.

"Daddy, I didn't mean to do it; I just wanted to help you get the car out. Are you going to spank me? Please, Daddy, I didn't—"

"*Quiet!*"

She was quiet, but immediately. "Molly, what on earth possessed you to do a thing like that? You know you're not supposed to touch the starter!"

"I was pretending, Daddy, like it was a summerine that could fly, the way Mewhu did."

Jack threaded his way through this extraordinary shambles of syntax. "Come here," he said sternly. She came, her paces half-size, her feet dragging, her hands behind her where her imagination told her they would do the most good. "I ought to whack you, you know."

"Yeah," she answered tremulously. "I guess you oughta. Not more'n a couple of times, huh, Daddy?"

Jack bit the insides of his cheeks for control, but couldn't make it. He grinned. *You little minx,* he thought. "Tell you what," he said gruffly, looking at the car. The garage was fortunately flimsy, and the few new dents on hood and fenders would blend well with the old ones. "You've got three good whacks coming to you. I'm going to add those on to your next spanking."

"Yes, Daddy," said Molly, her eyes big and chastened. She climbed into the back seat and sat, very straight and small, away back out of sight. Jack cleared away what wreckage he could, and then climbed in, started the old puddle-vaulter and carefully backed out of the damaged shed.

Mewhu was standing well clear, watching the groaning automobile with startled silver eyes. "Come on in," said Jack, beckoning. Mewhu backed off.

"Mewhu!" cried Molly, putting her head out the rear door. Mewhu said "Yowk," and came instantly. Molly opened the door and he climbed in, and Molly shouted with laughter when he crouched down on the floor, and made him get up on the seat. Jack pulled around the house, stopped, picked up Mewhu's jet rod, blew a kiss through the window to Iris, and they were off.

Forty minutes later they wheeled up to the airport after an ecstatic ride during which Molly had kept up a running fire of descriptive commentary on the wonders of a terrestrial countryside. Mewhu had goggled and ogled in a most satisfactory fashion, listening spellbound to the child—sometimes Jack would have sworn that the silver man understood everything she said—and uttering little shrieks, exclamatory mewings, and interrogative peeps.

"Now," said Jack, when he had parked at the field boundary, "you two stay in the car for a while. I'm going to speak to Mr. Zinsser and see if he'll come out and meet Mewhu. Molly, do you think that you can make Mewhu understand that he's to stay in the car, and out of sight? You see, if other people see him, they'll want to ask a lot of silly questions, and we don't want to embarrass him, do we?"

"No, Daddy. Mewhu'll be good. Mewhu," she said, turning to the silver man. She held his eyes with hers. His mustache swelled, rippled. "You'll be good, won't you, and stay out of sight?"

"Jeek," said Mewhu. "Jeek mereedy."

"He says you're the boss."

Jack laughed, climbing out. "He does, eh?" Did the child really know or was it mostly a game? "Be good, then. See you soon." Carrying the jet rod, he walked into the building.

Zinsser, as usual, was busy. The field was not large, but did a great deal of private-plane business, and as traffic manager, Zinsser had his hands full. He wrapped one of his pudgy, flexible hands around the phone he was using. "Hi, Garry! What's new out of this world?" he grated cheerfully. "Siddown. With you in a minute." He bumbled cheerfully into the telephone, grinning at Jack as he talked. Jack made himself as comfortable as patience permitted and waited until Zinsser hung up.

"Well now," said Zinsser, and the phone rang again.

Jack closed his open mouth in annoyance. Zinsser hung up and another bell rang. He picked up a field telephone from its hook on the side of his desk. "Zinsser. Yes—"

"Now that's enough," said Jack to himself. He rose, went to the door, closed it softly so that he was alone with the manager. He took the jet rod, and to Zinsser's vast astonishment, stood up on his desk, raised the rod high over his head, and stepped off. A hurricane screamed out of the jets. Jack, hanging by his hands from the rod as it lowered him gently through the air, looked over his shoulder. Zinsser's face looked like a red moon in a snow flurry, surrounded as it was by every interoffice memo for the past two weeks.

Anyway, the first thing he did when he could draw a breath was to hang up the phone.

"Thought that would do it," said Jack, grinning.

"You . . . you . . . what *is* that thing?"

"It's a dialectical polarizer," said Jack, alighting. "That is, it makes conversations possible with airport managers who won't get off the phone."

Zinsser was out of his chair and around the desk, remarkably light on his feet for a man his size. "Let me see that."

Jack handed it over.

"Look, Mewhu! Here comes a plane!"

Together they watched the Cub slide in for a landing, and squeaked at the little puffs of dust that were thrown up by the tires and flicked away by the slipstream.

"And there goes another one. It's gonna take off!" The little blue low-wing coupé taxied across the field, braked one wheel, swung in its own length and roared down toward them, lifting to howl away into the sky far over their heads.

"Eeeeeyow," droned Molly, imitating the sound of the motor as it passed overhead.

"S-s-s-sweeeeee!" hissed Mewhu, exactly duplicating the whine of control surfaces in the prop blast.

Molly clapped her hands and shrieked with delight. Another plane began to circle the field. They watched it avidly.

"Come on out and have a look at him," said Jack.

Zinsser looked at his watch. "I can't. All kidding aside, I got to stick by the phone for another half hour at the very least. Will he be all right out there? There's hardly anyone around."

"I think so. Molly's with him, and as I told you, they get along beautifully together. That's one of the things I want to have investigated—that telepathy angle." He laughed suddenly. "That Molly . . . know what she did this afternoon?" He told Zinsser about Molly's driving the car through the wrong end of the garage.

"The little hellion," chuckled Zinsser. "They'll all do it, bless 'em. At some time or other in his life, I think every kid climbs aboard something he doesn't know anything about and runs it wrong. My brother's kid went to work on the front lawn with his mother's vacuum cleaner the other day." He laughed. "To get back to what's-his-name—Mewhu, and this gadget of his. Jack, we've got to hang on to it. Do you realize that he and his clothes and this thing are the only clues we have as to what he is and where he came from?"

"I sure do. But listen—he's very intelligent. I'm sure he'll be able to tell us plenty."

"You can bet he's intelligent," said Zinsser. "He's probably above average on his planet. They wouldn't send just anyone on a trip like that. Jack, what a pity we don't have his ship!"

"Maybe it'll be back. What's your guess as to where he comes from?"

"Mars, maybe."

"Now, you know better than that. We know Mars has an atmosphere, but it's mighty tenuous. An organism the size of Mewhu would have to have enormous lungs to keep him going. No; Mewhu's used to an atmosphere pretty much like ours."

"That would rule Venus out."

"He wears clothes quite comfortably here. His planet must have not only pretty much the same atmosphere, but the same climate. He seems to be able to take most of our foods, though he is revolted by some of them—and aspirin sends him high as a kite. He gets what looks like a laughing drunk on when he takes it."

"You don't say. Let's see; it wouldn't be Jupiter, because he isn't built to take a gravity like that. And the outer planets are too cold, and Mercury is too hot." Zinsser leaned back in his chair and absently mopped his bald head. "Jack, this guy doesn't even come from this solar system!"

"Gosh. I guess you're right. Harry, what do you make of this jet gadget?"

"From the way you say it cuts wood . . . can I see that, by the way?" Zinsser asked.

"Sure." Garry went to work on the jet. He found the right studs to press simultaneously. The casing opened smoothly. He lifted out the active core of the device, and, handling it gingerly, sliced a small corner off Zinsser's desk top.

"That is the strangest thing I have ever seen," said Zinsser. "May I see it?"

He took it and turned it over in his hands. "There doesn't seem to be any fuel for it," he said, musingly.

"I think it uses air," said Jack.

"But what pushes the air?"

"Air," said Jack. "No—I'm not kidding. I think that in some way it disintegrates part of the air, and uses the energy released to activate a small jet. If you had a shell around this jet, with an intake at one end and a blast tube at the other, it would operate like a high-vacuum pump, dragging more air through."

"Or like an athodyd," said Zinsser. Garry's blood went cold as the manager sighted down into the jet orifice. "For heaven's sake don't push that button."

"I won't. Say—you're right. The tube's concentric. Now, how on earth could a disruption unit be as small and light as that?"

Jack Garry said, "I've been chewing on that all day. I have one answer. Can you take something that sounds really fantastic, so long as it's logical?"

"You know me," grinned Zinsser, waving at a long shelf of back number science-fiction magazines. "Go ahead."

"Well," said Jack carefully. "You know what binding energy is. The stuff that holds the nucleus of an atom together. If I understand my smattering of nuclear theory properly, it seems possible to me that a sphere of binding energy could be produced that would be stable."

"A sphere? With what inside it?"

"Binding energy—or maybe just nothing . . . space. Anyhow, if you surround that sphere with another, this one a force-field which is capable of penetrating the inner one, or of allowing matter to penetrate it, it seems to me that anything entering that balance of forces would be disrupted. An explosive pressure would be bottled up inside the inner sphere. Now if you bring your penetrating field in contact with the binding-energy sphere, the pressures inside will come blasting out. Incase the whole rig in a device which controls the amount of matter going in one side of the sphere and the amount of orifice allowed for the escape of energy, and incase that further in an outside shell which will give you a stream of air induced violently through it—like the vacuum pump you mentioned—and you have this." And he rapped on the little jet motor.

"Most ingenious," said Zinsser, wagging his head. "Even if you're wrong, it's an ingenious theory. What you're saying, you know, is that all we have to do to duplicate this device is to discover the nature of binding energy and then find a way to make it stay stably in spherical form. After which we figure out the nature of a field which can penetrate binding energy and allow any matter to do likewise—one way." He spread his hands. "That's all. Just learn to actually use the stuff that the long-hair boys haven't thought of theorizing about yet, and we're all set."

"Shucks," said Garry, "Mewhu will give us all the dope."

"I hope so. Jack, this can revolutionize the entire industrial world!"

"You're understating," grinned Jack.

The phone rang. Zinsser looked at his watch again. "There's my call." He sat down, answered the phone, and while he went on at great length to some high-powered character at the other end of the line, about bills of lading and charter service and interstate commerce restrictions, Jack lounged against the cut-off corner of the desk and dreamed. Mewhu—a superior member of a superior race, come to earth to lead struggling humanity out of its struggling, wasteful ways. He wondered what Mewhu was like at home among his strange people. Young, but very mature, he decided, and gifted in many ways—the pick of the crop, fit to be ambassador to a new and dynamic civilization like Earth's. And what about the ship? Having dropped Mewhu, had it and its pilot returned to the mysterious corner of the universe from which they had come? Or was it circling about somewhere in space, anxiously awaiting word from the adventurous ambassador?

Zinsser cradled his instrument and stood up with a sigh. "A credit to my will power," he said. "The greatest thing that has ever happened to me, and I stuck by the day's work in spite of it. I feel like a kid on Christmas Eve. Let's go have a look at him."

"Wheeeeyouwow!" screamed Mewhu as another rising plane passed over their heads. Molly bounced joyfully up and down on the cushions, for Mewhu was an excellent mimic.

The silver man slipped over the back of the driver's seat in a lithe movement, to see a little better around the corner of a nearby hangar. One of the Cubs had been wheeled into it, and was standing not far away, its prop ticking over.

Molly leaned her elbows on the edge of the seat and stretched her little neck so she could see, too. Mewhu brushed against her head and her hat fell off. He bent to pick it up and bumped his own head on the dashboard, and the glove compartment flew open. His strange pupils narrowed, and the nictitating membranes flickered over his eyes as he reached inside. The next thing Molly knew, he was out of the car and running over the parking area, leaping high in the air, mouthing strange noises, and stopping every few jumps to roll and beat with his good hand on the ground.

Horrified, Molly Garry left the car and ran after him. "Mewhu!" she cried. "Mewhu, come *back!*"

He cavorted toward her, his arms outspread. "W-r-r-row-w!" he shouted, rushing past her. Lowering one arm a little and raising the other like an airplane banking, he ran in a wide arc, leaped the little tarmac retaining wall and bounded out onto the hangar area.

Molly, panting and sobbing, stopped and stamped her foot. "Mewhu!" she croaked helplessly. "Daddy said—"

Two mechanics standing near the idling Cub looked around at a sound like a civet-cat imitating an Onondaga war whoop. What they saw was a long-legged, silver-gray apparition with a silver-white mustache, and slotted eyes, dressed in a scarlet robe that turned to indigo. Without a sound, moving as one man, they cut and ran. And Mewhu with one last terrible shriek of joy, leaped to the plane and disappeared inside.

Molly put her hands to her mouth and her eyes bugged. "Oh, Mewhu," she breathed. "Now you've done it." She heard pounding feet, turned. Her father was racing toward her, with Mr. Zinsser waddling behind. "Molly! Where's Mewhu?"

Wordlessly, she pointed at the Cub; and as if it were a signal, the little ship throttled up and began to crawl away from the hangars.

"Hey! Wait! Wait!" screamed Jack Garry uselessly, sprinting after the plane. He leaped the wall but misjudged it because of his speed. His toe hooked it and he sprawled slitheringly, jarringly on the tarmac. Zinsser and Molly ran to him, helped him up. Jack's nose was bleeding. He whipped out a handkerchief, looked out at the dwindling plane. "Mewhu!"

The little plane waddled across the field, bellowed suddenly with power. The tail came up, and it scooted away from them—cross wind, cross the runway. Jack turned to speak to Zinsser and saw the fat man's face absolutely stricken. He followed Zinsser's eyes and saw the other plane, the big six-place cabin job, coming in.

He had never felt so helpless in all his life. Those planes were going to collide. There was nothing anyone could do about it. He watched them, unblinking, almost detachedly. They were hurtling but they seemed to creep; the moment lasted forever. Then, with twenty feet altitude, Mewhu cut his gun and dropped a wing. The Cub slowed, leaned into the wind, and *side-slipped* so close under the cabin ship that another coat of paint on either craft would have meant disaster.

Jack didn't know how long he had been holding that breath, but it was agony when he let it out.

"Anyway, he can fly," breathed Zinsser.

"Of course he can fly," snapped Jack. "A prehistoric thing like an airplane would be child's play for him. Child's play."

"Oh, Daddy, I'm scared."

"I'm not," said Jack hollowly.

"Me, too," said Zinsser with an unconvincing laugh. "The plane's insured."

The Cub arrowed upward. At a hundred feet it went into a skidding turn, harrowing to watch, suddenly winged over and came shouting down at them. Mewhu buzzed them so close that Zinsser went flat on his face. Jack and Molly simply stood there, wall-eyed. An enormous cloud of dust obscured every thing for ninety interminable seconds. When they next saw the plane it was wobbling crazily at a hundred and fifty.

Suddenly Molly screamed piercingly and put her hands over her face.

"Molly! Kiddo, what is it?"

She flung her arms around his neck and sobbed so violently that he knew it was hurting her throat. "Stop it!" he yelled; and then, very gently, he asked, "What's the matter, darling?"

"He's scared. Mewhu's terrible, terrible scared," she said brokenly.

Jack looked up at the plane. It yawed, fell away on one wing.

Zinsser shouted, his voice cracking, "Gun her! Gun her! Throttle up, you idiot!"

Mewhu cut the gun.

Dead stick, the plane winged over and plunged to the ground. The impact was crushing.

Molly said, quite calmly, "All Mewhu's pictures have gone out now," and slumped unconscious to the ground.

They got him to the hospital. It was messy—all of it; picking him up, carrying him to the ambulance—

Jack wished fervently that Molly had not seen; but she had sat up and cried as they carried him past. He thought worriedly as he and Zinsser crossed and recrossed in their pacing of the waiting room, that he would have his hands full with the child when this thing was all over.

The resident physician came in, wiping his hands. He was a small man with a nose like a walnut meat. "Who brought that plane-crash case in here—you?"

"Both of us," said Zinsser.

"What . . . who is he?"

"A friend of mine. Is he . . . will he live?"

"How should I know?" snapped the doctor impatiently. "I have never in my experience—" He exhaled through his nostrils. "The man has two circulatory systems. Two *closed* circulatory systems, and a heart for each. All his arterial blood looks veinous—it's purple. How'd he happen to get hurt?"

"He ate half a box of aspirin out of my car," said Jack. "Aspirin makes him drunk. He swiped a plane and piled it up."

"Aspirin makes him—" The doctor looked at each of them in turn. "I won't ask if you're kidding me. Just to see that . . . that thing in there is enough to kid any doctor. How long has that splint been on his arm?"

Zinsser looked at Jack and Jack said "About eighteen hours."

"Eighteen *hours?*" The doctor shook his head. "It's so well knitted that I'd say eighteen days." Before Jack could say anything he added, "He needs a transfusion."

"But you can't! I mean . . . his blood—"

"I know. Took a sample to type it. I have two technicians trying to blend chemicals into plasma so we can approximate it. Both of 'em called me a liar. But he's got to have the transfusion. I'll let you know." He strode out of the room.

"There goes one bewildered medico."

"He's O.K.," said Zinsser. "I know him well. Can you blame him?"

"For feeling that way? Gosh no. Harry, I don't know what I'll do if Mewhu checks out."

"That fond of him?"

"Oh, it isn't only that. But to come so close to meeting a new culture, and then have it slip from our fingers like this—it's too much."

"That jet . . . Jack, without Mewhu to explain it, I don't think any scientist will be able to build another. It would be like . . . like giving a Damascus sword-smith some tungsten and asking him to draw it into filaments. There the jet would be, hissing when you shove it toward the ground, sneering at you."

"And that telepathy—what J. B. Rhine wouldn't give to be able to study it!"

"Yeah, and what about his origin?" Zinsser asked excitedly. "He isn't from this system. It means that he used an interstellar drive of some kind, or even that space-time warp the boys write about."

"He's got to live," said Jack. "He's got to, or there ain't no justice. There are too many things we've got to know, Harry! Look—he's here. That must mean that some more of his people will come some day."

"Yeah. Why haven't they come before now?"

"Maybe they have. Charles Fort—"

"Aw, look," said Zinsser, "don't let's get this thing out of hand."

The doctor came back. "I think he'll make it."

"Really?"

"Not really. Nothing real about that character. But from all indications, he'll be O.K. Responded very strongly. What does he eat?"

"Pretty much the same as we do, I think."

"You think. You don't seem to know much about him."

"I don't. He only just got here. No—don't ask me where from," said Jack. "You'll have to ask him."

The doctor scratched his head. "He's out of this world. I can tell you that. Obviously adult, but every fracture but one is a greenstick break; kind of thing you see on a three-year-old. Transparent membranes over his . . . what are you laughing at?" he asked suddenly.

Jack had started easily, with a chuckle, but it got out of control. He roared.

Zinsser said, "Jack! Cut it out. This is a hosp—"

Jack shoved his hand away. "I . . . I got to," he said helplessly and went off on another peal.

"You've got to what?"

"Laugh," said Jack, gasping. He sobered—he more than sobered. "It has to be funny, Harry. I won't let it be anything else."

"What the devil do you—"

"Look, Harry. We assumed a lot about Mewhu, his culture, his technology, his origin . . . we'll never know anything about it!"

"Why? You mean he won't tell us—"

"He won't tell us. I'm wrong. He'll tell us plenty. But it won't do any good. Here's what I mean. Because he's our size, because he obviously arrived in a spaceship, because he brought a gadget or two that's obviously the product of a highly advanced civilization, we believe that *he* produced the civilization; that he's a superior individual in his own place."

"Well, he must be."

"He must be? Harry, did Molly invent the automobile?"

"No, but—"

"But she drove one through the back of the garage."

Light began to dawn on Zinsser's moon face. "You mean—"

"It all fits! Remember when Mewhu figured out how to carry that heavy trapdoor of mine on the jet stick, and then left the problem half-finished? Remember his fascination with Molly's yo-yo? What about that peculiar rapport he has with Molly that he has with no one else? Doesn't that begin to look reasonable? Look at Iris' reaction to him—almost maternal, though she didn't know why."

"The poor little fellow," breathed Zinsser. "I wonder if he thought he was home when he landed?"

"Poor little fellow—sure," said Jack, and began to laugh again. "Can Molly tell you how an internal combustion engine works? Can she explain laminar flow on an airfoil?" He shook his head. "You wait and see. Mewhu will be able to tell us the equivalent of Molly's 'I rode in the car with Daddy and we went sixty miles an hour.'"

"But how did he get here?"

"How did Molly get through the back of my garage?"

The doctor shrugged his shoulders helplessly, "About that I don't know. But his biological reactions do look like those of a child—and if he is a child, then his rate of tissue restoration will be high, and I'll guarantee he'll live."

Zinsser groaned. "Much good will it do us—and him, poor kid. With a kid's inherent faith in any intelligent adult anywhere, he's probably been feeling happily sure we'd get him home somehow. Well —we haven't got what it takes, and won't have for a long, long time. We don't know enough to start duplicating that jet of his—and that was just a little kid's toy on his world."

"Daddy—"

"Molly! I thought Mother was—"

"Daddy, I jus' wannit you to take this to Mewhu." She held out her old, scuff-rimmed yo-yo. "Tellum I'm waiting. Tellum I'll play with him soon's he's better."

Jack Garry took the toy. "I'll tell him, honey."

GRAHAM DOAR

THE OUTER LIMIT

Patrolship S2J3, Galactic Guard, Sector K, reporting. . . . Pursuant to instructions from the Central Council: Planet 3, Star 5, Galaxy C, Sector K, has been placed under absolute quarantine. Notification to inhabitants made. Mission accomplished.

XEGLON, *Commanding.*

AT fifty thousand feet he began to feel the loss of power, the thinner air starving the oxygen-eating turbojets. Their thunderous whisper rose to a screaming whine.

His air speed dropped from six hundred to four-eighty in the while it took to pull the lever that dropped the jet assembly, white cloud of parachute mushrooming as the heavy engines plummeted earthward. He switched on the flow of lox and alky pressured by the nitrogen flasks under his seat. The liquid oxygen and alcohol sparked and caught, there was a hissing roar and he felt a sledge-hammer blow against his back and shoulders. Rocket No. 1 was firing, and his airspeed indicator whirled under the almost instantaneous acceleration, the sharklike ship leaping forward in a flashing upward glide.

This was the new one. The unknown. He'd flown her before, a dozen times, but not for speed and altitude, never at full power. Behind him, crowding the narrow fuselage, was fuel for ten minutes with all eight rockets firing full thrust. This was the new one and this was the day. He was going higher and faster than man had ever gone. He switched on No. 2.

He passed one hundred thousand feet at eighteen hundred miles an hour with only four rockets blasting. Counting slowly, his eyes glued to the clock on the instrument panel, he reached and turned No. 5 switch. Again the ship bucked, only slightly now, and the speed indicator rolled upward.

He was flying in absolute dead quiet. Only the sounds within the pressurized tiny cockpit reached his ears, the ticking of the clock, the beating of his heart, the small hissing of the nitrogen flow. The cataclysmic roar of his ship's passing formed miles in his wake, the mighty voice of the rockets was left far behind. He was traveling at nearly four times the speed of sound. He wondered what old terra firma would look like at this altitude. Jammed into the crowded cockpit, his lap full of instruments, his helmeted head almost touching the canopy, there was no way he could manage to look down. But he knew the clicking camera in the floor of his plane was making a record. He cut in the seventh rocket, wondering if the recording instruments were working.

The colonel wasn't going to believe this without proof. Mach 5—it was strictly a guess at this altitude—and still accelerating, still climbing.

He saw it just as he reached to switch on No. 8. He was pulling the ship in a wide circle, trying it for maneuverability at this altitude and speed. The ship jumped and side-slipped a bit when the last rocket fired. At that moment the sunlight glinted on some object far ahead and above him.

He didn't believe it. He knew all the standard explanations of the great flying-saucer plague—the runaway balloons, the planet Venus, hallucinations brought on by strain and weariness. Whatever this object was, this metallic ellipsoid turning slowly above him, it wasn't a ship. He knew that.

But he had six minutes' fuel left and with all eight rockets boosting him along, he could run rings around anything. A closer look wouldn't hurt. He pointed the shark's nose at the far-off gleam.

A long while ago the colonel had been worried. Now he was no longer worried. He had given up. He'd had the search planes out for hours now, looking for any sign of that double-damned X2JTO that had almost certainly killed his best pilot. The colonel wasn't kidding himself that the captain might have parachuted safely. You don't hit the silk at rocket speeds forty miles up. Radar reported the ship that high when the screen went blank.

The F-80 chase planes that had been sent up to observe the test had radioed in, almost immediately after he'd dropped the turbojet take-off assembly. They'd lost him about the time he cut in the fourth rocket. The ship was flying like a dream, they'd reported, but they couldn't keep him in sight.

The colonel looked at his watch and sighed. The search had been on for nine hours, and not even a nibble yet. It was hopeless. Sometime in the next few days—or weeks—reports would begin to drift in of pieces of the ship being picked up here and there. Maybe pieces of the pilot too. In the meantime, they'd build another one. And some flying fool would take it up. Death, the fear of death couldn't stop them. It never had and it never would. They had no fear, not that kind. *Thank God*, the colonel thought, *for the flying fools.* They had punched holes in the so-called sonic barrier and were beating their stubborn heads against the walls of space itself. He himself was getting old, the colonel realized. He himself was afraid of a great many things. Once he'd been one of the flying fools, but now the palms of his hands were wet at the thought of sending another of his pilots up in one of those skyrockets. He wondered if there was a drink left in the bottle he had in his desk, but it didn't seem worth the effort to look and see.

The telephone at his elbow tinkled sharply. He spoke quietly, holding his voice firm with an effort. "All right."

"Colonel! He's in!"

"Who is this speaking?"

"Staff Sergeant Smith, sir."

The colonel's voice was sharp now. "Have you been drinking, sergeant?"

"He's landing right now, sir. The tower sighted him just a minute ago. The ship looks all right."

He slammed down the phone and was through the door in three long strides. His driver had seen the plane. He spun the colonel's car to the door, motor roaring, and in a split second they were tearing across the field.

There was a drink left in the bottle after all. The colonel split it between two glasses and handed one to the pilot. The junior officer, both in age and rank, was not a big man, maybe an inch or two shorter than the six-foot colonel. He was lean, whipped by strenuous play and more strenuous work into one hundred and sixty-five pounds of bone and sinew. His normally good-natured, rather boyish face with the steel-blue eyes was now a yellowish purple, the hue that passes for pallor on a deeply tanned skin. The finely tuned nerves brought a quiver to the fingers that held a cigarette, and the golden-brown liquid shivered in the glass, but his grin was easy and the deep voice came out firm and low. "Sit down, Hank. This one will knock you over."

The colonel's answering grin was friendly, if uneasy, and he said, "Bill, I've called off the search, but I'd already shot the word to Washington. I've got to get an explanation on the wire soon, so let's have it."

"What's your idea about the flying saucers, Hank?"

"Not now, Bill. First things first. I want to know—I've got to know—how you stretched ten minutes' fuel to keep you in the air over ten hours."

"Believe me, this is it." The captain leaned forward in his chair. "One thing before I start to talk. Will you have the Geiger men run over that ship before it goes to the technicians?"

"What did you run into?"

"So help me, Hank, I don't know. I don't think its radioactivity, but we better know for sure."

The colonel reached one hand for the phone. "We'd better have you looked over, too, hadn't we?"

"No. No, I'll be all right. They said I'd be all right."

The colonel started to speak, but he checked himself and picked up the phone. He gave the orders for the Geiger team to inspect the ship for fission products, then added as an obvious afterthought, "After you complete your inspection, lieutenant, have that ship sealed. Whatever your findings, understand? Have the ship sealed, to be opened only on a direct order from me. . . . Right."

He hung up slowly, not turning back to face the pilot. His voice was tired as he spoke. "All right, Bill. This 'they' you speak of—that's going to be a little hard to get across." *If he's getting ready to feed me one of those men-from-Mars yarns,* he thought, *I should get the psychos in right now. But I know this boy. A night's sleep—he'll be all right.*

"Well, Hank, I chased me a flying saucer. And I caught it. Or rather it caught me." The captain finished his drink and placed the glass with gentle precision on the corner of the desk. "I was cruising nicely about two hundred thousand feet out at about four thousand m-p-h. I spotted —something, and decided to take a look at it. It must have been going at about half my speed. I caught up fast. It was—oh—egg-shaped and perfectly smooth. No visible openings anywhere. I made two passes looking it over and started back for a third. There was a humming sound—a kind of gentle vibration—and I blacked out. I was heading straight at the thing, Hank, and I felt this—sort of twang, as though I'd run into a harp string, and the—the black came down over me. I thought—I felt it coming for a split second—I thought—— Is there another drink left, Hank?"

Sweat glistened on the pilot's forehead. The colonel passed his own still-full glass across the desk. This was probably the wrong treatment, he thought, but the guy needed a drink.

The captain took only a small swallow, but some of the flutter went out of the strong, lean hands. "Hank, I thought it was going to be the biggest smash since Hiroshima. Well, it wasn't. I came to—inside their ship!"

The colonel spoke gently. "Bill, this is obviously a hell of a strain on you. And you'll have to run through it again, you know. Shall I call the—Major Donaldson in and let him hear it now?"

"The psychiatrist? Yeah, I guess he'll want to test my jerks. Well, Hank, if it's all the same to you, I'd like to put it off till tomorrow. I'd like to finish telling you, then go out and get good and drunk. Because, Hank, unless I miss my guess, I've just been tipped off to the way the world ends."

"Okay, Bill. But don't let Donaldson know you read Eliot or he'll certify you nuts. He thinks pilots read the comics."

"Thanks, Hank. Well, I came to, inside the ship, and I was surrounded by—let's call them men."

"The men from Mars, eh?"

A surge of color rode up the pilot's lean face. "Mars, Hank? No." He considered. He spoke slowly. "I hadn't thought—I couldn't quite grasp where—— Hank, this solar system of ours—it's a pretty big thing. I mean—you know—to us. They were trying to impress me with the importance, the absoluteness of their message, and they pointed out the terrific trouble they had gone to, the miracles of space navigation they'd had to perform in order to find us. Not our planet, Hank, but our sun! That great, blazing orb of unbearable brightness, Hank, became a pinpoint glimmer to them when nine tenths of their journey was completed. How far would that be, Hank? You tell me where they came from."

The colonel was reasonable. "Then how did they find us in the first place? What brought them here?"

"You know the old one about the man whose reach exceeds his grasp? That's us, Hank. All of us. We rang their bell, Hank. We tolled them in."

"Suppose you just tell it straight."

There was the faintest reminder of his rank in the colonel's voice. He was uneasy, he was tired and he liked this kid. It wasn't pleasant to watch this sort of thing, though he'd seen it before in these hot pilots. Let him talk it out, that might do the trick. Thank God, it was always temporary; nearly always.

"Right." Unconsciously the captain sat straighter in his chair. His tone became more clipped. "They looked—I don't know what they looked like. They were just—presences. There were a lot of them—I don't know how many. The inside of the ship was jammed completely full of incredibly intricate-looking machinery, and the noise was utterly deafening. After a few seconds I couldn't hear a sound. I—I just didn't believe it at first. Then—well, there it was. You had to believe it. I was angry, too—it seemed so—so belittling. But then suddenly I wasn't angry. There was nothing to strike at. Anyway, they seemed friendly, even gentle."

"Just one thing, Bill. If you couldn't hear anything, how did they speak to you? And in English, I suppose?"

"Funny." The pilot looked startled. "I hadn't thought of that. They didn't speak. They just—planted the ideas in my own head. It was just —suddenly, it was there—in my mind."

He never spoke a truer sentence, the colonel thought. He said gently, "Look, Bill. I'm sorry, but I'll have to pull a little rank. I'm getting Donaldson in."

Major Malcolm Donaldson, M.D., Ph.D., shifted his untidy bulk uneasily on the surface of the hard straight chair, took off his thick-lensed glasses and massaged his brows with a thumb and forefinger. Uncovered, his soft brown eyes looked tired and weak.

The colonel said, "Is that all clear, Donaldson?"

"Oh, sure. Sure, colonel." His voice was tenor in pitch, but strong and firm. "Go ahead, will you, Bill? Give us the rest of it." His brown eyes flashed a reassuring twinkle at the colonel.

"Right, sir." With the psychiatrist present, the captain was choosing his words carefully. "They knew, then, the danger as well as the utility of atomic power. They used to use it themselves, long ago; before they developed whatever it is they use now. They had their wars then; wars that almost destroyed their civilization. Now they have outlawed war throughout the sectors of space they patrol, and anywhere else they can reach. Wherever their detector system picks up traces of an atomic explosion, they send a patrol—with certain preventive powers. We've exploded—five, is it?—atomic bombs. Maybe seven. Plenty, anyway, for them to get a fix. They came. They found wars and rumors of wars. Factories busily turning out atomic weapons. So they quarantined us. This intergalactic board of health decided we were infected with a communicable disease. They sealed us off from the rest of space until we were well. That's good medical practice, isn't it, major?"

The major got up from his chair and came to stand beside the pilot, placing one pink hand on the sinewy wrist. The colonel started to speak, but the psychiatrist was first, firmly. "All right, Bill. Try to tell it straight—and keep the voice down, eh?"

There was silence for a moment, then the young captain began to speak again. "Right. Here it is, then. Out there—about a hundred miles out—they've spread a layer of—I don't know what to call it. I couldn't quite grasp—— Anyway, it's there, miles deep; and it's there to stay. When an atomic bomb is exploded anywhere on this earth and the mushroom cloud of radioactive particles rises up, fission products will infiltrate into this layer. Greatly dispersed, of course, only a few will ever get so high—but they've allowed for that. And that will be it. We will then have had it."

"Easy, Bill," said the major.

"Easy? Sure. The easiest thing you know. Because when the radio-activity in this layer of—whatever—rises above the normal level of cosmic activity, its particles will begin to fission. And, gentlemen and brothers, we will then have the damnedest galactic Fourth of July celebration of all time. In the time it takes that watch you're using to count my pulse, major, in the little piece of time it takes to tick just once—just once—this spinning globe will be a roaring ball of flame that will pale the sun. Colonel, your men from Mars will have to run for cover to keep from getting their hair singed. How do you like it, gentle-men?"

The rotund major fumbled a black case from his pocket and the overhead light struck a gleam from the hypodermic in his hand. "All right, Bill. Let's get your coat off and roll up your sleeve."

The pilot's breathing was harsh. He said, "We can forget about those atomic-powered spaceships, too, colonel. You see that, don't you? Unless we can figure out some way to shield the exhaust. On second thought, we won't last long enough for that to become a problem. Just forget it. That's best."

The colonel said, "Take it easy, Bill."

The major put a hand on his arm.

He shook it off. "No. That's the story. The whole thing. They fin-ished with me, I heard the harp twang again—and I was in the plane gliding back down. You saw me land. Now, colonel, with your permis-sion, I'm going over to the club and tie one on."

The colonel said, "No. Sorry, Bill, but not tonight. Let Donaldson give you the hypo."

"No. I've got a drink coming. Several drinks."

"Don't be an ass, Bill. I *can* make it an order. Go to bed, get some sleep. You've got leave coming, you can get as drunk as you like later."

The pilot stripped off his blouse silently. He said, watching the bright needle bite into his arm, "What are we going to do? I—I hadn't thought that far. What are we going to do?"

The colonel reached forward and laid a long hand on the lean forearm. "It's out of your hands now, Bill. For tonight, anyway. You don't have to worry about it. I'll draw up a summary of what you've told me; tomorrow we'll go over it together. The most we can do is make a report and try to push it right to the top. Well, that's my job, Bill. It's out of your hands. So you get some sleep, and tomorrow we'll go over it. Okay?"

"Okay." Suddenly he was tired. And the colonel would handle it. Good old Hank. The vision of a roaring, swirling mass of flame, the crackling apocalyptic thunder that he had conjured up in his mind was fading. It was still there, but faint now.

He waved a drowsy good night and stumbled outdoors.

The colonel walked after him, watched his progress toward his quarters. When the pilot was out of earshot, the colonel spoke to a soldier near the doorway, "Sergeant! Take a man and go to the captain's quarters. See him into bed and watch him all night."

"Yes, sir!"

"Keep your eye on his pistol. He's been under the hell of a strain."

"Yes, colonel. Nothing will happen, sir."

[Record for file . . . record for file. Xeglon, commanding Patrolship S2J3, to Sector Commander Zzyl, Galactic Guard, Sector K.

[Patrol Commander Pgot informed me that you requested this early, informal report on Mission S2K-C5-3 and I prepared it at once. The technical reports in detail prepared by the various teams involved in the operation will be in your hands shortly.

[Planet C5-3 was located by Patrol S2J about the 32nd time-period out of headquarters. Our nine ships went into an orbit at slow speed and confirmation of Central Council's report was found immediately. There were definite traces of fission products impregnating areas of the upper atmosphere. Commander Pgot designated this ship to complete the mission while he returned to station with the remainder of his patrol.

[Need for the quarantine having been established by our preliminary observations, our twofold problem was (1) its nature and duration and (2) communication of the necessary warning to the planet's inhabitants. The first was, of course, a matter of comprehensive but simple tests carried out by the technicians. The second was far more difficult, owing to the fact that the creatures employ a method of communication not heretofore found. Their range approaches zero and there is almost no directional factor. They do have a means of distance-communication by mechanically generated impulses or waves but, though these were not difficult to intercept, we failed entirely at interpreting them. Our earliest attempts at communication resulted in jamming and even destroying the nerve paths of the specimens we selected. Naturally, we attempted to choose the most highly organized and stable individuals, but, working over the necessary distance, selection was not easy. Obviously a landing was out of the question. We should have had to destroy thousands of them in order to seize one and might even have suffered some losses ourselves. You know the problem of regeneration with no greater facilities than our patrolships carry.

[Computing, on the Pheng scale, such observations as our psychoteam was able to make, we were led to expect an intelligence factor between four and five plus. Emotional stability, however, ran completely off the scale—at the minus end. In spite of the high intelligence level, their almost complete lack of social organization is thus explained.

[Through the really brilliant work of the team, we finally managed to locate an area where the stability factor ran to as much as plus eight over the norm we had established. Intelligence was not at the highest, but was also above the norm. To make it even simpler, the creatures were here engaged in testing operations with their aircraft, one-man ships that we observed making greater and greater speeds, climbing to higher and higher altitudes. Briefly, the time came when one of them reached a sufficient speed at a high enough altitude that we could use the scoop on him without much danger of injury.

[It was now that our psycho-men really distinguished themselves. With their previous observations added to estimations of brain convolutions and mass, they set up a mechanical hypnotor that established contact on the very first try. Only two serious blocks were encountered. One was a systemic syndrome resulting in increase of body temperature, increased speed and power of movement, and an almost complete stoppage of the intellectual processes. This seems to be an automatic reaction and is probably a survival factor in such a poorly organized society. It was easily overcome. The other block encountered was a complete mental rejection of the situation. Our team worked patiently at this for some time and were despairing of getting through when to our surprise, the creature broke it down himself.

[To judge from this one sample, they have an instinctive and involuntary censor that closes the mind to whatever is outside previous experience. Fortunately for them, this censor appears to be in constant conflict with such logic as they employ and is frequently defeated. Otherwise, of course, even such technological and sociological development as they enjoy would have been impossible.

[Having made contact, we fixed the creature's mind, implanting the necessary warning as to the nature of the quarantine, the reasons for it, the conditions under which it may be lifted. His grasp of the entire concept at last complete, we released him, close to the pick-up point, and traced him to the surface.

[In the meantime, tests had determined that Catalyst X, in a concentration of .003 negatively charged, would accomplish our task, remaining active for approximately one hundred of the planet's orbit-periods. This, being longer than the inhabitants' life cycle, should allow time for re-education and retraining of new generations—provided they heed our warning. Intermittent observation patrols and a renewal of the quarantine if need is determined are, of course, recommended.

[We proceeded now to sow the catalyst in the predetermined

depth and, mission accomplished, to depart for our station. Two time-periods out from the planet, we switch to space drive. Message ends. XEGLON.]

When the colonel turned back into the room, the major had resumed his seat. He was holding up the shining hypodermic needle, moving it to catch the glimmering reflections.

The colonel barked, "Put that thing away!"

"Certainly, colonel. Sorry."

"No, Donaldson. I'm sorry. I beg your pardon."

"Not at all, sir. It's damned tough, I know. He's one of the best."

The colonel sat, wearily. "He's *the* best, Donaldson. That combination of guts, loyalty and lightning reflexes comes about one in ten million. Oh, well. I've plenty of good men, as far as that goes. It's the kid himself I——How does it look to you?"

"I can't tell yet. It may be a week—six months—six years. It may be gone by tomorrow morning. I'll need a whole lot of time with him before I can say."

The colonel banged his fist on the desk. "If this thing holds up his promotion, I'll—I'll go to Washington personally! He's been due for major for six months now. He needs it too. His wife's having another baby, you know."

The psychiatrist nodded. "How many's that make?"

"It's his third."

"These boys run to large families for some reason. I've wondered about that. It's living on the ragged edge of danger that does it, I suppose. Ha!" His little snort of laughter made the colonel look up in surprise. "Sorry, colonel. It just occurred to me—if the captain's little fantasy were true and the word got around—brother! Would the population curve begin to shoot up! Or would it?" He was suddenly thoughtful.

The colonel said, "Well, Donaldson, we'd better get some sleep too."

The major stood up. "Right, colonel. It's going to be tough, telling his wife. Well, maybe it won't be necessary. He's a good strong boy, best nerves I've seen. I'd say things will be all right."

He wandered toward the doorway. He was reluctant to go and he wondered why. It was cozy in the little office. Outside it was dark and the desert cold was creeping down over the field. Suddenly the major wished it were daylight. He didn't want to see the stars.

He shrugged and said good night.

"Good night, Major Donaldson."

He turned, his hand on the open door. "Oh, colonel. There is one thing. It's outside my field, but I'm curious. How did he keep that plane in the air for ten hours—with only ten minutes' fuel?"

The two men stared at each other and, through the open door, the freezing desert cold began to seep into the little room.

Dorothy and John De Courcy

RAT RACE

LOIS MacDONALD opened the door of the laboratory. Her husband, Bruce, and Dr. Granas were studying something intently.

"It's six o'clock, Bruce," she called from the doorway.

Bruce looked up from the table. "Already?" he asked, surprised.

Dr. Granas stretched. "That's the way it is, Bruce. Time seems to slip through a man's fingers when he's doing something."

Bruce walked across the room. "Well, we might as well hear what he has to say and get it over with." He snapped on the televisor and walked back to the sink. The two men washed their hands and dried them, occasionally glancing at the screen.

The orchestra that had been playing vanished to be replaced by the solemn face of an announcer. "Ladies and Gentlemen. This is Malcolm Field, speaking to you from the United Nations Government Building in Geneva. Through the cooperation of the European Broadcasting Alliance, we bring you a special address by United States Delegate, Avery B. Clark."

The scene shifted and the usually tragic face of Delegate Clark appeared looking more dejected than usual. He cleared his throat.

"My fellow citizens. There are few of you, if any, who do not know of the momentous events of these last four days. You have heard, as did I, the surrender ultimatum of the Cafis. Yesterday, we experienced the type of warfare which we can expect if we are to resist.

"For one hour, it was as if our civilization did not exist and we were returned to the Stone Age. The official emissary of the Cafis explained the principle of this weapon and has shown how it is applied, yet none of our scientists, either professional or amateur, has been able to find a way to combat this weapon. The Cafis have informed us that this only one of many such weapons and each is equally potent.

"This is not war as we of earth have known war, but it is war none the less. The Cafis are an alien race and therefore a peculiar one. If they had wished, they could have attacked us without warning and by now, we would all be dead.

"My fellow delegates and I have felt the grave responsibility resting upon us and we have considered the facts carefully. If I were deciding for myself alone, I would say, fight! Fight to the end! I would have nothing of greater value to risk than my life and my honor. But, I have had to decide for you, for your wives, for your fathers and mothers, for your husbands and for your children.

"Therefore, I have made the only decision possible. It is the unanimous decision of the United Nations Government that we accept the ultimatum, 'surrender without condition.' The surrender will take effect at seven o'clock tonight, Eastern Standard Time. From then on, we will be subjects of the Galactic Empire of Cafis, and we will be expected to govern ourselves accordingly."

Delegate Clark paused, his lower lip trembling. "Good-by and God be with you," he finished hastily.

Bruce turned the televisor off. He looked at Granas and then at his wife. "Hello, fellow slaves," he said, grinning.

"It's not funny, Bruce!" Lois snapped and buried her face in her hands. Bruce went to her side and put his arms around her.

"I wonder what we do now?" Dr. Granas asked of no one in particular.

"I'm afraid I don't know, Uncle Bob," Bruce answered. "I haven't had much experience at this sort of thing."

"Is—isn't there something we can do?" Lois burst forth, desperately. "Maybe—maybe if there was more electricity—"

Dr. Granas shook his head. "If you were a scientist, Lois, you'd understand. This thing can't be beaten. You've seen condensers and you know how simple they are. The weapon of the Cafis is almost the same as a condenser. They created two electro-static fields of unimaginable intensity which encompassed the earth outside the atmosphere. This in turn, converted the earth into a non-unified stress field and isn't entirely understood."

"But—but how does it work?" Lois asked. "Surely there is some way to combat it!"

Dr. Granas smiled. "Well, any electrical activity, no matter how slight, acting in this field, instantly sets up a counter potential of almost equal pressure. It would take billions of horsepower to operate even the devices in the house. The earth simply hasn't got the available power to overcome this potential, and even if it did, we would be defeating ourselves in using it since the Cafis draw their power directly from the sun.

"Why, there would be such a tremendous amount of heat released here on earth that it would destroy all life within a matter of hours. Even if we surmounted that obstacle, the Cafis would be draining so much power from the sun that in a few weeks, it would become unstable and might even explode into a super-nova.

"We would then literally be jumping from the frying pan into the fire. There might be another way but we simply haven't the technology and knowledge to find it or use it. In a hundred years we might, but not now."

Lois nodded dejectedly. They just sat disconsolately in the laboratory. There was nothing to say; nothing to do but wait.

Finally, Dr. Granas glanced at the clock. "Thirty-eight more minutes of freedom," he sighed. "Thirty-eight more precious minutes and I have nothing to do."

Bruce roused himself. "Do you remember that bottle of Napoleon brandy you gave us two years ago?" Dr. Granas nodded. "Well, it seems to me," Bruce continued, "that it's still in the refrigerator."

Lois looked up. "It's still there, darling. Shall I get it?"

"I think it would be a good idea," Bruce said. "Take it into the living room, dear, and I'll get the goblets."

In the living room, Bruce carefully divided what was left of the brandy into three goblets. He set the bottle down and silently handed glasses to Lois and her Uncle Bob. They stood facing each other, Bruce slightly swirling the brandy in his glass.

Dr. Granas again glanced at the clock. "Ladies and gentlemen," he began, oratorically, "since this is my last twenty-seven minutes of freedom. I offer a toast. To the United Nations, to the United States, and to—tomorrow morning. May I wake up and find this is all a dream."

Lois bit her lip as the glasses tinkled. They fell silent again after the toast, each counting the minutes and having in them, thoughts too private to share.

Soon, Granas walked over to the televisor. He turned. "Shall I turn it on?" he asked, hesitantly.

"Let's wait until seven," Lois suggested. "We're free to do as we please until then."

"Maybe it would be better," Granas agreed. "I imagine the 'rats' will have us listening every day to propaganda broadcasts from now on."

"You're going to have to watch out for that word in the future, Uncle Bob," Bruce said. "They may be rodents but they're also our bosses."

Lois shuddered. "They do look like rats," she interposed. "I think they're horrible!"

Bruce replied, "You know, I think we're being illogical. They don't really look like rats. They don't have any fur. If it weren't for their teeth and that bottlelike shape, they could easily pass themselves off as men. We humans have some sort of a natural aversion for rodents, particularly rats, but after all, just because they're rodents instead of primates doesn't mean they are vicious. I think they've treated us quite well, so far."

"We still don't know what they're going to do," Dr. Granas said, caustically.

"I wonder how such a terrible life form happened to become a dominant animal?" Lois asked.

"Oh, it's logical enough," Dr. Granas answered. "It's really only an accident that a primate like man became dominant here. On the whole, rodentia are intelligent, and they are certainly prolific. By all rights they should have developed here. Even as it is, we have a great deal of trouble saving civilization from rats. They have lived with us everywhere and have practically defied our every attempt to get rid of them."

"Oh let's not talk about them any more," Lois exclaimed. "They make my skin crawl!"

"All right," Dr. Granas answered. "Maybe we should be watching the televisor. The Cafis will probably have plenty to say."

"I guess I'll go to bed," Lois said. "I don't think I could stand seeing those awful rat faces again."

Bruce kissed her. "I'll be up soon, dear, and don't worry. Everything will be all right."

Lois smiled and nodded her head, but Bruce could see that she wasn't convinced.

Dr. Granas waited until Lois was gone and then snapped on the televisor. A well-known commentator was reviewing the events of the preceding four days, augmented by recorded scenes.

". . . more than industrial paralysis. In homes and offices, these scenes were typical."

The scene shifted to show a young woman snapping on switches and plugging in appliances all over her house. Nothing worked. The scene changed to an office where a young man smilingly demonstrated an inoperative adding machine. The young man picked up a flashlight and snapped on the switch. Nothing happened.

The commentator's voice broke in. "These scenes are in no way exaggerated as you all know. Although we have not yet received the final reports, preliminary surveys show that all types of electrical equipment, no matter where situated, were blanked out during the one hour test yesterday.

"The Cafis emissary, Atis Tobe, declared that if the weapon had been stepped to a higher degree, it would have also prevented the travel of light and heat. Incidentally, we were able to make these recordings by using mechanical motion picture devices and so the stoppage had no effect."

He paused. "That's about all the time we have left. There will be further bulletins every hour unless the Cafis begin censorship of news. And now we take you to the New York News Bureau."

"Now what?" Dr. Granas asked.

"Good evening, ladies and gentlemen. This is Marvin Hill. Our New York News Bureau has become more or less the center of attention during the last twenty minutes. The Cafis Gan, Atis Tobe, has landed in New York and has requested a hookup for a nationwide broadcast. Reports are coming in indicating that similar broadcasts will take place in Europe and Asia. Official emissaries of the Cafis have established headquarters in London, Paris, Moscow, Madrid, Rome and Istanbul.

"We have a tentative report from Shanghai but it has not yet been verified. It appears that simultaneous broadcasts which will cover the whole world will begin in a very few minutes. Indications are that New York will be the new seat of government at least temporarily. We are preparing— That's the signal, ladies and gentlemen. We take you to the Municipal Building."

"I wish they wouldn't be so cheerful," Bruce muttered. "You'd think this was the Fourth of July or something!"

A new face appeared on the screen. "Good evening, ladies and gentlemen of the United States," the face intoned. "This is Kimball Trent. We are bringing you a special address by the Viceroy of the Cafis Empire, Atis Tobe." He paused, significantly. "Viceroy Tobe."

The face and shoulders of the Viceroy came into view. "So that's the number one rat," Dr. Granas mumbled. Bruce thought Atis Tobe was staring directly at Dr. Granas. At least, it looked as though he were. A man's voice was heard in the background. "You're on the air, Your Excellency."

"Thank you," the Viceroy said with a slight lisp. With beady eyes he stared from the screen and twitched his nose a little. The whiskers on the side of his nose were trimmed close and even, looking very much like an out-of-place mustache. His ears were small and except for the bulging forehead, he looked very much like a hairless rat. Even his voice was high pitched and somewhat squeaky.

"I bring greetings to the most recently acquired of the Cafis Empire. Although you have surrendered and are technically a subject race, may I assure you that your status is that of citizens in our great Empire."

"Soft soap!" Bruce growled.

"As fellow citizens," the Cafis Gan continued, "I feel we should understand one another. I am sure that a few of you are harboring some misconceptions regarding us. Possibly I do also regarding you. We have studied your planet for only four days and most of our energy and resources have been devoted to the study of your languages. It has been difficult but we have mastered them sufficiently to adequately express our desires. By induction, we have been able to formulate a reasonably accurate picture of the average inhabitant of this planet.

"That you are creatures of logic is obvious, since you have surrendered rather than tried to resist the inevitable. That you are civilized is plain, not only from your technology but from your attitude toward us, an alien race. Because of these things, I am safe in assuring you that you will soon be granted full citizenship in the Cafis Empire with all its rights and privileges."

Dr. Granas snorted. "He hasn't gathered what our attitude really is! His hide must be a foot thick!"

They listened to a glowing dissertation on the benefits of citizenship in the Cafis Empire. The inducements were purely intellectual and carried not even a residue of emotional appeal.

"Cold blooded little beggars!" the doctor growled.

"There are a few prerequisites to obtaining citizenship, however," the Viceroy went on, "but since these conditions are logically necessary, I confidently expect your full cooperation."

At this point, the Cafis Gan attempted a grin. Seldom had Bruce seen a more revolting spectacle. The Viceroy decided he had grinned enough and continued his speech.

"In order to coordinate technology, it is necessary that all scientists and technicians be registered. If then, you are engaged in one or more of the following professions, full or part time, you will go to the nearest center of local government and there leave your name, address and other such data as you will be asked by those in charge of the registration. Registration will begin tomorrow morning at eight o'clock and will continue until the registration is complete."

The Viceroy began reading off the names of various sciences, arts and crafts with monotonous intonations. When he reached 'Biologist,' Bruce stirred and mumbled something inaudibly. Shortly after that came 'Chemist.'

"I see I'm in this too," Dr. Granas sighed.

They listened while the Cafis Gan finished his list. Then he favored his audience with another smile. He laid down several more edicts which were not too restrictive and suggested that it was desirable that each person conduct himself in his most normal manner.

"Business as usual during altercations!" Dr. Granas gritted.

The Viceroy stopped speaking and turned his head. He made a motion to someone, and his face vanished to be replaced by that of a local announcer.

Dr. Granas reached over and switched off the televisor. "Well, Bruce, I wonder how many times a minute they would like to have us breathe!"

Bruce didn't move. He just stared at the blank screen.

"What do you think we should do now?" Dr. Granas asked.

Still Bruce didn't stir.

"What's the matter, boy? Are you hypnotized or something?"

"Huh? Oh. What did you say, Uncle Bob?"

"I said, are you hypnotized?"

"Ah—oh no. It was just that profile."

"Well," Granas smiled, "I can't say that it's any more repugnant than a full face view."

"No, I mean—" Bruce paused. "Oh, I don't know." He sighed. "Let it go."

"I've been thinking, Bruce. If we get downtown early tomorrow, we may not have to wait long to register."

"Yeah, I suppose so," Bruce answered, "but if you feel up to it, I'd like to do a little work tonight. The only thing we have to do is connect up the amplifying circuits."

"It's all right with me," Dr. Granas replied. "We can start testing tomorrow then."

"That reminds me," Bruce interrupted. "In order to energize the colloid, we'll have to feed a variable current into the input amplifier."

"Yes," Dr. Granas nodded. "The more variable, the better."

"Well, how about this idea," Bruce suggested. "Let's hook a microphone up to the input and stand it in front of the loudspeaker of the lab's televisor. That would really give us variation. We can keep it turned on low enough so it won't bother anyone."

"Sometimes, Bruce, you get the darnedest ideas," Dr. Granas chuckled. "I guess you're just naturally lazy. There's nothing like letting the broadcasting company energize the colloid for us!"

"Do you think it'll work?" Bruce asked.

"I don't see why not. There's nothing wrong with it."

The two men went into the laboratory and set to work on the final connections.

Forty-five minutes later, Bruce laid down his soldering iron. "Pretty much Goldburgish but the output is O.K."

"You all done?" Granas asked.

"Yup, she's all hooked up. Do you want me to help you?"

"No, I'm done too. The circulation pump looks kind of crude but I'll give it the 'Granas' personal guarantee."

Bruce walked over to a cabinet and took out a small microphone. As he walked back, he unwound the cord and plugged it into the calculator's input amplifying circuit. They finally got the microphone properly propped up in front of the televisor. As Granas tuned in a program, Bruce stuck two test leads into the innards of the tube circuit.

"A little more volume, Uncle Bob. There, that's about right."

Dr. Granas straightened and grinned. "Well, shall we go to bed and let the 'MacDonald automatic energizing system' do the work for us?"

Bruce stuck his ear next to the loudspeaker attached to the calculator's output.

"What do you expect to hear, Bruce?"

"Oh, nothing. I just couldn't resist it. By tomorrow we should have a pretty good echo coming through."

"I hope you're right, my boy," Dr. Granas replied. "If we don't, we will have wasted a lot of time and money."

"Under the present circumstances," Bruce said, slipping off his lab coat, "I don't see that it makes much difference how much money we lose."

"No use being bitter," Granas retorted. "It isn't going to do the Cafis any harm or you any good."

"I guess you're right," Bruce sighed.

The two men left the laboratory. Dr. Granas paused at the stairway. "You go ahead, Bruce. I forgot to shut the lights off."

"O.K. Good night."

"Pleasant dreams, fellow Roman!"

Bruce went upstairs. Lois was asleep so he undressed quietly and eased himself into bed.

Breakfast was a dismal ritual. Dr. Granas made two or three ineffectual attempts to relieve the oppression. Lois was obviously depressed, but Bruce seemed detached, preoccupied, and his face wore the same expression of philosophic calm it had the night before.

"What have I done? Why won't you talk to me?" Dr. Granas asked.

"I'm sorry, Uncle Bob," Lois sighed. "I don't mean to be rude."

"Oh, it isn't that," Granas smiled. "I know you aren't trying to be rude, but it worries me when you don't talk."

"Is a woman always supposed to be talking?" Lois asked, smiling.

"Of course not," Granas answered, "but I know you too well. You're letting this thing get you, and you can't hide it."

"I'm sorry I'm—just—oh—I guess I'm not used to being a slave!"

"I know it's unpleasant," Granas admitted, "but there's nothing we can do about it, and as people have always done, we'll just have to grin and bear it. Come on, Bruce! Stop brooding!" The older man laid a friendly hand on Bruce's shoulder.

"Huh?"

"I said, cheer up!"

Bruce sighed. "Oh, I'm not depressed. I've just been thinking."

"Well, you can do your thinking when we get back. It's almost time to leave. We want to get downtown before a line forms so we can get home earlier."

"Would you like some more coffee before you go?" Lois asked.

"I don't think so, dear," Bruce answered. "Uncle Bob is right."

"Bruce, you're getting to be a cynic, just like your father," Granas said.

"Maybe I am but I've got better reasons than he had."

Dr. Granas arose. "Let's get going. We can talk on the way to town."

Lois followed the two men into the hall. She took her coat out of the closet while Bruce was tying his tie.

"You aren't going too, are you?" Bruce asked.

"I most certainly am!" she replied.

"Oh, there isn't any necessity for that, darling. This is only a registration. We're only going downtown and we'll be right back."

"I don't trust them, any of them!" she stated. "If you go, I go too!"

Bruce opened his mouth to object, then, finding no logical reason, let it go. "All right, dear. Maybe we'll take in a show or something afterward."

"Not today, we won't!" Granas interposed. "It has taken us two years to build our calculator and today we're going to test it!"

"I'm not so sure I want to test it," Bruce replied, opening the door. "After all, our work is supposed to be dedicated to humanity. Now we'll be giving it to the rats."

"I doubt if we'll be giving much away, Bruce, but in any case, this might be valuable later on. Our calculator might find a method of counteracting that electro-stasis field of the rats."

"I don't see how!" Bruce commented as he slammed the car door.

Granas answered, "I don't mean ours. I mean a later development. Suppose in ten years from now, an electro-colloidal calculator built on our principle were given all the data on that stasis field, for example, a formula with an inoperative generator stated as part of the equation. Wouldn't the brain carry the formula to its logical conclusion? After all, an adding machine doesn't have to understand the term, two plus two."

"That's all just wishful thinking," Bruce replied. "A problem as complex as that would at least call for comprehension or awareness."

"It's only your mind that tells you that," Dr. Granas insisted. "In a sense, our colloid calculator does have awareness. There is always a continuous flow of impulses between all the cells, through the main inductors. You might say quite accurately that it thinks."

"Well, here we are," Bruce interrupted. "I'll let you two out and park the car."

"We'll wait in front of the building!" Lois called.

"All right!"

Ten minutes later, Bruce walked swiftly up to the entrance of the building. "I don't see a line waiting," Bruce smiled. "Have the rats lost their popularity so soon?"

"I wish you'd be serious, Bruce," Lois cautioned. "I don't think this is the least bit funny!"

"Maybe not, maybe not," Bruce replied as they walked into the building.

A policeman gave them directions and they soon found their way to the registration office. Dr. Granas picked out one of the interviewing desks at which no one was waiting. An oldish man was being interviewed by a uniformed Cafis.

"Shall I go first?" Granas asked. "Or do you want to?"

"It doesn't matter to me," Bruce shrugged. "Go ahead."

The oldish man arose and left the desk. Dr. Granas sat down in the chair and Bruce stood behind him.

The Cafis glanced up from the desk and looked at Bruce. "If you will have a chair over there, young man, I will be with you as soon as I have finished with this gentleman's interview."

"We work together," Dr. Granas remarked. "He might be able to give you information that I can't."

"I see," the Cafis said. "If you will draw up a chair, then, we will proceed." The rodent busied himself with some blanks then stared at Dr. Granas. "State your name, age and place of residence, please."

"Doctor Robert Granas, fifty-four, thirty-four-o-three Hudson Terrace."

"Your profession."

"Bio-chemist."

"By whom are you employed?"

"We are doing independent research."

"State the nature of it briefly, please."

"We are preparing a biological calculator utilizing a colloid substance which responds to electrical stimulae in known patterns. We—"

"Doctor, you are attempting to mislead us. You are making an artificial brain."

"Only by a very broad definition could you call it a brain, sir," Granas answered.

"Let me describe the device to you, Doctor," the Cafis said. "This device is fundamentally a tank, divided into tiny insulated compartments. Each compartment has a small opening between itself and all of its immediate neighbors. You have horizontal rods or wires and vertical rods or wires passing through the tank but not directly connected to the cells.

"It seems, by induction, these pick up the tiny impulses. You have an energizing solution slowly filtering through the colloid mass which forms the third pole of your primary electrical system. Connected to this are appropriate amplifiers, integrators and/or various other devices which utilize the output of the brain."

Dr. Granas listened to this recital open mouthed. "But—but—how could you know! How could you possibly know!!"

"From my position, Doctor Granas, it is quite simple but I am sorry that I can not tell you. I must, however, ask you to stop all work on this device. Our technicians will call at your laboratory this afternoon. You are not to do any further work until you receive their permission." Without waiting for a reply, he turned to Bruce. "Your name, age and place of residence, please."

"Bruce MacDonald, thirty-one, same address. I'm a biologist and I plan to leave here at once, return to our laboratory and work unceasingly until our device, as you call it, is finished! I wouldn't advise you or any of your friends to try and stop me."

"Mr. MacDonald. You are being irrational."

"And I plan to go right on being irrational! Any attempt at interference and I shall resort to violence. In case you don't realize what I mean, I will break bones and destroy lives if necessary!"

Bruce jerked the appalled Granas to his feet, and catching Lois by the arm, marched them out of the building. Lois was pale and Dr. Granas trembled a little. Bruce, however, took no notice of anything. Grimly, he led them up the street. No attempt was made to stop them. A few minutes later, they climbed into the car and drove homeward in silence.

As Bruce was unlocking the door, Lois whispered. "Bruce, why did you do it? Now they'll kill us all."

"I've been thinking about that," Bruce said, quietly. "I wondered if I'd made the biggest mistake of my life and possibly my last one—but I don't think so. The more I think about it, the more I'm sure I handled the situation in the only way possible."

"By losing your temper, I suppose!"

"And our lives in the balance!" Granas added.

"No, you two! They aren't going to do a thing to us!" Bruce answered. "I think—"

"And you'd better think fast too!" Granas interrupted, "because there's a car stopping out in front."

Lois dashed to the window. "Oh, Bruce, they've come!" she sobbed. "What'll we do!"

The trio fell silent as two of the aliens emerged from the car, said something to the human driver, and walked measuredly toward the door. Bruce opened it for them and they stepped in without comment. Granas' eyes widened as he recognized the face and dress of the Cafis Gan.

The Viceroy turned and faced Bruce. "I am the Cafis Gan. My name is Atis Tobe. You are, I believe, Bruce MacDonald."

"I am," Bruce admitted, trying not to smile.

"Something amuses you, Mr. MacDonald?" the observing Cafis asked.

"Yes," Bruce answered. "I'm more or less amused to see that I guessed correctly."

The Cafis Gan regarded him with an unwinking stare. "You have declined to follow our request to cease work."

"I have."

"You realize that you are being irrational then?"

"Your Excellency," Bruce began with a grin, "from your point of view, I am completely irrational but my behavior from the human standpoint is not only normal but you will encounter it in eighty percent of your subjects."

"That is impossible," Atis Tobe answered. "You are a civilized race. Such a thing will not be tolerated."

"You have only studied us for four days, Your Excellency," Bruce pointed out.

"True, but there are many indications of civilization. Your own device, for example."

"You have a point there," Bruce admitted, "but I have another device to show you." He reached into his pocket and took out an automatic.

Dr. Granas clenched his hands and Lois gasped. "Bruce, please!" she whispered, fervently.

"If I were to pull this bit of metal called the trigger, you would die instantly," Bruce said to the Cafis Gan.

"Assuming that is the truth, Mr. MacDonald, what does it prove?" The Cafis was annoyed.

"It proves, Your Excellency, that with us, destruction of life is a common thing."

Atis Tobe bent over and studied the revolver. "Did you make this?"

"No," Bruce answered. "Nearly every human possesses a gun and sometimes uses it. These are made in huge quantities, each one adapted to a specific purpose. This one is expressly designed for use on humans. It would work equally well on you also."

The Cafis Gan continued to stare at the gun. "What is the principle?"

"It's a simple heat engine," Bruce replied. "Chemical reaction generates a high gas pressure which forces a metal pellet through this tube. The velocity of the bit of metal or bullet will cause it to penetrate a body, rupturing its internal organs where it strikes."

Atis Tobe had apparently been practising his smile, for this one was not nearly so gruesome. "Your explanation, Mr. MacDonald, is most ingenious. For a moment, I almost believed you."

Bruce lined the gun up at point blank range and squeezed the trigger. The report was deafening in the small room. A metal insigne ripped off the shoulder of the uniform of the Cafis Gan. The Viceroy felt of the torn fabric and turned to look at the wall behind. It was almost imperceptible but Bruce detected a faint quiver in the rodent's talonlike hand.

"Almost you have convinced me," the Cafis said slowly.

"Lois," Bruce said. "Will you get that package from the butcher shop? It's in the refrigerator behind the milk."

"What?" Lois asked, confused.

"Get me our latest purchase from the butcher shop," Bruce repeated, distinctly.

Lois hurried to the kitchen and returned a moment later with a package wrapped in white paper. She extended it timidly to Bruce. He ripped it open with the muzzle of his automatic and removed a two inch thick, round steak from the wrapper. Slowly, Bruce extended the dripping steak to the Viceroy.

The rodent man recoiled a little. "A specimen, Mr. MacDonald?" he asked.

"No," Bruce replied, trying to leer. *"Food!"*

Atis Tobe winced and covered his eyes. In a moment he recovered his composure and turned to stare at Dr. Granas. "Is all this the truth?"

Granas nodded his head. "I'm afraid it is, Your Excellency."

"How horrible! How depraved!"

There was silence in the room as Bruce placed the steak back in its wrapper and handed it to Lois.

"I believe we have made a terrible mistake," the Cafis Gan said, weakly. "It is incredible that such barbarism can exist among thinking creatures!" His body twitched. He turned and walked to the door. In stupefied silence, the trio watched the two Cafis leave. The rodents paused at the car and stared at the human driver. Almost fearfully, they stepped in and drove off.

Lois turned from the window. "What are they going to do now?" she asked, wringing her hands.

"I imagine their full time occupation from now on will be leaving the earth and trying to forget it as soon as possible," Bruce answered, smiling.

Dr. Granas shook his head. "I don't understand this at all," he said. "What's going on?"

"It's quite simple, Uncle Bob," Bruce replied. "The Cafis thought we were civilized. In fact, I don't think they've ever come across an uncivilized race before."

"What do you mean, uncivilized!" Granas bristled.

"Civilization is a pretty relative term," Bruce answered. "To us, we are civilized. To the Cafis, however, we are monsters. You see, the Cafis don't kill. Their understanding of the term 'war' is a sort of a contest, certainly not bloodshed."

"But they're a conquering race!" Granas objected. "How can they do it without bloodshed?"

"I'm not entirely sure," Bruce replied, thoughtfully. "I'm only guessing, but so far my guesses have been pretty good. My theory is that the rest of their empire is much like themselves. You yourself remarked that it was only an accident that the rodents didn't become the predominant race here on earth."

"That's true," Dr. Granas admitted.

"I think we can assume, that up until now, the Cafis have only had to deal with races similar to themselves. When they came here, they carried on their warfare just as they always have done. I bet the rest of their empire considers them pretty ruthless conquerors."

"I don't see what you're getting at!" Granas exploded.

"I got the clue last night, Uncle Bob," Bruce continued, "when Atis Tobe turned his head. I thought about it for a long time and finally decided that I was right. I guessed that they were non-carnivores and were therefore unaccustomed to violence and bloodshed. It was so unheard of to them, that they didn't for one minute expect to find a carnivorous civilization.

"Look at how they conquered the earth. Not by killing! Their weapons are of a different type. They paralyze a civilization and give you a chance to nullify the weapon and if you can't do it, they win. If you can combat their weapon, then they think up a new one and on it goes until someone's resources are exhausted."

"Well—well—how did you know they were so peaceful?" Lois stammered. "Rats here on earth are vicious—and horrible!"

Bruce laughed. "Darling, that's what comes from jumping to conclusions. The Cafis are rodents to be sure, but as rodents go, rats are certainly not the most intelligent!"

"Well these rats are certainly intelligent!" Granas interrupted.

"Not rats, Uncle Bob," Bruce replied, grinning. "Beavers!"

"Not exactly," a loud voice boomed.

The trio stood frozen, staring at each other.

"W-h-a-t?" Granas said, weakly.

"I said, not exactly." The voice rumbled through the open door of the laboratory.

There was a momentary mad scramble as they all tried to go through the laboratory door at one time. Their eyes took in the empty room at a glance, then rested on the loudspeaker of the calculator. They waited, hardly breathing.

"Rabbits!" the calculator said.

Eric Frank Russell

DEAR DEVIL

THE first Martian vessel descended upon Earth with the slow, stately fall of a grounded balloon. It did resemble a large balloon in that it was spherical and had a strange buoyancy out of keeping with its metallic construction. Beyond this superficial appearance all similarity to anything Terrestrial ceased.

There were no rockets, no crimson venturis, no external projections other than several solaradiant distorting grids which boosted the ship in any desired direction through the cosmic field. There were no observation ports. All viewing was done through a transparent band running right around the fat belly of the sphere. The bluish, nightmarish crew were assembled behind that band, surveying the world with great multi-faceted eyes.

They gazed through the band in utter silence as they examined this world which was Terra. Even if they had been capable of speech they would have said nothing. But none among them had a talkative faculty in any sonic sense. At this quiet moment none needed it.

The scene outside was one of untrammelled desolation. Scraggy blue-green grass clung to tired ground right away to the horizon scarred by ragged mountains. Dismal bushes struggled for life here and there, some with the pathetic air of striving to become trees as once their ancestors had been. To the right, a long, straight scar through the grass betrayed the sterile lumpiness of rocks at odd places. Too rugged and too narrow ever to have been a road, it suggested no more than the desiccating remnants of a long-gone wall. And over all this loomed a ghastly sky.

Captain Skhiva eyed his crew, spoke to them with his sign-talking tentacle. The alternative was contact-telepathy which required physical touch.

"It is obvious that we are out of luck. We could have done no worse had we landed on the empty satellite. However, it is safe to go out. Anyone who wishes to explore a little while may do so."

One of them gesticulated back at him. "Captain, don't you wish to be the first to step upon this world?"

"It is of no consequence. If anyone deems it an honor, he is welcome to it." He pulled the lever opening both air-lock doors. Thicker, heavier air crowded in and pressure went up a little. "Beware of over-exertion," he warned as they went out.

Poet Fander touched him, tentacles tip to tip as he sent his thoughts racing through their nerve-ends. "This confirms all that we saw as we approached. A stricken planet far gone in its death throes. What do you suppose caused it?"

"I have not the remotest idea. I would like to know. If it has been smitten by natural forces, what might they do to Mars?" His troubled mind sent its throb of worry up Fander's contacting tentacle. "A pity that this planet had not been farther out instead of closer in; we might then have observed the preceding phenomena from the surface of Mars. It is so difficult properly to view this one against the Sun."

"That applies still more to the next world, the misty one," observed Poet Fander.

"I know it. I am beginning to fear what we may find there. If it proves to be equally dead, then we are stalled until we can make the big jump outward."

"Which won't be in our lifetimes."

"I doubt it," agreed Captain Skhiva. "We might move fast with the help of friends. We shall be slow—alone." He turned to watch his crew writhing in various directions across the grim landscape. "They find it good to be on firm ground. But what is a world without life and beauty? In a short time they will grow tired of it."

Fander said thoughtfully, "Nevertheless, I would like to see more of it. May I take out the lifeboat?"

"You are a songbird, not a pilot," reproved Captain Skhiva. "Your function is to maintain morale by entertaining us, not to roam around in a lifeboat."

"But I know how to handle it. Every one of us was trained to handle it. Let me take it that I may see more."

"Haven't we seen enough, even before we landed? What else is there to see? Cracked and distorted roads about to dissolve into nothingness. Ages-old cities, torn and broken, crumbling into dust. Shattered mountains and charred forests and craters little smaller than those upon the Moon. No sign of any superior life-form still surviving. Only the grass, the shrubs, and various animals, two or four-legged, that flee at our approach. Why do you wish to see more?"

"There is poetry even in death," said Fander.

"Even so, it remains repulsive." Skhiva gave a little shiver. "All right. Take the lifeboat. Who am I to question the weird workings of the non-technical mind?"

"Thank you, Captain."

"It is nothing. See that you are back by dusk." Breaking contact, he went to the lock, curled snakishly on its outer rim and brooded, still without bothering to touch the new world. So much attempted, so much done—for so poor reward.

He was still pondering it when the lifeboat soared out of its lock. Ex-pressionlessly, his multi-faceted eyes watched the energized grids change angle as the boat swung into a curve and floated away like a little bubble. Skhiva was sensitive to futility.

The crew came back well before darkness. A few hours were enough. Just grass and shrubs and child-trees straining to grow up. One had discovered a grassless oblong that once might have been the site of a dwelling. He brought back a small piece of its foundation, a lump of perished concrete which Skhiva put by for later analysis.

Another had found a small, brown, six-legged insect, but his nerve-ends had heard it crying when he picked it up, so hastily he had put it down and let it go free. Small, clumsily moving animals had been seen hopping in the distance, but all had dived down holes in the ground before any Martian could get near. All the crew were agreed upon one thing: the silence and solemnity of a people's passing was unendurable.

Fander beat the sinking of the Sun by half a time-unit. His bubble drifted under a great, black cloud, sank to ship-level, came in. The rain started a moment later, roaring down in frenzied torrents while they stood behind the transparent band and marvelled at so much water.

After a while, Captain Skhiva told them, "We must accept what we find. We have drawn a blank. The cause of this world's condition is a mystery to be solved by others with more time and better equipment. It is for us to abandon this graveyard and try the misty planet. We will take off early in the morning."

None commented, but Fander followed him to his room, made contact with a tentacle-touch.

"One could live here, Captain."

"I am not so sure of that." Skhiva coiled on his couch, suspending his tentacles on the various limb-rests. The blue sheen of him was reflected by the back wall. "In some places are rocks emitting alpha-sparks. They are dangerous."

"Of course, Captain. But I can sense them and avoid them."

"*You?*" Skhiva stared up at him.

"Yes, Captain. I wish to be left here."

"What?—in this place of appalling repulsiveness?"

"It has an all-pervading air of ugliness and despair," admitted Poet Fander. "All destruction is ugly. But by accident I have found a little beauty. It heartens me. I would like to seek its source."

"To what beauty do you refer?" Skhiva demanded.

Fander tried to explain the alien in non-alien terms.

"Draw it for me," ordered Skhiva.

Fander drew it, gave him the picture, said, "There!"

Gazing at it for a long time, Skhiva handed it back, mused awhile, then spoke along the other's nerves. "We are individuals with all the rights of individuals. As an individual, I don't think that picture sufficiently beautiful to be worth the tail-tip of a domestic *arlan*. I will admit that it is not ugly, even that it is pleasing."

"But, Captain—"

"As an individual," Skhiva went on, "you have an equal right to your opinions, strange though they may be. If you really wish to stay I cannot refuse you. I am entitled only to think you a little crazy." He eyed Fander again. "When do you hope to be picked up?"

"This year, next year, sometime, never."

"It may well be never," Skhiva reminded. "Are you prepared to face that prospect?"

"One must always be prepared to face the consequences of his own actions," Fander pointed out.

"True." Skhiva was reluctant to surrender. "But have you given the matter serious thought?"

"I am a non-technical component. I am not guided by thought."

"Then by what?"

"By my desires, emotions, instincts. By my inward feelings."

Skhiva said fervently, "The twin moons preserve us!"

"Captain, sing me a song of home and play me the tinkling harp."

"Don't be silly. I have not the ability."

"Captain, if it required no more than careful thought you would be able to do it?"

"Doubtlessly," agreed Skhiva, seeing the trap but unable to avoid it.

"There you are!" said Fander pointedly.

"I give up. I cannot argue with someone who casts aside the accepted rules of logic and invents his own. You are governed by notions that defeat me."

"It is not a matter of logic or illogic," Fander told him. "It is merely a matter of viewpoint. You see certain angles; I see others."

"For example?"

"You won't pin me down that way. I can find examples. For instance, do you remember the formula for determining the phase of a series tuned circuit?"

"Most certainly."

"I felt sure you would. You are a technician. You have registered it for all time as a matter of technical utility." He paused, staring at Skhiva. "I know that formula, too. It was mentioned to me, casually, many years ago. It is of no use to me—yet I have never forgotten it."

"Why?"

"Because it holds the beauty of rhythm. It is a poem."

Skhiva sighed and said, "I don't get it."

"*One upon R into omega L minus one upon omega C,*" recited Fander. "A perfect hexameter." He showed his amusement as the other rocked back.

After a while, Skhiva remarked, "It could be sung. One could dance to it."

"Same with this." Fander exhibited his rough sketch. "This holds beauty. Where there is beauty there once was talent—may still be talent for all we know. Where talent abides is also greatness. In the realms of greatness we may find powerful friends. We *need* such friends."

"You win." Skhiva made a gesture of defeat. "We leave you to your self-chosen fate in the morning."

"Thank you, Captain."

The same streak of stubbornness which made Skhiva a worthy commander induced him to take one final crack at Fander shortly before departure. Summoning him to his room, he eyed the poet calculatingly.

"You are still of the same mind?"

"Yes, Captain."

"Then does it not occur to you as strange that I should be so content to abandon this planet if indeed it does hold the remnants of greatness?"

"No."

"Why not?" Skhiva stiffened slightly.

"Captain, I think you are a little afraid because you suspect what I suspect: that there was no natural disaster. They did it themselves—to themselves."

"We have no proof of it," said Skhiva uneasily.

"No, Captain." Fander posed there without desire to add more.

"*If* this is their own sad handiwork," Skhiva commented at length, "what are our chances of finding friends among people so much to be feared?"

"Poor," admitted Fander. "But that—being the product of cold thought —means little to me. I am animated by warm hopes."

"There you go again, blatantly discarding reason in favor of an idle dream. Hoping, hoping, hoping—to achieve the impossible."

Fander said, "The difficult can be done at once; the impossible takes a little longer."

"Your thoughts make my orderly mind feel lopsided. Every remark is a flat denial of something that makes sense." Skhiva transmitted the sensation of a lugubrious chuckle. "Oh, well, we live and learn." He came forward, moving closer to the other. "All your supplies are assembled outside. Nothing remains but to bid you goodby."

They embraced in the Martian manner. Leaving the lock, Poet Fander watched the big sphere shudder and glide up. It soared without sound, shrinking steadily until it was a mere dot entering a cloud. A moment later it had gone.

He remained there, looking at the cloud, for a long, long time. Then he turned his attention to the load-sled holding his supplies. Climbing onto its tiny, exposed front seat, he shifted the control which energized the flotation-grids, let it rise a few feet. The higher the rise the greater the expenditure of power. He wished to conserve power; there was no knowing how long he might need it. So at low altitude and gentle pace he let the sled glide in the general direction of the thing of beauty.

Later, he found a dry cave in the hill on which his objective stood. It took him two days of careful, cautious raying to square its walls, ceiling and floor, plus half a day with a powered fan driving out silicate dust. After that, he stowed his supplies at the back, parked the sled near the front, set up a curtaining force-screen across the entrance. The hole in the hill was now home.

Slumber did not come easily that first night. He lay within the cave, a ropey, knotted thing of glowing blue with enormous, bee-like eyes, and found himself listening for harps that played sixty million miles away. His tentacle-ends twitched in involuntary search of the telepathic-contact songs that would go with the harps, and twitched in vain. Darkness grew deep and all the world a monstrous stillness held. His hearing organs craved for the eventide flip-flop of sand-frogs, but there were no frogs. He wanted the homely drone of night beetles, but none droned. Except for once when something faraway howled its heart at the Moon, there was nothing, nothing.

In the morning he washed, ate, took out the sled and explored the site of a small town. He found little to satisfy his curiosity, no more than mounds of shapeless rubble on ragged, faintly oblong foundations. It was a graveyard of long-dead domiciles, rotting, weedy, near to complete oblivion. A view from five hundred feet up gave him only one piece of information: the orderliness of outlines showed that these people had been tidy, methodical.

But tidiness is not beauty in itself. He came back to the top of his hill and sought solace with the thing that was beauty.

His explorations continued, not systematically as Skhiva would have performed them, but in accordance with his own mercurial whims. At times he saw many animals, singly or in groups, none resembling anything Martian. Some scattered at full gallop when his sled swooped over them. Some dived into groundholes, showing a brief flash of white, absurd tails. Others, four-footed, long-faced, sharp-toothed, hunted in gangs and bayed at him in concert with harsh, defiant voices.

On the seventieth day, in a deep, shadowed glade to the north, he spotted a small group of new shapes slinking along in single file. He recognized them at a glance, knew them so well that his searching eyes sent an immediate thrill of triumph into his mind. They were ragged, dirty and no more than half grown, but the thing of beauty had told him what they were.

Hugging the ground low, he swept around in a wide curve that brought him to the farther end of the glade. His sled sloped slightly into the drop as it entered the glade. He could see them better now, even the soiled pinkishness of their thin legs. They were moving away from him, with fearful caution, but the silence of his swoop gave them no warning.

The rearmost one of the stealthy file fooled him at the last moment. He was hanging over the side of the sled, tentacles outstretched in readiness to snatch the end one with the wild mop of yellow hair when, responding to some sixth sense, his intended victim threw itself flat.

His grasp shot past a couple of feet short and he got a glimpse of frightened gray eyes two seconds before a dexterous side-tilt of the sled enabled him to make good his loss by grabbing the less wary next in line.

This one was dark-haired, a bit bigger, and sturdier. It fought madly at his holding limbs while he gained altitude. Then suddenly, realizing the queer nature of its bonds, it writhed around and looked straight at him. The result was unexpected; it closed its eyes and went completely limp.

It was still limp when he bore it into the cave, but its heart continued to beat and its lungs to draw. Laying it carefully on the softness of his bed, he moved to the cave's entrance and waited for it to recover. Eventually it stirred, sat up, gazed confusedly at the facing wall. Its black eyes moved slowly around, taking in the surroundings. Then they saw Fander. They widened tremendously and their owner began to make high-pitched, unpleasant noises as it tried to back away through the solid wall. It screamed so much, in one rising throb after another, that Fander slithered out of the cave, right out of sight, and sat in the cold winds until the noises had died down.

A couple of hours later he made cautious reappearance to offer it food, but its reaction was so swift, hysterical and heart-rending that he dropped his load and hid himself as though the fear was his own. The food remained untouched for two full days. On the third, a little of it was eaten. Fander ventured within.

Although the Martian did not go near, the boy cowered away murmuring, "Devil! Devil!" His eyes were red, with dark discoloration beneath them.

"Devil!" thought Fander, totally unable to repeat the alien word, but wondering what it meant. He used his sign-talking tentacle in valiant effort to convey something reassuring. The attempt was wasted. The other watched its writhings half in fear, half with distaste, and showed complete lack of comprehension. He let the tentacle gently slither forward across the floor, hoping to make thought-contact. The other recoiled from it as from a striking snake.

"Patience," he reminded himself. "The impossible takes a little longer."

Periodically he showed himself with food and drink, and night-times he slept fitfully on the coarse, damp grass beneath lowering skies—while the prisoner who was his guest enjoyed the softness of the bed, the warmth of the cave, the security of the force-screen.

Time came when Fander betrayed an unpoetic shrewdness by using the other's belly to estimate the ripeness of the moment. When, on the eighth day, he noted that his food-offerings were now being taken regularly, he took a meal of his own at the edge of the cave, within plain sight, and observed that the other's appetite was not spoiled. That night he slept just within the cave, close to the force-screen, and as far from the boy as possible. The boy stayed awake late, watching him, always watching him, but gave way to slumber in the small hours.

A fresh attempt at sign-talking brought no better results than before, and the boy still refused to touch his offered tentacle. All the same, he was gaining ground slowly. His overtures still were rejected, but with less revulsion. Gradually, ever so gradually, the Martian shape was becoming familiar, almost acceptable.

The sweet savor of success was Fander's in the middle of the next day. The boy had displayed several spells of emotional sickness during which he lay on his front with shaking body and emitted low noises while his eyes watered profusely. At such times the Martian felt strangely helpless and inadequate. On this occasion, during another attack, he took advantage of the sufferer's lack of attention and slid near enough to snatch away the box by the bed.

From the box he drew his tiny electro-harp, plugged its connectors, switched it on, touched its strings with delicate affection. Slowly he began to play, singing an accompaniment deep inside himself. For he had no voice with which to sing out loud, but the harp sang it for him. The boy ceased his quiverings, sat up, all his attention upon the dexterous play of the tentacles and the music they conjured forth. And when he judged that at last the listener's mind was captured, Fander ceased with easy, quietening strokes, gently offered him the harp. The boy registered interest and reluctance. Careful not to move nearer, not an inch nearer, Fander offered it at full tentacle length. The boy had to take four steps to get it. He took them.

That was the start. They played together, day after day and sometimes a little into the night, while almost imperceptibly the distance between them was reduced. Finally they sat together, side by side, and the boy had not yet learned to laugh but no longer did he show unease. He could now extract a simple tune from the instrument and was pleased with his own aptitude in a solemn sort of way.

One evening as darkness grew, and the things that sometimes howled at the Moon were howling again, Fander offered his tentacle-tip for the hundredth time. Always the gesture had been unmistakable even if its motive was not clear, yet always it had been rebuffed. But now, now, five fingers curled around it in shy desire to please.

With a fervent prayer that human nerves would function just like Martian ones, Fander poured his thoughts through, swiftly, lest the warm grip be loosened too soon.

"Do not fear me. I cannot help my shape any more than you can help yours. I am your friend, your father, your mother. I need you as much as you need me."

The boy let go of him, began quiet, half-stifled whimpering noises. Fander put a tentacle on his shoulder, made little patting motions that he imagined were wholly Martian. For some inexplicable reason, this made matters worse. At his wits' end what to do for the best, what action to take that might be understandable in Terrestrial terms, he gave the problem up, surrendered to his instinct, put a long, ropey limb around the boy and held him close until the noises ceased and slumber came. It was then he realized the child he had taken was much younger than he had estimated. He nursed him through the night.

Much practice was necessary to make conversation. The boy had to learn to put mental drive behind his thoughts, for it was beyond Fander's power to suck them out of him.

"What is your name?"

Fander got a picture of thin legs running rapidly.

He returned it in question form. "Speedy?"

An affirmative.

"What name do you call me?"

An unflattering montage of monsters.

"Devil?"

The picture whirled around, became confused. There was a trace of embarrassment.

"Devil will do," assured Fander. He went on. "Where are your parents?"

More confusion.

"You must have had parents. Everyone has a father and mother, haven't they? Don't you remember yours?"

Muddled ghost-pictures. Grown-ups leaving children. Grown-ups avoiding children, as if they feared them.

"What is the first thing you remember?"

"Big man walking with me. Carried me a bit. Walked again."

"What happened to him?"

"Went away. Said he was sick. Might make me sick too."

"Long ago?"

Confusion.

Fander changed his aim. "What of those other children—have they no parents either?"

"All got nobody."

"But you've got somebody now, haven't you, Speedy?"

Doubtfully. "Yes."

Fander pushed it farther. "Would you rather have me, or those other children?" He let it rest a moment before he added, "Or both?"

"Both," said Speedy with no hesitation. His fingers toyed with the harp.

"Would you like to help me look for them tomorrow and bring them here? And if they are scared of me will you help them not to be afraid?"

"Sure!" said Speedy, licking his lips and sticking his chest out.

"Then," said Fander, "perhaps you would like to go for a walk today? You've been too long in this cave. Will you come for a walk with me?"

"Y'betcha!"

Side by side they went a short walk, one trotting rapidly along, the other slithering. The child's spirits perked up with this trip in the open; it was as if the sight of the sky and the feel of the grass made him realize at last that he was not exactly a prisoner. His formerly solemn features became animated, he made exclamations that Fander could not understand, and once he laughed at nothing for the sheer joy of it. On two occasions he grabbed a tentacle-tip in order to tell Fander something, performing the action as if it were in every way as natural as his own speech.

They got out the load-sled in the morning. Fander took the front seat and the controls; Speedy squatted behind him with hands gripping his harness-belt. With a shallow soar, they headed for the glade. Many small, white-tailed animals bolted down holes as they passed over.

"Good for dinner," remarked Speedy, touching him and speaking through the touch.

Fander felt sickened. Meat-eaters! It was not until a queer feeling of shame and apology came back at him that he knew the other had felt his revulsion. He wished he'd been swift to blanket that reaction before the boy could sense it, but he could not be blamed for the effect of so bald a statement taking him so completely unaware. However, it had produced another step forward in their mutual relationship—Speedy desired his good opinion.

Within fifteen minutes they struck lucky. At a point half a mile south of the glade Speedy let out a shrill yell and pointed downward. A small, golden-haired figure was standing there on a slight rise, staring fascinatedly upward at the phenomenon in the sky. A second tiny shape, with red but equally long hair, was at the bottom of the slope gazing in similar wonderment. Both came to their senses and turned to flee as the sled tilted toward them.

Ignoring the yelps of excitement close behind him, and the pulls upon his belt, Fander swooped, got first one, then the other. This left him with only one limb to right the sled and gain height. If the victims had fought he would have had his work cut out to make it. They did not fight. They shrieked as he snatched them and then relaxed with closed eyes.

The sled climbed, glided a mile at five hundred feet. Fander's attention was divided between his limp prizes, the controls and the horizon when suddenly a thunderous rattling sounded on the metal base of the sled, the entire framework shuddered, a strip of metal flew from its leading edge and things made whining sounds toward the clouds.

"Old Graypate," bawled Speedy, jigging around but keeping away from the rim. "He's shooting at us."

The spoken words meant nothing to the Martian and he could not spare a limb for the contact the other had forgotten to make. Grimly righting the sled, he gave it full power. Whatever damage it had suffered had not affected its efficiency; it shot forward at a pace that set the

ERIC FRANK RUSSELL

red and golden hair of the captives streaming in the wind. Perforce his landing by the cave was clumsy. The sled bumped down and lurched across forty yards of grass.

First things first. Taking the quiet pair into the cave, he made them comfortable on the bed, came out and examined the sled. There were half a dozen deep dents in its flat underside, two bright furrows angling across one rim. He made contact with Speedy.

"What were you trying to tell me?"

"Old Graypate shot at us."

The mind-picture burst upon him vividly and with electrifying effect: a vision of a tall, white-haired, stern-faced old man with a tubular weapon propped upon his shoulder while it spat fire upward. A white-haired old man! An adult!

His grip was tight on the other's arm. "What is this oldster to you?"

"Nothing much. He lives near us in the shelters."

Picture of a long, dusty concrete burrow, badly damaged, its ceiling marked with the scars of a lighting system which had rotted away to nothing. The old man living hermitlike at one end; the children at the other. The old man was sour, taciturn, kept the children at a distance, spoke to them seldom but was quick to respond when they were menaced. He had guns. Once he had killed many wild dogs that had eaten two children.

"People left us near shelters because Old Graypate was there, and had guns," informed Speedy.

"But why does he keep away from children? Doesn't he like children?"

"Don't know." He mused a moment. "Once told us that old people could get very sick and make young ones sick—and then we'd all die. Maybe he's afraid of making us die." Speedy wasn't very sure about it.

So there was some much-feared disease around, something contagious, to which adults were peculiarly susceptible. Without hesitation they abandoned their young at the first onslaught, hoping that at least the children would live. Sacrifice after sacrifice that the remnants of the race might survive. Heartbreak after heartbreak as elders chose death alone rather than death together.

Yet Graypate himself was depicted as very old. Was this an exaggeration of the child-mind?

"I must meet Graypate."

"He will shoot," declared Speedy positively. "He knows by now that you took me. He saw you take the others. He will wait for you and shoot."

"We will find some way to avoid that."

"How?"

"When these two have become my friends, just as you have become my friend, I will take all three of you back to the shelters. You can find Graypate for me and tell him that I am not as ugly as I look."

"I don't think you're ugly," denied Speedy.

The picture Fander got along with that gave him the weirdest sensation of pleasure. It was of a vague, shadowy but distorted body with a clear human face.

The new prisoners were female. Fander knew it without being told because they were daintier than Speedy and had the warm, sweet smell of females. That meant complications. Maybe they were mere children, and maybe they lived together in the shelter, but he was permitting none of that while they were in his charge. Fander might be outlandish by other standards but he had a certain primness. Forthwith he cut another and smaller cave for Speedy and himself.

Neither of the girls saw him for two days. Keeping well out of their sight, he let Speedy take them food, talk to them, prepare them for the shape of the thing to come. On the third day he presented himself for inspection at a distance. Despite forewarnings they went sheet-white, clung together, but uttered no distressing sounds. He played his harp a little while, withdrew, came back in the evening and played for them again.

Encouraged by Speedy's constant and self-assured flow of propaganda, one of them grasped a tentacle-tip next day. What came along the nerves was not a picture so much as an ache, a desire, a childish yearning. Fander backed out of the cave, found wood, spent the whole night using the sleepy Speedy as a model and fashioned the wood into a tiny, jointed semblance of a human being. He was no sculptor, but he possessed a natural delicacy of touch, and the poet in him ran through his limbs and expressed itself in the model. Making a thorough job of it, he clothed it in Terrestrial fashion, colored its face, fixed upon its features the pleasure-grimace which humans call a smile.

He gave her the doll the moment she awakened in the morning. She took it eagerly, hungrily, with wide, glad eyes. Hugging it to her unformed bosom, she crooned over it—and he knew that the strange emptiness within her was gone.

Though Speedy was openly contemptuous of this manifest waste of effort, Fander set to and made a second mannikin. It did not take quite as long. Practice on the first had made him swifter, more dexterous. He was able to present it to the other child by mid-afternoon. Her acceptance was made with shy grace, she held the doll close as if it meant more than the whole of her sorry world. In her thrilled concentration upon the gift, she did not notice his nearness, his closeness, and when he offered a tentacle, she took it.

He said, simply, "I love you."

Her mind was too untrained to drive a response, but her great eyes warmed.

Fander sat on the grounded sled at a point a mile east of the glade and watched the three children walk hand in hand toward the hidden shelters. Speedy was the obvious leader, hurrying them onward, bossing them with the noisy assurance of one who has been around and considers himself sophisticated. In spite of this, the girls paused at intervals to turn and wave to the ropey, bee-eyed thing they'd left behind. And Fander dutifully waved back, always using his signal-tentacle because it had not occurred to him that any tentacle would serve.

They sank from sight behind a rise of ground. He remained on the sled, his multi-faceted gaze going over his surroundings or studying the angry sky now threatening rain. The ground was a dull, dead gray-green all the way to the horizon. There was no relief from that drab color, not one shining patch of white, gold or crimson such as dotted the meadows of Mars. There was only the eternal gray-green and his own brilliant blueness.

Before long a sharp-faced, four-footed thing revealed itself in the grass, raised its head and howled at him. The sound was an eerily urgent wail that ran across the grasses and moaned into the distance. It brought others of its kind, two, ten, twenty. Their defiance increased with their numbers until there was a large band of them edging toward him with lips drawn back, teeth exposed. Then there came a sudden and undetectable flock-command which caused them to cease their slinking and spring forward like one, slavering as they came. They did it with the hungry, red-eyed frenzy of animals motivated by something akin to madness.

Repulsive though it was, the sight of creatures craving for meat— even strange blue meat—did not bother Fander. He slipped a control a notch, the flotation grids radiated, the sled soared twenty feet. So calm and easy an escape so casually performed infuriated the wild dog pack beyond all measure. Arriving beneath the sled, they made futile springs upward, fell back upon one another, bit and slashed each other, leaped again and again. The pandemonium they set up was a compound of snarls, yelps, barks and growls, the ferocious expressions of extreme hate. They exuded a pungent odor of dry hair and animal sweat.

Reclining on the sled in a maddening pose of disdain, Fander let the insane ones rave below. They raced around in tight circles shrieking insults at him and biting each other. This went on for some time and ended with a spurt of ultra-rapid cracks from the direction of the glade. Eight dogs fell dead. Two flopped and struggled to crawl away. Ten yelped in agony, made off on three legs. The unharmed ones flashed away to some place where they could make a meal of the escaping limpers. Fander lowered the sled.

Speedy stood on the rise with Graypate. The latter restored his weapon to the crook of his arm, rubbed his chin thoughtfully, ambled forward.

Stopping five yards from the Martian, the old Earthman again massaged his chin whiskers, then said, "It sure is the darnedest thing, just the darnedest thing!"

"No use talking *at* him," advised Speedy. "You've got to touch him, like I told you."

"I know, I know." Graypate betrayed a slight impatience. "All in good time. I'll touch him when I'm ready." He stood there, gazing at Fander with eyes that were very pale and very sharp. "Oh, well, here goes." He offered a hand.

Fander placed a tentacle-end in it.

"Jeepers, he's cold," commented Graypate, closing his grip. "Colder than a snake."

"He isn't a snake," Speedy contradicted fiercely.

"Ease up, ease up—I didn't say he is." Graypate seemed fond of repetitive phrases.

"He doesn't feel like one, either," persisted Speedy, who had never felt a snake and did not wish to.

Fander boosted a thought through. "I come from the fourth planet. Do you know what that means?"

"I ain't ignorant," snapped Graypate aloud.

"No need to reply vocally. I receive your thoughts exactly as you receive mine. Your responses are much stronger than the boy's and I can understand you easily."

"Humph!" said Graypate to the world at large.

"I have been anxious to find an adult because the children can tell me little. I would like to ask questions. Do you feel inclined to answer questions?"

"It depends," answered Graypate, becoming leery.

"Never mind. Answer them if you wish. My only desire is to help you."

"Why?" asked Graypate, searching around for a percentage.

"We need intelligent friends."

"Why?"

"Our numbers are small, our resources poor. In visiting this world and the misty one we've come near to the limit of our ability. But with assistance we could go farther. I think that if we could help you a time might come when you could help us."

Graypate pondered it cautiously, forgetting that the inward workings of his mind were wide-open to the other. Chronic suspicion was the keynote of his thoughts, suspicion based on life experiences and recent history. But inward thoughts ran both ways, and his own mind detected the clear sincerity in Fander's.

So he said, "Fair enough. Say more."

"What caused all this?" inquired Fander, waving a limb at the world.

"War," said Graypate. "The last war we'll ever have. The entire place went nuts."

"How did that come about?"

"You've got me there." Graypate gave the problem grave consideration. "I reckon it wasn't just any one thing; it was a multitude of things sort of piling themselves up."

"Such as?"

"Differences in people. Some were colored differently in their bodies, others in their ideas, and they couldn't get along. Some bred faster than others, wanted more room, more food. There wasn't any more room or more food. The world was full and nobody could shove in except by pushing another out. My old man told me plenty before he died, and he always maintained that if folk had had the hoss-sense to keep their numbers down there might not—"

"Your old man?" interjected Fander. "Your father? Didn't all this occur in your own lifetime?"

"It did not. I saw none of it. I am the son of the son of a survivor."

"Let's go back to the cave," put in Speedy, bored with this silent contact-talk. "I want to show him our harp."

They took no notice, and Fander went on, "Do you think there might be a lot of others still living?"

"Who knows?" Graypate was moody about it. "There isn't any way of telling how many are wandering around the other side of the globe, maybe still killing each other, or starving to death, or dying of the sickness."

"What sickness is this?"

"I couldn't tell what it is called." Graypate scratched his head confusedly. "My old man told me a few times, but I've long forgotten. Knowing the name wouldn't do me any good, see? He said his father told him that it was part of the war, it got invented and was spread deliberately —and it's still with us."

"What are its symptoms?"

"You go hot and dizzy. You get black swellings in the armpits. In forty-eight hours you're dead. Old ones get it first. The kids then catch it unless you make away from them mighty fast."

"It is nothing familiar to me," said Fander, unable to recognize cultured bubonic. "In any case, I'm not a medical expert." He eyed Graypate. "But you seem to have avoided it."

"Sheer luck," opined Graypate. "Or maybe I can't get it. There was a story going around during the war that some folk might develop immunity to it, durned if I know why. Could be that I'm immune, but don't count on it."

"So you keep your distance from these children?"

"Sure." He glanced at Speedy. "I shouldn't really have come along with this kid. He's got a lousy chance as it is without me increasing the odds."

"That is thoughtful of you," Fander put over softly. "Especially seeing that you must be lonely."

Graypate bristled and his thought-flow became aggressive. "I ain't grieving for company. I can look after myself, like I have done since my old man went away to curl up by himself. I'm on my own feet. So's every other guy."

"I believe that," said Fander. "You must pardon me—I'm a stranger here myself. I judged you by my own feelings. Now and again I get pretty lonely."

"How come?" demanded Graypate, staring at him. "You ain't telling me they dumped you and left you, on your own?"

"They did."

"Man!" exclaimed Graypate fervently.

Man! It was a picture resembling Speedy's conception, a vision elusive in form but firm and human in face. The oldster was reacting to what he considered a predicament rather than a choice, and the reaction came on a wave of sympathy.

Fander struck promptly and hard. "You see how I'm fixed. The companionship of wild animals is nothing to me. I need someone intelligent enough to like my music and forget my looks, someone intelligent enough to—"

"I ain't so sure we're that smart," Graypate chipped in. He let his gaze swing morbidly around the landscape. "Not when I see this graveyard and think of how it looked in grandpop's days."

"Every flower blooms from the dust of a hundred dead ones," answered Fander.

"What are flowers?"

It shocked the Martian. He had projected a mind-picture of a trumpet lily, crimson and shining, and Graypate's brain had juggled it around, uncertain whether it were fish, flesh or fowl.

"Vegetable growths, like these." Fander plucked half a dozen blades of blue-green grass. "But more colorful, and sweet-scented." He transmitted the brilliant vision of a mile-square field of trumpet lilies, red and glowing.

"Glory be!" said Graypate." We've nothing like those."

"Not here," agreed Fander. "Not here." He gestured toward the horizon. "Elsewhere may be plenty. If we got together we could be company for each other, we could learn things from each other. We could pool our ideas, our efforts, and search for flowers far away—also for more people."

"Folk just won't get together in large bunches. They stick to each other in family groups until the plague breaks them up. Then they abandon the kids. The bigger the crowd, the bigger the risk of someone contaminating the lot." He leaned on his gun, staring at the other, his thought-forms shaping themselves in dull solemnity. "When a guy gets hit he goes away and takes it on his own. The end is a personal contract between him and his God, with no witnesses. Death's a pretty private affair these days."

"What, after all these years? Don't you think that by this time the disease may have run its course and exhausted itself?"

"Nobody knows—and nobody's gambling on it."

"I would gamble," said Fander.

"You ain't like us. You mightn't be able to catch it."

"Or I might get it worse, and die more painfully."

"Mebbe," admitted Graypate, doubtfully. "Anyway, you're looking at it from a different angle. You've been dumped on your ownsome. What've you got to lose?"

"My life," said Fander.

Graypate rocked back on his heels, then said, "Yes, sir, that is a gamble. A guy can't bet any heavier than that." He rubbed his chin whiskers as before. "All right, all right, I'll take you up on that. You come right here and live with us." His grip tightened on his gun, his knuckles showing white. "On this understanding: the moment you feel sick you get out fast, and for keeps. If you don't, I'll bump you and drag you away myself, even if that makes me get it too. The kids come first, see?"

The shelters were far roomier than the cave. There were eighteen children living in them, all skinny with their prolonged diet of roots, edible herbs and an occasional rabbit. The youngest and most sensitive of them ceased to be terrified of Fander after ten days. Within four months his slithering shape of blue ropeyness had become a normal adjunct of their small, limited world.

Six of the youngsters were males older than Speedy, one of them much older but not yet adult. He beguiled them with his harp, teaching them to play, and now and again giving them ten-minute rides on the load-sled as a special treat. He made dolls for the girls, and queer, cone-shaped little houses for the dolls, and fan-backed chairs of woven grass for the houses. None of these toys were truly Martian in design, and none were Terrestrial. They represented a pathetic compromise within his imagination; the Martian notion of what Terrestrial models might have looked like had there been any in existence.

But surreptitiously, without seeming to give any less attention to the younger ones, he directed his main efforts upon the six older boys and Speedy. To his mind, these were the hope of the world—and of Mars. At no time did he bother to ponder that the non-technical brain is not without its virtues, or that there are times and circumstances when it is worth dropping the short view of what is practicable for the sake of the long view of what is remotely possible. So as best he could he concentrated upon the elder seven, educating them through the dragging months, stimulating their minds, encouraging their curiosity, and continually impressing upon them the idea that fear of disease can become a folk-separating dogma unless they conquered it within their souls.

He taught them that death is death, a natural process to be accepted philosophically and met with dignity—and there were times when he suspected that he was teaching them nothing, he was merely reminding them, for deep within their growing minds was the ancestral strain of Terrestrialism which had mulled its way to the same conclusions ten or twenty thousands of years before. Still, he was helping to remove this disease-block from the path of the stream, and was driving child-logic more rapidly toward adult outlook. In that respect he was satisfied. He could do little more.

In time, they organized group concerts, humming or making singing noises to the accompaniment of the harp, now and again improvising lines to suit Fander's tunes, arguing out the respective merits of chosen words until by process of elimination they had a complete song. As songs grew to a repertoire and singing grew more adept, more polished, Old Graypate displayed interest, came to one performance, then another, until by custom he had established his own place as a one-man audience.

One day the eldest boy, who was named Redhead, came to Fander and grasped a tentacle-tip. "Devil, may I operate your food-machine?"

"You mean you would like me to show you how to work it?"

"No, Devil, I know how to work it." The boy gazed self-assuredly into the other's great bee-eyes.

"Then how is it operated?"

"You fill its container with the tenderest blades of grass, being careful not to include roots. You are equally careful not to turn a switch before the container is full and its door completely closed. You then turn the red switch for a count of two hundred eighty, reverse the container, turn the green switch for a count of forty-seven. You then close both switches, empty the container's warm pulp into the end molds and apply the press until the biscuits are firm and dry."

"How have you discovered all this?"

"I have watched you make biscuits for us many times. This morning while you were busy, I tried it myself." He extended a hand. It held a biscuit. Taking it from him, Fander examined it. Firm, crisp, well-shaped. He tasted it. Perfect.

Redhead became the first mechanic to operate and service a Martian lifeboat's emergency premasticator. Seven years later, long after the machine had ceased to function, he managed to repower it, weakly but effectively, with dust that gave forth alpha sparks. In another five years he had improved it, speeded it up. In twenty years he had duplicated it and had all the know-how needed to turn out premasticators on a large scale. Fander could not have equalled this performance for, as a non-technician, he'd no better notion than the average Terrestrial of the principles upon which the machine worked, neither did he know what was meant by radiant digestion or protein enrichment. He could do little more than urge Redhead along and leave the rest to whatever inherent genius the boy possessed—which was plenty.

In similar manner, Speedy and two youths named Blacky and Big-ears took the load-sled out of his charge. On rare occasions, as a great privilege, Fander had permitted them to take up the sled for one-hour trips, alone. This time they were gone from dawn to dusk. Graypate mooched around, gun under arm, another smaller one stuck in his belt, going frequently to the top of a rise and scanning the skies in all directions. The delinquents swooped in at sunset, bringing with them a strange boy.

Fander summoned them to him. They held hands so that his touch would give him simultaneous contact with all three.

"I am a little worried. The sled has only so much power. When it is all gone there will be no more."

They eyed each other aghast.

"Unfortunately, I have neither the knowledge nor the ability to energize the sled once its power is exhausted. I lack the wisdom of the friends who left me here—and that is my shame." He paused, watching them dolefully, then went on, "All I do know is that its power does not leak away. If not used much, the reserves will remain for many years." Another pause before he added, "And in a few years you will be men."

Blacky said, "But, Devil, when we are men we'll be much heavier and the sled will use so much more power."

"How do you know that?" Fander put it sharply.

"More weight, more power to sustain it," opined Blacky with the air of one whose logic is incontrovertible. "It doesn't need thinking out. *It's obvious.*"

Very slowly and softly, Fander told him, "You'll do. May the twin moons shine upon you someday, for I know you'll do."

"Do what, Devil?"

"Build a thousand sleds like this one, or better—and explore the whole world."

From that time onward they confined their trips strictly to one hour, making them less frequently than of yore, spending more time poking and prying around the sled's innards.

Graypate changed character with the slow reluctance of the aged. Leastways, as two years then three rolled past, he came gradually out of his shell, was less taciturn, more willing to mix with those swiftly growing up to his own height. Without fully realizing what he was doing he joined forces with Fander, gave the children the remnants of Earthly wisdom passed down from his father's father. He taught the boys how to use the guns of which he had as many as eleven, some maintained mostly as a source of spares for others. He took them shell-hunting; digging deep beneath rotting foundations into stale, half-filled cellars in search of ammunition not too far corroded for use.

"Guns ain't no use without shells, and shells don't last forever."

Neither do buried shells. They found not one.

Of his own wisdom Graypate stubbornly withheld but a single item until the day when Speedy and Redhead and Blacky chivvied it out of him. Then, like a father facing the hangman, he gave them the truth about babies. He made no comparative mention of bees because there were no bees, nor of flowers because there were no flowers. One cannot analogize the non-existent. Nevertheless he managed to explain the matter more or less to their satisfaction, after which he mopped his forehead and went to Fander.

"These youngsters are getting too nosey for my comfort. They've been asking me how kids come along."

"Did you tell them?"

"I sure did." He sat down, staring at the Martian, his pale gray eyes bothered. "I don't mind giving in to the boys when I can't beat 'em off any longer, but I'm durned if I'm going to tell the girls."

Fander said, "I have been asked about this many a time before. I could not tell much because I was by no means certain whether you breed precisely as we breed. But I told them how *we* breed."

"The girls too?"

"Of course."

"Jeepers!" Graypate mopped his forehead again. "How did they take it?"

"Just as if I'd told them why the sky is blue or why water is wet."

"Must've been something in the way you put it to them," opined Graypate.

"I told them it was poetry between persons."

Throughout the course of history, Martian, Venusian or Terrestrial, some years are more noteworthy than others. The twelfth one after Fander's marooning was outstanding for its series of events each of which was pitifully insignificant by cosmic standards but loomed enormously in this small community life.

To start with, on the basis of Redhead's improvements to the premasticator, the older seven—now bearded men—contrived to repower the exhausted sled and again took to the air for the first time in forty months. Experiments showed that the Martian load-carrier was now slower, could bear less weight, but had far longer range. They used it to visit the ruins of distant cities in search of metallic junk suitable for the building of more sleds, and by early summer they had constructed another, larger than the original, clumsy to the verge of dangerousness, but still a sled.

On several occasions they failed to find metal but did find people, odd families surviving in under-surface shelters, clinging grimly to life and passed-down scraps of knowledge. Since all these new contacts were strictly human to human, with no weirdly tentacled shape to scare off the parties of the second part, and since many were finding fear of plague more to be endured than their terrible loneliness, many families returned with the explorers, settled in the shelters, accepted Fander, added their surviving skills to the community's riches.

Thus local population grew to seventy adults and four hundred children. They compounded with their plague-fear by spreading through the shelters, digging through half-wrecked and formerly unused expanses, and moving apart to form twenty or thirty lesser communities each one of which could be isolated should death reappear.

Growing morale born of added strength and confidence in numbers soon resulted in four more sleds, still clumsy but slightly less dangerous to manage. There also appeared the first rock house above ground, standing four-square and solidly under the gray skies, a defiant witness that mankind still considered itself a cut above the rats and rabbits. The community presented the house to Blacky and Sweetvoice, who had announced their desire to associate. An adult who claimed to know the conventional routine spoke solemn words over the happy couple before many witnesses, while Fander attended the groom as best Martian.

Toward summer's end Speedy returned from a solo sled-trip of many days, brought with him one old man, one boy and four girls, all of strange, outlandish countenance. They were yellow in complexion, had black hair, black, almond-shaped eyes, and spoke a language that none could understand. Until these newcomers had picked up the local speech, Fander had to act as interpreter, for his mind-pictures and theirs were independent of vocal sounds. The four girls were quiet, modest and very beautiful. Within a month Speedy had married one of them whose name was a gentle clucking sound which meant Precious Jewel Ling.

After this wedding, Fander sought Graypate, placed a tentacle-tip in his right hand. "There were differences between the man and the girl, distinctive features wider apart than any we know upon Mars. Are these some of the differences which caused your war?"

"I dunno. I've never seen one of these yellow folk before. They must live mighty far off." He rubbed his chin to help his thoughts along. "I only know what my old man told me and his old man told him. There were too many folk of too many different sorts."

"They can't be all that different if they can fall in love."

"Mebbe not," agreed Graypate.

"Supposing most of the people still in this world could assemble here, breed together, and have less different children; the children breed others still less different. Wouldn't they eventually become all much the same—just Earth-people?"

"Mebbe so."

"All speaking the same language, sharing the same culture? If they spread out slowly from a central source, always in contact by sled, continually sharing the same knowledge, same progress, would there be any room for new differences to arise?"

"I dunno," said Graypate evasively. "I'm not so young as I used to be and I can't dream as far ahead as I used to do."

"It doesn't matter so long as the young ones can dream it." Fander mused a moment. "If you're beginning to think yourself a back number you're in good company. Things are getting somewhat out of hand as far as I'm concerned. The onlooker sees the most of the game and perhaps that's why I'm more sensitive than you to a certain peculiar feeling."

"To what feeling?" inquired Graypate, eyeing him.

"That Terra is on the move once more. There are now many people where there were few. A house is up and more are to follow. They talk of six more. After the six they will talk of sixty, then six hundred, then six thousand. Some are planning to haul up sunken conduits and use them to pipe water from the northward lake. Sleds are being built. Premasticators will soon be built, and force-screens likewise. Children are being taught. Less and less is being heard of your plague and so far no more have died of it. I feel a dynamic surge of energy and ambition and genius which may grow with appalling rapidity until it becomes a mighty flood. I feel that I, too, am a back number."

"Bunk!" said Graypate. He spat on the ground. "If you dream often enough you're bound to have a bad one once in a while."

"Perhaps it is because so many of my tasks have been taken over and done better than I was doing them. I have failed to seek new tasks. Were I a technician I'd have discovered a dozen by now. Reckon this is as good a time as any to turn to a job with which you can help me."

"What is that?"

"A long, long time ago I made a poem. It was for the beautiful thing that first impelled me to stay here. I do not know exactly what its maker had in mind, nor whether my eyes see it as he wished it to be seen, but I have made a poem to express what I feel when I look upon his work."

"Humph!" said Graypate, not very interested.

"There is an outcrop of solid rock beneath its base which I can shave smooth and use as a plinth on which to inscribe my words. I would like to put them down twice: in the script of Mars and the script of Earth." Fander hesitated a moment, then went on. "Perhaps this is presumptuous of me, but it is many years since I wrote for all to read—and my chance may never come again."

Graypate said, "I get the idea. You want me to put down your notions in our writing so you can copy it."

"Yes."

"Give me your stylus and pad." Taking them, Graypate squatted on a rock, lowering himself stiffly, for he was feeling the weight of his years. Resting the pad on his knees, he held the writing instrument in his right hand while his left continued to grasp a tentacle-tip. "Go ahead."

He started drawing thick, laborious marks as Fander's mind-pictures came through, enlarging the letters and keeping them well separated. When he had finished he handed the pad over.

"Asymmetrical," decided Fander, staring at the queer letters and wishing for the first time that he had taken up the study of Earth-writing. "Cannot you make this part balance with that, and this with this?"

"It's what you said."

"It is your own translation of what I said. I would like it better balanced. Do you mind if we try again?"

They tried again. They made fourteen attempts before Fander was satisfied with the perfunctory appearance of letters and words he could not understand.

Taking the paper, he found his ray-gun, went to the base-rock of the beautiful thing and sheared the whole front to a flat, even surface. Adjusting his beam to cut a V-shaped channel one inch deep, he inscribed his poem on the rock in long, unpunctuated lines of neat Martian curli-cues. With less confidence and much greater care, he repeated the verse in Earth's awkward, angular hieroglyphics. The task took him quite a time and there were fifty people watching him when he finished. They said nothing. In utter silence they looked at the poem and at the beauti-ful thing, and were still standing there brooding solemnly when he went away.

One by one the rest of the community visited the site next day, going and coming with the air of pilgrims attending an ancient shrine. All stood there a long time, returned without comment. Nobody praised Fander's work, nobody damned it, nobody reproached him for alieniz-ing something wholly Earth's. The only effect—too subtle to be note-worthy—was a greater and still growing grimness and determination that boosted the already swelling Earth-dynamic.

In that respect, Fander wrought better than he knew.

A plague-scare came in the fourteenth year. Two sleds had brought back families from afar and within a week of their arrival the children sickened, became spotted.

Metal gongs sounded the alarm, all work ceased, the affected section was cut off and guarded, the majority prepared to flee. It was a threaten-ing reversal of all the things for which many had toiled so long: a de-structive scattering of the tender roots of new civilization.

Fander found Graypate, Speedy and Blacky, armed to the teeth, fac-ing a drawn-faced and restless crowd.

"There's most of a hundred folk in that isolated part," Graypate was telling them. "They ain't all got it. Maybe they won't get it. If they don't, it ain't so likely you'll go down either. We ought to wait and see. Stick around a bit."

"Listen who's talking," invited a voice in the crowd. "If you weren't immune you'd have been planted thirty-forty years ago."

"Same goes for near everybody," snapped Graypate. He glared around, his gun under one arm, his pale blue eyes bellicose. "I ain't much use at speechifying, so I'm just saying flatly that nobody goes before we know whether this really is the plague." He hefted his weapon in one hand, held it forward. "Anyone fancy himself at beating a bullet?"

The heckler in the audience muscled his way to the front. He was a swarthy man of muscular build, and his dark eyes looked belligerently into Graypate's. "While there's life there's hope. If we beat it we live to come back, when it's safe to come back, if ever—and you know it. So I'm calling your bluff, see?" Squaring his shoulders, he began to walk off.

Graypate's gun already was halfway up when he felt the touch of Fander's tentacle on his arm. He lowered the weapon, called after the escapee.

"I'm going into that cut-off section and the Devil is going with me.

We're running into things, not away from them. I never did like running away." Several of the audience fidgeted, murmured approval. He went on, "We'll see for ourselves just what's wrong. We mightn't be able to put it right, but we'll find out what's the matter."

The walker paused, turned, eyed him, eyed Fander, and said, "You can't do that."

"Why not?"

"You'll get it yourself—and a heck of a lot of use you'll be dead and stinking."

"What, and me immune?" cracked Graypate, grinning.

"The Devil will get it," hedged the other.

Graypate was about to retort, "What do *you* care?" but altered it slightly in response to Fander's contacting thoughts. He said, more softly, "Do you *care?*"

It caught the other off-balance. He fumbled embarrassedly within his own mind, avoided looking at the Martian, said lamely, "I don't see reason for any guy to take risks."

"He's taking them because *he* cares," Graypate gave back. "And I'm taking them because I'm too old and useless to give a darn."

With that, he stepped down, marched stubbornly toward the isolated section, Fander slithering by his side, tentacle in hand. The one who wished to flee stayed put, staring after them. The crowd shuffled uneasily, seemed in two minds whether to accept the situation and stick around, or whether to rush Graypate and Fander and drag them away. Speedy and Blacky made to follow the pair but were ordered off.

No adult sickened; nobody died. Children in the affected sector went one after another through the same routine of liverishness, high temperature and spots until the epidemic of measles had died out. Not until a month after the last case had been cured by something within its own constitution did Graypate and Fander emerge.

The innocuous course and eventual disappearance of this suspected plague gave the pendulum of confidence a push, swinging it farther. Morale boosted itself almost to the verge of arrogance. More sleds appeared, more mechanics serviced them, more pilots rode them. More people flowed in; more oddments of past knowledge came with them.

Humanity was off to a flying start with the salvaged seeds of past wisdom and the urge to do. The tormented ones of Earth were not primitive savages, but surviving organisms of a greatness nine-tenths destroyed but still remembered, each contributing his mite of know-how to restore at least some of those things which had been boiled away in atomic fires.

When, in the twentieth year, Redhead duplicated the premasticator, there were eight thousand stone houses standing around the hill. A community hall seventy times the size of a house, with a great green dome of copper, reared itself upon the eastward fringe. A dam held the lake to the north. A hospital was going up in the west. The nuances and energies and talents of fifty races had built this town and were still building it. Among them were ten Polynesians and four Icelanders and one lean, dusky child who was the last of the Seminoles.

Farms spread wide. One thousand heads of Indian corn rescued from a sheltered valley in the Andes had grown to ten thousand acres. Water buffaloes and goats had been brought from afar to serve in lieu of the horses and sheep that would never be seen again—and no man knew why one species survived while another did not. The horses had died; the water buffaloes lived. The canines hunted in ferocious packs; the felines had departed from existence. The small herbs, some tubers and a few seedy things could be rescued and cultivated for hungry bellies; but there were no flowers for the hungry mind. Humanity carried on, making do with what was available. No more than that could be done.

Fander was a back number. He had nothing left for which to live but his songs and the affection of the others. In everything but his harp and his songs the Terrans were way ahead of him. He could do no more than give of his own affection in return for theirs and wait with the patience of one whose work is done.

At the end of that year they buried Graypate. He died in his sleep, passing with the undramatic casualness of one who ain't much use at speechifying. They put him to rest on a knoll behind the community hall, and Fander played his mourning song, and Precious Jewel, who was Speedy's wife, planted the grave with sweet herbs.

In the spring of the following year Fander summoned Speedy and Blacky and Redhead. He was coiled on a couch, blue and shivering. They held hands so that his touch would speak to them simultaneously.

"I am about to undergo my *amafa*."

He had great difficulty in putting it over in understandable thought-forms, for this was something beyond their Earthly experience.

"It is an unavoidable change of age during which my kind must sleep undisturbed." They reacted as if the casual reference to his kind was a strange and startling revelation, a new aspect previously unthought-of. He continued, "I must be left alone until this hibernation has run its natural course."

"For how long, Devil?" asked Speedy, with anxiety.

"It may stretch from four of your months to a full year, or—"

"Or what?" Speedy did not wait for a reassuring reply. His agile mind was swift to sense the spice of danger lying far back in the Martian's thoughts. "Or it may never end?"

"It may never," admitted Fander, reluctantly. He shivered again, drew his tentacles around himself. The brilliance of his blueness was fading visibly. "The possibility is small, but it is there."

Speedy's eyes widened and his breath was taken in a short gasp. His mind was striving to readjust itself and accept the appalling idea that Fander might not be a fixture, permanent, established for all time. Blacky and Redhead were equally aghast.

"We Martians do not last forever," Fander pointed out, gently. "All are mortal, here and there. He who survives his *amafa* has many happy years to follow, but some do not survive. It is a trial that must be faced as everything from beginning to end must be faced."

"But—"

"Our numbers are not large," Fander went on. "We breed slowly and some of us die halfway through the normal span. By cosmic standards we are a weak and foolish people much in need of the support of the clever and the strong. You are clever and strong. Whenever my people visit you again, or any other still stranger people come, always remember that you are clever and strong."

"We are strong," echoed Speedy, dreamily. His gaze swung around to take in the thousands of roofs, the copper dome, the thing of beauty on the hill. "We are strong."

A prolonged shudder went through the ropey, bee-eyed creature on the couch.

"I do not wish to be left here, an idle sleeper in the midst of life, posing like a bad example to the young. I would rather rest within the little cave where first we made friends and grew to know and understand each other. Wall it up and fix a door for me. Forbid anyone to touch me or let the light of day fall upon me until such time as I emerge of my own accord." Fander stirred sluggishly, his limbs uncoiling with noticeable lack of sinuousness. "I regret I must ask you to carry me there. Please forgive me; I have left it a little late and cannot . . . cannot . . . make it by myself."

Their faces were pictures of alarm, their minds bells of sorrow. Running for poles, they made a stretcher, edged him onto it, bore him to the cave. A long procession was following by the time they reached it. As they settled him comfortably and began to wall up the entrance, the crowd watched in the same solemn silence with which they had looked upon his verse.

He was already a tightly rolled ball of dull blueness, with filmed eyes, when they fitted the door and closed it, leaving him to darkness and slumber. Next day a tiny, brown-skinned man with eight children, all hugging dolls, came to the door. While the youngsters stared huge-eyed at the door, he fixed upon it a two-word name in metal letters, taking great pains over his self-imposed task and making a neat job of it.

The Martian vessel came from the stratosphere with the slow, stately fall of a grounding balloon. Behind the transparent band its bluish, nightmarish crew were assembled and looking with great, multi-faceted eyes at the upper surface of the clouds. The scene resembled a pink-tinged snow-field beneath which the planet still remained concealed.

Captain Rdina could feel this as a tense, exciting moment even though his vessel had not the honor to be the first with such an approach. One Captain Skhiva, now long retired, had done it many years before. Nevertheless, this second venture retained its own exploratory thrill.

Someone stationed a third of the way around the vessel's belly came writhing at top pace toward him as their drop brought them near to the pinkish clouds. The oncomer's signalling tentacle was jiggling at a seldom used rate.

"Captain, we have just seen an object swoop across the horizon."

"What sort of an object?"

"It looked like a gigantic load-sled."

"It couldn't have been."

"No, Captain, of course not—but that is exactly what it appeared to be."

"Where is it now?" demanded Rdina, gazing toward the side from which the other had come.

"It dived into the mists below."

"You must have been mistaken. Long-standing anticipation can encourage the strangest delusions." He stopped a moment as the observation band became shrouded in the vapor of a cloud. Musingly, he watched the gray wall of fog slide upward as his vessel continued its descent. "That old report says definitely that there is nothing but desolation and wild animals. There is no intelligent life except some fool of a minor poet whom Skhiva left behind, and twelve to one he's dead by now. The animals may have eaten him."

"Eaten him? Eaten *meat?*' exclaimed the other, thoroughly revolted.

"Anything is possible," assured Rdina, pleased with the extreme to which his imagination could be stretched. "Except a load-sled. That was plain silly."

At which point he had no choice but to let the subject drop for the simple and compelling reason that the ship came out of the base of the cloud, and the sled in question was floating alongside. It could be seen in complete detail, and even their own instruments were responding to the powerful output of its numerous flotation-grids.

The twenty Martians aboard the sphere sat staring bee-eyed at this enormous thing which was half the size of their own vessel, and the forty humans on the sled stared back with equal intentness. Ship and sled continued to descend side by side, while both crews studied each other with dumb fascination which persisted until simultaneously they touched ground.

It was not until he felt the slight jolt of landing that Captain Rdina recovered sufficiently to look elsewhere. He saw the houses, the green-domed building, the thing of beauty poised upon its hill, the many hundreds of Earth-people streaming out of their town and toward his vessel.

None of these queer, two-legged life-forms, he noted, betrayed the slightest sign of revulsion or fear. They galloped to the tryst with a bumptious self-confidence which would still be evident any place the other side of the cosmos.

It shook him a little, and he kept saying to himself, again and again, "They're not scared—why should you be? They're not scared—why should you be?"

He went out personally to meet the first of them, suppressing his own apprehensions and ignoring the fact that many of them bore weapons. The leading Earthman, a big-built, spade-bearded two-legger, grasped his tentacle as to the manner born.

There came a picture of swiftly moving limbs. "My name is Speedy."

The ship emptied itself within ten minutes. No Martian would stay inside who was free to smell new air. Their first visit, in a slithering bunch, was to the thing of beauty. Rdina stood quietly looking at it, his crew clustered in a half-circle around him, the Earth-folk a silent audience behind.

It was a great rock statue of a female of Earth. She was broad-shouldered, full-bosomed, wide-hipped, and wore voluminous skirts that came right down to her heavy-soled shoes. Her back was a little bent, her head a little bowed, and her face was hidden in her hands, deep in her toil-worn hands. Rdina tried in vain to gain some glimpse of the tired features behind those hiding hands. He looked at her a long while before his eyes lowered to read the script beneath, ignoring the Earth-lettering, running easily over the flowing Martian curlicues:

> *Weep, my country, for your sons asleep,*
> *The ashes of your homes, your tottering towers.*
> *Weep, my country, O, my country, weep!*
> *For birds that cannot sing, for vanished flowers,*
> > *The end of everything,*
> > *The silenced hours.*
> *Weep! my country.*

There was no signature. Rdina mulled it through many minutes while the others remained passive. Then he turned to Speedy, pointed to the Martian script.

"Who wrote this?"

"One of your people. He is dead."

"Ah!" said Rdina. "That songbird of Skhiva's. I have forgotten his name. I doubt whether many remember it. He was only a very small poet. How did he die?"

"He ordered us to enclose him for some long and urgent sleep he must have, and—"

"The *amafa*," put in Rdina, comprehendingly. "And then?"

"We did as he asked. He warned us that he might never come out." Speedy gazed at the sky, unconscious that Rdina was picking up his sorrowful thoughts. "He has been there nearly two years and has not emerged." The eyes came down to Rdina. "I don't know whether you can understand me, but he was one of us."

"I think I understand." Rdina was thoughtful. He asked, "How long is this period you call nearly two years?"

They managed to work it out between them, translating it from Terran to Martian time-terms.

"It is long," pronounced Rdina. "Much longer than the usual *amafa*, but not unique. Occasionally, for no known reason, someone takes even longer. Besides, Earth is Earth and Mars is Mars." He became swift, energetic as he called to one of his crew. "Physician Traith, we have a prolonged *amafa* case. Get your oils and essences and come with me." When the other had returned, he said to Speedy, "Take us to where he sleeps."

Reaching the door to the walled-up cave, Rdina paused to look at the names fixed upon it in neat but incomprehensible letters. They read: DEAR DEVIL.

"What do those mean?" asked Physician Traith, pointing.

"Do not disturb," guessed Rdina carelessly. Pushing open the door, he let the other enter first, closed it behind him to keep all others outside.

They reappeared an hour later. The total population of the city had congregated outside the cave to see the Martians. Rdina wondered why they had not permitted his crew to satisfy their natural curiosity, since it was unlikely that they would be more interested in other things—such as the fate of one small poet. Ten thousand eyes were upon them as they came into the sunlight and fastened the cave's door. Rdina made contact with Speedy, gave him the news.

Stretching himself in the light as if reaching toward the sun, Speedy shouted in a voice of tremendous gladness which all could hear.

"He will be out again within twenty days."

At that, a mild form of madness seemed to overcome the two-leggers. They made pleasure-grimaces, piercing mouth-noises and some went so far as to beat each other.

Twenty Martians felt like joining Fander that same night. The Martian constitution is peculiarly susceptible to emotion.

PART FOUR

Adventures in Dimension

RALPH WILLIAMS

EMERGENCY LANDING

THE funny part about this is that Burke was perfectly sober. Not that
he is in the habit of coming on watch drunk, but then it just isn't the
sort of thing that happens to a sober person. I had the evening watch
that day, and when he relieved me at midnight he was absolutely
normal.

When I left he was settling down in the chief's chair with a detective story magazine. The CAA frowns on that—the magazine, I mean,
not the chief's chair—but most of us do read on duty, especially on the
mid-watch, because ordinarily there is nothing to do at an intermediate
landing field between midnight and eight but get out the weather once
an hour, and reading is about the only way to keep from getting sleepy.
But once in a while things do happen, which is why they keep a
twenty-four-hour watch at these places.

It must have been around one twenty that things began to happen
on this night. About that time Burke glanced up at the clock and decided it was time to start taking his weather—a job that wasn't likely
to prove very interesting, since conditions had been "ceiling and visibility unlimited" all evening, and the forecasts stubbornly maintained
that they could continue so—so he put aside his magazine and stepped
outside to read the thermometers. It was while he was spinning the
psychrometer crank and gazing around the sky for signs of cloudiness
that he saw this plane coming in.

When he first saw it, he says, it was just a dot of light sliding slowly
down the sky toward the field. The first thing that struck him as queer
about this ship was that he couldn't hear the engines, even though it
couldn't have been over half a mile from the west boundary. It seemed
to be gliding in, which was a very silly thing to do with nothing but
the boundary lights and beacon to guide by. Another thing, it was
strange that any plane at all would be landing here after dark, in good
weather, since there was none based at our field, and it was only about
once in a blue moon that we had a visitor. Burke wondered about that,

but then he remembered that he had to get his weather in the sequence, so he ran inside and put it on the wire.

By the time he could get to the window for another look, the stranger was just landing. He could see it more plainly now in the flashes from the beacon, and if it was a plane, it was like none he'd ever seen or even heard of. It looked more like an airship—only not like an airship either. This may sound silly, but Burke says if you can imagine a flying submarine, that is just what it looked like, and he should know, being ex-navy. He says it reminded him of the old gag the recruit instructors like to pull: If you were on guard and saw a battleship steaming across the parade ground, what would you do? It even had *U. S. Navy 1156* painted on its side in big black letters.

There was still no sound from the engines, but there was a faint blue exhaust from somewhere around its tail, and it was plain that the ship was under control—that is, if it really was there, and not just Burke's sins beginning to catch up with him. When it was about thirty yards from the watch house, this exhaust stopped, and it settled gently to the ground on two broad skis that ran the length of the ship. It drifted down like a feather, but when the weight came on those skis they sank a good three inches into the unsurfaced runway. Burke began to wonder about secret navy inventions, stratosphere planes, and stuff like that. Also he wondered whether he ought to call the chief, and decided not to, since the chief is apt to be cranky when someone wakes him up in the middle of the night and makes him drive the six miles from his home to the field. Burke compromised by making an entry in the log that *Navy 1156* had landed at 0141. Then he walked out to the ship and waited for someone to get out. When he got close enough, just to satisfy his own curiosity, he gave one of the ski struts a good hearty kick. It was solid enough, all right. He almost broke his toe.

There was a glassed-in compartment in the upper part of the nose that looked like the control room, and through the glass Burke could see someone in a blue coverall and flight cap fussing with some instruments. He was so busy watching this fellow that he didn't notice the door open behind him until a voice spoke almost over his shoulder.

"Hey," the voice said, "what's the name of this place?"

Burke spun around and looked up at an open door in the side of the ship and another man in the same blue coverall and flight cap. This one wore a web pistol belt, though, and a funny, bulky-looking pistol in the holster. He had a lieutenant's stripes on his shoulder and Burke automatically highballed him.

"Parker, sir," he answered, "Parker, North Dakota."

The lieutenant turned and relayed this information to someone back in the ship. Then he and Burke stared at each other. Burke was on the point of mustering up courage to ask what the score was when another man came into view. This was the one who had been in the control room, and Burke saw that he was a commander. He, too, stared curiously at Burke.

"Can we get some water here?"

"Sure." Burke indicated the pump, visible in the light from the open watch-house door. "Right over there."

The lieutenant eyed the pump doubtfully. "We might get it out of there in about a week," he said.

The commander jumped. "A week! My God, man, we have a mission to perform. We can't stay around here for a week. We have to be out by morning."

"Yes, sir, I know, but we're going to need a lot of water. Those Jennies will suck it up like a thousand-horse centrifugal when we hit that warp, or whatever it is."

"About how much?"

The lieutenant pulled a cigarette out of his pocket and lit it thoughtfully. "Well, we're almost dry now, and we'll need every drop we can carry. At least twenty-five thousand gallons."

The commander turned back to Burke. "How about it?" he demanded. "Can we get that much water around here?"

Burke mentally pictured a five-hundred-gallon tank, multiplied by fifty. That was a lot of water. He found himself agreeing with the lieutenant that it would be hardly feasible to get it out of the watch-house well, if a person was in a hurry.

"There's the river," he said, "but it'd be kind of hard to find in the dark."

"Never mind that. We'll pick it up in the visors. Which way?"

"South," Burke told him. "About five miles."

"Thanks."

For an instant longer they stared sharply at him, as if fascinated by his appearance, and he in turn began to realize that there was something obscurely alien about these people—nothing definite, just a hint of difference in the way they handled their words, a certain smooth precision in their movements. It made him vaguely uneasy, and he felt a distinct sense of relief when the commander turned and spoke to the lieutenant.

"Come on," he said. "Let's get her up."

The two officers disappeared into the ship. A seaman stepped into view and threw a switch and the door began silently to close. Burke suddenly remembered there were questions he wanted to ask.

"Hey," he shouted. "Wait a minute."

The door slid open a foot and the seaman's head popped out. "Stand clear," he warned. "If you're caught in the field when we start to go up, you'll go with us."

Before Burke could open his mouth to speak the face disappeared and the door closed again. Burke prudently retired to the watch-house porch.

Presently the ship lifted into the air, the exhaust flared out softly, and she spun on her tail and headed southward. Burke watched until the blue glow had faded out into the starry sky, then went inside and looked thoughtfully at the log. There are no regulations covering the landing of submarines at intermediate fields, and the CAA does not approve of unorthodox use of its facilities.

Finally he came to a decision and sat down to the typewriter.

"O152," he wrote. "*Navy 1156 took off.*"

GREEN PEYTON

THE SHIP THAT TURNED ASIDE

WE saw the lights our first evening out from New York. They grew in splendor until, for three of us, the voyage ended. For the others, they may still move sometimes in the sky. They have never been explained, not even by Pretloe, who found some reason for every other fantastic thing that happened.

Standing by the rail after dinner that first night, I watched them. The sea was a little rough, but most of our passengers were veterans. Nobody had retired except one old lady. We stood along the rail or walked about the deck, speaking to each other occasionally with that shyness peculiar to people who meet for the first time on board a ship—especially a small ship—the first day out. The man beside me was Pretloe, but I didn't know that then.

"Curious," he said. "They don't look like an ordinary display." I noted his soft, precise voice, and his traveler's accent—that slightly foreign but indistinguishable trick of speech which marks a linguist. I said:

"I've never seen the aurora borealis. I don't know why I haven't."

"I have," he said, "and it's different—not so definite as this." He pointed out to me the peculiarities of these lights. They lay in a narrow band across the sky, diagonal to our course but far down toward the east. They appeared very bright, and they had a sort of motion which couldn't be determined so far away. It became more evident during the next day or so, as we approached them. At first it was only a slight twinkling, such as stars appear to have. The lights didn't move. They looked more like the lights of a city the first night, and I heard passengers speculating as they went by, talking of zeppelins and floating cities.

Later on I tired of the lights. I took a few turns around the deck, and then went to my cabin. My companion was still watching, with a thoughtful expression, when I left.

The sea was rougher the next day, and rose perceptibly as night came on. There was little wind, though, and the sky seemed to be serene. After supper, we went up and found the lights there again. They were

---

closer tonight, and still directly in our path. None of us were worried, naturally, but we were curious. I watched them, alone, for some hours. I saw the man I had spoken to the night before, but he was immersed in his own thoughts.

The fourth night out we ran into the storm. The sea had been rising steadily, and tonight it was becoming actually dangerous. The ship pitched and rolled with difficulty through heavy seas that drenched the decks. We looked at the sky through occasional showers of spray. But the wind was still very moderate, and stars were visible at times through the dark, thin clouds that raced across the sky. It was as though the sea had been thrown into confusion by some curious and magnificent struggle going on far under its surface.

The lights were nearly overhead, and very bright. Tonight they were clear and distinct. They didn't touch the horizon. They seemed to appear out of nothingness down the sky in the south, and arched up to their most brilliant point over us, ahead. Then they went down again into nothingness to the north and east. It was oddly difficult to follow them at their ends, where they disappeared. It was as if they lost themselves in the distance, converging together; but whenever I tried to see where they ended, my eyes would return automatically to their center, overhead.

I met Pretloe again. I had not seen him during the day since we left port, except at meals. We were at different tables: he had his meals with the Captain. Tonight we were alone on deck. I had come up because I have a thoroughly disreputable preference for rough weather. Pretloe was watching the lights. I spoke to him, and he nodded. After a while he said:

"Do you notice how immovable those bands are? They seem to be fixed in the sky. They don't change position with the stars."

"I hadn't thought of that," I said. "Astronomy's not my line." Again he nodded.

"You see my point, though. And they're too sharply defined—more like physical objects in the sky than like bands of light."

I had noticed that. They had a certain rotundity, a perceptible effect of depth. They looked like long rods of a strange metal, heated white hot, and foreshortened by some indeterminable optical illusion. I could count an even dozen such rods. They appeared to be hundreds of miles overhead, but the clouds avoided them, thinning and dying out as they passed beneath. For the first time I had a vague feeling that something unknown and important was impending.

"You see that rod-like effect?" Pretloe was saying. I nodded. "I've had the impression for half an hour that they're turning over and over, very slowly, as on axes. Doesn't it seem so to you?"

I watched awhile, intently.

"I think I know what you mean," I said.

"Of course it may be only an illusion," Pretloe added.

We discussed the lights and watched them for several hours, until I found myself suddenly shivering with cold, and wet through to my skin. I turned away regretfully.

"This won't do," I said. "I'll have pneumonia if I don't go to my cabin." Pretloe retired a little to the shelter of a boat.

"I think I'll wait awhile," he said. "These lights have fascinated me."

I nodded good night to him, and left. It was hard even to move along the deck, with the ship tossing so. We had been issued life belts, but I didn't bother to put mine on. I got to bed with difficulty, and finally fell into a troubled sleep.

Hours later I sat up, suddenly awake. The ship was creaking and trembling and rocking in a confused medley of noise and motion. My trunk had come loose, and was pitching about the cabin in the midst of falling clothes and toilet articles. A brilliant bluish light streamed in through the porthole, lighting the cabin weirdly. My skin seemed to tingle and jump as if it were charged with electricity.

I rose hastily, snatched up my life belt, and ran out on deck. Most of the passengers were already there, comparatively quiet. I think they must have been overawed by the colossal majesty of the spectacle. The ship plunged desperately in the midst of the wildest sea I had ever encountered. Spray swept across the sky high over us, and from time to time waves battered against the side thunderously, rushing across the decks. There was obviously no possibility of launching a boat. Yet the little ship seemed to be holding its own somehow. The whole ocean surged about us with a strange appearance of lightness which we shared, riding it as though all at once gravity had been partly suspended.

The lights blazed above us, directly overhead. A bluish brilliance filled the sky and hovered about the ship and on the surface of the water. The ship quivered with it, and our bodies, the water, every object on deck seemed to be charged with electricity. There was an exhilaration in it for even the most alarmed spectators.

But nothing happened. After about an hour, the sea grew visibly quieter. The lights overhead dimmed a little, and the electric tension gradually diminished. A few stolid spirits went back to bed, and most of the women retired with obvious reluctance. The officers moved about on deck, assuring us that the worst was over, promising to have us called if anything more happened. I stayed on deck to watch.

After a while the sky grew paler, and the lights began to fade. I noticed that they had changed position and were now stretched, as well as I could see through the spray, from horizon to horizon, even and parallel, along our course—unless we had lost our course in the confusion. The sky was clouding over. The dawn, when it came, was gray and cold —sunless. I went back to my cabin at last for a few more hours of sleep.

There were few of us at breakfast that morning. There was an empty place at the Captain's table, and I took it. I wanted to hear his opinion of what had happened. He appeared haggard and sleepless, but shaven and neatly dressed as usual. After a brief greeting, he took his place and fell into a profound meditation which lasted until the meal was half finished. Then he shook his head slightly, and looked up. I suppose he felt that he must not neglect us.

"Mr. Pretloe," he said, addressing my fellow watcher of the past few nights, whose name I learned now for the first time, "what is your opinion of what happened this morning? You are a scientist."

"It's not my field precisely," Pretloe said thoughtfully. "I'm inclined to wonder whether any scientist could honestly have an opinion."

"What do you mean?"

"When we left New York, nothing was known of any such phenomenon in the sky, or I should have heard of it. It appeared our first night out, and it seems to have been connected definitely with the storm. Did you have any message from the shore?" The Captain frowned.

"None at all. We mentioned the lights in a report, but received no answer."

"And have had none this morning?"

"Unfortunately," said the Captain, "the radio is not working this morning." We stared at him, and he hastened to add, "Oh, it can't be anything serious—some minor electrical disturbance. As soon as we have it in order there's sure to be some explanation."

But Pretloe looked skeptical.

The radio remained silent. Although it was apparently unharmed, all the messages we tried to send seemed to fade out as they left the instrument; and nothing whatever could be heard in the receiver except a very faint noise like static from time to time. Eventually even that faded, and the sending apparatus ceased to work at all.

The day was dark, until late in the afternoon. I walked around the deck with Pretloe. The sea was subsiding rapidly, but there was no sign of the sun anywhere. A perpetual twilight obscured the sea, and there were lights in the saloon.

About noon, I happened to glance up and saw the Captain looking helplessly at his sextant. His eye caught mine, and he saw Pretloe. He beckoned for us to come up. As we approached, he came forward anxiously, and spoke to Pretloe.

"Mr. Pretloe," he said, "I don't want anything said to the other passengers about this, but I need your help."

"What's the trouble, Captain Weeks?"

"I can't find our course. There's not even a trace of the sun anywhere."

"But isn't the compass working?" said Pretloe.

"The needle just turns idly. None of the compasses are in order. All our electrical apparatus has been disturbed. Haven't you noticed how dim the lights are? Something is happening to our current."

"Can't your people find the trouble?"

"There doesn't seem to be any trouble except that nothing will work. My officers are worried to death. And I've no idea which way we're headed." He brought his fist down with nervous vexation against the rail. "It's uncanny," he muttered.

Pretloe said he'd take a look around.

"I doubt if I can help much," he added. "Your men probably know more about electrical apparatus than I do. You can get your bearings, of course, whenever the sky clears."

"If it ever *does* clear," said Captain Weeks, looking gloomily up toward the supposed place of the invisible sun.

Pretloe found nothing. I spent the afternoon reading. I dismissed the Captain's troubles as purely temporary. I wasn't in any hurry to get abroad. About sunset time, I looked up and saw Pretloe. The sky had practically cleared, and it was brighter than it had been at noon.

"Mr. Burton," Pretloe said. I rose, glad to have his company. But he was frowning anxiously, and went on. "Isn't it time for sunset by your watch?" I glanced at my wrist.

"The sun went down at six-thirty last night," I said. "I noticed particularly. It's six-fifteen now."

"And practically clear."

"Is anything the matter?"

"Nothing, except that there's not a sign of the sun anywhere."

"What?"

"The sun has completely disappeared." For a moment I was stunned. Then I grinned.

"But my dear fellow! That's ridiculous!" I said. Pretloe smiled wryly.

"You can look for yourself," he said.

I circled the ship with him. He was right. It was clear now; the sky was blue, with the faint tints of red that come at sunset. There was no sound anywhere but the throbbing of the engines: the special silence of twilight was approaching.

"But it's impossible, Mr. Pretloe," I protested. "I didn't mean to doubt you, but—why, I'm no astronomer, as I've told you, but even at that I know that anything happening to the sun would involve the earth too."

"You can see, though—it's gone," said Pretloe.

"Our clocks are wrong?"

"But it's daylight. We've had daylight for nearly an hour—full daylight, nearly clear. We haven't seen the sun. If it had gone down before the sky cleared, it would be dark now."

I thought dazedly. Dozens of fantastic ideas suggested themselves.

"Could we by any improbable means have gotten into the Arctic regions?"

"We'd still see the sun so long as there was daylight."

"Couldn't a mirage of some sort do it?"

"None that I have ever heard of. And notice—" he pointed to the deck, "even a mirage that would deceive the eye, if a mirage like this is conceivable, could hardly interfere with the physical laws of light. And there are no shadows."

I followed his pointing finger. I cast no shadow on the deck, nor did

Pretloe, nor did any of the chairs. The softest artificial arrangement of lights could not so completely have eliminated even the suggestion of a shadow.

Pretloe had just left the Captain. They had found no explanation. The Captain was waiting eagerly for a look at the stars. He didn't come to supper, and neither Pretloe nor I mentioned the impossible phenomenon of the sun's disappearance. The other passengers, for some reason, had observed nothing.

After supper we went on deck. Both Pretloe and I glanced up at the sky as we emerged into the open. It was nearly dark. Already several stars were faintly visible overhead. The light disappeared rapidly, and the stars came out one by one. It was a clear night.

I looked at Pretloe, and laughed with relief and amusement.

"Well, there they are," I said. "We shall find our course after all." And, for the first time, I realized how completely helpless we should have been if the stars also had disappeared.

"Will you come up with me to see Captain Weeks? I want to be sure he's satisfied." Pretloe said.

We found Captain Weeks on the bridge. He was looking up at the stars, motionless.

"Well, Captain," Pretloe said, "I suppose you've sighted your course all right by now?"

The Captain turned his head toward us slowly, as if he hadn't heard. "Eh?" he said tonelessly.

"Have you found the course again?"

"No." The Captain turned. He looked at us fixedly in the dark.

"What's that?" I said, not understanding. "Aren't the stars enough?" He shook his head.

"No," he said again. "Look at them."

We looked up at the stars obediently. They looked all right to me. But Pretloe, after a moment, exclaimed softly, "My God!" I turned to him helplessly.

"What is it?" I said. "I don't understand."

"Do you realize," said Pretloe, "that there's not a known constellation in the sky?"

Later that night the sinking lights had faded until they were nearly extinguished. Pretloe and I had been observed with Captain Weeks on the bridge. A group of passengers came up to us on deck to ask about the lights. Pretloe seemed a little at a loss what to say, but I explained:

"All the ship's electrical equipment has been disturbed by the storm this morning. I suppose the men will have it in shape again before long."

One middle-aged man, stout and red-faced, whom I had met earlier in the voyage and taken a drink or two with, said protestingly:

"But good Lord, Burton, how are we to get around without lights?"

"I'll speak to Captain Weeks about it," I said. And that is how I became, along with Pretloe, an official ambassador to the Captain and a member of his immediate group.

We saw him later. He had just sent officers in search of candles provided for just such an emergency. The three of us, Captain Weeks, Pretloe, and myself, gathered in the Captain's cabin for a discussion.

"Mr. Pretloe," the Captain said, "there's only one man on board who can make even a pretense of explaining what's happened today. You're the man." Pretloe shook his head.

"I'm afraid there's not even one man who can explain it, Captain," he said. "I've only one vague idea that could in any even faintly conceivable way account for these phenomena."

"What is it?"

"It's too impossible to mention. You'll laugh at me."

"My dear sir," the Captain said impatiently, "you haven't seen me laughing at the disappearance of the sun. Nor at the sudden discovery of some ten thousand new stars in the sky. If you've any idea at all about this, I want to hear it."

At that moment an officer arrived with candles for our cabin, which was nearly in darkness. Switching off the useless lights, Captain Weeks lit two of them and put them on the table. He gave orders that they were to be issued sparingly. There was no assurance that our lights would return before we reached port. Then he went to a cupboard and brought out a bottle, glasses, and some Seltzer water.

"Here's whisky if you want it, gentlemen," he said. And he went on, in a gloomy voice. "You see, don't you, how absolutely helpless I feel? I'm certain that we lost our course in the storm—you remember how those lights seemed to swing around? I've put the ship back on a course as nearly as possible what it should be if we have lost it in that manner. The lights lay approximately northeast and a little north. I'm sure we didn't turn completely about. So if we *did* turn, we must have ended on a northeast course. We should now be following a course that will take us a little south of England—to be on the safe side. If we didn't change, then we're headed for the Mediterranean and Africa.

"But I've no assurance," he added, "that we're headed toward Europe or Africa at all. All I can do is pick out certain of the new stars and hold a course by them, wherever it takes us to. Our stores can't last indefinitely. Unless we sight land more or less on time, I'll have to say something to the men and the passengers. I see grave trouble ahead of us."

Pretloe nodded.

"I've already reasoned most of that out as you put it," he said.

"And your theory?"

Pretloe paused a moment. Then he said, "You've heard of the fourth dimension?"

The Captain grew visibly paler. He nodded.

"It's theoretically possible that if some cataclysm had turned us aside into a fourth dimension we should no longer be able to see the sun or any known stars."

"But—" The Captain knit his brows, and thought for a moment. "I see," he said. "It sounds like madness. But the whole thing seems like madness." I was thinking too.

"But look here, Mr. Pretloe," I said, "isn't the weakness in your theory the same weakness you found in mine? How about the daylight?"

"Not necessarily," Pretloe said. "There are innumerable theories about the fourth dimension. But put it this way. Suppose the whole of our terrestrial phenomena took place in a thin section of the four dimensional universe. All our senses are fitted to perceive only in three directions. Then, if we got out of the section in which we belonged, we could no longer see the sun. But, so long as no actual obstruction existed between our portion and the rest of the universe, there would still be sunlight. The sun would be there still, but out of our line of vision."

"But how about shadows—if the sun were still there? You said——"

"I know. But the sun would cast a shadow also invisible to us. Look at it this way. Suppose, again, that we all lived on the earth's equator, and that everything on either side of the equator were invisible to us. Now, if an earthquake, say, tossed us a mile or so away from the equator, the sun would no longer be in our two dimensional line of vision (provided the sun strictly followed the equator) and it would cast just such an invisible shadow."

"That's clear enough," Captain Weeks said.

"Yes," I objected, "but wouldn't it be simple enough to turn around and go back again? Couldn't we just turn the ship toward the course we were following, and get back on it?"

Pretloe smiled.

"How would you go about it?" he asked. "In the one case, you would have no perception of a third dimension—all you could do would be to go on walking in a straight line for the rest of your life. In the other case —our case—the same principle applies. How are we to steer a course through the fourth dimension? We have neither senses nor instruments capable of pointing the way."

"If it was possible to get here, it must be possible to get back?"

"Theoretically, yes. But we'd have to learn how. It might take a cultured civilization having all facilities for research, hundreds of years to find that out. We have no such facilities."

"Consider this, too. If our equatorial man had landed facing northeast, he'd have had only to turn around, as you suggest, and retrace his steps to walk into the equator again. But he wouldn't know how to turn around or to deviate from a straight line. However, he could keep on walking until he encircled the globe. In that way he'd also get back. But he'd meet with a few difficult seas to cross.

"From the way those lights looked, I'm inclined to think they must have veered off at an angle somehow into the fourth dimension. In that case, no matter how we steer our course with regard to our own three dimensions, provided we have kept to our original direction in the fourth (and whether we do or not is beyond our control or knowledge), we have left our civilization some hundreds of miles behind us since the storm this morning. We don't know how to turn around, since that involves leaving temporarily our three dimensions.

"Theoretically, again, by continuing as we have started (providing always that the earth has a rotundity similar in the fourth dimension to its rotundity in the other three) we should in time come back to our starting point. This idea requires that we completely discard the Einstein theory of the fourth dimension, although in effect it comes to much the same thing. But there are probably obstructions as obvious as those which would face our equatorial man—seas, mountains, possibly variations in temperature, and certainly a loss of all sunlight for a time, as in our Arctic regions."

I nodded, my head whirling a little.

"I see that all right," I said.

I got up and poured myself a drink.

"Won't you have one, Captain?" But Captain Weeks shook his head. "Pretloe?"

"I'll have one," Pretloe said.

I made the drinks and sat down again, swallowing mine gratefully.

Captain Weeks cleared his throat.

"Your theory sounds plausible, Mr. Pretloe," he said. "Does it account for everything?" Pretloe smiled—coldly and quite collectedly.

"I don't claim that it does," he said. "I see nothing that renders it invalid, although it may ignore some things."

"How about those bands of light?"

"I don't pretend to explain those, Captain Weeks. It seemed to me that they were too regular, too—well, too *nice* looking to be quite natural. But they might be some normally rare natural phenomenon we've never come up against before. Or they might be the work of a secret experimenter. That's a wild idea, of course. Again, though, they might even be the work of a scientist in some civilization unknown to us, outside of our portion of the universe. I have no explanation for them. I doubt whether we shall ever find one."

"They seemed quite thoroughly visible," I said. "How would they have looked if they had crossed our course in the fourth dimension?"

"Frankly, I don't know. You remember how they faded off at the ends? I feel sure that they went into the fourth dimension at those points, if there's anything to my hypothesis. Except for that, I can't say."

It was growing late. I glanced at the clock.

"See here," I said, "you didn't sleep last night, did you, Captain?"

"No, I'm afraid I didn't," he said.

"We'd better go, then. We're in your hands, you know. You are automatically our leader, no matter what happens or what dangers we have to go through. You'd better get some sleep. Pretloe and I can talk to you again about this tomorrow."

The Captain nodded with a faint smile.

"I suppose you're right," he said. "I feel pretty helpless at the moment, but there's nothing to do but go ahead as we're going now until something turns up." He rose, and shook hands with us. "You've been a great help to me, both of you. I want you to come up as often as possible and talk things over."

Pretloe nodded.

"We'll be a sort of cabinet if you like," he said.

We took our leave, and went down to our cabins.

"It's strange, isn't it," Pretloe said as he left me, "that the stars look quite as natural as they ever looked before?" I agreed ruefully.

"The one thing I've noticed about life," I said, "is that the most fantastic things that ever happen to a man seem fairly normal at the time. It takes a poet or a writer of reminiscences to appreciate romance."

We had almost no trouble with the passengers. The ship's officers, of course, noticed quickly the disappearance of the familiar stars. We explained Pretloe's theory to Mr. Grady, the first mate, and he took care of the others. One or two members of the crew seemed to know what had happened, but Mr. Grady silenced them in time, and the rest remained as much in ignorance as the passengers. Most seamen, nowadays, are like skilled mechanics on land. They know thoroughly their own work. They may have idle speculations about life, but they are incurious. They are so accustomed to the sky that they never really see it. Many of them can't name more than two or three constellations, and those they never look for.

Both sailors and passengers, when they realized the disappearance of the sun and the moon, went wild with speculation. At first they were uneasy. Some were superstitious, and prophesied terrible events—another flood, or the end of the world. But superstition, too, is nearly dead even among sailors. After the first few days everyone was accustomed to the strange phenomena. Nothing happened. The sea was blue and serene, day after day. Nothing disturbed the silence of the cool, dark nights.

We met no ships. For the first time in many years I was able to recapture the expanding loneliness of the sea that had overwhelmed me so during my first crossings. I knew now, as I had felt then, that we were lost in a world from which, for all I could tell, the land had sunk down and disappeared, leaving only an endless waste of ocean, rising and falling with the tides, moving in unending long waves before the wind. There was a sort of peace, as well as a sort of dread, in knowing that we might never again come to land—that we might sail on into the east until a final twilight closed about us with a sea still quiet, still murmuring absently to itself, as it went by alongside of our rails.

We were due in Liverpool ten days after we left New York Harbor. The tenth day arrived without any sight of land, but Captain Weeks gave out the explanation that, due to the storm we had weathered, we had been delayed possibly several days. A few passengers grumbled, but that was all. Monday afternoon—the eleventh day—Pretloe and I were closeted with the Captain in his cabin.

"You see, gentlemen," he was saying, "this is our dilemma. We have considerable stores of food, but they will not last indefinitely. And so long as we are concealing from the passengers what seems to be our real situation, we can't put them on rations—that would alarm them, and force our hand. And the candles are running low. If they have to spend their evenings on a dark ship, Lord knows what ideas will come into their heads. I've found from experience that men are still primitive enough to feel uneasy in the dark."

We agreed, and he went on.

"If we don't sight land—some sort of land—within a day or so, we're going to have trouble."

"True enough," said Pretloe. "And do you expect to sight land?"

"Well, what do you think?"

"I see no assurance that we shall. On the other hand, I see no assurance that we shouldn't—sooner or later. If the ocean extends out into the fourth dimension on either side of what we called the world, it seems reasonable to suppose that the land does too. But we don't know our course, and we don't know at all how the land lies outside of our world. We may sight land today or tomorrow, we may sight it next week, or we may never sight it."

Captain Weeks nodded grimly.

"We have no data to go on. We know our own world, but not this one."

"Precisely," Pretloe said. "We can make certain assumptions. Others we can't make."

"Do you think there's any chance that this world is inhabited?" I asked.

"There's no way we can tell yet. There's no evidence of habitation."

"But your opinion?" said Captain Weeks. Pretloe shrugged.

"I doubt it. My opinion is that there must be something peculiar about our own stratum of the earth which renders it habitable. Otherwise, it appears to me that we should not be confined to such a thin three dimensional slice of what must be a vast, rich globe."

"What do you suppose that peculiarity could be?"

"It might be anything—perhaps something of which we are not even aware," Pretloe said. "We don't know what forces are operating on us in this waste land we have wandered into. Personally, I am inclined to suspect that the sun has something to do with it."

"The sun?" I exclaimed. "But how?"

"You know how necessary its light is to all plant and animal life. And you've seen plants turning their flowers and stems toward the sun as it moves across the sky during the day. It might be some instinctive attraction such as that.

"Our species originated most probably, you know, in the hot areas around the equator—under the sun. And it's still true that the hottest regions are the most densely populated. Then consider, too, how the ancient peoples all worshipped the sun, with rites and symbolisms that survive even now in our various church rituals, in our dream symbolisms, even in our subconscious daily motives and desires. Nobody has ever explained or understood fully the intense, varied, and mystic significances that the sun held for primitive peoples. Perhaps there was more to it than we realize—some definite and important kinship of animal life with the sun's path."

"And you think," I said, "that civilization has evolved in that narrow stratum because man needed the sun's occult influence?"

"Occult only in that we may not understand it entirely," Pretloe corrected me. "It seems probable enough that, because the sun is so necessary to us, our evolution has kept us in that one stratum and taken away from us any faculties which would have made us aware of these other reaches in the fourth dimension. Not needing any knowledge of them, we have, by the economy of nature, been left without the means of perceiving them. And it is possible that, if we should ever find a way of exploring into the fourth dimension, we shall evolve senses with which to understand it."

"How can you account, though," I said, "for the fact that our mechanical inventions—automobiles, ships, and so on—remain in our stratum with such docility? They have no instincts."

"For one thing," said Pretloe, "we keep them there. They work under our guidance. Again, too, if we could look at our world and our machines from an enlarged point of view that included a knowledge of the fourth dimension and its laws, we might find that there were other facts which made mechanics—at least our sort of mechanics—peculiar to our world. You remember that our lights have gone off, and the radio stopped working? That in itself is evidence that electricity must be non-existent outside of our world—unless there are other kinds of electricity unknown to us.

"I imagine that magnetism and electricity—about which, you know, we understand comparatively little except that they are related to each other—may be related also to the sun and the sun's path. It is not difficult to believe that the sun, following for millions of years one path around the earth in the fourth dimension, may in some way have affected it—magnetized it, so to speak—and given it the properties which make radio and electrical phenomena possible. It might be some such process, too, which gave us our metals with which to create machines. There may be no metals beyond our stratum. And it may be some such magnetism which creates a band of attraction to keep our ships and tools from blundering out of the world. All this is pure speculation, of course. But we haven't anything to work with except our speculations."

"True enough," said the Captain. "I remember——"

I don't know what he was remembering or what he would have said. At that moment there was a hasty rap on the door, and Mr. Grady, the mate, burst in. Breaking off with his remark, Captain Weeks turned and said:

"What is it, Mr. Grady?"

"We've just sighted land, sir."

"What!" The Captain leaped up, and Pretloe and I followed. "Are you sure?"

"Yes, sir."

We went out on the bridge. Captain Weeks examined the horizon carefully and then handed us his glasses. It was land, a long, flat line of blue, lying southeast of us. We watched it in silence for a while, absorbed in our speculations.

"Do you suppose it can be—?" Captain Weeks asked. But Pretloe shook his head regretfully.

"I'm afraid not, Captain Weeks," he said. "It may be inhabited, but I doubt whether it's any coast we've ever seen before." The Captain thought a moment. Then he looked at us soberly.

"This is our crisis, then," he said. "We'll have to tell the passengers. And the crew."

"Yes." I glanced down at the people promenading on the deck. They hadn't seen the land yet. They thought they were bound for Liverpool, to carry on their private businesses and pleasures, in which each of them was absorbed, enfolded and shut off like a chrysalis in its shell—a private world of his own. For most people the shell never opens except in death. These promenaders, perhaps, had counted the possibility of death as an unforetellable hazard of their voyage; but even death they had not imagined, because men never think of death as a reality. Now they were to face something more than death—a new life, the opening of the shell. From the moment when they should find themselves on land again, they would be no longer John Bealy, the lawyer, and Rudolph Cortez, the master of jazz, and Alicia Corey, the designer of dresses. They would be actors cast in new rôles, on a new stage. Nobody, not even themselves, could tell what they might become.

It was nearing twilight.

"We'll wait," Captain Weeks said. "Later on tonight we'll make for the coast. Tomorrow morning they'll wake and see it. Morning's the best time. We'll tell them then—after breakfast."

We went to supper, hiding our tense expectancy. Nobody observed that we had slackened speed to a bare few knots. We went to supper by candlelight.

I rose early, a long while before the other passengers, and went on deck. There we were, as Captain Weeks had promised us, cruising along the coast. The land rose abruptly out of the water, and out of little strips of sandy beach. It was a rocky coast, moderately high for the most part, occasionally dropping down toward the water's edge to form a small cove or a length of beach. It showed no signs of human life. There were trees, though, and bushes beyond the sand and at the top of the cliffs. Some distance back a forest began, rising gently to the summit of a low line of hills some miles inland. It was not a very picturesque coast. It looked as if there might be fertile soil on the slopes of the hills. There was something utterly simple and inviting about it. The sea was quite still; waves could be heard breaking unhurriedly on the beaches and against the rocks.

Captain Weeks was on the bridge. I went up and joined him. Sleep seemed to have refreshed him, and he turned to me with a smile less worried than it had been for days.

"You look better, Captain," I told him.

"I feel better," he admitted. "There's nothing to be gained by worrying now. We'll have to make the best of whatever turns up."

I asked him the question I had been pondering over before I fell asleep.

"Can we depend on the passengers? And the crew?"

"We can depend on the passengers. They seem to be intelligent people. As for the crew—well, it varies. They're good seamen. Some of them look like pretty rough customers, if it should come to trouble."

We examined the coast line again, Captain Weeks lending me his glasses.

"Looks deserted, eh?" he said. I nodded.

"Tell me, Captain," I said, "what resources have we for a Robinson Crusoe act?"

"I don't know. I've been wondering myself; but it's a complicated thing to start a settlement."

"Have we any tools?"

"A few of the rudimentary sort. There are axes, for instance—fire axes, you know. Of course we've hammers—nails—saws. I suppose we've all we'll need."

"Any books—technical books, I mean?"

"None except a few about navigation and ships' engines, and so on."

"Well, we can make out all right, anyhow?"

"Of course." Captain Weeks smiled, and his gray eyes grew hard. "A man doesn't *have* to have anything but his hands, you know."

We steamed on down the coast. We were approaching a point where the line broke and turned inland. A few miles beyond that it reappeared and went on, curving a little before us until it merged into the horizon.

"That looks like a harbor, doesn't it?" I said.

"Or a bay. Some sort of shelter. We'll hope it's navigable—as it should be."

I looked down and saw Pretloe. He was watching the coast line too, but after a moment he turned and came up. Already there were a few people on deck—a tall, middle-aged lawyer, John Bealy, the two daughters of Mr. Newton, the banker, and a couple of boys I didn't know. The boys were with Mr. Newton's daughters.

"How do they seem to take it, Mr. Pretloe?" Captain Weeks asked.

"They don't know yet. Mr. Bealy has just been assuring me that it doesn't look at all like England."

"And the young people?"

"Apparently don't care where they are."

We paced the bridge in silence, absorbed in thought. The break in the coast line was opening out into what seemed to be a large bay, extending for at least some miles inland. I more than half expected that we should any moment find smoke hovering over it, and see the first signs of a low sky-line such as cities have on the European water fronts. But the bay was deserted. There were no ships at anchor, no docks, no scattered houses nor people bathing.

It was time for breakfast. By now most of the passengers were up and clustered along the rail. We could hear the subdued sound of their voices. They were trying to place the coast, and its unfamiliar harbor. As we went down to breakfast, passing among them, they turned, one by one, and looked hesitantly at us. They wanted to question us, but none had the courage to intrude first. Captain Weeks bowed to them graciously, with a composed smile on his lips, and passed into the saloon. They followed, crowding about the door.

Our table—for by this time I had a regular place at the Captain's table—was the center of attention throughout breakfast. Captain Weeks announced briefly that he would have a statement to make in the main saloon later. We were all very quiet. Most of the passengers hurried through the meal, but the three of us, among a few others, ate in our usual leisurely fashion. We were conscious of an impending crisis, but we preferred to ignore it as long as we could.

I shan't attempt to describe all that took place during our meeting in the main saloon. Basically, it was a public review of the theory—now virtually accepted as fact—Pretloe had worked out for us some days earlier. The passengers sat around in groups and listened. At first they were too amazed and incredulous to appreciate fully how completely they had been cut off from all their old ties and associations. Later, as a realization of the magnitude and weirdness of the situation came to them, they were too overcome with a feeling of unreality to speak or even to think. Captain Weeks was very calm, very courteous, and he did his best to convey the impression that he meant to treat the whole thing in a matter-of-fact fashion. He assured them that we would work out plans and keep in mind the possibility of finding a way back into their world.

"But," he added, "it's better not to put too much hope in that. None of us is responsible for what has happened. If we all determine to cooperate with each other—as we shall have to do for our own salvation— we shall certainly be able to set up a new civilization which will endure and grow until, eventually, it can adequately replace the old. We have no alternative; and it is useless, of course, to mourn or question what has happened. It is an act of God." With that pious conclusion, he left. Pretloe and I followed.

Later he addressed the crew in much the same manner. By that time we were already advancing slowly into the harbor, being careful to take soundings for the depth. It was a long, wide bay, narrowing at the end opposite the sea into a river which looked navigable.

The three of us, as usual, gathered in Weeks' cabin to discuss plans. It was a fantastic thought, to me, that we were stranded here, like shipwrecks, on a deserted coast, but off completely from civilization, yet in possession of the one thing no other castaways in the history of the world had ever had—a ship.

"I suppose," Captain Weeks said, "the first thing we shall have to do will be to plant an American flag on the shore." Pretloe shrugged impatiently.

"Why?" he said. "It's about as inaccessible to development as any land I ever saw."

"Still—for form's sake?"

"It would be a futile gesture, since we can't ever hope to open communication again with our government. If we ever should—well, that will be another matter."

"Then what do you advise?" Pretloe smiled.

"It doesn't seem very important to me; but we might give the place a name. One that doesn't smack too strongly of any nation, so that we won't hurt the feelings of any foreigners we may have on board—we need every sort of amity. Then we'd better get on with the business of building a town. We'll make it our own territory for the present."

"Ours personally?"

"The ship's at large. And ours to apportion out so long as we're in command."

I made a suggestion.

"Wouldn't it be a good idea to define the sort of government we're having?"

"Oh, a republic, of course!" Captain Weeks said hastily.

"Or, perhaps, a dictatorship at first?" said Pretloe. "You, after all, are the logical leader. We know we can trust you. You can name a cabinet, and we'll work out our plans together. But we'll need some definite authority for the first few months. . . ."

I don't intend to set down here the details of that long conference. It was a perplexing task to make plans for a community so large as ours. We hardly finished with the preliminary discussions that morning. We agreed finally (with a smile) that it would be simple enough to call our new continent Leaguoa, after the League of Nations, and that plans for a permanent form of government could wait for the present. It seemed advisable for everybody to remain on board, until we had explored the immediate countryside and put up buildings. We could transfer them gradually to the land, and keep the ship as a stronghold against possible aggression by natives. There was very little else the ship would be good for until, perhaps, years later.

In the afternoon, immediately after dinner, we organized a party to go ashore and examine the land about the bay. I think the passengers, most of them, were still too dazed to understand what had happened. A few of them, especially the young people, took the whole thing as an adventure—which, I suppose, in a way it was. Mr. Newton's daughters wanted to go along, but of course Captain Weeks wouldn't hear of it. We took, instead, a Mr. James Folk, who had turned out to be a farmer from the West on his first vacation after twenty years of large scale farming, and the two husky boys I had seen with the Newton girls on the deck that morning. They were college boys of average intelligence, both of them sons of a retired financier who was on board—a Mr. Vance. We had some sailors with us, of course, and we carried revolvers.

We examined the margins of the bay on both sides for traces of habitation while the ship lay at anchor in the river's mouth. There were trees growing nearly to the water's edge, and thickening into a forest further back. The trees were tall and straight, but not very thick. Mr. Folk couldn't precisely identify them. We penetrated a mile or so into the forest, but discovered nothing.

We were on our way back to the ship, coming up the bay, when I made my discovery. The larger trees drew back a little from one point along the shore, as if there had once been a small clearing there, and some young trees had grown in their places, very slender and straight. I thought I saw something, a circular ring and dirty-white, lying under one of the large trees at the edge of the clearing. I left the others, in order to examine it. Nature doesn't grow many plants or animals that are smooth, ring-shaped and white.

It was a life preserver.

I called to the others, and carried it back to them. It had been hanging by a nail to the shore side of the tree's trunk. The cord supporting it had worn through. We carried it down to the water's edge and washed away the caked dry mud and dust that covered it; and underneath we found the inscription. On one side, of course, was the ship's name in faded letters:

THE PACIFIC, NEW YORK

On the other side, in smaller letters, and still more faded, a message had been written crudely with black paint and a brush:

Jamestown Bay, February 20, 1856. Food low. No relief in sight. Lost 23 days. 54 dead after mutiny. Heading south again.

We looked at each other in silence. 1856—and an American ship. We were not pioneers after all. Captain Weeks scratched his chin thoughtfully, with a puzzled frown.

"The *Pacific*," he murmured. "I've heard somewhere—" Then a light came into his eyes. "Of course! I remember!"

"What is it, Captain?" I asked.

"One of the famous missing ships," he said. "She sailed either from Liverpool or from New York—I've forgotten now—in January, 1856, and was never heard of again."

"A passenger ship?" Pretloe said.

"She carried about fifty passengers—and a cargo valued at two million dollars."

"That explains the mutiny, then."

"Of course. There was a crew of nearly fifty men."

"Was there a storm—anything to explain the disappearance?"

"Nothing at all—no storm worth mentioning. There have been other similar cases too. I've read of dozens, all authenticated. The *President* and the *City of Glasgow* were lost in the same way around 1850 between New York and Liverpool. A troopship, the *Lady Nugent,* was lost in the Bay of Bengal about the same time with a regiment of Indian troops aboard. H.M.S. *Wasp,* a warship, was lost in 1887 between Singapore and Hong Kong. None of these ships ever left any traces— there wasn't even any wreckage found in their vicinity. There were never any storms of undue proportions, and these were all fine, seaworthy vessels."

"Then," I said, realizing suddenly the significance of these accounts, "it is quite possible that we shall find other colonists nearby?"

"But hardly probable," Pretloe added. "Remember that they must have been bewildered by what had happened, as the *Pacific* seems to have been"—pointing to the life belt—"and probably went on cruising in search of a civilized port until their supplies gave out. They may have been damaged by storms. Smaller ships than ours, as these must have been, would have suffered severely in such a storm as we encountered, even if it were purely local. In any case, what course they were pursuing after their arrival in strange waters—with regard to the fourth dimension, I mean—may have depended always on chance. There may be hundreds of lost ships and colonies in isolated, unrelated three dimensional strata of the earth; but it's unlikely that we shall ever find another in ours."

"Still," said Captain Weeks, "it might be worth while to search some day, in so much as we've a ship at our command. Besides, we'll want to chart our new continent—Leaguoa." Pretloe nodded.

"Of course."

"And incidentally," I remarked, "it seems that our bay has been named for us—Jamestown Bay. I suppose after the first colonists in America." Pretloe smiled, and said:

"I'm glad they had the good sense not to mistake Plymouth for the first English colony in America."

It still puzzles me a little to recall how many of our passengers on that voyage were men and women of ability and imagination. It seemed that every soul on board, as soon as he had become adjusted to the change in his life, became at the same moment aware of a hundred suppressed ideals surging confusedly under the surface of his mind. We found ourselves in the midst of potential socialists, reformers, education-alists, Fathers of their Country. It was startling; and then I recalled the enthusiasm with which early English settlers in Virginia and New England had foreseen their visions becoming reality on a virgin soil. But I suppose our colonists have learned, as their fathers did, that a new land doesn't always make a new civilization. They have found that men, wherever they go, carry their old civilizations with them in their hearts —the old prejudices, the old virtues, the old blindnesses. A civilization is only the sum of many people's convictions.

But I was visionary like the rest. I like to think sometimes that possibly our visions are coming true. I can't take the time here to re-count in detail all the activity of my few weeks with the colony at the new city of Jamestown. Such an account would fill a lengthy volume. I want to give some idea, though, of what we were planning and what we might have accomplished.

Our idealists were of many sorts. Pretloe, for instance, was a scientist with a mind that had speculated on nearly every phase of human life. He was frantically determined that we should found and build a new civilization governed by scientific principles alone. No haphazard de-velopment, he insisted, would do—no vagaries resulting from the con-flict of personalities and emotions. For myself, I am an architect. I wanted a city designed from the beginning to care for the most im-probable degrees of future expansion. I wanted streets laid out and buildngs foreseen that might not become realities for hundreds of years, if ever.

John Bealy, the lawyer, and Charles Newton, the financier, both found themselves to be, without ever knowing it, socialists of a sort. They had discussed their political and economic ideals since their first intimation of what had happened. They discovered a profound con-viction that government ownership of business was necessary, in spite of the small fortunes they had privately accumulated in their own investments. They didn't know that this was socialism; they thought of socialism as a process of wandering about naked in the streets and pick-ing up whatever they saw and liked in store windows.

We had a young diplomat on board, Francis Wilson, who had been on his way to Paris as an attaché of the Embassy, with his wife and his young child. Wilson, like his illustrious namesake, had ideals in private which might have astonished his superiors at Washington. He believed in a world-state without tariff barriers or any barriers of language and custom. He frowned on all political systems. He wanted a govern-mental system under which all executives would be chosen by a method of examinations and intelligence tests, from the state gov-ernors up to the President. With John Bealy, Wilson felt that our whole legal and judicial systems should be developed by the best of compe-tent judges and legal authorities.

As to our practical work—it sounds like child's play compared with these ambitions. Captain Weeks added to the cabinet Bealy, Newton, and Wilson. He got out the crew and set them at cutting trees and building under the direction of his officers and the three students. The buildings were crude, of course, but sufficient for a beginning. A dock was built first, at a point where it was found the ship could come in fairly close to shore. I was drawing beautiful plans, in my leisure moments, of a future city. There was to be a traffic center around the harbor, with docks and termini for railroads and landing fields for airplanes—if we should ever live to build them. I had visions of an elevated drive around the harbor, and elevated streets for private automobile traffic. We *were* dreamers, weren't we?

We put up temporary houses. At the time of my departure a barracks for the crew had been built already—Weeks was imposing military life and discipline on them—and houses for all the married passengers and our only single woman passenger, Alicia Corey, whom I have mentioned earlier in this account. We had, of course, very few passengers —a little over two dozen. The stewardesses were given a house together. The ship was slowly stripped of its furnishings to fill the various buildings. They were luxurious fittings, and they looked very strange in the rude houses we had thrown up so quickly. We had, too, a building which served as a dining hall and a sort of lounge, with offices for ourselves, and a kitchen. Our idea, you see, was to dismantle the ship as soon as possible. Captain Weeks and his officers, I believe, had plans of their own for the ship, in order that it should be preserved in the best possible condition for the future.

There was a large and varied cargo on board. Ludicrous as it may appear, there were a number of automobiles and trucks, and two airplanes—the latter unassembled, of course. At the time I left, a hangar and a field were being planned for one of the planes. Besides these, there were innumerable other articles—phonographs, beds, bathroom fittings, machinery, etc.—which we used or intended to use as we needed them. We felt that we were entitled to these things under the circumstances, inasmuch as we saw no hope of returning them to their rightful owners. However, a number of the passengers, who were possessed of considerable fortunes, drew up a paper, which they gave Captain Weeks, assuming personal responsibility as a group for the entire cargo, the cost to be taken from their estates in case we should ever return.

In the meantime, our only immediate necessity which could not be readily supplied was food. Our rations were running low. A few wild fruits and berries were discovered in the surrounding woods, but not enough to satisfy the needs of a large group of people. James Folk, the farmer, was making a rapid survey of our resources for various crops. He foresaw the possibility of planting orchards with the fruit trees we had found in the woods. Besides that, he had found among the cargo a consignment of seeds. There was no great variety of these, though, and not enough of them to justify careless experimentation. In any case, it would obviously require months to sow and reap crops sufficient to meet even our most elementary needs. It was fortunately early in the summer, but we were looking forward to an unpleasant winter if other sources of food were not found. It was in one of our expeditions to discover whether there were any animals in the surrounding forests that Jim Grady, Pretloe, and I lost the colony.

The reason I have given even so brief an account of our activity lies in the fact that we were presented with what was, so far as I know, a unique problem. We were marooned there in that bay—marooned, too, is an apt word, for the ship was running low of fuel—and we were required to set up as quickly as possible a civilization that would give us as far as it could the comforts of civilization we had left. And our resources were, while limited, amazing for a band of castaways. The significance of our attempt is this, I think: that we were required to manufacture a machine-made civilization. We were the colonists of a new era, of an industrial period. And we went at our problem in a thoroughly business-like manner, with the organization and efficiency that modern business had taught us. The results, of course, are unknown to me now. But it was an experiment nobody had ever had the opportunity to make before.

Grady, Pretloe, and I had gone on several hunting expeditions before the final one which ended the adventure for us. We had found no signs of any life except a few rabbits and other small animals. It had become a matter of necessity to make a thorough search for larger game. So far we had penetrated only a few miles into the forest, being careful not to lose our way.

The final expedition was undertaken with great care. We intended to be gone about a week. We were provided, of course, with food, and we would get fresh water from the river or from any other sources we might find with which to fill our bottles. We carried guns, hatchets, and knives. With the hatchets we should have to mark or blaze our trail whenever we left the river. It was summer, so we carried few clothes and no bedding. Our only extra bodily protection was our raincoats. We had a coil of rope which might prove useful. Our intention was to strike up into the hills, following the river as far as we could.

One morning, after the early breakfast to which we had all become accustomed, we began our journey up the river. Before it disappeared behind a broad bend in the stream, I took one last look at the colony. More than anything else, it resembled the pictures you sometimes see of colonial settlements in Virginia. The row of little houses stretched along the side of the bay, with the big dining hall in the center, where the dock lay, and behind that the barracks. The ship was a fantastic touch. It had seemed a toy ship, leaving New York beside the *Majestic*. Now it looked gigantic, towering up above the long dock and the buildings. For the first time in days I noticed that it had no shadow; but I found that its absence didn't affect me so peculiarly as I might have expected. Mr. Newton's daughters and two or three other young women were swimming in the bay with Rudolph Cortez, the young jazz orchestra leader, who couldn't be persuaded to work. I turned away, and went on up the river.

The hills were not far away. We followed the first branch of the river that turned off on our side of the bank. It led us toward a pass through the hills. By late afternoon we had reached the beginning of the pass. Then a thunderstorm overtook us—the first real storm since that momentous evening our fourth night out from New York. We got out our raincoats and took shelter under the trees until the storm went by. I noted particularly that, while there were flashes of light accompanied by thunder, we saw no actual streaks of lightning. The thunder sounded rather distant.

It was dark afterward, and we couldn't go on without difficulty. We sat down on a big rock at the river's edge and watched the water passing under us, dark and sluggish and quiet, for an hour or so while we talked of our plans for the colony. Then, spreading the coats together on the cold ground, we fell asleep. We were too tired to mind the discomfort.

We were up early, ate our meager breakfast, and went on. The river wound about through the hills, narrowing. When it seemed to be turning back upon itself too much, we left it and started climbing. We had to mark our trail now with our hatchets, which slowed us up somewhat. But the forest was thinning all the time now as we went up, so that we didn't find it difficult to penetrate. Some while after lunch, we reached the summit of a low mountain. It dipped down again before us into a small valley. Beyond that it rose again to another line of hilltops, somewhat higher than these. We had seen no traces of animal life.

We went on. Darkness came as we were starting up the second range of hills. That night we slept on dry twigs beside a small fire that smouldered away during the night. We were no longer afraid that animals might molest us. We had little hope left of finding them. The stillness was profound and disturbing. There were few of the faint night sounds which make our evenings in the inhabited world, murmurous with hidden life. The silence there was the heavy silence of a vacuum, of a deaf man's world.

The following day we continued our climb. Early in the afternoon we reached the summit, leaving the forest behind except for a few scattered trees and the underbrush. Stretching out before us was a long plain, flat with tall grass waving gently in the wind. We went on.

Tired now, after our long climb, we plodded along with our eyes roving absently over the grass immediately around us. The grass was waist-high. It was late in the afternoon when I happened to raise my eyes and then pause. Some miles away, dim in the gathering twilight, and blurred like a dream, stood the apparition of a city. I rubbed my eyes, and smiled. Certainly there could be no city in front of us. But Pretloe and Grady had paused too, and were looking fixedly at it.

After a long silence, I managed to say breathlessly:

"What is it, Pretloe—a mirage?" He looked at me a moment doubtfully.

"A mirage?" he said. "Perhaps. . . ." Then, suddenly, he roused himself. "Come, we'd better hurry on before it's too dark."

We shouldered our rifles and went on, striding forward with long strides that felt all at once refreshed. As we walked, we watched the city looming up before us. The closer we came to it, the more doubtfully we watched it. It was peculiar—the distorted caricature of a city. I can see it still as we saw it in those few hurried minutes of walking. It's clear and distinct in my mind as I write. But I find that I can't describe with any words the strangeness of that startling apparition. Have you ever approached a little one-street village from the rear of the building along the street, and at twilight? It was something like that. We could see clearly many streets crossing each other, filled with traffic, squares and boulevards and buildings. And, somehow it seemed that we could see into the buildings, a confused mass of rooms and halls and moving people, people at rest, people coming in and going out. There were thousands of people everywhere, confused as if engaged in a gigantic struggle. But it seemed also that we saw the city in some indescribable fashion from *behind*. It was partly dark, partly hidden from us.

We were very close when a startled exclamation burst from Pretloe's lips—"My God!" Grady and I paused abruptly.

"What is it, Pretloe? What do you make of this?" Grady asked.

And Pretloe answered, his voice breaking a little: "Don't you see? It's Paris!"

We stood there in silence a moment, staring first at Pretloe, then at the distorted city. Suddenly we began to run breathlessly, shouting, and burst into the city. . . .

As if we had waked up from a dream and opened our eyes, we found ourselves standing on a street corner. The plain, with its tall grass waving in the wind, was gone. People moved about us, turning their heads curiously as they went by. Automobiles swept along the wide boulevard, quietly in the twilight. For a moment everything seemed very still. Then we became aware of the sound of many voices, and of the hooting of many horns. And at that moment, too, the lights were lighted up and down the boulevard, all together. It was night.

A gendarme approached us, and laid his hand gently on Grady's arm.

"Messieurs?" he said gently, questioningly. And Pretloe, relapsing unconsciously into French, muttered, "Mon Dieu! En vérité, c'est Paris!"

That's all. We gave out no statements to the press. We didn't care to see the inside of the sanitarium. We registered at an obscure hotel under assumed names, which we have been using ever since. The thing was simply too incredible to make public. Grady, a quietly observant and methodical fellow, had taken note of all the passengers and their names.

Together Grady and I got in touch with their attorneys, and explained in private what had happened. I don't suppose we were believed, but it was a reassurance of a sort. The attorneys presumably did whatever they felt it their duty to do. And Grady explained as well as he could to the owners of his ship. They fired him.

Before I left New York to straighten up my own affairs, I had a last talk with Pretloe at the hotel. He hadn't much to say.

"You can't expect me to explain it," was the sum of his remarks. "Somehow or other we are back, and that's all. My theory? Well, personally I'm getting a little tired of my theories. I'd like a little solid fact for a change. All I can suggest is that when we got out of our stratum we were completely adrift so far as the fourth dimension was concerned. For a while, probably, we left it behind. Then we must have drifted back. Or perhaps we never were very far away—just far enough away to make the radio and our lights useless. There's no way to tell. Somehow, at the end, we landed with our line (our three dimensional line) converging toward this one, like a straight line converging toward the equator we used to talk about. . . . I suppose the others will wander back, one by one." But, none have appeared.

I must make it clear that we never intended to desert them. You must imagine us as we were that afternoon in the twilight when we saw the distorted shape of Paris in front of us. We hadn't time to think. We saw it; something turned over frantically in our minds, and we ran. When we found ourselves standing on the street corner, in the midst of the crowds, it was too late. There was no way back.

Pretloe has lost himself in a maze of experiments. He is studying his physics all over again. He feels that, with even the meager data our experience gave us, we can eventually find some way back into the waste land where our colony is stranded. He talks of complicated instruments and machines in the rare letters I get from him. Personally, I think it's a waste of time. Besides, it's January now, and I don't know what they're doing for food. Probably they won't even survive.

New York, though, has palled on me of late, as it used to pall on me when I first left Virginia and came here. Secretly I've been wishing I were back in that adventure, with its ludicrous details and its heroic outlines. If Pretloe ever *does* work out his machines, and finds a way to rejoin them, I'll be with him. I can't forget the stillness, and the sea breaking gently on a shadowless beach.

PETER PHILLIPS

MANNA

TAKE best-quality synthetic protein. Bake it, break it up, steam it, steep it in sucrose, ferment it, add nut oil, piquant spices from the Indies, fruit juices, new flavors from the laboratory, homogenize it, hydrolize it, soak it in brine; pump in glutamic acid, balanced proportions of A, B_1, B_2, C, D, traces of calcium, copper and iron salts, an unadvertised drop of benzedrine; dehydrate, peptonize, irradiate, reheat in malt vapor under pressure compress, cut into mouth-sized chunks, pack in liquor from an earlier stage of the process—

Miracle Meal.

Everything the Body Needs to Sustain Life and Bounding Vitality, in the Most DEEE LISHUSSS Food Ever Devised. It will Invigorate You, Build Muscle, Brain, Nerve. Better than the Banquets of Imperial Rome, Renaissance Italy, Eighteenth Century France—All in One Can. The Most Heavenly Taste Thrills You Have Ever Experienced. Gourmets' Dream and Housewives' Delight. You Can Live On It. Eat it for Breakfast, Lunch, Dinner. You'll Never Get Tired of MIRACLE MEAL.

Ad cuts of Zeus contemptuously tossing a bowl of ambrosia over the edge of Mount Olympus and making a goggle-eyed grab for a can of Miracle Meal.

Studio fake-ups of Lucretia Borgia dropping a phial of poison and crying piously: "It Would Be a Sin to Spoil Miracle Meal."

Posters and night-signs of John Doe—or Bill Smith, or Henri Brun, or Hans Schmitt or Wei Lung—balancing precariously on a pyramided pile of empty M.M. cans, eyes closed, mouth pursed in slightly inane ecstasy as he finishes the last mouthful of his hundred-thousandth can.

You could live on it, certainly.

The publicity co-ordinator of the Miracle Meal Corporation chose the victim himself—a young man named Arthur Adelaide from Greenwich Village.

For a year, under the closest medical supervision and observation, Arthur ate nothing but Miracle Meal.

From this Miracle Meal Marathon, as it was tagged by video-print newssheets, he emerged smiling, twice the weight—publicity omitted to mention that he'd been half-starved to begin with—he'd been trying to live off pure art and was a bad artist—perfectly fit, and ten thousand dollars richer.

He was also given a commercial art job with M.M., designing new labels for the cans.

His abrupt death at the end of an eighty-story drop from his office window a week or two later received little attention.

It would be unreasonable to blame the cumulative effect of M.M., for Arthur was probably a little unbalanced to begin with, whereas M.M. was Perfectly Balanced—a Kitchen in a Can.

Maybe you could get tired of it. But not very quickly. The flavor was the secret. It was delicious yet strangely and tantalizingly indefinable. It seemed to react progressively on the taste-buds so that the tastes subtly changed with each mouthful.

One moment it might be *omelette au fine herbes,* the next, turkey and cranberry, then buckwheat and maple. You'd be through the can before you could make up your mind. So you'd buy another.

Even the can was an improvement on the usual plastic self-heater —shape of a small, shallow pie-dish, with a pre-impressed crystalline fracture in the plastic lid.

Press the inset button on the preheating unit at one side, and when the food was good and hot, a secondary chemical reaction in the unit released a fierce little plunger just inside the perimeter fracture. Slight steam pressure finished the job. The lip flipped off.

Come and get it. You eat right out of the can it comes in. Keep your fingers out, Johnny. Don't you see the hygiplast spoon in its moisture- and heat-repellent wrapper fixed under the lid?

The Rev. Malachi Pennyhorse did not eat Miracle Meal. Nor was he impressed when Mr. Stephen Samson, Site Advisor to the Corporation, spoke in large dollar signs of the indirect benefits a factory would bring to the district.

"Why here? You already have one factory in England. Why not extend it?"

"It's our policy, Reverend—"

"Not 'Reverend' young man. Call me Vicar. Or Mr. Pennyhorse. Or merely Pennyhorse— Go on."

"It's our policy, sir, to keep our factories comparatively small, site them in the countryside for the health of employees, and modify the buildings to harmonize with the prevailing architecture of the district. There is no interference with local amenities. All transport of employees, raw materials, finished product is by silent copter."

Samson laid a triphoto on the vicar's desk. "What would you say that was?"

Mr. Pennyhorse adjusted his pince-nez, looked closely. "Byzantine. Very fine. Around 500 A.D."

"And this—"

"Moorish. Quite typical. Fifteenth century."

Samson said: "They're our factories at Istanbul and Tunis respectively. At Allahabad, India, we had to put up big notices saying: 'This is not a temple or place of worship' because natives kept wandering in and offering-up prayers to the processing machines."

Mr. Pennyhorse glanced up quickly. Samson kept his face straight, added: "The report may have been exaggerated, but—you get the idea?"

The vicar said: "I do. What shape do you intend your factory to take in this village?"

"That's why I came to you. The rural district council suggested that you might advise us."

"My inclination, of course, is to advise you to go away and not return."

The vicar looked out of his study window at the sleepy, sun-washed village street, gables of the ancient Corn Exchange, paved market-place, lichened spire of his own time-kissed church; and, beyond, rolling Wiltshire pastures cradling the peaceful community.

The vicar sighed: "We've held out here so long—I hoped we would remain inviolate in my time, at least. However, I suppose we must consider ourselves fortunate that your corporation has some respect for tradition and the feelings of the . . . uh . . . 'natives.'"

He pulled out a drawer in his desk. "It might help you to understand those feelings if I show you a passage from the very full diary of my predecessor here, who died fifty years ago at the age of ninety-five—we're a long-lived tribe, we clergy. It's an entry he made one hundred years ago—sitting at this very desk."

Stephen Samson took the opened volume.

The century-old handwriting was as readable as typescript.

"*May 3, 1943. Long, interesting discussion with young American soldier, one of those who are billeted in the village. They term themselves G.I.'s. Told me countryside near his home in Pennsylvania not unlike our Wiltshire downs. Showed him round church. Said he was leaving soon, and added: 'I love this place. Nothing like my home town in looks, but the atmosphere's the same—old, and kind of comfortable. And I guess if I came back here a hundred years from now, it wouldn't have changed one bit.' An engaging young man. I trust he is right.*"

Samson looked up. Mr. Pennyhorse said: "That young man may have been one of your ancestors."

Samson gently replaced the old diary on the desk. "He wasn't. My family's Ohioan. But I see what you mean, and respect it. That's why I want you to help us. You will?"

"Do you fish?" asked the vicar, suddenly and irrelevantly.

"Yes, sir. Very fond of the sport."

"Thought so. You're the type. That's why I like you. Take a look at these flies. Seen anything like them? Make 'em myself. One of the finest trout streams in the country just outside the village. Help you? Of course I will."

"Presumption," said Brother James. He eased himself through a gray-stone wall by twisting his subexistential plane slightly, and leaned reflectively against a moonbeam that slanted through the branches of an oak.

A second habited and cowled figure materialized beside him. "Perhaps so. But it does my age-wearied heart a strange good to see those familiar walls again casting their shadows over the field."

"A mockery, Brother Gregory. A mere shell that simulates the outlines of our beloved Priory. Think you that even the stones are of that good, gray granite that we built with? Nay! As this cursed simulacrum was a-building, I warped two hands into the solid, laid hold of a mossy block, and by the saints, 'twas of such inconsequential weight I might have hurled it skyward with a finger. And within, is there aught which we may recognize? No chapel, no cloisters, no refectory—only long, geometrical rooms. And what devilries and unholy rites may not be centered about those strange mechanisms with which the rooms are filled?"

At the tirade, Brother Gregory sighed and thrust back his cowl to let the gracious moonbeams play on his tonsured head. "For an Untranslated One of some thousand years' standing," he said, "you exhibit a mulish ignorance, Brother James. You would deny men all advancement. I remember well your curses when first we saw horseless carriages and flying machines."

"Idols!" James snapped. "Men worship them. Therefore are they evil."

"You are so good, Brother James," Gregory said, with the heaviest sarcasm. "So good, it is my constant wonderment that you have had to wait so long for Translation Upwards. Do you think that Dom Penny-horse, the present incumbent of Selcor—a worthy man, with reverence for the past—would permit evil rites within his parish? You are a befuddled old anachronism, brother."

"That," said James, "is quite beyond sufferance. For you to speak thus of Translation, when it was your own self-indulgent pursuit of carnal pleasures that caused us to be bound here through the centuries!"

Brother Gregory said coldly: "It was not I who inveigled the daughter of Ronald the Wry-Neck into the kitchen garden, thus exposing the weak flesh of a brother to grievous temptation."

There was silence for a while, save for the whisper of a midnight breeze through the branches of the oak, and the muted call of a night-bird from the far woods.

Gregory extended a tentative hand and lightly touched the sleeve of James's habit. "The argument might proceed for yet another century and bring us no nearer Translation. Besides it is not such unbearable penance, my brother. Were we not both lovers of the earth, of this fair countryside?"

James shrugged. Another silence. Then he fingered his gaunt white cheeks. "What shall we do, Brother Gregory? Shall we—appear to them?"

Gregory said: "I doubt whether common warp manifestation would be efficacious. As dusk fell tonight, I overheard a conversation between Dom Pennyhorse and a tall, young-featured man who has been concerned in the building of this simulacrum. The latter spoke in one of the dialects of the Americas; and it was mentioned that several of the men who will superintend the working of the machines within will also be from the United States—for a time at least. It is not prudent to haunt Americans in the normal fashion. Their attitude towards such matters is notoriously—unseemly."

"We could polter," suggested Brother James.

Gregory replaced his cowl. "Let us review the possibilities, then," he said, "remembering that our subetheric energy is limited."

They walked slowly together over the meadow towards the resuscitated gray walls of the Selcor Prior. Blades of grass, positively charged by their passage, sprang suddenly upright, relaxed slowly into limpness as the charge leaked away.

They halted at the walls to adjust their planes of incidence and degree of tenuity, and passed inside.

The new Miracle Meal machines had had their first test run. The bearings on the dehydrator pumps were still warm as two black figures, who seemed to carry with them an air of vast and wistful loneliness, paced silently between rows of upright cylinders which shone dully in moonlight diffused through narrow windows.

"Here," said Gregory, the taller of the two, softly, "did we once walk the cloisters in evening meditation."

Brother James's broad features showed signs of unease. He felt more than mere nostalgia.

"Power—what are they using? Something upsets my bones. I am queasy, as when a thunderstorm is about to break. Yet there is no static."

Gregory stopped, looked at his hand. There was a faint blue aura at his fingertips. "Slight neutron escape," he said. "They have a small thorium-into-233 pile somewhere. It needs better shielding."

"You speak riddles."

Gregory said, with a little impatience: "You have the entire science section of the village library at your disposal at nightfall for the effort of a trifling polter, yet for centuries you have read nothing but the *Lives of the Saints*. So, of course, I speak riddles—to you. You are even content to remain in ignorance of the basic principles of your own structure and functioning, doing everything by traditional thought-rote and rule of thumb. But I am not so content; and of my knowledge, I can assure you that the radiation will not harm you unless you warp to solid and sit atop the pile when it is in full operation." Gregory smiled. "And then, dear brother, you would doubtless be so uncomfortable that you would dewarp before any harm could be done beyond the loss of a little energy that would be replaced in time. Let us proceed."

They went through three departments before Brother Gregory divined the integrated purpose of the vats, driers, conveyor-tubes, belts and containers.

"The end product, I'm sure, is a food of sorts," he said, "and by some quirk of fate, it is stored in approximately the position that was once occupied by our kitchen store—if my sense of orientation has not been bemused by these strange internal surroundings."

The test run of the assembly had produced a few score cans of Miracle Food. They were stacked on metal shelves which would tilt and gravity-feed them into the shaft leading up to the crating machine. Crated, they would go from there to the copter-loading bay on the roof.

Brother James reached out to pick up a loose can. His hand went through it twice.

"Polt, you dolt!" said Brother Gregory. "Or are you trying to be miserly with your confounded energy? Here, let me do it."

The telekineticized can sprang into his solid hands. He turned it about slightly increasing his infrared receptivity to read the label, since the storeroom was in darkness.

"Miracle Meal. Press Here."

He pressed, pressed again, and was closely examining the can when, after thirty seconds, the lid flipped off, narrowly missing his chin.

Born, and living, in more enlightened times, Brother Gregory's inquiring mind and insatiable appetite for facts would have made him a research worker. He did not drop the can. His hands were quite steady. He chuckled. He said: "Ingenious, very ingenious. See—the food is hot."

He warped his nose and back-palate into solid and delicately inhaled vapors. His eyes widened. He frowned, inhaled again. A beatific smile spread over his thin face.

"Brother James—warp your nose!"

The injunction, in other circumstances, might have been considered both impolite and unnecessary. Brother James was no beauty, and his big, blunt, snoutlike nose, which had been a flaring red in life, was the least prepossessing of his features.

But he warped it, and sniffed.

M.M. Sales Leaflet Number 14: It Will Sell By Its Smell Alone.

Gregory said hesitantly: "Do you think, Brother James, that we might—"

James licked his lips, from side to side, slowly. "It would surely take a day's accumulation of energy to hold digestive and alimentary in solid for a sufficient period. But—"

"Don't be a miser," said Gregory. "There's a spoon beneath the lid. Get a can for yourself. And don't bother with digestive. Teeth, palate and throat are sufficient. It would not digest in any case. It remains virtually unchanged. But going down—ah, bliss!"

It went down. Two cans.

"Do you remember, brother," said James, in a weak, reminiscing voice, "what joy it was to eat and be strengthened. And now to eat is to be weakened."

Brother Gregory's voice was faint but happy. "Had there been food of this character available before our First Translation, I doubt whether other desires of the flesh would have appealed to me. But what was our daily fare set on the refectory table: peas; lentils; cabbage soup; hard, tasteless cheese. Year after year—*ugh!*"

"Health-giving foods, murmured Brother James, striving to be right-eous even in his exhaustion. "Remember when we bribed the kitchener to get extra portions. Good trenchermen, we. Had we not died of the plague before our Priory became rich and powerful, then, by the Faith, our present bodies would be of greater girth."

"Forms, not bodies," said Gregory, insisting even in *his* exhaustion on scientific exactitudes. "Variable fields, consisting of open lattices of energy foci resolvable into charged particles—and thus solid matter—when they absorb energy beyond a certain stage. In other words, my dear ignorant brother, when we polt. The foci themselves—or rather the spaces between them—act as a limited-capacity storage battery for the slow accretion of this energy from cosmic sources, which may be con-trolled and concentrated in the foci by certain thought-patterns."

Talking was an increasing effort in his energy-low state.

"When we polt," he went on slowly, "we take up heat, air cools, live people get cold shivers; de-polt, give up heat, live people get clammy, cold-hot feeling; set up 'lectrostatic field, live peoples' hair stan's on end"—his voice was trailing into deep, blurred inaudibility, like a mechanical phonograph running down, but James wasn't listening any-way—"an' then when we get Translated Up'ards by The Power That Is, all the energy goes back where it came from an' we jus' become thought. Thassall. Thought. Thought, thought, thought, thought—"

The phonograph ran down, stopped. There was silence in the transit storeroom of the Selcor Priory Factory branch of the Miracle Meal Corporation.

For a while.

Then—

"THOUGHT!"

The shout brought Brother James from his uneasy, uncontrolled re-pose at the nadir of an energy balance.

"What is it?" he grumbled. "I'm too weak to listen to any of your theorizing."

"Theorizing! I have it!"

"Conserve your energies, brother, else will you be too weak even to twist yourself from this place."

Both monks had permitted their forms to relax into a corner of the storeroom, supine, replete in disrepletion.

Brother Gregory sat up with an effort.

"Listen, you attenuated conserve of very nothingness, I have a way to thwart, bemuse, mystify and irritate these crass philistines—and nothing so simple that a psychic investigator could put a thumb on us. What are we, Brother James?"

It was a rhetorical question, and Brother James had barely formulated his brief reply—"Ghosts"—before Brother Gregory, energized in a way beyond his own understanding by his own enthusiasm, went on: "Fields, in effect. Mere lines of force, in our un-polted state. What happens if we whirl? A star whirls. It has mass, rate of angular rotation, degree of compactness—therefore, gravity. Why? Because it has a field to start with. But we are our own fields. We need neither mass nor an excessive rate of rotation to achieve the same effect. Last week I grounded a high-flying wood-pigeon by whirling. It shot down to me through the air, and I'd have been buffeted by its pinions had I not stood aside. It hit the ground—not too heavily, by the grace of St. Barbara—recovered and flew away."

The great nose of Brother James glowed pinkly for a moment. "You fuddle and further weaken me by your prating. Get to your point, if you have such. And explain how we may do anything in our present unenergized state, beyond removing ourselves to a nexus point for recuperation."

Brother Gregory warped his own nose into solid in order to scratch its tip. He felt the need of this reversion to a life habit, which had once aided him in marshaling his thoughts.

"You think only of personal energy," he said scornfully. "We don't need that, to whirl. It is an accumulative process, yet we gain nothing, lose nothing. Matter is not the only thing we can warp. If you will only listen, you woof of unregenerate and forgotten flesh, I will try to explain without mathematics."

He talked.

After a while, Brother James's puzzled frown gave way to a faint smile. "Perhaps I understand," he said.

"Then forgive me for implying you were a moron," said Gregory. "Stand up, Brother James."

Calls on transatlantic tight-beam cost heavy. Anson Dewberry, Miracle Meal Overseas Division head, pointed this out to Mr. Stephen Samson three times during their conversation.

"Listen," said Samson at last, desperately, "I'll take no more delegation of authority. In my contract, it says I'm site adviser. That means I'm architect and negotiator, not detective or scientist or occulist. I offered to stay on here to supervise building because I happen to like the place. I like the pubs. I like the people. I like the fishing. But it wasn't in my contract. And I'm now standing on that contract. Building is finished to schedule, plant installed—your tech men, incidentally, jetted out of here without waiting to catch snags after the first runoff—and now I'm through. The machines are running, the cans are coming off—and if the copters don't collect, that's for you and the London office to bat your brains out over. And the Lord forgive that mess of terminal propositions," he added in lower voice. Samson was a purist in the matter of grammar.

Anson Dewberry jerked his chair nearer the scanner in his New York office. His pink, round face loomed in Samson's screen like that of an avenging cherub.

"Don't you have no gendarmes around that place?" Mr. Dewberry was no purist, in moments of stress. "Get guards on, hire some militia, check employees. Ten thousand cans of M.M. don't just evaporate."

"They do," Samson replied sadly. "Maybe it's the climate. And for the seventh time, I tell you I've done all that. I've had men packed so tightly around the place that even an orphan neutron couldn't get by. This morning I had two men from Scotland Yard gumming around. They looked at the machines, followed the assembly through to the transit storeroom, examined the electrolocks and mauled their toe-caps trying to boot a dent in the door. Then the top one—that is, the one who only looked half-asleep—said, 'Mr. Samson, sir, do you think it's . . . uh . . . possible . . . that . . . uh . . . this machine of yours . . . uh . . . goes into reverse when your . . . uh . . . backs are turned and . . . uh . . . sucks the cans back again?' "

Grating noises that might have been an incipient death rattle slid over the tight-beam from New York.

Samson nodded, a smirk of mock sympathy on his tanned, humor-wrinkled young face.

The noises ended with a gulp. The image of Dewberry thrust up a hesitant forefinger in interrogation. "Hey! Maybe there's something to that, at that—would it be possible?"

Samson groaned a little. "I wouldn't really know or overmuch care. But I have doubts. Meantime—"

"Right." Dewberry receded on the screen. "I'll jet a man over tonight. The best. From Research. Full powers. Hand over to him. Take some of your vacation. Design some more blamed mosques or tabernacles. Go fishing."

"A sensible suggestion," Samson said. "Just what I was about to do. It's a glorious afternoon here, sun a little misted, grass green, stream flowing cool and deep, fish lazing in the pools where the willow-shadows fall—"

The screen blanked. Dewberry was no purist, and no poet either.

Samson made a schoolkid face. He switched off the fluor lamps that supplemented the illumination from a narrow window in the supervisor's office—which, after studying the ground-plan of the original Selcor Priory, he had sited in the space that was occupied centuries before by the business sanctum of the Prior—got up from his desk and walked through a Norman archway into the sunlight.

He breathed the meadow-sweet air deeply, with appreciation.

The Rev. Malachi Pennyhorse was squatting with loose-jointed ease against the wall. Two fishing rods in brown canvas covers lay across his lap. He was studying one of the trout-flies nicked into the band of his ancient hat. His balding, brown pate was bared to the sun. He looked up.

"What fortune, my dear Stephen?"

"I convinced him at last. He's jetting a man over tonight. He told me to go fishing."

"Injunction unnecessary, I should imagine. Let's go. We shan't touch a trout with the sky as clear as this, but I have some float tackle for lazier sport." They set off across a field. "Are you running the plant today?"

Samson nodded his head towards a faint hum. "Quarter-speed. That will give one copter-load for the seventeen hundred hours collection, and leave enough over to go in the transit store for the night and provide Dewberry's man with some data. Or rather, lack of it."

"Where do you think it's going?"

"I've given up guessing."

Mr. Pennyhorse paused astride a stile and looked back at the gray bulk of the Priory. "I could guess who's responsible," he said, and chuckled.

"Uh? Who?"

Mr. Pennyhorse shook his head. "Leave that to your investigator."

A few moments later he murmured as if to himself: "What a haunt! Ingenious devils."

But when Stephen Samson looked at him inquiringly, he added: "But I can't guess where your cans have been put."

And he would say nothing more on the subject.

Who would deny that the pure of heart are often simple-minded? (The obverse of the proposition need not be argued.) And that cause-effect relations are sometimes divined more readily by the intuition of simpletons than the logic of scholars?

Brother Simon Simplex—Simple Simon to later legends—looked open-mouthed at the array of strange objects on the stone shelves of the kitchen storeroom. He was not surprised—his mouth was always open, even in sleep.

He took down one of the objects and examined it with mild curiosity. He shook it, turned it round, thrust a forefinger into a small depression. Something gave slightly, but there was no other aperture. He replaced it on the shelf.

When his fellow-kitchener returned, he would ask him the purpose of the objects—if he could remember to do so. Simon's memory was poor. Each time the rota brought him onto kitchen duty for a week, he had to be instructed afresh in the business of serving meals in the refectory: platter so, napkin thus, spoon here, finger bowls half-filled, three water pitchers, one before the Prior, one in the center, one at the foot of the table—"and when you serve, tread softly and do not breathe down the necks of the brothers."

Even now could he hear the slight scrape of benches on stone as the monks, with bowed heads, freshly washed hands in the sleeves of their habits, filed slowly into the refectory and took their seats at the long, oak table. And still his fellow-kitchener had not returned from the errand. Food was prepared—dared he begin to serve alone?

It was a great problem for Simon, brother in the small House of Selcor, otherwise Selcor Priory, poor cell-relation to the rich monastery of the Cluniac Order at Battle, in the year 1139 A.D.

Steam pressure in the triggered can of Miracle Meal did its work. The lid flipped. The aroma issued.

Simon's mouth nearly shut as he sniffed.

The calm and unquestioning acceptance of the impossible is another concommitant of simplicity and purity of heart. To the good and simple Simon the rising of the sun each morning and the singing of birds were recurrent miracles. Compared with these, a laboratory miracle of the year 2143 A.D. was as nothing.

Here was a new style of platter, filled with hot food, ready to serve. Wiser minds than his had undoubtedly arranged matters. His fellow-kitchener, knowing the task was thus simplified, had left him to serve alone.

He had merely to remove the covers from these platters and carry them into the refectory. To remove the covers—cause—effect—the intuition of a simple mind.

Simon carried fourteen of the platters to the kitchen table, pressed buttons and waited.

He was gravely tempted to sample the food himself, but all-inclusive Benedictine rules forbade kitcheners to eat until their brothers had been served.

He carried a loaded tray into the refectory where the monks sat in patient silence except for the one voice of the Reader who stood at a raised lectern and intoned from the *Lives of the Saints*.

Pride that he had been thought fit to carry out the duty alone made Simon less clumsy than usual. He served the Prior, Dom Holland, first, almost deftly; then the other brothers, in two trips to the kitchen.

A spicy, rich, titillating fragrance filled the refectory. The intoning of the *Lives of the Saints* faltered for a moment as the mouth of the Reader filled with saliva, then he grimly continued.

At Dom Holland's signal, the monks ate.

The Prior spooned the last drops of gravy into his mouth. He sat back. A murmur arose. He raised a hand. The monks became quiet. The Reader closed his book.

Dom Holland was a man of faith; but he did not accept miracles or even the smallest departures from routine existence without questioning. He had sternly debated with himself whether he should question

the new platters and the new food before or after eating. The aroma
decided him. He ate first.

Now he got up, beckoned to a senior monk to follow him, and paced
with unhurried calmness to the kitchen.

Simon had succumbed. He was halfway through his second tin.

He stood up, licking his fingers.

"Whence comes this food, my son?" asked Dom Holland, in sono-
rous Latin.

Simon's mouth opened wider. His knowledge of the tongue was confined to prayers.

Impatiently the Prior repeated the question in the English dialect
of the district.

Simon pointed, and led them to the storeroom.

"I looked, and it was here," he said simply. The words were to become
famed.

His fellow-kitchener was sought—he was found dozing in a warm
corner of the kitchen garden—and questioned. He shook his head.
The provisioner rather reluctantly disclaimed credit.

Dom Holland thought deeply, then gave instructions for a general
assembly. The plastic "platters" and the hygiplast spoons were carefully
examined. There were murmurs of wonderment at the workmanship.
The discussion lasted two hours.

Simon's only contribution was to repeat with pathetic insistence: "I
looked and it was there."

He realized dimly that he had become a person of some importance.

His face became a mask of puzzlement when the Prior summed up:

"Our simple but blessed brother, Simon Simplex, it seems to me,
has become an instrument or vessel of some thaumaturgical manifestation. It would be wise, however, to await further demonstration before
the matter is referred to higher authorities."

The storeroom was sealed and two monks were deputed as night-
guards.

Even with the possibility of a miracle on his hands, Dom Holland
was not prepared to abrogate the Benedictine rule of only one main
meal a day. The storeroom wasn't opened until early afternoon of the
following day.

It was opened by Simon, in the presence of the Prior, a scribe, the
provisioner, and two senior monks.

Released, a pile of Miracle Meal cans toppled forward like a crumbling cliff, slithering and clattering in noisy profusion around Simon's
legs, sliding over the floor of the kitchen.

Simon didn't move. He was either too surprised or cunningly aware
of the effectiveness of the scene. He stood calf-deep in cans, pointed
at the jumbled stack inside the storeroom, sloping up nearly to the stone
roof, and said his little piece:

"I look, and it is here."

"Kneel, my sons," said Dom Holland gravely, and knelt.

Manna.

And at a time when the Priory was hard-pressed to maintain even its own low standard of subsistence, without helping the scores of dispossessed refugees encamped in wattle shacks near its protecting walls.

The countryside was scourged by a combination of civil and foreign war. Stephen of Normandy against Matilda of Anjou for the British throne. Neither could control his own followers. When the Flemish mercenaries of King Stephen were not chasing Queen Matilda's Angevins back over the borders of Wiltshire, they were plundering the lands and possessions of nominal supporters of Stephen. The Angevins and the barons who supported Matilda's cause quite impartially did the same, then pillaged each other's property, castle against castle, baron against baron.

It was anarchy and free-for-all—but nothing for the ignored serfs, bondmen, villeins and general peasantry, who fled from stricken homes and roamed the countryside in bands of starving thousands. Some built shacks in the inviolate shadow of churches and monasteries.

Selcor Priory had its quota of barefoot, raggedly men, women and children—twelfth century Displaced Persons.

They were a headache to the Prior, kindly Dom Holland—until Simple Simon's Miracle.

There were seventy recipients of the first hand-out of Miracle Meal cans from the small door in the Priory's walled kitchen garden.

The next day there were three hundred, and the day after that, four thousand. Good news doesn't need radio to get around fast.

Fourteen monks worked eight-hour shifts for twenty-four hours, hauling stocks from the capacious storeroom, pressing buttons, handing out steaming platters to orderly lines of refugees.

Two monks, shifting the last few cans from the store, were suddenly buried almost to their necks by the arrival of a fresh consignment, which piled up out of thin air.

Providence, it seemed, did not depend solely upon the intervention of Simon Simplex. The Priory itself and all its inhabitants were evidently blessed.

The Abbot of Battle, Dom Holland's superior, a man of great girth and great learning visited the Priory. He confirmed the miracle—by studying the label on the can.

After several hours' work in the Prior's office, he announced to Dom Holland:

"The script presented the greatest difficulty. It is an extreme simplification of letter-forms at present in use by Anglo-Saxon scholars. The pertinent text is a corruption—if I may be pardoned the use of such a term in the circumstances—of the Latin 'miraculum' compounded with the word 'maél' from our own barbarous tongue—so, clearly, Miracle Meal!"

Dom Holland murmured his awe of this learning.

The Abbot added, half to himself: "Although why the nature of the manifestation should be thus advertised in repetitive engraving, when it is self-evident—" He shrugged. "The ways of Providence are passing strange."

Brother Gregory, reclining in the starlight near his favorite oak, said: "My only regret is that we cannot see the effect of our gift—the theoretical impact of a modern product—usually a weapon—on past ages is a well-tried topic of discussion and speculation among historians, scientists, economists and writers of fantasy."

Brother James, hunched in vague adumbration on a wall behind, said: "You are none of those things, else might you explain why it is that, if these cans have reached the period for which, according to your abstruse calculations, they were destined—an age in which we were both alive—we cannot remember such an event, or why it is not recorded in histories of the period."

"It was a time of anarchy, dear brother. Many records were destroyed. And as for our memories—well, great paradoxes of time are involved. One might as profitably ask how many angels may dance on the point of a pin. Now if you should wish to know how many atoms might be accommodated in a like position—"

Brother Gregory was adroit at changing the subject. He didn't wish to speculate aloud until he'd figured out all the paradox possibilities. He'd already discarded an infinity of time-streams as intellectually unsatisfying, and was toying with the concept of recurrent worlds—

"Dom Pennyhorse has guessed that it is our doing."

"What's that?"

Brother James repeated the information smugly.

Gregory said slowly: "Well, he is not—unsympathetic—to us."

"Assuredly, brother, we have naught to fear from him, nor from the pleasant young man with whom he goes fishing. But this young man was today in consultation with his superior, and an investigator is being sent from America."

"Psychic investigator, eh? Phooey. We'll tie him in knots," said Gregory complacently.

"I assume," said Brother James, with a touch of self-righteousness, "that these vulgar colloquialisms to which you sometimes have recourse are another result of your nocturnal reading. They offend my ear. 'Phooey,' indeed— No, this investigator is one with whom you will undoubtedly find an affinity. I gather that he is from a laboratory— a scientist of sorts."

Brother Gregory sat up and rubbed his tonsure thoughtfully. "That," he admitted, "is different." There was a curious mixture of alarm and eagerness in his voice. "There are means of detecting the field we employ."

An elementary electroscope was one of the means. An ionization indicator and a thermometer were others. They were all bolted firmly on

a bench just inside the storeroom. Wires led from them under the door
to a jury-rigged panel outside.

Sandy-haired Sidney Meredith of M.M. Research sat in front of the
panel on a folding stool, watching dials with intense blue eyes, chin
propped in hands.

Guards had been cleared from the factory. He was alone, on the
advice of Mr. Pennyhorse, who had told him: "If, as I suspect, it's the
work of two of my . . . uh . . . flock . . . two very ancient parishioners . . . they are more likely to play their tricks in the absence of a
crowd."

"I get it," Meredith had said. "Should be interesting."

It was.

He poured coffee from a thermos without taking his eyes from the
panel. The thermometer reading was dropping slowly. Ionization was
rising. From inside the store came the faint rasp of moving objects.

Meredith smiled, sighted a thumb-size camera, recorded the panel
readings. "This," he said softly, "will make a top feature in the *Journal*:
'The most intensive psychic and poltergeist phenomena ever recorded.
M.M.'s top tech trouble-shooter spikes spooks.'"

There was a faint snap beyond the door. Dials swooped back to
zero. Meredith quit smiling and daydreaming.

"Hey—play fair!" he called.

The whisper of a laugh answered him, and a soft, hollow whine, as
of a wind cycloning into outer space.

He grabbed the door, pulled. It resisted. It was like trying to break a
vacuum. He knelt, lit a cigarette, held it near the bottom of the nearly
flush-fitting door. A thin streamer of smoke curled down and was
drawn swiftly through the barely perceptible crack.

The soft whine continued for a few seconds, began to die away.

Meredith yanked at the door again. It gave, to a slight ingush of air.
He thrust his foot in the opening, said calmly into the empty blackness:
"When you fellers have quite finished—I'm coming in. Don't go away.
Let's talk."

He slipped inside, closed the door, stood silent for a moment. He
sniffed. Ozone. His scalp prickled. He scratched his head, felt the hairs
standing upright. And it was cold.

He said: "Right. No point in playing dumb or covering-up, boys."
He felt curiously ashamed of the platitudes as he uttered them. "I
must apologize for breaking in," he added—and meant it. "But this has
got to finish. And if you're not willing to—co-operate—I think I know
now how to finish it."

Another whisper of a laugh. And two words, faint, gently mocking:
"Do you?"

Meredith strained his eyes against the darkness. He saw only the
nerve-patterns in his own eyes. He shrugged.

"If you won't play—" He switched on a blaze of fluor lamps. The long steel shelves were empty. There was only one can of Miracle Meal left in the store.

He felt it before he saw it. It dropped on his head, clattered to the plastocrete floor. When he'd retrieved his breath, he kicked it savagely to the far end of the store and turned to his instruments.

The main input lead had been pulled away. The terminal had been loosened first.

He unclamped a wide-angle infrared camera, waited impatiently for the developrinter to act, pulled out the print.

And laughed. It wasn't a good line-caricature of himself, but it was recognizable, chiefly by the shock of unruly hair.

The lines were slightly blurred, as though written by a needlepoint of light directly on the film. There was a jumble of writing over and under it.

"Old English, I suppose," he murmured. He looked closer. The writing above the caricature was a de Sitter version of the Riemann-Christoffel tensor, followed in crabbed but readable modern English by the words: "Why reverse the sign? Do we act like anti-particles?"

Underneath the drawing was an energy tensor and a comment: "You will notice that magnetic momenta contribute a negative density and pressure."

A string of symbols followed, ending with an equals sign and a query mark. And another comment: "You'll need to take time out to balance this one."

Meredith read the symbols, then sat down heavily on the edge of the instrument bench and groaned. Time *out*. But Time was already out, and there was neither matter nor radiation in a de Sitter universe.

Unless—

He pulled out a notebook, started to scribble.

An hour later Mr. Pennyhorse and Stephen Samson came in.

Mr. Pennyhorse said: "My dear young fellow, we were quite concerned. We thought—"

He stopped. Meredith's blue eyes were slightly out of focus. There were beads of sweat on his brow despite the coolness of the storeroom. Leaves from his notebook and cigarette stubs littered the floor around his feet.

He jumped like a pricked frog when the vicar gently tapped his shoulder, and uttered a vehement cuss-word that startled even the broad-minded cleric.

Samson tutted.

Meredith muttered: "Sorry, sir. But I think I nearly had it."

"What, my son?"

Meredith looked like a ruffle-haired schoolboy. His eyes came back into focus. "A crossword puzzle clue," he said. "Set by a spook with a super-I.Q. Two quite irreconcilable systems of mathematics lumped together, the signs in an extended energy tensor reversed, merry hell played with a temporal factor—and yet it was beginning to make sense."

He smiled wryly. "A ghost who unscrews terminals before he breaks connections and who can make my brain boil is a ghost worth meeting."

Mr. Pennyhorse eased his pince-nez. "Uh . . . yes. Now, don't you think it's time you came to bed? It's four A.M. My housekeeper has made up a comfortable place on the divan in the sitting room." He took Meredith's arm and steered him from the store.

As they walked across the dewy meadows towards the vicarage, with the first pale streaks of dawn showing in the sky, Samson said: "How about the cans?"

"Time," replied Meredith vaguely, "will tell."

"And the guards?"

"Pay them off. Send them away. Keep the plant rolling. Fill the transit store tonight. And I want a freighter copter to take me to London University this afternoon."

Back in the transit store, the discarded leaves from Meredith's notebook fluttered gently upwards in the still air and disappeared.

Brother James said: "He is alone again."

They looked down on the sandy head of Sidney Meredith from the vantage point of a dehydrating tower.

"So I perceive. And I fear this may be our last uh . . . consignment to our erstwhile brothers," said Gregory thoughtfully.

"Why?"

"You will see. In giving him the clue to what we were doing, I gave him the clue to what we are, essentially."

They drifted down towards the transit store.

"After you, Brother James," said Brother Gregory with excessive politeness.

James adjusted his plane of incidence, started through the wall, and—

Shot backwards with a voiceless scream of agony.

Brother Gregory laughed. "I'm sorry. But that's why it will be our last consignment. Heterodyning is painful. He is a very intelligent fellow. The next time, he will take care to screen both his ultra-short generator and controls so that I cannot touch them."

Brother James recovered. "You . . . you use me as a confounded guinea pig! By the saints, you appear to have more sympathy with the man than with me!"

"Not more sympathy, my beloved brother, but certainly much more in common," Brother Gregory replied frankly. "Wait."

He drifted behind Meredith's back and poltered the tip of one finger to flick a lightly soldered wire from a terminal behind a switch. Meredith felt his scalp tingle. A pilot light on his panel blinked out.

Meredith got up from his stool, stretched lazily, grinned into the empty air. He said aloud: "Right. Help yourselves. But I warn you— once you're in, you don't come out until you agree to talk. I have a duplicate set and a built-in circuit-tester. The only way you can spike them is by busting tubes. And I've a hunch you wouldn't do that."

"No," James muttered. "You wouldn't. Let us go."

"No," Gregory answered. "Inside quickly—and whirl. Afterwards I shall speak with him. He is a youth of acute sensibilities and gentleness, whose word is his bond."

Gregory urged his fellow-monk to the wall. They passed within.

Meredith heard nothing, until a faint whine began in the store. He waited until it died away, then knocked on the door. It seemed, crazily, the correct thing to do.

He went into the darkness. "You there?"

A low and pleasant voice, directionless: "Yes. Why didn't you switch on your duplicate generator?"

Meredith breathed deep. "I didn't think it would be necessary. I feel we understand each other. My name is Sidney Meredith."

"Mine is Gregory of Ramsbury."

"And your—friend?"

"James Brasenose. I may say that he disapproves highly of this conversation."

"I can understand that. It is unusual. But then, you're a very unusual . . . un—"

" 'Ghost' is the common term, Mr. Meredith. Rather inadequate, I think, for supranormal phenomena which are, nevertheless, subject to known laws. Most Untranslated spirits remain quite ignorant of their own powers before final Translation. It was only by intensive reading and thought that I determined the principles and potentialities of my construction."

"Anti-particles?"

"According to de Sitter," said Brother Gregory, "that is what we should be. But we are not mere mathematical expressions. I prefer the term 'energy foci.' From a perusal of the notes you left behind yesterday morning—and, of course, from your use of ultra-short waves tonight—it seems you struck the correct train of deduction immediately. Incidentally, where did you obtain the apparatus at such short notice?"

"London University."

Brother Gregory sighed. "I should like to visit their laboratories. But we are bound to this area by a form of moral compulsion that I cannot define or overcome. Only vicariously, through the achievements of others, may I experience the thrill of research."

"You don't do so badly," Meredith said. He was mildly surprised that he felt quite so sane and at ease, except for the darkness. "Would you mind if we had a light?"

"I must be semipolted—or warped—to speak with you. It's not a pleasant sight—floating lungs, larynx, palate, tongue and lips. I'd feel uncomfortable for you. We might appear for you later, if you wish."

"Right. But keep talking. Give me the how and the why. I want this for my professional journal."

"Will you see that the issue containing your paper is placed in the local library?"

"Surely," Meredith said. "Two copies."

"Brother James is not interested. Brother James, will you kindly stop whispering nonsense and remove yourself to a nexus point for a while. I intend to converse with Mr. Meredith. Thank you."

The voice of Brother Gregory came nearer, took on a slightly professorial tone. "Any massive and rotating body assumes the qualities of magnetism—or rather, gravitic, one-way flux—by virtue of its rotation, and the two quantities of magnetic momentum and angular momentum are always proportional to one another, as you doubtless know."

Meredith smiled inwardly. A lecture on elementary physics from a ghost. Well—maybe not so elementary. He remembered the figures that he'd sweated over. But he could almost envisage the voice of Brother Gregory emanating from a black-gowned instructor in front of a classroom board.

"Take a star," the voice continued. "Say 78 Virginis—from whose flaming promontories the effect was first deduced a hundred years ago —and put her against a counter-whirling star of similar mass. What happens? Energy warp, of the kind we use every time we polt. But something else happens—did you infer it from my incomplete expression?"

Meredith grinned. He said: "Yes. Temporal warp."

"Oh." There was a trace of disappointment in the voice.

Meredith added quickly: "But it certainly gave me a headache figuring it out."

Gregory was evidently mollified by the admission. "Solids through time," he went on. "Some weeks ago, calculating that my inherent field was as great in certain respects as that of 78 Virginis, I whirled against a longitudinal line, and forced a stone back a few days—the nearest I could get to laboratory confirmation. Knowing there would be a logical extension of the effect if I whirled against a field as strong as my own, I persuaded Brother James to co-operate with me—and you know the result."

"How far back?"

"According to my mathematics, the twelfth century, at a time when we were—alive. I would appreciate your views on the paradoxes involved."

Meredith said: "Certainly. Let's go over your math together first. If it fits in with what I've already figured, perhaps I'll have a suggestion to make. You appreciate, of course, that I can't let you have any more cans?"

"Quite. I must congratulate your company on manufacturing a most delicious comestible. If you will hand me the roll of infrared film from your camera, I can make my calculations visible to you on the emulsion in the darkness. Thank you. It is a pity," Gregory murmured, "that we could not see with our own eyes what disposal they made of your product in the days of our Priory."

When, on the morning of a certain bright summer day in 1139, the daily consignment of Miracle Meal failed to arrive at Selcor Priory, thousands of disappointed refugees went hungry.

The Prior, Dom Holland—who, fortunately for his sanity or at least his peace of mind, was not in a position to separate cause from effect—attributed the failure of supply to the lamentable departure from grace and moral standards of two of the monks.

By disgracing themselves in the kitchen garden with a female refugee, he said, they had obviously rendered the Priory unfit to receive any further miraculous bounty.

The abject monks, Brother Gregory and Brother James, were severely chastised and warned in drastic theological terms that it would probably be many centuries before they had sufficiently expiated their sins to attain blessedness.

On the morning of another bright summer day, the Rev. Malachi Pennyhorse and Stephen Samson were waiting for Sidney Meredith in the vicar's comfortable study.

Meredith came in, sank into a century-old leather easy-chair, stretched his shoes, damp with dew from the meadow grass, towards the flames. He accepted a glass of whiskey gratefully, sipped it.

He said: "The cans are there. And from now on, they stay in the transit store until the copters collect."

There was an odd note of regret in his voice.

Samson said: "Fine. Now maybe you'll tell us what happened yesterday."

Mr. Pennyhorse said: "You . . . uh . . . liked my parishioners, then?"

Meredith combined a smile and a sigh. "I surely did. That Brother Gregory had the most intense and dispassionate intellectual curiosity of anyone I ever met. He nearly grounded me on some aspects of energy mathematics. I could have used him in my department. He'd have made a great research man. Brother James wasn't a bad old guy, either. They appeared for me—"

"How did you get rid of them?" Samson interrupted.

"They got rid of themselves. Gregory told me how, by whirling against each other with gravitic fields cutting, they drew the cans into a vortex of negated time that threw them way back to the twelfth century. After we'd been through his math, I suggested they whirl together."

"What—and throw the cans ahead?"

"No. Themselves, in a sense, since they precipitated a future, hoped-for state. Gregory had an idea what would happen. So did I. He'd only discovered the effect recently. Curiosity got the better of him. He had to try it out straight away. They whirled together. The fields reinforced, instead of negated. Enough in-going energy was generated to whoop their own charges well above capacity and equilibrium. They just—went. As Gregory would put it—they were Translated."

"Upwards, I trust," said Mr. Pennyhorse gently.

"Amen to that," said Samson.

Upwards—

Pure thought, unbound, Earth-rid, roaming free amid the wild bright stars—

Thought to Thought, over galactic vastnesses, wordless, yet swift and clear, before egos faded—

"Why didn't I think of this before? We might have Translated ourselves centuries ago."

"But then we would never have tasted Miracle Meal."

"That is a consideration," agreed the Thought that had been Brother Gregory.

"Remember our third can?" came the Thought that had been Brother James.

But there was no reply. Something of far greater urgency and interest than memories of Miracle Meal had occurred to the Thought that had been Brother Gregory.

With eager curiosity, it was spiraling down into the heart of a star to observe the integration of helium at first hand.

Noel Loomis

THE LONG DAWN

THE man was called Chark. He was seven feet tall, and had tremendous shoulders. His skin was bronzed; his stomach was lean and flat. He was naked.

He stood up straight and looked around the time-vault. In the faint glow of radioactive light he could see the female in her bed of moss. She was still sleeping in spite of her broken back, and he was glad. But the child near her was beginning to move restlessly. Chark wheeled and went quickly to the opening. Lagh, the tyrannosaur, followed him.

He stopped for a moment just outside the steel-and-lead door. Then he stepped out upon a great slab of granite. His night-seeing eyes swept the mountain above and behind the vault. He saw no danger there, and turned his attention to the valley below, listening with ultra-keen ears for the lumbering of a quarrelsome stegosaur, testing the wind for the rank stench of a hungry phrysonoma.

His ears detected running water at a distance, but he could not find the organic dankness of Jurassic mud or the fetid lizard-smell that always had hung over the Great Salt Marsh. The world must have changed, and he could only hope that Man had changed along with it, for the better.

He studied the valley. Five hundred feet down was a meadow, and a quarter of a mile away, almost where Old Grak had once had his laboratory, was a small group of buildings. Chark watched them for a moment. There were lights in the buildings. He raised his eyes. Far off was a great cluster of tiny twinkling lights as if many buildings had been built in a group.

Chark looked again at the first buildings. Then he stepped lightly down from the rock and vanished into the darkness. The tyrannosaur followed. A moment later he stood in the meadow, looking up a little slope toward the small group of buildings. His hair, black and straight, was long at the sides but clipped above his eyes. He stood alert but unafraid and watched for movement while he tested gently with ultra-sensitive perceptions to determine what sort of creatures might be inside the buildings.

Chark was hungry—ravenously hungry, for he had been in the time-vault, along with the female and the young one, and Lagh the tyrannosaur and Sala the pterodactyl, for a hundred million years, and during that time he had been awakened to eat only two times. In the vault, his body-processes had been extremely slow, but he had been there a long time.

In the tall, square building on his left, he knew at once, were men. He could feel their emanations more clearly even than his peculiarly developed eyes could see the building against the stars. In the other buildings, which were bigger, were other mammals—all of them, if he could still judge after these long years, being of unfamiliar species.

Chark's night-seeing eyes came to a small building. His lips parted and his mouth worked hungrily. There were birds in that building. He could detect their restless, fluttery minds. But in spite of his hunger, he took an instant to note that Man was now building shelters for mammals and birds. That was good; perhaps Man finally had reached a period of selflessness.

Chark started forward, then paused. The development of mammalian life was an unexpected turn—especially so with the apparent total absence of reptilian forms. He'd better be cautious.

But Lagh, the great tyrannosaur at his side, was impatient. The big saurian's gizzard was grinding on bare stones, and his jaws were working nervously. Chark felt sorry for him, because Lagh's fifteen-ton body demanded a lot of food. But still Chark held him back. They were strangers in a strange world, and Chark didn't want to do anything precipitous that might give modern man a bad impression of him and his companions. Lagh's brain was whimpering but he obeyed.

Over Chark's head Sala, the twenty-foot pterodactyl, swooped up and down excitedly on her leathery wings, waiting for the word, for Sala was hungry too. Chark sent her an emanation of reassurance. He listened with his mind for another instant, then he started forward again. Lagh lumbered behind. Sala fluttered into a long forward glide.

After the first few strides, Chark moved ahead at full speed. He covered the two hundred yards in an incredibly short time, and entered the bird-building. It was very small. He had to double up to get through the door.

The birds were roosting in a huge cluster. They were fully feathered, which itself was astonishing. Most of the birds Chark had known were covered with a leathery skin, like Sala. At most, they had a few tail and wing feathers.

These were fat, too—not tough and stringy. They made an awful squawking when he grabbed them. He got two and started eating one. Then something made him uneasy.

He heard the tyrannosaur crunch into a big animal that squealed horribly for a moment, and the pterodactyl seized something that went "baa" so loudly and so continuously that he could trace Sala's flight by the sound.

Chark was glad they had found food; especially for Lagh. The big tyrannosaur could eat five hundred pounds of meat a day. Chark bit into the bird again. He was glad, too, that Sala had minded him and stayed away from the building that contained the men, for Sala might think she was still back in the Jurassic Era where men fought each other and all animals and the only rule was to attack.

Chark felt a presence, and stopped chewing, with the bird in his hand halfway to his mouth. Then he turned back to the opening through which he had come. A light caught him full in its beam. He felt sudden consternation from a man, then danger.

He leaped toward the opening. He brushed the light from the man's hand and pushed him over as he went, doubled up, through the door. He heard a great noise and saw an instantaneous brilliant flash, something like the explosion of his own first atomic bomb, but millions of times smaller.

Three things he learned in going through the opening: this man wore clothes, and he had a bomb of some sort, perhaps a very tiny atom bomb, although Old Grak, the director of research in the marsh when Chark had left the Jurassic Era, had assured them that atomic fission could not be induced with small amounts; also, Man was a weakling. If the man Chark had brushed aside was a representative specimen, Chark could move ten times faster and probably with many times his strength.

So Chark, running at half-speed and easily leaping all the obstructions in his way, although once he came down in the herd of animals that made oinking sounds, met Lagh and Sala in a little grove a mile away. Lagh was noisily devouring his meal, bones and all, and Sala was tearing hers into the strips which she gulped unprettily.

Chark finished the second bird and patted his stomach. He was ready to sleep until daylight, but first he had to find a place to hide Lagh. He followed the sound of the running water and came to a small river. He took them along the bank until they found a deep pool fringed with tall marsh-grass. Lagh was getting sleepy now that he was full, and so he obeyed readily. He got down in the water until only his head was above the surface, and that was well hidden by the grass.

There were trees on the shore, and Sala could stay in the top of a big one. Chark himself could drape his arms and legs over a couple of limbs and sleep quite comfortably.

He was well pleased. He had found Man—Man with a culture of some sort, apparently, for he built large buildings where many could live to-gether. It was far different from a hundred million years before, when every man had to sleep in a secret cave camouflaged with brush to hide it from other men, or in the top of a great fern so that anyone who might come near would sway the fronds and awaken him in time for de-fense. Chark slept well, for now he felt that at last he would find help for the female back in the time-vault on the mountainside. . . .

The sun was barely up when Chark was awakened by the yapping of a dozen small mammals moving across the meadow with completely in-comprehensible circuitousness. There were men behind them, so Chark started down. He would take no chance on Lagh and Sala. If those two should get into a fight with the men, the men might be injured—and severely.

Lagh was out of the pool, dripping mud and water, when Chark jumped to the ground. Lagh was big, and he looked bigger in the morning sun. Lagh was fifteen tons of the deadliest fighting machine on Earth. His three-toed hind legs were enormous; his torso and an ex-tremely heavy tail served to balance each other, for Lagh walked upright on his hind legs. He stood twelve feet high, with tiny front legs folded across his chest, a short neck and a too-large, bony head fitted with great jaws and fearsome teeth. He was covered with overlapping horny scales. He was afraid of nothing and his one mode of conduct was typi-cally Jurassic: attack.

He attacked for food and whenever he considered it necessary in self-defense, but even in these matters he was amenable to Chark. When Lagh was less than half-grown, Chark had pulled him out of the mud one day where he had been trampled by a herd of angry brontosaurs, and Lagh, in almost embarrassing gratitude, had attached himself to Chark so strongly that he would roam the fern-forest within sight of the laboratory all day waiting for Chark to come from work, and then he would guard him all night.

Now, when Lagh himself was facing unknown danger, he stood un-certainly and looked down at Chark. Chark ordered him back into the pool. Lagh went, but when he had sunk into the mud and water until nothing showed above the surface but his protruding eyes, he looked at Chark and there was a whimper of fear in his mind—not fear for himself but for Chark.

Chark smiled briefly and reassured the saurian. Then he cautioned Sala to stay in the trees. Sala would probably obey him, and Lagh would too—as long as he could. But when the tyrannosaur got hungry again, he'd be nervous. Chark promised them both that he would be back by night and help them get something to eat; he walked out to meet the men. Certainly, he thought, men must now live in a world free from fear, to judge by the loudness of their voices across half a mile of meadow.

The sun felt good on his broad back. Suddenly the dogs began yapping more and started toward him. The men also yelled at each other, and Chark frowned. He did not know if he would like a civilization where everyone made so much noise with his mouth.

The dogs ran up to him, but it required only a very small mind-command to quiet them. They lay down in a circle around him. The men suddenly became quiet too, and Chark caught emanations of fright from them. He quieted their fears and strode up to them. He stood there and smiled, towering over them by two heads. He wondered why these men were so small.

Chark searched their minds fleetingly. There was a feeling he didn't understand. Then one of them, staring at Chark, said to a smaller man: "Billy, you run back to the house and tell your mother to get the girls inside." The smaller one ran back. A fat-stomached man with a metallic star-shaped ornament fastened to the strange clothing he wore, walked forward. Chark felt admiration for the little man, who was obviously puny but who didn't seem as scared as the others.

"I'm the sheriff," the man said. "What do you know about them great big chicken-tracks?"

He pointed. Chark saw the three-toed tracks of Lagh's enormous hind feet, but he wasn't ready yet to explain. There was too much hostility present. He did not answer.

A thin, wrinkled man whispered in the sheriff's ear. Chark felt like smiling, for he read the man's mind before the man whispered the words. "It was him eating a chicken—raw!"

The sheriff began to look uncomfortable. He looked Chark up and down, and sighed. "If I was as husky a specimen as you, I might go in for nudism myself," he observed. Then he turned, businesslike. "You better come along with me."

Chark went. They led him back to the farmyard. The sheriff gave him a blanket, and Chark put it around himself to please the sheriff. If they were concerned that he might get cold, he'd humor them, although it was silly, in a way, for back in the Jurassic Era Man had developed a tough, thick skin in place of fur.

The sheriff opened a machine and invited Chark to get inside. It was a little small for Chark, so obviously all men were small now. It was a nice machine, but Chark did not think Old Grak would have approved its apparent complexity.

"You better put him in front, Sheriff, and I'll ride in the back seat with a shotgun," said the wrinkled man. "Somehow I don't like his looks—a feller like him running around naked and eating live chickens."

"Never mind." The sheriff did not seem perturbed. "I won't have any trouble with him."

Chark did not know what a shotgun was. He sensed that it was a weapon, and he thought these men might be surprised to know what a strong weapon it would take to injure him.

He liked riding in the car, though it was noisy. Noise seemed to be characteristic of this age. The car went very fast—faster even than Lagh could run. They followed a hard-surfaced path for some miles until they came to a large group of buildings arranged in rows with paths between the rows. This pleased him, for it meant that men had learned to trust each other in very large groups.

They stopped before a stone building, and got out. Chark was taken to an opening not high enough for him to go through without bending, and presently he faced a white-haired man with tiny pieces of glass before his eyes, apparently to assist his eyesight; he sat behind a large book. He stared at Chark for a moment and swallowed.

"Quite a physical specimen, eh?" he said admiringly, and for an instant Chark let the muscles ripple along his arms. The judge's eyes popped wider. "But that's no excuse for running around like that," he said, and started writing.

"Name?" he said.

Chark waited.

"Name?" The man sounded impatient.

Chark spoke. "Chark."

"How do you spell it?"

Chark put it in the man's mind.

"First name?"

"Chark."

"Okay. Chark Chark. Where you from?"

Chark had to dig deep into the man's subconscious to find the words he needed. "The Jurassic Era," he said.

The judge looked grim. "Where'd you come from, mister? And no wisecracks."

"From the mountain." Chark pointed.

The judge raised his eyebrows. "From the mountain, eh? Makin' any moonshine up there?"

Chark smiled and shook his head. No, he had had nothing to do with the moon up there.

"Okay. The charge is disorderly conduct." He looked contemplatively at Chark. "Can't very well plead anything but guilty." He wrote in the big book and then looked up. "Ten dollars and costs." Chark said nothing.

"Or ten days," the judge said. Chark did not answer. "Okay, then. Take him away, Sheriff."

The sheriff looked hopefully at Chark. Chark read the sheriff's mind quite easily. In fact, he could have done that from the sheriff's eyes. He followed.

The sheriff led him into a small room walled by steel bars. He closed the steel door and did something to it, and Chark knew he had locked it. Then the sheriff wiped his brow.

Chark was amused. Those puny bars—he could twist those into spirals. He could have controlled the judge, but he did not want to interfere in Man's new social structure. He sat down and waited. Soon they would send their scientists to see him. Back in the Jurassic Era, Old Grak would have been here before now.

But at noon the sheriff brought around a big plate of food. Chark gulped it. The sheriff said, "Tried to find you some clothes, but there ain't any big enough in town. Guess you'll have to use the blanket."

Chark didn't bother. He was quite comfortable. He lay down on the floor and took a nap while he was waiting for the scientists.

He awoke with a start. It was dark. He was hungry again, and it struck him with a pang of conscience that he had ordered Sala and Lagh to stay hidden and had promised to be back by night and help them find something to eat.

He took hold of two of the iron bars and pushed them apart. The space they made wasn't wide enough for his chest, so he twisted them off entirely and spread two more. He leaped through and walked down the corridor to the light.

The sheriff was just coming in from outside. He stared at Chark and said, "Did you pick the lock?"

Chark ignored the question. "I want to see your scientists," he said. "And please hurry." He wanted to establish contact, and then he would hurry back to help Sala and Lagh find food.

The sheriff looked at him. "I'll see what I can do," he said pleadingly, "if you'll go back in the cell and stay there."

Chark went back. He trusted the sheriff, but he thought about Lagh and how hungry the big tyrannosaur would get, and he was worried. He knew the female back in the time-vault would be getting hungry too, but she would behave. Anyway, a human could go hungry for days without doing anything impetuous.

It was the female's broken back that worried Chark most. With the time-vault open again, she would undoubtedly be awake and her broken back could cause a great deal of pain. He wished the scientists would come so he could learn how to care for it properly.

Old Grak had had the greatest intellect of the Jurassic Era, but he had refused to let anyone spend time learning anything about the human body. "If one gets sick," he said, "it means he's a weakling and should die. The race won't get to be a strong species if we preserve the weak." And so Chark, with no knowledge of anatomy or medicine, had been helpless with the female's injury. Now he wished the scientists would hurry.

But it was an hour before anyone came. Then it was a serious-looking young fellow. Chark searched his mind at once and knew there was no technical knowledge there that would help him. Still Chark was interested, because the young man's mind was worried. Chark answered questions while he searched the fellow's mind a little further.

"I'm Henderson, reporter for the *Tribune*," the young man said. "Is that your real name—Chark Chark?"

"Chark," said Chark.

"Where you from?"

"The Jurassic Era."

The reporter squinted at him for a moment. "Well, what town are you from?"

"No town," said Chark. "From the Great Salt Marsh. I was a research worker in Grak's laboratory; nuclear physics."

The reporter shrugged, and Chark saw that he did not believe. "Okay, if that's your tale, mister." He sighed. "You look like good material for a story. Big enough for two ordinary men, Weissmuller build, Palm Beach bronze, and waging a one-man war against the high price of white shirts—to say nothing of pants and shoes. Say—" his brow wrinkled—"how did you ever learn anything about the Jurassic Era?" His eyes began to brighten. "Maybe you're a professor or something. Do you suppose I've got a case of amnesia on my hands? Now where could you be from? No seven-foot professors have been reported missing lately—certainly not from the university. Maybe some small college somewhere."

Chark touched his mind lightly, and the reporter looked speculative. "You know, I think I almost believe you—only a reporter has to have better sense than that. Tell you what I'm going to do. There's something here. I'm going to write this as a feature, just the way you gave it to me. The Old Man can't object to that."

"Will you get me an audience with your scientists?" asked Chark. "Now—tonight?"

The reporter looked sympathetic but he shook his head. "You'd never get to see any of the big-shots at the natural history museum this time of night. Wait. What kind of scientists do you mean?"

"Men interested in chemistry, physics, astronomy—but especially—" he searched the young man's mind quickly—"a man versed in medicine."

"Well, the top man in physics in this part of the country is Dr. Phillips, head of the physics department at the U., and he's tough. You wouldn't get him out of the house after supper to see a tyrannosaur parade down the middle of Main Street preceded by fourteen motorcycle cops and a South Sea island drum majorette—with a flying escort of pterodactyls, since you mentioned the Jurassic Era. No, sir, old Dr. Phillips doesn't believe in anything that he hasn't seen—not even his own grandmother. Why do you want to see a physician?" he asked suddenly. "You don't look sick."

"I want information," said Chark patiently.

"Well, okay, I'll see what I can do. What do you want—a specialist or what?"

"I want information about a broken back," said Chark, "and I must have it tonight."

Chark saw that the reporter was not over-impressed. Chark could have changed his mind, but he didn't want to be arbitrary. He wanted to convince him.

"You are in trouble," Chark said softly.

The reporter nodded absently. "Yeah. The Old Man doesn't like the way I brush my teeth. I get in his hair."

"Especially," said Chark, "since you printed the article about Professor E. M. Stanley and his new theory of two-dimensional matter."

The reporter looked up. "You read the papers, I see."

"Your friend, Professor Stanley, is an assistant in the physics department at the university and has just written for his doctor's degree a thesis putting forth the theory that space and time are the only two absolute substances in the universe."

The reporter was unimpressed. "The only thing wrong there," he said, "is that my friend is a she."

"What do you mean—'she'?" asked Chark.

The reporter's eyes widened, but Chark required him to answer. "A female, you dope. Didn't you ever hear of a female professor?"

Chark shook his head slowly, wonderingly. The world had indeed changed.

"So I guess you're not very psychic, after all." The reporter sounded disappointed.

"And this Dr. Phillips," Chark went on, groping hard in the reporter's mind for the words, "is her department head. He protested to your publisher against the publication of what he termed a 'crackpot theory' by one of his instructors."

The reporter looked at Chark. "How did you know that?"

"Dr. Phillips has received many letters of protest from all over the world, and he has complained. Also your publisher has severely reprimanded you for publishing unverified information and has ordered you to get any further such stories approved by Dr. Phillips, which, you are firmly convinced, means that you never will get another such story printed, for, in your own words, Phillips is an old battleaxe."

The reporter was staring at Chark. "Hey, wait a minute. I never said that to anybody—not even to Ellen."

"It is in your mind," said Chark, unperturbed. "Furthermore, your friend's theory is correct. The only material thing is space, and the only thing that makes space display different forms is time. Time causes frequency and different frequencies make different substances. All time is the same, and all space is propagated at the same velocity, but time folds back on itself, and the number of folds determines the frequency and therefore the final substance of space—which becomes energy or matter."

The reporter's mouth was open. "That's what I was trying to put across in my story, but I bungled it. You did it better. Who are you anyway?"

"I am Chark from the Jurassic Era."

The reporter wiped sweat from his forehead. "Damned if I couldn't almost believe you—now." He looked at the bars that Chark had twisted aside. "If you'd explain that, maybe, I could—"

Chark reached out with one hand. He grasped a half-inch bar and turned his hand slowly. With a great screech of tortured metal, the bar stretched and then broke.

The reporter swallowed hard. He looked closely at the bar. Then he shook his head. "It's a good trick. How'd you do it?"

Chark sighed. Men could be very difficult, it seemed. "Why does your friend not prove her theory with mathematics?" he asked.

"That's a good point. The truth—which I couldn't print—is that the only electronic calculator available to her is under the direction of Dr. Phillips, and he won't let her use it. This figuring would take several lifetimes to do by hand, so that's out. It could be done in five hours on the brain, but Dr. Phillips insists there isn't time for her to work on such a 'fantastic' problem." Henderson sounded sarcastic.

"It is possible," said Chark, "that I can help, if I can talk to your friend."

"Tell you what. I'll call Ellen, and I'll try to get hold of somebody to listen to your story, whatever it is. How's that?"

"Good," said Chark. "But please hurry. Tonight."

He sat back to wait. Telepathically, now that he had established connection with the young man, he was able to follow him to the Tribune Building and into the Old Man's office. The Old Man reminded Chark of Grak, for when he saw the reporter he roared at him.

"Where have you been for the last two hours?"

"Working on a story," the reporter said quietly, "about a man who claims he's from the Jurassic Era."

The Old Man's face turned purple. "If that story you wrote about Professor Stanley wasn't enough— And then I find out today that Stanley is a woman—a *young* woman. That explains everything."

Chark was quite puzzled at that speech.

"Half an hour ago," the Old Man went on, "a leg-man came in with a story about fresh tyrannosaur tracks out in the country somewhere. A paleontologist at the U. examined them and said they seemed to be the real thing." The Old Man exploded. "They even had one of my high-priced photographers out there to take pictures. What am I running around here—a newspaper or an insane asylum? Now you come up with a man from the Mesozoic Age. Now look, Henderson. I'm a patient man, but when you and our girl-friend deliberately conspire to get my goat, it's too much. Guild or no Guild, I'll fire you if this kind of thing happens again."

Chark admired Henderson. The reporter's face was red, but he kept his tongue. Chark felt sorry for the Old Man, because he was so much like Old Grak.

Henderson left, and Chark, tired from the strain of projecting his

mind so far, let him go and sat back to wait. He hoped it wouldn't take
too long, for it was worrying him to think about the female back in the
time-vault. Her back must be very painful by now. Twice had they
been awakened in the last hundred million years, and each time Chark
had tried desperately to find medical help, but each time he had failed.
On both occasions she had been very patient and had not even whimpered, but Chark had seen the suffering in her eyes and it had been hard
for him to take. This time he was determined to get help.

Perhaps it had been a mistake to try to save her, after all. Old Grak
had said, when she fell out of the big moa-tree and lay writhing in the
tall grass, "Let her alone. She'll die before sundown."

Chark had heard the ominous thump as she hit the ground; he had
heard her first cry of pain and had seen the anguish in her eyes. A sudden inexplicable impulse to go to her had come over him, but while he
was debating that strange feeling and trying to reconcile it with Grak's
rule against wasting time on the unfit, Grak himself had come up behind him and reminded him of his duties.

For a few hours after the accident Chark went ahead with his work in
the laboratory. All of the five or six hundred men in the Great Salt
Marsh worked in the laboratory, on problems directed by Grak. The
laboratory was a huge building of glass and steel and lead for shielding
against hard radiation, built on the only large area of high ground in
the marsh. When a man was working in it, during the daytime, he was
safe, for one of the two rules that governed the Grak outfit was: no fighting in the laboratory. The other was: no help to the unfit.

So Chark tried not to think of the female. His was a problem that
would take several years, for he was studying each element to determine the rate of energy flow at the instant a neutrino triggered a meso-
tron into the reverse field that held the nucleus together. The neutrino,
of course, traveling at the compound square of the speed of light—c
square squared—was indetectable, and the creation of mesotrons involved considerable apparatus and a very thorough knowledge of dimensional mechanics, so that Chark soon became absorbed in his work and
forgot even to look outside until the middle of the afternoon when the
steam began to rise in clouds from the marsh.

Then he remembered the female. He went to the window and saw
her still in the grass. Her face was contorted but she made no sound.
The baby, after which she had crawled out on a rotten limb, had been
in her arms when she fell, and was unhurt. Chark saw the female's lips,
dry and beginning to crack, and he felt that same feeling of sympathy
that he had felt when she dropped. It was stronger in him now because
he realized it was the same feeling she had had when she went after the
baby—a desire to help.

That was a strange emotion for a Grak man. In Chark's hundred or
more years in the laboratory he had never seen it before. He had felt it,
and he had watched for it in others, but he had not seen it, and, know-

ing the immutable law, he had never shown it. But now he recognized it in another, and the fact that they two had it, and that they were the only ones, seemed to require that they should stand together.

He shut off the great electrostatic generator. He got a glass beaker and went to the fresh-water spring. He filled the beaker with cool water and took it to the female. She saw him, and her eyes were big, and strangely wet.

She took the beaker and drank it dry. Chark saw that she was young and strongly built. It was a pity that she had fallen. He turned back to the laboratory.

Grak was waiting for him outside the laboratory. "Is your work no longer important, that you waste time on the unfit?"

Chark studied Grak but he hardly saw him. He was turning over a great many unusual thoughts in his mind. "She needed water," he said slowly.

Grak roared. "Let her die! She's no good. She's helpless. You can't clutter up civilization with a lot of cripples."

Chark saw more Grakmen coming. Muz, the bully, and Gor, his henchman, were in the van. Chark backed to the wall.

Grak glared at him. His voice lowered. "You're showing soft emotions, Chark—emotions that I never have seen in a man, but only in a female with young."

"I wonder if that is so bad," said Chark, watching the semicircle fill up around him. "Is there to be nothing for Man but hunger, mating, fear, and the incessant quest for knowledge?"

"Mental achievement," said Old Grak, talking now like a man to an inferior, "is the only worth-while thing. There is no place in civilization for the soft emotions."

Chark answered steadily, "The so-called 'soft' emotions are all that distinguish us from the dinosaurs."

Grak snarled. "The mind is the distinguishing feature."

"Even the dinosaur has a brain," Chark pointed out. "Some have two brains."

Grak snorted. "You think a brontosaur could figure out atomic fission?"

"Not a brontosaur, no. But take Lagh. Give him a hundred million years to develop. Or take Sala, the pterodactyl. Either one of them can evolve to where Man is now. I say that Man must keep on evolving, and that sentiment is the next step."

Grak exploded at that. "Our methods are harsh but they are just," he roared. "We have kept the racial stock at a high level."

"True. Not more than one out of ten men survives to maturity because no one will help an unfortunate. That is why there are only scattered small groups of men over the world today—less than six hundred thousand on Earth."

"And you think we need more?"

Chark hesitated. "No, perhaps not. But we owe something to those

whom we create, and they too may have much to contribute to Man."
He paused, and then went on with renewed vigor, looking squarely
into the impassive brown faces around him. "Is Man always to live in
fear?" asked Chark. "Should he not expect help when he needs it
rather than sharp teeth in his neck when he isn't looking?"

He glared at them, fifty men of the Great Salt Marsh. Their cold eyes
showed no understanding. "I am backed against a wall because I do
not trust anyone." He smiled grimly. "No one attacks me from the front
because no one dares. If any one of you felt himself my equal, he would
try to kill me." He snorted. "We call ourselves civilized, but we do not
care for our young. The female lying there in the sun is the only one I
have ever seen who was concerned enough for her young to risk her
own body. We cannot even live in herds like the diplodoci. We meet, we
work in the laboratory, and we separate. Each one hides away for the
night. We are not civilized. Mentality has no bearing on civilization.
We are savages!"

It was the supreme insult, to say that to Old Grak, the physicist.
Grak's wrinkled face turned pale, his great chest filled and expanded.
His eyes were like knifeblades, and Chark waited for the rush that
would bring them all on him. But Grak looked at Chark's great shoulders, and changed his mind. They were well developed, these men of
the Salt Marsh, but Chark was stronger and quicker than any of them.
So they were cautious.

Grak scowled and went back to his work, and again Chark, waiting
with his back to the wall until the last man should leave, felt that
strange emotion. He felt sorry now for Old Grak, who was a hundred
years past the prime of his life and no longer able to avenge an insult.

Chark went back to the generator. He was a little ashamed, too. He
was the one who had made Old Grak back down—and he was stronger
and younger. It wasn't right.

Old Grak had the finest brain of the Jurassic Era. He had marked
many milestones in physics. Grak's theory of inverse atomic structure
to explain the incongruities in atomic physics had superseded the old
shell theory of electrons; Grak had been the first to explain why a magnetic field would attract or repel; Grak was the one who had advanced
and proved the theory that there were only two basics in creation: space
and time, and that all matter and all energy were products of those
two in varied forms.

Yes, Grak had a fine brain, but no trust in men and no trustworthiness
—nothing that tended to make life comfortable. Chark wondered if
perhaps comfort was not to be desired as much as knowledge.

There was tension in the laboratory. Chark knew that Grak was
watching for an opportunity to kill. Chark didn't mind that, but he did
mind the looks that began to come from the others. He spent the rest
of the day in constant alertness. Someone here would soon be killed.

He was cautious, and his great strength made the others cautious and
kept them at a distance. But by evening he had come to a decision. As

soon as it was dark he took some fresh clams to the female under the moa-tree. Then he went to the warehouse and gathered supplies. He carried them to the mountain, and such was his strength and speed that within a few hours he had an enormous quantity of material.

He spent the rest of the night digging a cave in the solid granite with explosives. The mountain was carefully chosen. He lined the cave with lead and installed a thorium-activated relay. He gathered herbs to induce catalepsy, and just before dawn he connected a temperature-regulator with the radiation from the relay. Then he set the relay to open the vault at whatever time in the future it might detect enough hard radiation to indicate that man had begun to use atomic fission in quantities.

As the sun came up over the marsh, and steam began to rise in place of fog, Chark surveyed his night's work and found it good. Then he went back to the laboratory. He faced Grak and announced:

"I am leaving, Grak. I have prepared a time-vault and am going into the long sleep. I am taking the female and her young with me, since that is the only way I can save them. We shall go into a future civilization and rebuild the race, teaching and instilling into it the sentiments that we have and that you do not recognize."

Triumph glowed suddenly in Grak's opaque eyes. "You are a coward," he said. "You are afraid and you are running from me."

Chark stiffened. "Old man," he said, "keep your tongue." He looked at the waiting faces behind Grak. "I am afraid of no man and no combination of men, but if I stay, I shall have to kill some of you, and that is waste. I do not belong in this era, because I do not believe in killing. Therefore I am leaving."

He backed away. At the door he turned. He heard Grak's growl and turned in time to meet the old man's rush, the great yellow fangs seeking his jugular vein.

Grak was no match for Chark. Chark met him, parried him once, twice, and when he saw the ring of men closing in he killed Grak. They would have overwhelmed him by sheer weight if he had not, so he bit Grak's neck cleanly in two and tossed the body away, showing his independence by refusing even to eat it.

That also was taken as a sign of weakness by Muz, the bully, and Gor. The two rushed Chark, one from each side. There was a moment of whirling legs and arms, flashing brown bodies. There were cracking bones, and then the two bodies, of Muz and Gor, followed Grak's carcass through the air, both with their necks bitten through.

Then Chark was gone. He stopped to snatch up the female and her young and carry them to the vault. He sent out mental commands for Lagh and Sala, for they were known to be his friends. Worse, they had in the past responded to Chark's friendliness with some show of "soft" emotions on their own part. Their lives now would be worth little around the marsh.

In an hour the great dinosaur and the big pterodactyl came up the mountain. Chark took them into the vault. He made the female comfortable in a bed of moss, and set about sealing the vault against the weather and against time. Once it was sealed, the Grakmen would waste no more time on him. They would be busy protecting themselves from one another. And with luck the vault would last a long time, for it was not located near a geological fault. . . .

In less than a thousand years the vault had opened. The descendants of the Grakmen had started fighting each other with atomic explosives.

Chark by that time was faced with a new problem. The female was in pain. She did not whimper, but anguish showed on her face when she tried to move. If she was to live, she should be relieved. But that was beyond Chark's knowledge. With all his mentality, Chark had no knowledge of anatomy and was helpless. He set out to find a man who might have that knowledge, but was unsuccessful. He barely got back to the vault with Lagh and Sala, and water and mollusks for the female and her young, before the marsh was devastated by a lithium bomb.

It was a predicament to which there seemed but one answer. They must go back to sleep. That would arrest the pain and any other trouble that might develop in the female's back, and probably the next time they were awakened, Man would have some knowledge of his own body. . . .

The second period of sleep was a long one. On awakening, Chark looked twice when the graph on his relay showed nearly a hundred million years. He opened the vault and went out hopefully. Surely in such a very long time Man must have developed the knowledge he needed.

But he was disappointed. Man was still primitive; socially he was a little advanced, because he lived in groups, but mentally he had lost ground. His language was crude. He still lived in caves. He took care of his females and his young, but not of weaklings. He still had not studied the human body—but he had studied the atom. He was experimenting with fission. Astonishing, thought Chark, how that one thing—the secret of matter and energy—was a perpetual challenge to Man.

In this caveman culture, Man had learned fission empirically. He didn't know how it happened and didn't think about it. He only knew that he could produce energy from matter. Perhaps his knowledge came from incredibly ancient legends handed down from the Jurassic Era. At any rate, Man was playing with cosmic fire. It burned him. The known world and its few centers of society again were destroyed, and the few not killed by the blasts or the subsequent radiation fled into the forests and the mountains to start new lines of the species.

Once again Chark retreated into the vault with his companions, sorely troubled because each time the vault opened for a few days the female's pain grew worse. Chark was afraid that one more time would be the last unless he could get help. Wouldn't Man ever turn from destruction to helping Man?

The next time he was awakened, the slow-motion graph on his relay showed it was only twenty thousand years later. Now it was an even hundred million years from the time of Grak.

This time the female did not awaken at once. So Chark got Lagh and Sala and they set out together. It was when he saw the artificial buildings that he was encouraged. If Man had developed enough to live in communities, he must have developed also a knowledge of treating injuries.

And so a few hours later, Chark, finding himself in a strange world with strange ideas and customs, and not wanting to offend, allowed them to imprison him. But now, waiting for their scientists, he was beginning to get impatient. He hoped Henderson (what a long name!) would hurry and bring the physician as he had promised.

After an hour Henderson was back. "I've brought my friend, Miss Stanley," he told Chark. "Maybe you'd better pull the blankets around you."

Chark complied. Then Henderson disappeared. Chark felt feminine emanations. Henderson came back, opening the door for the female, who came through the first. Chark stared. She too was clothed, but at once he liked her calm and her kindness and her logic. A quick glimpse into her mind astonished him. She was much better versed in science than Henderson. But best of all, Chark liked the warmness of her radiations and the glowing aura that they caused in Henderson's mind. Chark paused in wonderment. This was something like the feeling he had for the female back in the vault; but this was more highly developed.

She put her arm through the bars, and Chark made a quick search of her mind to find that she expected him to shake hands. "So you're from the Jurassic Era," she said, and there was no skepticism in her voice. She turned to Henderson and said, "I like him."

Henderson said, "I do too."

Like, she had said. That was an odd concept. There was no equivalent word in Chark's vocabulary, but he knew it was akin to the feeling she and Henderson had for each other. Now Chark himself felt warm and glowy, and he positively squirmed when she smiled at him. Then he remembered his own female. "Can you get a physician?" he asked.

"I'd like to ask some questions first," she said. "What do you know about my two-substance theory?"

Chark said, "Old Grak evolved that theory, a hundred million years ago. I am familiar with his postulates."

She looked at him thoughtfully, and Chark saw that she was trying to believe in him. He said, "Why not do it this way. Let g sub a equal the gravitational constant for the nucleus of the atom." He was searching her mind for her own symbols. "Now, take your Rydberg wave number." He went on, not working the problems, but explaining them to her in her own terms, and substituting symbols for the answers to the equations.

She listened raptly, but finally she interrupted. "I can't follow you there." She had been making written notes, but now she looked up. "You are speaking of n-dimensional continua as if they were physically real. Our science isn't ready for that."

He searched her mind for an instant. Then he said, "Your two-substance universe has come too soon. What you need as a foundation is dimensional mechanics. It would be the next logical step after your present wave mechanics. How long have you had wave mechanics?"

"Since about nineteen twenty-five," she said. "Thirty years."

"Then you're ready," he told her. "And it's simple enough—an extension of the quantum theory. There isn't really much difference between quantum mechanics and wave mechanics, when you know the basic principles. A dimension consists of electromagnetic energy folded back on itself in fantastic shapes, and other dimensions are merely complications or consolidations. Keep your pencil ready and I will give you some formulae. Grak had worked out the system to the twenty-fifth dimension before I killed him."

She stared an instant, but he started talking and she started writing. Presently he said, "There it is. Using the dimensional formulae as a base, you can prove your substance postulate."

"But these equations! It would take five hundred years to work them out. In half an hour you've laid out enough math to keep a dozen men busy for a lifetime. If I had access to an electronic calculator—"

Chark said, "Let Dr. Phillips do it for you."

"Oh, that's impossible. He won't even let me use the brain."

"Don't worry," Chark assured her. "Describe the steps of the problem as I have described them to you, advance your dimensional mechanics ideas, and give the mathematical answer that I have given you—and he will do the rest."

"He's right," said Henderson gleefully. "The doc will have to work it out in self-defense. He won't know how *you* did it, but he'll sneak it through the 'brain' to see if you're right."

Her eyes were glowing. "How can I ever thank you?"

"You can get me an audience with a physician," said Chark.

"You wanted to talk to scientists, too," she said softly. "Well, I'll get them for you. I'll get them tonight." She turned to Henderson. "Jim," she said, "I do believe he came from the Jurassic Era."

Chark was pleased.

He was even more pleased when, an hour later, the sheriff came for him. "I don't know how she did it," the sheriff said. "Here it is eleven o'clock at night and you're going up to the museum for a conference. I didn't think you could get the museum open this time of night with an atomic bomb." He led Chark outside. "Better wrap that blanket around you."

Fifteen minutes later they walked into a high-ceiling room in the Paleontology Section of the museum.

There were Henderson and Miss Stanley, and Henderson introduced the others: Dr. Phillips, head of the physics department at the University's School of Technology; Mr. Jameson, in charge of Paleontology at the museum; Mr. Swinburne, who occupied a chair in anthropology at the University; and Dr. Radke, an instructor in the medical college. Chark had to search Henderson's mind fast to understand these terms, but when he did he knew that Henderson and Miss Stanley had done well; they had brought him their topmost scientists. Chark was impatient to search the physician's mind, but he must be polite and answer their questions on physics and mechanics first.

Dr. Phillips looked at Chark, and the sourness of his face reminded Chark very much of Old Grak.

Miss Stanley said confidently, "He's from the Jurassic Era, doctor."

Phillips snorted. "Nonsense. He just needs a haircut."

"Ask him about wave mechanics," Miss Stanley suggested.

Phillips gave her a terrible scowl. "Miss Stanley, I came here because you promised proof of your fantastic theory on substances, and frankly, I came more to give you a chance to expose yourself than for anything else. I'll say more. If this turns out to be a fiasco, as it is bound to, I shall use my influence in the graduate school to see that your petition for a doctor's degree is tabled."

Miss Stanley turned white, and Chark felt sorry for her. But he kept quiet and waited.

Dr. Radke, a medium-sized man, very calm and capable-looking, approached Chark, and at that moment a door opened and another female entered with a notebook. She stood behind Radke. Very convenient, thought Chark. In this modern civilization a man even had someone else to remember for him.

Radke looked up at Chark. "Height, about seven-one," he said, and the female made queer marks in her notebook. "Weight, I'd put at two-forty. Brownish skin. No distinguishing scars or deformities. No abnormalities. Quite the reverse, in fact. A magnificent specimen of homo sapiens." He looked at Chark thoughtfully. "Or *is* he homo sapiens?"

Chark didn't pay much attention to him, for he was busy searching the physician's mind and finding out all he needed to know about anatomy and especially about a broken back. It was encouraging. He thought now that he knew what was wrong. Two of the vertebrae, at a bad angle, were pinching the spinal cord and causing paralysis of the lower body. He had principally to straighten out the bend, and the female would recover.

"Miss Lasky, will you take Mr. Swinburne's notes as he goes?"

Swinburne, a tall man with penetrating eyes and a husky, drawling voice, said, "That's quite a brain-case, wouldn't you say, doctor? It would appear to have a capacity of twenty-eight or twenty-nine hundred cubic centimeters, I would say."

Radke looked up. "I thought you'd notice that. I hesitated to say. Isn't the largest brain on record something like twenty-two hundred C.C.'s?"

Swinburne nodded. "Yes—and still I'd swear this one will go close to three thousand."

"You should know. You've been looking at brain-cases all your life." Radke chuckled slightly.

"The odd part is," said Swinburne thoughtfully, "the head-shape is definitely dolichocephalic, which you hardly expect to find under the circumstances. And there's a puzzler: the brain-case and the absence of jutting eyebrows eliminates this man from any prehistoric species of our knowledge, but the skull is brachyfacial—like a Cro-Magnard. Handsome beast, all right. Observe that heavy lower jaw. That isn't compatible with any of our fossils." Swinburne was truly puzzled. "Neanderthal man, for instance, didn't have any chin at all." He went on. "Note that very high forehead. It looks as if Nature has played one of her best tricks in this man. How can you reconcile his physique with that enormous brain?"

Jameson said, "I believe you claim a familiarity with the Jurassic Era. Do you mind if I ask a few questions?"

"Not at all," said Chark.

"Where's your home?"

"In the Great Salt Marsh."

"Where did you vote?"

"Vote?" asked Chark.

"Sure. When you elected the head man."

Chark bared his strong white teeth. "We elected the head man with these."

Jameson blinked. Then he said, "How did you get here from the Jurassic?"

"In a time-vault," said Chark.

"Where is it?"

"Up on the mountain."

"Isn't it destroyed now?"

"No."

"Think you can find it?"

"I know I can," said Chark.

"That was the age of reptiles. I suppose you know all about dinosaurs of various descriptions."

"I am familiar with many species."

"You didn't happen to bring any fossils with you?"

"I did better than that," said Chark. "I brought a tyrannosaur—alive."

Now Jameson smiled. Chark saw that he did not believe. Jameson said, "We have few fossil remains that give us any information about that era, but we have here at the museum a man who has devoted his life to a study of them. Perhaps you can verify his findings. Can you tell me what you had in the Jurassic? Just a few items, let's say. Start with the crinoids. Maybe we can find a common ground here."

"Do you mind," Chark asked apologetically, "if I search your mind to put it in your own words?"

Jameson smiled. "Not at all."

Chark said, slowly and carefully, "We had a small crinoid echinoderm which you call pentacrinus. Then we had pelecypods which you know as gryphea and trigonia, a cone-shaped gastropod—pleurotomaria, you call it. I might add that we had quite a representation of trilobites, which you may not have discovered. They—"

But Jameson was staring at him. "Wickert did not announce that until yesterday," he said slowly. "It is the first time that anyone ever has found trilobites as late as the Jurassic. How did you know that?"

Chark smiled. "I was there," he said simply.

Jameson looked at Phillips and shook his head wonderingly. "I check," he said.

The fat-stomached sheriff said, "See how strong he is."

Radke looked thoughtful. "We haven't any weights."

Jameson said, "Here's a broom. A couple of you take hold and see how easily he can twist it out of your hands. I have a hunch—"

Chark lifted it out of Radke's hands as if he was lifting a feather.

Then they all took hold—everybody but Phillips and Miss Stanley. Chark took hold of the round piece in the middle and with no effort twisted a piece a foot long out of the middle of it.

There was silence.

"How high can you jump?" asked Radke.

Chark looked at the ceiling. It was about three times his height. He crouched and sprang, holding the blanket with one hand. He thumped the ceiling and dropped back softly.

Radke's eyes were bulging. "Brotherrr!" he said. "Whatever it is, I'm in on it. You can talk about abnormalities all you want to, but this isn't abnormal. This is a superman!"

He began to put away his tape-measure. "We're wasting time here. Tomorrow I'll have him out at the clinic."

Phillips growled. "How could a man from the Jurassic Era know anything about atomic fission?"

"Are we so superior?" asked Jameson softly. "You read the story about the Euphrates. Archaeologists dug up a layer from an agrarian culture eight thousand years old, then a deeper one of a herdsman culture, still another of a cave culture, and finally a layer of fused green glass, just like what was left on the desert by the first atom bomb in New Mexico."

Phillips motioned to the others, and they all went off in a corner to talk.

Chark thought he heard shouting down the street. But Phillips' voice rose in the room. "I tell you it's quite impossible. I don't know where he's from, but certainly not from the Mesozoic."

The shouting now seemed to be in the street under the museum. It grew in volume. Weren't these noisy humans ever quiet?

The sheriff was at a window. He looked, and Chark felt amazement flood the man's mind. "Hey, professor!" His eyes were distended. "They've got the biggest animal in the world down there!"

Jameson jumped to a window. He took one look and shouted, "It's a *tyrannosaur!*"

"You're crazy," Phillips growled. He turned to the window. He looked and then turned around and quietly slumped to the floor with his hands crossed on his chest.

Chark had been so busy watching the antics of the professor that he had not realized what they were saying. Now it struck him. He made the window in one great leap and looked down.

Crawling along the street was one of the machines with a huge flat top. On its top was the mangled, bloody body of Lagh, with his oversize head twisted under him at a gruesome angle.

A man standing beside the body saw the sheriff in the window and shouted, "It was stealin' a hog out of Gleason's farmyard! The boys got him with a bazooka!"

Chark felt a great pang of grief. Lagh was dead. And it hurt Chark because he was responsible. If he had returned in time, Lagh wouldn't have been killed.

Chark stood straight and tall, hard and strong. He started to leave.

"Hey, wait a minute," said the sheriff.

Chark did not stop but as he approached the door the sheriff pulled a small object from his clothing somewhere and pointed it at him. Chark sucked in a deep breath and hardened his muscles at the spot on his stomach where the sheriff was aiming. The small object made a loud noise and a flash.

Chark felt something hit him. It struck with great force and even the mighty Chark, stopping it abruptly, was pushed back almost off-balance. The thing that hit him, a small piece of very hot lead, shaped like the end of a man's thumb according to the way Chark saw it before it hit, flattened itself against the steel-hard spot on his stomach and dropped to the floor with a small thud.

The sheriff's eyes opened ludicrously wider. His hand, holding the weapon, went limp.

"Say," said the sheriff. "What's going on here?"

Chark looked at him and a little wave of mirth—or the nearest thing to mirth that Chark knew anything about—came in his mind. He fixed his eyes on the little sheriff and said, "Go."

The sheriff turned and marched out.

At that instant Henderson seemed to come alive. He snatched his hat and snapped at Miss Stanley, "Tyrannosaur. Got to get a picture. Got to write a story about Chark here."

Chark remembered then he had a duty. He went into Phillips' mind and made sure that the professor would approve Miss Stanley's application for a degree, whatever that was. It would save Miss Stanley trouble and it would save embarrassment for the professor.

Then Chark went out after the sheriff.

They didn't get very far before a crowd gathered around them. Chark was controlling the sheriff, hoping to get away peacefully, but he heard a nasal voice, "That's the feller that was in my henhouse last night!"

Chark looked around. He felt the threatening emotions in the white faces turned on him. There were too many for him to use hypnosis. He decided to run.

It would have been difficult for any man to follow him, for he covered the first hundred yards in something like three seconds.

He went through town at that speed, and then he set out in a long, fast lope that brought him to the tree where Sala, the pterodactyl, had been.

Sala was there. Her mind was still filled with fright, for she had been close enough to feel Lagh's death-agonies. She fluttered clumsily to the ground, and when Chark touched her she was trembling.

Chark soothed her, then he set out for the mountain. . . .

It was early morning when at last he sat down to rest in the doorway of the time-vault. He had spent some time making the female comfortable, and now he knew that she would get well and it made him feel pleased. She was sleeping now, for he had given her the herb-tea. He sat there, watching the sky, his nostrils testing every gust of wind.

He noticed the black clouds then. There would be a storm.

Then he saw something unexpected. Half a dozen of the moving machines were coming toward the mountain.

The first few drops of rain came in a swirl of wind. The clouds rolled over the mountain and it was dark. The lightning began to indicate a leveling of potentials, and thunder crashed among the rocks. A fitting scene for an exit, thought Chark, trying to follow the men down below.

He caught the perturbations in Sala's mind and looked up. She was flying above him in short, excited bursts. All of Chark's eleven senses were taut. His keen eyes penetrated the blackness.

He knew when they broke out into the clearing a hundred yards below. He heard them yelling when they saw Sala, and heard a shot. He gave Sala a sharp command. She swooped down and into the mouth of the vault. Reluctantly he got up and went inside.

He closed the door and sealed it. He set off the tiny explosion that would shower down rocks to hide the door. In the utter darkness he set the opening mechanism. He stretched out on the moss by the side of the female and prepared to sleep.

He had found medical help in 1954, but sympathy and understanding were sketchy. Man still retained a good deal of the savage. It wasn't the right period for Chark and the female to try to build a new civilization.

How long, he wondered, would they sleep this time? Would it be again for a hundred million years? And in that time would Man change as little as he had since the Jurassic?

Sala was settling down in her nest. Her great leathery wings were folded in around her. Chark sent her a thought of assurance. The female was sleeping soundly beside him. Chark was glad. He relaxed. Perhaps the next time the vault opened, it would be to a world where they all could live in peace.

———————

T. L. SHERRED

E FOR EFFORT

THE captain was met at the airport by a staff car. Long and fast it sped. In a narrow, silent room the general sat, ramrod-backed, tense. The major waited at the foot of the gleaming steps shining frostily in the night air. Tires screamed to a stop and together the captain and the major raced up the steps. No words of greeting were spoken. The general stood quickly, hand outstretched. The captain ripped open a dispatch case and handed over a thick bundle of papers. The general flipped them over eagerly and spat a sentence at the major. The major disappeared and his harsh voice rang curtly down the outside hall. The man with glasses came in and the general handed him the papers. With jerky fingers the man with glasses sorted them out. With a wave from the general the captain left, a proud smile on his weary young face. The general tapped his fingertips on the black glossy surface of the table. The man with glasses pushed aside crinkled maps, and began to read aloud.

> Dear Joe:
> I started this just to kill time, because I got tired of just looking out the window. But when I got almost to the end I began to catch the trend of what's going on. You're the only one I know that can come through for me, and when you finish this you'll know why you must.
> I don't know who will get this to you. Whoever it is won't want you to identify a face later. Remember that, and please, Joe —*hurry!*
>
>   Ed

It all started because I'm lazy. By the time I'd shaken off the sandman and checked out of the hotel every seat in the bus was full. I stuck my bag in a dime locker and went out to kill the hour I had until the next bus left. You know the bus terminal: right across from the Book-Cadillac and the Statler, on Washington Boulevard near Michigan Avenue. Michigan Avenue. Like Main in Los Angeles, or maybe Sixty-third in its present state of decay in Chicago, where I was going. Cheap movies, pawnshops and bars by the dozens, a penny arcade or two, restaurants that feature hamburg steak, bread and butter and coffee for forty cents. Before the War, a quarter.

I like pawnshops. I like cameras, I like tools, I like to look in windows crammed with everything from electric razors to sets of socket wrenches to upper plates. So, with an hour to spare, I walked out Michigan to Sixth and back on the other side of the street. There are a lot of Chinese and Mexicans around that part of town, the Chinese running the restaurants and the Mexicans eating Southern Home Cooking. Between Fourth and Fifth I stopped to stare at what passed for a movie. Store windows painted black, amateurish signs extolling in Spanish: "Detroit premiere . . . cast of thousands . . . this week only . . . ten cents—" The few 8x10 glossy stills pasted on the windows were poor blowups, spotty and wrinkled; pictures of mailed cavalry and what looked like a good-sized battle. All for ten cents. Right down my alley.

Maybe it's lucky that history was my major in school. Luck it must have been, certainly not cleverness, that made me pay a dime for a seat in an undertaker's rickety folding chair imbedded solidly—although the only other customers were a half-dozen Sons of the Order of Tortilla—in a cast of second-hand garlic. I sat near the door. A couple of hundred watt bulbs dangling naked from the ceiling gave enough light for me to look around. In front of me, in the rear of the store, was the screen, what looked like a white-painted sheet of beaverboard, and when over my shoulder I saw the battered sixteen millimeter projector I began to think that even a dime was no bargain. Still, I had forty minutes to wait.

Everyone was smoking. I lit a cigarette and the discouraged Mexican who had taken my dime locked the door and turned off the lights, after giving me a long, questioning look. I'd paid my dime, so I looked right back. In a minute the old projector started clattering. No film credits, no producer's name, no director, just a tentative flicker before a closeup of a bewhiskered mug labeled Cortez. Then a painted and feathered Indian with the title of Guatemotzin, successor to Montezuma; an aerial shot of a beautiful job of model-building tagged Ciudad de Mejico, 1521. Shots of old muzzle-loaded artillery banging away, great walls spurting stone splinters under direct fire, skinny Indians dying violently with the customary gyrations, smoke and haze and blood. The photography sat me right up straight. It had none of the scratches and erratic cuts that characterize an old print, none of the fuzziness, none of the usual mugging at the camera by the handsome hero. There wasn't any handsome hero. Did you ever see one of these French pictures, or a Russian picture, and note the reality and depth brought out by working on a small budget that can't afford famed actors? This, what there was of it, was as good, or better.

It wasn't until the picture ended with a pan shot of a dreary desolation that I began to add two and two. You can't, for pennies, really have a cast of thousands, or sets big enough to fill Central Park. A mock-up, even, of a thirty-foot wall costs enough to irritate the auditors, and there had been a lot of wall. That didn't fit with the bad editing and lack of sound track, not unless the picture had been made in the old silent days. And I knew it hadn't by the color tones you get with pan film. It looked like a well-rehearsed and badly planned newsreel.

The Mexicans were easing out and I followed them to where the discouraged one was rewinding the reel. I asked him where he got the print. "I haven't heard of any epics from the press agents lately, and it looks like a fairly recent print."

He agreed that it was recent, and added that he'd made it himself. I was polite to that, and he saw that I didn't believe him and straightened up from the projector.

"You don't believe that, do you?" I said that I certainly did, and I had to catch a bus. "Would you mind telling me why, exactly why?" I said that the bus— "I mean it. I'd appreciate it if you'd tell me just what's wrong with it."

"There's nothing wrong with it," I told him. He waited for me to go on. "Well, for one thing, pictures like that aren't made for the sixteen millimeter trade. You've got a reduction from a thirty-five millimeter master." I gave him a few of the other reasons that separate home movies from Hollywood. When I finished he smoked quietly for a minute.

"I see." He took the reel off the projector spindle and closed the case. "I have beer in the back." I agreed beer sounded good, but the bus— well, just one. From in back of the beaverboard screen he brought paper cups and a Jumbo bottle. With a whimsical "Business suspended" he closed the open door and opened the bottle with an opener screwed on the wall. The store had likely been a grocery or restaurant. There were plenty of chairs. Two we shoved around and relaxed companionably. The beer was warm.

"You know something about this line," he said tentatively.

I took it as a question and laughed. "Not too much. Here's mud." And we drank. "Used to drive a truck for the Film Exchange." He was amused at that.

"Stranger in town?"

"Yes and no. Mostly yes. Sinus trouble chased me out and relatives bring me back. Not any more, though; my father's funeral was last week." He said that was too bad, and I said it wasn't. "He had sinus, too." That was a joke, and he refilled the cups. We talked awhile about Detroit climate.

Finally he said, rather speculatively, "Didn't I see you around here last night? Just about eight." He got up and went after more beer.

I called after him. "No more beer for me." He brought a bottle anyway, and I looked at my watch. "Well, just one."

"Was it you?"

"Was it me what?" I held out my paper cup.

"Weren't you around here—"

I wiped foam off my mustache. "Last night? No, but I wish I had. I'd have caught my bus. No, I was in the Motor Bar last night at eight. And I was still there at midnight."

He chewed his lip thoughtfully. "The Motor Bar. Just down the street?" And I nodded. "The Motor Bar. Hm-m-m." I looked at him. "Would you like . . . sure, you would." Before I could figure out what he was talking about he went to the back and from behind the beaverboard screen rolled out a big radio-phonograph and another Jumbo bottle. I held the bottle against the light. Still half full. I looked at my watch. He rolled the radio against the wall and lifted the lid to get at the dials.

"Reach behind you, will you? The switch on the wall." I could reach the switch without getting up, and I did. The lights went out. I hadn't expected that, and I groped at arm's length. Then the lights came on again, and I turned back, relieved. But the lights weren't on; I was looking at the street!

Now, all this happened while I was dripping beer and trying to keep my balance on a tottering chair—the street moved, I didn't and it was day and it was night and I was in front of the Book-Cadillac and I was going into the Motor Bar and I was watching myself order a beer and I knew I was wide awake and not dreaming. In a panic I scrabbled off the floor, shedding chairs and beer like an umbrella while I ripped my nails feeling frantically for that light switch. By the time I found it— and all the while I was watching myself pound the bar for the barkeep —I was really in fine fettle, just about ready to collapse. Out of thin air right into a nightmare. At last I found the switch.

The Mexican was looking at me with the queerest expression I've ever seen, like he'd baited a mousetrap and caught a frog. Me? I suppose I looked like I'd seen the devil himself. Maybe I had. The beer was all over the floor and I barely made it to the nearest chair.

"What," I managed to get out, "what was that?"

The lid of the radio went down. "I felt like that too, the first time. I'd forgotten."

My fingers were too shaky to get out a cigarette, and I ripped off the top of the package. "I said, what was that?"

He sat down. "That was you, in the Motor Bar, at eight last night." I must have looked blank as he handed me another paper cup. Automatically I held it out to be refilled.

"Look here—" I started.

"I suppose it is a shock. I'd forgotten what I felt like the first time I . . . I don't care much any more. Tomorrow I'm going out to Phillips Radio." That made no sense to me, and I said so. He went on.

"I'm licked. I'm flat broke. I don't give a care any more. I'll settle for cash and live off the royalties." The story came out, slowly at first, then faster until he was pacing the floor. I guess he was tired of having no one to talk to.

His name was Miguel Jose Zapata Laviada. I told him mine; Lefko. Ed Lefko. He was the son of sugar beet workers who had emigrated from Mexico somewhere in the Twenties. They were sensible enough not to quibble when their oldest son left the back-breaking Michigan fields to seize the chance provided by a NYA scholarship. When the scholarship ran out, he'd worked in garages, driven trucks, clerked in stores, and sold brushes door-to-door to exist and learn. The Army cut short his education with the First Draft to make him a radar technician, the Army had given him an honorable discharge and an idea so nebulous as to be almost merely a hunch. Jobs were plentiful then, and it wasn't too hard to end up with enough money to rent a trailer and fill it with Army surplus radio and radar equipment. One year ago he'd finished what he'd started, finished underfed, underweight, and overexcited. But successful, because he had it.

"It" he installed in a radio cabinet, both for ease in handling and for camouflage. For reasons that will become apparent, he didn't dare apply for a patent. I looked "it" over pretty carefully. Where the phonograph turntable and radio controls had been were vernier dials galore. One big one was numbered 1 to 24, a couple were numbered 1 to 60, and there were a dozen or so numbered 1 to 25, plus two or three with no numbers at all. Closest of all it resembled one of these fancy radio or motor testers found in a super super-service station. That was all, except that there was a sheet of heavy plywood hiding whatever was installed in place of the radio chassis and speaker. A perfectly innocent cache for—

Daydreams are swell. I suppose we've all had our share of mental wealth or fame or travel or fantasy. But to sit in a chair and drink warm beer and realize that the dream of ages isn't a dream any more, to feel like a god, to know that just by turning a few dials you can see and watch anything, anybody, anywhere, that has ever happened—it still bothers me once in a while.

I know this much, that it's high frequency stuff. And there's a lot of mercury and copper and wiring of metals cheap and easy to find, but what goes where, or how, least of all, why, is out of my line. Light has mass and energy, and that mass always loses part of itself and can be translated back to electricity, or something. Mike Laviada himself says that what he stumbled on and developed was nothing new, that long before the War it had been observed many times by men like Compton and Michelson and Pfeiffer, who discarded it as a useless laboratory effect. And, of course, that was before atomic research took precedence over everything.

When the first shock wore off—and Mike had to give me another demonstration—I must have made quite a sight. Mike tells me I couldn't sit down. I'd pop up and gallop up and down the floor of that ancient store kicking chairs out of my way or stumbling over them, all the time gobbling out words and disconnected sentences faster than my tongue could trip. Finally it filtered through that he was laughing at me. I didn't see where it was any laughing matter, and I prodded him. He began to get angry.

"I know what I have," he snapped. "I'm not the biggest fool in the world, as you seem to think. Here, watch this," and he went back to the radio. "Turn out the light." I did, and there I was watching myself at the Motor Bar again, a lot happier this time. "Watch this."

The bar backed away. Out in the street, two blocks down to the City Hall. Up the steps to the Council Room. No one there. Then Council was in session, then they were gone again. Not a picture, not a projection of a lantern slide, but a slice of life about twelve feet square. If we were close, the field of view was narrow. If we were further away, the background was just as much in focus as the foreground. The images, if you want to call them images, were just as real, just as lifelike as looking in the doorway of a room. Real they were, three-dimensional, stopped by only the back wall or the distance in the background. Mike was talking as he spun the dials, but I was too engrossed to pay much attention.

I yelped and grabbed and closed my eyes as you would if you were looking straight down with nothing between you and the ground except a lot of smoke and a few clouds. I winked my eyes open almost at the end of what must have been a long racing vertical dive, and there I was, looking at the street again.

"Go any place up to the Heaviside Layer, go down as deep as any hole, anywhere, any time." A blur, and the street changed into a glade of sparse pines. "Buried treasure. Sure. Find it, with what?" The trees disappeared and I reached back for the light switch as he dropped the lid of the radio and sat down.

"How are you going to make any money when you haven't got it to start?" No answer to that from me. "I ran an ad in the paper offering to recover lost articles; my first customer was the Law wanting to see my private detective's license. I've seen every big speculator in the country sit in his office buying and selling and making plans; what do you think would happen if I tried to peddle advance market information? I've watched the stock market get shoved up and down while I had barely the money to buy the paper that told me about it. I watched a bunch of Peruvian Indians bury the second ransom of Atuahalpa; I haven't the fare to get to Peru, or the money to buy the tools to dig." He got up and brought two more bottles. He went on. By that time I was getting a few ideas.

"I've watched scribes indite the books that burnt at Alexandria; who would buy, or who would believe me, if I copied one? What would happen if I went over to the Library and told them to rewrite their histories? How many would fight to tie a rope around my neck if they knew I'd watched them steal and murder and take a bath? What sort of a padded cell would I get if I showed up with a photograph of Washington, or Caesar? Or Christ?"

I agreed that it was all probably true, but—

"Why do you think I'm here now? You saw the picture I showed for a dime. A dime's worth, and that's all, because I didn't have the money to buy film or to make the picture as I knew I should." His tongue began to get tangled. He was excited. "I'm doing this because I haven't the money to get the things I need to get the money I'll need—" He was so disgusted he booted a chair halfway across the room. It was easy to see that if I had been around a little later, Phillips Radio would have profited. Maybe I'd have been better off, too.

Now, although always I've been told that I'd never be worth a hoot, no one has ever accused me of being slow for a dollar. Especially an easy one. I saw money in front of me, easy money, the easiest and the quickest in the world. I saw, for a minute, so far in the future with me on top of the heap, that my head reeled and it was hard to breathe.

"Mike," I said, "let's finish that beer and go where we can get some more, and maybe something to eat. We've got a lot of talking to do." So we did.

Beer is a mighty fine lubricant; I have always been a pretty smooth talker, and by the time we left the gin mill I had a pretty good idea of just what Mike had on his mind. By the time we'd shacked up for the night behind that beaverboard screen in the store, we were full-fledged partners. I don't recall our even shaking hands on the deal, but that partnership still holds good. Mike is ace high with me, and I guess it's the other way around, too. That was six years ago; it only took me a year or so to round some of the corners I used to cut.

Seven days after that, on a Tuesday, I was riding a bus to Grosse Pointe with a full briefcase. Two days after that I was riding back from Grosse Pointe in a shiny taxi, with an empty briefcase and a pocketful of folding money. It was easy.

"Mr. Jones—or Smith—or Brown—I'm with Aristocrat Studios, Personal and Candid Portraits. We thought you might like this picture of you and . . . no, this is just a test proof. The negative is in our files. . . . Now, if you're really interested, I'll be back the day after tomorrow with our files. . . . I'm sure you will, Mr. Jones. Thank you, Mr. Jones. . . ."

Dirty? Sure. Blackmail is always dirty. But if I had a wife and family and a good reputation, I'd stick to the roast beef and forget the Roquefort. Very smelly Roquefort, at that. Mike liked it less than I did. It took some talking, and I had to drag out the old one about the ends justifying the means, and they could well afford it, anyway. Besides, if there was a squawk, they'd get the negatives free. Some of them were pretty bad.

So we had the cash; not too much, but enough to start. Before we took the next step there was plenty to decide. There are a lot of people who live by convincing millions that Sticko soap is better. We had a harder problem than that: we had, first, to make a salable and profitable product, and second, we had to convince many, many millions that our "Product" was absolutely honest and absolutely accurate. We all know that if you repeat something long enough and loud enough many—or most—will accept it as gospel truth. That called for publicity on an international scale. For the skeptics who know better than to accept advertising, no matter how blatant, we had to use another technique. And since we were going to get certainly only one chance, we had to be right the first time. Without Mike's machine the job would have been impossible; without it the job would have been unnecessary.

A lot of sweat ran under the bridge before we found what we thought —and we still do!—the only workable scheme. We picked the only possible way to enter every mind in the world without a fight; the field of entertainment. Absolute secrecy was imperative, and it was only when we reached the last decimal point that we made a move. We started like this.

First we looked for a suitable building, or Mike did, while I flew east, to Rochester, for a month. The building he rented was an old bank. We had the windows sealed, a flossy office installed in the front—the bullet-proof glass was my idea—air conditioning, a portable bar, electrical wiring of whatever type Mike's little heart desired, and a blond secretary who thought she was working for M-E Experimental Laboratories. When I got back from Rochester I took over the job of keeping happy the stone masons and electricians, while Mike fooled around in our suite in the Book where he could look out the window at his old store. The last I heard, they were selling snake oil there. When the Studio, as we came to call it, was finished, Mike moved in and the blonde settled down to a routine of reading love stories and saying no to all the salesmen that wandered by. I left for Hollywood.

I spent a week digging through the files of Central Casting before I was satisfied, but it took a month of snooping and some under-the-table cash to lease a camera that would handle Trucolor film. That took the biggest load from my mind. When I got back to Detroit the big view camera had arrived from Rochester, with a truckload of glass color plates. Ready to go.

We made quite a ceremony of it. We closed the Venetian blinds and I popped the cork on one of the bottles of champagne I'd bought. The blond secretary was impressed; all she'd been doing for her salary was to accept delivery of packages and crates and boxes. We had no wine glasses, but we made no fuss about that. Too nervous and excited to drink any more than one bottle, we gave the rest to the blonde and told her to take the rest of the afternoon off. After she left—and I think she was disappointed at breaking up what could have been a good party— we locked up after her, went into the studio itself, locked up again and went to work.

I've mentioned that the windows were sealed. All the inside wall had been painted dull black, and with the high ceiling that went with that old bank lobby, it was impressive. But not gloomy. Midway in the studio was planted the big Trucolor camera, loaded and ready. Not much could we see of Mike's machine, but I knew it was off to the side, set to throw on the back wall. Not *on* the wall, understand, because the images produced are projected into the air, like the meeting of the rays of two searchlights. Mike lifted the lid and I could see him silhouetted against the tiny lights that lit the dials.

"Well?" he said expectantly.

I felt pretty good just then, right down to my billfold.

"It's all yours, Mike." A switch ticked over. There he was. There was a youngster, dead twenty-five hundred years, real enough, almost, to touch. Alexander. Alexander of Macedon.

Let's take that first picture in detail. I don't think I can ever forget what happened in the next year or so. First we followed Alexander through his life, from beginning to end. We skipped, of course, the little things he did, jumping ahead days and weeks and years at a time. Then we'd miss him, or find that he'd moved in space. That would mean we'd have to jump back and forth, like the artillery firing bracket or ranging shots, until we found him again. Helped only occasionally by his published lives, we were astounded to realize how much distortion had crept into his life. I often wonder why legends arise about the famous. Certainly their lives are as startling or appalling as fiction. And unfortunately we had to hold closely to the accepted histories. If we hadn't, every professor would have gone into his corner for a hearty sneer. We couldn't take that chance. Not at first.

After we knew approximately what had happened and where, we used our notes to go back to what had seemed a particularly photogenic section and work on that awhile. Eventually we had a fair idea of what we were actually going to film. Then we sat down and wrote an actual script to follow, making allowance for whatever shots we'd have to double in later. Mike used his machine as the projector, and I operated the Trucolor camera at a fixed focus, like taking moving pictures of a movie. As fast as we finished a reel it would go to Rochester for processing, instead of one of the Hollywood outfits that might have done it cheaper. Rochester is so used to horrible amateur stuff that I doubt if anyone ever looks at anything. When the reel was returned we'd run it ourselves to check our choice of scenes and color sense and so on.

For example, we had to show the traditional quarrels with his father, Philip. Most of that we figured on doing with doubles, later. Olympias, his mother, and the fangless snakes she affected, didn't need any doubling, as we used an angle and amount of distance that didn't call for actual conversation. The scene where Alexander rode the bucking horse no one else could ride came out of some biographer's head, but we thought it was so famous we couldn't leave it out. We dubbed the close-ups later, and the actual horseman was a young Scythian who hung around the royal stables for his keep. Roxanne was real enough, like the rest of the Persian's wives that Alexander took over. Luckily most of them had enough poundage to look luscious. Philip and Parmenio and the rest of the characters were heavily bearded, which made easy the necessary doubling and dubbing-in the necessary speech. (If you ever saw them shave in those days, you'd know why whiskers were popular.)

The most trouble we had with the interior shots. Smoky wicks in a bowl of lard, no matter how plentiful, were too dim even for fast film. Mike got around that by running the Trucolor camera at a single frame a second, with his machine paced accordingly. That accounts for the startling clarity and depth of focus we got from a lens well stopped down. We had all the time in the world to choose the best possible scenes and camera angles; the best actors in the world, expensive camera booms, or repeated retakes under the most exacting director couldn't compete with us. We had a lifetime from which to choose.

Eventually we had on film about eighty per cent of what you saw in the finished picture. Roughly we spliced the reels together and sat there entranced at what we had actually done. Even more exciting, even more spectacular than we'd dared to hope, the lack of continuity and sound didn't stop us from realizing that we'd done a beautiful job. We'd done all we could, and the worst was yet to come. So we sent for more champagne and told the blonde we had cause for celebration. She giggled.

"What are you doing in there, anyway?" she asked. "Every salesman who comes to the door wants to know what you're making."

I opened the first bottle. "Just tell them you don't know."

"That's just what I've been telling them. They think I'm awfully dumb." We all laughed at the salesmen.

Mike was thoughtful. "If we're going to do this sort of thing very often, we ought to have some of these fancy hollow-stemmed glasses."

The blonde was pleased with that. "And we could keep them in my bottom drawer." Her nose wrinkled prettily. "These bubbles— You know, this is the only time I've ever had champagne, except at a wedding, and then it was only one glass."

"Pour her another," Mike suggested. "Mine's empty, too." I did. "What did you do with those bottles you took home last time?"

A blush and a giggle. "My father wanted to open them, but I told him you said to save it for a special occasion."

By that time I had my feet on her desk. "This is the special occasion, then," I invited. "Have another, Miss . . . what's your first name, anyway? I hate being formal after working hours."

She was shocked. "And you and Mr. Laviada sign my checks every week! It's Ruth."

"Ruth. Ruth." I rolled it around the piercing bubbles, and it sounded all right.

She nodded. "And your name is Edward, and Mr. Laviada's is Migwell. Isn't it?" And she smiled at him.

"*Migell*." He smiled back. "An old Spanish custom. Usually shortened to Mike."

"If you'll hand me another bottle," I offered, "shorten Edward to Ed." She handed it over.

By the time we got to the fourth bottle we were as thick as bugs in a rug. It seems that she was twenty-four, free, white, and single, and loved champagne.

"But," she burbled fretfully, "I wish I knew what you were doing in there all hours of the day and night. I know you're here at night sometimes because I've seen your car out in front."

Mike thought that over. "Well," he said a little unsteadily, "we take pictures." He blinked one eye. "Might even take pictures of you if we were approached properly."

I took over. "We take pictures of models."

"Oh, no."

"Yes. Models of things and people and what not. Little ones. We make it look like it's real." I think she was a trifle disappointed.

"Well, now I know, and that makes me feel better. I sign all those bills from Rochester and I don't know what I'm signing for. Except that they must be film or something."

"That's just what it is; film and things like that."

"Well, it bothered me— No, there's two more behind the fan."

Only two more. She had a capacity. I asked her how she would like a vacation. She hadn't thought about a vacation just yet.

I told her she'd better start thinking about it. "We're leaving day after tomorrow for Los Angeles, Hollywood."

"The day after tomorrow? Why—"

I reassured her. "You'll get paid just the same. But there's no telling how long we'll be gone, and there doesn't seem to be much use in your sitting around here with nothing to do."

From Mike, "Let's have that bottle." And I handed it to him. I went on.

"You'll get your checks just the same. If you want, we'll pay you in advance so—"

I was getting full of champagne, and so were we all. Mike was humming softly to himself, happy as a taco. The blonde, Ruth, was having a little trouble with my left eye. I knew just how she felt, because I was having a little trouble watching where she overlapped the swivel chair. Blue eyes, sooo tall, fuzzy hair. Hm-m-m. All work and no play— She handed me the last bottle.

Demurely she hid a tiny hiccup. "I'm going to save all the corks— No I won't either. My father would want to know what I'm thinking of, drinking with my bosses."

I said it wasn't a good idea to annoy your father. Mike said why fool with bad ideas, when he had a good one. We were interested. Nothing like a good idea to liven things up.

Mike was expansive as the very devil. "Going to Los Angeles."

We nodded solemnly.

"Going to Los Angeles to work."

Another nod.

"Going to work in Los Angeles. What will we do for pretty blond girl to write letters?"

Awful. No pretty blonde to write letters and drink champagne. Sad case.

"Gotta hire somebody to write letters anyway. Might not be blonde. No blondes in Hollywood. No good ones, anyway. So—"

I saw the wonderful idea, and finished for him. "So we take pretty blonde to Los Angeles to write letters!"

What an idea that was! One bottle sooner and its brilliancy would have been dimmed. Ruth bubbled like a fresh bottle and Mike and I sat there, smirking like mad.

"But I can't! I couldn't leave day after tomorrow just like that—!"

Mike was magnificent. "Who said day after tomorrow? Changed our minds. Leave right now."

She was appalled. "Right now! Just like that?"

"Right now. Just like that." I was firm.

"But—"

"No buts. Right now. Just like that."

"Nothing to wear—"

"Buy clothes any place. Best ones in Los Angeles."

"But my hair—"

Mike suggested a haircut in Hollywood, maybe?

I pounded the table. It felt solid. "Call the airport. Three tickets."

She called the airport. She intimidated easy.

The airport said we could leave for Chicago any time on the hour, and change there for Los Angeles. Mike wanted to know why she was wasting time on the telephone when we could be on our way. Holding up the wheels of progress, emery dust in the gears. One minute to get her hat.

"Call Pappy from the airport."

Her objections were easily brushed away with a few word-pictures of how much fun there was to be had in Hollywood. We left a sign on the door, "Gone to Lunch—Back in December," and made the airport in time for the four o'clock plane, with no time left to call Pappy. I told the parking attendant to hold the car until he heard from me and we made it up the steps and into the plane just in time. The steps were taken away, the motors snorted, and we were off, with Ruth holding fast her hat in an imaginary breeze.

There was a two-hour layover in Chicago. They don't serve liquor at the airport, but an obliging cab driver found us a convenient bar down the road, where Ruth made her call to her father. Cautiously we stayed away from the telephone booth, but from what Ruth told us, he must have read her the riot act. The bartender didn't have champagne, but

gave us the special treatment reserved for those that order it. The cab
driver saw that we made the liner two hours later.

In Los Angeles we registered at the Commodore, cold sober and
ashamed of ourselves. The next day Ruth went shopping for clothes for
herself, and for us. We gave her the sizes and enough money to soothe
her hangover. Mike and I did some telephoning. After breakfast we sat
around until the desk clerk announced a Mr. Lee Johnson to see us.

Lee Johnson was the brisk professional type, the high-bracket salesman. Tall, rather homely, a clipped way of talking. We introduced ourselves as embryo producers. His eyes brightened when we said that. His
meat.

"Not exactly the way you think," I told him. "We have already eighty
per cent or better of the final print."

He wanted to know where he came in.

"We have several thousand feet of Trucolor film. Don't bother asking
where or when we got it. This footage is silent. We'll need sound and,
in places, speech dubbed in."

He nodded. "Easy enough. What condition is the master?"

"Perfect condition. It's in the hotel vault right now. There are gaps in
the story to fill. We'll need quite a few male and female characters. And
all of these will have to do their doubling for cash, and not for screen
credit."

Johnson raised his eyebrows. "And why? Out here screen credit is
bread and butter."

"Several reasons. This footage was made—never mind where—with
the understanding that film credit would favor no one."

"If you're lucky enough to catch your talent between pictures you
might get away with it. But if your footage is worth working with, my
boys will want screen credit. And I think they're entitled to it."

I said that was reasonable enough. The technical crews were essential, and I was prepared to pay well. Particularly to keep their mouths
closed until the print was ready for final release. Maybe even after that.

"Before we go any further," Johnson rose and reached for his hat,
"let's take a look at that print. I don't know if we can—"

I knew what he was thinking. Amateurs. Home movies. Feelthy peek-
chures, mebbe?

We got the reels out of the hotel safe and drove to his laboratory, out
Sunset. The top was down on his convertible and Mike hoped audibly
that Ruth would have sense enough to get sport shirts that didn't itch.

"Wife?" Johnson asked carelessly.

"Secretary," Mike answered just as casually. "We flew in last night
and she's out getting us some light clothes." Johnson's estimation of us
rose visibly.

A porter came out of the laboratory to carry the suitcase containing
the film reels. It was a long, low building, with the offices at the front
and the actual laboratories tapering off at the rear. Johnson took us in

the side door and called for someone whose name we didn't catch. The anonymous one was a projectionist who took the reels and disappeared into the back of the projection room. We sat for a minute in the soft easy-chairs until the projectionist buzzed ready. Johnson glanced at us and we nodded. He clicked a switch on the arm of his chair and the overhead lights went out. The picture started.

It ran a hundred and ten minutes as it stood. We both watched Johnson like a cat at a rathole. When the tag end showed white on the screen he signaled with the chairside buzzer for lights. They came on. He faced us.

"Where did you get that print?"

Mike grinned at him. "Can we do business?"

"Do business?" He was vehement. "You bet your life we can do business. We'll do the greatest business you ever saw!"

The projection man came down. "Hey, that's all right. Where'd you get it?"

Mike looked at me. I said, "This isn't to go any further."

Johnson looked at his man, who shrugged. "None of my business."

I dangled the hook. "That wasn't made here. Never mind where."

Johnson rose and struck, hook, line and sinker. "Europe! Hm-m-m. Germany. No, France. Russia, maybe. Einstein, or Eisenstein, or whatever his name is?"

I shook my head. "That doesn't matter. The leads are all dead, or out of commission, but their heirs . . . well, you get what I mean."

Johnson saw what I meant. "Absolutely right. No point taking any chances. Where's the rest—?"

"Who knows? We were lucky to salvage that much. Can do?"

"Can do." He thought for a minute. "Get Bernstein in here. Better get Kessler and Marrs, too." The projectionist left. In a few minutes Kessler, a heavy-set man, and Marrs, a young, nervous chain-smoker, came in with Bernstein, the sound man. We were introduced all around and Johnson asked if we minded sitting through another showing.

"Nope. We like it better than you do."

Not quite. Kessler and Marrs and Bernstein, the minute the film was over, bombarded us with startled questions. We gave them the same answers we'd given Johnson. But we were pleased with the reception, and said so.

Kessler grunted. "I'd like to know who was behind that camera. Best I've seen, by Cripes, since 'Ben Hur.' Better than 'Ben Hur.' The boy's good."

I grunted right back at him. "That's the only thing I can tell you. The photography was done by the boys you're talking to right now. Thanks for the kind word."

All four of them stared.

Mike said, "That's right."

"Hey, hey!" from Marrs. They all looked at us with new respect. It felt good.

Johnson broke into the silence when it became awkward. "What's next on the score card?"

We got down to cases. Mike, as usual, was content to sit there with his eyes half closed, taking it all in, letting me do all the talking.

"We want sound dubbed in all the way through."

"Pleasure," said Bernstein.

"At least a dozen, maybe more, of speaking actors with a close resemblance to the leads you've seen."

Johnson was confident. "Easy. Central Casting has everybody's picture since the Year One."

"I know. We've already checked that. No trouble there. They'll have to take the cash and let the credit go, for reasons I've already explained to Mr. Johnson."

A moan from Marrs. "I bet I get that job."

Johnson was snappish. "You do. What else?" to me.

I didn't know. "Except that we have no plans for distribution as yet. That will have to be worked out."

"Like falling off a log." Johnson was happy about that. "One look at the rushes and United Artists would spit in Shakespeare's eye."

Marrs came in. "What about the other shots? Got a writer lined up?"

"We've got what will pass for the shooting script, or will have in a week or so. Want to go over it with us?"

He'd like that.

"How much time have we got?" interposed Kessler. "This is going to be a job. When do we want it?" Already it was "we."

"Yesterday is when we want it," snapped Johnson, and he rose. "Any ideas about music? No? We'll try for Werner Janssen and his boys. Bernstein, you're responsible for that print from now on. Kessler, get your crew in and have a look at it. Marrs, you'll go with Mr. Lefko and Mr. Laviada through the files at Central Casting at their convenience. Keep in touch with them at the Commodore. Now, if you'll step into my office, we'll discuss the financial arrangements—"

As easy as all that.

Oh, I don't say that it was easy work or anything like that, because in the next few months we were playing Busy Bee. What with running down the only one registered at Central Casting who looked like Alexander himself—he turned out to be a young Armenian who had given up hope of ever being called from the extra lists and had gone home to Santee—casting and rehearsing the rest of the actors and swearing at the costumers and the boys who built the sets, we were kept hopping. Even Ruth, who had reconciled her father with soothing letters, for once earned her salary. We took turns shooting dictation at her until we had a script that satisfied Mike and myself and young Marrs, who turned out to be a fox on dialogue.

What I really meant is that it was easy, and immensely gratifying, to crack the shell of the tough boys who had seen epics and turkeys come and go. They were really impressed by what we had done. Kessler was disappointed when we refused to be bothered with photographing the rest of the film. We just batted our eyes and said that we were too busy, that we were perfectly confident that he would do as well as we. He outdid himself, and us. I don't know what we would have done if he had asked us for any concrete advice. I suppose, when I think it all over, that the boys we met and worked with were so tired of working with the usual mine-run Grade B's, that they were glad to meet someone that knew the difference between glycerin tears and reality and didn't care if it cost two dollars extra. They had us placed as a couple of city slickers with plenty on the ball. I hope.

Finally it was all over with. We all sat in the projection room; Mike and I, Marrs and Johnson, Kessler and Bernstein, and all the lesser technicians that had split up the really enormous amount of work that had been done watched the finished product. It was terrific. Everyone had done his work well. When Alexander came on the screen, he was Alexander the Great. (The Armenian kid got a good bonus for that.) All that blazing color, all that wealth and magnificence and glamor seemed to flare right out of the screen and sear across your mind. Even Mike and I, who had seen the original, were on the edge of our seats.

The sheer realism and magnitude of the battle scenes, I think, really made the picture. Gore, of course, is glorious when it's all make-believe and the dead get up to go to lunch. But when Bill Mauldin sees a picture and sells a breathless article on the similarity of infantrymen of all ages—well, Mauldin knows what war is like. So did the infantrymen throughout the world who wrote letters comparing Alexander's Arbela to Anzio and the Argonne. The weary peasant, not stolid at all, trudging and trudging into mile after mile of those dust-laden plains and ending as a stinking, naked, ripped corpse peeping from under a mound of flies isn't any different when he carries a sarissa instead of a rifle. That we'd tried to make obvious, and we succeeded.

When the lights came up in the projection room we knew we had a winner. Individually we shook hands all around, proud as a bunch of penguins, and with chests out as far. The rest of the men filed out and we retired to Johnson's office. He poured a drink all around and got down to business.

"How about releases?"

I asked him what he thought.

"Write your own ticket," he shrugged. "I don't know whether or not you know it, but the word has already gone around that you've got something."

I told him we'd had calls at the hotel from various sources, and named them.

"See what I mean? I know those babies. Kiss them out if you want to keep your shirt. And while I'm at it, you owe us quite a bit. I suppose you've got it."

"We've got it."

"I was afraid you would. If you didn't, I'd be the one that would have your shirt." He grinned, but we all knew he meant it. "All right, that's settled. Let's talk about release.

"There are two or three outfits around town that will want a crack at it. My boys will have the word spread around in no time; there's no point in trying to keep them quiet any longer. I know—they'll have sense enough not to talk about the things you want off the record. I'll see to that. But you're top dog right now. You got loose cash, you've got the biggest potential gross I've ever seen, and you don't have to take the first offer. That's important, in this game."

"How would you like to handle it yourself?"

"I'd like to try. The outfit I'm thinking of needs a feature right now, and they don't know I know it. They'll pay and pay. What's in it for me?"

"That," I said, "we can talk about later. And I think I know just what you're thinking. We'll take the usual terms and we don't care if you hold up whoever you deal with. What we don't know won't hurt us." That's what he was thinking, all right. That's a cutthroat game out there.

"Good. Kessler, get your setup ready for duplication."

"Always ready."

"Marrs, start the ball rolling on publicity . . . what do you want to do about that?" to us.

Mike and I had talked about that before. "As far as we're concerned," I said slowly, "do as you think best. Personal publicity, O.K. We won't look for it, but we won't dodge it. As far as that goes, we're the local yokels making good. Soft pedal any questions about where the picture was made, without being too obvious. You're going to have trouble when you talk about the nonexistent actors, but you ought to be able to figure out something."

Marrs groaned and Johnson grinned. "He'll figure out something."

"As far as technical credit goes, we'll be glad to see you get all you can, because you've done a swell job." Kessler took that as a personal compliment, and it was. "You might as well know now, before we go any further, that some of the work came right from Detroit." They all sat up at that.

"Mike and I have a new process of model and trick work." Kessler opened his mouth to say something but thought better of it. "We're not going to say what was done, or how much was done in the laboratory, but you'll admit that it defies detection."

About that they were fervent. "I'll say it defies detection. In the game this long and process work gets by me . . . where—"

"I'm not going to tell you that. What we've got isn't patented and won't be, as long as we can hold it up." There wasn't any griping there. These men knew process work when they saw it. If they didn't see it, it was good. They could understand why we'd want to keep a process that good a secret.

"We can practically guarantee there'll be more work for you to do later on." Their interest was plain. "We're not going to predict when, or make any definite arrangement, but we still have a trick or two in the deck. We like the way we've been getting along, and we want to stay that way. Now, if you'll excuse us, we have a date with a blonde."

Johnson was right about the bidding for the release. We—or rather Johnson—made a very profitable deal with United Amusement and the affiliated theaters. Johnson, the bandit, got his percentage from us and likely did better with United. Kessler and Johnson's boys took huge ads in the trade journals to boast about their connections with the Academy Award Winner. Not only the Academy, but every award that ever went to any picture. Even the Europeans went overboard. They're the ones that make a fetish of realism. They knew the real thing when they saw it, and so did everyone else.

Our success went to Ruth's head. In no time she wanted a secretary. At that, she needed one to fend off the screwballs that popped out of the woodwork. So we let her hire a girl to help out. She picked a good typist, about fifty. Ruth is a smart girl, in a lot of ways. Her father showed signs of wanting to see the Pacific, so we raised her salary on condition he'd stay away. The three of us were having too much fun.

The picture opened at the same time in both New York and Hollywood. We went to the premiere in great style with Ruth between us, swollen like a trio of bullfrogs. It's a great feeling to sit on the floor, early in the morning, and read reviews that make you feel like floating. It's a better feeling to have a mintful of money. Johnson and his men were right along with us. I don't think he could have been too flush in the beginning, and we all got a kick out of riding the crest.

It was a good-sized wave, too. We had all the personal publicity we wanted, and more. Somehow the word was out that we had a new gadget for process photography, and every big studio in town was after what they thought would be a mighty economical thing to have around. The studios that didn't have a spectacle scheduled looked at the receipts of "Alexander" and promptly scheduled a spectacle. We drew some very good offers, Johnson said, but we made a series of long faces and broke the news that we were leaving for Detroit the next day, and to hold the fort awhile. I don't think he thought we actually meant it, but we did. We left the next day.

Back in Detroit we went right to work, helped by the knowledge that we were on the right track. Ruth was kept busy turning away the countless would-be visitors. We admitted no reporters, no salesmen, no one. We had no time. We were using the view camera. Plate after plate we sent to Rochester for developing. A print of each was returned to us and the plate was held in Rochester for our disposal. We sent to New York for a representative of one of the biggest publishers in the country. We made a deal.

Your main library has a set of the books we published, if you're interested. Huge heavy volumes, hundreds of them, each page a razor-sharp blowup from an 8x10 negative. A set of those books went to every major library and university in the world. Mike and I got a real kick out of solving some of the problems that have had savants guessing for years. In the Roman volume, for example, we solved the trireme problem with a series of pictures, not only the interior of a trireme, but a line-of-battle quinquereme. (Naturally, the professors and amateur yachtsmen weren't convinced at all.) We had a series of aerial shots of the City of Rome taken a hundred years apart, over a millennium. Aerial views of Ravenna and Londinium, Palmyra and Pompeii, of Eboracum and Byzantium. Oh, we had the time of our lives! We had a volume for Greece and for Rome, for Persia and for Crete, for Egypt and for the Eastern Empire. We had pictures of the Parthenon and the Pharos, pictures of Hannibal and Caractacus and Vercingetorix, pictures of the Walls of Babylon and the building of the pyramids and the palace of Sargon, pages from the Lost Books of Livy and the plays of Euripedes. Things like that.

Terrifically expensive, a second printing sold at cost to a surprising number of private individuals. If the cost had been less, historical interest would have become even more the fad of the moment.

When the flurry had almost died down, some Italian digging in the hitherto-unexcavated section of ash-buried Pompeii, dug right into a tiny buried temple right where our aerial shot had showed it to be. His budget was expanded and he found more ash-covered ruins that agreed with our aerial layout, ruins that hadn't seen the light of day for almost two thousand years. Everyone promptly wailed that we were the luckiest guessers in captivity; the head of some California cult suspected aloud that we were the reincarnations of two gladiators named Joe.

To get some peace and quiet Mike and I moved into our studio, lock, stock, and underwear. The old bank vault had never been removed, at our request, and it served well to store our equipment when we weren't around. All the mail Ruth couldn't handle we disposed of, unread; the old bank building began to look like a well-patronized soup kitchen. We hired burly private detectives to handle the more obnoxious visitors and subscribed to a telegraphic protective service. We had another job to do, another full-length feature.

We still stuck to the old historical theme. This time we tried to do what Gibbon did in the Decline and Fall of the Roman Empire. And, I think, we were rather successful, at that. In four hours you can't completely cover two thousand years, but you can, as we did, show the cracking up of a great civilization, and how painful the process can be. The criticism we drew for almost ignoring Christ and Christianity was unjust, we think, and unfair. Very few knew then, or know now, that we had included, as a kind of trial balloon, some footage of Christ Himself, and His times. This footage we had to cut. The Board of Review, as you know, is both Catholic and Protestant. They—the Board—went right up in arms. We didn't protest very hard when they claimed our "treatment" was irreverent, indecent, and biased and inaccurate "by any Christian standard. Why," they wailed, "it doesn't even look like Him."

And they were right; it didn't. Not any picture *they* ever saw. Right then and there we decided that it didn't pay to tamper with anyone's religious beliefs. That's why you've never seen anything emanating from us that conflicted even remotely with the accepted historical, sociological, or religious features of Someone Who Knew Better. That Roman picture, by the way—but not accidentally—deviated so little from the textbooks you conned in school that only a few enthusiastic specialists called our attention to what they insisted were errors. We were still in no position to do any mass rewriting of history, because we were unable to reveal just where we got our information.

Johnson, when he saw the Roman epic, mentally clicked high his heels. His men went right to work, and we handled the job as we had the first. One day Kessler got me in a corner, dead earnest.

"Ed," he said, "I'm going to find out where you got that footage if it's the last thing I ever do."

I told him that some day he would.

"And I don't mean some day, either; I mean right now. That bushwa about Europe might go once, but not twice. I know better, and so does everyone else. Now, what about it?"

I told him I'd have to consult Mike and I did. We were up against it. We called a conference.

"Kessler tells me he has troubles. I guess you all know what they are." They all knew.

Johnson spoke up. "He's right, too. We know better. Where did you get it?"

I turned to Mike. "Want to do the talking?"

A shake of his head. "You're doing all right."

"All right." Kessler hunched a little forward and Marrs lit another cigarette. "We weren't lying and we weren't exaggerating when we said the actual photography was ours. Every frame of film was taken right here in this country, within the last few months. Just how—I won't mention why or where—we can't tell you just now." Kessler snorted in disgust. "Let me finish.

"We all know that we're cashing in, hand over fist. And we're going to cash in some more. We have, on our personal schedule, five more pictures. Three of that five we want you to handle as you did the others. The last two of the five will show you both the reason for all the childish secrecy, as Kessler calls it, and another motive that we have so far kept hidden. The last two pictures will show you both our motives and our methods; one is as important as the other. Now—is that enough? Can we go ahead on that basis?"

It wasn't enough for Kessler. "That doesn't mean a thing to me. What are we, a bunch of hacks?"

Johnson was thinking about his bank balance. "Five more. Two years, maybe four."

Marrs was skeptical. "Who do you think you're going to kid that long? Where's your studio? Where's your talent? Where do you shoot your exteriors? Where do you get your costumes and your extras? In one single shot you've got forty thousand extras, if you've got one! Maybe you can shut *me* up, but who's going to answer the questions that Metro and Fox and Paramount and RKO have been asking? Those boys aren't fools, they know their business. How do you expect me to handle any publicity when I don't know what the score is, myself?"

Johnson told him to pipe down for a while and let him think. Mike and I didn't like this one bit. But what could we do—tell the truth and end up in a strait-jacket?

"Can we do it this way?" he finally asked. "Marrs, these boys have an in with the Soviet Government. They work in some place in Siberia, maybe. Nobody gets within miles of there. No one ever knows what the Russians are doing—"

"Nope!" Marrs was definite. "Any hint that these came from Russia and we'd all be a bunch of Reds. Cut the gross in half."

Johnson began to pick up speed. "All right, not from Russia. From one of these little republics fringed around Siberia or Armenia or one of those places. They're not Russian-made films at all. In fact, they've been made by some of these Germans and Austrians the Russians took over and moved after the War. The war fever has died down enough for people to realize that the Germans knew their stuff occasionally. The old sympathy racket for these refugees struggling with faulty equipment, lousy climate, making super-spectacles and smuggling them out under the nose of the Gestapo or whatever they call it—That's it!"

Doubtfully, from Marrs: "And the Russians tell the world we're nuts, that they haven't got any loose Germans?"

That, Johnson overrode. "Who reads the back pages? Who pays any attention to what the Russians say? Who cares? They might even think we're telling the truth and start looking around their own backyard for something that isn't there! All right with you?" to Mike and myself.

I looked at Mike and he looked at me.

"O.K. with us."

"O.K. with the rest of you? Kessler? Bernstein?"

They weren't too agreeable, and certainly not happy, but they agreed to play games until we gave the word.

We were warm in our thanks. "You won't regret it."

Kessler doubted that very much, but Johnson eased them all out, back to work. Another hurdle leaped, or sidestepped.

"Rome" was released on schedule and drew the same friendly reviews. "Friendly" is the wrong word for reviews that stretched ticket line-ups blocks long. Marrs did a good job on the publicity. Even that chain of newspapers that afterward turned on us so viciously fell for Marrs' word wizardry and ran full-page editorials urging the reader to see "Rome."

With our third picture, "Flame Over France," we corrected a few misconceptions about the French Revolution, and began stepping on a few tender toes. Luckily, however, and not altogether by design, there 'happened to be in power in Paris a liberal government. They backed us to the hilt with the confirmation we needed. At our request they released a lot of documents that had hitherto conveniently been lost in the cavernous recesses of the Bibliotheque Nationale. I've forgotten the name of whoever happened to be the perennial pretender to the French throne. At, I'm sure, the subtle prodding of one of Marrs' ubiquitous publicity men, the pretender sued us for our whole net, alleging the defamation of the good name of the Bourbons. A lawyer Johnson dug up for us sucked the poor chump into a courtroom and cut him to bits. Not even six cents damages did he get. Samuels, the lawyer, and Marrs drew a good-sized bonus, and the pretender moved to Honduras.

Somewhere around this point, I believe, did the tone of the press begin to change. Up until then we'd been regarded as crosses between Shakespeare and Barnum. Since long obscure facts had been dredged into the light, a few well-known pessimists began to wonder *sotto voce* if we weren't just a pair of blasted pests. "Should leave well enough alone." Only our huge advertising budget kept them from saying more.

I'm going to stop right here and say something about our personal life while all this was going on. Mike kept in the background pretty well, mostly because he wanted it that way. He let me do all the talking and stick my neck out while he sat in the most comfortable chair in sight. I yelled and I argued and he just sat there; hardly ever a word coming out of that dark-brown pan, certainly never an indication showing that behind those polite eyebrows there was a brain—and a sense of humor and wit—faster and as deadly as a bear trap. Oh, I know we played around, sometimes with a loud bang, but we were, ordinarily, too busy and too preoccupied with what we were doing to waste any time. Ruth, while she was with us, was a good dancing and drinking partner. She was young, she was almost what you'd call beautiful, and she seemed to like being with us. For a while I had a few ideas about her that might have developed into something serious. We both—I should say, all three of us—found out in time that we looked at a lot of things too differently. So we weren't too disappointed when she signed with Metro. Her contract meant what she thought was all the fame and money and happiness in the world, plus the personal attention she was doubtless entitled to have. They put her in Class B's and serials and she, financially, is better off than she ever expected to be. Emotionally, I don't know. We heard from her sometime ago, and I think she's about due for another divorce. Maybe it's just as well.

But let's get away from Ruth. I'm ahead of myself, anyway. All this time Mike and I had been working together, our approach to the final payoff had been divergent. Mike was hopped on the idea of making a better world, and doing that by making war impossible. "War," he often said, "war of any kind is what has made man spend most of his history in merely staying alive. Now, with the atom to use, he has within himself the seed of self-extermination. So help me, Ed, I'm going to do my share of stopping that, or I don't see any point in living. I mean it!"

He did mean it. He told me that in almost the same words the first day we met. Then, I tagged that idea as a pipe dream picked up on an empty stomach. I saw his machine only as a path to a luxurious and personal Nirvana, and I thought he'd soon be going my way. I was wrong.

You can't live, or work, with a likable person without admiring some of the qualities that make that person likable. Another thing; it's a lot easier to worry about the woes of the world when you haven't any yourself. It's a lot easier to have a conscience when you can afford it. When I donned the rose-colored glasses half my battle was won; when I realized how grand a world this *could* be, the battle was over. That was about the time of "Flame Over France," I think. The actual time isn't important. What *is* important is that, from that time on, we became the tightest team possible. Since then about the only thing we differed on was the time to knock off for a sandwich. Most of our leisure time, what we had of it, was spent in locking up for the night, rolling out the portable bar, opening just enough beer to feel good, and relaxing. Maybe, after one or two, we might diddle the dials of the machine, and go rambling.

Together we'd been everywhere and seen everything. It might be a good night to check up on François Villon, that faker, or maybe we might chase around with Haroun-el-Rashid. (If there was ever a man born a few hundred years too soon, it was that careless caliph.) Or if we were in a bad or discouraged mood we might follow the Thirty Years' War for a while, or if we were real raffish we might inspect the dressing rooms at Radio City. For Mike the crackup of Atlantis had always had an odd fascination, probably because he was afraid that man would do it again, now that he's rediscovered nuclear energy. And if I dozed off he was quite apt to go back to the very Beginning, back to the start of the world as we know it now. (It wouldn't do any good to tell you what went before *that*.)

When I stop to think, it's probably just as well that neither of us married. We, of course, had hopes for the future, but we were both tired of the whole human race; tired of greedy faces and hands. With a world that puts a premium on wealth and power and strength, it's no wonder what decency there is stems from fear of what's here now, or fear of what's hereafter. We had seen so much of the hidden actions of the world—call it snooping, if you like—that we learned to disregard the surface indications of kindness and good. Only once did Mike and I ever look into the private life of someone we knew and liked and respected. Once was enough. From that day on we made it a point to take people as they seemed. Let's get away from that.

The next two pictures we released in rapid succession; the first "Freedom for Americans," the American Revolution, and "The Brothers and the Guns," the American Civil War. Bang! Every third politician, a lot of so-called "educators," and all the professional patriots started after our scalps. Every single chapter of the DAR, the Sons of Union Veterans, and the Daughters of the Confederacy pounded their collective heads against the wall. The South went frantic; every state in the Deep South and one state on the border flatly banned both pictures, the second because it was truthful, and the first because censorship is a contagious disease. They stayed banned until the professional politicians got wise. The bans were revoked, and the choke-collar and string-tie brigade pointed to both pictures as horrible examples of what some people actually believed and thought, and felt pleased that someone had given them an opportunity to roll out the barrel and beat the drums that sound sectional and racial hatred.

New England was tempted to stand on its dignity, but couldn't stand the strain. North of New York both pictures were banned. In New York state the rural representatives voted en bloc, and the ban was clamped on statewide. Special trains ran to Delaware, where the corporations were too busy to pass another law. Libel suits flew like confetti, and although the extras blared the filing of each new suit, very few knew that we lost not one. Although we had to appeal almost every suit to higher courts, and in some cases request a change of venue which was seldom granted, the documentary proof furnished by the record cleared us once we got to a judge, or series of judges, with no fences to mend.

It was a mighty rasp we drew over wounded ancestral pride. We had shown that not all the mighty had haloes of purest gold, that not all the Redcoats were strutting bullies—nor angels, and the British Empire, except South Africa, refused entry to both pictures and made violent passes at the State Department. The spectacle of Southern and New England congressmen approving the efforts of a foreign ambassador to suppress free speech drew hilarious hosannahs from certain quarters. H. L. Mencken gloated in the clover, doing loud nip-ups, and the newspapers hung on the triple-horned dilemma of anti-foreign, pro-patriotic, and quasi-logical criticism. In Detroit the Ku Klux Klan fired an anemic cross on our doorstep, and the Friendly Sons of St. Patrick, the NAACP, and the WCTU passed flattering resolutions. We forwarded the most vicious and obscene letters—together with a few names and addresses that hadn't been originally signed—to our lawyers a? d the Post Office Department. There were no convictions south of Illinois.

Johnson and his boys made hay. Johnson had pyramided his bets into an international distributing organization, and pushed Marrs into hiring every top press agent either side of the Rockies. What a job they did! In no time at all there were two definite schools of thought that overflowed into the public letter boxes. One school held that we had no business raking up old mud to throw, that such things were better left forgotten and forgiven, that nothing wrong had ever happened, and if it had, we were liars anyway. The other school reasoned more to our liking. Softly and slowly at first, then with a triumphant shout, this fact began to emerge; such things had actually happened, and could happen again, were possibly happening even now; had happened because twisted truth had too long left its imprint on international, sectional, and racial feelings. It pleased us when many began to agree, with us, that it is important to forget the past, but that it is even more important to understand and evaluate it with a generous and unjaundiced eye. That was what we were trying to bring out.

The banning that occurred in the various states hurt the gross receipts only a little, and we were vindicated in Johnson's mind. He had dolefully predicted loss of half the national gross because "you can't tell the truth in a movie and get away with it. Not if the house holds over three hundred." Not even on the stage? "Who goes to anything but a movie?"

So far things had gone just about as we'd planned. We'd earned and received more publicity, favorable and otherwise, than anyone living. Most of it stemmed from the fact that our doing had been newsworthy. Some, naturally, had been the ninety-day-wonder material that fills a thirsty newspaper. We had been very careful to make our enemies in the strata that can afford to fight back. Remember the old saw about knowing a man by the enemies he makes? Well, publicity was our ax. Here's how we put an edge on it.

I called Johnson in Hollywood. He was glad to hear from us. "Long time no see. What's the pitch, Ed?"

"I want some lip readers. And I want them yesterday, like you tell your boys."

"Lip readers? Are you nuts? What do you want with lip readers?"

"Never mind why. I want lip readers. Can you get them?"

"How should I know? What do you want them for?"

"I said, can you get them?"

He was doubtful. "I think you've been working too hard."

"Look—"

"Now, I didn't say I couldn't. Cool off. When do you want them? And how many?"

"Better write this down. Ready? I want lip readers for these languages: English, French, German, Russian, Chinese, Japanese, Greek, Belgian, Dutch and Spanish."

"*Ed Lefko, have you gone crazy?*"

I guess it didn't sound very sensible, at that. "Maybe I have. But those languages are essential. If you run across any who can work in any other language, hang on to them. I might need them, too." I could see him sitting in front of his telephone, wagging his head like mad. Crazy. The heat must have got Lefko, good old Ed. "Did you hear what I said?"

"Yes, I heard you. If this is a rib—"

"No rib. Dead serious."

He began to get mad. "Where you think I'm going to get lip readers, out of my hat?"

"That's your worry. I'd suggest you start with the local School for the Deaf." He was silent. "Now, get this into your head; this isn't a rib, this is the real thing. I don't care what you do, or where you go, or what you spend—I want those lip readers in Hollywood when we get there or I want to know they're on the way."

"When are you going to get here?"

I said I wasn't sure. "Probably a day or two. We've got a few loose ends to clean up."

He swore a blue streak at the inequities of fate. "You'd better have a good story when you do—" I hung up.

Mike met me at the studio. "Talk to Johnson?" I told him, and he laughed. "Does sound crazy, I suppose. But he'll get them, if they exist and like money. He's the Original Resourceful Man."

I tossed my hat in a corner. "I'm glad this is about over. Your end caught up?"

"Set and ready to go. The films and the notes are on the way, the real estate company is ready to take over the lease, and the girls are paid up to date, with a little extra."

I opened a bottle of beer for myself. Mike had one. "How about the office files? How about the bar, here?"

"The files go to the bank to be stored. The bar? Hadn't thought about it."

The beer was cold. "Have it crated and send it to Johnson."

We grinned, together. "Johnson it is. He'll need it."

I nodded at the machine. "What about that?"

"That goes with us on the plane as air express." He looked closely at me. "What's the matter with you—jitters?"

"Nope. Willies. Same thing."

"Me, too. Your clothes and mine left this morning."

"Not even a clean shirt left?"

"Not even a clean shirt. Just like—"

I finished it. "—the first trip with Ruth. A little different, maybe."

Mike said slowly, "A lot different." I opened another beer. "Anything you want around here, anything else to be done?" I said no. "O.K. Let's get this over with. We'll put what we need in the car. We'll stop at the Courville Bar before we hit the airport."

I didn't get it. "There's still beer left—"

"But no champagne."

I got it. "O.K. I'm dumb, at times. Let's go."

We loaded the machine into the car, and the bar, left the studio keys at the corner grocery for the real estate company, and headed for the airport by way of the Courville Bar. Ruth was in California, but Joe had champagne. We got to the airport late.

Marrs met us in Los Angeles. "What's up? You've got Johnson running around in circles."

"Did he tell you why?"

"Sounds crazy to me. Couple of reporters inside. Got anything for them?"

"Not right now. Let's get going."

In Johnson's private office we got a chilly reception. "This better be good. Where do you expect to find someone to lipread in Chinese? Or Russian, for that matter?"

We all sat down. "What have you got so far?"

"Besides a headache?" He handed me a short list.

I scanned it. "How long before you can get them here?"

An explosion. "How long before I can get them here? Am I your errand boy?"

"For all practical purposes you are. Quit the fooling. How about it?" Marrs snickered at the look on Johnson's face.

"What are you smirking at, you moron?" Marrs gave in and laughed outright, and I did, too. "Go ahead and laugh. This isn't funny. When I called the State School for the Deaf they hung up. Thought I was some practical joker. We'll skip that.

"There's three women and a man on that list. They cover English, French, Spanish, and German. Two of them are working in the East, and I'm waiting for answers to telegrams I sent them. One lives in Pomona and one works for the Arizona School for the Deaf. That's the best I could do."

We thought that over. "Get on the phone. Talk to every state in the union if you have to, or overseas."

Johnson kicked the desk. "And what are you going to do with them, if I'm that lucky?"

"You'll find out. Get them on planes and fly them here, and we'll talk turkey when they get here. I want a projection room, not yours, and a good bonded court reporter."

He asked the world to appreciate what a life he led.

"Get in touch with us at the Commodore." To Marrs: "Keep the reporters away for a while. We'll have something for them later." Then we left.

Johnson never did find anyone who could lipread Greek. None, at least, that could speak English. The expert on Russian he dug out of Ambridge, in Pennsylvania, the Flemish and Holland Dutch expert came from Leyden, in the Netherlands, and at the last minute he stumbled upon a Korean who worked in Seattle as an inspector for the Chinese Government. Five women and two men. We signed them to an ironclad contract drawn by Samuels, who now handled all our legal work, I made a little speech before they signed.

"These contracts, as far as we've been able to make sure, are going to control your personal and business life for the next year, and there's a clause that says we can extend that period for another year if we so desire. Let's get this straight. You are to live in a place of your own, which we will provide. You will be supplied with all necessities by our buyers. Any attempt at unauthorized communication will result in abrogation of the contract. Is that clear?

"Good. Your work will not be difficult, but it will be tremendously important. You will, very likely, be finished in three months, but you will be ready to go any place at any time at our discretion, naturally at our expense. Mr. Sorenson, as you are taking this down, you realize that this goes for you, too." He nodded.

"Your references, your abilities, and your past work have been thoroughly checked, and you will continue under constant observation. You will be required to verify and notarize every page, perhaps every line, of your transcripts, which Mr. Sorenson here will supply. Any questions?"

No questions. Each was getting a fabulous salary, and each wanted to appear eager to earn it. They all signed.

Resourceful Johnson bought for us a small rooming house, and we paid an exorbitant price to a detective agency to do the cooking and cleaning and chauffeuring required. We requested that the lipreaders refrain from discussing their work among themselves, especially in front of the house employees, and they followed instructions very well.

One day, about a month later, we called a conference in the projection room of Johnson's laboratory. We had a single reel of film.

"What's that for?"

"That's the reason for all the cloak-and-dagger secrecy. Never mind calling your projection man. This I'm going to run through myself. See what you think of it."

They were all disgusted. "I'm getting tired of all this kid stuff," said Kessler.

As I started for the projection booth I heard Mike say, "You're no more tired of it than I am."

From the booth I could see what was showing on the downstairs screen, but nothing else. I ran through the reel, rewound, and went back down.

I said, "One more thing, before we go any further, read this. It's a certified and notarized transcript of what has been read from the lips of the characters you just saw. They weren't, incidentally, 'characters,' in that sense of the word." I handed the crackling sheets around, a copy for each. "Those 'characters' are real people. You've just seen a newsreel. This transcript will tell you what they were talking about. Read it. In the trunk of the car Mike and I have something to show you. We'll be back by the time you've read it."

Mike helped me carry in the machine from the car. We came in the door in time to see Kessler throw the transcript as far as he could. He bounced to his feet as the sheets fluttered down.

He was furious. "What's going on here?" We paid no attention to him, nor to the excited demands of the others until the machine had been plugged into the nearest outlet.

Mike looked at me. "Any ideas?"

I shook my head and told Johnson to shut up for a minute. Mike lifted the lid and hesitated momentarily before he touched the dials. I pushed Johnson into his chair and turned off the lights myself. The room went black. Johnson, looking over my shoulder, gasped. I heard Bernstein swear softly, amazed.

I turned to see what Mike had shown them.

It was impressive, all right. He had started just over the roof of the laboratory and continued straight up in the air. Up, up, up, until the city of Los Angeles was a tiny dot on a great ball. On the horizon were the Rockies. Johnson grabbed my arm. He hurt.

"What's that? What's that? Stop it!" He was yelling. Mike turned off the machine.

You can guess what happened next. No one believed their eyes, nor Mike's patient explanation. He had to twice turn on the machine again, once going far back into Kessler's past. Then the reaction set in.

Marrs smoked one cigarette after another, Bernstein turned a gold pencil over and over in his nervous fingers, Johnson paced like a caged tiger, and burly Kessler stared at the machine, saying nothing at all. Johnson was muttering as he paced. Then he stopped and shook his fist under Mike's nose.

"Man! Do you know what you've got there? Why waste time playing around here? Can't you see you've got the world by the tail on a downhill pull? If I'd ever known this—"

Mike appealed to me. "Ed, talk to this wildman."

I did. I can't remember exactly what I said, and it isn't important. But I did tell him how we'd started, how we'd plotted our course, and what we were going to do. I ended by telling him the idea behind the reel of film I'd run off a minute before.

He recoiled as though I were a snake. "You can't get away with that! You'd be hung—if you weren't lynched first!"

"Don't you think we know that? Don't you think we're willing to take that chance?"

He tore his thinning hair. Marrs broke in. "Let me talk to him." He came over and faced us squarely.

"Is this on the level? You going to make a picture like that and stick your neck out? You're going to turn that . . . that thing over to the people of the world?"

I nodded. "Just that."

"And toss over everything you've got?" He was dead serious, and so was I. He turned to the others. "He means it!"

Bernstein said, "Can't be done!"

Words flew. I tried to convince them that we had followed the only possible path. "What kind of a world do you want to live in? Or don't you want to live?"

Johnson grunted. "How long do you think we'd live if we ever made a picture like that? You're crazy! I'm not. I'm not going to put by head in a noose."

"Why do you think we've been so insistent about credit and responsibility for direction and production? You'll be doing only what we hired you for. Not that we want to twist your arm, but you've made a fortune, all of you, working for us. Now, when the going gets heavy, you want to back out!"

Marrs gave in. "Maybe you're right, maybe you're wrong. Maybe you're crazy, maybe I am. I always used to say I'd try anything once. Bernie, you?"

Bernstein was quietly cynical. "You saw what happened in the last war. This might help. I don't know if it will. I don't know—but I'd hate to think I didn't try. Count me in!"

Kessler?

He swiveled his head. "Kid stuff! Who wants to live forever? Who wants to let a chance go by?"

Johnson threw up his hands. "Let's hope we get a cell together. Let's all go crazy." And that was that.

We went to work in a blazing drive of mutual hope and understanding In four months the lipreaders were through. There's no point in detailing here their reactions to the dynamite they daily dictated to Sorenson. For their own good we kept them in the dark about our final purpose, and when they were through we sent them across the border into Mexico, to a small ranch Johnson had leased. We were going to need them later.

While the print duplicators worked overtime Marrs worked harder. The press and the radio shouted the announcement that, in every city of the world we could reach, there would be held the simultaneous premieres of our latest picture. It would be the last we needed to make. Many wondered aloud at our choice of the word "needed." We whetted curiosity by refusing any advance information about the plot, and Johnson so well infused their men with their own now-fervent enthusiasm that not much could be pried out of them but conjecture. The day we picked for release was Sunday. Monday, the storm broke.

I wonder how many prints of that picture are left today. I wonder how many escaped burning or confiscation. Two World Wars we covered, covered from the unflattering angles that, up until then, had been represented by only a few books hidden in the dark corners of libraries. We showed and *named* the war-makers, the cynical ones who signed and laughed and lied, the blatant patriots who used the flare of headlines and the ugliness of atrocity to hide behind their flag while life turned to death for millions. Our own and foreign traitors were there, the hidden ones with Janus faces. Our lipreaders had done their work well; no guesses these, no deduced conjectures from the broken records of a blasted past, but the exact words that exposed treachery disguised as patriotism.

In foreign lands the performances lasted barely the day. Usually, in retaliation for the imposed censorship, the theaters were wrecked by the raging crowds. (Marrs, incidentally, had spent hundreds of thousands bribing officials to allow the picture to be shown without previous censorship. Many censors, when that came out, were shot without trial.) In the Balkans, revolutions broke out, and various embassies were stormed by mobs. Where the film was banned or destroyed written versions spontaneously appeared on the streets or in coffee-houses. Bootlegged editions were smuggled past customs guards, who looked the other way. One royal family fled to Switzerland.

Here in America it was a racing two weeks before the Federal Government, prodded into action by the raging of press and radio, in an unprecedented move closed all performances "to promote the common welfare, insure domestic tranquillity, and preserve foreign relations." Murmurs—and one riot—rumbled in the Midwest and spread until it was realized by the powers that be that something had to be done, and done quickly, if every government in the world were not to collapse of its own weight.

We were in Mexico, at the ranch Johnson had rented for the lipreaders. While Johnson paced the floor, jerkily fraying a cigar, we listened to a special broadcast of the attorney general himself:

". . . furthermore, this message was today forwarded to the government of the United States of Mexico. I read: 'The government of the United States of America requests the immediate arrest and extradition of the following:

"'Edward Joseph Lefkowicz, known as Lefko.'" First on the list. Even a fish wouldn't get into trouble if he kept his mouth shut.

"'Miguel Jose Zapata Laviada.'" Mike crossed one leg over the other.

"'Edward Lee Johnson.'" He threw his cigar on the floor and sank into a chair.

"'Robert Chester Marrs.'" He lit another cigarette. His face twitched.

"'Benjamin Lionel Bernstein.'" He smiled a twisted smile and closed his eyes.

"'Carl Wilhelm Kessler.'" A snarl.

"These men are wanted by the government of the United States of America, to stand trial on charges ranging from criminal syndicalism, incitement to riot, suspicion of treason—"

I clicked off the radio. "Well?" to no one in particular.

Bernstein opened his eyes. "The rurales are probably on their way. Might as well go back and face the music—" We crossed the border at Juarez. The FBI was waiting.

Every press and radio chain in the world must have had coverage at that trial, every radio system, even the new and imperfect television chain. We were allowed to see no one but our lawyer. Samuels flew from the West Coast and spent a week trying to get past our guards. He told us not to talk to reporters, if we ever saw them.

"You haven't seen the newspapers? Just as well— How did you ever get yourselves into this mess, anyway? You ought to know better."

I told him.

He was stunned. "Are you all crazy?"

He was hard to convince. Only the united effort and concerted stories of all of us made him believe that there was such a machine in existence. (He talked to us separately, because we were kept isolated.) When he got back to me he was unable to think coherently.

"What kind of defense do you call that?"

I shook my head. "No. That is, we know that we're guilty of practically everything under the sun if you look at it one way. If you look at it another—"

He rose. "Man, you don't need a lawyer, you need a doctor. I'll see you later. I've got to get this figured out in my mind before I can do a thing."

"Sit down. What do you think of this?" And I outlined what I had in mind.

"I think . . . I don't know what I think. I don't know. I'll talk to you later. Right now I want some fresh air." And he left.

As most trials do, this one began with the usual blackening of the defendant's character, or lack of it. (The men we'd blackmailed at the beginning had long since had their money returned, and they had sense enough to keep quiet. That might have been because they'd received a few hints that there might still be a negative or two lying around. Compounding a felony? Sure.) With the greatest of interest we sat in that great columned hall and listened to a sad tale.

We had, with malice aforethought, libeled beyond repair great and unselfish men who had made a career of devotion to the public weal, imperiled needlessly relations traditionally friendly by falsely reporting mythical events, mocked the courageous sacrifices of those who had *dulce et gloria mori,* and completely unset everyone's peace of mind. Every new accusation, every verbal lance drew solemn agreement from the dignitary-packed hall. Against someone's better judgment, the trial had been transferred from the regular courtroom to the Hall of Justice. Packed with influence, brass, and pompous legates from over the world, only the congressmen from the biggest states, or with the biggest votes were able to crowd the newly installed seats. So you can see it was a hostile audience that faced Samuels when the defense had its say. We had spent the previous night together in the guarded suite to which we had been transferred for the duration of the trial, perfecting, as far as we could, our planned defense. Samuels has the arrogant sense of humor that usually goes with supreme self-confidence, and I'm sure he enjoyed standing there among all those bemedaled and bejowled bigwigs, knowing the bombshell he was going to hurl. He made a good grenadier. Like this:

"We believe there is only one defense possible, we believe there is only one defense necessary. We have gladly waived, without prejudice, our inalienable right of trial by jury. We shall speak plainly and bluntly, to the point.

"You have seen the picture in question. You have remarked, possibly, upon what has been called the startling resemblance of the actors in that picture to the characters named and portrayed. You have remarked possibly, upon the apparent verisimilitude to reality. That I will mention again. The first witness will, I believe, establish the trend of our rebuttal of the allegations of the prosecution." He called the first witness.

"Your name, please?"

"Mercedes Maria Gomez."

"A little louder, please."

"Mercedes Maria Gomez."

"Your occupation?"

"Until last March I was a teacher at the Arizona School for the Deaf. Then I asked for and obtained a leave of absence. At present I am under personal contract to Mr. Lefko."

"If you see Mr. Lefko in this courtroom, Miss . . . Mrs.—"

"Miss."

"Thank you. If Mr. Lefko is in this court will you point him out? Thank you. Will you tell us the extent of your duties at the Arizona School?"

"I taught children born totally deaf to speak. And to read lips."

"You read lips yourself, Miss Gomez?"

"I have been totally deaf since I was fifteen."

"In English only?"

"English and Spanish. We have . . . had many children of Mexican descent."

Samuels asked for a designated Spanish-speaking interpreter. An officer in the back immediately volunteered. He was identified by his ambassador, who was present.

"Will you take this book to the rear of the courtroom, sir?" To the Court: "If the prosecution wishes to examine that book, they will find that it is a Spanish edition of the Bible." The prosecution didn't wish to examine it.

"Will the officer open the Bible at random and read aloud?" He opened the Bible at the center and read. In dead silence the Court strained to hear. Nothing could be heard the length of that enormous hall.

Samuels: "Miss Gomez. Will you take these binoculars and repeat, to the Court, just what the officer is reading at the other end of the room?"

She took the binoculars and focused them expertly on the officer, who had stopped reading and was watching alertly. "I am ready."

Samuels: "Will you please read, sir?"

He did, and the Gomez woman repeated aloud, quickly and easily, a section that sounded as though it might be anything at all. I can't speak Spanish. The officer continued to read for a minute or two.

Samuels: "Thank you, sir. And thank you, Miss Gomez. Your pardon, sir, but since there are several who have been known to memorize the Bible, will you tell the Court if you have anything on your person that is written, anything that Miss Gomez has had no chance of viewing?" Yes, the officer had. "Will you read that as before? Will you, Miss Gomez—"

She read that, too. Then the officer came to the front to listen to the court reporter read Miss Gomez' words.

"That's what I read," he affirmed.

Samuels turned her over to the prosecution, who made more experiments that served only to convince that she was equally good as an interpreter and lipreader in either language.

In rapid succession Samuels put the rest of the lipreaders on the stand. In rapid succession they proved themselves as able and as capable as Miss Gomez, in their own linguistic specialty. The Russian from Ambridge generously offered to translate into his broken English any other Slavic language handy, and drew scattered grins from the press box. The Court was convinced, but failed to see the purpose of the exhibition. Samuels, glowing with satisfaction and confidence, faced the Court.

"Thanks to the indulgence of the Court, and despite the efforts of the distinguished prosecution, we have proved the almost amazing accuracy of lipreading in general, and these lipreaders in particular." One Justice absently nodded in agreement. "Therefore, our defense will be based on that premise, and on one other which we have had until now found necessary to keep hidden—the picture in question was and is definitely not a fictional representation of events of questionable authenticity. Every scene in that film contained, not polished professional actors, but the original person named and portrayed. Every foot, every inch of film was not the result of an elaborate studio reconstruction but an actual collection of pictures, an actual collection of newsreels—if they can be called that—edited and assembled in story form!"

Through the startled spurt of astonishment we heard one of the prosecution: "That's ridiculous! No newsreel—"

Samuels ignored the objections and the tumult to put me on the stand. Beyond the usual preliminary questions I was allowed to say things my own way. At first hostile, the Court became interested enough to overrule the repeated objections that flew from the table devoted to the prosecution. I felt that at least two of the Court, if not outright favorable, were friendly. As far as I can remember, I went over the maneuvers of the past years, and ended something like this:

"As to why we arranged the cards to fall as they did; both Mr. Laviada and myself were unable to face the prospect of destroying his discovery, because of the inevitable penalizing of needed research. We were, and we are, unwilling to better ourselves or a limited group by the use and maintenance of secrecy, if secrecy were possible. As to the only other alternative," and I directed this straight at Judge Bronson, the well-known liberal on the bench, "since the last war all atomic research and activity has been under the direction of a Board nominally civilian, but actually under the 'protection and direction' of the Army and Navy. This 'direction and protection,' as any competent physicist will gladly attest, has proved to be nothing but a smothering blanket serving to conceal hidebound antiquated reasoning, abysmal ignorance, and inestimable amounts of fumbling. As of right now, this country, or any country that was foolish enough to place any confidence in the rigid regime of the military mind, is years behind what would otherwise be the natural course of discovery and progress in nuclear and related fields.

"We were, and we are, firmly convinced that even the slightest hint of the inherent possibilities and scope of Mr. Laviada's discovery would have meant, under the present regime, instant and mandatory confiscation of even a supposedly secure patent. Mr. Laviada has never applied for a patent, and never will. We both feel that such a discovery belongs not to an individual, a group, or corporation, or even to a nation, but to the world and those who live in it.

"We know, and are eager and willing to prove, that the domestic and external affairs not only of this nation but of every nation are influenced, sometimes controlled, by esoteric groups warping political theories and human lives to suit their own ends." The Court was smothered in sullen silence, thick and acid with hate and disbelief.

"Secret treaties, for example, and vicious, lying propaganda have too long controlled human passions and made men hate; honored thieves have too long rotted secretly in undeserved high places. The machine can make treachery and untruth impossible. It *must,* if atomic war is not to sear the face and fate of the world.

"Our pictures were all made with that end in view. We needed, first, the wealth and prominence to present to an international audience what we knew to be the truth. We have done as much as we can. From now on, this Court takes over the burden we have carried. We are guilty of no treachery, guilty of no deceit, guilty of nothing but deep and true humanity. Mr. Laviada wishes me to tell the Court and the world that he has been unable till now to give his discovery to the world, free to use as it wills."

The Court stared at me. Every foreign representative was on the edge of his seat waiting for the Justices to order us shot without further ado, the sparkling uniforms were seething, and the pressmen were racing their pencils against time. The tension dried my throat. The speech that Samuels and I had rehearsed the previous night was strong medicine. Now what?

Samuels filled the breach smoothly. "If the Court pleases; Mr. Lefko has made some startling statements. Startling, but certainly sincere, and certainly either provable or disprovable. And proof it shall be!"

He strode to the door of the conference room that had been allotted us. As the hundreds of eyes followed him it was easy for me to slip down from the witness stand, and wait, ready. From the conference room Samuels rolled the machine, and Mike rose. The whispers that curdled the air seemed disappointed, unimpressed. Right in front of the Bench he trundled it.

He moved unobtrusively to one side as the television men trained their long-snouted cameras. "Mr. Laviada and Mr. Lefko will show you . . . I trust there will be no objection from the prosecution?" He was daring them.

One of the prosecution was already on his feet. He opened his mouth hesitantly, but thought better, and sat down. Heads went together in conference as he did. Samuels was watching the Court with one eye, and the courtroom with the other.

"If the Court pleases, we will need a cleared space. If the bailiff will . . . thank you, sir." The long tables were moved back, with a raw scraping. He stood there, with every eye in the courtroom glued on him. For two long breaths he stood there, then he spun and went to his table. "Mr. Lefko." And he bowed formally. He sat.

The eyes swung to me, to Mike, as he moved to his machine and stood there silently. I cleared my throat and spoke to the Bench as though I did not see the directional microphones trained at my lips.

"Justice Bronson."

He looked steadily at me and then glanced at Mike. "Yes, Mr. Lefko?"

"Your freedom from bias is well known." The corners of his mouth went down as he frowned. "Will you be willing to be used as proof that there can be no trickery?" He thought that over, then nodded slowly. The prosecution objected, and was waved down. "Will you tell me exactly where you were at any given time? Any place where you are absolutely certain and can verify that there were no concealed cameras or observers?"

He thought. Seconds. Minutes. The tension twanged, and I swallowed dust. He spoke quietly. "1918. November 11th."

Mike whispered to me. I said, "Any particular time?"

Justice Bronson looked at Mike. "Exactly eleven. Armistice time." He paused, then went on. "Niagara Falls. Niagara Falls, New York."

I heard the dials tick in the stillness, and Mike whispered again. I said, "The lights should be off." The bailiff rose. "Will you please watch the left wall, or in that direction? I think that if Justice Kassel will turn a little . . . we are ready."

Bronson looked at me, and at the left wall. "Ready."

The lights flicked out overhead and I heard the television crews mutter. I touched Mike on the shoulder. "Show them, Mike!"

We're all showmen at heart, and Mike is no exception. Suddenly out of nowhere and into the depths poured a frozen torrent. Niagara Falls. I've mentioned, I think, that I've never got over my fear of heights. Few people ever do. I heard long, shuddery gasps as we started straight down. Down, until we stopped at the brink of the silent cataract, weird in its frozen majesty. Mike had stopped time at exactly eleven, I knew. He shifted to the American bank. Slowly he moved along. There were a few tourists standing in almost comic attitudes. There was snow on the ground, flakes in the air. Time stood still, and hearts slowed in sympathy.

Bronson snapped, "Stop!"

A couple, young. Long skirts, high-buttoned army collar, dragging army overcoat, facing, arms about each other. Mike's sleeve rustled in the darkness and they moved. She was sobbing and the soldier was smiling. She turned away her head, and he turned it back. Another couple seized them gayly, and they twirled breathlessly.

Bronson's voice was harsh. "That's enough!" The view blurred for seconds.

Washington. The White House. The President. Someone coughed like a small explosion. The President was watching a television screen. He jerked erect suddenly, startled. Mike spoke for the first time in Court.

"That is the President of the United States. He is watching the trial that is being broadcast and televised from this courtroom. He is listening to what I am saying right now, and he is watching, in his television screen, as I use my machine to show him what he was doing one second ago."

The President heard those fateful words. Stiffly he threw an unconscious glance around his room at nothing and looked back at his screen in time to see himself do what he just had done, one second ago. Slowly, as if against his will, his hand started toward the switch of his set.

"Mr. President, don't turn off that set." Mike's voice was curt, almost rude. "You must hear this, you of all people in the world. You must understand!

"This is not what we wanted to do, but we have no recourse left but to appeal to you, and to the people of this twisted world." The President might have been cast in iron. "You must see, you must understand that you have in your hands the power to make it impossible for green-born war to be bred in secrecy and rob man of his youth or his old age or whatever he prizes." His voice softened, pleaded. "That is all we have to say. That is all we want. That is all anyone could want, ever." The President, unmoving, faded into blackness. "The lights, please." And almost immediately the Court adjourned. That was over a month ago.

Mike's machine has been taken from us, and we are under military guard. Probably it's just as well we're guarded. We understand there have been lynching parties, broken up only as far as a block or two away. Last week we watched a white-haired fanatic scream about us, on the street below. We couldn't catch what he was shrieking, but we did catch a few air-borne epithets.

"Devils! Anti-Christs! Violation of the Bible! Violations of this and that!" Some, right here in the city, I suppose, would be glad to build a bonfire to cook us right back to the flames from which we've sprung. I wonder what the various religious groups are going to do now that the truth can be seen. Who can read lips in Aramaic, or Latin, or Coptic? And is a mechanical miracle a miracle?

This changes everything. We've been moved. Where, I don't know, except that the weather is warm, and we're on some type of military reservation, by the lack of civilians. Now we know what we're up against. What started out to be just a time-killing occupation, Joe, has turned out to be a necessary preface to what I'm going to ask you to do. Finish this, and then move fast! We won't be able to get this to you for a while yet, so I'll go on for a bit the way I started, to kill time. Like our clippings:

TABLOID:

. . . Such a weapon cannot, must not be loosed in unscrupulous hands. The last professional production of the infamous pair proves what distortions can be wrested from isolated and misunderstood events. In the hands of perpetrators of heretical isms, no property, no business deal, no personal life could be sacrosanct, no foreign policy could be . . .

TIMES:

. . . colonies stand with us firmly. . . liquidation of the Empire . . . white man's burden . . .

LE MATIN:

. . . rightful place . . . restore proud France . . .

PRAVDA:

. . . democratic imperialist plot . . . our glorious scientist ready to announce . . .

NICHI-NICHI:

. . . incontrovertibly prove divine descent . . .

LA PRENSA:

. . . oil concessions . . . dollar diplomacy . . .

DETROIT JOURNAL:

. . . under our noses in a sinister fortress on East Warren . . . under close Federal supervision . . . perfection by our production-trained technicians a mighty aid to law-enforcement agencies . . . tirades against politicians and business common-sense carried too far . . . tomorrow revelations by . . .

L'OSSERVATORE ROMANO:

Council of Cardinals . . . announcement expected hourly . . .

JACKSON STAR-CLARION:

. . . proper handling will prove the fallacy of race equality . . .

Almost unanimously the press screamed; Pelger frothed, Winchell leered. We got the surface side of the situation from the press. But a military guard is composed of individuals, hotel room must be swept by maids, waiters must serve food, and a chain is as strong— We got what we think the truth from those who work for a living.

There are meetings on street corners and in homes, two great veterans' groups have arbitrarily fired their officials, seven governors have resigned, three senators and over a dozen representatives have retired with "ill health," and the general temper is ugly. International travelers report the same of Europe, Asia is bubbling, and transport planes with motors running stud the airports of South America. A general whisper is that a Constitutional Amendment is being rammed through to forbid the use of any similar instrument by any individual, with the manufacture and leasing by the Federal government to law-enforcement agencies or financially responsible corporations suggested; it is whispered that motor caravans are forming throughout the country for a Washington march to demand a decision by the Court on the truth of our charges; it is generally suspected that all news disseminating services are under direct Federal—Army—control; wires are supposed to be sizzling with petitions and demands to Congress, which are seldom delivered.

One day the chambermaid said: "And the whole hotel might as well close up shop. The whole floor is blocked off, there're MP's at every door, and they're clearing out all the other guests as fast as they can be moved. The whole place wouldn't be big enough to hold the letters and wires addressed to you, or the ones that are trying to get in to see you. Fat chance they have," she added grimly. "The joint is lousy with brass."

Mike glanced at me and I cleared my throat. "What's your idea of the whole thing?"

Expertly she spanked and reversed a pillow. "I saw your last picture before they shut it down. I saw all your pictures. When I wasn't working I listened to your trial. I heard you tell them off. I never got married because my boy friend never came back from Burma. Ask *him* what he thinks." And she jerked her head at the young private who was supposed to keep her from talking. "Ask him if he wants some bunch of stinkers to start him shooting at some other poor chump. See what he says, and then ask me if I want an atom bomb dropped down my neck just because some chiselers want more than they got." She left suddenly, and the soldier left with her. Mike and I had a beer and went to bed. Next week the papers had headlines a mile high.

U.S. KEEPS MIRACLE RAY
CONSTITUTION
AMENDMENT
AWAITS STATES OKAY
LAVIADA-LEFKO FREED

We were freed all right, Bronson and the President being responsible for that. But the President and Bronson don't know, I'm sure, that we were rearrested immediately. We were told that we'll be held in "protective custody" until enough states have ratified the proposed constitutional amendment. The Man Without a Country was in what you might call "protective custody," too. We'll likely be released the same way he was.

We're allowed no newspapers, no radio, allowed no communication coming or going, and we're given no reason, as if that were necessary. They'll never, never let us go, and they'd be fools if they did. They think that if we can't communicate, or if we can't build another machine, our fangs are drawn, and when the excitement dies, we fall into oblivion, six feet of it. Well, we can't build another machine. But, communicate?

Look at it this way. A soldier is a soldier because he wants to serve his country. A soldier doesn't want to die unless his country is at war. Even then death is only a last resort. And war isn't necessary any more, not with our machine. In the dark? Try to plan or plot in absolute darkness, which is what would be needed. Try to plot or carry on a war without putting things in writing. O.K. Now—

The Army has Mike's machine. The Army has Mike. They call it military expediency, I suppose. Bosh! Anyone beyond the grade of moron can see that to keep that machine, to hide it, is to invite the world to attack, and attack in self-defense. If every nation, or if every man, had a machine, each would be equally open, or equally protected. But if only one nation, or only one man can see, the rest will not long be blind. Maybe we did this all wrong. God knows that we thought about it often. God knows we did our best to make an effort at keeping man out of his own trap.

There isn't much time left. One of the soldiers guarding us will get this to you, I hope, in time.

A long time ago we gave you a key, and hoped we would never have to ask you to use it. But now is the time. That key fits a box at the Detroit Savings Bank. In that box are letters. Mail them, not all at once, or in the same place. They'll go all over the world, to men we know, and have watched well; clever, honest, and capable of following the plans we've enclosed.

But you've got to hurry! One of these bright days someone is going to wonder if we've made more than one machine. We haven't, of course. That would have been foolish. But if some smart young lieutenant gets hold of that machine long enough to start tracing back our movements they'll find that safety deposit box, with the plans and letters ready to be scattered broadside. You can see the need for haste—if the rest of the world, or any particular nation, wants that machine bad enough, they'll fight for it. And they will! They must! Later on, when the Army gets used to the machine and its capabilities, it will become obvious to everyone, as it already has to Mike and me, that, with every plan open to inspection as soon as it's made, no nation or group of nations would have a chance in open warfare. So if there is to be an attack, it will have to be deadly, and fast, and sure. Please God that we haven't shoved the world into a war we tried to make impossible. With all the atom bombs and rockets that have been made in the past few years—*Joe, you've got to hurry!*

GHQ TO 9TH ATTK GRP

Report report report report report report report report report report

CMDR 9TH ATTK GRP TO GHQ

BEGINS: No other manuscript found. Searched body of Lefko immediately upon landing. According to plan Building Three untouched. Survivors insist both were moved from Building Seven previous day defective plumbing. Body of Laviada identified definitely through fingerprints. Request further instructions. ENDS

GHQ TO CMDR 32ND
SHIELDED RGT

BEGINS: Seal area Detroit Savings Bank. Advise immediately condition safety deposit boxes. Afford coming technical unit complete cooperation. ENDS

LT.COL. TEMP. ATT.
32ND SHIELDED RGT

BEGINS: Area Detroit Savings Bank vaporized direct hit. Radioactivity lethal. Impossible boxes or any contents survive. Repeat, direct hit. Request permission proceed Washington Area. ENDS

GHQ. TO LT. COL. TEMP. ATT.
32ND SHIELDED RGT

BEGINS: Request denied. Sift ashes if necessary regardless cost. Repeat, regardless cost. ENDS

GHQ. TO ALL UNITS REPEAT
ALL UNITS

BEGINS: Lack of enemy resistance explained misdirected atom rockets seventeen miles SSE Washington. Lone survivor completely destroyed special train claims all top officials left enemy capital two hours preceding attack. Notify local governments where found necessary and obvious cessation hostilities. Occupy present areas Plan Two. Further orders follow. ENDS

PART FIVE

Far Traveling

FLETCHER PRATT

THE ROGER BACON FORMULA

I MET the old man as the result of three beers and an argument. I never even knew his name. He may be one of the greatest scientists alive; he may even not have been human; and in either of these cases, I would hold through him the key to an almost infinite enrichment of the human spirit. On the other hand, he may merely have been one of those people of whom the law takes a justifiably dim view, and in that case, it wouldn't even do for me to be inquiring after him. I work in a bank, and it would be as much as my job is worth.

So all I have is a rather incredible story. All right, I admit I wouldn't believe it myself if somebody else told it. But just listen, will you? You can check if you want to.

It starts in one of those restaurant-bars in Greenwich Village, where they have booths opposite the bar, a radio that goes all the time, and as little light as possible. The gang used to meet there because it was less depressing than getting together in anyone's furnished room and just about as cheap as long as you stuck to beer. It was a good gang, even if most of them were a bunch of lousy Reds—or thought they were in those days. I noticed that with most of them, the closer they got to fifty bucks a week, the farther they got from the party line. That was the dividing line, fifty per; once they hit it, they were all through as Commies.

At the time I'm telling about, it was different, and I was practically the only one who blew a fuse whenever the name of Karl Marx was mentioned. They used to gang up on me, with a lot of scientific terms, and they knew most of the arguments I used, so I was always having to

Originally this tale appeared under a joint byline, Irvin Lester and Fletcher Pratt. Mr. Pratt, well-known naval historian and commentator on things maritime, reports that Irvin Lester was "a newspaper man with whom I was working at the time the story was written, and we always used a dual byline. It's so long ago that I can't be certain at this date whether he actually had a hand in this one or not, but I suspect not. He died about 1928 or 1929. . . ." In any event, Mr. Pratt has completely rewritten the story for use in this anthology, so that by now it is entirely his.

think up new ones. On this night I'm talking about, I'd been doing a little reading, so I let them have it with something about Roger Bacon, the medieval friar, you know, who did so much monkeying around both with philosophy and the physical sciences. "Go on, look him up some time," I told them. "You'll find that every real argument of the Marxian dialectic has been anticipated and answered before it was ever written down. Marx was just ignoramus enough not to know that he was digging up dead rats."

That let things loose, especially as none of them really knew any more about Roger Bacon than I did, and for that matter, they hadn't read Marx at first hand, either. We all talked loud enough to keep down the noise of the radio and to try to keep down each other, so that after about the third beer, the bartender came around and told us to pipe down a little. I had had my fun by that time, so I tried to change the subject to something safe, like baseball, and when the rest wouldn't, I got up and went home.

Or started for home. I was just going around the corner when this old man sidled up to me. "Pardon me, sir," he said apologetically.

The Village is full of panhandlers. I glanced at him for long enough to see that he was very short, had white hair and no hat, and a tear in his coat. I said, "Sorry, chum, I haven't got any money."

"I don't want money," he said. "It's about—that is, I heard you mention Roger Bacon."

I looked at him again then. He had a kind of pear-shaped head with a little fluffy crown of hair on the top of it, and a rim of more hair around over the ears, and the longest and thinnest hands I ever saw on a human being. The tendons stood out on the backs of those hands and made it look as though there were no flesh between them at all. I said, "I'm afraid I'm really not much of a Bacon student."

He looked so disappointed that I thought he was going to burst into tears. I tried to comfort him with, "But I do think the Bacon manuscripts are remarkable productions, whether they are forged or not."

"Forged?," he said, his voice going up thinly. "I don't . . . Oh, you mean the Parma manuscripts, the ones Newbold tried to translate when he achieved such curiously correct results by the wrong method. But those only describe annular eclipses and plant reproduction. They are the least part of the work. If the world had listened to the full doctrine of Roger Bacon, it would be six centuries further along the path of civilization."

"Do you think so?" I said. This sounded like the beginning of one of the arguments of the gang.

"I know it! Can you spare a few moments to come up to my place? I have something that will interest any student of Roger Bacon. There are so few."

If there is one thing the Village has more of than panhandlers, it is nuts, but the night was young and the old bird sounded so wistful that it was hard to turn him down. Besides, even a nut can be interesting.

I let him lead me around a couple of corners to Bank Street and up interminable flights of stairs in a rickety building to where he flung open a door on an attic room of surprising size.

Its layout resembled the tower of a medieval alchemist more than anything it could have been designed for. There was a long library table in black wood, stained and scarred, on which stood a genuine alembic, which had been abandoned to distill some pungent liquid over a low flame. All around about the alembic was a furious litter of papers, chemical apparatus and bottled reagents. A cabinet opposite held rolls of something that appeared to be sheepskin; there was a sextant on the cot, and a telescope stood by the window. To complete the picture, a huge armillary sphere occupied the corner of the room between the cot and the telescope.

I realized the old duffer was talking in his piping voice: "—the unity of all the sciences, Roger Bacon's greatest contribution to human knowledge. Your modern specialists are only beginning to realize that every experimenter must understand other sciences before he can begin to deal with his own. What would the zoologist do without a knowledge of some chemistry, the chemist without geology, and the geologist without physics? Science is all one. I will show—"

He was at the cabinet, producing one of the sheepskin rolls. It was covered with the crabbed and illegible writing of the Middle Ages, made more illegible still by the wear and tear of centuries.

"A genuine Roger Bacon. You know there are some years following his stay in Paris that have never been accounted for publicly? Ha! Certainly you do not know that he spent them at Citeaux, the headquarters of the order to which he belonged. I have been to Citeaux. I found them restoring the place after the damage caused by the war. Fortunate circumstance that you—that we have wars. The vaults had been damaged by shellfire; it was easy to search among them and gather —these!" He waved one of his skeleton-like hands toward the sheepskin rolls. "The greatest of Roger Bacon's works."

"But didn't the French government—?" I asked.

"French government! What does any government that represents only a tiny portion of the world know about something that affects the whole? The French government never heard of the manuscripts. I saw to that." He chuckled.

"What did you find in them?" I asked.

"Everything. What would you say to an absolutely flat statement of the nebular hypothesis? An exposition of nuclear theory?"

"It must be wonderful. Is that all in there?" I was not quite sure what he was talking about, but I knew enough to know I should be startled.

"All that and more. Didn't I tell you that Bacon made discoveries that the rest of the world has not yet grasped? Here, look at this—" He shoved one of the sheepskins into my hand. "Wait, you do not know how to read the script. I have the same thing written out and translated." He fumbled among the papers on the laboratory table and handed me one. His own writing was almost as bad as the medieval script, but I managed to make out something like this:

"*De Transpositio mentis*: He that would let hys spirit vade within the launds of fay and fell shall drinke of the drogge mandragoreum till he bee sight out of eye, sowne out of ear, speache out of lips and time out of minde. Lapped in lighte shall he then fare toe many a straunge and horrid earthe beyond the bounds of ocean and what he seeth there shall astounde him much; yet shall he return withouten any hurt."

"What do you make of it?" said the old man.

"That he was probably a drug addict," I said, frankly. "Mandragora is fairly well known—was well known even in the Middle Ages, I presume."

"You are as bad as the rest," said the old man. "I had hoped that a Bacon scholar—look, you're missing all the essentials. You people here never believe in anything but yourselves. Now, look again. He doesn't say 'mandragora' but 'mandragoreum' and it's not a copyist's error, because it's written in Bacon's own hand. Note also that he titles it 'the transposition of the mind.' He never imagined, as drug addicts do, that his body was performing strange things. What Roger Bacon is telling us there is that there is a drug which will bring about the dissociation of the mind from the body which seems to occur under hypnotism, but 'withouten any hurt.' Also he says 'lapped in lighte,' which is more than a hint of employing the force and speed of light. Modern science has not attained anything like that yet. I told you Bacon was ahead not only of his time, but of ours. Moreover—" here he gave me a quick glance "—in another place, I found the formula for compounding his drug mandragoreum, and I can assure you that it is nothing like mandragora. I have even used it myself; it produces a certain ionization among the cells of the inner brain by action on the pineal—but you probably don't understand; you are willing to remain earthbound."

I looked at him, trying to figure out what he was driving at. Was he suggesting that I try out this mandragoreum of his? And why me? Surely, if there were anything in it—

"You doubt me? I grant it sounds incredible. Your scientists, as they call themselves, would laugh. But here, try it for yourself. It is the authentic mandragoreum of Bacon." He seized the flask into which the alembic had discharged its contents and thrust it into my hand.

I hesitated, sniffing. The odor was rather pleasant than otherwise, spicy as though it were some form of liqueur. When I touched a drop of it to my tongue, the flavor confirmed this diagnosis. So genial a beverage could hardly be dangerous. And after all, he believed me a fellow student of Roger Bacon. I seated myself in the one chair the room afforded, and sipped.

At once room and surroundings were blotted out in an immense burst of light, so brilliant that I closed my eyes to shield them from it. When I opened them again, the light was still there all about me, but it seemed to be gathering into me from an outside source, as though my own body were draining it away to leave everything else dark. At the same time there was a wonderful sensation of lightness and freedom.

As my eyes became accustomed to the surrounding dimness, I perceived to my astonishment that I was no longer in the room. There was no trace of a room; I was out under the winter sky, floating along over the lights of New York like a cloud. Beneath and behind me a long trail of phosphorescence like a comet's tail led back to the roof of one of the buildings, I supposed that from which I had come. It was not a hallucination; I have been over New York in a plane, and everything was in the right position and right proportions. I was actually seeing New York from the air; but that phosphorescent trail held me like a tether, I could not get free from it, nor go farther. I felt someone touching my hand, and as the light around me seemed to burn down, there was another flash, and I was back in the room.

The old man with the long hands was smiling into my face.

"An experience, is it not?" he said. "You did not drink enough to gain the full effect. Would you care to try again? Mandragoreum is not easy to make, but I have enough for you."

This time I tilted my head back and took a long pull from the flask.

Again the unbearable flash of light, a sense of swift motion. When I opened my eyes, New York City was far beneath, receding into the distance as I seemed to gather speed. The long cord of light that had bound me to the room trailed off behind me; but either its farther end became so small as to be invisible or I had taken enough of the drug altogether to break the connection. In the single glance backward that my speed allowed, I could not even tell toward what part of the city it led.

Clear and bright as I rose, Venus hung like a lamp against the vault of the sky. If I could direct my course, I decided it would be thither, to the most mysterious of the planets. Old Friar Bacon had promised that his drug would "let hys spirit vade . . . toe many a straunge and horrid earthe beyond the bounds of ocean," and surely Venus met such a definition better than any other place.

I looked back. The earth seemed to be beneath me, fading to a black ball, on which land and sea were just barely visible in the darkness. My speed was still mounting. Suddenly I reached the limit of the earth's shadow; the sun flashed blazingly from behind it, and I beheld the skies as no one on earth has ever seen them—except perhaps Roger Bacon. The nearer planets stood out like so many phases of the moon against the intense blackness of space. The moon itself was a tiny crescent, just visible at the outer edge of the sun, on whose huge disk the earth had sunk to a black spot; yet I found that I could bear to look directly into that glare.

When I turned to look ahead again, however, it was as though my sense of direction had shifted. Venus, growing from the size of a moon to that of a great shield of silver, was no longer overhead, but beneath me, and I was diving downward to a whirling, tossing mass of clouds that reflected the sunlight with dazzling brilliance. Now it was a sea of clouds that seemed to take the shape of a bowl; I reached them, cleft the radiant depths, and at once was in a soundless and almost lightless mass of mist, with no knowledge of my direction except that I seemed to be following the straight course that had brought me here.

The cloud-banks lifted behind me, and I experienced a sense of deep disappointment, for below I saw nothing but an endless ocean, heaving slowly under the heavy groundswell and dotted with drops of rain from the clouds I had just left. The planet of mystery was all one vast ocean, then, inhabited by fishes if by anything, and we men of earth were the only intelligent form of life in the solar system, after all.

I found that I could direct my flight by moving my shoulders and arms, but as I soared across the Venerian ocean, my progress was much slower than it had ever been before. I can only explain this now by the fact that much of the sun's light was cut off by the omnipresent clouds. Roger Bacon's drug undoubtedly makes use of some property of light, that form of energy which is so little understood. I do not know what it can be and my scientific friends laugh at the idea.

But that is wandering from my story. At the time, the slowness of this exploratory voyage gave me no special concern, except that it was becoming monotonous until I perceived in the distance a place where the clouds seemed to touch the surface of the sea. I moved toward it; it soon became clear that this was not the clouds coming down but a thin mist rising up like steam from the surface of a patch of land. But what a land!

It was a water-logged swamp, out of which coiled a monstrous vegetation of a sickly yellow hue, quite without any touch of the green of earthly growths. Here were gigantic mushrooms, that must have been twenty or thirty feet tall; long, slender reedlike stems that burst out at the top into spreading tangles of branches; huge fungus growths of bulbous shape, and a vinelike form that twisted and climbed around and over the reed-trees and giant fungi.

There was no clear line where shore and sea met. The swamp began with a tangle of branches reaching out of the ocean and the growths simply became larger and more dense as one progressed. But at last the ground seemed to be rising; I could catch glimpses of something that was not water among the trunks and vines.

It had occurred to me that where there was such abundant vegetable life, there might be something animal, but up to this point I had seen no sign of anything that might move by its own will under the ceaselessly falling rain and rising mist. But at last I caught sight of a growth resembling the round balls of the fungoids, but too large and too regular to be a fungus. I swung my shoulders toward it; it was a huge ball that seemed made of some material harder and more permanent than the vegetation amid which it rose. I circled the ball; at one side, low down, there was the only opening, a door of some sort. It stood open.

I slid in. The room in which I found myself was very dim and my progress was slow. The light was a kind of phosphorescence like that on the sea at night, issuing from some invisible source. I looked round; I was in a vast hall, whose ceiling vaulted upward until it reached a vertical wall at the other end. From the looks of the outside I had not realized that it was so large. There was no other architectural feature in the place save a hole in the center of the floor, set round with a curbing of some sort.

Slanting toward this with some difficulty of movement, I saw that the hole was a wide well, with the sheen of water visible below. Down into this well went a circular staircase, the stairs of which were broad and fitted with low risers.

From behind the vertical wall at the far end, I was conscious of, rather than heard, a confused shouting, and as I drew near to it I saw that it was pierced by several doors, like the one I had entered by, very thick and heavy. These doors bore horizontal rods which I took to be the Venerian equivalent of doorknobs, and over the terminations of the rods were a series of slits which I took to be approximations of keyholes. I do not know of any sight that would have pleased me more at the moment. Something of the order of cave-men could conceivably have set up such a building; savages might have dug the well and lined it with stairs; but only a fairly intelligent and fairly well-civilized form of life would have doors that locked. We were not alone in the solar system after all.

One of the doors toward the end was open; I drifted through. I don't know what I expected to find inside, but what I did find was beyond any expectation. It was another hall, larger if anything than the first, but not as high, since it was roofed over about halfway up. At each corner a circular staircase, with the same wide, low steps as the well ran up to pierce this ceiling.

The room was filled with an endless range of tables, wide and low, like those in a kindergarten. They were composed of a shimmering metal which may very well have been silver, though it may also have been some alloy of which I am ignorant. At these tables, in high-backed chair-like seats of the same metal sat rows of—the people of Venus. They were busy eating and talking together, like a terrestrial crowd in a busy cafeteria, and their babble was the noise I had sensed.

The Venerians bore a cartoonist's resemblance to seals. They had the same short, barrel-like body, surmounted by the same long, narrow head, but the muzzle had grown back to a face and the forehead was high enough to contain a brain of at least the size of our own. The nostrils were wide and very high, so that the eyes were almost behind them. There were no outer ears, but a pair of holes, low down and toward the back, I took to be orifices for hearing.

The legs of the Venerians are pillar-like muscular appendages, short and terminating in flat, spiny feet, webbed between the four toes. I may mention here that while swimming they trail these feet behind them, using them both for propulsion and changes of direction.

The greatest shock was to see their arms—or rather, the appendages that served them for arms, since they really had no arms at all. Instead there were tentacles in groups; two groups beginning at the place where the short, thick neck joined the trunk, on the sides, and a third, smaller set springing from the center of the back, high up. These tentacles reached nearly to the floor when a full-grown Venerian was standing at his height of nearly four feet. Each of the three groups contained four tentacles; all the tentacles were prehensile and capable of independent action, giving the Venerian not only an excellent grip on anything, but also the power of picking up as many as twelve objects at a time. I am inclined to think that the tentacles at the back were less functional than the rest; only once did I see a Venerian use one of them.

The Venerians in the hall were entirely innocent of clothing, and all were covered with rough, coarse hair, except for their faces, and of course, the tentacles. Most of them were wearing a type of bandolier, or belt, supported by a strap around the neck, and in turn carrying a series of pocket-like pouches, held shut by clasps. When a Venerian wished to open one, he thrust two of his tentacles into slits in the clasps; I do not know how they operated.

Some of them carried weapons in their belts; short spears or knife-blades, with the handles set T-shape for better grasping in Venerian tentacles. There were also what I later found to be explosive weapons, with a tube springing out from the T-shaped handle. Every tool and weapon was of metal; clearly there could be little wood in this world where the clouds were never broken.

The Venerians were eating with little metal spades, sharpened at the outer end for cutting. Their food came up to them from beneath, through the tables, when they pulled handles set in front of them. The food itself seemed to be the same throughout the hall, some kind of stew, with solids floating in sauces.

I had come in to find the meal nearly over, with Venerians all over the room rising to leave the table and move down the hall with quick, shambling steps. I followed a pair of the weapon-bearers who were talking animatedly together. They went straight to the door into the other hall, crossed it to the well, which they descended till they were about waist-deep, then turned suddenly and dived. I hesitated, then followed; in my envelope of light there was no sense of wetness, and below I found the well turning into a long underwater passage, lit by the same dim radiance that illuminated the hall.

The dimness made it difficult for me to keep up with the Venerians, who were evidently water-livers as we are creatures of the land, for they were amazing swimmers. Abruptly the passage widened, and the light became enough stronger for me to catch up with the pair ahead.

They directed their course upward through the water, came to the surface (where I saw we were well beyond the swamp belt) and took fresh gulps of air through their elevated nostrils. Then, diving beneath the surface again, they coasted along slowly. I caught a flash of something silvery ahead in the water. So did the Venerians. One of them snatched the tube-weapon from his belt, the other jerked out his spear; both swam faster.

Their quarry was a huge fish, its head and body covered with scaly plates. A long tail projected backward from this coat of mail and two big paddles hung near the beast's head. I'm no biologist, but I just happen to have taken my girl to the museum one afternoon, and we saw something just like it. I remember kidding about the tag, which described it as an "ostracoderm."

It had seen the Venerians, and evidently had a well-developed respect for them, for it fled down the watery path like an arrow—but not fast enough.

The Venerian with the spear gained more rapidly than his companion, heading the fish off with its barbed point, and herding it around. The other lifted his tubed weapon; there were two muffled thuds, like the blows of a padded hammer, and the seven-foot fish wavered, then stopped, its paddles moving convulsively. The Venerian with the spear ranged alongside dodged the reflex swing of the long tail, and thrust his weapon in where the bony plate of the head met the cuirass of the body. The big fish heaved once more, then slowly began to sink, but the two Venerians, each wrapping his tentacles round the fish's tail, began to tow him back toward the hall of the well.

Neither of them rose to the surface during all this period. They were marvellously adapted to staying under water.

They were evidently regular, professional hunters by the manner in which they went about their business. It occurred to me that a race which could divide labor in this fashion, which could produce the explosive weapons, and organize life with the ingenuity shown in the common dining-hall, with its ingenious arrangements for service of food, must possess other and interesting establishments of some kind in the swampy land that represented continents on this planet.

Filled with a desire to see them, I took to the air once more and hurried back to the building. The door was still open, and the hall held an assortment of Venerians, some merely standing and talking, some diving into the well to swim off somewhere, and some passing through the portal out into the jungle of fungi. I had seen the sea-hunters; now I followed a party of those who remained on the surface.

They blinked as the brighter light of the out-of-doors struck their eyes, and I wondered what they would do in the dazzling illumination of an earthly day. After a moment or two to accustom their eyes to the light, they struck out up the gentle slope behind the ball-shaped building. The vegetation was a perfect tangle, and I wondered how the Venerians would manage if they left the path they were following until I saw one of them blunder against the trunk of one of the yellow trees. It was all of twenty-five feet high, but his impact sent it crashing to the ground as though it were made of tissue-paper.

The slope became steeper as the Venerians pushed on, kicking the big, soft stems out of their way when they had fallen to block the path. At last the track encountered a buttress of outcropping stone, the first I had seen on the planet. The Venerians paused. Two of them produced tube-weapons from their belts and, walking with some care, took the lead in the group, which had suddenly grown silent.

What were they afraid of? Some grisly amphibian monster of the swamps, I fancy. At all events, one of them suddenly lifted his weapon and fired it in among the crowding growths. I caught a glimpse of a pair of huge eyes, heard the thud of the fall of a big mushroom and that was all. The Venerians with the weapons crouched and peered; there were a few words, and then they pushed on again. On that steaming planet, the ordinary individual must live far closer to the terrors of the beast-world than he does on earth.

The Venerians followed their path down a little dip till it ended at another bulbous building like the hall of the food and the well. Its door was open; within it had the same cold and feeble illumination as the other. All about the outer room of this place were shelves filled with tools, and a Venerian in attendance. At the back another of the thick doors gave on a room in which I glimpsed pulsating machinery. They were that high up the scale.

The party I had followed received tools from the attendant in the outer hall, and came out again, following another path to the hillside behind. There, where a cliff towered out of the swamp, they entered a hole that had been dug in the stony face of the hill, and drawing from the pouches at their belts some balls that emitted the same light I had seen indoors, they plunged in.

I followed them. It was injudicious, no doubt, but I only found that out later. At the time, I had only noticed that my movements were sometimes faster, sometimes slower, and I had not worked out the rationale of what turned out to be a very dangerous business. It also turned out to be an interesting business, though one that had no particular meaning for me, and has not had since.

It was a mine. The Venerians worked it by means of a shafted tool, which is attached by a metal cord to a box about two feet square, the box standing on the floor behind the miner and evidently furnishing the power for the operation. At the working end of the shafted head is a circle of metal teeth, and beneath the teeth a basket of woven metal. The Venerian presses the tool against the rock he is mining. The teeth spring into motion with the pressure, the rock is pulverized and falls into the basket as a powder. When the basket is filled, the miner takes it to the power box, empties it in and pulls a small rod. Immediately, the box emits a strong red glow, and in a minute or two a bar of shining metal is discharged at the back, and a little ball of waste material falls beside it.

When a pile of the metal bars has accumulated, the miner picks them up and carries them back to the tool-hall, where he turns them in, receiving in exchange a metal token which he deposits in one of his pouches.

I watched the Venerian miners carefully and for a long while, hoping to learn the secret of their power box. Eventually, I thought something would go wrong with one of them, or it would need a re-charge, and the miner would open it. If I could get an inkling of that, and tell it to some of my engineering friends, it would not only be a proof of my strange experience, but it might also be worth—well, a great deal.

So much interested in the project did I become, that I failed to notice the passage of time, and during one of the miner's visits to the hall of the machines, as I waited for him to return, I suddenly realized that it had grown dark. The miner, too, seemed to be gone for an extraordinarily long time. If he had finished his assigned task for the day, there was no sense remaining where I was. I started to leave—and found I could not move an inch.

It was at this point I realized the implications of the fact that Roger Bacon's drug enabled the use of the power of light. There was no light; and there I was, bound by motionlessness, as though in a nightmare; marooned on a planet millions of miles from home, from my own body even, and with no means of returning. I could hear the crash of some beast through the vegetation and the patter of the eternal Venerian rain. That was all; I was alone.

At such moments, in spite of the statements of some writers, one does not rave and storm, or review the mistakes of a past life. I thought of my body back in the room on Bank Street, Earth, and what the old man would do as it sat there in the chair, lifelessly. Would he dare to call the police or a doctor? Would he try to dispose of part of "me"? Was there any antidote to the drug mandragoreum that he could apply? Suppose I finally obtained some kind of release, with the coming of the Venerian dawn, and came rushing home to find my body beneath the waters of the Hudson or on a dissecting table in the New York morgue?

Or perhaps I would remain as a disembodied brain there on Venus throughout eternity? The creatures of this planet had taken no notice of me, and I had made no attempt to communicate with them. Could I if I wished? It was a pretty academic problem. I remembered Jack London's remark that the blackest thing in nature was a hole in a box. That was what I was in—a hole in a box.

From that point, I turned to wondering how long it would be before dawn on Venus. For all I knew it might not come for fifty or sixty hours—quite enough time for anything on earth to happen to my body.

It would begin to need nourishment, even if nothing more drastic happened to it. There it sat, in what resembled a hypnotic trance. How long could people stay alive in such a state? I tried to remember and could not recall ever having heard anywhere. Every time I tried to review my knowledge on the subject it turned out to be too sketchy to be helpful.

I was aroused from this reverie by a grunting sound like that made by a wallowing pig, and looking toward the mouth of the cave, saw a pair of phosphorescent eyes gleaming at the entrance. Apparently the animal, who had no outline in that absolute black, was disturbed by the smell of the place, for the grunts changed into a grinding bellow and it backed out. Perhaps I could communicate with the Venerians after all—provided my mind did not die with my distant body.

Followed another series of grunts, and the sound of heavy footsteps, followed by angry snarls. Then came the sound of heavy bodies hurled about. Two of the Venerian beasts were fighting outside my prison. Of all the events of that journey, this one stands out most clearly; the quarrel of those two Venerian monsters, whose shape I did not even know, snarling and biting each other under the rain, while I hung in the cave without the power of motion.

The battle trailed off to one side and ended in grunting moans, which in turn faded into a sound suggestive of eating. One of the invisible beasts had evidently been victorious and was celebrating—noisily. Finally this sound also ceased, and there was only the steady beat of the rain.

It seemed to grow heavier, and I began to wonder how that mattered on a planet where it was always raining. Far in the distance, I heard the roll of thunder; and I noted without really thinking about it that they had thunderstorms on Venus as well as on earth.

The rain fell harder; again came the peal of thunder, and as it rolled I could see lightning flickering, far in the distance. A new, wild hope rose in me. Lightning was light; if one of those flashes came near enough—

For a time it seemed that it would not. The lightning flashed away among the distant clouds, the thunder continued to boom, but the storm seemed about to pass off to one side and away from me. I was just giving up hope when there were simultaneously a terrific crash and a dazzling burst of lightning across the door of the cave.

With a twist of the shoulders, I was out and riding. It was as dark as before out there, but I was now in the open, where I could travel on any flash of lightning that came, and I did, in a long series of jerking leaps. Another flash—I was among the clouds. Another—I was more than halfway through them. I believed I could see the stars of space beyond. Another flash below me, and I was at last out of the atmosphere of that grim and slimy planet and riding the ether in the light of the stars.

When I reached the earth and the room on Bank Street, dawn was just coming up behind the skyscrapers. I felt cold and numb all over; the old man was standing in the center of the room, looking at me anxiously.

"Thank God!" he said, as I opened my eyes and moved a palsied hand. "I had begun to fear that you could not make the return trip, and I would have to look for you—although that is very difficult for a person of my constitution."

"I need some coffee," was all I said; and as I looked at him, I noticed how very much he resembled the Venerians I had seen.

"Was it an interesting journey?" he asked.

"Wonderful; but I need some coffee," I repeated. "I'll tell you about it later."

I staggered out and down the stairs. And that's just the trouble about my story. There wasn't any later.

For after I fumbled through a day's work at the bank, I got to thinking about things, and I wasn't quite sure whether I wanted to go back there again alone; that is, until I had talked to someone else about it. When I did summon up nerve enough to go back, a couple of evenings later, I found there wasn't any name beside the top button in the row in the hall, and nobody answered the bell when I rang. So I pushed the button marked "Super" and a fat woman with scraggly hair came out.

As I remarked before, I didn't even know the old man's name. "Who lives on the top floor?" I asked.

"Nobody," she said. "Not now, anyway." She gave me a suspicious look. "If you're another one of them G-men, I want to see your badge."

So there it is. I went away. I'm not a G-man, I don't want them looking for me when I have to work in a bank. It could be that the old man gave me some kind of dope, and that he was mixed up in the racket somehow. I don't know. But if he was, why did he have all those old rolls of sheepskin up there? They were genuine, all right. And any scientific people I've talked to since say that my description of Venus is just about what it would look like. Me, I just don't know.

LESTER DEL REY

THE WINGS OF NIGHT

"DAMN all Martians!" Fats Welch's thin mouth bit out the words with all the malice of an offended member of a superior race. "Here we are, loaded down with as sweet a high-rate cargo of iridium as ever came out

Copyright, 1942, in the U. S. A. and Great Britain, by Street and Smith Publications, Inc. Reprinted by permission of Street and Smith Publications, Inc., the Scott Meredith Literary Agency and the author, from *Astounding Science Fiction*, March, 1942.

of the asteroids, just barely over the Moon, and that injector starts mis-metering again. If I ever see that bulbous Marshy—"

"Yeah." Slim Lane groped back with his right hand for the flexible-shaft wrench, found it, and began wriggling and grunting forward into the mess of machinery again. "Yeah. I know. You'll make mince meat out of him. Did you ever figure that maybe you were making your own trouble? That maybe Martians are people after all? Lyro Bmachis told you it would take two days to make the overhaul of the injector control hookup, so you knocked him across the field, called his ancestors dirty dogs, and gave him just eight hours to finish repairs. Now you expect his rush job to be a labor of love for you— Oh, skip it, Fats, and give me the screwdriver."

What was the use? He'd been over it all with Fats a dozen times before, and it never got him anywhere. Fats was a good rocket man, but he couldn't stretch his imagination far enough to forget the hogwash the Reconstruction Empire was dishing out about the Destiny of Man and the Divine Plan whereby humans were created to exploit all other races. Not that it would do Fats much good if he did. Slim knew the value of idealism—none better.

He'd come out of college with a bad dose of it and an inherited fortune big enough for three men, filled with the old crusading spirit. He'd written and published books, made speeches, interviewed administrators, lobbied, joined and organized societies, and been called things that weren't complimentary. Now he was pushing freight from Mars to Earth for a living, quarter owner of a space-worn freighter. And Fats, who'd come up from a tube cleaner without the help of ideals, owned the other three quarters.

Fats watched him climb out of the hold. "Well?"

"Nothing. I can't fix it—don't know enough about electronics. There's something wrong with the relays that control the time interval, but the indicators don't show where, and I'd hate to experiment out here."

"Make it to Earth—maybe?"

Slim shook his head. "I doubt it, Fats. Better set us down on Luna somewhere, if you can handle her that far. Then maybe we can find out what's wrong before we run out of air."

Fats had figured as much and was already braking the ship down, working against the spasmodic flutter of the blasts, and swearing at the effects of even the Moon's weak gravity. But the screens showed that he was making progress toward the spot he'd chosen—a small flat plain with an area in the center that seemed unusually clear of debris and pockmarks.

"Wish they'd at least put up an emergency station out here," he muttered.

"They had one once," Slim said. "But nobody ever goes to Luna, and there's no reason for passenger ships to land there; takes less fuel for them to coast down on their fins through Earth's atmosphere than to jet down here. Freighters like us don't count, anyway. Funny how regular and flat that place is; we can't be over a mile up, and I don't see even a meteor scar."

"Luck's with us, then. I'd hate to hit a baby crater and rip off a tube or poke a hole in the shell." Fats glanced at the radio altimeter and fall indicator. "We're gonna hit plenty hard. If— Hey, what the deuce?"

Slim's eyes flicked to the screen just in time to see the flat plain split into two halves and slide smoothly out from under them as they seemed about to touch it; then they were dropping slowly into a crater of some sort, seemingly bottomless and widening out rapidly; the roar of the tubes picked up suddenly. Above them, the overscreens showed a pair of translucent slides closing together again. His eyes stared at the height indicator, neither believing nor doubting.

"Hundred and sixty miles down, and trapped in! Tube sounds show air in some amount, at least, even up here. This crazy trap can't be here; there's no reason for it."

"Right now, who cares? We can't go through that slide up there again, so we go down and find out, I guess. Damn, no telling what kind of landing field we'll find when we reach bottom." Fats' lack of excess imagination came in handy in cases like this. He went about the business of jockeying down the enormous crater as if he were docking at York port, too busy with the uncertain blast to worry about what he might find at the bottom. Slim gazed at him in wonder, then fell back to staring at the screens for some indication of the reason behind this obviously artificial trap.

Lhin scratched idly through the pile of dirt and rotten shale, pried out a thin scrap of reddened stone his eyes had missed the first time, and rose slowly to his feet. The Great Ones had been good to him, sending a rockslide just when the old beds were wearing thin and poor from repeated digging. His sensitive nostrils told him there was magnesium, ferrous matter, and sulphur in abundance, all more than welcome. Of course, he'd hoped there might be copper, even as little as the end of his finger, but of that there seemed no sign. And without copper—

He shrugged the thought aside as he had done a thousand times before, and picked up his crude basket, now filled half with broken rock and half with the lichenlike growth that filled this end of the crater. One of his hands ground a bit of rottenstone together with shreds of lichen and he popped the mixture into his mouth. Grace to the Great Ones who had sent the slide; the pleasant flavor of magnesium tickled his tongue, and the lichens were full-flavored from the new richness of the soil around them. Now, with a trace of copper, there would have been nothing left to wish for.

With a rueful twitch of his supple tail, Lhin grunted and turned back toward his cave, casting a cursory glance up at the roof of the cavern. Up there, long miles away, a bright glare lanced down, diffusing out as it pierced through the layers of air, showing that the long lunar day was nearing noon, when the sun would lance down directly through the small guarding gate. It was too high to see, but he knew of the covered opening where the sloping walls of the huge valley ended and the roof began. Through all the millennia of his race's slow defeat, that great roof had stood, unsupported except for the walls that stretched out around in a circle of perhaps fifty miles diameter, strong and more lasting than even the crater itself; the one abiding monument to the greatness that had been his people's.

He knew without having to think of it, that the roof was artificial, built when the last thin air was deserting the Moon, and the race had sought a final refuge here in the deepest crater, where oxygen could be trapped and kept from leaking away. In a vague way, he could sense the ages that had passed since then and wonder at the permanence of the domed roof, proof against all time.

Once, as the whole space about him testified, his had been a mighty race. But time had worked on them, aging the race as it had individuals, removing the vigor of their youth and sending in the slow creepers of hopelessness. What good was existence here, cooped up in one small colony, away from their world? Their numbers had diminished and some of their skill had gone from them. Their machines had crumbled and vanished, unreplaced, and they had fallen back to the primitive, digging out the rocks of the crater walls and the lichens they had cultured to draw energy from the heat and radioactive phosphorescence of the valley instead of sunlight. Fewer young were planted each year, and of the few, a smaller percentage proved fertile, so that their original million fell to thousands, then to hundreds, and finally to a few grubbing individuals.

Only then had they awakened to the danger of extinction, to find it too late. There had been three elders when Lhin was grown, his seed being the only fertile one. Now the elders were gone long years since, and Lhin had the entire length and breadth of the crater to himself. And life was a long series of sleeps and food forages, relieved only by the same thoughts that had been in his mind while his dead world turned to the light and away more than a thousand times. Monotony had slowly killed off his race, but now that its work was nearly done, it had ended. Lhin was content with his type of life; he was habituated, and immune to boredom.

His feet had been moving slowly along with the turning of his thoughts, and he was out of the valley proper, near the door of the shelter carved into the rocky walls which he had chosen from the many as his home. He munched another mouthful of rock and lichen and let the diffused sunlight shine on him for a few minutes more, then turned into the cave. He needed no light, since the rock walls about had all been rendered radioactive in the dim youth of his race, and his eyes were adapted to wide ranges of light conditions. He passed quickly through the outer room, containing his woven lichen bed and few simple furnishings, and back into the combination nursery and workshop, an illogical but ever-present hope drawing him back to the far corner.

But, as always, it was reasonless. The box of rich earth, pulped to a fine loam and watered carefully, was barren of life. There was not even the beginnings of a small red shoot to awaken him to hope for the future. His seed was infertile, and the time when all life would be extinct was growing near. Bitterly he turned his back on the nursery bed.

So little lacking, yet so much! A few hundred molecules of copper salt to eat, and the seeds he grew would be fertile; or those same copper molecules added to the water would render the present seeds capable of growing into vigorous manhood—or womanhood; Lhin's people carried both male and female elements within each member, and could grow the seeds that became their children either alone or with another. So long as one member of the race lived, as many as a hundred young a year could be reared in the carefully tended incubating soil—if the vital hormone containing copper could be made.

But that, it seemed, was not to be. Lhin went over his laboriously constructed apparatus of hand-cut rock bowls and slender rods bound together into tubes, and his hearts were heavy within him. The slow fire of dried lichen and gummy tar burned still, and slow, drop by drop, liquid oozed from the last tube into a bowl. But even in that there was no slightest odor of copper salts. Well, he had tried that and failed. The accumulation of years of refining had gone into the water that kept the nursery soil damp, and in it there had been too little of the needed mineral for life. Almost dispassionately he threw the permanent metal rolls of his race's science back into their cylinders and began disassembling the chemical part of his workshop.

That meant the other solution, harder, and filled with risks, but necessary now. Somewhere up near the roof, the records indicated, there was copper in small amounts, but well past the breathable concentration of air. That meant a helmet and tanks for compressed air, long with hooks and grapples to bridge the eroded sections of the old trail and steps leading up, instruments to detect the copper, and a pump to fill the tanks. Then he must carry many tanks forward, cache them, and go up to make another cache, step by step, until his supply line would reach the top and—perhaps—he could find copper for a new beginning.

He deliberately avoided thinking of the time required and the chances of failure. His foot came down on the little bellows and blue flames licked up from his crude forge as he drew out the hunks of refined metal and began heating them to malleability. Even the shaping of it by hand to the patterns of the ancient records was almost impossible, and yet, somehow, he must accomplish it correctly. His race must not die!

He was still working doggedly hours later when a high-pitched note shot through the cave. A meteor, coming into the fields around the sealing slides of the roof, and a large one! In all Lhin's life there had been none big enough to activate the warning screens, and he had doubted that the mechanism, though meant to be ageless and draw Sun power until the Sun died, was still functioning. As he stood staring at the door senselessly, the whistling note came again.

Now, unless he pressed his hand over the inductance grid, the automatic forces would come into play, twisting the meteor aside and beyond the roof. But he gave no thought to that as he dashed forward and slapped his fingers against the grilled panel. It was for that he had chosen this rock house, once the quarters of the Watchers who let the few scouting rockets of dim past ages in and out. A small glow from the grid indicated the meteor was through, and he dropped his hand, letting the slides close again.

Then he waited impatiently for it to strike, moving out to the entrance. Perhaps the Great Ones were kind and were answering his prayers at last. Since he could find no copper here, they were sending a token from outer space to him, and who knew what fabulous amounts it might contain—perhaps even as much as he could hold in one hand! But why hadn't it struck? He scanned the roof anxiously, numb with a fear that he had been too late and the forces had thrown it aside.

No, there was a flare above—but surely not such as a meteor that size should make as it sliced down through the resisting air! A sharp stinging whine hit his ears finally, flickering off and on; and that was not the sound a meteor would logically make. He stared harder, wondering, and saw that it was settling downward slowly, not in a sudden rush, and that the flare struck down instead of fading out behind. That meant—could only mean—intelligent control! A rocket!

Lhin's mind spun under the shock, and crazy ideas of his ancestors' return, of another unknown refuge, of the Great Ones' personal visit slid into his thoughts. Basically, though, he was severely logical, and one by one he rejected them. This machine could not come from the barren moon, and that left only the fabled planet lying under the bottom of his world, or those that wandered around the Sun in other orbits. Intelligence there?

His mind slid over the records he had read, made when his ancestors had crossed space to those worlds, long before the refuge was built. They had been unable to colonize, due to the oppressive pull of gravity, but they had observed in detail. On the second planet were only squamous things that slid through the water and curious fronds on the little dry land; on his own primary, gigantic beasts covered the globe, along with growth rooted to the ground. No intelligence on those worlds. The fourth, though, was peopled by more familiar life, and like his own evolutionary forerunners, there was no division into animal and vegetable, but both were present in all. Ball-shaped blobs of life had already formed into packs, guided by instinct, with no means of communication. Yet, of the other worlds known, that seemed the most probable as a source of intelligence. If, by some miracle, they came from the third, he abandoned hope; the blood lust of that world was too plainly written in the records, where living mountainlike beasts tore at others through all the rolls of etched pictures. Half filled with dread, half with anticipation, he heard the ship land somewhere near, and started toward it, his tail curved tightly behind him.

He knew, as he caught sight of the two creatures outside the opened
lock of the vessel, that his guess had been wrong. The creatures were
bifurcate, like himself, though massive and much larger, and that meant
the third world. He hesitated, watching carefully as they stared about,
apparently keenly enjoying the air around them. Then one spoke to the
other, and his mind shook under a new shock.

The articulation and intonation were intelligent, but the sounds were
a meaningless babble. Speech—that! It must be, though the words held
no meaning. Wait—in the old records. Slha the Freethinker had touched
on some such thought; he had written of remote days when the Lunar-
ites had had no speech and postulated that they had invented the sounds
and given them arbitrary meaning, and that only by slow ages of use had
they become instinctive in the new-grown infants—had even dared to
question that the Great Ones had ordered speech and sound meanings
as the inevitable complement of intelligence. And now, it seemed, he
was right. Lhin groped up through the fog of his discovery and tightened his thoughts into a beam.

Again, shock struck at him. Their minds were hard to reach, and once
he did find the key and grope forward into their thoughts, it was apparent that they could not read his! Yet they were intelligent. But the one
on whom his thoughts centered noticed him finally, and grabbed at the
other. The words were still harsh and senseless, but the general meaning reached the Moon man. "Fats, what's that?"

The other turned and stared at Lhin's approach. "Dunno. Looks like
a scrawny three-foot monkey. Reckon it's harmless?"

"Probably, maybe even intelligent. It's a cinch no band of political
refugees built this place—nonhuman construction. Hi there!" The one
who thought of himself as Slim—massive though he appeared—turned
to the approaching Lunarite. "What and who are you?"

"Lhin," he answered, noting surprised pleasure in Slim's mind. "Lhin
—me Lhin."

Fats grunted. "Guess you're right, Slim. Seems to savvy you. Wonder
who came here and taught him English."

Lhin fumbled clumsily, trying to pin down the individual sounds to
their meanings and remember them. "No sahffy Enlhish. No who came
here. You—" He ran out of words and drew nearer, making motions
toward Slim's head, then his own. Surprisingly, Slim got it.

"He means he knows what we're thinking, I guess. Telepathy."

"Yeah? Marshies claim they can do it among themselves, but I never
saw one read a human mind. They claim we don't open up right. Maybe
this Ream monkey's lying to you."

"I doubt it. Take another look at the radioactivity meter in the viability tester—men wouldn't come here and go home without spreading the
good word. Anyway, his name isn't Ream—Lean comes closer to the
sound he made, though we'll never get it right." He half sent a thought
to Lhin, who dutifully pronounced his name again. "See? His liquid
isn't . . . it's a glottal stop. And he makes the final consonant a labial,

though it sounds something like our dental. We can't make sounds like that. Wonder how intelligent he is."

He turned back into the ship before Lhin could puzzle out some kind of answer, and was out a moment later with a small bundle under his arm. "Space English code book," he explained to Fats. "Same as they used to teach the Martians English a century ago."

Then to Lhin: "Here are the six hundred most useful words of our language, organized, so it'll beat waiting for you to pick them up bit by bit. You look at the diagramed pictures while I say and think the word. Now. One—w-uh-nn; two—t-ooo. Getting it?"

Fats watched them for a while, half amused, then grew tired of it. "O. K., Slim, you molly-coddle the native awhile and see what you learn. I'm going over to the walls and investigate that radioactive stuff until you're ready to start repairs. Wish radios weren't so darned limited in these freighters and we could get a call through."

He wandered off, but Lhin and Slim were hardly aware of it. They were going through the difficult task of organizing a means of communication, with almost no common background, which should have been worse than impossible in terms of hours. Yet, strange as the word associations and sounds were, and odd as their organization into meaningful groups, they were still only speech, after all. And Lhin had grown into life with a highly complex speech as natural to him as breathing. He twisted his lips over the sounds and nailed the meanings down in his mind, one by one, indelibly.

Fats finally found them in Lhin's cave, tracing them by the sound of their voices, and sat down to watch, as an adult might watch a child playing with a dog. He bore Lhin no ill will, but neither could he regard the Moon man as anything but some clever animal, like the Martians or the primitives of Venus; if Slim enjoyed treating them as equals, let him have his way for the time.

Lhin was vaguely conscious of those thoughts and others more disturbing, but he was too wrapped up in the new experience of having some living mind to communicate with, after nearly a century of being alone with himself. And there were more important things. He wriggled his tail, spread his arms, and fought over the Earth sounds while Slim followed as best he could.

Finally the Earth man nodded. "I think I get it. All of them have died off except you, and you don't like the idea of coming to a dead end. Um-m-m. I wouldn't either. So now you hope these Great Ones of yours —we call 'em God—have sent us down here to fix things up. How?"

Lhin beamed, his face contorting into a furrowed grimace of pleasure before he realized Slim misinterpreted the gesture. Slim meant well. Once he knew what was needed, perhaps he would even give the copper gladly, since the old records showed that the third world was richest of all in minerals.

"Nra is needed. Life comes from making many simple things one not-simple thing—air, drink stuff, eat stuff, all that I have, so I live. But to begin the new life, Nra is needed. It makes things begin. The seed has no life—with Nra it lives. But I had no word."

He waited impatiently while Slim digested that. "Sort of a vitamin or hormone, something like Vitamin E_6, eh? Maybe we could make it, but—"

Lhin nodded. Surely the Great Ones were kind. His hearts were warm as he thought of the many seeds carefully wrapped and stored that could be made to grow with the needed copper. And now the Earth man was willing to help. A little longer and all would be well.

"No need to make," he piped happily. "Simple stuff. The seed or I can make, in us. But we need Nra to make it. See." He pulped a handful of rock from the basket lying near, chewed it carefully, and indicated that it was being changed inside him.

Fats awoke to greater attention. "Do that again, monkey!" Lhin obliged, curious to note that they apparently ate nothing other life had not prepared for them. "Darn. Rocks—just plain rocks—and he eats them. Has he got a craw like a bird, Slim?"

"He digests them. If you've read of those half-plant, half-animal things the Martians came from, you'll know what his metabolism's like. Look, Lhin, I take it you mean an element. Sodium, calcium, chlorine? No, I guess you have all those. Iodine, maybe? Hm-m-m." He went over a couple of dozen he could imagine having anything to do with life, but copper was not among them, by accident, and a slow fear crept up into the Lunarite's thoughts. This strange barrier to communication—would it ruin all?

He groped for the answer—and relaxed. Of course, though no common word existed, the element itself was common in structure. Hurriedly he flipped the pages of the code book to a blank one and reached for the Earth man's pencil. Then, as Slim and Fats stared curiously, he began sketching in the atomic structure of copper, particle by particle, from the center out, as the master physicists of his race had discovered it to be.

It meant nothing to them! Slim handed the paper back, shaking his head. "Fella, if I'm right in thinking that's a picture of some atom, we've got a lot to learn back on Earth. *Wheoo!*"

Fats twisted his lips. "If that's an atom, I'm a fried egg. Come on, Slim, it's sleepy time and you've fooled away half a day. Anyhow, I want to talk that radioactive business over with you. It's so strong it'd cook us in half an hour if we weren't wearing these portable nullifiers —yet the monkey seems to thrive on it. I got an idea."

Slim came back from his brown study and stared at his watch. "Darn it! Look, Lhin, don't give up yet; we'll talk all this over tomorrow again. But Fats is right; it's time for us to sleep. So long, fella."

Lhin nodded a temporary farewell in his own tongue and slumped back on his rough bed. Outside, he heard Fats extolling a scheme of some kind for getting out the radioactives with Lhin's help, somehow, and Slim's protesting voice. But he paid no attention. The atomic structure had been right, he knew, but they were only groping toward it in their science, and their minds knew too little of the subject to enable them to grasp his pictures.

Chemical formulas? Reactions that would eliminate others, one by one? If they were chemists, perhaps, but even Slim knew too little for that. Yet, obviously, unless there was no copper on Earth, there was an answer somewhere. Surely the Great Ones whom they called God would never answer generations of faithful prayer with a mockery! There was an answer, and while they slept, he would find it, though he had to search through every record roll for clues.

Hours later he was trudging across the plain toward the ship, hope again high. The answer, once found, was simple. All elements formed themselves into families and classes. Slim had mentioned sodium, and copper was related in the more primitive tables, such as Earth might use. More important, its atomic number was twenty-nine by theory elementary enough for any race that could build rockets.

The locks were open, and he slipped through both, the wavering half-formed thoughts of the men leading him to them unerringly. Once in their presence, he stopped, wondering about their habits. Already he had learned that what held true for his people was not necessarily the rule with them, and they might not approve of his arousing a sleeper. Finally, torn between politeness and impatience, he squatted on the metal floor, clutching the record roll, his nostrils sampling the metals around him. Copper was not there; but he hadn't expected so rare an element, though there were others here that he failed completely to recognize and guessed were among the heavy ones almost lacking on the Moon.

Fats gurgled and scrimmaged around with his arms, yawned, sat up, still half asleep. His thoughts were full of some Earth person of the female element which Lhin had noted was missing in these two, and what he'd do "when he got rich." Lhin was highly interested in the thought pictures until he realized that it would be best not to intrude on these obviously secret things. He withdrew his mind just as the man noted him.

Fats was never at his best while waking up. He came to his feet with a bellow and grabbed for something. "Why, you sneaking little monkey! Trying to sneak up and cut our—"

Lhin squealed and avoided the blow that would have left him a shapeless blob, uncertain of how he had offended, but warned by caution to leave. Physical fear was impossible to him—too many generations had grown and died with no need of it. But it came as a numbing shock that these beings would actually kill another intelligent person. Was life so cheap on Earth?

"Hey! Hey, Fats, stop it!" Slim had awakened at the sound of the commotion, and a hasty glance showed Lhin that he was holding the other's arms. "Lay off, will you? What's going on?"

But now Fats was fully awake and calming down. He dropped the metal bar and grinned wryly. "I dunno. I guess he meant all right, but he was sitting there with that metal thing in his hands, staring at me, and I figured he meant to cut my throat or something. I'm all right now. Come on back, monkey; it's all right."

Slim let his partner go and nodded at Lhin. "Sure, come back, fella. Fats has some funny ideas about nonhumans, but he's a good-hearted sort, on the whole. Be a good doggie and he won't kick you—he might even scratch your ears."

"Nuts." Fats was grinning, good nature restored. He knew Slim meant it as a crack, but it didn't bother him; what was wrong with treating Marshies and monkeys like what they were? "Whatcha got there, monkey? More pictures that mean nothing?"

Lhin nodded in imitation of their assent gesture and held out the roll to Slim; Fats' attitude was no longer unfriendly, but he was an unknown quantity, and Slim seemed the more interested. "Pictures that mean much, I hope. Here is Nra, twenty-nine, under sodium."

"Periodic table," Slim told Fats. "At least, it looks like one. Get me the handbook, will you? Hm-m-m. Under sodium, No. 29. Sodium, potassium, copper. And it's No. 29, all right. That it, Lhin?"

Lhin's eyes were blazing with triumph. Grace to the Great Ones. "Yes, it is copper. Perhaps you have some? Even a gram, perhaps?"

"A thousand grams, if you like. According to your notions, we're lousy with the stuff. Help yourself."

Fats cut in. "Sure, monkey, we got copper, if that's the stuff you've been yelling about. What'll you pay for it?"

"Pay?"

"Sure, give in return. We help you; you help us. That's fair, isn't it?"

It hadn't occurred to Lhin, but it did seem fair. But what had he to give? And then he realized what was in the man's mind. For the copper, he was to work, digging out and purifying the radioactives that gave warmth and light and life to the crater, so painfully brought into being when the place was first constructed, transmuted to meet the special needs of the people who were to live there. And after him, his sons and their sons, mining and sweating for Earth, and being paid in barely enough copper to keep Earth supplied with laborers. Fats' mind filled again with dreams of the other Earth creature. For that, he would doom a race to life without pride or hope or accomplishment. Lhin found no understanding in it. There were so many of those creatures on Earth—why should his enslavement be necessary?

Nor was enslavement all. Eventually, doom was as certain that way as the other, once Earth was glutted with the radioactives, or when the supply here dropped below the vital point, great as the reserve was. He shuddered under the decision forced upon him.

Slim's hand fell on his shoulder. "Fats has things slightly wrong, Lhin. Haven't you, Fats?"

There was something in Slim's hand, something Lhin knew dimly was a weapon. The other man squirmed, but his grin remained.

"You're touched, Slim, soft. Maybe you believe all this junk about other races' equality, but you won't kill me for it. I'm standing pat—I'm not giving away my copper."

And suddenly Slim was grinning, too, and putting the weapon back. "O. K., don't. Lhin can have my share. There's plenty on the ship in forms we can spare, and don't forget I own a quarter of it."

Fats' thoughts contained no answer to that. He mulled it over slowly, then shrugged. Slim was right enough about it, and could do as he wanted with his share. Anyhow— "O. K. Have it your way. I'll help you pry it off wherever it is, or dig it out. How about that wire down in the engine locker?"

Lhin stood silently watching them as they opened a small locker and rummaged through it, studying the engines and controls with half his mind, the other half quivering with ecstasy at the thought of copper— not just a handful, but all he could carry, in pure form, easily turned into digestible sulphate with acids he had already prepared for his former attempt at collecting it. In a year, the crater would be populated again, teeming with life. Perhaps three or four hundred sons left, and as they multiplied, more and yet more.

A detail of the hookup he was studying brought that part of his mind uppermost, and he tugged at Slim's trouser leg. "That . . . that . . . is not good, is it?"

"Huh? No, it isn't, fella. That's what brought us here. Why?"

"Then, without radioactives, I can pay. I will fix it." A momentary doubt struck him. "That is to pay, is it not?"

Fats heaved a coil of wonderful-smelling wire out of the locker, wiped off sweat, and nodded. "That's to pay, all right, but you let those things alone. They're bad enough, already, and maybe even Slim can't fix it."

"I can fix."

"Yeah. What school did you get your degree in electronics from? Two hundred feet in this coil, makes fifty for him. You gonna give it all to him, Slim?"

"Guess so." Slim was looking at Lhin doubtfully, only half watching as the other measured and cut the wire. "Ever touched anything like that before, Lhin? Controls for the ion feed and injectors are pretty complicated in these ships. What makes you think you can do it—unless your people had things like this and you studied the records."

Lhin fought for words as he tried to explain. His people had had nothing like that—their atomics had worked from a different angle, since uranium was almost nonexistent on the Moon, and they had used a direct application of it. But the principles were plain to him, even from what he could see outside; he could feel the way it worked in his head.

"I feel. When I first grew, I could fix that. It is the way I think, not the way I learn, though I have read all the records. For three hundred million years, my people have learned it—now I feel it."

"Three hundred million years! I knew your race was old when you told me you were born talking and reading, but—galloping dinosaurs!"

"My people saw those things on your world, yes," Lhin assured him solemnly. "Then I shall fix?"

Slim shook his head in confusion and handed over a tool kit without another word. "Three hundred million years, Fats, and during almost all that time they were farther ahead than we are now. Figure that one out. When we were little crawling things living off dinosaur eggs, they were flitting from planet to planet—only I don't suppose they could stay very long; six times normal gravity for them. And now, just because they had to stay on a light world and their air losses made them gather here where things weren't normal, Lhin's all that's left."

"Yeah, and how does that make him a mechanic?"

"Instinct. In the same amount of time, look at the instincts the animals picked up. He has an instinct for machinery; he doesn't know all about it, probably, but he can instinctively feel how a thing should work. Add to that the collection of science records he was showing me and the amount of reading he's probably done, and there should be almost nothing he couldn't do to a machine."

There wasn't much use in arguing, Fats decided, as he watched what was happening. The monkey either fixed things or they never would leave. Lhin had taken snips and disconnected the control box completely; now he was taking that to pieces, one thing at a time. With a curious deftness, he unhooked wires, lifted out tubes, uncoupled transformers.

It seemed simple enough to him. They had converted energy from the atomic fuel, and they used certain forces to ionize matter, control the rate of ionization, feed the ions to the rocket tubes, and force them outward at high speed through helices. An elementary problem in applied electronics to govern the rate and control the ionization forces.

With small quick hands he bent wires into coils, placed other coils in relation, and coupled a tube to the combination. Around the whole, other coils and tubes took shape, then a long feeder connected to the pipe that carried the compound to be ionized, and bus bars to the energy intake. The injectors that handled the feeding of ions were needlessly complicated, but he let them alone, since they were workable as they were. It had taken him less than fifteen minutes.

"It will now work. But use care when you first try it. Now it makes all work, not a little as it did before."

Slim inspected it. "That all? What about this pile of stuff you didn't use?"

"There was no need. It was very poor. Now it is good." As best he could, he explained to Slim what happened when it was used now; before, it would have taken a well-trained technician to describe, even with the complicated words at his command. But what was there now was the product of a science that had gone beyond the stumbling complications of first attempts. Something was to be done, and was done, as simply as possible. Slim's only puzzle was that it hadn't been done that way in the first place—a normal reaction, once the final simplification is reached. He nodded.

"Good. Fats, this is the business. You'll get about 99.99% efficiency now, instead of the 20% maximum before. You're all right, Lhin."

Fats knew nothing of electronics, but it had sounded right as Lhin explained, and he made no comment. Instead, he headed for the control room. "O. K., we'll leave here, then. So long, monkey."

Slim gathered up the wire and handed it to Lhin, accompanying him to the air lock. On the ground as the locks closed, the Moon man looked up and managed an Earth smile. "I shall open the doors above for you to go through. And you are paid, and all is fair, not so? Then—so long, Slim. The Great Ones love you, that you have given my people back to me."

" 'Dios," Slim answered, and waved, just before the doors came shut. "Maybe we'll be back sometime and see how you make out."

Back at the cave, Lhin fondled the copper and waited for the sounds the rockets would make, filled with mixed emotions and uncertainties. The copper was pure ecstasy to him, but there were thoughts in Fats' mind which were not all clear. Well, he had the copper for generations to come; what happened to his people now rested on the laps of the Great Ones.

He stood outside the entrance, watching the now-steady rocket blast upward and away, carrying with it the fate of his race. If they told of the radioactives, slavery and extinction. If they remained silent, perhaps a return to former greatness, and passage might be resumed to other planets, long deserted even at the height of their progress; but now planets bearing life and intelligence instead of mere jungles. Perhaps, in time, and with materials bought from other worlds with ancient knowledge, even a solution that would let them restore their world to its ancient glory, as they had dreamed before hopelessness and the dark wings of a race's night had settled over them.

As he watched, the rocket spiraled directly above him, cutting the light off and on with a shadow like the beat of wings from the mists of antiquity, when winged life had filled the air of the Moon. An omen, perhaps, those sable wings that reached up and passed through the roof as he released the slides, then went skimming out, leaving all clear behind. But whether a good omen or ill, he had not decided.

He carried the copper wire back to the nursery.

And on the ship, Slim watched Fats wiggle and try to think, and there was amusement on his face. "Well, was he good? As good as any human, perhaps?"

"Yeah. All right, better. I'll admit anything you want. He's as good as I am—maybe he's better. That satisfy you?"

"No." Slim was beating the iron while it was hot. "What about those radioactives?"

Fats threw more power into the tubes, and gasped as the new force behind the rockets pushed him back into his seat. He eased up gently, staring straight ahead. Finally he shrugged and turned back to Slim.

"O. K., you win. The monkey keeps his freedom and I keep my lip buttoned. Satisfied?"

"Yeah." Slim was more than satisfied. To him, also, things seemed an omen of the future, and proof that idealism was not altogether folly. Some day the wings of dark prejudice and contempt for others might lift from all Earth's Empire, as they were lifting from Fats' mind. Perhaps not in his time, but eventually; and intelligence, not race, would rule.

"Well satisfied, Fats," he said. "And you don't need to worry about losing too much. We'll make all the money we can ever spend from the new principles of Lhin's hookup; I've thought of a dozen applications already. What do you figure on doing with your share?"

Fats grinned. "Be a damned fool. Help you start your propaganda again and go around kissing Marshies and monkeys. Wonder what our little monkey's thinking."

Lhin wasn't thinking, then; he'd solved the riddle of the factors in Fats' mind, and he knew what the decision would be. Now he was making copper sulphate, and seeing dawn come up where night had been. There's something beautiful about any dawn, and this was very lovely to him.

CLIFFORD D. SIMAK

DESERTION

FOUR men, two by two, had gone into the howling maelstrom that was Jupiter and had not returned. They had walked into the keening gale—or rather, they had loped, bellies low against the ground, wet sides gleaming in the rain.

For they did not go in the shape of men.

Now the fifth man stood before the desk of Kent Fowler, head of Dome No. 3, Jovian Survey Commission.

Under Fowler's desk, old Towser scratched a flea, then settled down to sleep again.

Harold Allen, Fowler saw with a sudden pang, was young—too young. He had the easy confidence of youth, the straight back and straight eyes, the face of one who never had known fear. And that was strange. For men in the domes of Jupiter did know fear—fear and humility. It was hard for Man to reconcile his puny self with the mighty forces of the monstrous planet.

"You understand," said Fowler, "that you need not do this. You understand that you need not go."

It was formula, of course. The other four had been told the same thing, but they had gone. This fifth one, Fowler knew, would go too. But suddenly he felt a dull hope stir within him that Allen wouldn't go.

"When do I start?" asked Allen.

There was a time when Fowler might have taken quiet pride in that answer, but not now. He frowned briefly.

"Within the hour," he said.

Allen stood waiting, quietly.

"Four other men have gone out and have not returned," said Fowler. "You know that, of course. We want you to return. We don't want you going off on any heroic rescue expedition. The main thing, the only thing, is that you come back, that you prove man can live in a Jovian form. Go to the first survey stake, no farther, then come back. Don't take any chances. Don't investigate anything. Just come back."

Allen nodded. "I understand all that."

"Miss Stanley will operate the converter," Fowler went on. "You need have no fear on that particular point. The other men were converted without mishap. They left the converter in apparently perfect condition. You will be in thoroughly competent hands. Miss Stanley is the best qualified conversion operator in the Solar System. She had had experience on most of the other planets. That is why she's here."

Allen grinned at the woman and Fowler saw something flicker across Miss Stanley's face—something that might have been pity, or rage—or just plain fear. But it was gone again and she was smiling back at the youth who stood before the desk. Smiling in that prim, schoolteacherish way she had of smiling, almost as if she hated herself for doing it.

"I shall be looking forward," said Allen, "to my conversion."

And the way he said it, he made it all a joke, a vast, ironic joke.

But it was no joke.

It was serious business, deadly serious. Upon these tests, Fowler knew, depended the fate of men on Jupiter. If the tests succeeded, the resources of the giant planet would be thrown open. Man would take over Jupiter as he already had taken over the other smaller planets. And if they failed—

If they failed, Man would continue to be chained and hampered by the terrific pressure, the greater force of gravity, the weird chemistry of the planet. He would continue to be shut within the domes, unable to set actual foot upon the planet, unable to see it with direct, unaided vision, forced to rely upon the awkward tractors and the televisor, forced to work with clumsy tools and mechanisms or through the medium of robots that themselves were clumsy.

For Man, unprotected and in his natural form, would be blotted out by Jupiter's terrific pressure of fifteen thousand pounds per square inch, pressure that made Terrestrial sea bottoms seem a vacuum by comparison.

Even the strongest metal Earthmen could devise couldn't exist under pressure such as that, under the pressure and the alkaline rains that forever swept the planet. It grew brittle and flaky, crumbling like clay, or it ran away in little streams and puddles of ammonia salts. Only by stepping up the toughness and strength of that metal, by increasing its electronic tension, could it be made to withstand the weight of thousands of miles of swirling, choking gases that made up the atmosphere. And even when that was done, everything had to be coated with tough quartz to keep away the rain—the bitter rain that was liquid ammonia.

Fowler sat listening to the engines in the sub-floor of the dome. Engines that ran on endlessly, the dome never quiet of them. They had to run and keep on running. For if they stopped, the power flowing into the metal walls of the dome would stop, the electronic tension would ease up and that would be the end of everything.

Towser roused himself under Fowler's desk and scratched another flea, his leg thumping hard against the floor.

"Is there anything else?" asked Allen.

Fowler shook his head. "Perhaps there's something you want to do," he said. "Perhaps you—"

He had meant to say write a letter and he was glad he caught himself quick enough so he didn't say it.

Allen looked at his watch. "I'll be there on time," he said. He swung around and headed for the door.

Fowler knew Miss Stanley was watching him and he didn't want to turn and meet her eyes. He fumbled with a sheaf of papers on the desk before him.

"How long are you going to keep this up?" asked Miss Stanley and she bit off each word with a vicious snap.

He swung around in his chair and faced her then. Her lips were drawn into a straight, thin line, her hair seemed skinned back from her forehead tighter than ever, giving her face that queer, almost startling death-mask quality.

He tried to make his voice cool and level. "As long as there's any need of it," he said. "As long as there's any hope."

"You're going to keep on sentencing them to death," she said. "You're going to keep marching them out face to face with Jupiter. You're going to sit in here safe and comfortable and send them out to die."

"There is no room for sentimentality, Miss Stanley," Fowler said, trying to keep the note of anger from his voice. "You know as well as I do why we're doing this. You realize that Man in his own form simply cannot cope with Jupiter. The only answer is to turn men into the sort of things that can cope with it. We've done it on the other planets.

"If a few men die, but we finally succeed, the price is small. Through the ages men have thrown away their lives on foolish things, for foolish reasons. Why should we hesitate, then, at a little death in a thing as great as this?"

Miss Stanley sat stiff and straight, hands folded in her lap, the lights shining on her graying hair and Fowler, watching her, tried to imagine what she might feel, what she might be thinking. He wasn't exactly afraid of her, but he didn't feel quite comfortable when she was around. Those sharp blue eyes saw too much, her hands looked far too competent. She should be somebody's Aunt sitting in a rocking chair with her knitting needles. But she wasn't. She was the top-notch conversion unit operator in the Solar System and she didn't like the way he was doing things.

"There is something wrong, Mr. Fowler," she declared.

"Precisely," agreed Fowler. "That's why I'm sending young Allen out alone. He may find out what it is."

"And if he doesn't?"

"I'll send someone else."

She rose slowly from her chair, started toward the door, then stopped before his desk.

"Some day," she said, "you will be a great man. You never let a chance go by. This is your chance. You knew it was when this dome was picked for the tests. If you put it through, you'll go up a notch or two. No matter how many men may die, you'll go up a notch or two."

"Miss Stanley," he said and his voice was curt, "young Allen is going out soon. Please be sure that your machine—"

"My machine," she told him, icily, "is not to blame. It operates along the co-ordinates the biologists set up."

He sat hunched at his desk, listening to her footsteps go down the corridor.

What she said was true, of course. The biologists had set up the co-ordinates. But the biologists could be wrong. Just a hairbreadth of difference, one iota of digression and the converter would be sending out something that wasn't the thing they meant to send. A mutant that might crack up, go haywire, come unstuck under some condition or stress of circumstance wholly unsuspected.

For Man didn't know much about what was going on outside. Only what his instruments told him was going on. And the samplings of those happenings furnished by those instruments and mechanisms had been no more than samplings, for Jupiter was unbelievably large and the domes were very few.

Even the work of the biologists in getting the data on the Lopers, apparently the highest form of Jovian life, had involved more than three years of intensive study and after that two years of checking to make sure. Work that could have been done on Earth in a week or two. But work that, in this case, couldn't be done on Earth at all, for one couldn't take a Jovian life form to Earth. The pressure here on Jupiter couldn't be duplicated outside of Jupiter and at Earth pressure and temperature the Lopers would simply have disappeared in a puff of gas.

Yet it was work that had to be done if Man ever hoped to go about Jupiter in the life form of the Lopers. For before the converter could change a man to another life form, every detailed physical characteristic of that life form must be known—surely and positively, with no chance of mistake.

Allen did not come back.

The tractors, combing the nearby terrain, found no trace of him, unless the skulking thing reported by one of the drivers had been the missing Earthman in Loper form.

The biologists sneered their most accomplished academic sneers when Fowler suggested the co-ordinates might be wrong. Carefully they pointed out, the co-ordinates worked. When a man was put into the converter and the switch was thrown, the man became a Loper. He left the machine and moved away, out of sight, into the soupy atmosphere.

Some quirk, Fowler had suggested; some tiny deviation from the thing a Loper should be, some minor defect. If there were, the biologists said, it would take years to find it.

And Fowler knew that they were right.

So there were five men now instead of four and Harold Allen had walked out into Jupiter for nothing at all. It was as if he'd never gone so far as knowledge was concerned.

Fowler reached across his desk and picked up the personal file, a thin sheaf of papers neatly clipped together. It was a thing he dreaded but a thing he had to do. Somehow the reason for these strange disappearances must be found. And there was no other way than to send out more men.

He sat for a moment listening to the howling of the wind above the dome, the everlasting thundering gale that swept across the planet in boiling, twisting wrath.

Was there some threat out there, he asked himself? Some danger they did not know about? Something that lay in wait and gobbled up the Lopers, making no distinction between Lopers that were *bona fide* and Lopers that were men? To the gobblers, of course, it would make no difference.

Or had there been a basic fault in selecting the Lopers as the type of life best fitted for existence on the surface of the planet? The evident intelligence of the Lopers, he knew, had been one factor in that determination. For if the thing Man became did not have capacity for intelligence, Man could not for long retain his own intelligence in such a guise.

Had the biologists let that one factor weigh too heavily, using it to offset some other factor that might be unsatisfactory, even disastrous? It didn't seem likely. Stiffnecked as they might be, the biologists knew their business.

Or was the whole thing impossible, doomed from the very start? Conversion to other life forms had worked on other planets, but that did not necessarily mean it would work on Jupiter. Perhaps Man's intelligence could not function correctly through the sensory apparatus provided Jovian life. Perhaps the Lopers were so alien there was no common ground for human knowledge and the Jovian conception of existence to meet and work together.

Or the fault might lie with Man, be inherent with the race. Some mental aberration which, coupled with what they found outside, wouldn't let them come back. Although it might not be an aberration, not in the human sense. Perhaps just one ordinary human mental trait, accepted as commonplace on Earth, would be so violently at odds with Jovian existence that it would blast all human intelligence and sanity.

Claws rattled and clicked down the corridor. Listening to them, Fowler smiled wanly. It was Towser coming back from the kitchen, where he had gone to see his friend, the cook.

Towser came into the room, carrying a bone. He wagged his tail at Fowler and flopped down beside the desk, bone between his paws. For a long moment his rheumy old eyes regarded his master and Fowler reached down a hand to ruffle a ragged ear.

"You still like me, Towser?" Fowler asked and Towser thumped his tail.

"You're the only one," said Fowler. "All through the dome they're cussing me. Calling me a murderer, more than likely."

He straightened and swung back to the desk. His hand reached out and picked up the file.

Bennett? Bennett had a girl waiting for him back on Earth.

Andrews? Andrews was planning on going back to Mars Tech just as soon as he earned enough to see him through a year.

Olson? Olson was nearing pension age. All the time telling the boys how he was going to settle down and grow roses.

Carefully, Fowler laid the file back on the desk.

Sentencing men to death. Miss Stanley had said that, her pale lips scarcely moving in her parchment face. Marching men out to die while he, Fowler, sat here safe and comfortable.

They were saying it all through the dome, no doubt, especially since Allen had failed to return. They wouldn't say it to his face, of course. Even the man or men he called before this desk and told they were the next to go, wouldn't say it to him.

They would only say: "When do we start?" For that was formula.

But he would see it in their eyes.

He picked up the file again. Bennett, Andrews, Olson. There were others, but there was no use in going on.

Kent Fowler knew that he couldn't do it, couldn't face them, couldn't send more men out to die.

He leaned forward and flipped up the toggle on the intercommunicator.

"Yes, Mr. Fowler."

"Miss Stanley, please."

He waited for Miss Stanley, listening to Towser chewing half-heartedly on the bone. Towser's teeth were getting bad.

"Miss Stanley," said Miss Stanley's voice.

"Just wanted to tell you, Miss Stanley, to get ready for two more."

"Aren't you afraid," asked Miss Stanley, "that you'll run out of them? Sending out one at a time, they'd last longer, give you twice the satisfaction."

"One of them," said Fowler, "will be a dog."

"A dog!"

"Yes, Towser."

He heard the quick, cold rage that iced her voice. "Your own dog! He's been with you all these years—"

"That's the point," said Fowler. "Towser would be unhappy if I left him behind."

It was not the Jupiter he had known through the televisor. He had expected it to be different, but not like this. He had expected a hell of ammonia rain and stinking fumes and the deafening, thundering tumult of the storm. He had expected swirling clouds and fog and the snarling flicker of monstrous thunderbolts.

He had not expected the lashing downpour would be reduced to drifting purple mist that moved like fleeing shadows over a red and purple sward. He had not even guessed the snaking bolts of lightning would be flares of pure ecstasy across a painted sky.

Waiting for Towser, Fowler flexed the muscles of his body, amazed at the smooth, sleek strength he found. Not a bad body, he decided, and grimaced at remembering how he had pitied the Lopers when he glimpsed them through the television screen.

For it had been hard to imagine a living organism based upon ammonia and hydrogen rather than upon water and oxygen, hard to believe that such a form of life could know the same quick thrill of life that humankind could know. Hard to conceive of life out in the soupy maelstrom that was Jupiter, not knowing, of course, that through Jovian eyes it was no soupy maelstrom at all.

The wind brushed against him with what seemed gentle fingers and he remembered with a start that by Earth standards the wind was a roaring gale, a two-hundred-mile an hour howler laden with deadly gases.

Pleasant scents seeped into his body. And yet scarcely scents, for it was not the sense of smell as he remembered it. It was as if his whole being was soaking up the sensation of lavender—and yet not lavender. It was something, he knew, for which he had no word, undoubtedly the first of many enigmas in terminology. For the words he knew, the thought symbols that served him as an Earthman would not serve him as a Jovian.

The lock in the side of the dome opened and Towser came tumbling out—at least he thought it must be Towser.

He started to call to the dog, his mind shaping the words he meant to say. But he couldn't say them. There was no way to say them. He had nothing to say them with.

For a moment his mind swirled in muddy terror, a blind fear that eddied in little puffs of panic through his brain.

How did Jovians talk? How—

Suddenly he was aware of Towser, intensely aware of the bumbling, eager friendliness of the shaggy animal that had followed him from Earth to many planets. As if the thing that was Towser had reached out and for a moment sat within his brain.

And out of the bubbling welcome that he sensed, came words.

"Hiya, pal."

Not words really, better than words. Thought symbols in his brain, communicated thought symbols that had shades of meaning words could never have.

"Hiya, Towser," he said.

"I feel good," said Towser. "Like I was a pup. Lately I've been feeling pretty punk. Legs stiffening up on me and teeth wearing down to almost nothing. Hard to mumble a bone with teeth like that. Besides, the fleas give me hell. Used to be I never paid much attention to them. A couple of fleas more or less never meant much in my early days."

"But . . . but—" Fowler's thoughts tumbled awkwardly. "You're talking to me!"

"Sure thing," said Towser. "I always talked to you, but you couldn't hear me. I tried to say things to you, but I couldn't make the grade."

"I understood you sometimes," Fowler said.

"Not very well," said Towser. "You knew when I wanted food and when I wanted a drink and when I wanted out, but that's about all you ever managed."

"I'm sorry," Fowler said.

"Forget it," Towser told him. "I'll race you to the cliff."

For the first time, Fowler saw the cliff, apparently many miles away, but with a strange crystalline beauty that sparkled in the shadow of the many-colored clouds.

Fowler hesitated. "It's a long way—"

"Ah, come on," said Towser and even as he said it he started for the cliff.

Fowler followed, testing his legs, testing the strength in that new body of his, a bit doubtful at first, amazed a moment later, then running with a sheer joyousness that was one with the red and purple sward, with the drifting smoke of the rain across the land.

As he ran the consciousness of music came to him, a music that beat into his body, that surged throughout his being, that lifted him on wings of silver speed. Music like bells might make from some steeple on a sunny, springtime hill.

As the cliff drew nearer the music deepened and filled the universe with a spray of magic sound. And he knew the music came from the tumbling waterfall that feathered down the face of the shining cliff.

Only, he knew, it was no waterfall, but an ammonia-fall and the cliff was white because it was oxygen, solidified.

He skidded to a stop beside Towser where the waterfall broke into a glittering rainbow of many hundred colors. Literally many hundred, for here, he saw, was no shading of one primary to another as human beings saw, but a clear-cut selectivity that broke the prism down to its last ultimate classification.

"The music," said Towser.

"Yes, what about it?"

"The music," said Towser, "is vibrations. Vibrations of water falling."

"But, Towser, you don't know about vibrations."

"Yes, I do," contended Towser. "It just popped into my head."

Fowler gulped mentally. "Just popped!"

And suddenly, within his own head, he held a formula—the formula for a process that would make metal to withstand the pressure of Jupiter.

He stared, astounded, at the waterfall and swiftly his mind took the many colors and placed them in their exact sequence in the spectrum. Just like that. Just out of blue sky. Out of nothing, for he knew nothing either of metals or of colors.

"Towser," he cried. "Towser, something's happening to us!"

"Yeah, I know," said Towser.

"It's our brains," said Fowler. "We're using them, all of them, down to the last hidden corner. Using them to figure out things we should have known all the time. Maybe the brains of Earth things naturally are slow and foggy. Maybe we are the morons of the universe. Maybe we are fixed so we have to do things the hard way."

And, in the new sharp clarity of thought that seemed to grip him, he knew that it would not only be the matter of colors in a waterfall or metals that would resist the pressure of Jupiter, he sensed other things, things not yet quite clear. A vague whispering that hinted of greater things, of mysteries beyond the pale of human thought, beyond even the pale of human imagination. Mysteries, fact, logic built on reasoning. Things that any brain should know if it used all its reasoning power.

"We're still mostly Earth," he said. "We're just beginning to learn a few of the things we are to know—a few of the things that were kept from us as human beings, perhaps because we were human beings. Because our human bodies were poor bodies. Poorly equipped for thinking, poorly equipped in certain senses that one has to have to know. Perhaps even lacking in certain senses that are necessary to true knowledge."

He stared back at the dome, a tiny black thing dwarfed by the distance.

Back there were men who couldn't see the beauty that was Jupiter. Men who thought that swirling clouds and lashing rain obscured the face of the planet. Unseeing human eyes. Poor eyes. Eyes that could not see the beauty in the clouds, that could not see through the storms. Bodies that could not feel the thrill of trilling music stemming from the rush of broken water.

Men who walked alone, in terrible loneliness, talking with their tongue like Boy Scouts wigwagging out their messages, unable to reach out and touch one another's mind as he could reach out and touch Towser's mind. Shut off forever from that personal, intimate contact with other living things.

He, Fowler, had expected terror inspired by alien things out here on the surface, had expected to cower before the threat of unknown things, had steeled himself against disgust of a situation that was not of Earth.

But instead he had found something greater than Man had ever known. A swifter, surer body. A sense of exhilaration, a deeper sense of life. A sharper mind. A world of beauty that even the dreamers of the Earth had not yet imagined.

"Let's get going," Towser urged.

"Where do you want to go?"

"Anywhere," said Towser. "Just start going and see where we end up. I have a feeling . . . well, a feeling—"

"Yes, I know," said Fowler.

For he had the feeling, too. The feeling of high destiny. A certain sense of greatness. A knowledge that somewhere off beyond the horizons lay adventure and things greater than adventure.

Those other five had felt it, too. Had felt the urge to go and see, the compelling sense that here lay a life of fullness and of knowledge.

That, he knew, was why they had not returned.

"I won't go back," said Towser.

"We can't let them down," said Fowler.

Fowler took a step or two, back toward the dome, then stopped.

Back to the dome. Back to that aching, poison-laden body he had left. It hadn't seemed aching before, but now he knew it was.

Back to the fuzzy brain. Back to muddled thinking. Back to the flapping mouths that formed signals others understood. Back to eyes that now would be worse than no sight at all. Back to squalor, back to crawling, back to ignorance.

"Perhaps some day," he said, muttering to himself.

"We got a lot to do and a lot to see," said Towser. "We got a lot to learn. We'll find things—"

Yes, they could find things. Civilizations, perhaps. Civilizations that would make the civilization of Man seem puny by comparison. Beauty and more important—an understanding of that beauty. And a comradeship no one had ever known before—that no man, no dog had ever known before.

And life. The quickness of life after what seemed a drugged existence.

"I can't go back," said Towser.

"Nor I," said Fowler.

"They would turn me back into a dog," said Towser.

"And me," said Fowler, "back into a man."

ROBERTSON OSBORNE

CONTACT, INCORPORATED

ON the thirty-third day out of Earth Central, the *Special Agent* heterodyned itself out of w-space and re-entered the normal continuum. The little 1400-ton vessel fell free toward the fifth planet of Procyon for half an hour before planetary drive was applied to slow it into an orbit.

Allan Stuart, linguist, in this maiden mission of CONTACT, INCORPORATED, felt seasick again during the period of free fall. Of the six men aboard, he was the only one who hadn't spent at least one hitch in the Solar System Patrol. He was doggedly trying to steady his nerves by floating a row of dictionaries in midair when the intercom startled him. It was the voice of James Gordon, ship's captain and head of the new firm.

"All hands! We start spiraling in shortly and we should land on Azura in about five hours. Nestor, relieve White in the drive room. The rest of you come on up to Control for a final briefing."

The bony little linguist sighed, put away his books, and unstrapped himself. Nausea made him hiccup. Detouring sadly around the intricate day-old wreckage of what had been a beautiful cephaloid unit, he swung stiffly out of the lab. In the corridor he had to squeeze past a badly torn-up wall. Dan Rogers, one of the two planetary scouts, shut off a welding torch and coasted along with him.

"Little old piece of nickel-iron sure raised heck, didn't it, Mr. Stuart?" drawled the scout. "Come out into normal space for two minutes to get a bearing, and—WHAM!" He propelled himself along with the effortless efficiency of a man accustomed to doing without gravity.

Stuart, correcting course with some difficulty, took a moment to answer. "Hm? Oh, the meteor! Yes, indeed it did. My leg is still stiff,

---

First published under the title "Action on Azura," this story was originally called "Contact, Incorporated" by the author, as a gesture of obligation to Will Jenkins, whose Murray Leinster story, "First Contact," served as the inspiration for this one. "First Contact," which appeared in *The Best of Science Fiction*, dealt with the incredible difficulties encountered by two alien civilizations—ours and another —in getting in touch with each other *in mid-space*. Mr. Osborne writes: " 'Contact, Incorporated' was inspired by the problem set forth in Leinster's great 'First Contact,' " and it was for that reason, obviously, that a title so closely allied to Leinster's was the author's own choice. It is used here at his request.

and of course half my equipment is just junk now. But I guess we were rather fortunate at that, since none of us was killed. All the way to Procyon . . . three point four parsecs. Dear me!" He clucked, shaking his head, and wondered again how the other five men in the crew could take these things so casually.

He drifted into the control room with Rogers and hovered near the desk. Brettner, the other scout, came in playing some outlandish sort of guitar; White, engineer and assistant astrogator, joined him in a final caterwauling chorus of "The Demon of Demos."

The ship's captain swung his chair to face them, his angular face folding into a responsive grin. Then he waved a teletape at the four men and looked more serious.

"Here's Patrol's latest summary of the situation," he announced. "Still no response from Procyon V, otherwise known as Azura. No activity in the ruined cities. No further clashes with traders, because the traders have given up. However, the natives are still taking pot-shots from the woods at any scouting parties that dare to sit down on the planet. Every attempt at contact is fiercely rejected.

"The Patrol lads, naturally, are forbidden to shoot back, at least until they find out what this is all about . . . which, of course, is where our own little expedition of specialists comes in. Incidentally, it seems fairly certain the natives know nothing of radio, so we'll be safe in using microwave to feel our way down in the dark."

He accepted a cigarette from Rogers and nodded toward a month-old report titled: Unofficial Data as of 31 October 2083; Procyon V (Azura).

"I know we have precious little to go in there with, but that's the situation. A million credits from Earth Central, if we establish friendly contact." He smoked awhile, gray eyes on the ceiling. Then, as nobody spoke, he added: "The Patrol has had two more skirmishes, not far from here, with what we've called the Invader culture. None of their ships has been captured, but it's fairly certain they're the same vicious crowd we've fought near Rigel, Alpha Centauri, and so on. They seem to be heading this way again slowly. Here . . ."

He handed out half a dozen photographs of strange-looking spacecraft. They're undoubtedly the gang that blew hell out of Azura a few years ago, before we got here, and gave the natives such a violent dislike of strangers. The Invader's weapons are somewhat inferior to ours, but he apparently has the considerable advantage of having superior position in regard to bases . . . particularly around here. The patrol simply can't stand up to a determined attack in this region unless a base is made available, preferably on Azura."

Brettner said, softly, "That's what we're really after, isn't it? Nobody's handing us a million credits just for cultural purposes."

The leader of the expedition nodded. "Yep. Once we talk to these Azurans, I think we can convince them we all have a common enemy.

An enemy who seems to enjoy smashing things just for fun. I have a hunch the Azurans expect the Invaders back, too . . . that might account for their apparent determination to remain hidden." He reached for the log. "Incidentally, what's the latest on the damage situation?"

Stuart shook his head unhappily and brushed hair out of his eyes. "One cephaloid is completely ruined. It was the one I had trained to translate into Universal Speech from whatever other language would be fed into it later. I was going to teach it what Azuran I could pick up and use it as a direct interpreter. We have to use Universal Speech, you see, because cephaloids simply can't handle homonyms such as 'see' and 'sea,' or 'threw' and 'through.' However," his worried look lessened, "the multiple analyzer is all right. And the stand-by, originally conditioned only for generalized language response, has been restrained in Universal Speech and will learn Azuran from the analyzer."

He managed a feeble smile. "After all, the natives are manlike, and we know they had a city culture much like ours, so there is a good possibility of our finding mutually intelligible symbols. And we know what their language sounds like, thanks to the trader who got away with a recording."

White spoke up. "I hope you weren't counting too much on the portable teleview, Mr. Stuart. It's a total loss. So is the long-range microphone. It's going to be tough to study their language at a distance." He looked at Gordon. "The ship is okay, chief, except for the debris we're still cutting away. All the animals are dead; I guess you knew that. And all we've salvaged from the jeep is the power unit and one repulsor. We'll have to walk where we can't use the scout-ship."

Brettner, when the captain looked at him, said quietly: "We're awful low on food. Just about enough to get us back, with three or four days to spare. Can't we eat any of this Azuran stuff?"

Gordon shook his head. "The water and air are all right, but there's no food for us down there. Good thing, in a way."

He laughed at the surprised expressions. "All Terrestrial life is based on complexes of iron, magnesium, or copper, but Azuran life seems to be built on cobalt complexes. Consequently both sides are immune to the diseases of the other. You remember the terrible plagues that hit the Terrestrial port areas in the old days, and the grim effects of our landings on Alpha Centauri III and Proxima II. But the biostat labs report that Terrestrial and Azuran tissue cultures have only a toxic effect on each other . . . no parasitic viability whatever."

He looked up at the chronometer. "About time to begin our spiral, if we're to land before daybreak in that area we picked out. Let's get some sleep. White, you'll relieve me for a couple of hours, soon as we've established our trajectory."

Stuart, on the way out, picked up the sheaf of papers summarizing what was known about Azura. He strapped into his bunk absent-mindedly and lay there trying to visualize his first non-solar planet. Many kinds of intelligent animals, the reports agreed. Evidently a mutation leading to intelligence had occurred quite early in the diversification of the animal phyla.

One of the traders, said the report, claimed he had even learned to converse in a limited way with what he called monkey-rats. These had about the intelligence of a five-year-old human, and displayed the group cooperation common to many Azuran forms.

Too bad the trader hadn't been able to stay there longer. He had finally found some of the natives, just at the time they had found him. He was preparing to leave his ship and accept their thanks for the fine gifts he had set out, when gifts, trees, and nearby boulders began to blow up all around. He had taken off without further discussion.

Four other traders and three Patrol ships had failed. A small freighter, landing to make emergency repairs, had disappeared. The only weapon the natives had, apparently, was a disrupter of some sort, with a range of only two or three kilometers. But the wreckage of the cities showed plainly that the Invaders had used weapons of the same type as Earth's, probably with a range of hundreds of kilometers. That meant—

He awoke, struggling, as if from a nightmare. The klaxon was sounding off, jarring his teeth. Gordon's slightly nasal voice came over the loudspeaker: "Landing stations, everybody. We're sitting down in fifteen minutes."

The linguist hastily unfastened his safety belts, rolled out, and scrambled into primary space gear. "Secondary equipment?" he asked Rogers, who was getting dressed beside him.

"Naw, no armor. Leave your oxygen off, too. This is a Class E planet, just like home."

Stuart scrambled down to the control room and strapped himself in beside the stern-view screen. He could hear White and Brettner in the drive room, sleepily arguing about who had mislaid the coffee jug. Such nonchalance! he thought. Trembling with excitement, he nearly dropped his camera. "I wonder how soon I can get some pictures," he muttered. "If I could only photograph our landing . . . that would really liven up the next meeting of the Philological Society!" He had already taken over a hundred pictures of the expedition, and his hobby was the subject of much ribbing from the rest of the six-man corporation.

Gordon looked over from the control board and interrupted his thoughts. "Stuart! See anything out there?"

A dial over the linguist's head indicated only a hundred meters to go. His screen showed a dark landscape, illuminated by two of the four moons. "Tree directly below," he announced. "Better move to the red side about twenty meters."

The vessel shifted slightly and eased down smoothly under Gordon's practised handling. Relays clacked; the drive hummed softly.

Suddenly a rough branch scraped along the side, making metallic echoes in the double walls. Seconds later the ship settled with a gritty crunching. A few kicks of the drive leveled it off.

There was profound silence for a moment after the drive died away. Someone yelled "Wahoo!" Then Rogers came clattering down the ladder. He beckoned to Stuart, who was already climbing out of the seat eagerly.

"Time for the landing party," said the scout. He eyed the camera. "Remember now, play your cards close to your chest. Don't go skittering off to take pictures. First we patrol once around the ship, then we get the camouflage nets pegged down, right away. Then we sit tight 'til we've had a good look around in daylight."

As they approached the arms locker, they found Nestor drawing out three blast rifles. He held out two of them. "Your weapons, gentlemen," said the chubby engineer, bowing. "I'm guarding the airlock while you're out there. And next time we cut cards for this little privilege, I'm going to shuffle the deck myself. Six years in the Patrol before this trip, and I've been first-to-land only once in my life!"

The linguist smiled, feeling his taut nerves relax a bit. He pushed the Outside Test button beside the lock at the end of the corridor. A green light flashed. "Air's already been okayed," Nestor told him.

Stuart pushed another button. The inner door withdrew from its permoid gasket and swung aside. The three men clanked into the echoing airlock chamber, where a touch on a third stud slid shut the inner door and opened the outer.

The night lay mysterious before them, full of exotic odors, unfamiliar sounds, and double shadows. The slender linguist clambered like an eager monkey down the fin rungs and stood inhaling deeply.

He was adjusting his camera when Rogers whispered in his ear, "Come on, let's make a tour around the clearing." Into his microphone, the scout reported: "Beginning our circuit, chief. Circling counterclockwise."

Rifles unslung, the two began walking cautiously. They had gone about halfway, and Stuart was studying the two moons, when his feet were abruptly yanked out from under him and he fell to the ground. The patch of pinkish grass under him seemed to ripple, rolling him over and over helplessly until he was brought up against a rounded hummock. Before he could struggle to his feet, he came floundering back again to be dumped at the edge of the patch. Sitting up dazedly, he found Rogers looking for something to shoot at.

"What the devil happened?" whispered the scout. Gordon's voice came over the earphones: "What's going on down there? All I can hear up here in the turret is grunts and whispers, but what I see sure looks screwy!"

Stuart got up lamely, rubbing his sore leg. "I was sniffed at and rejected, in a manner of speaking," he answered. "Watch." He drew his hand gun, which happened to be the most convenient thing, and tossed it on the animated grass before the flabbergasted scout could stop him. Immediately it was whisked away to the central hump, brushed with feelers, and sent tumbling back to his feet. "A most intriguing experience," murmured the linguist, studying the pink grass with his head cocked to one side. "I shall have to try it again when there's more time." He picked up the gun and limped away on patrol.

Rogers, with an expression of surprised scorn and amusement on his handsome face, explained briefly to Gordon what had happened. As he caught up with Stuart, he glanced toward the nose of the *Special Agent*. "See anything yet, chief?"

In the nose turret, two gun barrels continued their sweep. "Nope," came back Gordon's voice. There's a broad prairie just beyond the trees on the 'East' side of this clearing, if you remember. Plain as day in this double moonlight. Almost looks like my home state, except for a few hills of that phosphorescent coral rock. Maybe—HEY! Some kind of critters running toward the hills! About five kilometers away. Flashes . . ." He broke off, as if absorbed in watching.

The two men on the ground slowly continued their patrol, listening intently. In about fifteen seconds, above the faint rustling of the leaves in the pre-dawn breeze, they heard far-off snarling roars, mingled with crackling explosions. Almost total silence followed, as if the whole forest were listening. "All quiet," Gordon reported after a while. "Must have been what the traders called hell-cats, attacking some native settlement. Looks like we made a fair guess about where to find some natives."

"We also know where they keep some of their popguns," added Rogers sarcastically.

Gordon's voice chuckled. "Patrol says the only known weapon has an apparent range of two or three kilometers at most, and probably is not portable."

The scout looked skeptical. "Patrol says," he repeated sourly. "Apparently, probably, maybe. I notice our old buddies haven't cared to get within a hundred kilometers of said popgun."

When the tour around the ship had been completed, Rogers looked up. "Okay, chief. Ready for the nets."

Far up in the nose appeared a black hole. White climbed out and spread a conical camouflage net over the nose. Then he ducked back into the ship. "Here comes the first strip," said Gordon. "I hope this gimmick works!" A slot opened behind the skirt of the conical net, and a sheet of neolon camouflage unrolled downward. Rogers seized the bundle of stakes at its lower end and had the strip pegged down in a few seconds, with willing but ineffectual help from the inexperienced Stuart.

"All right so far," the scout reported. Another strip came down. Stuart grabbed the stakes, then put them down to rearrange the rifle slung across his back. Suddenly there was a blur of movement and the stakes disappeared around a fin.

Rogers, carrying the rubber mallet, walked up and nudged him.

"Come on! Dawn's about to break, laddie. What are you staring at?" His own eyes widened as the bundle of stakes came back and dropped near his feet. He whipped out a flashlight and revealed a pair of "monkey-rats" scurrying away. He laughed and shook his head. "Things around here have a cockeyed way of putting back what they don't want. I suppose these fellers were after metal, like Venus blacksmith lizards."

The two men resumed working, and at length the entire ship was tented. Not long after they had finished, the light was strong enough to show the beady-eyed little monkey-rats sitting nearby, watching curiously. The fearless creatures, as large as cocker spaniels, were an indeterminate red-gray in color, four-legged, and had two six-fingered tentacles where Stuart expected a muzzle. Bright black eyes looked out from under bony ridges. The monkey-rats carried short spears, and seemed to have pouches slung on their backs.

"Too bad we can't feed 'em," murmured the scout. "I bet we can make friends with them. We better explore a little more, though, first." Stuart strolled with him to where a narrow neck of turf led from the clearing out to the prairie. A brook followed this little alley into the woods.

Rogers pointed to the near bank, where a miniature scaffolding of bright orange and blue matchsticks stood a few centimeters high. "Construction plant," said the linguist, remembering a trader's description. Nearby were three mossbacks, looking like turtles with tufts of green on their backs. "Possibly symbiotic," Stuart thought to himself. The creatures dabbled their forelegs in the water and blinked sleepily.

The monkey-rats, following the men, apparently discovered the mossbacks just then; there was a sudden squirrel-like chittering sound as one of them pointed with a tentacle. Immediately two small spears flashed through the early morning light and chunked into one of the mossbacks. The creature squawked once and fell over; its companions looked at it stupidly for a moment, then dove clumsily into the brook. The monkey-rats dashed over to their prey, seized it with their tentacles, and began to hustle it toward the nearby trees.

Without warning, a sky-colored creature like a hawk swooped over them and dropped a rock. One of the monkey-rats was hit in the leg and fell sprawling. The other whistled with rage and hurled an ineffectual spear. The hawk came back a moment later and began to bomb them with more rocks. The injured one was being half-carried by its companion, and both were screaming angrily.

Rogers scowled at the battle. "Looks like he doesn't want to leave his friend," he growled. Suddenly he whipped out a hunting-knife, aimed for an imperceptible split second, and let fly. The hawk was slashed open down the belly from head to tail. It flopped heavily onto the patch of pink grass, snapping with vicious gray teeth in dying hatred. The uninjured monkey-rat ran to retrieve the knife.

The two men went to look at the wounded one and found it dragging a bleeding hind leg. It seemed especially shocking to Stuart, somehow, that the blood was red, although of a more brilliant shade than that of Terrestrial mammals. The creature turned to face the men, waving a spear defensively and shrilling for help. Its companion came charging up with the knife and two spears. The two forms of life eyed each other for a moment.

"Here's your opportunity to make friends with them," urged Gordon over the radio. "They seem accustomed to manlike beings. Maybe they can be of some use to us. Worth trying, anyway."

The scout squatted and made soothing sounds. Stuart backed away a few steps, so as to represent less of a threat, and began taking pictures as unobtrusively as possible.

Rogers studied the situation in a moment, then extended his empty hands, palms up, in response to a whispered suggestion from the semanticist. Both monkey-rats cocked their heads and watched him sharply, murmuring to each other.

Moving slowly as Stuart directed, the scout tore a strip of bandage from his first-aid packet and allowed it to be examined. He reached for one of the wooden spears, needle-tipped with something like obsidian, but it was withdrawn hastily. He broke off a small branch from a nearby bush and tried to splint the broken leg. The creature squealed and snapped at him, but neither monkey-rat threatened him with a weapon. They seemed more curious than afraid.

Nonplussed for a moment, the Earthman whistled softly, thinking. "Give them your other knife," suggested Stuart. The scout drew it out and dropped it hastily before a spear could be launched at him.

Two knives! The creatures examined them with obvious pleasure, testing the blades and inspecting them closely. Again Rogers reached out; this time his touch was tolerated. "Warm-blooded," he said quietly into his microphone. "Feels like two bones in the upper leg." He succeeded in straightening the limb and tying it up. Then he pantomimed carrying the victim and pointed into the woods. The other monkey-rat pushed the injured one toward him and made tentacle motions which evidently meant "yes." He picked up the one with the broken leg, carried it a short distance into the woods, and set it down. The other followed, bristling with knives and spears. Stuart came behind at a discreet distance, observing carefully and making notes. Occasionally he snapped a picture.

The scout poured some water into the palm of his hand and offered it. The injured animal shot out a tubular orange tongue and sucked up the water. The two men were trying to establish further communication when suddenly their earphones crackled.

"You men outside! Stand by the neck of the clearing! There's been some shooting over near those coral rocks, and here comes a native hell-for-leather with three hell-cats after him. Heading for the clearing, I think. Try to catch him . . . he seems to be unarmed. We'll get out and hold off the hell-cats from up here!"

Rogers was belly-down in the grass at one side of the entrance before Gordon finished talking. Stuart dashed after him, noticing absently as he passed the pink grass that it was churning and enveloping the carcass of the dead hawk. He reached the edge of the clearing and took up a position across the brook from Rogers. He could see nothing but dust through the grass and heavy scrub. The canteen gouged into his flank, and his holster seemed caught in a root. He struggled to get the blast rifle unslung from his back, wishing for the twentieth time that he had had at least a little experience at this sort of thing. Just one hitch in the Patrol, for instance . . .

The radio broke in on his whispered swearing. "You might have to do some shooting down there. These machine-guns may not stop all the hell-cats dead in their tracks, but I don't want to use anything bigger . . . no use letting the neighborhood know what we've got."

A few seconds later the native came pounding desperately through the alley into the clearing. "Hold him!" yelled the scout. Stuart sprang to his feet with a leveled rifle and confronted the astounded humanoid, who collided with a tree and stopped. Nestor came dodging out through the nets to cover the prisoner with another gun. The brilliant red manlike creature, obviously understanding the weapons, still tried to edge away from the squalling roars of the hell-cats not far behind on the prairie.

The twin sixty-millimeter guns in the nose burst out with a clatter. The noise of the exploding projectiles was deafening. Clumps of dirt and scrub flew high into the air. Then Nestor's blast rifle roared once, sharply.

Abruptly there was silence. The Azuran had obviously discovered the ship behind the camouflage; he stared at it, blinked, and stared again, as though in disbelief. Stuart began taking pictures of him. "No more cats," came Gordon's voice. "They were bunched up and Nestor got 'em all. Ah, I notice our new friend has seen through the camouflage net."

The native's reaction was sudden, unexpected. He shuddered and slumped to the ground, a picture of dejection. His tentacles were limp. Nothing would induce him to communicate. At length Stuart offered water; the native suddenly arose, as if in a hopeless rage, knocked the canteen aside, and kicked the linguist's injured leg. Then the red being sank to the ground again.

"Damn!" growled Stuart through clenched teeth. He rubbed his leg. "I suppose he thinks we're the Invaders, coming back to ravage his people again. Either he never saw the Invaders himself, or we happen to resemble them. Or maybe the terror of the invasion was so great that a serious semantic confusion exists, labelling all strangers as Bad. Well, at any rate, I'll have to go through some semantic analysis to establish any rapport at all." Meditating on the problem, he sent Nestor back to the ship for drawing materials, and bent over to retrieve the canteen. The native immediately knocked him flat and fled into the woods.

Rogers started after the Azuran, unslinging his gun, but Gordon spoke up from the airlock, where he had been about to climb down to the ground. "Dan! Get out of those woods, you half-wit! Let him go; you can't possibly catch him. Anyway, we may be able to see where he goes, if he breaks out into open country again. White, will you keep an eye on the edge of the woods from up there? Be ready to man the 'scope. I'll be right up."

Nestor sat down beside the linguist a few minutes later and held out a cup of fragrant coffee. "Here, Mr. Stuart. I figured you guys could use breakfast better than drawing materials right now. Feel okay?"

Stuart sipped and nodded gratefully. "Mmm. Yes, fine, thanks."

The plump little flight engineer handed him a sandwich. "You're due for relief about now anyway. The boss and I will be out here, and White and Brettner inside. You and Rogers can sleep awhile."

The linguist leaned back against a tree and lit a cigarette. "Has the native showed up again?" he asked his microphone.

White answered. "Yeah. He high-tailed it across the prairie and disappeared among the coral rocks. Chief says for you to come in, Stuart; he wants to know what you found out."

Stuart picked up his rifle, canteen, camera, and cup. He wondered vaguely, as he trudged wearily over to the ship, how he had gotten so tired. Then he realized that, like the others, he had gotten only five hours' sleep in the past two nights. Procyon was yellow-white and hot on his back, even through the netting, as he clambered up the fin rungs. He felt sleepy.

In the captain's crowded little cabin he dropped into a chair and yawned. Gordon stretched, scratching lazily, and grinned at him. "Bored, on your first day ashore?"

The linguist smiled ruefully. "Tired, yes, but hardly bored. I don't mind admitting the first few hours have been rather disappointing. We had a native right here, I stood face to face with him, and we even saved his life . . . well, no use yowling about it. I presume he's gone off to warn the others now. Our element of surprise, as you fellows say, is lost." He brushed the hair out of his eyes. "What shall we do about it, Gordon?"

The leader drummed on the desk awhile. "I dunno. This sort of situation was never covered in Patrol courses. Maybe the General Staff studies this stuff, but I was just a line officer, like the other guys. If you remember, we figured we'd sort of make up our operations plan as we went along. You probably know as much about it as we do, from all your reading. Nothing predictable about any of this; we just have to react to whatever develops. What would you suggest?"

"Um. Well, I've a half-formed scheme for—er, seizing the bull by the horns. The natives are certain to react immediately, either by attacking us or by disappearing again. I feel that we should assume the initiative as soon as possible, without waiting for them to maneuver one of their weapons within range of us."

"How do we assume the initiative?"

"Yes, exactly—how?" The semanticist shook his head. "I'll have to sleep on it at least a little while, Gordon. Right now I feel unable to think. But somehow we have to convey to the Azurans the knowledge that we are friendly. We'll have to find some way of representing the idea to them."

"Drop leaflets," suggested Gordon, wryly. "Or put up one of those billboards they used to have all over a hundred years ago. Everybody in the universe must have become accustomed to some kind of advertising by now!" He laughed heartily. "Okay, Stuart. Go fall into your bunk. Let's hope you wake up with a good idea!"

The thoughtful little language expert got up to leave. "Billboard. Billboard . . . there may be something in that, even if you were joking."

His musings were broken off by the alarm bell and the intercom's squawk. "All hands! Battle stations! Chief, three natives just popped up from a hole in the ground about two hundred meters away. Strong radar indication."

As Stuart ran down to his post at the airlock, he heard Gordon's calm voice from the intercom. "All right, Brettner. Keep them covered, but don't fire."

At the lock, the linguist remembered to punch the personnel buttons as the men climbed in, out of breath and swearing. He pushed the stud beside his own name last and shut the lock as the "All Aboard" shone green.

Gordon spoke again, apparently to someone in the control room with him. "They've evidently lugged a disrupter or something along a tunnel. Seem to have a couple of big beasts of burden carrying a gadget . . . looks like one of those old pack howitzers. Let's wait 'til they get it nearly assembled, so we can get an idea of——hup! Let's GO!"

Stuart had forgotten to buckle his safety straps. He just had time to grab a stanchion when the violent acceleration tripled his weight and nearly threw him to the floor. No more than a heartbeat later, there was a muffled boom from outside the ship, and a section of blazing tree went rocketing past the glassite window.

After a few seconds' acceleration he felt the ship take on a horizontal component. The pressure eased off. He got up from his hands and knees and adjusted the periscope controls until he got a view of the ground. There was a group of burning trees several kilometers below, sliding rapidly to the east. Several times the scenery shifted rapidly as the ship zigzagged.

As he swung the 'scope, Stuart was thunderstruck to discover a hole blasted in the edge of a fin, not four meters away from where he stood. Shreds of charred camouflage netting fluttered in tangled strings.

On the intercom, White's voice broke the tense silence. "Gimme that again, slowly, somebody. What happened, anyway?"

Gordon answered. "That must have been a tunnel they came out of, right at the edge of the woods. Maybe they use it to get home if hellcats happen to catch them out on the prairie. That fellow we caught today was probably heading for it, hoping to lose the cats in the woods first."

After a moment, he added, "Anyway, they showed up with a heavy weapon and nearly got us. Patrol guessed wrong about its portability, and I guessed wrong about its operation."

Stuart commented, "Good thing someone happened to be on duty in the turret, and we were able to take off on such short notice."

"*Happened!*" barked the captain. "Mr. Stuart, that's the first rule of *any* ship landing on territory listed as 'unsafe,' and it 'happens' to be Rules Seven through Sixteen of the Patrol Regulations!"

Brettner eased the linguist's embarrassment by changing the subject a little. "Did you all see the colossal helpers they had carrying that weapon? Must be what the traders called heffalumps . . . I thought the pictures were fakes. Those critters practically did the shooting themselves, and they were talking to the natives! This is some planet—everybody talks to everybody except us!"

Gordon spoke again. "White, I want you to rig up a mosaic alarm with controls in the turret, Number One Lock, and control room . . . before tonight, if possible. Jury-rig it, just so it goes off when anything larger than a mossback moves near the ship. Get as much range as you can."

"That means dismantling the space-probe and comparator, boss. Not enough spare checkerboards to scan three hundred and sixty degrees with a decent vertical coverage. And for stereo-perception, so the thing can discriminate between a nearby leaf and a far-away heffalump——"

"All right, do the best you can. Can you hook it up with an infra-red snooper for night work? I don't believe the natives can see infra-red . . . I hope. Procyon's a little farther toward the blue than Sol is."

"I'll see what I can do. Can't get very good resolution with the electro-optical stuff we have for infra-red. We had to weed out four tons, you know, and the Hollmann scanners are three and a half parsecs back, in our shop."

Stuart noticed that the ship's course had steadied. A look through the 'scope showed the recently abandoned clearing now swinging under the stern again, far below. He was about to take a picture of it when Gordon called him.

"Stuart, will you go to the drive room and give Nestor a hand? He's scanning the area with microwave, and I want you to use the stern-view telescope. Those characters may have decided to go back to their base without using the tunnel; maybe we can keep out of sight and get a good fix on where they hole up."

The linguist retracted the periscope and saw to it that the guard plates slid over the outer lens. Then he dodged through the radiation trap into the darkened drive room. He was wondering how to strap himself into the seat without taking off all his photographic gear, when Nestor, peering into the radar screen, snapped his fingers.

"Got a blip, Gordon," said the engineer with supressed excitement.

"One metallic object about the size of a foot-locker, maybe a little bigger. Boy, do those rocks show up! Must be nearly all metal."

In a moment the leader answered. "I believe I see something. Awkward angle, though, on this turret telescope. How about you, Stuart?"

"No, frankly, I——"

Gordon cut in. "What magnification are you using?"

"Let me see . . . all I can get—sixty-four diameters."

"Too much; cut it down to twelve. Center your 'scope. Now look at the crosshair grids. Find the lower part of F-7; you should see something around there."

"More likely F-6 from here," put in Nestor. "That's where my indication is."

"Oh, yes! I see them. Three natives and two . . . my goodness, those heffalumps *are* big! Almost as big as elephants!"

Gordon answered, "Yes, and apparently considerably more useful. Well, keep a sharp watch on the group. Let me know where they go, and be sure you mark the spot on a large-scale sketch or photo. I've got to send off a report to Patrol; we're keeping them posted on every development."

"Like a bomb-defusing squad," said Nestor hollowly. "The next crew will take up where we left off, see?"

The ship, swinging slowly ahead of the little raiding party, came to a stop about six kilometers above and slightly beyond the coral rocks.

White spoke over the intercom. "I don't think they'll see us here. We're in the sun. But keep yourselves strapped in, gang; we're going to move in a hurry if they point that thing at us. You guys below let me know if they do anything suspicious. I can't see too much on the control room screens."

In the drive room, the power hummed softly. Relays clicked occasionally as the minutes passed. The creatures on the ground entered a faint trail winding among the hills of bright coral rock. Now and then one of the heffalumps stopped and adjusted the load on his back, using the middle two of his six limbs. Nestor nudged the language expert's arm.

"Looks like they're getting close to home. Better get set to take some pictures."

Stuart nodded, having already picked up a plate magazine, and loaded the camera box on the side of the telescope. He adjusted the controls from time to time with nervous delicacy, occasionally tapping the shutter button. Suddenly he switched to higher magnification, exclaiming, "There they go! Into that cave!" He took three pictures in rapid succession at different magnifications. He also banged his nose hard on the eyepiece, and wondered some hours later how it came to be so tender.

There was a clatter of feet on the steel ladder. Gordon came running over to him, an unfinished report in one hand and a half-eaten hamburger in the other. "Lessee," he demanded.

The linguist showed him. Only the cave mouth could be seen now, black in the hot sunlight. It was halfway up a hill of dense coral, and was protected from the front by another hill.

The chief took a bite of hamburger and grinned at Stuart. "This is a bit of luck," he said happily through the mouthful. "We wouldn't have found that hideout in ten years if they hadn't taken a potshot at us!"

Nestor exhaled cigarette smoke, looking cynical. "Swell. What do we do now? Wave a hankie at them?"

Gordon's expression became less cheerful. "We don't know yet. Things have moved a little fast. But whatever we do, we'll have to get it done fast. You guys might as well know now what came in a little while ago on the radio." He drew a deep breath. "An Invader base has been discovered—within striking distance of this area. It's a jolt, of course, but at least we've finally discovered a base of theirs. Earth Central says either we close this deal in four days or the planet will have to be taken over the hard way."

Stuart shook his head sadly, thinking of the already-ruined cities below. "Our little firm had better live up to its name," he said.

Gordon nodded. "A task force is already on the way."

Brettner had come cat-footed down the ladder. "There's one way to hustle things up," he growled, patting his hip holster. "I wish you'd let me blister their stern-plates a little. Little old Frontier Lawyer here would teach 'em some manners right now!"

Stuart repressed a shudder.

The captain strode over and confronted the scout with a frown. "That's what we're here to avoid, Mr. Brettner, and you know it. Our weapons are purely for defense, and there'd be hell raised if we harmed any natives. If we got out of here alive, we'd lose our million credits and all our expenses, as well as being tried for unauthorized warlike acts." He sounded hoarse with fatigue and irritation. "Get over any belligerent ideas you may have. That goes for all of you—at least on this trip."

He looked sternly at the group a moment, then nodded toward the ladder. "Let's go have a conference. Nestor, will you stay here and keep a sharp eye on that hideout?"

The chubby engineer leaned back in the seat, swung the eyepiece over into a comfortable position, and sighed. "Yeah, all right. Somebody better bring me some food before long, though. I'm dying."

Up in the "conference room," the men gathered about Gordon at the controls. He checked the autopilot and sat drumming his fingers on the desk. Finally he looked squarely at the language expert. "Mr. Stuart . . . it seems fairly obvious now that the outcome of this entire expedition depends almost solely on you. You're the one who knows how to convey ideas, probably as well as any human being alive, according to the information we got before we asked you to join us. All the rest of us can do is run this ship and make like space-fighters."

He raised a hand at Stuart's beginning protest, and went on. "Let me finish my little speech. You're trained for this sort of thing, even if you do lack non-Terrestrial experience. You figured out the elements of the Alpha Centauri II and IV languages from nothing but sound movies, a few years back. Now, what I'm getting at is this: you tell us what has to be done, and we'll try to figure out a way to do it. We're starting from scratch, of course; that meteor, by a million-to-one chance, ruined all our previous plans."

Stuart pulled at his ear a moment. "Well, all those plans were designed to give me at least the minimum amount of observation I'd need to prepare a friendly message. Now, while my stock of Azuran symbols is still zero, we've gained some information. It's too bad we lost the horses and bloodhounds, for the combination can't be beaten when it's a matter of finding someone in hiding. However, we do know where at least three natives are. And personally, I don't regret it a bit that I'll not make use of those hasty riding lessons."

He paused, and White spoke up. "Even if we do know where some of them are, I don't see how we can use Plan One. How can we set up hidden microphones and telicons, when the ruddy natives live in a cave?"

Brettner, looking disgusted, added, "Even when we catch one of the critters by dumb luck, he won't talk. Trained not to. And that tears up the second plan."

The captain nodded. "And our third scheme . . . to watch and wait, using long-range equipment, and play for the breaks. That sure seemed like a flexible plan. But of course it was blown all over the Milky Way along with our food. Anyway, the news from Patrol makes speed essential."

There was glum silence for a while. Then Rogers offered, "There must be some way we can use our knowledge of where at least three of them are hiding—even if the place is defended with a natural barricade and a souped-up pack howitzer."

After a thoughtful moment, the little language expert cleared his throat hesitantly. "Er—I should like to suggest something . . ." They all looked at him, making him feel rather self-conscious, but he went on. "You said something about an old-fashioned billboard, Gordon, that got me thinking. I have a good many pictures of the expedition and our activities—" he reddened, remembering the frequent ribbings about his photographic activity "—and I can make a few sketches for the rest of it. You see, I was thinking we could sneak down there at night and leave a series of pictures where the natives would find them in the morning."

He was talking rapidly now, full of steam, pacing back and forth. "The pictures would show that we are *not* the Invaders, that we are friendly—I took pictures of Rogers helping the monkey-rats, for instance—and then we could have a couple of pictures of Terrestrials and Azurans exchanging gifts." He stopped, embarrassed, wondering whether his scheme sounded naive to these practical men. "It—it's been tried before with considerable success . . . in some cases."

Gordon thought it over awhile, rubbing the stubble on his cheeks. "Might work," he mused aloud. "What about setting up an automatic-sequence gimmick of some kind, controlled from here while we watch their reaction with a telescope? We could turn the pages, see? . . . or should we just tack up a string of pictures along the path?"

Rogers sat forward. "Machine might be better, if we can rig it up soon enough. Separate pictures might get blown away or something, for all we know, or some kind of critter might destroy 'em."

Stuart stopped pacing and squinted at the ceiling. "Yes, I like the machine. We could include a little pick-up unit so I could record and analyze their comments, knowing just what they were looking at. That would really help a lot." He snapped his fingers, struck with inspiration. "What about ending the little show with a real surprise? A gift that would really demonstrate our good intentions?"

What did he consider a suitable gift?

"A blast rifle!" he answered boldly.

"What the devil!" exclaimed Gordon. The others indicated various degrees of consternation. They stared at Stuart as if he had suggested turning pirate. But he showed a firmness that was new to them—and to himself.

"Nothing else will do the trick as simply and surely," he insisted. "In the first place, their most desperate need, as they see it right now, is probably an efficient but simple weapon of some sort, capable of being enlarged into a heavy defensive piece of great range. I understand our blast rifle is such a weapon. I believe they live in absolute terror of another attack, and they apparently have little or no technology left with which to prepare for such an attack. Hence their going underground."

He paused to let the point sink in. "And in the second place, it seems reasonable to believe they would understand our good intentions from such a gift. Surely they will see that no one planning an aggressive move is going to arm his intended victims first! Their behavior certainly indicates that they are accustomed to direct action, rather than to Machiavellian subtleties of plot and counter-plot."

Nestor stuck out a skeptical lower lip. "How will they know we're making a gesture that means anything? I mean, they still might figure the gun is just a little toy in our league, and that we're not running any risk at all by giving it to them."

Stuart hesitated before replying. He nodded in appreciation of intelligent analysis. "That's a difficult point which will have to be worked out later . . . possibly on the spot. First of all, we shall have to establish contact. It will also be necessary to show them we have a defensive screen, too—which they would doubtless be overjoyed to have—and that we are willing to turn it off and trust them. It will be a delicate and intriguing problem in psycho-logic."

Rogers shook his head and laughed a little. "It sounds as cockeyed as 'Uncle Willie' Ulo's stories about Sirius V. But, so help me, I believe it'd work!" All at once his expression changed, and he looked hard at the expert. "One thing, though, mister. I know I wouldn't care for the job! Who's going to be the guinea-pig and go down for the first little chat with them?"

Stuart smiled thinly. "Who will bell the cat, eh? Another fair question. Well, I shall set up the apparatus, and of course I intend to try out its effect, too. I shall confront the natives myself after they have received our picture message and the gun."

The others protested, but there was a stubborn set to his jaw. "After all," he explained later to Gordon, "while you fellows have been acquiring glamor, so to speak, I've been leading a rather dull life. I intend to have at least one little fling at dangerous living. Besides, I'm the only really expendable man in the crew . . . the rest of you are necessary to the operation of the *Special Agent*. And anyway, I'm only here because I know something about communicating ideas. This is part of my job, if anything is."

The rest of the day and a major part of the night, except for brief catnaps, were spent in fabricating the device which Gordon designed to Stuart's specifications. Even White's work on the mosaic alarm was suspended. The linguist planned, sketched, and worked with his photographs for ten hours before allowing himself to rest. He had done all he could with his part of the project, and decided to lend a hand in the shop . . . but first he would massage the leg which had been so painfully gouged when the meteor struck. He sat down to ease the ache, and promptly fell asleep.

When they woke him three hours later, his machine was ready. In his meticulous way, he had made careful notes of the picture sequence, and the other five members of Contact, Incorporated had arranged everything as indicated. He examined the device sleepily, rubbing the back of his neck and yawning. "Looks okay," he grunted. "Controls tested? Good. Nice job, very nice." Still blinking, he helped carry the makeshift metal-and-plastic assembly into the scout ship in Number Three Lock.

Brettner climbed in and sat down next to him at the controls. "Sort of a lucky thing for us this old planet has four moons," grinned the scout. "All four were in the sky until a few minutes ago. Too much light for us to pussyfoot around on the surface, so you and I had a chance for a nap. Now there's only two . . . just enough for us to work by. We'll have to hustle though."

A few minutes later, under Brettner's skillful handling, the little ship settled to a quick, silent landing about two kilometers from the cave. The scout got out and began unloading the apparatus. Stuart, now fully alert, held a low-voiced radio conversation with Gordon. "Still no sign of any activity?"

The captain's voice was blurred with fatigue. "No, nothing, except some infra-red indications of large animals to the south. We'll keep you informed. For Pete's sake, be careful."

The linguist, nervous as he was, chuckled. "Good of you to remind us." He put on his bone-conduction earpiece, throat-mike, and all the other gear designed for planets with breathable atmospheres. Clambering out of the little vessel, he joined Brettner. The two men helped each other with the slings of their backpacks, locked up the ship, and started off.

Stuart had to run occasionally to keep up with the other's easy, practised stride. The extra rifle and his half of the apparatus jounced and dug into his back. Occasionally he heard Brettner whisper into his mike, asking for directions. The compass was useless near the iron-bearing coral rocks.

Like the scout, Stuart had studied the route in advance, but traversing it in the dark was a grimly different matter. The double shadows of the two moons were confusing and made him stumble. Once a sensitive bush of some kind shuddered and drew back with a moan when he grasped it for support. He shuddered and brushed sweat off his face and sleeve. What did anyone know, after all, about the number of dangerous organisms this planet harbored? Carnivorous plants, for instance, or even animals, might not have sense enough to avoid iron complexes such as human blood . . .

Something soft beneath his foot shrieked horribly in the night and slid away. He went down on one knee, but waved when Brettner turned as if to help him up. "I'm letting this get me," he thought angrily. He got up and jogged along again, trying to imitate the scout's powerful stride.

Abruptly they came upon the trail. They had just started along it when a warning came from the *Special Agent*. "One of those animals on the prairie must have picked up your scent. Probably a hell-cat. Sloping off toward the trail now. Ye gods! . . . he must be doing sixty kilometers! Now he's slowing . . . you should see him about a hundred meters ahead in a few seconds. He's sneaking onto the trail."

The linguist's heart thudded as he crouched in shadow with the scout. "What do we do, Brettner?" he whispered.

"Have to use this," the other replied, hauling out a wide-barrelled, clumsy looking Texas Slugger. "Picked up this sweetheart on Callisto, but I only got three shells." He aimed down the path through an offset sight. "Don't get behind this, laddie."

In the moonlight farther up the trail, a sinuous beast like a huge armor-plated cat glided out from the brush. It opened jaws a meter wide, showing double rows of dull green phosphorescent teeth, and began to lope toward the men. The scout fired when it was less than sixty meters away, and a rocket-propelled projectile hissed out toward it. A few meters out, the 2000-G drive of the projectile cut in, and the missile crashed into the hell-cat with terrible impact.

The creature was a hollow mass of pulp almost instantaneously. The only sounds had been the brief hiss of the rocket, the even shorter crackling of the accelerated drive, and an earth-shuddering crunch when the device had struck a wall of rock beyond the beast. Apparently these had not alarmed the other nocturnal creatures about, for the various animal cries went on as before.

"Come on," said the scout, resuming the trail. "We got to hurry." Stuart followed, wrinkling his nose at the horrible stench of the dead animal. Nearby, a brightly glowing hole in the rock showed where the missile had buried itself and disintegrated.

By the time the men reached their objective, a little trailside clearing just out of sight from the cave, the language expert was thoroughly winded. It was some satisfaction to him to note that the scout was sweating heavily too. Brettner unshouldered his equipment, took a sip of water from his canteen, and moved up the path a few meters to keep watch on the cave. The opening glowed less brightly than the luminescent rock around it.

Stuart worked as rapidly as he could in the moonlight and ghostly shine of the hill. His footing was uncertain on the irregular coral. Twice he stopped and crouched, rifle ready, as his sensitive ears detected a change in the pattern of night sounds. A wild assortment of odors drifted with the faint breeze; once a friendly little creature smelling like fragrant Scotch offered him a pebble and giggled. In his anxious haste, the linguist dropped two bolts into the twisted crevices of the rock, and he began to feel he was having a nightmare.

When the assembly was nearly completed, Nestor warned over the radio, "Better step on it, guys. We can see daylight coming from up here. You have about half an hour to get away." By the time the device was operating satisfactorily, there was enough light to see clearly. The two men on the ground picked up the tools and canteens hastily and hurried back along the trail.

They had gone about halfway when a stone the size of a baseball landed with a vicious clank on the scout's headgear. He swore softly and sagged against a bush, fighting dizzily to stay on his feet. Stuart snatched up a smaller rock and hurled it at the attacking stone-hawk, which was banking into another dive in the dim morning light. The stone smashed one wing. The creature spun and flopped through the air, screaming and gobbling, until it crashed into a tree and fell dead.

Brettner shook his head and grinned ruefully. "Good thing I got a wooden head . . . Yeah, I'm okay." He examined the dent in his helmet, and spit contemptuously at the dead hawk. "That's some arm you've got, mister," he added respectfully.

Stuart examined his arm, pleased. "Used to pitch on the varsity," he explained. "Did you hear the mouthings of that vicious bird? He was swearing at us, I'm sure!" He resumed the march, wondering absently whether all these Azuran creatures spoke basically the same language. From what little he had been able to observe, it seemed likely.

It was almost full daylight when they reached their scout ship.

"Come on up," Nestor told them. "No sign of activity around the cave yet, but you better keep between it and the sun just in case somebody peeks." Brettner took off immediately.

Ten minutes later Stuart was seated at his apparatus, stuffing breakfast food into his mouth and feeling very tired. "Been making this stuff for a hundred and fifty years," he grumbled to himself, chewing doggedly, "and it's still lousy." Suddenly he dropped his spoon and adjusted the view-screen controls. Gordon walked in, buttoning up his dungarees and yawning. "Brother," said the chief, "when we get back we're going to sleep for two weeks!" He looked at the busy linguist and was immediately wide awake. "What's up?"

Stuart pointed to the screen. "Native just peeked out." He reached over toward one of the cephaloids, mindless brains with tremendous memory and associative power, and began flipping switches. Activating solution flowed through the microcellular colloid; little lights on a panel winked on as the surface potentials reached operating level.

The linguist glanced briefly at the screen. "I guess there's time to show you one of its little tricks, just to warm it up," he said. He sang, in Universal Speech, a couple of ribald verses of "The Venus of Venus," then touched a switch. Immediately the song came back at him through a little speaker, but in English—and with the unmistakable drawl of Rogers. "I conditioned it a few minutes ago with his voice," explained Stuart. He was delighted with Gordon's reaction of incredulous astonishment. "It's really a wonderful mechanism, Gordon. It—oops! There's a native!"

He jabbed hastily at the "Primary Condition" stud, erasing the song and the accent, and switched on the remote control for the picture sequence. He handed Gordon a headset. "Will you monitor the pickup, please? The rest of this stuff will keep me busy." He fell silent, watching the screen.

Gordon reached over and switched on the movie camera set up beside him to record the scene.

Three scarlet natives had come out of the cave. They stood in a patch of brilliant sunlight, swinging their middle limbs about and playing with a sassy little monkey-rat as men would with a fox terrier. At length they picked up what seemed to be a crossbow and several spears, slung bundles across their sloping shoulders, and started down the trail. They walked slowly, spears at the ready, and were obviously alert. Frequently they glanced up, or paused as if listening.

Rounding a turn, the lead native stopped abruptly, leaped back and dropped flat. The other two dropped almost simultaneously. The leader motioned cautiously for his companions to crawl forward; he pointed with a tentacular upper limb toward the picture sequence machine gleaming in the morning light. On it was showing a picture of a native, enlarged from Stuart's picture of his temporary "prisoner."

The semanticist had evidently made a good guess in alien psychology, for no hostile move was made toward the machine. The natives lay there studying it, making occasional guarded gestures to each other. They stiffened as the next picture flipped into view. It was a Terrestrial family with two children. It was the picture Stuart kept beside his bunk, and was the best thing he could think of to put across the concept of a peaceful people.

Still no hostile move. No sounds, either, except the background chirping and jabbering of other animals.

Anxiously, Stuart fussed with his controls. He flipped to the next picture and a dozen after that without getting an audible response. The natives were shown views of Terrestrial life, New York and the space-port, the *Special Agent,* and two views of the receding Earth.

Then the linguist tried one of his sketches. It showed a globular ship, such as the Invaders were believed to have used, attacking the Terrestrial ship. In the following sketches, the Earth ship was damaged, but managed to destroy the other.

One of the natives was evidently jolted into comment at this point. "Aru!" came distinctly over the loudspeaker. Stuart immediately murmured "Picture Fifteen" in Universal Speech into his microphone. He beamed at Gordon, relaxed a little, and hit the sequence button again.

The next set of pictures showed the approach to Azura, the landing, and Rogers' kindly treatment of the monkey-rats. Again a comment came from the middle native, evidently younger and less well-trained. This time he uttered several syllables, which the cephaloid duly absorbed. The rear native thwacked him across the back angrily. Stuart bounced in his seat with silent glee. He made microscopic adjustments to the analyzer and continued the show.

Behind him, the door opened quietly. Rogers came in with some breakfast for Gordon. The scout raised his eyebrows inquiringly; the chief winked and nodded at the screen, holding up a hand in the "okay" gesture. Stuart looked around at them, his finger hesitating over the sequence button. He shut off his mike for a moment. "This is one of the parts I'm dubious about. We swing into our sales talk here. Man sees native, puts down gun, and approaches peacefully. Then they exchange gifts."

He pushed the stud thoughtfully. "If the response to this is favorable, do you think we ought to go ahead with the rest?"

The chief frowned. "Sure. Why not?"

"Well . . . I suppose it would be foolish to stop now. I don't have enough material yet to prepare a verbal message, and they seem to be understanding this one anyway. On the other hand . . . they might not like this. It shows us helping them to rebuild a city, and giving them weapons." He lit a cigarette and hit the button again. "They might wonder what we want in return."

Gordon put down his coffee and scratched his chin. "Well, I don't think we ought to revise our plans now, Stuart. I think they'd be glad to offer us a base, in return for protection. We might as well go ahead."

The linguist nodded. The minutes passed as he continued the series of pictures. After a while he opened his mouth to say something, but was interrupted by a gabble of sounds from the pickup unit. The natives were pointing upward and discussing something. Pilot lights on the cephaloid hookup showed that the material was being received, passed back and forth for analysis, and stored away. Stuart threw in a key word now and then to identify the picture being shown.

"It's clear that they understand," he whispered. "Now for the clincher. We help them fight off the Invaders. I hope they don't get the idea that our presence would make another Invader attack more likely."

He continued to push the stud every twenty or thirty seconds, lips moving as he counted. When the counter showed the end of the sequence approaching, he nodded in satisfaction. The natives were still talking to each other. "Good thing we've got these cephaloids," Stuart whispered. "An electronic analyzer could never sort out the three voices. Nor could any linguist alive, for that matter."

Once again he paused, finger hovering. "This is where we show them pictures of a blast rifle, how to use it, and so on—and then the magic box opens and we give them one." His whisper was faint, and he swallowed. "Should I go ahead?" He seemed to be asking himself.

Gordon studied him a few seconds. "Play it your own way, Stuart. The risk is yours, so the decision ought to be."

The linguist put out his cigarette with trembling fingers. "Yes . . . I realize that I talked you into letting me go ahead with my own plan. But . . . you see . . . well, I've never done anything especially brave or dangerous, as all you fellows have. The plan *might* be made to work out without my actually going down there in person. I've been wondering what you would say if I . . . backed out."

The chief got up and clapped him on the back, awkwardly. "Why, not a thing, Stuart. Wouldn't say a word. A man's personal project is his own, in this kind of business. Long as it doesn't affect the welfare of anyone else, he can volunteer for, or refuse, any job."

Stuart smiled slowly and sat up straight. "Then I'll go ahead. I just wanted to be sure I could have backed out if I'd wanted to. If I do something worthwhile, I want it to be without compulsion." He punched the sequence button vigorously, while the chief stared at him with amused respect. He grinned back at Gordon. "Sit down, Captain, and keep an eye on the natives."

Gordon sat, applying his attention to the scene on the ground. "Think they'll get this part?"

"They certainly ought to. I even made a sketch of a native destroying a hell-cat with my new gun." After a few minutes of attentive study by the three natives, the series was finished. The language expert reached over and depressed a different stud without hesitation. "There it is. A nice little blast rifle, practically new!"

The screen showed the front of a box falling open under the sequence machine. The three Azurans raised their heads and stared. Then they looked up at the sky, and back at the box. Their conversation was excited, not at all hushed.

Finally the leader sent the third native around in a flanking move, equipped with the crossbow. When the new position had been taken up, the three studied the situation and seemed to discuss its various aspects. Suddenly, while the flanker held a bead on the machine, the one who had been in the lead stood up and advanced warily toward the proffered gun. He studied it at close range, after looking over the scene carefully.

Abruptly he laid down his spear and seized the blast rifle. He remained crouching, obviously waiting for something to happen. When nothing did, he straightened up and began to examine the weapon. He turned to the last picture, still showing on the machine, and carefully conformed his tentacles around the gunstock as indicated. Then he looked about, as if seeking a target.

A large, brilliant blue tree about twenty meters away seemed to be his choice. He spent a moment getting the sights lined up and then pulled the trigger.

The entire lower half of the tree disappeared in a tremendous explosion of steam and splinters. The upper part of it came smashing down, as did great sections of others directly behind the target.

The stunned native staggered to his feet, still clutching the gun, and cooed at it lovingly. His two companions came running up, whistling and gabbling with excitement. They were allowed to take the gun up on the hill and try it out—at more distant targets. Several trees and a good-sized rock disappeared with a noisy violence that was obviously satisfactory.

The leader remained with the picture machine and began to examine it. He jumped, startled, when Stuart flipped one more sketch into view. It showed the little scout ship about to land. After the native had studied it awhile, Stuart gave him the last one. This was a sketch of the linguist himself, stepping out of the scout ship and greeting a waiting Azuran.

The reaction to this was immediate and positive. Shrill commands sent the smaller native into ambush in the shrubbery; the other came running down the hill, handed over the gun, and fled to the cave. The leader, still watching the sky, squatted down to wait, rifle beside him. After a moment he took something out of his knapsack and apparently began to munch on it. Twice he snatched up the gun and sighted through it, as though practising.

Stuart frowned at the screen. "They seem to understand I'm about to visit them, but they're not convinced they can trust visitors. No reason why they should be, I suppose." He disconnected the pickup unit from the cephaloid circuit.

Gordon cocked his head to one side reflectively. "Well, I don't think the situation is too bad. You've seen how cautious they are . . . they must have been very badly scared when their cities were destroyed. Perfectly natural. It's also evident they're not fundamentally warlike; their behavior shows an absence of military background. Even a couple of traders noticed that, by the way, over on the other side of the planet last year."

The linguist shook his head reprovingly. "Let's avoid semantic confusions when we can, Gordon. Their behavior does not fit in with *your* notion of military background. We have no right to say what it connotes *in their culture.*"

The captain acknowledged the reasonableness of this statement with a smile and left him to the solitude he needed. He began the task of receiving the material the cephaloids had assimilated, feeding in associations of "probable general context" with the natives' comments regarding each picture. He laughed to himself as he realized that a certain amount of projection of his own notions was inevitable.

Such was the tremendous power of the cephaloids, and the delicate, almost intuitive skill of his handling, that the major part of the analysis was complete in little more than an hour. He switched the controls to "Translate, Univ. Sp. to Other." Indicator needles shifted and steadied as the surface potentials readjusted in the semiliving colloids.

Then, before proceeding further, he asked the captain to join him again. When Gordon was seated, the expert smiled wryly at him. "This is usually considered very poor procedure, but there's only one word I can be fairly sure of as a check on this thing. It seems reasonable that, when the middle native exclaimed 'Aru!,' he meant 'Good!!' That was when we destroyed the attacking ship, if you remember . . . a little fiction which I shall have to explain to them later." Into the microphone he said, in Universal Speech, "Good. That is good."

"Aru. Aru naa lo," replied the loudspeaker.

Stuart, though he relaxed a little then, lost no time. It took him only a few minutes to memorize several phrases which the jelly-and-silver translator gave him. By the time Brettner had the little scout ship warmed up for him, Stuart was prepared to tell the natives, "Peace! I come in peace. Your people and my people have the same enemy. Therefore let us be friends and work together. We shall give you large and strong weapons."

He turned to leave the lab, but stopped to squint once more at the screen. Only the native with the gun was visible, still grimly waiting. The linguist finished buckling on his gear with nervous fingers. "They look awfully well-disciplined to me," he murmured to himself. "Wish I felt a little more nonchalant about this!" He clumped down the passageway to Number Three Lock, where he met Brettner climbing out of the scout ship.

Brettner slapped him on the back, saying, "She's all wound up. Good luck, chum. Keep away from the girlies, hear?" From the control room, Rogers shouted gaily, "Send us a postcard, laddie. One of them Venus-type!" The two scouts guffawed heartily. Gordon looked out and waved at him.

The linguist climbed into the control seat, laughing in spite of himself. He waved at Brettner, shut the inner door, and opened the outer. A monitor light showed green. "Ready," he told the intercom. He was surprised at how steady his voice and hands were.

"Cast off!" came Gordon's voice.

He touched the "Release" button and felt himself flung away from the *Special Agent*. He boosted his little vessel around a semicircle several kilometers in diameter, as he had been instructed, so the position of the big ship would not be given away when he approached the ground. He overmodulated the drive then, to make plenty of noise, and headed directly for the waiting native. Over a suitable grassy spot, he waited until he was sure the Azuran had seen him; then he eased down slowly, careful not to make any sudden moves.

He landed with the nose about ten degrees too low, settled with a rolling bump, and opened the port as soon as he could manage. He mumbled to himself a bit, practising his little speech. Then he stepped out.

The blast rifle looked like a ninety-millimeter projector. It scowled viciously at his abdomen from only twenty paces away. He swallowed several times and managed a trembly little smile.

The native continued to inspect him sourly through the peepsight. A tentacle seemed to twitch impatiently at the trigger.

"After all," the linguist thought rapidly, "a facial expression such as a smile is probably meaningless to him. I shall have to make a more significant sign, as in that sketch." He unbuckled his holster belt and carefully laid it to one side, handguns and all. Still no response.

He walked forward halfway to the native, holding up his open hands. He recited his speech, then, and stood waiting.

With his first words, the other's attitude changed. The gun was lowered slowly while the native stared at him with big, black, disk-like eyes. He stared back, examining the bright red native with interest. Long feet, with two toes like pincers; heavily muscled legs; middle limbs like arms, with short, powerful hands of a sort; two six-fingered tentacles growing out from the sides of the head—

One of the middle limbs reached out and tugged at his arm experimentally. The native said something evidently meaning "Come along." Stuart walked along with him, reporting "Okay, so far," into his radio. The two beings walked up to the entrance to the cave, from where the scout ship could just be seen. Suddenly the smaller native sprang out of the brush and backed the linguist against a tree, holding the crossbow almost at his throat. The first native whirled, aimed the blast rifle at the scout ship, and fired. There was a flash at the ship's bow, and a deep gash was blasted into the metal.

"Aru!" said the natives.

Stuart's earphone crackled, but the signal was weak. "What's going on?" came Gordon's voice, faintly. "Get away from them and we'll blow them to smithereens!"

He tried to think clearly. "I don't know how to get away," he realized miserably. "Never had any of that combat training." He found the native with the blast rifle chattering at him; the other had withdrawn the crossbow from his throat. "I'm all right," he reported weakly. He listened to the native a moment, then added, "This is rather puzzling, though. They actually seem friendly. I believe one of them is telling me that we're friends now."

"That lousy iron hill you're on is killing your signal, Stuart. I can hardly hear you. You're in plain sight, though, through the telescope. Shall we come after you?"

The natives were pulling at the linguist's arm, urging him toward the cave. "No, keep out of sight awhile," he shouted, shaking his head. "I believe they want me to come with them."

The reply from the *Special Agent* was unintelligble. Stuart allowed the Azurans to guide him into the cave; he was not surprised to find it the end of a long tunnel through the coral. Two other natives came running past and took up positions as guards just inside the entrance.

The phosphorescent material of the hill itself supplied a feeble light. There seemed to be an alarm system of some sort, for handles were set into small square boxes on the walls every fifty meters or so.

During the hour-long walk, Stuart learned bits of the natives' language. If one could apply the hitherto universally valid criteria of the Linguistic Academy, he decided, this language represented a long history of high culture and philosophical achievement. He found the idea encouraging.

He was already constructing simple sentences when the tunnel turned sharply and entered a small cave. It was really an underground room, he noticed, with several corridors leading away. One of his guides pulled a lever; a moment later a dozen other natives entered the room. With them was a monkey-rat, sporting Rogers' two hunting knifes; it pointed to the linguist and chattered shrilly. The linguist recognized one of the Azurans as the one he had caught. The first to enter, however, seemed considerably older than the rest. Stuart guessed he was a high official.

The elderly one approached the Earthman and held out his tentacles to the sides. It seemed to mean something. There was a short, tense silence.

"Of course!" exclaimed Stuart to himself. "The gesture of peaceful intent: showing the absence of weapons!" He held up his hands, likewise empty, and repeated his speech.

There were murmurs of "Aru!" around him. Unobtrusive weapons were unobtrusively lowered. Sketching materials were brought to the official: sheets of something like parchment, and a reed which exuded an inky substance through a fine hole. Two blocks of what seemed to be extraordinarily soft wood were carried in; the official sat down, somewhat in human fashion, and motioned the language expert to do likewise.

The "conversation" lasted almost two hours. Stuart, by sketching and using a few words, explained his mission. The natives seemed to understand; judging by their awareness of the outer universe, they had considerable scientific knowledge. He guessed, though, that their technology was more biological than mechanical. They knew where the Invaders were from, what they had looked like, and how some of their mechanisms had operated. But Azuran culture, never warlike, had been unable to strike back, and had been so badly smashed that there had been no opportunity to use the captured knowledge.

"They nearly destroyed my people," explained the official with words and pictures. "We were many millions. Now only thousands. We saved what we could and hid underground, scattered. For five years we have struggled to stay alive. Now we are regaining our strength and can think of building again. But always we must be ready for the Invaders. They killed for nothing or for amusement. Took nothing except specimens; apparently they wanted nothing here but sport. They simply attacked without warning one day, all over the planet, and hunted us for fifty-four days. Then they disappeared. We caught a few live ones outside their ships by trickery, and we captured two small ships the same way. But in our difficulty we have had little time to investigate the ships."

"Where are the captured creatures?" asked Stuart.

"Oh, they did not live long." The other's manner did not indicate regret. "They needed high temperature and a special atmosphere to stay alive, and of course we had inadequate means to care for them. We made very thorough biological studies of them, however." He shook his tentacles, as if in disgust. "They were remarkably unpleasant. Colorless, and gritty to the touch. Completely hateful. They used to throw dissected specimens of our people out of their ships; sometimes live people were dropped."

He nodded toward the blast rifle. "You are good to offer weapons. From certain records we found, we believe the enemy will return soon. I understand your need for a base here. I can speak for my people . . . what is left of them. We accept your offer. Come down again tomorrow to the clearing in your big ship. Our highest leader will be present, and a treaty will be made."

Abruptly, thus, the interview was over. The old native was obviously tired. The linguist got to his feet, intending to express his pleasure at the outcome. He had his mouth open, and it stayed that way when the blast rifle was suddenly thrust into his hands. The official, who had handed it to him, put a tentacle on his shoulder in what Stuart recognized as a gesture of friendship.

The linguist grinned, put his hand on the other's shoulder, and handed back the weapon.

There was a great din of whistling and cries of "Aru! Aru naa lo!"
It became a sort of cheer, with a crowd of natives following Stuart and
his three guides back down the tunnel. The old official stood and
watched them go.

Back in the daylight, the linguist was startled to discover that
Procyon was low in the sky and that night was near. He hurried down
the path toward his scout ship to get away from the iron hill. Hastily
he switched on his radio. Before he could catch his breath enough to
talk, he heard White's voice.

"Hey, I see him! There he is, chief; there's the little guy!" Sounds of
the drive being activated came through the earphone.

Gordon's voice cut in. "You okay, Stuart?"

"Yes, yes, I'm all right. Come on down—peaceably."

"What's the deal?"

"They're convinced. They'll have their president, or whatever, here
in the morning to sign a treaty with us."

"WHAT?!"

A moment later the big ship landed with a silent rush, flattening out
a large expanse of scrub. The ground crunched under it. A dozen wide-
eyed natives watched from a respectful distance.

The lower port flew open; Gordon and Rogers came scrambling down
the ladder. The two men came running over, handguns swinging heavily
at their sides. The turret guns were trained on the hill before the cave.

"Is this on the level?" demanded Gordon.

"Yes. I'll explain later, after I've had some sleep."

The captain's eye fell on the scout ship. "Looks like your ship will
navigate all right," he said, still out of breath. "Probably have to replace the autopilot and tracker, though. But why in blazes did they
take a shot at it? And why wasn't your defensive field on?"

The linguist kicked a pebble. "I forgot to ask them why they did that.
I guess they figured my gesture of offering a weapon didn't mean much
unless I was vulnerable to the weapon myself. Or maybe they felt that,
if I came in good faith, I'd come without protection. Anyway, they
didn't want to shoot me just to find out, so they tested it on the ship
and decided I was—er, on the level. If it *had* been on, they'd probably
have shot me immediately with the crossbow. Or maybe they'd have
figured out what the glow was and shot me without testing it. Then
they'd have gone back in the tunnel and sealed it up for good."

He suddenly laughed aloud, face alight with pleasure and surprised
realization, "For the first time on this trip, I'm glad I've never had any
military experience! If I'd been well-trained, that field would have
been turned on!"

Gordon's strained face relaxed. He looked at Stuart in awe, and put an
arm around his shoulders. After a moment he said, musingly, "What
do we do next? We've got to get back, but we also ought to see this
through when the brass gets here."

Stuart's reply was prompt. "You go back. Leave me food for a couple of days and tell Patrol to bring me what I need for a long stay. I'll see this thing through."

"Can I take a picture of you tomorrow with the Azuran big chief? It'd look swell in the papers back home." Gordon's tone was bantering.

The linguist looked him in the eye. "I wish you would," he said, soberly.

FREDRIC BROWN

ARENA

CARSON opened his eyes, and found himself looking upward into a flickering blue dimness.

It was hot, and he was lying on sand, and a sharp rock embedded in the sand was hurting his back. He rolled over to his side, off the rock, and then pushed himself up to a sitting position.

"I'm crazy," he thought. "Crazy—or dead—or something." The sand was blue, bright blue. And there wasn't any such thing as bright blue sand on Earth or any of the planets.

Blue sand.

Blue sand under a blue dome that wasn't the sky nor yet a room, but a circumscribed area—somehow he knew it was circumscribed and finite even though he couldn't see to the top of it.

He picked up some of the sand in his hand and let it run through his fingers. It trickled down onto his bare leg. *Bare?*

Naked. He was stark naked, and already his body was dripping perspiration from the enervating heat, coated blue with sand wherever sand had touched it.

But elsewhere his body was white.

He thought: Then this sand is really blue. If it seemed blue only because of the blue light, then I'd be blue also. But I'm white, so the sand *is* blue. *Blue sand.* There isn't any blue sand. There isn't any place like this place I'm in.

Sweat was running down in his eyes.

It was hot, hotter than hell. Only hell—the hell of the ancients—was supposed to be red and not blue.

But if this place wasn't hell, what was it? Only Mercury, among the planets, had heat like this and this wasn't Mercury. And Mercury was some four billion miles from—

It came back to him then, where he'd been. In the little one-man scouter, outside the orbit of Pluto, scouting a scant million miles to one side of the Earth Armada drawn up in battle array there to intercept the Outsiders.

That sudden strident nerve-shattering ringing of the alarm bell when the rival scouter—the Outsider ship—had come within range of his detectors—

No one knew who the Outsiders were, what they looked like, from what far galaxy they came, other than that it was in the general direction of the Pleiades.

First, sporadic raids on Earth colonies and outposts. Isolated battles between Earth patrols and small groups of Outsider spaceships; battles sometimes won and sometimes lost, but never to date resulting in the capture of an alien vessel. Nor had any member of a raided colony ever survived to describe the Outsiders who had left the ships, if indeed they had left them.

Not a too-serious menace, at first, for the raids had not been too numerous or destructive. And individually, the ships had proved slightly inferior in armament to the best of Earth's fighters, although somewhat superior in speed and maneuverability. A sufficient edge in speed, in fact, to give the Outsiders their choice of running or fighting, unless surrounded.

Nevertheless, Earth had prepared for serious trouble, for a showdown, building the mightiest armada of all time. It had been waiting now, that armada, for a long time. But now the showdown was coming.

Scouts twenty billion miles out had detected the approach of a mighty fleet—a showdown fleet—of the Outsiders. Those scouts had never come back, but their radiotronic messages had. And now Earth's armada, all ten thousand ships and half-million fighting spacemen, was out there, outside Pluto's orbit, waiting to intercept and battle to the death.

And an even battle it was going to be, judging by the advance reports of the men of the far picket line who had given their lives to report—before they had died—on the size and strength of the alien fleet.

Anybody's battle, with the mastery of the solar system hanging in the balance, on an even chance. A last and *only* chance, for Earth and all her colonies lay at the utter mercy of the Outsiders if they ran that gauntlet—

Oh yes. Bob Carson remembered now.

Not that it explained blue sand and flickering blueness. But that strident alarming of the bell and his leap for the control panel. His frenzied fumbling as he strapped himself into the seat. The dot in the visiplate that grew larger.

The dryness of his mouth. The awful knowledge that this was *it*. For him, at least, although the main fleets were still out of range of one another.

This, his first taste of battle. Within three seconds or less he'd be victorious, or a charred cinder. Dead.

Three seconds—that's how long a space-battle lasted. Time enough to count to three, slowly, and then you'd won or you were dead. One hit completely took care of a lightly armed and armored little one-man craft like a scouter.

Frantically—as, unconsciously, his dry lips shaped the word "One" —he worked at the controls to keep that growing dot centered on the crossed spiderwebs of the visiplate. His hands doing that, while his right foot hovered over the pedal that would fire the bolt. The single bolt of concentrated hell that had to hit—or else. There wouldn't be time for any second shot.

"Two." He didn't know he'd said that, either. The dot in the visiplate wasn't a dot now. Only a few thousand miles away, it showed up in the magnification of the plate as though it were only a few hundred yards off. It was a sleek, fast little scouter, about the size of his.

And an alien ship, all right.

"Thr—" His foot touched the bolt-release pedal—

And then the Outsider had swerved suddenly and was off the cross-hairs. Carson punched keys frantically, to follow.

For a tenth of a second, it was out of the visiplate entirely, and then as the nose of his scouter swung after it, he saw it again, diving straight toward the ground.

The ground?

It was an optical illusion of some sort. It *had* to be, that planet—or whatever it was—that now covered the visiplate. Whatever it was, it couldn't be there. Couldn't possibly. There *wasn't* any planet nearer than Neptune three billion miles away—with Pluto around on the opposite side of the distant pinpoint sun.

His *detectors! They* hadn't shown any object of planetary dimensions, even of asteroid dimensions. They still didn't.

So it couldn't be there, that whatever-it-was he was diving into, only a few hundred miles below him.

And in his sudden anxiety to keep from crashing, he forgot even the Outsider ship. He fired the front braking rockets, and even as the sudden change of speed slammed him forward against the seat straps, he fired full right for an emergency turn. Pushed them down and *held* them down, knowing that he needed everything the ship had to keep from crashing and that a turn that sudden would black him out for a moment.

It did black him out.

And that was all. Now he was sitting in hot blue sand, stark naked but otherwise unhurt. No sign of his spaceship and—for that matter— no sign of *space*. That curve overhead wasn't a sky, whatever else it was.

He scrambled to his feet.

Gravity seemed a little more than Earth-normal. Not much more.

Flat sand stretching away, a few scrawny bushes in clumps here and there. The bushes were blue, too, but in varying shades, some lighter than the blue of the sand, some darker.

Out from under the nearest bush ran a little thing that was like a lizard, except that it had more than four legs. It was blue, too. Bright blue. It saw him and ran back again under the bush.

He looked up again, trying to decide what was overhead. It wasn't exactly a roof, but it was dome-shaped. It flickered and was hard to look at. But definitely, it curved down to the ground, to the blue sand, all around him.

He wasn't far from being under the center of the dome. At a guess, it was a hundred yards to the nearest wall, if it was a wall. It was as though a blue hemisphere of *something*, about two hundred and fifty yards in circumference, was inverted over the flat expanse of the sand.

And everything blue, except one object. Over near a far curving wall there was a red object. Roughly spherical, it seemed to be about a yard in diameter. Too far for him to see clearly through the flickering blueness. But, unaccountably, he shuddered.

He wiped sweat from his forehead, or tried to, with the back of his hand.

Was this a dream, a nightmare? This heat, this sand, that vague feeling of horror he felt when he looked toward the red thing?

A dream? No, one didn't go to sleep and dream in the midst of a battle in space.

Death? No, never. If there were immortality, it wouldn't be a senseless thing like this, a thing of blue heat and blue sand and a red horror.

Then he heard the voice—

Inside his head he heard it, not with his ears. It came from nowhere or everywhere.

"*Through spaces and dimensions wandering,*" rang the words in his mind, "*and in this space and this time I find two peoples about to wage a war that would exterminate one and so weaken the other that it would retrogress and never fulfill its destiny, but decay and return to mindless dust whence it came. And I say this must not happen.*"

"Who . . . what are you?" Carson didn't say it aloud, but the question formed itself in his brain.

"*You would not understand completely. I am—*" There was a pause as though the voice sought—in Carson's brain—for a word that wasn't there, a word he didn't know. "*I am the end of evolution of a race so old the time can not be expressed in words that have meaning to your mind. A race fused into a single entity, eternal—*

"*An entity such as your primitive race might become*"—again the groping for a word—"*time from now. So might the race you call, in your mind, the Outsiders. So I intervene in the battle to come, the battle between fleets so evenly matched that destruction of both races will result. One must survive. One must progress and evolve.*"

"One?" thought Carson. "Mine, or—?"

"*It is in my power to stop the war, to send the Outsiders back to their galaxy. But they would return, or your race would sooner or later follow them there. Only by remaining in this space and time to intervene constantly could I prevent them from destroying one another, and I cannot remain.*

"*So I shall intervene now. I shall destroy one fleet completely without loss to the other. One civilization shall thus survive.*"

Nightmare. This had to be nightmare, Carson thought. But he knew it wasn't.

It was too mad, too impossible, to be anything but real.

He didn't dare ask *the* question—*which?* But his thoughts asked it for him.

"*The stronger shall survive,*" said the voice. "*That I can not—and would not—change. I merely intervene to make it a complete victory, not*"—groping again—"*not Pyrrhic victory to a broken race.*

"*From the outskirts of the not-yet battle I plucked two individuals, you and an Outsider. I see from your mind that in your early history of nationalisms battles between champions, to decide issues between races, were not unknown.*

"*You and your opponent are here pitted against one another, naked and unarmed, under conditions equally unfamiliar to you both, equally unpleasant to you both. There is no time limit, for here there is no time. The survivor is the champion of his race. That race survives.*"

"But—" Carson's protest was too inarticulate for expression, but the voice answered it.

"*It is fair. The conditions are such that the accident of physical strength will not completely decide the issue. There is a barrier. You will understand. Brain-power and courage will be more important than strength. Most especially courage, which is the will to survive.*"

"But while this goes on, the fleets will—"

"*No, you are in another space, another time. For as long as you are here, time stands still in the universe you know. I see you wonder whether this place is real. It is, and it is not. As I—to your limited understanding—am and am not real. My existence is mental and not physical. You saw me as a planet; it could have been as a dustmote or a sun.*

"*But to you this place is now real. What you suffer here will be real. And if you die here, your death will be real. If you die, your failure will be the end of your race. That is enough for you to know.*"

And then the voice was gone.

Again he was alone, but not alone. For as Carson looked up, he saw that the red thing, the red sphere of horror which he now knew was the Outsider, was rolling toward him.

Rolling.

It seemed to have no legs or arms that he could see, no features. It rolled across the blue sand with the fluid quickness of a drop of mercury. And before it, in some manner he could not understand, came a paralyzing wave of nauseating, retching, horrid hatred.

Carson looked about him frantically. A stone, lying in the sand a few feet away, was the nearest thing to a weapon. It wasn't large, but it had sharp edges, like a slab of flint. It looked a bit like blue flint.

He picked it up, and crouched to receive the attack. It was coming fast, faster than he could run.

No time to think out how he was going to fight it, and how anyway could he plan to battle a creature whose strength, whose characteristics, whose method of fighting he did not know? Rolling so fast, it looked more than ever like a perfect sphere.

Ten yards away. Five. And then it stopped.

Rather, it *was stopped*. Abruptly the near side of it flattened as though it had run up against an invisible wall. It bounced, actually bounced back.

Then it rolled forward again, but more slowly, more cautiously. It stopped again, at the same place. It tried again, a few yards to one side.

There was a barrier there of some sort. It clicked, then, in Carson's mind. That thought projected into his mind by the Entity who had brought them there: "—accident of physical strength will not completely decide the issue. There is a barrier."

A force-field, of course. Not the Netzian Field, known to Earth science, for that glowed and emitted a crackling sound. This one was invisible, silent.

It was a wall that ran from side to side of the inverted hemisphere; Carson didn't have to verify that himself. The Roller was doing that; rolling sideways along the barrier, seeking a break in it that wasn't there.

Carson took half a dozen steps forward, his left hand groping out before him, and then his hand touched the barrier. It felt smooth, yielding, like a sheet of rubber rather than like glass. Warm to his touch, but no warmer than the sand underfoot. And it was completely invisible, even at close range.

He dropped the stone and put both hands against it, pushing. It seemed to yield, just a trifle. But no farther than that trifle, even when he pushed with all his weight. It felt like a sheet of rubber backed up by steel. Limited resiliency, and then firm strength.

He stood on tiptoe and reached as high as he could and the barrier was still there.

He saw the Roller coming back, having reached one side of the arena. That feeling of nausea hit Carson again, and he stepped back from the barrier as it went by. It didn't stop.

But did the barrier stop at ground level? Carson knelt down and burrowed in the sand. It was soft, light, easy to dig in. At two feet down the barrier was still there.

The Roller was coming back again. Obviously, it couldn't find a way through at either side.

There must be a way through, Carson thought. *Some* way we can get at each other, else this duel is meaningless.

But no hurry now, in finding that out. There was something to try first. The Roller was back now, and it stopped just across the barrier, only six feet away. It seemed to be studying him, although for the life of him, Carson couldn't find external evidence of sense organs on the thing. Nothing that looked like eyes or ears, or even a mouth. There was though, he saw now, a series of grooves—perhaps a dozen of them altogether, and he saw two tentacles suddenly push out from two of the grooves and dip into the sand as though testing its consistency. Tentacles about an inch in diameter and perhaps a foot and a half long.

But the tentacles were retractable into the grooves and were kept there except when in use. They were retracted when the thing rolled and seemed to have nothing to do with its method of locomotion. That, as far as Carson could judge, seemed to be accomplished by some shifting—just *how* he couldn't even imagine—of its center of gravity.

He shuddered as he looked at the thing. It was alien, utterly alien, horribly different from anything on Earth or any of the life forms found on the other solar planets. Instinctively, somehow, he knew its mind was as alien as its body.

But he had to try. If it had no telepathic powers at all, the attempt was foredoomed to failure, yet he thought it had such powers. There had, at any rate, been a projection of something that was not physical at the time a few minutes ago when it had first started for him. An almost tangible wave of hatred.

If it could project that, perhaps it could read his mind as well, sufficiently for his purpose.

Deliberately, Carson picked up the rock that had been his only weapon, then tossed it down again in a gesture of relinquishment and raised his empty hands, palms up, before him.

He spoke aloud, knowing that although the words would be meaningless to the creature before him, speaking them would focus his own thoughts more completely upon the message.

"Can we not have peace between us?" he said, his voice sounding strange in the utter stillness. "The Entity who brought us here has told us what must happen if our races fight—extinction of one and weakening and retrogression of the other. The battle between them, said the Entity, depends upon what we do here. Why can not we agree to an external peace—your race to its galaxy, we to ours?"

Carson blanked out his mind to receive a reply.

It came, and it staggered him back, physically. He actually recoiled several steps in sheer horror at the depth and intensity of the hatred and lust-to-kill of the red images that had been projected at him. Not as articulate words—as had come to him the thoughts of the Entity—but as wave upon wave of fierce emotion.

For a moment that seemed an eternity he had to struggle against the mental impact of that hatred, fight to clear his mind of it and drive out the alien thoughts to which he had given admittance by blanking his own thoughts. He wanted to retch.

Slowly his mind cleared as, slowly, the mind of a man wakening from nightmare clears away the fear-fabric of which the dream was woven. He was breathing hard and he felt weaker, but he could think.

He stood studying the Roller. It had been motionless during the mental duel it had so nearly won. Now it rolled a few feet to one side, to the nearest of the blue bushes. Three tentacles whipped out of their grooves and began to investigate the bush.

"O. K.," Carson said, "so it's war then." He managed a wry grin. "If I got your answer straight, peace doesn't appeal to you." And, because he was, after all, a quiet young man and couldn't resist the impulse to be dramatic, he added. "To the death!"

But his voice, in that utter silence, sounded very silly, even to himself. It came to him, then, that this *was* to the death. Not only his own death or that of the red spherical thing which he now thought of as the Roller, but death to the entire race of one or the other of them. The end of the human race, if he failed.

It made him suddenly very humble and very afraid to think that. More than to think it, to *know* it. Somehow, with a knowledge that was above even faith, he knew that the Entity who had arranged this duel had told the truth about its intentions and its powers. It wasn't kidding.

The future of humanity depended upon *him*. It was an awful thing to realize, and he wrenched his mind away from it. He had to concentrate on the situation at hand.

There had to be some way of getting through the barrier, or of killing through the barrier.

Mentally? He hoped that wasn't all, for the Roller obviously had stronger telepathic powers than the primitive, undeveloped ones of the human race. Or did it?

He had been able to drive the thoughts of the Roller out of his own mind; could it drive out his? If its ability to project were stronger, might not its receptivity mechanism be more vulnerable?

He stared at it and endeavored to concentrate and focus all his thoughts upon it.

"Die," he thought. *"You are going to die. You are dying. You are—"*

He tried variations on it, and mental pictures. Sweat stood out on his forehead and he found himself trembling with the intensity of the effort. But the Roller went ahead with its investigation of the bush, as utterly unaffected as though Carson had been reciting the multiplication table.

So *that* was no good.

He felt a bit weak and dizzy from the heat and his strenuous effort at concentration. He sat down on the blue sand to rest and gave his full attention to watching and studying the Roller. By close study, perhaps, he could judge its strength and detect its weaknesses, learn things that would be valuable to know when and if they should come to grips.

It was breaking off twigs. Carson watched carefully, trying to judge just how hard it worked to do that. Later, he thought, he could find a similar bush on his own side, break off twigs of equal thickness himself, and gain a comparision of physical strength between his own arms and hands and those tentacles.

The twigs broke off hard; the Roller was having to struggle with each one, he saw. Each tentacle, he saw, bifurcated at the tip into two fingers, each tipped by a nail or claw. The claws didn't seem to be particularly long or dangerous. No more so than his own fingernails, if they were let to grow a bit.

No, on the whole, it didn't look too tough to handle physically. Unless, of course, that bush was made of pretty tough stuff. Carson looked around him and, yes, right within reach was another bush of indentically the same type.

He reached over and snapped off a twig. It was brittle, easy to break. Of course, the Roller might have been faking deliberately but he didn't think so.

On the other hand, where was it vulnerable? Just how would he go about killing it, if he got the chance? He went back to studying it. The outer hide looked pretty tough. He'd need a sharp weapon of some sort. He picked up the piece of rock again. It was about twelve inches long, narrow, and fairly sharp on one end. If it chipped like flint, he could make a serviceable knife out of it.

The Roller was continuing its investigations of the bushes. It rolled again, to the nearest one of another type. A little blue lizard, many-legged like the one Carson had seen on his side of the barrier, darted out from under the bush.

A tentacle of the Roller lashed out and caught it, picked it up. Another tentacle whipped over and began to pull legs off the lizard, as coldly and calmly as it had pulled twigs off the bush. The creature struggled frantically and emitted a shrill squealing sound that was the first sound Carson had heard here other than the sound of his own voice.

Carson shuddered and wanted to turn his eyes away. But he made himself continue to watch; anything he could learn about his opponent might prove valuable. Even this knowledge of its unnecessary cruelty. Particularly, he thought with a sudden vicious surge of emotion, this knowledge of its unnecessary cruelty. It would make it a pleasure to kill the thing, if and when the chance came.

He steeled himself to watch the dismembering of the lizard, for that very reason.

But he felt glad when, with half its legs gone, the lizard quit squealing and struggling and lay limp and dead in the Roller's grasp.

It didn't continue with the rest of the legs. Contemptuously it tossed the dead lizard away from it, in Carson's direction. It arced through the air between them and landed at his feet.

It had come through the barrier! The barrier wasn't there any more!

Carson was on his feet in a flash, the knife gripped tightly in his hand, and leaped forward. He'd settle this thing here and now! With the barrier gone—

But it wasn't gone. He found that out the hard way, running head on into it and nearly knocking himself silly. He bounced back, and fell.

And as he sat up, shaking his head to clear it, he saw something coming through the air toward him, and to duck it, he threw himself flat again on the sand, and to one side. He got his body out of the way, but there was a sudden sharp pain in the calf of his left leg.

He rolled backward, ignoring the pain, and scrambled to his feet. It was a rock, he saw now, that had struck him. And the Roller was picking up another one now, swinging it back gripped between two tentacles, getting ready to throw again.

It sailed through the air toward him, but he was easily able to step out of its way. The Roller, apparently, could throw straight, but not hard nor far. The first rock had struck him only because he had been sitting down and had not seen it coming until it was almost upon him.

Even as he stepped aside from that weak second throw, Carson drew back his right arm and let fly with the rock that was still in his hand. If missiles, he thought with sudden elation, can cross the barrier, then two can play at the game of throwing them. And the good right arm of an Earthman—

He couldn't miss a three-foot sphere at only four-yard range, and he didn't miss. The rock whizzed straight, and with a speed several times that of the missiles the Roller had thrown. It hit dead center, but it hit flat, unfortunately, instead of point first.

But it hit with a resounding thump, and obviously it hurt. The Roller had been reaching for another rock, but it changed its mind and got out of there instead. By the time Carson could pick up and throw another rock, the Roller was forty yards back from the barrier and going strong.

His second throw missed by feet, and his third throw was short. The Roller was back out of range—at least out of range of a missile heavy enough to be damaging.

Carson grinned. That round had been his. Except—

He quit grinning as he bent over to examine the calf of his leg. A jagged edge of the stone had made a pretty deep cut, several inches long. It was bleeding pretty freely, but he didn't think it had gone deep enough to hit an artery. If it stopped bleeding of its own accord, well and good. If not, he was in for trouble.

Finding out one thing, though, took precedence over that cut. The nature of the barrier.

He went forward to it again, this time groping with his hands before him. He found it; then holding one hand against it, he tossed a handful of sand at it with the other hand. The sand went right through. His hand didn't.

Organic matter versus inorganic? No, because the dead lizard had gone through it, and a lizard, alive or dead, was certainly organic. Plant life? He broke off a twig and poked it at the barrier. The twig went through, with no resistance, but when his fingers gripping the twig came to the barrier, they were stopped.

He couldn't get through it, nor could the Roller. But rocks and sand and a dead lizard—

How about a live lizard? He went hunting, under bushes, until he found one, and caught it. He tossed it gently against the barrier and it bounced back and scurried away across the blue sand.

That gave him the answer, in so far as he could determine it now. The screen was a barrier to living things. Dead or inorganic matter could cross it.

That off his mind, Carson looked at his injured leg again. The bleeding was lessening, which meant he wouldn't need to worry about making a tourniquet. But he should find some water, if any was available, to clean the wound.

Water—the thought of it made him realize that he was getting awfully thirsty. He'd *have* to find water, in case this contest turned out to be a protracted one.

Limping slightly now, he started off to make a full circuit of his half of the arena. Guiding himself with one hand along the barrier, he walked to his right until he came to the curving sidewall. It was visible, a dull blue-gray at close range, and the surface of it felt just like the central barrier.

He experimented by tossing a handful of sand at it, and the sand reached the wall and disappeared as it went through. The hemispherical shell was a force-field, too. But an opaque one, instead of transparent like the barrier.

He followed it around until he came back to the barrier, and walked back along the barrier to the point from which he'd started.

No sign of water.

Worried now, he started a series of zigzags back and forth between the barrier and the wall, covering the intervening space thoroughly.

No water. Blue sand, blue bushes, and intolerable heat. Nothing else.

It must be his imagination, he told himself angrily, that he was suffering *that* much from thirst. How long had he been here? Of course, no time at all, according to his own space-time frame. The Entity had told him time stood still out there, while he was here. But his body processes went on here, just the same. And according to his body's reckoning, how long had he been here? Three or four hours, perhaps. Certainly not long enough to be suffering seriously from thirst.

But he was suffering from it; his throat dry and parched. Probably the intense heat was the cause. It was *hot!* A hundred and thirty Fahrenheit, at a guess. A dry, still heat without the slightest movement of air.

He was limping rather badly, and utterly fagged out when he'd finished the futile exploration of his domain.

He stared across at the motionless Roller and hoped it was as miserable as he was. And quite possibly it wasn't enjoying this, either. The Entity had said the conditions here were equally unfamiliar and equally uncomfortable for both of them. Maybe the Roller came from a planet where two-hundred degree heat was the norm. Maybe it was freezing while he was roasting.

Maybe the air was as much too thick for it as it was too thin for him. For the exertion of his explorations had left him panting. The atmosphere here, he realized now, was not much thicker than that on Mars.

No water.

That meant a deadline, for him at any rate. Unless he could find a way to cross that barrier or to kill his enemy from this side of it, thirst would kill him, eventually.

It gave him a feeling of desperate urgency. He *must* hurry.

But he made himself sit down a moment to rest, to think.

What was there to do? Nothing, and yet so many things. The several varieties of bushes, for example. They didn't look promising, but he'd have to examine them for possibilities. And his leg—he'd have to do something about that, even without water to clean it. Gather ammunition in the form of rocks. Find a rock that would make a good knife.

His leg hurt rather badly now, and he decided that came first. One type of bush had leaves—or things rather similar to leaves. He pulled off a handful of them and decided, after examination, to take a chance on them. He used them to clean off the sand and dirt and caked blood, then made a pad of fresh leaves and tied it over the wound with tendrils from the same bush.

The tendrils proved unexpectedly tough and strong. They were slender, and soft and pliable, yet he couldn't break them at all. He had to saw them off the bush with the sharp edge of a piece of the blue flint. Some of the thicker ones were over a foot long, and he filed away in his memory, for future reference, the fact that a bunch of the thick ones, tied together, would make a pretty serviceable rope. Maybe he'd be able to think of a use for rope.

Next, he made himself a knife. The blue flint *did* chip. From a foot-long splinter of it, he fashioned himself a crude but lethal weapon. And of tendrils from the bush, he made himself a rope-belt through which he could thrust the flint knife, to keep it with him all the time and yet have his hands free.

He went back to studying the bushes. There were three other types. One was leafless, dry, brittle, rather like a dried tumbleweed. Another was of soft, crumbly wood, almost like punk. It looked and felt as though it would make excellent tinder for a fire. The third type was the most nearly woodlike. It had fragile leaves that wilted at a touch, but the stalks, although short, were straight and strong.

It was horribly, unbearably hot.

He limped up to the barrier, felt to make sure that it was still there. It was.

He stood watching the Roller for a while. It was keeping a safe distance back from the barrier, out of effective stone-throwing range. It was moving around back there, doing something. He couldn't tell what it was doing.

Once it stopped moving, came a little closer, and seemed to concentrate its attention on him. Again Carson had to fight off a wave of nausea. He threw a stone at it and the Roller retreated and went back to whatever it had been doing before.

At least he could make it keep its distance.

And, he thought bitterly, a devil of a lot of good *that* did him. Just the same, he spent the next hour or two gathering stones of suitable size for throwing, and making several neat piles of them, near his side of the barrier.

His throat burned now. It was difficult for him to think about anything except water.

But he *had* to think about other things. About getting through that barrier, under or over it, getting *at* that red sphere and killing it before this place of heat and thirst killed him first.

The barrier went to the wall upon either side, but how high and how far under the sand?

For just a moment, Carson's mind was too fuzzy to think out how he could find out either of those things. Idly, sitting there in the hot sand —and he didn't remember sitting down—he watched a blue lizard crawl from the shelter of one bush to the shelter of another.

From under the second bush, it looked out at him.

Carson grinned at it. Maybe he was getting a bit punch-drunk, because he remembered suddenly the old story of the desert-colonists on Mars, taken from an older desert story of Earth— "Pretty soon you get so lonesome you find yourself talking to the lizards, and then not so long after that you find the lizards talking back to you—"

He should have been concentrating, of course, on how to kill the Roller, but instead he grinned at the lizard and said, "Hello, there."

The lizard took a few steps toward him. "Hello," it said.

Carson was stunned for a moment, and then he put back his head and roared with laughter. It didn't hurt his throat to do so, either; he hadn't been *that* thirsty.

Why not? Why should the Entity who thought up this nightmare of a place not have a sense of humor, along with the other powers he had? Talking lizards, equipped to talk back in my own language, if I talk to them— It's a nice touch.

He grinned at the lizard and said, "Come on over." But the lizard turned and ran away, scurrying from bush to bush until it was out of sight.

He was thirsty again.

And he had to *do* something. He couldn't win this contest by sitting here sweating and feeling miserable. He had to *do* something. But what?

Get through the barrier. But he couldn't get through it, or over it.

But was he certain he couldn't get under it? And come to think of it, didn't one sometimes find water by digging? Two birds with one stone—

Painfully now, Carson limped up to the barrier and started digging, scooping up sand a double handful at a time. It was slow, hard work because the sand ran in at the edges and the deeper he got the bigger in diameter the hole had to be. How many hours it took him, he didn't know, but he hit bedrock four feet down. Dry bedrock; no sign of water.

And the force-field of the barrier went down clear to the bedrock. No dice. No water. Nothing.

He crawled out of the hole and lay there panting, and then raised his head to look across and see what the Roller was doing. It must be doing something back there.

It was. It was making something out of wood from the bushes, tied together with tendrils. A queerly shaped framework about four feet high and roughly square. To see it better, Carson climbed up onto the mound of sand he had excavated from the hole, and stood there staring.

There were two long levers sticking out of the back of it, one with a cup-shaped affair on the end of it. Seemed to be some sort of a catapult, Carson thought.

Sure enough, the Roller was lifting a sizable rock into the cup-shaped outfit. One of his tentacles moved the other lever up and down for a while, and then he turned the machine slightly as though aiming it and the lever with the stone flew up and forward.

The stone arced several yards over Carson's head, so far away that he didn't have to duck, but he judged the distance it had traveled, and whistled softly. He couldn't throw a rock that weight more than half that distance. And even retreating to the rear of his domain wouldn't put him out of range of that machine, if the Roller shoved it forward almost to the barrier.

Another rock whizzed over. Not quite so far away this time.

That thing could be dangerous, he decided. Maybe he'd better do something about it.

Moving from side to side along the barrier, so the catapult couldn't bracket him, he whaled a dozen rocks at it. But that wasn't going to be any good, he saw. They had to be light rocks, or he couldn't throw them that far. If they hit the framework, they bounced off harmlessly. And the Roller had no difficulty, at that distance, in moving aside from those that came near it.

Besides, his arm was tiring badly. He ached all over from sheer weariness. If he could only rest awhile without having to duck rocks from that catapult at regular intervals of maybe thirty seconds each—

He stumbled back to the rear of the arena. Then he saw even that wasn't any good. The rocks reached back there, too, only there were longer intervals between them, as though it took longer to wind up the mechanism, whatever it was, of the catapult.

Wearily he dragged himself back to the barrier again. Several times he fell and could barely rise to his feet to go on. He was, he knew, near the limit of his endurance. Yet he didn't dare stop moving now, until and unless he could put that catapult out of action. If he fell asleep, he'd never wake up.

One of the stones from it gave him the first glimmer of an idea. It struck upon one of the piles of stones he'd gathered together near the barrier to use as ammunition, and it struck sparks.

Sparks. Fire. Primitive man had made fire by striking sparks, and with some of those dry crumbly bushes as tinder—

Luckily, a bush of that type was near him. He broke it off, took it over to the pile of stones, then patiently hit one stone against another until a spark touched the punklike wood of the bush. It went up in flames so fast that it singed his eyebrows and was burned to an ash within seconds.

But he had the idea now, and within minutes he had a little fire going in the lee of the mound of sand he'd made digging the hole an hour or two ago. Tinder bushes had started it, and other bushes which burned, but more slowly, kept it a steady flame.

The tough wirelike tendrils didn't burn readily; that made the fire-bombs easy to make and throw. A bundle of faggots tied about a small stone to give it weight and a loop of the tendril to swing it by.

He made half a dozen of them before he lighted and threw the first. It went wide, and the Roller started a quick retreat, pulling the catapult after him. But Carson had the others ready and threw them in rapid succession. The fourth wedged in the catapult's framework, and did the trick. The Roller tried desperately to put out the spreading blaze by throwing sand, but its clawed tentacles would take only a spoonful at a time and his efforts were ineffectual. The catapult burned.

The Roller moved safely away from the fire and seemed to concentrate its attention on Carson and again he felt that wave of hatred and nausea. But more weakly; either the Roller itself was weakening or Carson had learned how to protect himself against the mental attack.

He thumbed his nose at it and then sent it scuttling back to safety by throwing a stone. The Roller went clear to the back of its half of the arena and started pulling up bushes again. Probably it was going to make another catapult.

Carson verified—for the hundredth time—that the barrier was still operating, and then found himself sitting in the sand beside it because he was suddenly too weak to stand up.

His leg throbbed steadily now and the pangs of thirst were severe. But those things paled beside the utter physical exhaustion that gripped his entire body.

And the heat.

Hell must be like this, he thought. The hell that the ancients had believed in. He fought to stay awake, and yet staying awake seemed futile, for there was nothing he could do. Nothing, while the barrier remained impregnable and the Roller stayed back out of range.

But there must be *something*. He tried to remember things he had read in books of archaeology about the methods of fighting used back in the days before metal and plastic. The stone missile, that had come first, he thought. Well, that he already had.

The only improvement on it would be a catapult, such as the Roller had made. But he'd never be able to make one, with the tiny bits of wood available from the bushes—no single piece longer than a foot or so. Certainly he could figure out a mechanism for one, but he didn't have the endurance left for a task that would take days.

Days? But the Roller had made one. Had they been here days already? Then he remembered that the Roller had many tentacles to work with and undoubtedly could do such work faster than he.

And besides, a catapult wouldn't decide the issue. He had to do better than that.

Bow and arrow? No; he had tried archery once and knew his own ineptness with a bow. Even with a modern sportsman's durasteel weapon, made for accuracy. With such a crude, pieced-together outfit as he could make here, he doubted if he could shoot as far as he could throw a rock, and knew he couldn't shoot as straight.

Spear? Well, he *could* make that. It would be useless as a throwing weapon at any distance, but would be a handy thing at close range, if he ever got to close range.

And making one would give him something to do. Help keep his mind from wandering, as it was beginning to do. Sometimes now, he had to concentrate awhile before he could remember why he was here, why he had to kill the Roller.

Luckily he was still beside one of the piles of stones. He sorted through it until he found one shaped roughly like a spearhead. With a smaller stone he began to chip it into shape, fashioning sharp shoulders on the sides so that if it penetrated it would not pull out again.

Like a harpoon? There was something in that idea, he thought. A harpoon was better than a spear, maybe, for this crazy contest. If he could once get it into the Roller, and had a rope on it, he could pull the Roller up against the barrier and the stone blade of his knife would reach through that barrier, even if his hands wouldn't.

The shaft was harder to make than the head. But by splitting and joining the main stems of four of the bushes, and wrapping the joints with the tough but thin tendrils, he got a strong shaft about four feet long, and tied the stone head in a notch cut in the end.

It was crude, but strong.

And the rope. With the thin tough tendrils he made himself twenty feet of line. It was light and didn't look strong, but he knew it would hold his weight and to spare. He tied one end of it to the shaft of the harpoon and the other end about his right wrist. At least, if he threw his harpoon across the barrier, he'd be able to pull it back if he missed.

Then when he had tied the last knot and there was nothing more he could do, the heat and the weariness and the pain in his leg and the dreadful thirst were suddenly a thousand times worse than they had been before.

He tried to stand up, to see what the Roller was doing now, and found he couldn't get to his feet. On the third try, he got as far as his knees and then fell flat again.

"I've got to sleep," he thought. "If a showdown came now, I'd be helpless. He could come up here and kill me, if he knew. I've got to regain some strength."

Slowly, painfully, he crawled back away from the barrier. Ten yards, twenty—

The jar of something thudding against the sand near him waked him from a confused and horrible dream to a more confused and more horrible reality, and he opened his eyes again to blue radiance over blue sand.

How long had he slept? A minute? A day?

Another stone thudded nearer and threw sand on him. He got his arms under him and sat up. He turned around and saw the Roller twenty yards away, at the barrier.

It rolled away hastily as he sat up, not stopping until it was as far away as it could get.

He'd fallen asleep too soon, he realized, while he was still in range of the Roller's throwing ability. Seeing him lying motionless, it had dared come up to the barrier to throw at him. Luckily, it didn't realize how weak he was, or it could have stayed there and kept on throwing stones.

Had he slept long? He didn't think so, because he felt just as he had before. Not rested at all, no thirstier, no different. Probably he'd been there only a few minutes.

He started crawling again, this time forcing himself to keep going until he was as far as he could go, until the colorless, opaque wall of the arena's outer shell was only a yard away.

Then things slipped away again—

When he awoke, nothing about him was changed, but this time he knew that he had slept a long time.

The first thing he became aware of was the inside of his mouth; it was dry, caked. His tongue was swollen.

Something was wrong, he knew, as he returned slowly to full awareness. He felt less tired, the stage of utter exhaustion had passed. The sleep had taken care of that.

But there was pain, agonizing pain. It wasn't until he tried to move that he knew that it came from his leg.

He raised his head and looked down at it. It was swollen terribly below the knee and the swelling showed even halfway up his thigh. The plant tendrils he had used to tie on the protective pad of leaves now cut deeply into the swollen flesh.

To get his knife under that imbedded lashing would have been impossible. Fortunately, the final knot was over the shin bone, in front, where the vine cut in less deeply than elsewhere. He was able, after an agonizing effort, to untie the knot.

A look under the pad of leaves told him the worst. Infection and blood poisioning, both pretty bad and getting worse.

And without drugs, without cloth, without even *water*, there wasn't a thing he could do about it.

Not a thing, except *die,* when the poison had spread through his system.

He knew it was hopeless, then, and that he'd lost.

And with him, humanity. When he died here, out there in the universe he knew, all his friends, everybody, would die too. And Earth and the colonized planets would be the home of the red, rolling, alien Outsiders. Creatures out of nightmare, things without a human attribute, who picked lizards apart for the fun of it.

It was the thought of that which gave him courage to start crawling, almost blindly in pain, toward the barrier again. Not crawling on hands and knees this time, but pulling himself along only by his arms and hands.

A chance in a million, that maybe he'd have strength left, when he got there, to throw his harpoon-spear just *once,* and with deadly effect, if—on another chance in a million—the Roller would come up to the barrier. Or if the barrier was gone, now.

It took him years, it seemed, to get there.

The barrier wasn't gone. It was as impassable as when he'd first felt it.

And the Roller wasn't at the barrier. By raising up on his elbows, he could see it at the back of its part of the arena, working on a wooden framework that was a half-completed duplicate of the catapult he'd destroyed.

It was moving slowly now. Undoubtedly it had weakened, too.

But Carson doubted that it would ever need that second catapult. He'd be dead, he thought, before it was finished.

If he could attract it to the barrier, now, while he was still alive— He waved an arm and tried to shout, but his parched throat would make no sound.

Or if he could get through the barrier—

His mind must have slipped for a moment, for he found himself beating his fists against the barrier in futile rage, and made himself stop.

He closed his eyes, tried to make himself calm.

"Hello," said the voice.

It was a small, thin voice. It sounded like—

He opened his eyes and turned his head. It *was* a lizard.

"Go away," Carson wanted to say. "Go away; you're not really there, or you're there but not really talking. I'm imagining things again."

But he couldn't talk; his throat and tongue were past all speech with the dryness. He closed his eyes again.

"Hurt," said the voice. "Kill. Hurt—kill. Come."

He opened his eyes again. The blue ten-legged lizard was still there. It ran a little way along the barrier, came back, started off again, and came back.

"Hurt," it said. "Kill. Come."

Again it started off, and came back. Obviously it wanted Carson to follow it along the barrier.

He closed his eyes again. The voice kept on. The same three meaningless words. Each time he opened his eyes, it ran off and came back.

"Hurt. Kill. Come."

Carson groaned. There would be no peace unless he followed the blasted thing. Like it wanted him to.

He followed it, crawling. Another sound, a high-pitched squealing, came to his ears and grew louder.

There was something lying in the sand, writhing, squealing. Something small, blue, that looked like a lizard and yet didn't—

Then he saw what it was—the lizard whose legs the Roller had pulled off, so long ago. But it wasn't dead; it had come back to life and was wriggling and screaming in agony.

"Hurt," said the other lizard. "Hurt. Kill. Kill."

Carson understood. He took the flint knife from his belt and killed the tortured creature. The live lizard scurried off quickly.

Carson turned back to the barrier. He leaned his hands and head against it and watched the Roller, far back, working on the new catapult.

"I could get that far," he thought, "if I could get through. If I could get through, I might win yet. It looks weak, too. I might—"

And then there was another reaction of black hopelessness, when pain snapped his will and he wished that he were dead. He envied the lizard he'd just killed. It didn't have to live on and suffer. And he did. It would be hours, it might be days, before the blood poisoning killed him.

If only he could use that knife on himself—

But he knew he wouldn't. As long as he was alive, there was the millionth chance—

He was straining, pushing on the barrier with the flat of his hands, and he noticed his arms, how thin and scrawny they were now. He must really have been here a long time, for days, to get as thin as that.

How much longer now, before he died? How much more heat and thirst and pain could flesh stand?

For a little while he was almost hysterical again, and then came a time of deep calm, and a thought that was startling.

The lizard he had just killed. *It had crossed the barrier, still alive.* It had come from the Roller's side; the Roller had pulled off its legs and then tossed it contemptuously at him and it had come through the barrier. He'd thought, because the lizard was dead.

But it hadn't been dead; it had been unconscious.

A live lizard couldn't go through the barrier, but an unconscious one could. The barrier was not a barrier, then, to living flesh, but to conscious flesh. It was a *mental* projection, a *mental* hazard.

And with that thought, Carson started crawling along the barrier to make his last desperate gamble. A hope so forlorn that only a dying man would have dared try it.

No use weighing the odds of success. Not when, if he didn't try it, those odds were infinitely to zero.

He crawled along the barrier to the dune of sand, about four feet high, which he'd scooped out in trying—how many days ago?—to dig under the barrier or to reach water.

That mound was right at the barrier, its farther slope half on one side of the barrier, half on the other.

Taking with him a rock from the pile nearby, he climbed up to the top of the dune and over the top, and lay there against the barrier, his weight leaning against it so that if the barrier were taken away he'd roll on down the short slope, into the enemy territory.

He checked to be sure that the knife was safely in his rope belt, that the harpoon was in the crook of his left arm and that the twenty-foot rope fastened to it and to his wrist.

Then with his right hand he raised the rock with which he would hit himself on the head. Luck would have to be with him on that blow; it would have to be hard enough to knock him out, but not hard enough to knock him out for long.

He had a hunch that the Roller was watching him, and would see him roll down through the barrier, and come to investigate. It would think he was dead, he hoped—he thought it had probably drawn the same deduction about the nature of the barrier that he had drawn. But it would come cautiously. He would have a little time—

He struck.

Pain brought him back to consciousness. A sudden, sharp pain in his hip that was different from the throbbing pain in his head and the throbbing pain in his leg.

But he had, thinking things out before he had struck himself, anticipated that very pain, even hoped for it, and had steeled himself against awakening with a sudden movement.

He lay still, but opened his eyes just a slit, and saw that he had guessed rightly. The Roller was coming closer. It was twenty feet away and the pain that had awakened him was the stone it had tossed to see whether he was alive or dead.

He lay still. It came closer, fifteen feet away, and stopped again. Carson scarcely breathed.

As nearly as possible, he was keeping his mind a blank, lest its telepathic ability detect consciousness in him. And with his mind blanked out that way, the impact of its thoughts upon his mind was nearly soul-shattering.

He felt sheer horror at the utter *alienness*, the *differentness* of those thoughts. Things that he felt but could not understand and could never express, because no terrestrial language had words, no terrestrial mind had images to fit them. The mind of a spider, he thought, or the mind of a praying mantis or a Martian sand-serpent, raised to intelligence and put in telepathic rapport with human minds, would be a homely familiar thing, compared to this.

He understood now that the Entity had been right: Man or Roller, and the universe was not a place that could hold them both. Farther apart than god and devil, there could never be even a balance between them.

Closer. Carson waited until it was only feet away, until its clawed tentacles reached out—

Oblivious to agony now, he sat up, raised and flung the harpoon with all the strength that remained to him. Or he thought it was all; sudden final strength flooded through him, along with a sudden forgetfulness of pain as definite as a nerve block.

As the Roller, deeply stabbed by the harpoon, rolled away, Carson tried to get to his feet to run after it. He couldn't do that; he fell, but kept crawling.

It reached the end of the rope, and he was jerked forward by the pull of his wrist. It dragged him a few feet and then stopped. Carson kept on going, pulling himself toward it hand over hand along the rope.

It stopped there, writhing tentacles trying in vain to pull out the harpoon. It seemed to shudder and quiver, and then it must have realized that it couldn't get away, for it rolled back toward him, clawed tentacles reaching out.

Stone knife in hand, he met it. He stabbed, again and again, while those horrid claws ripped skin and flesh and muscle from his body.

He stabbed and slashed, and at last it was still.

A bell was ringing, and it took him a while after he'd opened his eyes to tell where he was and what it was. He was strapped into the seat of his scouter, and the visiplate before him showed only empty space. No Outsider ship and no impossible planet.

The bell was the communications plate signal; someone wanted him to switch power into the receiver. Purely reflex action enabled him to reach forward and throw the lever.

The face of Brander, captain of the *Magellan,* mother-ship of his group of scouters, flashed into the screen. His face was pale and his black eyes glowed with excitement.

"*Magellan* to Carson," he snapped. "Come on in. The fight's over. We've won!"

The screen went blank; Brander would be signaling the other scouters of his command.

Slowly, Carson set the controls for the return. Slowly, unbelievingly, he unstrapped himself from the seat and went back to get a drink at the cold-water tank. For some reason, he was unbelievably thirsty. He drank six glasses.

He leaned there against the wall, trying to think.

Had it happened? He was in good health, sound, uninjured. His thirst had been mental rather than physical; his throat hadn't been dry. His leg—

He pulled up his trouser leg and looked at the calf. There was a long white scar there, but a perfectly healed scar. It hadn't been there before. He zipped open the front of his shirt and saw that his chest and abdomen were criss-crossed with tiny, almost unnoticeable, perfectly healed scars.

It *had* happened.

The scouter, under automatic control, was already entering the hatch of the mother-ship. The grapples pulled it into its individual lock, and a moment later a buzzer indicated that the lock was air-filled. Carson opened the hatch and stepped outside, went through the double door of the lock.

He went right to Brander's office, went in, and saluted.

Brander still looked dizzily dazed. "Hi, Carson," he said. "What you missed! What a show!"

"What happened, sir?"

"Don't know, exactly. We fired one salvo, and their whole fleet went up in dust! Whatever it was jumped from ship to ship in a flash, even the ones we hadn't aimed at and that were out of range! The whole fleet disintegrated before our eyes, and we didn't get the paint of a single ship scratched!

"We can't even claim credit for it. Must have been some unstable component in the metal they used, and our sighting shot just set it off. Man, oh man, too bad you missed all the excitement."

Carson managed to grin. It was a sickly ghost of a grin, for it would be days before he'd be over the mental impact of his experience, but the captain wasn't watching, and didn't notice.

"Yes, sir," he said. Common sense, more than modesty, told him he'd be branded forever as the worst liar in space if he ever said any more than that. "Yes, sir, too bad I missed all the excitement."

Jerry Shelton

CULTURE

BLOODSON was fat. He was also big. Big and fat—physically and financially. His huge body slouched motionless behind the immense black desk as the two stumbling men were brought in. Coldly, Bloodson watched the men, feet dragging, start the long trip toward him across the dazzling white floor. Effective!

Bloodson's small eyes blinked once as a stomach twinge sent him the pain message that already his newly installed stomach was developing the usual ulcers. His fourth stomach. This time he would accept no more excuses from the surgical staff. Punishment regardless—as soon as these men were efficiently dealt with of course.

The men halted wearily. No—not wearily. Bloodson tensed. No—these men were something else. Something—extra. Bloodson felt the back of his mind groping hurriedly down into the deeper thought channels, searching swiftly for something as precedent. His nape hairs tingled as the mental processes spewed forth nothing. So there *was* something unusually wrong here. He, too, could feel it. His psycho-medics—the fools—had reported that much before they gave up. Well, he'd show his bungling staff why he *was* Bloodson.

His brain narrowed. Analyze: The men just stood there. Their ripped gray uniforms showed the violence with which all insignia had been removed. BLOODSON EXPLORATORY ENTERPRISES insignia. Faces: gray. Eyes: dull—no—unfocused. Breathing: slow. Tension: arms, fingers limp. Severe nervous shock—perhaps. Bloodson's nostrils flared. Only the shorter one showed anything: just the slow twitching of a muscle in his right cheek.

Bloodson took a flashing glance at the notes on his desk, then leaned his massive bulk forward and—his exquisite chair squeaked! It was terrifying—that squeak. In the unbelievable vastness of that soaring room of polished beauty and efficiency—that squeak sawed the nerves. Effective! Bloodson knew.

And at the proper instant, he followed with the one word, "Why?" Softly.

The word slithered across the sleek twenty feet of desk at the two men like an amorous serpent.

The cheek muscle of the shorter gray-faced man stopped for an instant—and then continued twitching. Slowly and rhythmically. The

Jerry Shelton is a professional accordionist and orchestra leader in Chicago—certainly one of the most unusual occupations pursued by any science fiction writer.

silence deepened. The room was motionless except for the cheek muscle.

Bloodson frowned. He moved his head to stare deep into the un-focused eyes of the shorter one. Instantly, his mind reeled under the smashing impact of something that brought a quick sweat to his arm-pits. Locked there—behind those two visual windows was a brain fro-zen in the tortured pattern of something too horrible for a human mind to bear. The fuses in that mind had burnt out under the terrible over-load, leaving the helpless brain imprisoned in a swirling, chaotic jumble. Bloodson shivered, and snatched at his tottering reason. Attack!

He exploded. A mountain of flesh with a whipping saw-edged voice: "Do you men want me to have you psychoed?" Powerful as thunder crashes, rolling and booming, his amplified words smashed at the two men, bouncing off to boom heavily against the distant walls of that vast room. "What explanation can you possibly offer? An entire expedition; millions of credits; years of work—all lost—except for you two stubborn, silent men."

Bloodson's voice dropped. "And the lives of the expedition. How many? If you won't talk"—the voice roared—"I have ways of *making* you talk. You killed nine of the men with your own hands! Why?"

The men stood there.

"What happened to the other men you didn't kill?"

Silence.

"I warn you—" Bloodson's voice was ominous. "I had a Keybell neuro-recorder on that ship. I can have you psychoed. I can have my psycho-medics reconstruct what happened. But I warn you—the drain of nervous energy from your bodies will make you blithering idiots for years to come. *Will* you talk?"

Silence.

Bloodson's teeth made an audible sound. Grinding. "Psycho them."

On the instant, the room light dimmed and men approached wheel-ing a machine. Heavy and squat. Pneumatic chairs swelled up out of the floor and the gray-faced men were forced into them as neat robed medics hurried up unreeling thin shining wires from the Keybell.

The short one's cheek muscle twitched rapidly as the flashing scal-pels and tiny clamps inserted the trailing wires in the proper places. His jaw worked. Up and down. But no words came. His wooden-faced companion submitted, heedless of what the medics were doing to him.

Pressure of a switch; a low hum; and a pinkish milk-white cloud so-lidified in the center of the room. Vague images swirled and flickered. Jumbled voices—disjointed thoughts vibrated the room.

"You can do better than that," snapped Bloodson. "What am I pay-ing you medics for?"

The swirling mist brightened and suddenly snapped into crystal-clear reality. Three dimensional. The interior of a spaceship—a group of men—and a young voice interlocked with a developing thought tendril of worry—

"—somehow there must be an explanation behind all this." Hardwick tried to ignore the hunger biting at his stomach and at the same time to make his voice sound convincing. "It's merely a missing factor that must be found." The growing worry nagged at him—Junior Command was an alarming thing when it unexpectedly turned into Senior Command complete with an emergency not in the books. "That missing factor means our survival or—"

Benton interrupted. "If you were going to say 'survival or not'—I'd change it to 'survival or we'll all go psycho!' Huh?" Benton's sharp face looked around as if expecting a laugh. Not a man laughed. Faces were grim.

Hardwick held on to his overstrung nerves. "Let me finish, Benton. The scouting parties should return any moment. If they have found no trace of Captain Houseworth or the others, then we must consider them —dead." He sensed the level stares of the crew. "And that passes the command definitely to me."

Hardwick looked each man in the eye. These men were irritable. Their enforced thirty-period diet of concentrates had played havoc with their nervous systems. And the fact that they knew he, acting as Senior Command, was just as green to deep space as they were, didn't exactly help things either. They also knew that an immediate attempt had to be made to force out into the open the unseen, unguessed *something* that seemed to brood over this space-buried planet. He searched carefully for signs of open resentment to the fact that they realized their lives rested in his accurate judgment of the situation—and what must be done without delay. *Now!*

He felt a brief surge of confidence. He could detect no open resentment—yet. The next move was up to him.

Hardwick took a long breath. "Now"—he turned to the oil-splattered engineer—"what about the engines?"

The engineer sounded weary. "The same. I've explained to everybody until I'm sick of saying it. Those engines were in perfect working order until the third waking period after we landed. They just stopped. That's all. They are still perfect—except they won't work. Do you understand me?" His voice rose. "Every stinking tube and coil I've taken apart and put back half-a-dozen times. Everything's perfect. Except—"

"Except they don't work," finished Benton, dryly. 'And how much longer can we function on the emergency batteries alone? Four more waking periods is tops. We won't have to worry about eating concentrates. That's *my* guess. Huh?"

Hardwick gave Benton a long look. "If our hydroponics hadn't disappeared, we wouldn't be eating concentrates. Those ponics were your responsibility and you've offered no satisfactory explanation as yet."

Benton shrugged. "I still don't see how those stupid, naked natives could have stolen forty tons of ponic tanks. Too big. Too heavy. The lock was guarded—or wasn't it? I'm not psychic. They don't seem to eat anyhow. We don't know yet if they *do* eat, or if they do, where they get it. No agriculture; no industries—all they seem to do is play. What a stupid—"

Metal-shod feet clanked through the open starboard lock. "*Something* around here isn't so stupid!" It was Doc Marshal, the medic. "Other scouting party back yet?" Wassel, the language expert, shouldered in past Marshal's bulky figure and sat down on the tool locker with a metallic thump.

Hardwick shook his head. "Did you find the captain or the men?"

A shadow flitted across Marshal's firm-jawed face. "No," bluntly. Then his face softened. "That makes you the skipper for sure, lad. Organization is your specialty, so you should do all right. Luck to you." He flexed his massive shoulders. "But we investigated that smaller black temple in the valley."

"And scared the blazes out of our well-balanced, beautifully integrated minds. Eh—Doc?" This from Wassel.

The slender sociologist in the corner stirred irritably. "If you will remember, I originally insisted that it is dangerous to interfere with any civilization's temple of religion or to try to contact their females."

"Who said anything specific about religion or women?" countered Marshal. "What did we know about their religion or their women? Where are their females anyhow? Whoever heard of a race consisting *only* of males between the apparent ages of ten and fifty? Where are the kids? Where are the old ones?"

"Or the women?" rumbled Wassel from where he rested.

"A moment," cut in Hardwick smoothly. "While it is true we are the first expedition in this star cluster, I still don't think sociological problems should concern us too much. It was our luck and should be our good fortune to have discovered a planet rich in coal deposits. We've tried to trade fairly with these natives for their hydrocarbons which are so precious to our laboratories. Our mechanos have filled the ship's hold to capacity. Despite the fact they don't seem interested in payment—we will leave just payment, regardless."

"If we leave," said Benton softly.

The sociologist shot Benton a dark look. "We are discussing sociological considerations more important than a temporary emergency."

"Temporary?" Benton's jaw dropped.

The thin sociologist ignored him. "I admit that it is decidedly a departure from the norm for a humanoid race to not appear interested in gainful trade—or acceptance of gifts. These natives have upset me more than I care to admit. I've offered them everything from gaudy trinkets to sub-ether communicators. They are not interested. Therefore"—he put his fingertips together—"regardless of what we might leave as payment, assuming we take the coal, *if* the payment has no value to them—we are stealing the coal." He leaned back in his corner. "That is my point and I might add that it could be a clue toward that missing factor you mentioned."

Benton sniffed. "My bet is that the engines would start if we put that coal back where the mechanos got it. Might be something religious. Then maybe we'd get off this space-forsaken hunk of dirt. Although I don't see how in blazes they could mess up our engines like this. And I'm hungry." He looked at Wassel. "If we could find out where or how *they* eat . . . hey, Wassel . . . how about it? Why don't *you* ask them for a handout?"

Lips tight, Wassel said in a slow voice: "I am a qualified expert at analyzing, understanding and speaking any language—given time. Any language—"

"Except this one," said Benton.

"Benton," Wassel jumped to his feet. "If you don't quit interrupting people—"

"At ease," mocked Benton. "Everything's fine. In ten periods you've learned fifty-three words and seven gestures."

"He did his best," said Hardwick steadily. Then to Doc Marshal, "What about that temple? What scared you?"

Marshal took a long breath before he answered. "We weren't exactly scared, we were just—" He groped for a word.

"We don't believe it," said Wassel in a flat voice.

Hardwick felt a slow chill settle on his heart.

"That's all we need," exploded the engineer. "More things we can't believe. Our skipper vanishes into nothing out of a locked control room. Men go for walks and don't come back. We don't know their language—we don't know their religion—we don't know anything—the ponics are gone—and my perfect engines won't work."

"What's getting into him?" snapped Benton. "While he sits here safe in the ship tinkering with a lot of tubes—we've all been out there floundering around deliberately trying to find something that will flatten our ears down if we do. I say give the coal back—"

Hardwick felt a curious sense of detachment as the hot words and accusations crackled back and forth in the cramped quarters. Let them argue. Let them talk. Somehow—somewhere, their anger-stimulated minds were going to find the thread they had all missed. A thread that could be captured and dragged out into the open where these usually cold scientific minds could logically weave it into the larger unseen, unguessed pattern. Nerves were reaching the breaking point. You couldn't blame the men. The helplessness of trying to find something to fight and not finding it was unnerving to the finest of nervous systems. Especially nerves connected to growling stomachs.

Something had to be done. He was now Senior Command beyond a doubt—and the men looked to him for organization. Hardwick felt very young and troubled as he let his mind spiral back down into the room noise.

Marshal was speaking: "—as soon as we reached the door of the smaller black temple in the valley we stopped and checked the fuses on our blasters. The natives we had passed, as usual, practically ignored us."

"Up to this moment," broke in Wassel, "none of us had ventured inside a temple"—he nodded toward the sociologist—"in accordance with his ideas. We hadn't found a trace of the skipper, and Doc was in a frenzy of curiosity after seeing a native with an injured arm walk into that temple and then walk out a few moments later—perfectly healed. That's strong stuff to take without a look-see. Eh—Doc?"

Doc Marshal grunted.

"Besides," Wassel straightened up, "although limited by the small vocabulary I had picked up—I nevertheless had spent the entire previous waking period questioning one native whose attention I was lucky enough to hold. It was difficult as their language is coupled with gestures."

"Wait until you hear this," interjected Marshal. "It'll blast you."

"Well—I tried to find out what was meant by this sign," Wassel gestured, "accompanied by the long double-vowel sound." He looked around as if prepared for disbelief. "It means 'Going to Heaven'!"

"What?" The question came automatically in several voices.

"Yes—as far as I can understand—those natives merely live for the time until they go to a place which would be the same in our comprehension as—Heaven!" Wassel looked around the room nervously. *"But they also return!* Evidently they do it quite often. Go to Heaven and return to wait impatiently for the next time. When I pressed the native for more detailed information as to why and how the process took place he became vague—something about: *You had to come and get yourself."*

There was a dead silence. Wassel looked around.

Hardwick could sense the men—their minds already filled to the bursting point with contradictions—trying to digest that astounding bit of information—and then rejecting it. Their nerves, meanwhile, pulled a shade tighter.

Hardwick said quietly, "What happened inside, Doc?"

Wassel flushed a deep red. "I see"—the words came out heavily—"you don't think I correctly interpreted—"

"Forget it," interrupted Marshal. "I'll tell them something just as bad. I'll be brief. Inside the temple were a lot of gadgets we couldn't understand. So I'll skip that. We waited. Pretty soon, two natives came in carrying another one between them. He was a mess—looked as if he had been mangled somehow. Well—they pushed open a red door at the far end and carried him in. Then they walked out and shut the door. They waited," Doc Marshal closed his eyes. "Whatever went on behind that red door I don't know, but a moment later that native walked out perfectly well."

A pause.

"That's all?" breathed the engineer in a hushed voice.

"That's all," said Wassel bluntly.

The room was silent save for the hiss of the emergency air circulation system.

Benton broke in sarcastically. "I don't suppose you even tried to look behind that door?"

Hardwick snapped himself to the alert. "Would you, Benton?"

Benton flustered, "Why . . . of course . . . I would have—"

"That's fine." Hardwick felt his duty of command give him strength. "Put on your body armor—that's what you and I are going to do."

Hardwick's further orders were interrupted as Miller returned from his scouting trip. He was alone. He walked through the air lock like a dead man. White-faced. Wordlessly he passed through the stunned group and continued to his quarters.

"Miller—" Hardwick's tone was sharp. And as Miller continued aft, stumbling heedlessly down the passageway, he motioned to Benton. "Get him."

Miller was brought back. He sat down like an automaton.

Hardwick felt prickles start up his back. "Where are Thompkins and McKesson?"

Miller began to shake his head from side to side. Slowly. But no words sounded. Long racking sobs began to twist him double. His eyes were dry. His mouth drooled wet. Roughly, Doc slapped him, but Miller continued to sob—long racking sobs as if his throat would burst.

Hardwick fought to steady his voice as he said: "Miller's one of our best men. What could do that to him?"

Marshal frowned and began to question Miller in a quiet voice until the words came, haltingly: "Outside . . . Thompkins . . . almost here . . . and then—" Miller shuddered. The voice stopped.

"Quick," rapped Hardwick, "see if Thompkins is outside. Find him."

When they dragged in what once must have been Thompkins, Hardwick clenched his hands until the nails dug deep into his palms. He saw the shocked crew turning away—sickened—trying desperately to control themselves. The engineer leaned over, ill, while Benton stared wide-eyed, saying, "Get it out of here."

Hardwick had to force himself to look at the motionless thing on the deck. Twisted, torn, mangled—the body looked—yes—looked as if something tremendous and irresistible had forced half of it inside out. Only half of it—that was what made it so revolting. Like a child's glove. A wet trail, splotched with crimson, indicated mutely the direction of the air lock.

Something cracked inside Hardwick's brain. "Enough!" he roared, "we've had enough of this. All men into their full battle armor—we're going to settle this or blast every stinking temple to ruins. Marshal— you and Wassel find out from Miller exactly what happened. Find out about McKesson—drug him if you have to—but get it out and tape it. I'll want to hear it before we leave. Now jump! On the double!"

That did it. The verbal explosion did it. The men moved swiftly, each to a job he had been trained for. This was something they could understand and relish. Action at last after endless waiting. Hardwick's orders rolled from the loudspeakers throughout. The ship vibrated to the thud of running feet, excited voices, the clank of body armor and the breaking out of battle equipment.

The assembly klaxon blared, and the men jammed the tiny room forward of the lock.

Hardwick counted them, ". . . twelve—thirteen. A baker's dozen. All right, men. This is it. We've been trying to handle this thing in a civilized way according to the book some brass hat writes sitting at a desk. By following the book we lost four men. That's four men too many. We've tried to think this thing through to learn what to fight— well, now we'll *find* it! Marshal, play the tape you got from Miller."

The men were silent and attentive as Miller's halting voice, drug- deadened, filled the room: "Three of us . . . up to biggest temple . . . top of the hill . . . Black . . . five miles square . . . five miles high . . . I guess . . . got to the door . . . big door or opening . . . yes . . . opening . . . McKesson volunteered to go in." A long pause. "He . . . went in the blackness . . . and . . . his torch and radio call just winked off—" Pause. "We waited long time . . . decided best return to ship . . . almost here when a wind and rustling noise . . . something came down . . . could see Thompkins struggle and some- thing . . . twisted and turned him until . . . until—" A longer pause while Doc Marshal's voice was heard to say, "Might as well give him another shot." Then Miller: "Must have fainted because when I came to, I saw . . . I saw—" The sobbing started again.

Hardwick switched off the tape. "That's it, men—whatever it is. We'll take a look at that temple first. Take along two semiportable blasters and extra-heavy duty fuses. Let's go."

The men marched, close formation, with a semiportable blaster wheeling front and rear through the town and past the outskirts. With- out the heavy duty blasters the party could have reached the temple with the aid of their suit repulsors in a tenth of the time. But the walk- ing felt good to their ship-cramped muscles. The naked natives they passed only favored them with brief stares. The late afternoon sun glinted dully on their formidable battle armor as they climbed the hill to the square black temple. Far below, their ship dwindled until it resembled a tiny gold needle.

Hardwick halted before the opening. The building—if it was a build- ing—was a solid black without seam or blemish. It erupted, squat and massive, five miles up into the air. What substance composed its walls he didn't try to guess or why or how or when such a building was built. The opening was only noticeable by being blacker than the walls. Experimentally, he flicked on his powerful hand torch and was sur- prised to see the opening swallow the intense beam like space itself. The opening seemed to be several hundred yards wide and about half a mile high. He couldn't be sure. What reason could a race of naked natives have for a thing like this?

With the men watching, Hardwick approached the opening and carefully thrust the head of his battle-ax into the blackness. It just disappeared. He felt nothing. He withdrew the weapon and examined it critically. Perfect. Careful to keep clear of the black veil—it seemed a veil—he again thrust the ax through and lowered it until it touched something solid at what should be floor level. He straightened up and drew back. As he turned, he noticed the setting sun was withdrawing before long black shadows that were slowly swallowing the ship in the valley beneath. A chill developed unaccountably. The Powers of Darkness? Hardwick muttered irritably at himself. He was being silly. The men were waiting.

"Hardwick!" It was a voice, full of alarm, crackling in over his headset. The men were running toward him and pointing at something behind his back.

He swung around, both hands tense on the handle of his heavy battle-ax. Something was stepping through the veil. It was a native. Bronzed and bare of any clothing. The native walked toward them, mouthing words and making gestures. In some sort of a way, Hardwick felt that he should know this native. As if he had known him somewhere.

The native walked over to Benton and said in perfect Earthian: "Well . . . I didn't think I looked that surprised. Come along now—"

Marshal gasped. "He speaks Earthian. Why, he looks like—"

"Seize him," ripped Hardwick as the native took the open-mouthed unresisting Benton by the arm and led him toward the dark opening.

One of the gunners whipped up his blaster and the native's eyes widened in alarm. "Don't," he screamed as the blaster leveled, "you don't understand . . . don't—"

The blast caught him deep in the shoulder and spun him around, hanging desperately on to Benton who seemed dazed by the nearness of the blast.

Dashing forward, Hardwick saw the native, with a last agonized gesture, push the numbed Benton through the yawning opening into the engulfing darkness.

Hardwick and Marshal were on the native in a flash, dragging him away from the veil.

"You speak Earthian," gritted Hardwick, "now we've got one of you. What goes on?"

"He looks like Benton," cut in Marshal.

The native rolled his head helplessly, his voice weak. "I am Benton." The voice faded and the eyelids fluttered.

Hardwick gasped. He looked close. It was true—it was Benton. A different Benton. Skin bronzed from head to foot. Slightly older, perhaps. Bare feet callused.

The bronzed Benton licked his dry lips and tried to gather strength. *"Remember Wassel said you had to come get yourself to go to Heaven?"* His voice rattled and the eyes dimmed. "I've been in Heaven—lots of women. Beautiful women and lots of kids—*my* kids. Was going to explain . . . only . . . you—" A long quiver started to run through the body. "Don't go back . . . they—"

Benton was dead.

Hardwick was startled to see Doc Marshal straighten up suddenly. His face was drained of all blood. Silver white. His voice thick, he said, "Let's get back to the ship."

"No," Hardwick was firm. "I'm going in there and see what—"

"It won't do any good," said Marshal dully. "I've got to get back to the ship. I've got to. Then I'll know for sure." He flicked on the warming button to his suit repulsors. "I'm going now. Coming, Wassel?"

Hardwick's mind rocked. This was unthinkable! He was in command—or wasn't he? Could Marshal be turning yellow? Anger blazed within him. "I'm going in there."

"If you wish," said Marshal tonelessly, "but it won't do any good. I'll know for sure when I get to the ship." He pushed his throttle open and soared swishing up into the night.

Wassel looked at Hardwick keenly. "Should I go with him? Think he needs me?"

"He needs something." Sickened, Hardwick turned away. "The rest of us can handle this." He didn't even look up as he heard Wassel's body whistle up and up in a long looping flight down toward the ship. He felt empty.

Hardwick pulled at his scattered emotions. This was no time for a letdown. "You—Taylor. Hook up to my belt cable and you to Gregor and so on down the line. I'm going in as far as a cable length. If my radio cuts out—don't enter unless I give three tugs. If I pull once—pull me out. Quickly. If you want me to come out, pull twice and then pull me out anyhow. Got it?"

The men moved about their duties quietly, their glowing hand torches and shining battle dress giving them the appearance of gnomes. Hardwick shook himself. He must get a better grip on his nerves or he would be imagining things. He tried a short laugh. The laugh sounded like a grunt. Or did he need to imagine things? Hadn't enough happened already?

Slowly, carefully, he approached the black curtain. It drank the beam of his torch. No reflection. He pushed his battle-ax through. Nothing— then his arm. No sensation. Now, tensely, he inched his foot into the blackness. It seemed solid. Now he was almost inside—almost—

Instantly, blackness. Hardwick shivered but began a slow sliding, inching progress deeper into the blackness. His headset was dead. Not even the hiss of static. He mustn't get lost. The thought made him whirl in the direction of the opening behind him. Nothing—panic seized him and he was about to grope for the belt cable when without warning he was jerked viciously from his feet. His mind spun as he felt himself hurtle through space to crash heavily on a hard surface.

Hardwick opened his eyes. He was outside! Sprawling on the ground. Everything was a chaos. Dimly he could see the men firing rapidly in all directions. Firing at something he couldn't see. And didn't understand. His mind snarled inside his skull. The eternal stumbling and fumbling and waiting now seemed ended. Something was happening. He started to run over to where one of the semiportable blasters was spitting intolerable flashes into the dark sky—and stumbled over a body. Automatically he dropped his glare shield to absorb the blinding flashes from the blaster and saw it was the crushed and mangled body of Taylor. The strong cable was snapped from the beltlike thread. That tremendous jerk—his temples pounded—had pulled him out. But what had done *that* to Taylor. A few feet away he saw another body flattened and impressed into the hard soil as if from the blow of a gigantic maul.

Overhead, things swirled and whirled. His straining eyes couldn't quite catch an image in definite focus. The men were drawn together in a tight ring—back to back—their blasters flashing upward in futile-seeming blasts. The impressions, the thoughts, the incoming scenes all washed into his mind as a gigantic overwhelming wave. Almost in the same instant, he gave the command to return to the ship, dropped his cable and flicked on his repulsor. He waited until the last man had cleared and then put on full acceleration for the distant ship.

The air sighed at his body armor as Hardwick, every muscle tense, eyes wide, waited for something to happen to him. The wind whistled. Vague things brushed him—or did he imagine it? His knee hurt.

The ship swelled in size as he dropped swiftly. He could see tiny figures tumbling into the open lock. The lighted opening yawned—swallowed him—the lock clanged. He was inside!

"Sit down, Hardwick." The voice was weary. Weary as death.

Hardwick turned.

Doc Marshal faced him. He held a blaster cocked at full aperture. Stunned, Hardwick stood there.

"Sit down. I don't think outside will bother us now that we are back to where we are supposed to stay like good little boys." Marshal twitched the blaster. "Pardon this thing—but first I must know how all of you will feel about what I have to say. It's not pleasant."

Hardwick hardly heard his words. He had noticed a faint familiar throbbing beneath his feet. Why—that meant the engines were functioning again. That meant they could move once again. He galvanized into action. "The engines . . . we're leaving—"

"HOLD IT!" It was Marshal holding the blaster dead on him. "We're not going anywhere."

The words just skittered across Hardwick's mind for an interval before his brain accepted the unbelievable knowledge his ears brought.

"Not . . . going . . . anywhere?" Hardwick heard himself say the meaningless words and his mind tightened. "Seize him, men. We're getting out of here."

Not a man moved. Their eyes were riveted on the blaster held so steadily.

For the first time Hardwick noticed that Wassel was standing slightly behind and to the right of Marshal. His eyes held an expression that made Hardwick wince. He looked at Doc Marshal and there, too, was a look of hopeless, utter defeat.

Hardwick sat down.

"That's better." Marshal said it almost gently and then his voice shook as he continued. "I'm sorry, Hardwick. I'm sorry for everybody. I'm even sorry for myself." He took a breath and seemed trying to form a sentence. Finally, he managed: "If we are the men I think we are—we are all dead men!"

Hardwick's nerves jumped. He had to deal with this situation psychologically. Doc Marshal, his old friend, must have cracked up. He tried to relax and say in a calm voice: "Now look, Doc, put down that blaster and let's start from the beginning."

Marshal smiled grayly. "There is no beginning now—this is the end." He tightened his grip on the weapon. "So don't think you can talk me into putting this thing down. This is the finish for all of us. I've talked it over with Wassel, told him what I'd analyzed and he agrees. Right, Wassel?"

It was the look on Wassel's face and the utterly hopeless way that he nodded that gave Hardwick his first grave doubt. Wassel's eyes held a message. A dreadful message. What had they discovered to pull the backbone out of men such as they? What had they decided?

Hardwick thought darkly. Let Marshal talk all he wanted to, but the first unwary instant—he—Hardwick, would get that blaster and then he would see. But he must be swift, as Doc was an expert with a blaster.

Marshal went on: "Hardwick, during your brief assumption of Senior Command, it is my opinion you did your best. I'm sure the men feel the same. You were under a tremendous strain. No one could ask a man for more. You did all right."

Hardwick's heart missed three beats. What did Doc mean by saying: *did* and *were? That was as if his command was past tense!* What did Doc mean? "Explain yourself," he burst out. "This is mutiny!"

Doc Marshal shook his head. "It is far more than mere mutiny. But I am putting the responsibility solely on my own head. And my main responsibility is seeing to it that you all either kill yourselves"—he looked around the suddenly hushed circle—"or I'll kill all of you—to a man!"

Hardwick could hear his own mind repeating that astounding message word for word—over and over—like a recording tape. It didn't make sense. The engines were working again—

Words tumbled out of Wassel. "Don't you see? The rabbits!" His voice shrilled. "Just like the rabbits and guinea pigs in Doc's laboratory."

Doc Marshal's tired voice cut in: "Like my rabbits." He paused as if he had to mentally lift a great weight. Then: "Hardwick, I have a laboratory full of animals back there. I breed them for laboratory purposes. Experiments, toxins, cultures, vitamins. Things we humans breed for our own selfish purposes. I don't keep the male rabbits with the female rabbits. The rabbits don't know who built their pens. Or why. They don't know how food magically appears or from where. They don't know how they are healed. Time to them is surely different from time to us. They don't know how one rabbit is miraculously transported from one pen to another. It must be rabbit heaven for a healthy male when he is put into a pen full of—"

"STOP IT!" Hardwick was astounded to realize it had been his own voice that had blurted that command. His entire being retreated from the realization that was trying to get a foothold in his brain. He said dully, "All those humanoids out there are nothing more than—" He couldn't finish. "Then why don't we get out of here?"

As if off in a distance he could hear the other men clamoring. Angrily.

Marshal blanketed the noise. "Wait—my original statement was that *if we are the men I think we are—we are all dead men!*" He went on swiftly. "The human race—our civilization could never accept the knowledge we now have. Think what a devastating realization it would be to our civilization to know it was nothing but a race of—wild rabbits that hadn't been discovered. Humans could never face the fact that a race existed so far superior to them that they were nothing but animals used in experiments."

Wassel broke in: "After all, it's not so unthinkable that . . . higher life forms might need . . . higher life forms than rabbits to breed their own cultures necessary to protect themselves against"—he shrugged wearily—"something deadly to them?"

Doc Marshal said, "If you were raising white rabbits and discovered that unaccountably some . . . black rabbits had somehow wandered into the pens . . . what would you do?" He didn't wait for an answer. "At first you would make certain they didn't get away. Then you would remove a few specimens and examine—dissect a few—analyze their food supply—and then what would you do?"

"Try to scare them back to where they came from." Hardwick said it listlessly. "Try to catch the rest of the bunch."

"Exactly," said Marshal. "When we got back to the ship I knew that that was what is expected of us."

"The engines were working again," said Wassel.

Marshal's image faded into focus on Hardwick's spinning brain. The blaster was steady and Marshal went on: "Whatever is out there, found out what it wanted to know. Now it wants us to go back where we came from. Catch the rest of the bunch perhaps—we don't know. We can't

hope to explain or beg. It wouldn't even recognize us as thinking creatures to its way of reasoning. Us, our civilization, this ship, is probably
kid's stuff. But there is one thing it probably doesn't know and that is
man's—our civilization's eternal willingness to"—the voice faltered for an
instant, then steadied—"sacrifice everything—life itself, for the preservation of the race. It was inevitable, as our race expanded, that sooner or
later we would stick our necks out too far. Run into something so utterly far beyond our own development that it couldn't be handled in
ordinary ways. This is it. But I think we can handle it."

The engineer cracked immediately like a strip of metal bent too far.
His voice babbled and pleaded and cursed. "Let's get out of here."

It began to infect the other men. Hardwick could feel it. He felt
strangely distant, but he could feel the growing mob instinct. The wild
desire to get away from something it couldn't understand. The room
was a bedlam of shouting voices. If Marshal was right—this then was
death for all of them. And him. Perhaps Marshal was being too hasty.
Overwrought. Perhaps he had missed something. But if Marshal was
right, then he was right one thousand percent. They had to die rather
than return and take the chance of whatever was out there discovering
their unthinkably distant civilization. Hardwick had a smothering sensation. Even a civilization as powerful as this unknown thing that hung
over them couldn't hope to find their home planet in the uncounted
billions of suns unless they led the way home. Or could it?

Abruptly he found himself thinking that Marshal was right. But no
—he must get that blaster and convince Marshal to wait until—he didn't
know what. He snapped alert as the engineer roared:

"Why kill ourselves? I ain't gonna kill myself and you ain't gonna kill
me! So what do you think of that? I say let's get out of here." His body
was tensing visibly.

Marshal's face became a mask of pain as he looked at the engineer.
"If the thing sees we don't leave or thinks we are trying to give it the
slip, who knows what it could do? Who knows what it could learn from
our brain channels if we forced it? If it already hasn't." He swung the
blaster. "I'm sorry—believe me." And shot him.

In that instant, Hardwick leaped for the blaster—and in that floating
split second, as his body hurtled through the air, he knew he was too
late.

He saw Marshal's distended eyes and the flaring mouth of the blaster
swing toward him as in a dream. Time seemed to stop and he was suspended in midair. The muzzle flared. Bright.

The intolerable blow smashed him. His mind filled with swirling
blackness spotted with spinning flashes of red pain. Dimly he heard
Marshal say, "How do the rest of you men want it? It's got to be
done."

Then he must have fainted for when he felt himself coming back
and up as from a great distance all was quiet except for Marshal saying, "—am sorry about Hardwick. There was no other way."

Hardwick struggled against the weakness. He must let Marshal know. His throat managed to whisper, "Right . . . Doc . . . it's all right—" and then Hardwick felt his mind going over the edge of darkness and he knew Doc Marshal was right. As his mind slipped down and down it thought bitterly—so this is death—blackness. And the thoughts and consciousness that had been Hardwick glimmered faintly and went out.

Marshal's stooping figure straightened up from Hardwick's lifeless body. He looked at Wassel. "I liked Hardwick." His voice choked. "And now that leaves you and me—"

The figures of the two men suddenly flickered and the walls of the spaceship wavered as a thick milky whiteness swirled around and—

Bloodson's frightened eyes stared at the now fuzzy and jumbled three-dimensional images, and then at the two silent gray-faced men in the pneumatic chairs.

"Marshal," he croaked. "Wassel—you fools. Why did you try . . . how did you two men bring back that entire ship all by—"

"WITHDRAWING!" cut in the alien thought. "ENOUGH. SUGGEST PERMITTING CULTURE TO BREED UNMOLESTED. USELESS FOR OUR PURPOSES. INDIVIDUAL INITIATIVE AND INSTINCT OF RACIAL PRESERVATION TOO HIGHLY DEVELOPED. RETENTION OF KNOWLEDGE OF OUR EXISTENCE FORBIDDEN. SUGGEST DISINFECTING LOCAL AREA. WITHDRAWING."

Terror-stricken, Bloodson watched one of the gray-clad figures collapse like a deflated balloon and the other figure rise from the chair withdrawing a strange-looking instrument.

"No—" gasped Bloodson. "No—" And then he sagged in his exquisite chair waiting for he knew not what.

PART SIX

World of Tomorrow

JULES VERNE

IN THE YEAR 2889

LITTLE though they seem to think of it, the people of this twenty-ninth century live continually in fairyland. Surfeited as they are with marvels, they are indifferent in presence of each new marvel. To them all seems natural. Could they but duly appreciate the refinements of civilization in our day; could they but compare the present with the past, and so better comprehend the advance we have made! How much fairer they would find our modern towns, with populations amounting sometimes to 10,000,000 souls; their streets 300 feet wide, their houses 100 feet in height; with a temperature the same in all seasons; with their lines of aërial locomotion crossing the sky in every direction! If they would but picture to themselves the state of things that once existed, when through muddy streets rumbling boxes on wheels, drawn by horses—yes, by horses!—were the only means of conveyance. Think of the railroads of the olden time, and you will be able to appreciate the pneumatic tubes through which to-day one travels at the rate of 100 miles an hour. Would not our contemporaries prize the telephone and the telephote more highly if they had not forgotten the telegraph?

Singularly enough, all these transformations rest upon principles which were perfectly familiar to our remote ancestors, but which they disregarded. Heat, for instance, is as ancient as man himself; electricity was known 3000 years ago, and steam 1100 years ago. Nay, so early as ten centuries ago it was known that the differences between the several chemical and physical forces depend on the mode of vibration of the etheric particles, which is for each specifically different. When at last the kinship of all these forces was discovered, it is simply astounding

As far as is known this amusing prophecy by one of the fathers of modern science fiction has never been reprinted in English since its original appearance in *The Forum*, New York, in February, 1889. . . . One curious circumstance about its translation bears repeating. When first published in the French language, the names of the two newspaper owners were completely different from those used in the English translation. The nineteenth century journalist was called James Gordon Bennett, and his paper was *The New York Herald*. His descendant's name was Francis Bennett, and he ran the *Earth Herald*. The editors of *The Forum*, obviously not wanting to become involved in any dispute with the Bennett family (James Gordon died in 1872), simply changed the names to Smith. It is a pleasure to set the record straight, even at this late date.

that 500 years should still have to elapse before men could analyze and describe the several modes of vibration that constitute these differences. Above all, it is singular that the mode of reproducing these forces directly from one another, and of reproducing one without the others, should have remained undiscovered till less than a hundred years ago. Nevertheless, such was the course of events, for it was not till the year 2792 that the famous Oswald Nier made this great discovery.

Truly was he a great benefactor of the human race. His admirable discovery led to many another. Hence is sprung a pleiad of inventors, its brightest star being our great Joseph Jackson. To Jackson we are indebted for those wonderful instruments—the new accumulators. Some of these absorb and condense the living force contained in the sun's rays; others, the electricity stored in our globe; others again, the energy coming from whatever source, as a waterfall, a stream, the winds, etc. He, too, it was that invented the transformer, a more wonderful contrivance still, which takes the living force from the accumulator, and, on the simple pressure of a button, gives it back to space in whatever form may be desired, whether as heat, light, electricity, or mechanical force, after having first obtained from it the work required. From the day when these two instruments were contrived is to be dated the era of true progress. They have put into the hands of man a power that is almost infinite. As for their applications, they are numberless. Mitigating the rigors of winter, by giving back to the atmosphere the surplus heat stored up during the summer, they had revolutionized agriculture. By supplying motive power for aërial navigation, they have given to commerce a mighty impetus. To them we are indebted for the continuous production of electricity without batteries or dynamos, of light without combustion or incandescence, and for an unfailing supply of mechanical energy for all the needs of industry.

Yes, all these wonders have been wrought by the accumulator and the transformer. And can we not to them also trace, indirectly, this latest wonder of all, the great "Earth Chronicle" building in 253d Avenue, which was dedicated the other day? If George Washington Smith, the founder of the Manhattan "Chronicle," should come back to life today, what would he think were he to be told that this palace of marble and gold belongs to his remote descendant, Fritz Napoloen Smith, who, after thirty generations have come and gone, is owner of the same newspaper which his ancestor established!

For George Washington Smith's newspaper has lived generation after generation, now passing out of the family, anon coming back to it. When, 200 years ago, the political center of the United States was transferred from Washington to Centropolis, the newspaper followed the government and assumed the name of Earth Chronicle. Unfortunately, it was unable to maintain itself at the high level of its name. Pressed on all sides by rival journals of a more modern type, it was continually in danger of collapse. Twenty years ago its subscription list contained but a few hundred thousand names, and then Mr. Fritz

Napoleon Smith bought it for a mere trifle, and originated telephonic journalism.

Every one is familiar with Fritz Napoleon Smith's system—a system made possible by the enormous development of telephony during the last hundred years. Instead of being printed, the Earth Chronicle is every morning spoken to subscribers, who, in interesting conversations with reporters, statesmen, and scientists, learn the news of the day. Furthermore, each subscriber owns a phonograph, and to this instrument he leaves the task of gathering the news whenever he happens not to be in a mood to listen directly himself. As for purchasers of single copies, they can at a very trifling cost learn all that is in the paper of the day at any of the innumerable phonographs set up nearly everywhere.

Fritz Napoleon Smith's innovation galvanized the old newspaper. In the course of a few years the number of subscribers grew to be 85,-000,000 and Smith's wealth went on growing, till now it reaches the almost unimaginable figure of $10,000,000,000. This lucky hit has enabled him to erect his new building, a vast edifice with four *façades*, each 3,250 feet in length, over which proudly floats the hundred-starred flag of the Union. Thanks to the same lucky hit, he is to-day king of newspaperdom; indeed, he would be king of all the Americans, too, if Americans could ever accept a king. You do not believe it? Well, then, look at the plenipotentiaries of all nations and our own ministers themselves crowding about his door, entreating his counsels, begging for his approbation, imploring the aid of his all-powerful organ. Reckon up the number of scientists and artists that he supports, of inventors that he has under his pay.

Yes, a king is he. And in truth his is a royalty full of burdens. His labors are incessant, and there is no doubt at all that in earlier times any man would have succumbed under the overpowering stress of the toil which Mr. Smith has to perform. Very fortunately for him, thanks to the progress of hygiene, which, abating all the old sources of unhealthfulness, has lifted the mean of human life from 37 up to 52 years, men have stronger constitutions now than heretofore. The discovery of nutritive air is still in the future, but in the meantime men to-day consume food that is compounded and prepared according to scientific principles, and they breathe an atmosphere freed from the microorganisms that formerly used to swarm in it; hence they live longer than their forefathers and know nothing of the innumerable diseases of olden times.

Nevertheless, and notwithstanding these considerations, Fritz Napoleon Smith's mode of life may well astonish one. His iron constitution is taxed to the utmost by the heavy strain that is put upon it. Vain the attempt to estimate the amount of labor he undergoes; an example alone can give an idea of it. Let us then go about with him for one day as he attends to his multifarious concernments. What day? That matters little; it is the same every day. Let us then take at random September 25th of this present year 2889.

This morning Mr. Fritz Napoleon Smith awoke in very bad humor. His wife having left for France eight days ago, he was feeling disconsolate. Incredible though it seems, in all the ten years since their marriage, this is the first time that Mrs. Edith Smith, the professional beauty, has been so long absent from home; two or three days usually suffice for her frequent trips to Europe. The first thing that Mr. Smith does is to connect his phonotelephote, the wires of which communicate with his Paris mansion. The telephote! Here is another of the great triumphs of science in our time. The transmission of speech is an old story; the transmission of images by means of sensitive mirrors connected by wires is a thing but of yesterday. A valuable invention indeed, and Mr. Smith this morning was not niggard of blessings for the inventor, when by its aid he was able distinctly to see his wife notwithstanding the distance that separated him from her. Mrs. Smith, weary after the ball or the visit to the theater the preceding night, is still abed, though it is near noontide at Paris. She is asleep, her head sunk in the lace-covered pillows. What? She stirs? Her lips move. She is dreaming perhaps? Yes, dreaming. She is talking, pronouncing a name—his name— Fritz! The delightful vision gave a happier turn to Mr. Smith's thoughts. And now, at the call of imperative duty, light-hearted he springs from his bed and enters his mechanical dresser.

Two minutes later the machine deposited him all dressed at the threshold of his office. The round of journalistic work was now begun. First he enters the hall of the novel-writers, a vast apartment crowned with an enormous transparent cupola. In one corner is a telephone, through which a hundred Earth Chronicle *littérateurs* in turn recount to the public in daily installments a hundred novels. Addressing one of these authors who was waiting his turn, "Capital! Capital! my dear fellow," said he, "your last story. The scene where the village maid discusses interesting philosophical problems with her lover shows your very acute power of observation. Never have the ways of country folk been better portrayed. Keep on, my dear Archibald, keep on! Since yesterday, thanks to you, there is a gain of 5000 subscribers."

"Mr. John Last," he began again, turning to a new arrival, "I am not so well pleased with your work. Your story is not a picture of life; it lacks the elements of truth. And why? Simply because you run straight on to the end; because you do not analyze. Your heroes do this thing or that from this or that motive, which you assign without ever a thought of dissecting their mental and moral natures. Our feelings, you must remember, are far more complex than all that. In real life every act is the resultant of a hundred thoughts that come and go, and these you must study, each by itself, if you would create a living character. 'But,' you will say, 'in order to note these fleeting thoughts one must know them, must be able to follow them in their capricious meanderings.' Why, any child can do that, as you know. You have simply to make use of hypnotism, electrical or human, which gives one a two-fold being, setting free the witness-personality so that it may see, understand,

and remember the reasons which determine the personality that acts. Just study yourself as you live from day to day, my dear Last. Imitate your associate whom I was complimenting a moment ago. Let yourself be hypnotized. What's that? You have tried it already? Not sufficiently, then, not sufficiently!"

Mr. Smith continues his round and enters the reporters' hall. Here 1500 reporters, in their respective places, facing an equal number of telephones, are communicating to the subscribers the news of the world as gathered during the night. The organization of this matchless service has often been described. Besides his telephone, each reporter, as the reader is aware, has in front of him a set of commutators, which enable him to communicate with any desired telephotic line. Thus the subscribers not only hear the news but see the occurrences. When an incident is described that is already past, photographs of its main features are transmitted with the narrative. And there is no confusion withal. The reporters' items, just like the different stories and all the other component parts of the journal, are classified automatically according to an ingenious system, and reach the hearer in due succession. Furthermore, the hearers are free to listen only to what specially concerns them. They may at pleasure give attention to one editor and refuse it to another.

Mr. Smith next addresses one of the ten reporters in the astronomical department—a department still in the embryonic stage, but which will yet play an important part in journalism.

"Well, Cash, what's the news?"

"We have phototelegrams from Mercury, Venus, and Mars."

"Are those from Mars of any interest?"

"Yes, indeed. There is a revolution in the Central Empire."

"And what of Jupiter?" asked Mr. Smith.

"Nothing as yet. We cannot quite understand their signals. Perhaps ours do not reach them."

"That's bad," exclaimed Mr. Smith, as he hurried away, not in the best of humor, toward the hall of the scientific editors. With their heads bent down over their electric computers, thirty scientific men were absorbed in transcendental calculations. The coming of Mr. Smith was like the falling of a bomb among them.

"Well, gentlemen, what is this I hear? No answer from Jupiter? Is it always to be thus? Come, Cooley, you have been at work now twenty years on this problem, and yet——"

"True enough," replied the man addressed. "Our science of optics is still very defective, and though our mile-and-three-quarter telescopes——"

"Listen to that, Peer," broke in Mr. Smith, turning to a second scientist. "Optical science defective! Optical science is your specialty. But," he continued, again addressing William Cooley, "failing with Jupiter, are we getting any results from the moon?"

"The case is no better there."

"This time you do not lay the blame on the science of optics. The moon is immeasurably less distant than Mars, yet with Mars our communication is fully established. I presume you will not say that you lack telescopes?"

"Telescopes? Oh no, the trouble here is about—inhabitants!"

"That's it," added Peer.

"So, then, the moon is positively uninhabited?" asked Mr. Smith.

"At least," answered Cooley, "on the face which she presents to us. As for the opposite side, who knows?"

"Ah, the oppostie side! You think, then," remarked Mr. Smith, musingly, "that if one could but——"

"Could what?"

"Why, turn the moon about-face."

"Ah, there's something in that," cried the two men at once. And indeed, so confident was their air, they seemed to have no doubt as to the possibility of success in such an undertaking.

"Meanwhile," asked Mr. Smith, after a moment's silence, "have you no news of interest to-day?"

"Indeed we have," answered Cooley. "The elements of Olympus are definitely settled. That great planet gravitates beyond Neptune at the mean distance of 11,400,799,642 miles from the sun, and to traverse its vast orbit takes 1311 years, 294 days, 12 hours, 43 minutes, 9 seconds."

"Why didn't you tell me that sooner?" cried Mr. Smith. "Now inform the reporters of this straightway. You know how eager is the curiosity of the public with regard to these astronomical questions. That news must go into to-day's issue."

Then, the two men bowing to him, Mr. Smith passed into the next hall, an enormous gallery upward of 3200 feet in length, devoted to atmospheric advertising. Every one has noticed those enormous advertisements reflected from the clouds, so large that they may be seen by the populations of whole cities or even of entire countries. This, too, is one of Mr. Fritz Napoleon Smith's ideas, and in the Earth Chronicle building a thousand projectors are constantly engaged in displaying upon the clouds these mammoth advertisements.

When Mr. Smith to-day entered the sky-advertising department, he found the operators sitting with folded arms at their motionless projectors, and inquired as to the cause of their inaction. In response, the man addressed simply pointed to the sky, which was of a pure blue. "Yes," muttered Mr. Smith, "a cloudless sky! That's too bad, but what's to be done? Shall we produce rain? That we might do, but is it of any use? What we need is clouds, not rain. Go," said he, addressing the head engineer, "go see Mr. Samuel Mark, of the meteorological division of the scientific department, and tell him for me to go to work in earnest on the question of artificial clouds. It will never do for us to be always thus at the mercy of cloudless skies!"

Mr. Smith's daily tour through the several departments of his newspaper is now finished. Next, from the advertisement hall he passes to the reception chamber, where the ambassadors accredited to the American government are awaiting him, desirous of having a word of counsel or advice from the all-powerful editor. A discussion was going on when he entered. "Your Excellency will pardon me," the French Ambassador was saying to the Russian, "but I see nothing in the map of Europe that requires change. 'The North for the Slavs?' Why, yes, of course; but the South for the Latins. Our common frontier, the Rhine, it seems to me, serves very well. Besides, my government, as you must know, will firmly oppose every movement, not only against Paris, our capital, or our two great prefectures, Rome and Madrid, but also against the kingdom of Jerusalem, the dominion of Saint Peter, of which France means to be the trusty defender."

"Well said!" exclaimed Mr. Smith. "How is it," he asked, turning to the Russian ambassador, "that you Russians are not content with your vast empire, the most extensive in the world, stretching from the banks of the Rhine to the Celestial Mountains and the Kara-Korum, whose shores are washed by the Frozen Ocean, the Atlantic, the Mediterranean, and the Indian Ocean? Then, what is the use of threats? Is war possible in view of modern inventions—asphyxiating shells capable of being projected a distance of 60 miles, an electric spark of 90 miles, that can at one stroke annihilate a battalion; to say nothing of the plague, the cholera, the yellow fever, that the belligerents might spread among their antagonists mutually, and which would in a few days destroy the greatest armies?"

"True," answered the Russian; "but can we do all that we wish? As for us Russians, pressed on our eastern frontier by the Chinese, we must at any cost put forth our strength for an effort toward the west."

"Oh, is that all? In that case," said Mr. Smith, "the thing can be arranged. I will speak to the Secretary of State about it. The attention of the Chinese government shall be called to the matter. This is not the first time that the Chinese have bothered us."

"Under these conditions, of course——" And the Russian ambassador declared himself satisfied.

"Ah, Sir John, what can I do for you?" asked Mr. Smith as he turned to the representative of the people of Great Britain, who till now had remained silent.

"A great deal," was the reply. "If the Earth Chronicle would but open a campaign on our behalf——"

"And for what object?"

"Simply for the annulment of the Act of Congress annexing to the United States the British islands."

Though, by a just turn-about of things here below, Great Britain has become a colony of the United States, the English are not yet reconciled to the situation. At regular intervals they are ever addressing to the American government vain complaints.

"A campaign against the annexation that has been an accomplished fact for 150 years!" exclaimed Mr. Smith. "How can your people suppose that I would do anything so unpatriotic?"

"We at home think that your people must now be sated. The Monroe Doctrine is fully applied; the whole of America belongs to the Americans. What more do you want? Besides, we will pay for what we ask."

"Indeed!" answered Mr. Smith, without manifesting the slightest irritation. "Well, you English will ever be the same. No, no, Sir John, do not count on me for help. Give up our fairest province, Britain? Why not ask France generously to renounce possession of Africa, that magnificent colony the complete conquest of which cost her the labor of 800 years? You will be well received!"

"You decline! All is over then!" murmured the British agent sadly. "The United Kingdom falls to the share of the Americans; the Indies to that of——"

"The Russians," said Mr. Smith, completing the sentence.

"Australia——"

"Has an independent government."

"Then nothing at all remains for us!" sighed Sir John, downcast.

"Nothing?" asked Mr. Smith, laughing. "Well, now, there's Gibraltar!"

With this sally the audience ended. The clock was striking twelve, the hour of breakfast. Mr. Smith returns to his chamber. Where the bed stood in the morning a table all spread comes up through the floor. For Mr. Smith, being above all a practical man, has reduced the problem of existence to its simplest terms. For him, instead of the endless suites of apartments of the olden time, one room fitted with ingenious mechanical contrivances is enough. Here he sleeps, takes his meals, in short, lives.

He seats himself. In the mirror of the phonotelephote is seen the same chamber at Paris which appeared in it this morning. A table furnished forth is likewise in readiness here, for notwithstanding the difference of hours, Mr. Smith and his wife have arranged to take their meals simultaneously. It is delightful thus to take breakfast *tête-à-tête* with one who is 3000 miles or so away. Just now, Mrs. Smith's chamber has no occupant.

"She is late! Woman's punctuality! Progress everywhere except there!" muttered Mr. Smith as he turned the tap for the first dish. For like all wealthy folk in our day, Mr. Smith has done away with the domestic kitchen and is a subscriber to the Grand Alimentation Company, which sends through a great network of tubes to subscribers' residences all sorts of dishes, as a varied assortment is always in readiness. A subscription costs money, to be sure, but the *cuisine* is of the best, and the system has this advantage, that it does away with the pestering race of the *cordons-bleus*. Mr. Smith received and ate, all alone, the *hors-d'œuvre, entrées, rôti,* and *legumes* that constituted the repast. He was just finishing the dessert when Mrs. Smith appeared in the mirror of the telephote.

"Why, where have you been?" asked Mr. Smith through the telephone.

"What! You are already at the desert? Then I am late," she exclaimed, with a winsome *naïveté*. "Where have I been, you ask? Why, at my dress-maker's. The hats are just lovely this season! I suppose I forgot to note the time, and so am a little late."

"Yes, a little," growled Mr. Smith; "so little that I have already quite finished breakfast. Excuse me if I leave you now, but I must be going."

"Oh certainly, my dear; good-by till evening."

Smith stepped into his air-coach, which was in waiting for him at a window. "Where do you wish to go, sir?" inquired the coachman.

"Let me see; I have three hours," Mr. Smith mused. "Jack, take me to my accumulator works at Niagara."

For Mr. Smith has obtained a lease of the great falls of Niagara. For ages the energy developed by the falls went unutilized. Smith, applying Jackson's invention, now collects this energy, and lets or sells it. His visit to the works took more time than he had anticipated. It was four o'clock when he returned home, just in time for the daily audience which he grants to callers.

One readily understands how a man situated as Smith is must be beset with requests of all kinds. Now it is an inventor needing capital; again it is some visionary who comes to advocate a brilliant scheme which must surely yield millions of profit. A choice has to be made between these projects, rejecting the worthless, examining the questionable ones, accepting the meritorious. To this work Mr. Smith devotes every day two full hours.

The callers were fewer to-day than usual—only twelve of them. Of these, eight had only impracticable schemes to propose. In fact, one of them wanted to revive painting, an art fallen into desuetude owing to the progress made in color-photography. Another, a physician, boasted that he had discovered a cure for nasal catarrh! These impracticables were dismissed in short order. Of the four projects favorably received, the first was that of a young man whose broad forehead betokened his intellectual power.

"Sir, I am a chemist," he began, "and as such I come to you."

"Well!"

"Once the elementary bodies," said the young chemist, "were held to be sixty-two in number; a hundred years ago they were reduced to ten; now only three remain irresolvable, as you are aware."

"Yes, yes."

"Well, sir, these also I will show to be composite. In a few months, a few weeks, I shall have succeeded in solving the problem. Indeed, it may take only a few days."

"And then?"

"Then, sir, I shall simply have determined the absolute. All I want is money enough to carry my research to a successful issue."

"Very well," said Mr. Smith. "And what will be the practical outcome of your discovery?"

"The practical outcome? Why, that we shall be able to produce easily all bodies whatever—stone, wood, metal, fibers——"

"And flesh and blood?" queried Mr. Smith, interrupting him. "Do you pretend that you expect to manufacture a human being out and out?"

"Why not?"

Mr. Smith advanced $100,000 to the young chemist, and engaged his services for the Earth Chronicle laboratory.

The second of the four successful applicants, starting from experiments made so long ago as the nineteenth century and again and again repeated, had conceived the idea of removing an entire city all at once from one place to another. His special project had to do with the city of Granton, situated, as everybody knows, some fifteen miles inland. He proposes to transport the city on rails and to change it into a watering-place. The profit, of course, would be enormous. Mr. Smith, captivated by the scheme, bought a half-interest in it.

"As you are aware, sir," began applicant No. 3, "by the aid of our solar and terrestrial accumulators and transformers, we are able to make all the seasons the same. I propose to do something better still. Transform into heat a portion of the surplus energy at our disposal; send this heat to the poles; then the polar regions, relieved of their snow-caps, will become a vast territory available for man's use. What think you of the scheme?"

"Leave your plans with me, and come back in a week. I will have them examined in the meantime."

Finally, the fourth announced the early solution of a weighty scientific problem. Every one will remember the bold experiment made a hundred years ago by Dr. Nathaniel Faithburn. The doctor, being a firm believer in human hibernation—in other words, in the possibility of our suspending our vital functions and of calling them into action again after a time—resolved to subject the theory to a practical test. To this end, having first made his last will and pointed out the proper method of awakening him; having also directed that his sleep was to continue a hundred years to a day from the date of his apparent death, he unhesitatingly put the theory to the proof in his own person. Reduced to the condition of a mummy, Dr. Faithburn was coffined and laid in a tomb. Time went on. September 25th, 2889, being the day set for his resurrection, it was proposed to Mr. Smith that he should permit the second part of the experiment to be performed at his residence this evening.

"Agreed. Be here at ten o'clock," answered Mr. Smith; and with that the day's audience was closed.

Left to himself, feeling tired, he lay down on an extension chair. Then, touching a knob, he established communication with the Central Concert Hall, whence our greatest *maestros* send out to subscribers

their delightful successions of accords determined by recondite alge-
braic formulas. Night was approaching. Entranced by the harmony,
forgetful of the hour, Smith did not notice that it was growing dark. It
was quite dark when he was aroused by the sound of a door opening.
"Who is there?" he asked, touching a commutator.

Suddenly, in consequence of the vibrations produced, the air became
luminous.

"Ah! you, Doctor?"

"Yes," was the reply. "How are you?"

"I am feeling well."

"Good! Let me see your tongue. All right! Your pulse. Regular! And
your appetite?"

"Only passably good."

"Yes, the stomach. There's the rub. You are over-worked. If your
stomach is out of repair, it must be mended. That requires study. We
must think about it."

"In the meantime," said Mr. Smith, "you will dine with me."

As in the morning, the table rose out of the floor. Again, as in the
morning, the *potage, rôti, ragoûts,* and *legumes* were supplied through
the food-pipes. Toward the close of the meal, phonotelephotic communication was made with Paris. Smith saw his wife, seated alone at the
dinner-table, looking anything but pleased at her loneliness.

"Pardon me, my dear, for having left you alone," he said through the
telephone. "I was with Dr. Wilkins."

"Ah, the good doctor!" remarked Mrs. Smith, her countenance lighting up.

"Yes. But, pray, when are you coming home?"

"This evening."

"Very well. Do you come by tube or by air-train?"

"Oh, by tube."

"Yes; and at what hour will you arrive?"

"About eleven, I suppose."

"Eleven by Centropolis time, you mean?"

"Yes."

"Good-by, then, for a little while," said Mr. Smith as he severed
communication with Paris.

Dinner over, Dr. Wilkins wished to depart. "I shall expect you at
ten," said Mr. Smith. "To-day, it seems, is the day for the return to life
of the famous Dr. Faithburn. You did not think of it, I suppose. The
awakening is to take place here in my house. You must come and see.
I shall depend on your being here."

"I will come back," answered Dr. Wilkins.

Left alone, Mr. Smith busied himself with examining his accounts—
a task of vast magnitude, having to do with transactions which involve
a daily expenditure of upward of $800,000. Fortunately, indeed, the
stupendous progress of mechanic art in modern times makes it comparatively easy. Thanks to the Piano Electro-Reckoner, the most com-

plex calculations can be made in a few seconds. In two hours Mr. Smith completed his task. Just in time. Scarcely had he turned over the last page when Dr. Wilkins arrived. After him came the body of Dr. Faithburn, escorted by a numerous company of men of science. They commenced work at once. The casket being laid down in the middle of the room, the telephote was got in readiness. The outer world, already notified, was anxiously expectant, for the whole world could be eyewitnesses of the performance, a reporter meanwhile, like the chorus in the ancient drama, explaining it all *viva voce* through the telephone.

"They are opening the casket," he explained. "Now they are taking Faithburn out of it—a veritable mummy, yellow, hard, and dry. Strike the body and it resounds like a block of wood. They are now applying heat; now electricity. No result. These experiments are suspended for a moment while Dr. Wilkins makes an examination of the body. Dr. Wilkins, rising, declares the man to be dead. 'Dead!' exclaims every one present. 'Yes,' answers Dr. Wilkins, 'dead!' 'And how long has he been dead?' Dr. Wilkins makes another examination. 'A hundred years,' he replies."

The case stood just as the reporter said. Faithburn was dead, quite certainly dead! "Here is a method that needs improvement," remarked Mr. Smith to Dr. Wilkins, as the scientific committee on hibernation bore the casket out. "So much for that experiment. But if poor Faithburn is dead, at least he is sleeping," he continued. "I wish I could get some sleep. I am tired out, Doctor, quite tired out! Do you not think that a bath would refresh me?"

"Certainly. But you must wrap yourself up well before you go out into the hall-way. You must not expose yourself to cold."

"Hall-way? Why, Doctor, as you well know, everything is done by machinery here. It is not for me to go to the bath; the bath will come to me. Just look!" and he pressed a button. After a few seconds a faint rumbling was heard, which grew louder and louder. Suddenly the door opened, and the tub appeared.

Such, for this year of grace 2889, is the history of one day in the life of the editor of the Earth Chronicle. And the history of that one day is the history of 365 days every year, except leap-years, and then of 366 days—for as yet no means has been found of increasing the length of the terrestrial year.

RAY BRADBURY

FOREVER AND THE EARTH

AFTER seventy years of writing short stories that never sold, Mr. Henry William Field arose one night at 11:30 and burned ten million words. He carried the manuscripts downstairs through his dark old mansion and threw them into the furnace.

"That's that," he said, and thinking about his lost art and his misspent life, he put himself to bed, among his rich antiques. "My mistake was in ever trying to picture this wild world of 2257 A.D. The rockets, the atom wonders, the travels to planets and double suns. Nobody can do it. Everyone's tried. All of our modern authors have failed."

Space was too big for them, and rockets too swift, and atomic science too instantaneous, he thought. But at least the other writers, while failing, had been published, while he, in his idle wealth, had used the years of his life for nothing.

After an hour of feeling this way, he fumbled through the night rooms to his library and switched on a green hurricane lamp. At random, from a collection untouched in fifty years, he selected a book. It was a book three centuries yellow and three centuries brittle, but he settled into it and read hungrily until dawn. . . .

At nine o'clock, Henry William Field rushed from his library, called his servants, televised lawyers, friends, scientists, litterateurs.

"Come at once!" he cried.

Within the hour, a dozen people hurried into the study where Henry William Field sat, very disreputable and hysterical with an odd, feeding joy, unshaven and feverish. He clutched a thick book in his brittle arms and laughed if anyone even said good morning.

"Here you see a book," he said at last, holding it out, "written by a giant, a man born in Asheville, North Carolina, in the year 1900. Long gone to dust, he published four huge novels. He was a whirlwind. He lifted up mountains and collected winds. He left a trunk of pencilled manuscripts behind when he lay in bed at Johns Hopkins Hospital in Baltimore in the year 1938, on September 15th, and died of pneumonia, an ancient and awful disease."

They looked at the book.

Look Homeward, Angel.

He drew forth three more. *Of Time and the River. The Web and the Rock. You Can't Go Home Again.*

"By Thomas Wolfe," said the old man. "Three centuries cold in the North Carolina earth."

"You mean you've called us simply to see four books by a dead man?" his friends protested.

"More than that! I've called you because I feel Tom Wolfe's the man, the necessary man, to write of space, of time, huge things like nebulae and galactic war, meteors and planets; all the dark things he loved and put on paper were like this. He was born out of his time. He needed really big things to play with and never found them on Earth. He should have been born this afternoon instead of one hundred thousand mornings ago."

"I'm afraid you're a bit late," said Professor Bolton.

"I don't intend to be late!" snapped the old man. "I will *not* be frustrated by reality. You, professor, have experimented with time-travel. I expect you to finish your time machine this month. Here's a check, a blank check, fill it in. If you need more money, ask for it. You've done *some* traveling already, haven't you?"

"A few years, yes, but nothing like centuries——"

"We'll *make* it centuries! You others—" he swept them with a fierce and shining glance "—will work with Bolton. I *must* have Thomas Wolfe."

"What!" They fell back before him.

"Yes," he said. "That's the plan. Wolfe is to be brought to me. We will collaborate in the task of describing the flight from Earth to Mars, as only he could describe it!"

They left him in his library with his books, turning the dry pages, nodding to himself. "Yes. Oh, dear Lord, yes, Tom's the boy, Tom is the *very* boy for this."

The month passed slowly. Days showed a maddening reluctance to leave the calendar, and weeks lingered on until Mr. Henry William Field began to scream silently.

At the end of the month, Mr. Field awoke one midnight. The phone was ringing. He put his hand out in the darkness.

"Yes?"

"This is Professor Bolton calling."

"Yes, Bolton?"

"I'll be leaving in an hour," said the voice.

"Leaving? Leaving where? Are you quitting? You can't do that!"

"Please, Mr. Field, leaving means *leaving*."

"You mean, you're actually going?"

"Within the hour."

"To 1938? To September 15th?"

"Yes!"

"You're sure you've the date written down? You'll arrive before he dies? Be sure of it! Good Lord, you'd better get there a good hour before his death, don't you think?"

"A good hour."

"I'm so excited I can't hold the phone. Good luck, Bolton. Bring him through safely!"

"Thank you, sir. Goodbye."

The phone clicked.

Mr. Henry William Field lay through the ticking night. He thought of Tom Wolfe as a lost brother to be lifted intact from under a cold, chiseled stone, to be restored to blood and fire and speaking. He trembled each time he thought of Bolton whirling on the time wind back to other calendars and other faces.

Tom, he thought, faintly, in the half-awake warmth of an old man calling after his favorite and long-gone child, Tom, where are you tonight, Tom? Come along now, we'll help you through, you've got to come, there's need of you. I couldn't do it, Tom, none of us here can. So the next best thing to doing it myself, Tom, is helping you to do it. You can play with rockets like jackstraws, Tom, and you can have the stars, like a handful of crystals. Anything your heart asks, it's here. You'd like the fire and the travel, Tom, it was made for you. Oh, we've a pale lot of writers today, I've read them all, Tom, and they're not like you. I've waded in libraries of their stuff and they've never touched space, Tom; we need *you* for that! Give an old man his wish then, for God knows I've waited all my life for myself or some other to write the really great book about the stars, and I've waited in vain. So, whatever you are tonight, Tom Wolfe, make yourself tall. It's that book you were going to write. It's that good book the critics said was in you when you stopped breathing. Here's your chance, will you do it, Tom? Will you listen and come through to us, will you do that tonight, and be here in the morning when I wake? Will you, Tom?

His eyelids closed down over the fever and the demand. His tongue stopped quivering in his sleeping mouth.

The clock struck four.

Awakening to the white coolness of morning, he felt the excitement rising and welling in himself. He did not wish to blink, for fear that the thing which awaited him somewhere in the house might run off and slam a door, gone forever. His hands reached up to clutch his thin chest.

Far away . . . footsteps . . .

A series of doors opened and shut. Two men entered the bedroom. Field could hear them breathe. Their footsteps took on identities. The first steps were those of a spider, small and precise: Bolton. The second steps were those of a big man, a large man, a heavy man.

"Tom?" cried the old man. He did not open his eyes.

"Yes," said the voice, at last.

Tom Wolfe burst the seams of Field's imagination, as a huge child bursts the lining of a too-small coat.

"Tom Wolfe, let me look at you!" If Field said it once he said it a dozen times as he fumbled from bed, shaking violently. "Put up the blinds, for God's sake, I want to see this! Tom Wolfe, is that *you?*"

Tom Wolfe looked down from his tall thick body, with big hands out to balance himself in a world that was strange. He looked at the old man and the room and his mouth was trembling.

"You're just as they said you were, Tom!"

Thomas Wolfe began to laugh and the laughing was huge, for he must have thought himself insane or in a nightmare, and he came to the old man and touched him and he looked at Professor Bolton and felt of himself, his arms and legs, he coughed experimentally and touched his own brow. "My fever's gone," he said. "I'm not sick any more."

"Of course not, Tom."

"What a night," said Tom Wolfe. "It hasn't been easy. I thought I was sicker than any man ever was. I felt myself floating and I thought, this is fever. I felt myself traveling, and thought, I'm dying fast. A man came to me. I thought, this is the Lord's messenger. He took my hands. I smelled electricity. I flew up and over, and I saw a brass city. I thought, I've arrived. This is the city of heaven, there is the Gate! I'm numb from head to toe, like someone left in the snow to freeze. I've got to laugh and do things or I might think myself insane. You're not God, are you? You don't look like him."

The old man laughed. "No, no, Tom, not God, but playing at it. I'm Field." He laughed again. "Lord, listen to me. I said it as if you should know who Field is. Field, the financier, Tom, bow low, kiss my ring-finger. I'm Henry Field, I like your work. I brought you here. Come here."

The old man drew him to an immense crystal window.

"Do you see those lights in the sky, Tom?"

"Yes, sir."

"Those fireworks?"

"Yes."

"They're not what you think, son. It's not July Fourth, Tom. Not in the usual way. Every day's Independence Day now. Man has declared his Freedom from Earth. Gravitation without representation has been overthrown. The Revolt has long since been successful. That green Roman Candle's going to Mars. That red fire, that's the Venus rocket. And the others, you see the yellow and the blue? Rockets, all of them!"

Thomas Wolfe gazed up like an immense child caught amid the colorized glories of a July evening when the set-pieces are awhirl with phosphorous and glitter and barking explosion.

"What year is this?"

"The year of the rocket. Look here." And the old man touched some flowers that bloomed at his touch. The blossoms were like blue and white fire. They burned and sparkled their cold, long petals. The blooms were two feet wide, and they were the color of an autumn moon. "Moon-flowers," said the old man. "From the other side of the moon." He brushed them and they dripped away into a silver rain, a shower of white sparks, on the air. "The year of the rocket. That's a title for you, Tom. That's why we brought you here, we've need of you. You're the only man could handle the sun without being burnt to a ridiculous cinder. We want you to juggle the sun, Tom, and the stars, and whatever else you see on your trip to Mars."

"Mars?" Thomas Wolfe turned to seize the old man's arm, bending down to him, searching his face in unbelief.

"Tonight. You leave at six o'clock."

The old man held a fluttering pink ticket on the air, waiting for Tom to think to take it.

It was five in the afternoon. "Of course, of course I appreciate what you've done," cried Thomas Wolfe.

"Sit down, Tom. Stop walking around."

"Let me finish, Mr. Field, let me get through with this, I've got to say it."

"We've been arguing for hours," pleaded Mr. Field, exhaustedly.

They had talked from breakfast until lunch until tea, they had wandered through a dozen rooms and ten dozen arguments, they had perspired and grown cold and perspired again.

"It all comes down to this," said Thomas Wolfe, at last. "I can't stay here, Mr. Field. I've got to go back. This isn't my time. You've no right to interfere—"

"But, I—"

"I was amidst my work, my best was yet to come, and now you hurry me off three centuries. Mr. Field, I want you to call Mr. Bolton back. I want you to have him put me in his machine, whatever it is, and return me to 1938, my rightful place and year. That's all I ask of you."

"But, don't you *want* to see Mars?"

"With all my heart. But I know it isn't for me. It would throw my writing off. I'd have a huge handful of experience that I couldn't fit into my other writing when I went home."

"You don't understand, Tom, you don't understand at all."

"I understand that you're selfish."

"Selfish? Yes," said the old man. "For myself, and for others, very selfish."

"I want to go home."

"Listen to me, Tom."

"Call Mr. Bolton."

"Tom, I don't want to have to tell you this. I thought I wouldn't have to, that it wouldn't be necessary. Now, you leave me only this alternative." The old man's right hand fetched hold of a curtained wall, swept back the drapes revealing a large white screen, and dialed a number, a series of numbers, the screen flickered into vivid color, the lights of the room darkened, darkened, and a graveyard took line before their eyes.

"What are you doing?" demanded Wolfe, striding forward, staring at the screen.

"I don't like this at all," said the old man. "Look there."

The graveyard lay in mid-afternoon light, the light of summer. From the screen drifted the smell of summer earth, granite, and the odor of a nearby creek. From the trees, a bird called. Red and yellow flowers nodded among the stones, and the screen moved, the sky rotated, the old man twisted a dial for emphasis, and in the center of the screen, growing large, coming closer, yet larger, and now filling their senses was a dark granite mass and Thomas Wolfe, looking up in the dim room, ran his eyes over the chiseled words, once, twice, three times, gasped, and read again, for there was his name:

THOMAS WOLFE.

And the date of his birth and the date of his death, and the flowers and green ferns smelling sweetly on the air of the cold room.

"Turn it off," he said.

"I'm sorry, Tom."

"Turn it off, turn it off! I don't believe it."

"It's there."

The screen went black and now the entire room was a midnight vault, a tomb, with the last faint odor of flowers.

"I didn't wake up again," said Thomas Wolfe.

"No. You died that September of 1938."

"I never finished my book."

"It was edited for you, by others who went over it, carefully."

"I didn't finish my work, I didn't finish my work."

"Don't take it so badly, Tom."

"How else can I take it?"

The old man didn't turn on the lights. He didn't want to see Tom there. "Sit down, boy." No reply. "Tom?" No answer. "Sit down, son; will you have something to drink?" For answer there was only a sigh and a kind of brutal moaning. "Good Lord," said Tom, "it's not fair. I had so much left to do, it's not fair." He began to weep quietly.

"Don't do that," said the old man. "Listen. Listen to me. You're still alive, aren't you? Here? Now? You still *feel*, don't *you?*"

Thomas Wolfe waited for a minute and then he said, "Yes."

"All right, then." The old man pressed forward on the dark air. "I've brought you here, I've given you another chance, Tom. An extra month or so. Do you think I haven't grieved for you? When I read your books and saw your gravestone there, three centuries worn by rains and wind, boy, don't you imagine how it killed me to think of your talent gone away? Well, it did! It killed me, Tom. And I spent my money to find a way to you. You've got a respite, not long, not long at all. Professor Bolton says that, with luck, he can hold the channels open through time for eight weeks. He can keep you here that long, and only that long. In that interval, Tom, you must write the book you've wanted to write—no, not the book you were working on for them, son, no, for they're dead and gone and it can't be changed. No, this time it's a book for us, Tom, for us the living, that's the book we want. A book you can leave with us, for you, a book bigger and better in every way than anything you ever wrote; say you'll *do* it, Tom, say you'll forget about that stone and that hospital for eight weeks and start to work for us, will you, Tom, will you?"

The lights came slowly on. Tom Wolfe stood tall at the window, looking out, his face huge and tired and pale. He watched the rockets on the sky of early evening. "I imagine I don't realize what you've done for me," he said. "You've given me a little more time, and time is the thing I love most and need, the thing I always hated and fought against, and the only way I can show my appreciation is by doing as you say." He hesitated. "And when I'm finished, then what?"

"Back to your hospital in 1938, Tom."

"Must I?"

"We can't change time. We borrowed you for five minutes. We'll return you to your hospital cot five minutes after you left it. That way, we upset nothing. It's all been written. You can't hurt us in the future by living here now with us, but, if you refused to go back, you could hurt the past, and resultantly, the future, make it into some sort of chaos."

"Eight weeks," said Thomas Wolfe.

"Eight weeks."

"And the Mars rocket leaves in an hour?"

"Yes."

"I'll need pencils and paper."

"Here they are."

"I'd better go get ready. Goodbye, Mr. Field."

"Good luck, Tom."

Six o'clock. The sun setting. The sky turning to wine. The big house quiet. The old man shivering in the heat until Professor Bolton entered. "Bolton, how is he getting on, how was he at the port; tell me?"

Bolton smiled. "What a monster he is, so big, they had to make a special uniform for him! You should've seen him, walking around, lifting up everything, sniffing like a great hound, talking, his eyes looking at everyone, excited as a ten-year-old!"

"God bless him, oh, God bless him! Bolton, can you keep him here as long as you say?"

Bolton frowned. "He doesn't belong here, you know. If our power should falter, he'd be snapped back to his own time, like a puppet on a rubber band. We'll try and keep him, I assure you."

"You've got to, you understand, you can't let him go back until he's finished with his book. You've—"

"Look," said Bolton. He pointed to the sky. On it was a silver rocket.

"Is that him?" asked the old man.

"That's Tom Wolfe," replied Bolton. "Going to Mars."

"Give 'em hell, Tom, give 'em hell!" shouted the old man, lifting both fists.

They watched the rocket fire into space.

By midnight, the story was coming through.

Henry William Field sat in his library. On his desk was a machine that hummed. It repeated words that were being written out beyond the Moon. It scrawled them in black pencil, in facsimile of Tom Wolfe's fevered hand a million miles away. The old man waited for a pile of them to collect and then he seized them and read them aloud to the room where Bolton and the servants stood listening. He read the words about space and time and travel, about a large man and a large journey and how it was in the long midnight and coldness of space, and how a man could be hungry enough to take all of it and ask for more. He read the words that were full of fire and thunder and mystery.

Space was like October, wrote Thomas Wolfe. He said things about its darkness and its loneliness and man so small in it. The eternal and timeless October, was one of the things he said. And then he told of the rocket itself, the smell and the feel of the metal of the rocket, and the sense of destiny and wild exultancy to at last leave Earth behind, all problems and all sadnesses, and go seeking a bigger problem and a bigger sadness. Oh, it was fine writing, and it said what had to be said about space and man and his small rockets out there alone.

The old man read until he was hoarse, and then Bolton read, and then the others, far into the night, when the machine stopped transcribing words and they knew that Tom Wolfe was in bed, then, on the rocket, flying to Mars, probably not asleep, no, he wouldn't sleep for hours yet, no, lying awake, like a body the night before a circus, not believing the big jewelled black tent is up and the circus is on, with ten billion blazing performers on the high wires and the invisible trapezes of space.

"There," breathed the old man, gentling aside the last pages of the first chapter. "What do you think of that, Bolton?"

"It's good."

"Good, hell!" shouted Field. "It's wonderful! Read it again, sit down, read it again, damn you!"

It kept coming through, one day following another, for ten hours at a time. The stack of yellow papers on the floor, scribbled on, grew immense in a week, unbelievable in two weeks, absolutely impossible in a month.

"Listen to this!" cried the old man, and read.

"And this!" he said.

"And this chapter here, and this little novel here, it just came through, Bolton, titled *The Space War*, a complete novel on how it feels to fight a space war. Tom's been talking to people, soldiers, officers, men, veterans of space. He's got it all here. And here's a chapter called The Long Midnight, and here's one on the Negro colonization of Mars, and here's a character sketch of a Martian, absolutely priceless!"

Bolton cleared his throat. "Mr. Field?"

"Yes, yes, don't bother me."

"I've some bad news, sir."

Field jerked his grey head up. "What? The time element?"

"You'd better tell Wolfe to hurry his work. The connection may break some time this week," said Bolton, softly.

"I'll give you another million dollars if you keep it going!"

"It's not money, Mr. Field. It's just plain physics right now. I'll do everything I can. But you'd better warn him, is all I say."

The old man shriveled away into his chair and was small. "But you can't take him away from me now, not when he's doing so well. You should see the outline he sent through, an hour ago, the stories, the sketches. Here, here's one on spatial tides, another on meteors. Here's a short novel begun called *Thistledown and Fire*—"

"I'm sorry."

"If we lose him now, can we get him again?"

"I'd be afraid to tamper too much."

The old man was frozen. "Only one thing to do then. Arrange to have Wolfe type his work, if possible, or dictate it, to save time, rather than have him use pencil and paper, he's got to use a machine of some sort. See to it!"

The machine ticked away by the hour into the night and into the dawn and through the day. The old man slept only in faint dozes, blinking awake when the machine stuttered to life, and all of space and travel and existence came to him through the mind of another:

"*. . . the great starred meadows of space . . .*"

The machine jumped.

"Keep at it, Tom, show them!" The old man waited.

The phone rang.

It was Bolton.

"We can't keep it up, Mr. Field. The time contact will fade some time in the next minute."

"Do something!"

"I can't."

The teletype chattered. In a cold fascination, in a horror, the old man watched the black lines form.

"*. . . the Martian cities, immense and unbelievable, as numerous as stones thrown from some great mountain in a rushing and incredible avalanche, resting at last in shining mounds . . .*"

"Tom!" cried the old man.

"Now," said Bolton, on the phone.

The teletype hesitated, typed a word, and fell silent.

"Tom!" screamed the old man.

He shook the teletype.

"It's no use," said the telephone voice. "He's gone. I'm shutting off the Time Machine."

"No! Leave it on!"

"But—"

"You heard me—leave it! We're not sure he's gone."

"He is. It's no use, we're wasting energy."

"Waste it, then!"

He slammed the phone down.

He turned to the teletype, to the unfinished sentence.

"Come on, Tom, they can't get rid of you that way, you won't let them, will you, boy, come on. Tom, show them, you're big, you're bigger than time or space or their damned machines, you're strong and you've a will like iron, Tom, show them, don't let them send you back!"

The teletype snapped one key.

The old man bleated. "Tom! You *are* there, aren't you? Can you still write? Write, Tom, keep it coming, as long as you keep it rolling, Tom, they *can't* send you back!"

"The," typed the machine.

"More, Tom, more!"

"Odors of," clacked the machine.

"Yes?"

"Mars," typed the machine, and paused. A minute's silence. The machine spaced, skipped a paragraph, and began:

The odors of Mars, the cinnamons and cold spice winds, the winds of cloudy dust and winds of powerful bone and ancient pollen—

"Tom, you're still alive!"

For answer the machine, in the next ten hours, slammed out six chapters of *Flight Before Fury* in a series of fevered explosions.

"Today makes six weeks, Bolton, six whole weeks, Tom gone, on Mars, through the Asteroids. Look here, the manuscripts. Ten thousand words a day, he's driving himself, I don't know when he sleeps, or if he eats, I don't care, he doesn't either, he only wants to get it done, because he knows the time is short."

"I can't understand it," said Bolton. "The power failed because our relays wore out. It took us three days to manufacture and replace the particular channel relays necessary to keep the Time Element steady and yet Wolfe hung on. There's a personal factor here, Lord knows what, we didn't take into account. Wolfe lives here, in this time, when he *is* here, and can't be snapped back, after all. Time isn't as flexible as we imagined. We used the wrong simile. It's not like a rubber band. More like osmosis; the penetration of membranes by liquids, from Past to Present, but we've got to send him back, can't keep him here, there'd be a void there, a derangement. The one thing that really keeps him here now is himself, his drive, his desire, his work. After it's over he'll go back as naturally as pouring water from a glass."

"I don't care about reasons, all I know is Tom is finishing it. He has the old fire and description, and something else, something more, a searching of values that supersede time and space. He's done a study of a woman left behind on Earth while the brave rocket heroes leap into space that's beautiful, objective and subtle; he calls it *Day of the Rocket,* and it is nothing more than an afternoon of a typical suburban housewife who lives as her ancestral mothers lived, in a house, raising her children, her life not much different from a cavewoman's, in the midst of the splendor of science and the trumpetings of space projectiles; a true and steady and subtle study of her wishes and frustrations. Here's another manuscript called *The Indians,* in which he refers to the Martians as Cherokees and Iroquois and Blackfoots, the Indian nations of space, destroyed and driven back. Have a drink, Bolton, have a drink!"

Tom Wolfe returned to Earth at the end of eight weeks.

He arrived in fire as he had left in fire, and his huge steps were burned across space, and in the library of Henry William Field's house were towers of yellow paper, with lines of black scribble and type on them, and these were to be separated out into the six sections of a masterwork that, through endurance, and a knowing that the sands were dwindling from the glass, had mushroomed day on day.

Tom Wolfe came back to Earth and stood in the library of Henry William Field's house and looked at the massive outpourings of his heart and his hand and when the old man said, "Do you want to read it, Tom?" he shook his great head and replied, putting back his thick mane of dark hair with his big pale hand, "No. I don't dare start on it. If I did, I'd want to take it home with me. And I can't do that, can I?"

"No, Tom, you can't."

"No matter *how* much I wanted to?"

"No, that's the way it is. You never wrote another novel in that year, Tom. What was written here must stay here, what was written there must stay there. There's no touching it."

"I see." Tom sank down into a chair with a great sigh. "I'm tired. I'm mightily tired. It's been hard, but it's been good. What day is it?"

"This is the sixtieth day."

"The *last* day?"

The old man nodded and they were both silent awhile.

"Back to 1938 in the stone cemetery," said Tom Wolfe, eyes shut. "I don't like that. I wish I didn't know about that, it's a horrible thing to know." His voice faded and he put his big hands over his face and held them tightly there.

The door opened. Bolton let himself in and stood behind Tom Wolfe's chair, a small phial in his hand.

"What's that?" asked the old man.

"An extinct virus. Pneumonia. Very ancient and very evil," said Bolton. "When Mr. Wolfe came through, I had to cure him of his illness, of course, which was immensely easy with the techniques we know today, in order to put him in working condition for his job, Mr. Field. I kept this pneumonia culture. Now that he's going back, he'll have to be reinoculated with the disease."

"Otherwise?"

Tom Wolfe looked up.

"Otherwise, he'd get well, in 1938."

Tom Wolfe arose from his chair. "You mean, get well, walk around, back there, be well, and cheat the mortician?"

"That's what I mean."

Tom Wolfe stared at the phial and one of his hands twitched. "What if I destroyed the virus and refused to let you inoculate me?"

"You can't do that!"

"But—supposing?"

"You'd ruin things."

"What things?"

"The pattern, life, the way things are and were, the things that can't be changed. You can't disrupt it. There's only one sure thing, you're to die, and I'm to see to it."

Wolfe looked at the door. "I could run off, go back by myself."

"We control the machine. You wouldn't get out of the house. I'd have you back here, by force, and inoculated. I anticipated some such trouble when the time came; there are five men waiting down below. One shout from me—you see, it's useless. There, that's better. Here now."

Wolfe had moved back and now had turned to look at the old man and the window and this huge house. "I'm afraid I must apologize. I don't want to die. So very much I don't want to die."

The old man came to him and shook his hand. "Think of it this way; you've had two more months than anyone could expect from life, and you've turned out another book, a last book, a new book, think of that, and you'll feel better."

"I want to thank you for this," said Thomas Wolfe, gravely. "I want to thank both of you. I'm ready." He rolled up his sleeve. "The inoculation."

And while Bolton bent to his task, with his free hand Thomas Wolfe pencilled two black lines across the top of the first manuscript and went on talking:

"There's a passage from one of my old books, "he said, scowling to remember it. ". . . of wandering forever and the earth . . . Who owns the Earth? Did we want the Earth? that we should wander on it? Did we need the Earth that we were never still upon it? Whoever needs the Earth shall have the Earth; he shall be upon it, he shall rest within a little place, he shall dwell in one small room forever . . ."

Wolfe was finished with the remembering.

"Here's my last book," he said, and on the empty yellow paper facing it he blocked out vigorous huge black letters with pressures of the pencil: Forever and the Earth, by Thomas Wolfe.

He picked up a ream of it and held it tightly in his hands, against his chest, for a moment. "I wish I could take it back with me. It's like parting with my son." He gave it a slap and put it aside and immediately thereafter gave his quick hand into that of his employer, and strode across the room, Bolton after him, until he reached the door where he stood framed in the late afternoon light, huge and magnificent. "Good-bye, goodbye!" he cried.

The door slammed. Tom Wolfe was gone.

They found him wandering in the hospital corridor.

"Mr. Wolfe!"

"What?"

"Mr. Wolfe, you gave us a scare, we thought you were gone!"

"Gone?"

"Where did you go?"

"Where? Where?" He let himself be led through the midnight corridors. "Where? Oh, if I *told* you where, you'd never believe."

"Here's your bed, you shouldn't have left it."

Deep into the white death bed, which smelled of pale, clean mortality awaiting him, a mortality which had the hospital odor in it; the bed which, as he touched it, folded him into fumes and white starched coldness.

"Mars, Mars," whispered the huge man, late at night. "My best, my very best, my really fine book, yet to be written, yet to be printed, in another year, three centuries away . . ."

"You're tired."

"Do you really think so?" murmured Thomas Wolfe. "Was it a dream? Perhaps. A good dream."

His breathing faltered. Thomas Wolfe was dead.

In the passing years, flowers are found on Tom Wolfe's grave. And this is not unusual, for many people travel to linger there. But these flowers appear each night. They seem to drop from the sky. They are the color of an autumn moon, their blossoms are immense and they burn and sparkle their cold, long petals in a blue and white fire. And when the dawn wind blows they drip away into a silver rain, a shower of white sparks on the air. Tom Wolfe has been dead many, many years, but these flowers never cease. . . .

––––––

Permission to quote from "Of Time and the River" gratefully acknowledged to Charles Scribner's Sons.

JOHN D. MACDONALD

THE MINIATURE

AS Jedediah Amberson stepped through the bronze, marble and black-glass doorway of the City National Bank on Wall Street, he felt the strange jar. It was, he thought, almost a tremor. Once he had been in Tepoztlan, Mexico, on a Guggenheim grant, doing research on primitive barter systems, and during the night a small earthquake had awakened him.

This was much the same feeling. But he stood inside the bank and heard the unruffled hum of activity, heard no shouts of surprise. And, even through the heavy door he could hear the conversation of passers-by on the sidewalk.

He shrugged, beginning to wonder if it was something within himself, some tiny constriction of blood in the brain. It had been a trifle like that feeling which comes just before fainting. Jedediah Amberson had fainted once.

Fumbling in his pocket for the checkbook, he walked, with his long loose stride, over to a chest-high marble counter. He hadn't been in the main office of the bank since he had taken out his account. Usually he patronized the branch near the University, but today, finding himself in the neighborhood and remembering that he was low on cash, he had decided to brave the gaudy dignity of the massive institution of finance.

For, though Jed Amberson dealt mentally in billions, and used such figures familiarly in dealing with his classes in economics, he was basically a rather timid and uncertain man and he had a cold fear of the scornful eyes of tellers who might look askance at the small check he would present at the window.

He made it out for twenty dollars, five more than he would have requested had he gone to the familiar little branch office.

Jedediah Amberson was not a man to take much note of his surroundings. He was, at the time, occupied in writing a text, and the problems it presented were so intricate that he had recently found himself walking directly into other pedestrians and being snatched back onto the curb by helpful souls who didn't want to see him truck-mashed before their eyes. Just the day before he had gone into his bedroom in

---

mid-afternoon to change his shoes and had only awakened from his
profound thoughts when he found himself, clad in pajamas, brushing
his teeth before the bathroom mirror.

He took his place in the line before a window. He was mentally ex-
trapolating the trend line of one of J. M. Keynes' debt charts when a
chill voice said, "Well!"

He found that he had moved up to the window itself and the teller
was waiting for his check. He flushed and said, "Oh! Sorry." He tried
to push the check under the grill, but it fluttered out of his hand. As
he stooped to get it, his hat rolled off.

At last recovering both hat and check, he stood up, smiled painfully
and pushed the check under the grill.

The young man took it, and Jed Amberson finally grew aware that he
was spending a long time looking at the check. Jed strained his neck
around and looked to see if he had remembered to sign it. He had.

Only then did he notice the way the young man behind the window
was dressed. He wore a deep wine-colored sports shirt, collarless and
open at the throat. At the point where the counter bisected him, Jedediah could see that the young man wore green-gray slacks with at least
a six-inch waistband of ocher yellow.

Jed had a childlike love of parties, sufficient to overcome his chronic
self-consciousness. He said, in a pleased tone, "Ah, some sort of festival?"

The teller had a silken wisp of beard on his chin. He leaned almost
frighteningly close to the grill, aiming the wisp of beard at Amberson
as he gave him a careful scrutiny.

"We are busy here," the teller said. "Take your childish little game
across street and attempt it on them."

Though shy, Jedediah was able to call on hidden stores of indignation when he felt himself wronged. He straightened slowly and said,
with dignity, "I have an account here and I suggest you cash my check
as quickly and quietly as possible."

The teller glanced beyond Jedediah and waved the silky beard in a
taut half circle, a "come here" gesture.

Jedediah turned and gasped as he faced the bank guard. The man
wore a salmon-pink uniform with enormously padded shoulders. He
had a thumb hooked in his belt, his hand close to the plastic bowl of
what seemed to be a child's bubble pipe.

The guard jerked his other thumb toward the door and said, "Ride
off, honorable sir."

Jedediah said, "I don't care much for the comic-opera atmosphere of
this bank. Please advise me of my balance and I will withdraw it all and
put it somewhere where I'll be treated properly."

The guard reached out, clamped Jed's thin arm in a meaty hand and
yanked him in the general direction of the door. Jed intensely disliked
being touched or pushed or pulled. He bunched his left hand into a
large knobby fist and thrust it with vigor into the exact middle of the
guard's face.

The guard grunted as he sat down on the tile floor. The ridiculous bubble pipe came out, and was aimed at Jed. He heard no sound of explosion, but suddenly there was a large cold area in his middle that felt the size of a basketball. And when he tried to move, the area of cold turned into an area of pain so intense that it nauseated him. It took but two tiny attempts to prove to him that he could achieve relative comfort only by standing absolutely still. The ability to breathe and to turn his eyes in their sockets seemed the only freedom of motion left to him.

The guard said, tenderly touching his puffed upper lip, "Don't drop signal, Harry. We can handle this without flicks." He got slowly to his feet, keeping the toy weapon centered on Jedediah.

Other customers stood at a respectful distance, curious and interested. A fussy little bald-headed man came trotting up, carrying himself with an air of authority. He wore pastel-blue pajamas with a gold medallion over the heart.

The guard stiffened. "Nothing we can't handle, Mr. Greenbush."

"Indeed!" Mr. Greenbush said, his voice like a terrier's bark. "Indeed! You seem to be creating enough disturbance at this moment. Couldn't you have exported him more quietly?"

"Bank was busy," the teller said. "I didn't notice him till he got right up to window."

Mr. Greenbush stared at Jedediah. He said, "He looks reasonable enough, Palmer. Turn it off."

Jed took a deep, grateful breath as the chill area suddenly departed. He said weakly, "I demand an explanation."

Mr. Greenbush took the check the teller handed him and, accompanied by the guard, led Jed over to one side. He smiled in what was intended to be a fatherly fashion. He said, glancing at the signature on the check, "Mr. Amberson, surely you must realize, or your patrons must realize, that City National Bank is not sort of organization to lend its facilities to inane promotional gestures."

Jedediah had long since begun to have a feeling of nightmare. He stared at the little man in blue pajamas. "Promotional gestures?"

"Of course, my dear fellow. For what other reason would you come here dressed as you are and present this . . . this document."

"Dressed?" Jed looked down at his slightly baggy gray suit, his white shirt, his blue necktie and cordovan shoes. Then he stared around at the customers of the bank who had long since ceased to notice the little tableau. He saw that the men wore the sort of clothes considered rather extreme at the most exclusive of private beaches. He was particularly intrigued by one fellow who wore a cerise silk shirt, open to the waist, emerald green shorts to his knees, and calf-length pink nylons.

The women, he noticed, all wore dim shades of deep gray or brown, and a standard costume consisting of a halter, a short flared skirt that ended just above the knees and a knit cap pulled well down over the hair.

Amberson said, "Uh. Something special going on."

"Evidently. Suppose you explain."

"Me explain! Look, I can show you identification. I'm an Associate Professor of Economics at Columbia and I—" He reached for his hip pocket. Once again the ball of pain entered his vitals. The guard stepped over to him, reached into each of his pockets in turn, handed the contents to Mr. Greenbush.

Then the pressure was released. "I am certainly going to give your high-handed procedures here as much publicity as I can," Jed said angrily.

But Greenbush ignored him. Greenbush had opened his change purse and had taken out a fifty-cent piece. Greenbush held the coin much as a superstitious savage would have held a mirror. He made tiny bleating sounds. At last he said, his voice thin and strained, "Nineteen forty-nine mint condition! What do you want for it?"

"Just cash my check and let me go," Jed said wearily. "You're all crazy here. Why shouldn't this year's coins be in mint condition?"

"Bring him into my office," Greenbush said in a frenzy.

"But I—" Jed protested. He stopped as the guard raised the weapon once more. Jed meekly followed Greenbush back through the bank. He decided that it was a case of mistaken identity. He could call his department from the office. It would all be straightened out, with apologies.

With the door closed behind the two of them, Jed looked around the office. The walls were a particularly liverish and luminescent yellow-green. The desk was a block of plastic balanced precariously on one slim pedestal no bigger around then a lead pencil. The chairs gave him a dizzy feeling. They looked comfortable, but as far as he could see, they were equipped only with front legs. He could not see why they remained upright.

"Please sit there," Greenbush said.

Jed lowered himself into the chair with great caution. It yielded slightly, then seemed to clasp him with an almost embarrassing warmth, as though he sat on the pneumatic lap of an exceptionally large woman.

Greenbush came over to him, pointed to Jed's wristwatch and said, "Give me that, too."

"I didn't come for a loan," Jed said.

"Don't be ass. You'll get all back."

Greenbush sat behind his desk, with the little pile of Jed's possessions in front of him. He made little mumbling sounds as he prodded and poked and pried. He seemed very interested in the money. He listened to the watch tick and said, "Mmm. Spring mechanical."

"No. It runs on atomic power," Jed said bitterly. Greenbush didn't answer.

From the back of Jed's wallet, Greenbush took the picture of Helen. He touched the glossy surface, said, "Two-dimensional."

After what seemed an interminable period, Mr. Greenbush leaned back, put the tips of his fingers together and said, "Amberson, you are fortunate that you contacted me."

"I can visualize two schools of thought on that," Jed said stiffly.

Greenbush smiled. "You see, Amberson, I am coin collector and also antiquarian. It is possible National Museum might have material to equip you, but their stuff would be obviously old. I am reasonable man, and I know there must be explanation for all things." He fixed Jed with his sharp bright eyes, leaned slowly forward and said, "How did you get here?"

"Why, I walked through your front door." Jed suddenly frowned. "There was a strange jar when I did so. A dislocation, a feeling of being violently twisted in here." He tapped his temple with a thin finger.

"That's why I say you are fortunate. Some other bank might have had you in deviate ward by now where they'd be needling out slices of your frontal lobes."

"Is it too much to ask down here to get a small check cashed?"

"Not too much to ask in nineteen forty-nine, I'm sure. And I am ready to believe you are product of nineteen forty-nine. But, my dear Amberson, this is year eighty-three under Gradzinger calendar."

"For a practical joke, Greenbush, this is pretty ponderous."

Greenbush shrugged, touched a button on the desk. The wide draperies slithered slowly back from the huge window. "Walk over and take look, Amberson. Is that your world?"

Jed stood at the window. His stomach clamped into a small tight knot which slowly rose up into his throat. His eyes widened until the lids hurt. He steadied himself with his fingertips against the glass and took several deep, aching breaths. Then he turned somehow and walked, with knees that threatened to bend both ways, back to the chair. The draperies rustled back into position.

"No," Jed said weakly, "this isn't my world." He rubbed his forehead with the back of his hand, finding there a cold and faintly oily perspiration. "I had two classes this morning. I came down to look up certain documents. Everything was fine. And then I came in . . . how . . ."

Greenbush pursed his lips. "How? Who can say? I'm banker, not temporal tech. Doubtless you'd like to return to your own environment. I will signal Department of Temporal Technics at Columbia where you were employed so many years ago. . . ."

"That particular phraseology, Mr. Greenbush, I find rather disturbing."

"Sorry." Greenbush stood up. "Wait here. My communicator is deranged. I'll have to use other office."

"Can't we go there? To the University?"

"I wouldn't advise it. In popular shows I've seen on subject, point of entry is always important. I rather postulate they'll assist you back through front door."

Greenbush was at the office door. Jed said, "Have—have you people sent humans back and forth in time?"

"No. They send neutrons and gravitons or something like those. Ten minutes in future or ten minutes in past. Very intricate. Enormous energy problem. Way over my head."

While Greenbush was gone, Jed methodically collected his belongings from the desk and stowed them away in his pockets. Greenbush bustled in and said, "They'll be over in half hour with necessary equipment. They think they can help you."

Half an hour. Jed said, "As long as I'm here, I wonder if I could impose? You see, I have attempted to predict certain long-range trends in monetary procedures. Your currency would be—"

"Of course, my dear fellow! Of course! Kindred interest, etc. What would you like to know?"

"Can I see some of your currency?"

Greenbush shoved some small pellets of plastic across the desk. They were made from intricate molds. The inscription was in a sort of shorthand English. "Those are universal, of course," Greenbush said.

Two of them were for twenty-five cents and the other for fifty cents. Jed was surprised to see so little change from the money of his own day.

"One hundred cents equals dollar, just as in your times," Greenbush said.

"Backed by gold, of course," Jed said.

Greenbush gasped and then laughed. "What ludicrous idea! Any fool with public-school education has learned enough about transmutation of elements to make five tons of gold in afternoon, or of platinum or zinc or any other metal or alloy of metal you desire."

"Backed by a unit of power? An erg or something?" Jed asked with false confidence.

"With power unlimited? With all power anyone wants without charge? You're not doing any better, Amberson."

"By a unit share of national resources maybe?" Jed asked hollowly.

"National is obsolete word. There are no more nations. And world resources are limitless. We create enough for our use. There is no depletion."

"But currency, to have value, must be backed by something," Jed protested.

"Obviously!"

"Precious stones?"

"Children play with diamonds as big as baseballs," Greenbush said. "Speaking as economist, Amberson, why was gold used in your day?"

"It was rare, and, where obtainable, could not be obtained without a certain average fixed expenditure of man hours. Thus it wasn't really the metal itself, it was the man hours involved that was the real basis. Look, now you've got me talking in the past tense."

"And quite rightly. Now use your head, Mr. Amberson. In world where power is free, resources are unlimited and no metal or jewel is rare, what is one constant, one user of time, one external fixity on which monetary system could be based?"

Jed almost forgot his situation as he labored with the problem. Finally he had an answer, and yet it seemed so incredible that he hardly dared express it. He said in a thin voice, "The creation of a human being is something that probably cannot be shortened or made easy. Is—is human life itself your basis?"

"Bravo!" Greenbush said. "One hundred cents in dollar, and five thousand dollars in HUC. That's brief for Human Unit of Currency."

"But that's slavery! That's—why, that's the height of inhumanity!"

"Don't sputter, my boy, until you know facts."

Jed laughed wildly. "If I'd made my check out for five thousand they'd have given me a—a person!"

"They'd have given you certificate entitling you to HUC. Then you could spend that certificate, you see."

"But suppose I wanted the actual person?"

"Then I suppose we could have obtained one for you from World Reserve Bank. As matter of fact, we have one in our vault now."

"In your vault!"

"Where else would we keep it? Come along. We have time."

The vault was refrigerated. The two armed attendants stood by while Greenbush spun the knob of the inner chamber, slid out the small box. It was of dull silver, and roughly the size of a pound box of candy. Greenbush slid back the grooved lid and Jed, shuddering, looked down through clear ice to the tiny, naked, perfect figure of an adult male, complete even to the almost invisible wisp of hair on his chest.

"Alive?" Jed asked.

"Naturally. Pretty well suspended, of course." Greenbush slid the lid back, replaced the box in the vault and led the way back to the office.

Once again in the warm clasp of the chair, Jed asked, with a shaking voice, "Could you give me the background on—this amazing currency?"

"Nothing amazing about it. Technic advances made all too easily obtainable through lab methods except living humans. There, due to growth problems and due to—certain amount of nontechnic co-operation necessary, things could not be made easily. Full-sized ones were too unwieldy, so lab garcons worked on size till they got them down to what you see. Of course, they are never brought up to level of consciousness. They go from birth bottle to suspension chambers and are held there until adult and then refrigerated and boxed."

Greenbush broke off suddenly and said, "Are you ill?"

"No. No, I guess not."

"Well, when I first went to work for this bank, HUC was unit worth twenty thousand dollars. Then lab techs did some growth acceleration work—age acceleration, more accurate—and that brought price down and put us into rather severe inflationary period. Cup of java went up to dollar and it stayed there ever since. So World Union stepped in and made it against law to make any more refinements in HUC production. That froze it at five thousand. Things have been stable ever since."

"But they're living, human beings!"

"Now you sound like silly Anti-HUC League. My boy, they wouldn't exist were it not for our need for currency base. They never achieve consciousness. We, in banking business, think of them just as about only manufactured item left in world which cannot be produced in afternoon. Time lag is what gives them their value. Besides, they are no longer in production, of course. Being economist, you must realize overproduction of HUC's would put us back into inflationary period."

At that moment the girl announced that the temporal techs had arrived with their equipment. Jed was led from the office out into the bank proper. The last few customers were let out as the closing hour arrived.

The men from Columbia seemed to have no interest in Jed as a human being. He said hesitantly to one, smiling shyly, "I would think you people would want to keep me here so your historians could do research on me."

The tech gave him a look of undisguised contempt. He said, "We know all to be known about your era. Very dull period in world history."

Jed retired, abashed, and watched them set up the massive silvery coil on the inside of the bank door.

The youngest tech said quietly, "This is third time we've had to do this. You people seem to wander into sort of rhythm pattern. Very careless. We had one failure from your era. Garcon named Crater. He wandered too far from point of entry. But you ought to be all opt."

"What do I have to do?"

"Just walk through coil and out door. Adjustment is complicated. If we don't use care you might go back into your own era embedded up to your eyes in pavement. Or again, you might come out forty feet in air. Don't get unbalanced."

"I won't," Jed said fervently.

Greenbush came up and said, "Could you give me that coin you have?"

The young technician turned wearily and said, "Older, he has to leave with everything he brought and he can't take anything other with him. We've got to fit him into same vibratory rhythm. You should know that."

"It is such nice coin," Greenbush sighed.

"If I tried to take something with me?" Jed asked.

"It just wouldn't go, gesell. You would go and it would stay."

Jed thought of another question. He turned to Greenbush. "Before I go, tell me. Where are the HUC's kept?"

"In refrigerated underground vault at place called Fort Knox."

"Come on, come on, you. Just walk straight ahead through coil. Don't hurry. Push door open and go out onto street."

Jed stood, faintly dizzy, on the afternoon sidewalk of Wall Street in Manhattan. A woman bounced off him, snarled, "Fa godsake, ahya goin' uh comin'!" Late papers were tossed off a truck onto the corner.

Jed tiptoed over, looked cautiously and saw that the date was Tuesday, June 14th, 1949.

The further the subway took him uptown, the more the keen reality of the three quarters of an hour in the bank faded. By the time he reached his own office, sat down behind his familiar desk, it had become like a fevered dream.

Overwork. That was it. Brain fever. Probably wandered around in a daze. Better take it easy. Might fade off into a world of the imagination and never come back. Skip the book for a month. Start dating Helen again. Relax.

He grinned slowly, content with his decision. "HUC's, indeed!" he said.

Date Helen tonight. Better call her now. Suddenly he remembered that he hadn't cashed a check, and he couldn't take Helen far on a dollar.

He found the check in his pocket, glanced at it, and then found himself sitting rigid in the chair. Without taking his eyes from the check, he pulled open the desk drawer, took out the manuscript entitled, "Probable Bases of Future Monetary Systems," tore it in half and dropped it in the wastebasket.

His breath whistled in pinched nostrils. He heard, in his memory, a voice saying, "You would go and it would stay."

The check was properly made out for twenty dollars. But he had used the ink supplied by the bank. The check looked as though it had been written with a dull knife. The brown desk top showed up through the fragile lace of his signature.

FRITZ LEIBER, JR.

SANITY

"COME in, Phy, and make yourself comfortable."

The mellow voice—and the suddenly dilating doorway—caught the general secretary of the World playing with a blob of greenish gasoid, squeezing it in his fist and watching it ooze between his fingers in spatulate tendrils that did not dissipate. Slowly, crookedly, he turned his head. World Manager Carrsbury became aware of a gaze that was at once oafish, sly, vacuous. Abruptly the expression was replaced by a nervous smile. The thin man straightened himself, as much as his habitually drooping shoulders would permit, hastily entered, and sat down on the extreme edge of a pneumatically form-fitting chair.

He embarrassedly fumbled the blob of gasoid, looking around for a convenient disposal vent or a crevice in the upholstery. Finding none, he stuffed it hurriedly into his pocket. Then he repressed his fidgetings by clasping his hands resolutely together, and sat with downcast eyes.

"How are you feeling, old man?" Carrsbury asked in a voice that was warm with a benign friendliness.

The general secretary did not look up.

"Anything bothering you, Phy?" Carrsbury continued solicitously. "Do you feel a bit unhappy, or dissatisfied, about your . . . er . . . transfer, now that the moment has arrived?"

Still the general secretary did not respond. Carrsbury leaned forward across the dully silver, semi-circular desk and, in his most winning tones, urged, "Come on, old fellow, tell me all about it."

The general secretary did not lift his head, but he rolled up his strange, distant eyes until they were fixed directly on Carrsbury. He shivered a little, his body seemed to contract, and his bloodless hands tightened their interlocking grip.

"I know," he said in a low, effortful voice. "You think I'm insane."

Carrsbury sat back, forcing his brows to assume a baffled frown under the mane of silvery hair.

"Oh, you needn't pretend to be puzzled," Phy continued, swiftly now that he had broken the ice. "You know what that word means as well as I do. Better—even though we both had to do historical research to find out.

"Insane," he repeated dreamily, his gaze wavering. "Significant departure from the norm. Inability to conform to basic conventions underlying all human conduct."

"Nonsense!" said Carrsbury, rallying and putting on his warmest and most compelling smile. "I haven't the slightest idea of what you're talking about. That you're a little tired, a little strained, a little distraught—that's quite understandable, considering the burden you've been carrying, and a little rest will be just the thing to fix you up, a nice long vacation away from all this. But as for your being . . . why, ridiculous!"

"No," said Phy, his gaze pinning Carrsbury. "You think I'm insane. You think all my colleagues in the World Management Service are insane. That's why you're having us replaced with those men you've been training for ten years in your Institute of Political Leadership—ever since, with my help and connivance, you became World manager."

Carrsbury retreated before the finality of the statement. For the first time his smile became a bit uncertain. He started to say something, then hesitated and looked at Phy, as if half hoping he would go on.

But that individual was once again staring rigidly at the floor.

Carrsbury leaned back, thinking. When he spoke it was in a more natural voice, much less consciously soothing and fatherly.

"Well, all right, Phy. But look here, tell me something, honestly. Won't you—and the others—be a lot happier when you've been relieved of all your responsibilities?"

Phy nodded somberly. "Yes," he said, "we will . . . but"—his face became strained—"you see—"

"But—?" Carrsbury prompted.

Phy swallowed hard. He seemed unable to go on. He had gradually slumped toward one side of the chair, and the pressure had caused the green gasoid to ooze from his pocket. His long fingers crept over and kneaded it fretfully.

Carrsbury stood up and came around the desk. His sympathetic frown, from which perplexity had ebbed, was not quite genuine.

"I don't see why I shouldn't tell you all about it now, Phy," he said simply. "In a queer sort of way I owe it all to you. And there isn't any point now in keeping it a secret . . . there isn't any danger—"

"Yes," Phy agreed with a quick bitter smile, "you haven't been in any danger of a *coup d'état* for some years now. If ever we should have revolted, there'd have been"—his gaze shifted to a point in the opposite wall where a faint vertical crease indicated the presence of a doorway —"your secret police."

Carrsbury started. He hadn't thought Phy had known. Disturbingly, there loomed in his mind a phrase: *the cunning of the insane.* But only for a moment. Friendly complacency flooded back. He went behind Phy's chair and rested his hands on the sloping shoulders.

"You know, I've always had a special feeling toward you, Phy," he said, "and not only because your whims made it a lot easier for me to become World manager. I've always felt that you were different from the others, that there were times when—" He hesitated.

Phy squirmed a little under the friendly hands. "When I had my moments of sanity?" he finished flatly.

"Like now," said Carrsbury softly, after a nod the other could not see. "I've always felt that sometimes, in a kind of twisted, unrealistic way, you *understood*. And that has meant a lot to me. I've been alone, Phy, dreadfully alone, for ten whole years. No companionship anywhere, not even among the men I've been training in the Institute of Political Leadership—for I've had to play a part with them too, keep them in ignorance of certain facts, for fear they would try to seize power over my head before they were sufficiently prepared. No companionship anywhere, except for my hopes—and for occasional moments with you. Now that it's over and a new regime is beginning for us both, I can tell you that. And I'm glad."

There was a silence. Then—Phy did not look around, but one lean hand crept up and touched Carrsbury's. Carrsbury cleared his throat. Strange, he thought, that there could be even a momentary rapport like this between the sane and the insane. But it was so.

He disengaged his hands, strode rapidly back to his desk, turned.

"I'm a throwback, Phy," he began in a new, unused, eager voice. "A throwback to a time when human mentality was far sounder. Whether my case was due chiefly to heredity, or to certain unusual accidents of environment, or to both, is unimportant. The point is that a person had been born who was in a position to criticize the present state of mankind in the light of the past, to diagnose its condition, and to begin its cure. For a long time I refused to face the facts, but finally my researches—especially those in the literature of the twentieth century—left me no alternative. The mentality of mankind had become —aberrant. Only certain technological advances, which had resulted in making the business of living infinitely easier and simpler, and the fact that war had been ended with the creation of the present world state, were staving off the inevitable breakdown of civilization. But only staving it off—delaying it. The great masses of mankind had become what would once have been called hopelessly neurotic. Their leaders had become . . . you said it first, Phy . . . insane. Incidentally, this latter phenomenon—the drift of psychological aberrants toward leadership—has been noted in all ages."

He paused. Was he mistaken, or was Phy following his words with indications of a greater mental clarity than he had ever noted before, even in the relatively nonviolent World secretary? Perhaps—he had often dreamed wistfully of the possibility—there was still a chance of saving Phy. Perhaps, if he just explained to him clearly and calmly—

"In my historical studies," he continued, "I soon came to the conclusion that the crucial period was that of the Final Amnesty, concurrent with the founding of the present world state. We are taught that at that time there were released from confinement millions of political prisoners—and millions of others. Just who were those others? To this question, our present histories gave only vague and platitudinous answers. The semantic difficulties I encountered were exceedingly obstinate. But I kept hammering away. Why, I asked myself, have such words as insanity, lunacy, madness, psychosis, disappeared from our vocabulary—and the concepts behind them from our thought? Why has the subject 'abnormal psychology' disappeared from the curricula of our schools? Of greater significance, why is our modern psychology strikingly similar to the field of abnormal psychology as taught in the twentieth century, and to that field alone? Why are there no longer, as there were in the twentieth century, any institutions for the confinement and care of the psychologically aberrant?"

Phy's head jerked up. He smiled twistedly. "Because," he whispered slyly, "everyone's insane now."

The cunning of the insane. Again that phrase loomed warningly in Carrsbury's mind. But only for a moment. He nodded.

"At first I refused to make that deduction. But gradually I reasoned out the why and wherefore of what had happened. It wasn't only that a highly technological civilization had subjected mankind to a wider and more swiftly-tempoed range of stimulations, conflicting suggestions, mental strains, emotional wrenchings. In the literature of twentieth century psychiatry there are observations on a kind of psychosis that results from success. An unbalanced individual keeps going so long as he is fighting something, struggling toward a goal. He reaches his goal—

and goes to pieces. His repressed confusions come to the surface, he realizes that he doesn't know what he wants at all, his energies hitherto engaged in combatting something outside himself are turned against himself, he is destroyed. Well, when war was finally outlawed, when the whole world became one unified state, when social inequality was abolished . . . you see what I'm driving at?"

Phy nodded slowly. "That," he said in a curious, distant voice, "is a very interesting deduction."

"Having reluctantly accepted my main premise," Carrsbury went on, "everything became clear. The cyclic six-months' fluctuations in a world credit—I realized at once that Morgenstern of Finance must be a manic-depressive with a six-months' phase, or else a dual personality with one aspect a spendthrift, the other a miser. It turned out to be the former. Why was the Department of Cultural advancement stagnating? Because Manager Hobart was markedly catatonic. Why the boom in extraterrestrial Research? Because McElvy was a euphoric."

Phy looked at him wonderingly. "But naturally," he said, spreading his lean hands, from one of which the gasoid dropped like a curl of green smoke.

Carrsbury glanced at him sharply. He replied, "Yes, I know that you and several of the others have a certain warped awareness of the differences between your . . . personalities, though none whatsoever of the basic aberration involved in them all. But to get on. As soon as I realized the situation, my course was marked out. As a sane man, capable of entertaining fixed realistic purposes, and surrounded by individuals of whose inconsistencies and delusions it was easy to make use, I was in a position to attain, with time and tact, any goal at which I might aim. I was already in the Managerial Service. In three years I became World manager. Once there, my range of influence was vastly enhanced. Like the man in Archimedes' epigram, I had a place to stand from which I could move the world. I was able, in various guises and on various pretexts, to promulgate regulations the actual purpose of which was to soothe the great neurotic masses by curtailing upsetting stimulations and introducing a more regimented and orderly program of living. I was able, by humoring my fellow executives and making the fullest use of my greater capacity for work, to keep world affairs staggering along fairly safely—at least stave off the worst. At the same time I was able to begin my Ten Years' Plan—the training, in comparative isolation, first in small numbers, then in larger, as those instructed could in turn become instructors, of a group of prospective leaders carefully selected on the basis of their relative freedom from neurotic tendencies."

"But that—" Phy began rather excitedly, starting up.

"But what?" Carrsbury inquired quickly.

"Nothing," muttered Phy dejectedly, sinking back.

"That about covers it," Carrsbury concluded, his voice suddenly grown a little duller. "Except for one secondary matter. I couldn't afford to let myself go ahead without any protection. Too much depended on me. There was always the risk of being wiped out by some ill-co-ordinated but none the less effective spasm of violence, momentarily uncontrollable by tact, on the part of my fellow executives. So, only because I could see no alternative, I took a dangerous step. I created"—his glance strayed toward the faint crease in the side wall —"my secret police. There is a type of insanity known as paranoia, an exaggerated suspiciousness involving delusions of persecution. By means of the late twentieth century Rand technique of hypnotism, I inculcated a number of these unfortunate individuals with the fixed idea that their lives depended on me and that I was threatened from all sides and must be protected at all costs. A distasteful expedient, even though it served its purpose. I shall be glad, very glad to see it discontinued. You can understand, can't you, why I had to take that step?"

He looked questioningly at Phy—and became aware with a shock that that individual was grinning at him vacuously and holding up the gasoid between two fingers.

"I cut a hole in my couch and a lot of this stuff came out," Phy explained in a thick naïve voice. "Ropes of it got all over my office. I kept tripping." His fingers patted at it deftly, sculpturing it into the form of a hideous transparent green head, which he proceeded to squeeze out of existence. "Queer stuff," he rambled on, "rarefied liquid. Gas of fixed volume. And all over my office floor, tangled up with the furniture."

Carrsbury leaned back and shut his eyes. His shoulders slumped. He felt suddenly a little weary, a little eager for his day of triumph to be done. He knew he shouldn't be despondent because he had failed with Phy. After all, the main victory was won. Phy was the merest of side issues. He had always known that, except for flashes, Phy was hopeless as the rest. Still—

"You don't need to worry about your office floor, Phy," he said with a listless kindliness. "Never any more. Your successor will have to see about cleaning it up. Already, you know, to all intents and purposes, you have been replaced."

"That's just it!" Carrsbury started at Phy's explosive loudness. The World secretary jumped up and strode toward him, pointing an excited hand. "That's what I came to see you about! That's what I've been trying to tell you! I can't be replaced like that! None of the others can, either! It won't work! You can't do it!"

With a swiftness born of long practice, Carrsbury slipped behind his desk. He forced his features into that expression of calm, smiling benevolence of which he had grown unutterably weary.

"Now, now, Phy," he said brightly, soothingly, "if I can't do it, of course I can't do it. But don't you think you ought to tell me why? Don't you think it would be very nice to sit down and talk it all over and you tell me why?"

Phy halted and hung his head, abashed.

"Yes, I guess it would," he said slowly, abruptly falling back into the low, effortful tones. "I guess I'll have to. I guess there just isn't any other way. I had hoped, though, not to have to tell you everything." The last sentence was half question. He looked up wheedlingly at Carrsbury. The latter shook his head, continuing to smile. Phy went back and sat down.

"Well," he finally began, gloomily kneading the gasoid, "it all began when you first wanted to be World manager. You weren't the usual type, but I thought it would be kind of fun—yes, and kind of helpful." He looked up at Carrsbury. "You've really done the World a lot of good in quite a lot of ways, always remember that," he assured him. "Of course," he added, again focusing the tortured gasoid, "they weren't exactly the ways you thought."

"No?" Carrsbury prompted automatically. *Humor him. Humor him.* The wornout refrain droned in his mind.

Phy sadly shook his head. "Take those regulations you promulgated to soothe people—"

"Yes?"

"—they kind of got changed on the way. For instance, your prohibition, regarding reading tapes, of all exciting literature . . . oh, we tried a little of the soothing stuff you suggested at first. Everyone got a great kick out of it. They laughed and laughed. But afterwards, well, as I said, it kind of got changed—in this case to a prohibition of all *unexciting* literature."

Carrsbury's smile broadened. For a moment the edge of his mind had toyed with a fear, but Phy's last remark had banished it.

"Every day I coast past several reading stands," Carrsbury said gently. "The fiction tapes offered for sale are always in the most chastely and simply colored containers. None of those wild and lurid pictures that one used to see everywhere."

"But did you ever buy one and listen to it? Or project the visual text?" Phy questioned apologetically.

"For ten years I've been a very busy man," Carrsbury answered. "Of course I've read the official reports regarding such matters, and at times glanced through sample résumés of taped fiction."

"Oh, sure, that sort of official stuff," agreed Phy, glancing up at the wall of tape files beyond the desk. "What we did, you see, was to keep the monochrome containers but go back to the old kind of contents. The contrast kind of tickled people. Remember, as I said before, a lot of your regulations have done good. Cut out a lot of unnecessary noise and inefficient foolishness, for one thing."

That sort of official stuff. The phrase lingered unpleasantly in Carrsbury's ears. There was a trace of irrepressible suspicion in his quick over-the-shoulder glance at the tiered tape files.

"Oh, yes," Phy went on, "and that prohibition against yielding to unusual or indecent impulses, with a long listing of specific categories.

It went into effect all right, but with a little rider attached: 'unless you really want to.' That seemed absolutely necessary, you know." His fingers worked furiously with the gasoid. "As for the prohibition of various stimulating beverages—well, in this locality they're still served under other names, and an interesting custom has grown up of behaving very soberly while imbibing them. Now when we come to that matter of the eight-hour working day—"

Almost involuntarily, Carrsbury had got up and walked over to the outer wall. With a flip of his hand through an invisible U-shaped beam, he switched on the window. It was as if the outer wall had disappeared. Through its near-perfect transparency, he peered down with fierce curiosity past the sleekly gleaming façades to the terraces and parkways below.

The modest throngs seemed quiet and orderly enough. But then there was a scurry of confusion—a band of people, at this angle all tiny heads with arms and legs, came out from a shop far below and began to pelt another group with what looked like foodstuffs. While, on a side parkway, two small ovoid vehicles, seamless drops of silver because their vision panels were invisible from the outside, butted each other playfully. Someone started to run.

Carrsbury hurriedly switched off the window and turned around. Those were just off-chance occurrences, he told himself angrily. Of no real statistical significance whatever. For ten years mankind had steadily been trending toward sanity despite occasional relapses. He'd seen it with his own eyes, seen the day-by-day progress—at least enough to know. He'd been a fool to let Phy's ramblings affect him—only tired nerves had made that possible.

He glanced at his timepiece.

"Excuse me," he said curtly, striding past Phy's chair, "I'd like to continue this conversation, but I have to get along to the first meeting of the new Central Managerial Staff."

"Oh but you can't!" Instantly Phy was up and dragging at his arm. "You just can't do it, you know! It's impossible!"

The pleading voice rose toward a scream. Impatiently Carrsbury tried to shake loose. The seam in the side wall widened, became a doorway. Instantly both of them stopped struggling.

In the doorway stood a cadaverous giant of a man with a stubby dark weapon in his hand. Straggly black beard shaded into gaunt cheeks. His face was a cruel blend of suspicion and fanatical devotion, the first directed along with the weapon at Phy, the second—and the somnambulistic eyes—at Carrsbury.

"He was threatening you?" the bearded man asked in a harsh voice, moving the weapon suggestively.

For a moment an angry, vindictive light glinted in Carrsbury's eyes. Then it flicked out. What could he have been thinking, he asked himself. This poor lunatic World secretary was no one to hate.

"Not at all, Hartman," he remarked calmly. "We were discussing something and we became excited and allowed our voices to rise. Everything is quite all right."

"Very well," said the bearded man doubtfully, after a pause. Reluctantly he returned his weapon to its holster, but he kept his hand on it and remained standing in the doorway.

"And now," said Carrsbury, disengaging himself, "I must go."

He had stepped on to the corridor slidewalk and had coasted halfway to the elevator before he realized that Phy had followed him and was plucking timidly at his sleeve.

"You can't go off like this," Phy pleaded urgently, with an apprehensive backward glance. Carrsbury noted that Hartman had also followed —an ominous pylon two paces to the rear. "You must give me a chance to explain, to tell you why, just like you asked me."

Humor him. Carrsbury's mind was deadly tired of the drone, but mere weariness prompted him to dance to it a little longer. "You can talk to me in the elevator," he conceded, stepping off the slidewalk. His finger flipped through a U-beam and a serpentine movement of light across the wall traced the elevator's obedient rise.

"You see, it wasn't just that matter of prohibitory regulations," Phy launched out hurriedly. "There were lots of other things that never did work out like your official reports indicated. Departmental budgets for instance. The reports showed, I know, that appropriations for Extraterrestrial Research were being regularly slashed. Actually, in your ten years of office, they increased tenfold. Of course, there was no way for you to know that. You couldn't be all over the world at once and see each separate launching of supra-stratospheric rockets."

The moving light became stationary. A seam dilated. Carrsbury stepped into the elevator. He debated sending Hartman back. Poor babbling Phy was no menace. Still—*the cunning of the insane.* He decided against it, reached out and flipped the control beam at the sector which would bring them to the hundredth and top floor. The door snipped softly shut. The cage became a surging darkness in which floor numerals winked softly. Twenty-one. Twenty-two. Twenty-three.

"And then there was the Military Service. You had it sharply curtailed."

"Of course I did." Sheer weariness stung Carrsbury into talk. "There's only one country in the world. Obviously, the only military requirement is an adequate police force. To say nothing of the risks involved in putting weapons into the hands of the present world population."

"I know," Phy's answer came guiltily from the darkness. "Still, what's happened is that, unknown to you, the Military Service has been increased in size, and recently four rocket squadrons have been added."

Fifty-seven. Fifty-eight. *Humor him.* "Why?"

"Well, you see we've found out that Earth is being reconnoitered. Maybe from Mars. Maybe hostile. Have to be prepared. We didn't tell you . . . well, because we were afraid it might excite you."

The voice trailed off. Carrsbury shut his eyes. How long, he asked himself, how long? He realized with dull surprise that in the last hour people like Phy, endured for ten years, had become unutterably weary to him. For the moment even the thought of the conference over which he would soon be presiding, the conference that was to usher in a sane world, failed to stir him. Reaction to success? To the end of a ten years' tension?

"Do you know how many floors there are in this building?"

Carrsbury was not immediately conscious of the new note in Phy's voice, but he reacted to it.

"One hundred," he replied promptly.

"Then," asked Phy, "just where are we?"

Carr opened his eyes to the darkness. One hundred twenty-seven, blinked the floor numeral. One hundred twenty-eight. One hundred twenty-nine.

Something cold dragged at Carrsbury's stomach, pulled at his brain. He felt as if his mind were being slowly and irresistibly twisted. He thought of hidden dimensions, of unsuspected holes in space. Something remembered from elementary physics danced through his thoughts: If it were possible for an elevator to keep moving upward with uniform acceleration, no one inside an elevator could determine whether the effects they were experiencing were due to acceleration or to gravity—whether the elevator were standing motionless on some planet or shooting up at ever-increasing velocity through free space.

One hundred forty-one. One hundred forty-two.

"Or as if you were rising through consciousness into an unsuspected realm of mentality lying above," suggested Phy in his new voice, with its hint of gentle laughter.

One hundred forty-six. One hundred forty-seven. It was slowing now. One hundred forty-nine. One hundred fifty. It had stopped.

This was some trick. The thought was like cold water in Carrsbury's face. Some cunning childish trick of Phy's. An easy thing to hocus the numerals. Carrsbury groped irascibly about in the darkness, encountered the slick surface of a holster, Hartman's gaunt frame.

"Get ready for a surprise," Phy warned from close at his elbow.

As Carrsbury turned and grabbed, bright sunlight drenched him, followed by a griping, heart-stopping spasm of vertigo.

He, Hartman, and Phy, along with a few insubstantial bits of furnishings and controls, were standing in the air fifty stories above the hundred-story summit of World Managerial Center.

For a moment he grabbed frantically at nothing. Then he realized they were not falling and his eyes began to trace the hint of walls and ceiling and floor and, immediately below them, the ghost of a shaft.

Phy nodded. "That's all there is to it," he assured Carrsbury casually. "Just another of those charmingly odd modern notions against which you have legislated so persistently—like our incomplete staircases and roads to nowhere. The Buildings and Grounds Committee decided to extend the range of the elevator for sightseeing purposes. The shaft was made air-transparent to avoid spoiling the form of the original building and to improve the view. This was achieved so satisfactorily that an electronic warning system had to be installed for the safety of passing airjets and other craft. Treating the surfaces of the cage like windows was an obvious detail."

He paused and looked quizzically at Carrsbury. "All very simple," he observed, "but don't you find a kind of symbolism in it? For ten years now you've been spending most of your life in that building below. Every day you've used this elevator. But not once have you dreamed of these fifty extra stories. Don't you think that something of the same sort may be true of your observations of other aspects of contemporary social life?"

Carrsbury gaped at him stupidly.

Phy turned to watch the growing speck of an approaching aircraft. "You might look at it too," he remarked to Carrsbury, "for it's going to transport you to a far happier, more restful life."

Carrsbury parted his lips, wet them. "But—" he said, unsteadily. "But—"

Phy smiled. "That's right, I didn't finish my explanation. Well, you might have gone on being World manager all your life, in the isolation of your office and your miles of taped official reports and your occasional confabs with me and the others. Except for your Institute of Political Leadership and your Ten-Year-Plan. That upset things. Of course, we were as much interested in it as we were in you. It had definite possibilities. We hoped it would work out. We would have been glad to retire from office if it had. But, most fortunately, it didn't. And that sort of ended the whole experiment."

He caught the downward direction of Carrsbury's gaze.

"No," he said, "I'm afraid your pupils aren't waiting for you in the conference chamber on the hundredth story. I'm afraid they're still in the Institute." His voice became gently sympathetic. "And I'm afraid that it's become . . . well . . . a somewhat different sort of institute."

Carrsbury stood very still, swaying a little. Gradually his thoughts and his will power were emerging from the waking nightmare that had paralyzed them. *The cunning of the insane*—he had neglected that trenchant warning. In the very moment of victory—

No! He had forgotten Hartman! This was the very emergency for which that counterstroke had been prepared.

He glanced sideways at the chief member of his secret police. The black giant, unconcerned by their strange position, was glaring fixedly at Phy as if at some evil magician from whom any malign impossibility could be expected.

Now Hartman became aware of Carrsbury's gaze. He divined his thought.

He drew his dark weapon from its holster, pointed it unwaveringly at Phy.

His black-bearded lips curled. From them came a hissing sound. Then, in a loud voice, he cried, "You're dead, Phy! I disintegrated you."

Phy reached over and took the weapon from his hand.

"That's another respect in which you completely miscalculated the modern temperament," he remarked to Carrsbury, a shade argumentatively. "All of us have certain subjects on which we're a trifle unrealistic. That's only human nature. Hartman's was his suspiciousness—a weakness for ideas involving plots and persecutions. You gave him the worst sort of job—one that catered to and encouraged his weaknesses. In a very short time he became hopelessly unrealistic. Why for years he's never realized that he's been carrying a dummy pistol."

He passed it to Carrsbury for inspection.

"But," he added, "give him the proper job and he'd function well enough—say something in creation of exploration or social service. Fitting the man to the job is an art with infinite possibilities. That's why we had Morgenstern in Finance—to keep credit fluctuating in a safe, predictable rhythm. That's why a euphoric is made manager of Extraterrestrial Research—to keep it booming. Why a catatonic is given Cultural Advancement—to keep it from tripping on its face in its haste to get ahead."

He turned away. Dully, Carrsbury observed that the aircraft was hovering close to the cage and sidling slowly in.

"But in that case why—" he began stupidly.

"Why were you made World manager?" Phy finished easily. "Isn't that fairly obvious? Haven't I told you several times that you did a lot of good, indirectly? You interested us, don't you see? In fact, you were practically unique. As you know, it's our cardinal principle to let every individual express himself as he wants to. In your case, that involved letting you become World manager. Taken all in all it worked out very well. Everyone had a good time, a number of constructive regulations were promulgated, we learned a lot—oh, we didn't get everything we hoped for, but one never does. Unfortunately, in the end, we were forced to discontinue the experiment."

The aircraft had made contact.

"You understand, of course, why that was necessary?" Phy continued hurriedly, as he urged Carrsbury toward the opening port. "I'm sure you must. It all comes down to a question of sanity. What is sanity—now, in the twentieth century, any time? Adherence to a norm. Conformity to certain basic conventions underlying all human conduct. In our age, departure from the norm has become the norm. Inability to conform has become the standard of conformity. That's quite clear, isn't it? And it enables you to understand, doesn't it, your own case and that of your proteges? Over a long period of years you persisted in adhering to a norm, in conforming to certain basic conventions. You were completely unable to adapt yourself to the society around you. You could only pretend—and your proteges wouldn't have been able to do even that. Despite our many engaging personal characteristics, there was obviously only one course of action open to us."

In the port Carrsbury turned. He had found his voice at last. It was hoarse, ragged. "You mean that all these years you've just been *humoring* me?"

The port was closing. Phy did not answer the question.

As the aircraft edged out, he waved farewell with the blob of green gasoid.

"It'll be very pleasant where you're going," he shouted encouragingly. "Comfortable quarters, adequate facilities for exercise, and a complete library of twentieth century literature to while away your time."

He watched Carrsbury's rigid face, staring whitely from the vision port, until the aircraft had diminished to a speck.

Then he turned away, looked at his hands, noticed the gasoid, tossed it out the open door of the cage, studied its flight for a few moments, then flicked the downbeam.

"I'm glad to see the last of that fellow," he muttered, more to himself than to Hartman, as they plummeted toward the roof. "He was beginning to have a very disturbing influence on me. In fact, I was beginning to fear for my"—his expression became suddenly vacuous—"sanity."

C. M. KORNBLUTH

THE ONLY THING WE LEARN

THE professor, though he did not know the actor's phrase for it, was counting the house—peering through a spyhole in the door through which he would in a moment appear before the class. He was pleased with what he saw. Tier after tier of young people, ready with notebooks and styli, chattering tentatively, glancing at the door against which his nose was flattened, waiting for the pleasant interlude known as "Archaeo-Literature 203" to begin.

The professor stepped back, smoothed his tunic, crooked four books in his left elbow and made his entrance. Four swift strides brought him to the lectern and, for the thousandth-odd time, he impassively swept the lecture hall with his gaze. Then he gave a wry little smile. Inside, for the thousandth-odd time, he was nagged by the irritable little thought that the lectern really ought to be a foot or so higher.

The irritation did not show. He was out to win the audience, and he did. A dead silence, the supreme tribute, gratified him. Imperceptibly, the lights of the lecture hall began to dim and the light on the lectern to brighten.

He spoke.

"Young gentlemen of the Empire, I ought to warn you that this and the succeeding lectures will be most subversive."

There was a little rustle of incomprehension from the audience—but by then the lectern light was strong enough to show the twinkling smile about his eyes that belied his stern mouth, and agreeable chuckles sounded in the gathering darkness of the tiered seats. Glow-lights grew bright gradually at the students' tables, and they adjusted their notebooks in the narrow ribbons of illumination. He waited for the small commotion to subside.

"Subversive—" He gave them a link to cling to. "Subversive because I shall make every effort to tell both sides of our ancient beginnings with every resource of archaeology and with every clue my diligence has discovered in our epic literature.

"There *were* two sides, you know—difficult though it may be to believe that if we judge by the Old Epic alone—such epics as the noble and tempestuous *Chant of Remd*, the remaining fragments of *Krall's Voyage*, or the gory and rather out-of-date *Battle for the Ten Suns*." He paused while styli scribbled across the notebook pages.

"The Middle Epic is marked, however, by what I might call the rediscovered ethos." From his voice, every student knew that that phrase, surer than death and taxes, would appear on an examination paper. The styli scribbled. "By this I mean an awakening of fellow-feeling with the Home Suns People, which had once been filial loyalty to them when our ancestors were few and pioneers, but which turned into contempt when their numbers grew.

"The Middle Epic writers did not despise the Home Suns People, as did the bards of the Old Epic. Perhaps this was because they did not have to—since their long war against the Home Suns was drawing to a victorious close.

"Of the New Epic I shall have little to say. It was a literary fad, a pose, and a silly one. Written within historic times, the some two score pseudo-epics now moulder in their cylinders, where they belong. Our ripening civilization could not with integrity work in the epic form, and the artistic failures produced so indicate. Our genius turned to the lyric and to the unabashedly romantic novel.

"So much, for the moment, of literature. What contribution, you must wonder, have archaeological studies to make in an investigation of the wars from which our ancestry emerged?

"Archaeology offers—one—a check in historical matter in the epics—confirming or denying. Two—it provides evidence glossed over in the epics—for artistic or patriotic reasons. Three—it provides evidence which has been lost, owing to the fragmentary nature of some of the early epics."

All this he fired at them crisply, enjoying himself. Let them not think him a dreamy litterateur, nor, worse, a flat precisionist, but let them be always a little off-balance before him, never knowing what came next, and often wondering, in class and out. The styli paused after heading Three.

"We shall examine first, by our archaeo-literary technique, the second book of the *Chant of Remd*. As the selected youth of the Empire, you know much about it, of course—much that is false, some that is true and a great deal that is irrelevant. You know that Book One hurls us into the middle of things, aboard ship with Algan and his great captain, Remd, on their way from the triumph over a Home Suns stronghold, the planet Telse. We watch Remd on his diversionary action that splits the Ten Suns Fleet into two halves. But before we see the destruction of those halves by the Horde of Algan, we are told in Book Two of the battle for Telse."

He opened one of his books on the lectern, swept the amphitheater again and read sonorously.

> "Then battle broke
> And high the blinding blast
> Sight-searing leaped
> While folk in fear below
> Cowered in caverns
> From the wrath of Remd—

"Or, in less sumptuous language, one fission bomb—or a stick of time-on-target bombs—was dropped. An unprepared and disorganized populace did not take the standard measure of dispersing, but huddled foolishly to await Algan's gunfighters and the death they brought.

"One of the things you believe because you have seen them in notes to elementary-school editions of *Remd* is that Telse was the fourth planet of the star, Sol. Archaeology denies it by establishing that the fourth planet—actually called Marse, by the way—was in those days weather-roofed at least, and possibly atmosphere-roofed as well. As potential warriors, you know that one does not waste fissionable material on a roof, and there is no mention of chemical explosives being used to crack the roof. Marse, therefore, was not the locale of *Remd*, Book Two.

"Which planet was? The answer to that has been established by X-radar, differential decay analyses, video-coring and every other resource of those scientists still quaintly called 'diggers.' We know and can prove that Telse was the *third* planet of Sol. So much for the opening of the attack. Let us jump to Canto Three, the Storming of the Dynastic Palace.

> "Imperial purple wore they
> Fresh from the feast
> Grossly gorged
> They sought to slay—

"And so on. Now, as I warned you, Remd is of the Old Epic, and makes no pretense at fairness. The unorganized huddling of Telse's population was read as cowardice instead of poor A.R.P. The same is true of the Third Canto. Video-cores show on the site of the palace a hecatomb of dead in once-purple livery, but also shows impartially that they were not particularly gorged and that digestion of their last meals had been well advanced. They didn't give such a bad accounting of themselves, either. I hesitate to guess, but perhaps they accounted for one of our ancestors apiece and were simply outnumbered. The study is not complete.

"That much we know." The professor saw they were tiring of the terse scientist and shifted gears. "But if the veil of time were rent that shrouds the years between us and the Home Suns People, how much more would we learn? Would we despise the Home Suns People as our frontiersman ancestors did, or would we cry: 'This is our spiritual home —this world of rank and order, this world of formal verse and exquisitely patterned arts'?"

If the veil of time were rent—?

We can try to rend it . . .

Wing Commander Arris heard the clear jangle of the radar net alarm as he was dreaming about a fish. Struggling out of his too-deep, too-soft bed, he stepped into a purple singlet, buckled on his Sam Browne belt with its holstered .45 automatic and tried to read the radar screen. Whatever had set it off was either too small or too distant to register on the five-inch C.R.T.

He rang for his aide, and checked his appearance in a wall-mirror while waiting. His space tan was beginning to fade, he saw, and made a mental note to get it renewed at the parlor. He stepped into the corridor as Evan, his aide, trotted up—younger, browner, thinner, but the same officer type that made the Service what it was, Arris thought with satisfaction.

Evan gave him a bone-cracking salute, which he returned. They set off for the elevator that whisked them down to a large, chilly, dark underground room where faces were greenly lit by radar screens and the lights of plotting tables. Somebody yelled "Attention!" and the tecks snapped. He gave them "At ease" and took the brisk salute of the senior teck, who reported to him in flat, machine-gun delivery:

"Object-becoming-visible-on-primary-screen-sir."

He studied the sixty-inch disk for several seconds before he spotted the intercepted particle. It was coming in fast from zenith, growing while he watched.

"Assuming it's now traveling at maximum, how long will it be before it's within striking range?" he asked the teck.

"Seven hours, sir."

"The interceptors at Idlewild alerted?"

"Yessir."

Arris turned on a phone that connected with Interception. The boy at Interception knew the face that appeared on its screen, and was al-ready capped with a crash helmet.

"Go ahead and take him, Efrid," said the wing commander.

"Yessir!" and a punctilious salute, the boy's pleasure plain at being known by name and a great deal more at being on the way to a fight that might be first-class.

Arris cut him off before the boy could detect a smile that was forming on his face. He turned from the pale lumar glow of the sixty-incher to enjoy it. Those kids—when every meteor was an invading dreadnaught, when every ragged scouting ship from the rebels was an armada!

He watched Efrid's squadron soar off on the screen and then he retreated to a darker corner. This was his post until the meteor or scout or whatever it was got taken care of. Evan joined him, and they silently studied the smooth, disciplined functioning of the plot room, Arris with satisfaction and Evan doubtless with the same. The aide broke silence, asking:

"Do you suppose it's a Frontier ship, sir?" He caught the wing commander's look and hastily corrected himself: "I mean rebel ship, sir, of course."

"Then you should have said so. Is that what the junior officers generally call those scoundrels?"

Evan conscientiously cast his mind back over the last few junior messes and reported unhappily: "I'm afraid we do, sir. We seem to have got into the habit."

"I shall write a memorandum about it. How do you account for that very peculiar habit?"

"Well, sir, they do have something like a fleet, and they did take over the Regulus Cluster, didn't they?"

What had got into this incredible fellow, Arris wondered in amazement. Why, the thing was self-evident! They had a few ships—accounts differed as to how many—and they had, doubtless by raw sedition, taken over some systems temporarily.

He turned from his aide, who sensibly became interested in a screen and left with a murmured excuse to study it very closely.

The brigands had certainly knocked together some ramshackle league or other, but— The wing commander wondered briefly if it could last, shut the horrid thought from his head, and set himself to composing mentally a stiff memorandum that would be posted in the junior officer's mess and put an end to this absurd talk.

His eyes wandered to the sixty-incher, where he saw the interceptor squadron climbing nicely toward the particle—which, he noticed, had become three particles. A low crooning distracted him. Was one of the tecks singing at work? It couldn't be!

It wasn't. An unsteady shape wandered up in the darkness, murmuring a song and exhaling alcohol. He recognized the Chief Archivist, Glen.

"This is Service country, mister," he told Glen.

"Hullo, Arris," the round little civilian said, peering at him. "I come down here regularly—regularly against regulations—to wear off my regular irregularities with the wine bottle. That's all right, isn't it?"

He was drunk and argumentative. Arris felt hemmed in. Glen couldn't be talked into leaving without loss of dignity to the wing commander, and he couldn't be chucked out because he was writing a biography of the chamberlain and could, for the time being, have any head in the palace for the asking. Arris sat down unhappily, and Glen plumped down beside him.

The little man asked him.

"Is that a fleet from the Frontier League?" He pointed to the big screen. Arris didn't look at his face, but felt that Glen was grinning maliciously.

"I know of no organization called the Frontier League," Arris said. "If you are referring to the brigands who have recently been operating in Galactic East, you could at least call them by their proper names." Really, he thought—civilians!

"So sorry. But the brigands should have the Regulus Cluster by now, shouldn't they?" he asked, insinuatingly.

This was serious—a grave breach of security. Arris turned to the little man.

"Mister, I have no authority to command you," he said measuredly. "Furthermore, I understand you are enjoying a temporary eminence in the non-service world which would make it very difficult for me to—ah —tangle with you. I shall therefore refer only to your altruism. How did you find out about the Regulus Cluster?"

"Eloquent!" murmured the little man, smiling happily. "I got it from Rome."

Arris searched his memory. "You mean Squadron Commander Romo broke security? I can't believe it!"

"No, commander. I mean Rome—a place—a time—a civilization. I got it also from Babylon, Assyria, the Mogul Raj—every one of them. You don't understand me, of course."

"I understand that you're trifling with Service security and that you're a fat little, malevolent, worthless drone and scribbler!"

"Oh, commander!" protested the archivist. "I'm not so little!" He wandered away, chuckling.

Arris wished he had the shooting of him, and tried to explore the chain of secrecy for a weak link. He was tired and bored by this harping on the Fron—on the brigands.

His aide tentatively approached him. "Interceptors in striking range, sir," he murmured.

"Thank you," said the wing commander, genuinely grateful to be back in the clean, etched-line world of the Service and out of that blurred, water-color, civilian land where long-dead Syrians apparently retailed classified matter to nasty little drunken warts who had no business with it. Arris confronted the sixty-incher. The particle that had become three particles was now—he counted—eighteen particles. Big ones. Getting bigger.

He did not allow himself emotion, but turned to the plot on the interceptor squadron.

"Set up Lunar relay," he ordered.

"Yessir."

Half the plot room crew bustled silently and efficiently about the delicate job of applied relativistic physics that was 'lunar relay.' He knew that the palace power plant could take it for a few minutes, and he wanted to see. If he could not believe radar pips, he might believe a video screen.

On the great, green circle, the eighteen—now twenty-four—particles neared the thirty-six smaller particles that were interceptors, led by the eager young Efrid.

"Testing Lunar relay, sir," said the chief teck.

The wing commander turned to a twelve-inch screen. Unobtrusively, behind him, tecks jockeyed for position. The picture on the screen was something to see. The chief let mercury fill a thick-walled, ceramic tank. There was a sputtering and contact was made.

"Well done," said Arris. "Perfect seeing."

He saw, upper left, a globe of ships—what ships! Some were Service jobs, with extra turrets plastered on them wherever there was room. Some were orthodox freighters, with the same porcupine-bristle of weapons. Some were obviously home-made crates, hideously ugly—and as heavily armed as the others.

Next to him, Arris heard his aide murmur, "It's all wrong, sir. They haven't got any pick-up boats. They haven't got any hospital ships. What happens when one of them gets shot up?"

"Just what ought to happen, Evan," snapped the wing commander. "They float in space until they desiccate in their suits. Or if they get grappled inboard with a boat hook, they don't get any medical care. As I told you, they're brigands, without decency even to care for their own." He enlarged on the theme. "Their morale must be insignificant compared with our men's. When the Service goes into action, every rating and teck knows he'll be cared for if he's hurt. Why, if we didn't have pick-up boats and hospital ships the men wouldn't—" He almost finished it with "fight," but thought, and lamely ended—"wouldn't like it."

Evan nodded, wonderingly, and crowded his chief a little as he craned his neck for a look at the screen.

"Get the hell away from here!" said the wing commander in a restrained yell, and Evan got.

The interceptor squadron swam into the field—a sleek, deadly needle of vessels in perfect alignment, with its little cloud of pick-ups trailing, and farther astern a white hospital ship with the ancient red cross.

The contact was immediate and shocking. One of the rebel ships lumbered into the path of the interceptors, spraying fire from what seemed to be as many points as a man has pores. The Service ships promptly riddled it and it should have drifted away—but it didn't. It kept on fighting. It rammed an interceptor with a crunch that must have killed every man before the first bulwark, but aft of the bulwark the ship kept fighting.

It took a torpedo portside and its plumbing drifted through space in a tangle. Still the starboard side kept squirting fire. Isolated weapon blisters fought on while they were obviously cut off from the rest of the ship. It was a pounded tangle of wreckage, and it had destroyed two interceptors, crippled two more, and kept fighting.

Finally, it drifted away, under feeble jets of power. Two more of the fantastic rebel fleet wandered into action, but the wing commander's horrified eyes were on the first pile of scrap. It was going *somewhere*—

The ship neared the thin-skinned, unarmored, gleaming hospital vessel, rammed it amidships, square in one of the red crosses, and then blew itself up, apparently with everything left in its powder magazine, taking the hospital ship with it.

The sickened wing commander would never have recognized what he had seen as it was told in a later version, thus:

> "The crushing course they took
> And nobly knew
> Their death undaunted
> By heroic blast
> The hospital's host
> They dragged to doom
> Hail! Men without mercy
> From the far frontier!"

Lunar relay flickered out as overloaded fuses flashed into vapor. Arris distractedly paced back to the dark corner and sank into a chair.

"I'm sorry," said the voice of Glen next to him, sounding quite sincere. "No doubt it was quite a shock to you."

"Not to you?" asked Arris bitterly.

"Not to me."

"Then how did they do it?" the wing commander asked the civilian in a low, desperate whisper. "They don't even wear .45's. Intelligence says their enlisted men have hit their officers and got away with it. They *elect* ship captains! Glen, what does it all mean?"

"It means," said the fat little man with a timbre of doom in his voice, "that they've returned. They always have. They always will. You see, commander, there is always somewhere a wealthy, powerful city, or nation, or world. In it are those whose blood is not right for a wealthy, powerful place. They must seek danger and overcome it. So they go out —on the marshes, in the desert, on the tundra, the planets, or the stars.

Being strong, they grow stronger by fighting the tundra, the planets or the stars. They—they change. They sing new songs. They know new heroes. And then, one day, they return to their old home.

"They return to the wealthy, powerful city, or nation or world. They fight its guardians as they fought the tundra, the planets or the stars—a way that strikes terror to the heart. Then they sack the city, nation or world and sing great, ringing sagas of their deeds. They always have. Doubtless they always will."

"But what shall we do?"

"We shall cower, I suppose, beneath the bombs they drop on us, and we shall die, some bravely, some not, defending the palace within a very few hours. But you will have your revenge."

"How?" asked the wing commander, with haunted eyes.

The fat little man giggled and whispered in the officer's ear. Arris irritably shrugged it off as a bad joke. He didn't believe it. As he died, drilled through the chest a few hours later by one of Algan's gunfighters, he believed it even less.

The professor's lecture was drawing to a close. There was time for only one more joke to send his students away happy. He was about to spring it when a messenger handed him two slips of paper. He raged inwardly at his ruined exit and poisonously read from them:

"I have been asked to make two announcements. One, a bulletin from General Sleg's force. He reports that the so-called Outland Insurrection is being brought under control and that there is no cause for alarm. Two, the gentlemen who are members of the S.O.T.C. will please report to the armory at 1375 hours—whatever that may mean—for blaster inspection. The class is dismissed."

Petulantly, he swept from the lectern and through the door.

DAMON KNIGHT

NOT WITH A BANG

TEN months after the last plane passed over, Rolf Smith knew beyond doubt that only one other human being had survived. Her name was Louise Oliver, and he was sitting opposite her in a department-store cafe in Salt Lake City. They were eating canned Vienna sausages and drinking coffee.

Sunlight struck through a broken pane, lying like a judgment on the cloudy air of the room. Inside and outside, there was no sound; only a stifling rumor of absence. The clatter of dishware in the kitchen, the heavy rumble of streetcars: never again. There was sunlight; and silence; and the watery, astonished eyes of Louise Oliver.

He leaned forward, trying to capture the attention of those fishlike eyes for a second. "Darling," he said, "I respect your views, naturally. But I've got to make you see that they're impractical."

She looked at him with faint surprise, then away again. Her head shook slightly: No. *No, Rolf. I will not live with you in sin.*

Smith thought of the women of France, of Russia, of Mexico, of the South Seas. He had spent three months in the ruined studios of a radio station in Rochester, listening to the voices until they stopped. There had been a large colony in Sweden, including an English cabinet minister. They reported that Europe was gone. Simply gone; there was not an acre that had not been swept clean by radioactive dust. They had two planes and enough fuel to take them anywhere on the Continent; but there was nowhere to go. Three of them had the plague; then eleven; then all.

There had been a man and his wife in Kenya. Only two bombs had fallen in Africa, but one was bacterial. That had probably been a mistake, the Kenya man thought; there was no military reason for wiping out a hundred million Negroes.

There was a bomber pilot who had fallen near a government radio in Palestine. He did not last long, because he had broken some bones in the crash; but he had seen the vacant waters where the Pacific Islands should have been. It was his guess that the Arctic ice-fields had been bombed. He did not know whether that had been a mistake or not.

There were no reports from Washington, from New York, from London, Paris, Moscow, Chungking, Sydney. You could not tell who had been destroyed by disease, who by the dust, who by bombs.

Smith himself had been a laboratory assistant in a team that was trying to find an antibiotic for the plague. His superiors had found one that worked sometimes, but it was a little too late. When he left, Smith took along with him all there was of it—forty ampoules, enough to last him for years.

Louise had been a nurse in a genteel hospital near Denver. According to her, something rather odd had happened to the hospital as she was approaching it the morning of the attack. She was quite calm when she said this, but a vague look came into her eyes and her shattered expression seemed to slip a little more. Smith did not press her for an explanation.

Like himself, she had found a radio station which still functioned, and when Smith discovered that she had not contracted the plague, he agreed to meet her. She was, apparently, naturally immune. There must have been others, a few at least; but the bombs and the dust had not spared them.

It seemed very awkward to Louise that not one Protestant minister was left alive.

The trouble was, she really meant it. It had taken Smith a long time to believe it, but it was true. She would not sleep in the same hotel with him, either; she expected, and received, the utmost courtesy and decorum. Smith had learned his lesson. He walked on the outside of the rubble-heaped sidewalks; he opened doors for her, when there were still doors; he held her chair; he refrained from swearing. He courted her.

Louise was forty or thereabouts, at least five years older than Smith, He often wondered how old she thought she was. The shock of seeing whatever it was that had happened to the hospital, the patients she had cared for, had sent her mind scuttling back to her childhood. She tacitly admitted that everyone else in the world was dead, but she seemed to regard it as something one did not mention.

A hundred times in the last three weeks, Smith had felt an almost irresistible impulse to break her thin neck and go his own way. But there was no help for it; she was the only woman in the world, and he needed her. If she died, or left him, he died. *Old bitch!* he thought to himself furiously, and carefully kept the thought from showing on his face.

"Louise, honey," he told her gently, "I want to spare your feelings as much as I can. You know that."

"Yes, Rolf," she said, staring at him with the face of a hypnotized chicken.

Smith forced himself to go on. "We've got to face the facts, unpleasant as they may be. Honey, we're the only man and the only woman there are. We're like Adam and Eve in the Garden of Eden."

Louise's face took on a slightly disgusted expression. She was obviously thinking of fig-leaves.

"Think of the generations unborn," Smith told her, with a tremor in his voice. *Think about me for once. Maybe you're good for another ten years, maybe not.* Shuddering, he thought of the second stage of the disease—the helpless rigidity, striking without warning. He'd had one such attack already, and Louise had helped him out of it. Without her, he would have stayed like that till he died, the hypodermic that would save him within inches of his rigid hand. He thought desperately, *If I'm lucky, I'll get at least two kids out of you before you croak. Then I'll be safe.*

He went on, "God didn't mean for the human race to end like this. He spared us, you and me, to—" He paused; how could he say it without offending her? "Parents" wouldn't do—too suggestive. "—to carry on the torch of life," he ended. There. That was sticky enough.

Louise was staring vaguely over his shoulder. Her eyelids blinked regularly, and her mouth made little rabbit-like motions in the same rhythm.

Smith looked down at his wasted thighs under the tabletop. *I'm not strong enough to force her,* he thought. *Christ, if I were strong enough!*

He felt the futile rage again, and stifled it. He had to keep his head, because this might be his last chance. Louise had been talking lately, in the cloudy language she used about everything, of going up in the mountains to pray for guidance. She had not said, "alone," but it was easy enough to see that she pictured it that way. He had to argue her around before her resolve stiffened. He concentrated furiously, and tried once more.

The pattern of words went by like a distant rumbling. Louise heard a phrase here and there; each of them fathered chains of thought, binding her revery tighter. "Our duty to humanity . . ." Mama had often said—that was in the old house on Waterbury Street of course, before Mama had taken sick—she had said, "Child, your duty is to be clean, polite, and God-fearing. Pretty doesn't matter. There's a plenty of plain women that have got themselves good, Christian husbands."

Husbands . . . To have and to hold . . . Orange blossoms, and the bridesmaids; the organ music. Through the haze, she saw Rolf's lean, wolfish face. Of course, he was the only one she'd ever get; *she* knew that well enough. Gracious, when a girl was past twenty-five, she had to take what she could get.

But I sometimes wonder if he's really a nice *man*, she thought.

". . . in the eyes of God . . ." She remembered the stained-glass windows in the old First Episcopalian Church, and how she always thought God was looking down at her through that brilliant transparency. Perhaps He was still looking at her, though it seemed sometimes that He had forgotten. Well, of course she realized that marriage customs changed, and if you couldn't have a regular minister. . . . But it was really a shame, an outrage almost, that if she were actually going to marry this man, she couldn't have all those nice things . . . There wouldn't even be any wedding presents. Not even that. But of course Rolf would give her anything she wanted. She saw his face again, noticed the narrow black eyes staring at her with ferocious purpose, the thin mouth that jerked in a slow, regular tic, the hairy lobes of the ears below the tangle of black hair.

He oughtn't to let his hair grow so long, she thought, *it isn't quite decent*. Well, she could change all that. If she did marry him, she'd certainly make him change his ways. It was no more than her duty.

He was talking now about a farm he'd seen outside town—a good big house and a barn. There was no stock, he said, but they could get some later. And they'd plant things, and have their own food to eat, not go to restaurants all the time.

She felt a touch on her hand, lying pale before her on the table. Rolf's brown, stubby fingers, black-haired above and below the knuckles, were touching hers. He had stopped talking for a moment, but now he was speaking again, still more urgently. She drew her hand away.

He was saying, ". . . and you'll have the finest wedding dress you ever saw, with a bouquet. Everything you want, Louise, everything . . ."

A wedding dress! And flowers, even if there couldn't be any minister! Well, why hadn't the fool said so before?

Rolf stopped halfway through a sentence, aware that Louise had said quite clearly, "Yes, Rolf, I will marry you if you wish."

Stunned, he wanted her to repeat it, but dared not ask, "What did you say?" for fear of getting some fantastic answer, or none at all. He breathed deeply. He said, "Today, Louise?"

She said, "Well, *today* . . . I don't know quite . . . Of course, if you think you can make all the arrangements in time, but it does seem . . ."

Triumph surged through Smith's body. He had the advantage now, and he'd ride it. "Say you will, dear," he urged her; "say yes, and make me the happiest man . . ."

Even then, his tongue balked at the rest of it; but it didn't matter. She nodded submissively. "Whatever you think best, Rolf."

He rose, and she allowed him to kiss her pale, sapless cheek. "We'll leave right away," he said. "If you'll excuse me for just a minute, dear?"

He waited for her "Of course" and then left her, making footprints in the furred carpet of dust down toward the end of the room. Just a few more hours he'd have to speak to her like that, and then, in her eyes, she'd be committed to him forever. Afterwards, he could do with her as he liked—beat her when he pleased, submit her to any proof of his scorn and revulsion, use her. Then it would not be too bad, being the last man on Earth—not bad at all. She might even have a daughter . . .

He found the washroom door and entered. He took a step inside, and froze, balanced by a trick of motion, upright but helpless. Panic struck at his throat as he tried to turn his head and failed; tried to scream, and failed. Behind him, he was aware of a tiny click as the door, cushioned by the hydraulic check, shut forever. It was not locked; but its other side bore the warning: MEN.